THE MALLEN
NOVELS

Catherine Cookson

THE MALLEN NOVELS

The Mallen Streak
The Mallen Girl
The Mallen Litter

LONDON   NEW YORK SYDNEY TORONTO

This edition published 1992
by BCA by arrangement with
William Heinemann Ltd

The Mallen Streak first published in Great Britain 1973
© Catherine Cookson 1973

The Mallen Girl first published in Great Britain 1974
© Catherine Cookson 1973

The Mallen Litter first published in Great Britain 1974
© Catherine Cookson 1974

The Mallen Novels first published in one volume 1979

CN 1741

Printed in England by Clays Ltd, St Ives plc

THE MALLEN
STREAK

PART ONE

Thomas Mallen

I

HIGH BANKS HALL showed its sparsely-windowed back to beautiful woodland and the town of Allendale in the far distance, whilst its buttressed and emblazoned and many-windowed face looked out over formal gardens on to mountainous land, so austere and wild that even its short summer beauty brought no paeans of praise except from those who had been bred within the rigours of its bosom.

Away to the south lay Nine Banks Peel; to the north was the lovely little West Allen village of Whitfield; but staring the Hall straight in the face were the hills, for most part bare and barren and rising to miniature mountains which, on this day, Tuesday, the twenty-fifth of February, 1851, were thickly crusted with snow, not white, but pale pink, being tinged for the time being by the straining rays of a weak sun.

The Hall was fronted by a terrace bordered by an open balustrade, its parapet festooned with stone balls, and each pillar at the top of the steps which led to the drive was surmounted by a moss-stained naked Cupid.

The doors to the house were double and of black oak studded with large iron nails which gave the impression that it had withstood the attack of a fusillade of bullets. Over the door was a coat of arms composed of three shields, above it a Latin inscription had been cut into the stone which roughly translated read: *Man is compassionate because he gave God a mother.*

At first the inscription appeared to have religious connotations, but when dissected it proved to many to be blasphemous.

Thomas Wigmore Mallen, who built the Hall in 1767, had himself composed the inscription and had explained to those interested the deep significance of the motto, which was that God, in the first place, had been created of man's need, and the need had been brought about by the frightening mystery of both birth and death; more so the latter.

5

And knowing that no man came into the world except through woman, man felt compelled to be compassionate towards the omnipotent image he had created. Therefore, even in pagan times, even before Christ was heard of, man had given to his particular deity a mother; but with this difference: she was always untouched by man, a virgin who could nevertheless give birth.

Thomas Wigmore Mallen was an avowed atheist and the devil took his soul. Everyone knew this when he was found stone dead seated against a tree with not a mark on him, his horse cropping gently by his side.

It was said, among the hills, that the Mallen streak began with Thomas Wigmore Mallen, but then no one hereabouts had known his forbears for he had hailed from away in the Midlands. However, it wasn't long before he had spread his mark around the vicinity of his new house. No matter what colour the hair of a male Mallen the white streak started from the crown and thrust its wiry way down to the left temple.

Strangely, the streak never left its mark on the women of the family, and again not on all the males either. But it was noted that the Mallen men who bore the streak did not usually reach old age, nor did they die in their beds.

Yet the present owner of the Hall, Thomas Richard Mallen, nicknamed Turk by his friends, seemed to be an exception, for he was hale and hearty at fifty-five, and on this day his voice could be heard booming through the length of the house, calling on his guests to get ready and to have sport while it lasted, for in two days' time the hare-hunting season would end.

The guests had not come to the Hall merely to join the hare hunt, most of them had been there for the past three days. They had come originally for the wedding of Thomas's daughter, his only daughter by his second marriage.

More than half the county, they said, had been invited to the wedding, for it wasn't every day that a Northumberland miss married an Italian count, even if a poor one; and Thomas Mallen had gone out of his way to show the foreigner how things were done in England, especially in the north-east of England.

The festivities had gone on for two full days . . . and nights; only an hour ago four carriages had rumbled away, their occupants hardly able to stand on their feet. And this went for the women too. When Thomas Mallen entertained, he entertained. Mallen was a man, everybody said so. Could he not drink three men under the table? And had he not fathered more brats in the countryside than his bulls had heifers? Some mothers, it was said, were for ever dyeing their youngsters' hair with tea, but some children, one here and one there, seemed to be proud of the white tuft, and the evidence of this had just now been brought to Thomas by his son, Dick.

Dick Mallen was twenty-three years old and in looks a younger replica of his father, but in character there were divergent traits, for there was no streak of kindness in Dick Mallen. Thomas could forgive and forget, life was too short to bear the inconvenience of malice. Not so Dick Mallen; Dick always repaid the slightest slur with interest, creating an opportunity to get rid of the debt, which might have been only a disdainful look, or a snub. Yet a snub to young Mallen was worse than a blow; it indicated condemnation not only of himself, but also of the house. Both Mallens were laws unto themselves; whosoever dare question that law – and there were many in the county who did, a few openly, but the majority slyly – would be brought to book by the sole male heir to High Banks Hall.

Thomas's two sons by his first marriage had died, the second of them only last year, since when Dick Mallen had gambled more, drunk more, and whored more, three very expensive pastimes, and over the last three days he had excelled himself at all three. Now prancing down the main staircase with very little sway to his gait, for he, too, could hold his drink, he paused and shouted into the throng below, which looked for all the world like a hunt meeting without the horses.

'D'you hear me, Father! He's arrived; your hill nipper's arrived. I glimpsed him from the gallery.' He thrust his arm backwards.

Most of the faces down below were turned upwards, and the ruddy countenance of Thomas Mallen was split wide in a grin, showing a mouthful of blunt teeth with only two gaps to the side, and he cried back at his son, 'Has he now? He's early; the passes are still snowed up. Well! well!' He now turned to the dozen or so men and women about him. 'Do you hear that? My hill nipper has arrived, earlier than ever this year. November when last he came, wasn't it?' He was looking across the hall now at his son who was threading his way towards him.

'Nearer December.' Dick Mallen pulled a face at a friend and dug him in the ribs with his elbow, and the friend, William Lennox, who could claim relationship with another of that name who was Lord of the Bedchamber to Prince Albert, pushed his young host in the shoulder, then flung his head back and laughed aloud.

In his twenty-eight years William Lennox had stayed in all types of country houses but he would swear that he had never stayed in one quite like this where everything was as good as a play. He turned now to a man at his side who was thrusting down a dog from his thigh, and said, 'What do you think of that, eh? He wasn't lying in his boast, his bastards do risk the mountains just to get a peep at him.'

7

Carl Breton-Weir merely answered with a tight smile, thinking cynically that this house appeared like a factory for the manufacture of bastards of all kinds. If it wasn't that tonight he meant to recuperatate with good interest all the money he had purposely lost to his host and his friends, he would leave now. But tomorrow, if all went well, he would go, good and early. And he wouldn't be sorry to see the back of them all; coarse bores, every one of them. They afforded him amusement at first but one quickly tired of this kind of amusement.... Where were they going now? And these damn dogs all over the place. 'Get down! Get down!' He flung the dog from him.

'She likes you; she likes you, Carl.' Dick Mallen was laughing at him now. 'You must have a smell about you she recognises.'

At this there were great guffaws from the men and open titters from the four women present. Kate Armstrong, an overweight woman in her late forties, decked, even in her outdoor garb, with jewellery, one piece of which would have kept six of her husband's miners for a year, slapped out at her daughter Fanny, who at twenty-eight was still unmarried and could, they said, tell a joke as good as any man, saying, 'That Dick. That Dick ... I tell you!'

There was Jane Ferrier, small, fat and as giggly as a girl, which mannerism sat odd on her forty-three years. Her husband, John, owned a number of glass works in Newcastle, and to see the extent of their wealth you had to visit their home and be blinded by the chandeliers.

Then there was Maggie Headley. She had a name for being careful with the grocery bills, although her husband, Ralph, owned not only a brewery and a candle factory, but a coal mine also.

Among the men present was Headley's son, John, and his close friend, Pat Ferrier, both happy men at the moment, for they had made enough out of their friend and host and his London guests during the last two nights to keep them in pin money for some considerable time.

'Where was he, in the same place?' Thomas was again calling to his son, and Dick Mallen, who was making for the hall door, cried back to him, 'Aye, the same place. I wonder his legs don't give out by the time he reaches there.'

'Seven miles over and seven miles back he has to go; done it since he was that high.' Thomas measured a distance of four feet from the ground. 'An' I can't get near the beggar. And he won't speak, not a word. Skites off; that is after he's had a good look at me.' He gave an exaggerated heave to his chest and preened himself, and his voice now couldn't be heard for the laughter. 'Come on, come on, we'll change our route, we'll go round by the Low Fields.'

The whole party now swarmed out on to the terrace, where, below on the broad drive, three keepers were waiting. Led now by Thomas, they went through the gardens, skirted the lake, crossed in single file the narrow bridge over the stream that led to the River Allen, then bunched together again and, with the exception of the keepers, laughing and shouting to each other, they stumbled over the stretch of valley called the Low Fields, which edged the north boundary of the estate, and so came to a ridge of shale hills.

After rounding the foot of the hills they were brought to an abrupt stop by Thomas, who was standing, his arm outstretched, pointing.

Before them, about twenty yards distant, a zig-zag pathway cutting up the side of steep hill met up with the lower mountain road which at this time of the year was the only passable road between Alston and Whitfield. At the foot of the mountain and to the right of this pathway was a high peak of rock, accessible to the ordinary climber from one side only, and on top of the rock sat a boy.

From this distance the boy looked to be about twelve years old. His thin body was dressed warmly, not in the rough working-man's style, nor yet was his dress like that of the gentry, but his greatcoat had a collar to it which was turned up about his ears. He wore no cap and his hair, from this distance, looked jet black.

The whole company looked up towards him and he down at them.

'Why don't you rush him?' It was a quiet voice from behind, and Thomas answered as quietly, 'We tried it. He's as fast as the hare itself; he could skid down from that rock quicker than I can say Jack Robinson.'

'Have you never got any nearer to him?'

'Never. But one of these days, one of these days.'

'Where does he come from?'

'Oh, over the mountain, near Carr Shield.'

'Well, you could go and see him when the weather's fine. Haven't you thought of it?'

Thomas Mallen turned round and gazed at the speaker; his blue eyes were bright and laughing as he said, 'Yes, yes, I've thought of it; but then –' he spread one hand wide '– if I were to visit all my streaks I'd have no time for my estate. Now would I?' Both hands were held out in appeal now and as the laughter rang over the mountain and echoed into the next valley the boy suddenly disappeared from view, and they didn't see him make for the pass although they stood for some time scanning the hills before them.

9

2

I T HAD SNOWED for two days, thawed a little, then frozen, and the five guests left in the house had skated on the lake. They were Frank Armstrong, his wife Kate and daughter, Fanny, and Dick Mallen's two friends, William Lennox and Carl Breton-Weir.

Thomas Mallen had allowed his two nieces, Barbara and Constance Farrington, to join the company. It had been a great day for the children for they were seldom, if ever, allowed to mingle with the guests. When Thomas was at home alone, which wasn't very often, he had the children brought down in the afternoon to share his dinner, and he would laugh and joke with them and make funny remarks about their governess, Miss Brigmore. The two girls loved their Uncle Thomas; he was the only man in their lives and they had lived under his care for six years now, having been brought to the Hall when Barbara was four and Constance one year old. They were the children of his stepsister who had, against repeated warnings by him, married one Michael Farrington, a man with only one asset, charm. Michael Farrington had deserted his wife when she was carrying his second child but Thomas had known nothing of this until he had received a letter from her telling him that she was near death and begging him to take into his care her two small children. It says much for the man that he immediately made the journey to London and spent two days with her before she died. Then he brought the children from what, to him, were appalling lodgings, back to the Hall.

First, he engaged a nurse for them and then a governess. The nurse had long since gone, but the governess, Miss Brigmore, was still with them, and Barbara was now ten and Constance seven years old.

The children's world consisted of six rooms at the top of the east wing of the house, from which they descended by a back staircase once a day, if the weather was clement, to the world below, accompanied on such journeys by Mary Peel, the nursery attendant. If the coast was clear and Mrs Brydon the housekeeper, or Mr Tweedy the steward, or

10

Mr Dunn the butler, weren't about, Mary would take them through the kitchen and let them stop and have a cheery word with the cook and kitchen staff, and receive titbits in the form of rich sticky ginger-fingers, or a hot yeasty cake split and filled with jam and cream, two delicacies which were forbidden by Miss Brigmore, who was a believer in plain fare for children.

The children adored Mary Peel and in a way looked upon her as a mother figure. Of course, they both knew that Mary was very common and of no account; all the staff in the house were of no account, at least those below Brown, who was their Uncle Thomas's valet, and Taylor, who was Uncle Dick's valet. But they were aware that even these two personages did not come any way near Miss Brigmore's station. Their governess, they knew, was someone apart from the rest of the staff. Miss Brigmore had not stated this in words, but her manner left no one in doubt about it.

The girls had never experienced such pleasure as the afternoon spent on the ice. They squealed and laughed and caused great amusement as they fell on their bottoms and clung to the legs of first one escort and then the other. Barbara fell in love with Mr Weir and Constance with Mr Lennox, because both these gentlemen went out of their way to initiate them into the art of skating. Their Uncle Thomas, too, did his share in their coaching; only Uncle Dick did not take his turn with them for he skated constantly with Miss Fanny Armstrong.

On the side of the lake they ate hot chops which they held in a napkin, and their Uncle Thomas let them sip from his pewter tankard. The drink was hot and stinging and they coughed and their eyes watered and everybody laughed. It was a wonderful, glorious day.

They were still under the spell and talking about it at half-past six when Miss Brigmore retired to her room to have her supper. This was the only part of the day, with the exception of their exercise time, or when they were in bed, that they were free of Miss Brigmore's presence; but even now they weren't alone, for Mary Peel sat with them. But Mary didn't count. They could say what they liked in front of Mary; being with Mary was as good as being by themselves. Even when she joined in their conversation, as now, it didn't matter.

'No right to talk about Mr Armstrong in that manner, Miss Barbara,' she said, lifting her eyes from one of their night-dresses, the front of which she was herring-boning.

'Well I don't like him, Mary.'

'What's there to dislike about him? He's a fine man; he owns a mine, a big mine, away . . . away over the hills.'

'How far?'

'Oh, a long way, Miss Constance; a place I've never seen, near the

11

city, they say; beyond the Penny Hills, and that's a mighty long distance.'

'Have you to be rich before you can be good, Mary?'

'Ah! Miss Barbara, fancy asking a question like that: have you to be rich afore you can be good?'

'Well, you said he was a good man.'

'Well, so he is, according to his lights.'

'What lights?'

'Oh, Miss Constance, don't keep asking me questions I can't answer. Sufficient it be he's a lifelong friend of the master's, an' that should be enough for anybody.'

'Is it true that Miss Fanny is going to marry Uncle Dick?'

Mary now turned her head sharply and looked at the thin, dark girl sitting to one side of the round table, her paint brush poised over a piece of canvas, and she asked sharply, 'How did you come to hear that, Miss Barbara?'

'Little pigs have got big ears.' This came from the fair child sitting opposite, and the two girls leant across the table towards each other and giggled.

'Little pigs have got big ears' was a saying constantly on Mary's lips, and now she reprimanded them sternly, saying, 'Aye; well, little pigs have their ears cut off sometimes when they hear too much.'

'But is she, Mary?'

'You know as much about it as me, Miss Barbara.'

'I don't, Mary. You know everything.'

Mary Peel tightened her lips to suppress a smile, then said in mock harshness, 'I know this much, as soon as Miss Brigmore enters that door I'll tell her to smack your backsides.'

Again they were leaning across the table. They knew that Mary didn't like Miss Brigmore and that whenever she could she opposed her; as for Mary giving them away in anything, they would have sooner believed that Miss Brigmore's God was a figment of the imagination, like the ogres in fairy tales.

'When are the Armstrongs going home?' Barbara now asked.

'The morrow, as far as I know.'

'Oh.' Both the children now sat straight up in their chairs, but it was Barbara who said, 'That means that tonight there'll be carry-on and high jinks and divils fagarties.'

Mary Peel rose hastily to her feet and, coming to the table, she looked fearfully from one to the other, saying under her breath, 'If Miss Brigmore hears you comin' out with anythin' like that, you know what'll happen, not only to you, but to me. An' I'm warnin' you, for she'll have me kept downstairs and then you could have anybody up here, Nancy Wright, or Kate Steel.'

'Oh no! no!' They both grabbed at her hands, crying softly, 'We were only teasing, Mary.' Barbara looked up into the round, homely face which to her was both old and young because twenty-seven was a very great age for anyone to be, and she said, 'We like your sayings, Mary, we think they're nice, much better than Miss Brigmore's.'

Mary nodded grimly from one to the other. 'Well, I can tell you this much, Miss Brigmore wouldn't agree with you. And how do you know anyway about the ... about the divils, I mean carry-on?'

'Oh –' they looked at each other and grinned impishly '– we sometimes get up and creep down to the gallery. We hid in the armour box last week. It's a good job it was empty.'

'Oh my God!' The words came as a faint whisper through Mary's fingers, which she was holding tightly over her mouth. Then giving her attention wholly to Barbara, she whispered, 'Look you, Miss Barbara, look, now promise you'll not do it again. Promise? . . . In the armour box! How in the name of God did you get the lid up, child?'

'Well, it was very heavy but we managed to get in. But we couldn't get out.'

'You couldn't get out?' Mary had dropped her hand from her mouth and she gaped at them for a moment before she asked under her breath, 'Well, how did you then?'

'We knocked on the lid and called, and Waite opened it.'

'Waite?'

'Yes.' They were both nodding at her.

'What did he say?'

'He just said what you said.'

Mary screwed her brows up trying to recollect what she had said, and when she seemed to be finding some difficulty Constance put in with a smile, 'He said, "Oh my God!"'

Mary sat down suddenly on the third chair at the table and, picking up the corner of her long white apron, she passed it round her face before leaning towards them and again saying, 'Promise me on God's honour you'll not do anything like that again. . . . Now come on, promise?'

It was Connie who nodded her promise straightaway, but Barbara remained quiet, and Mary said, 'Aw, Miss Barbara.'

'Well, I cannot promise you, Mary, 'cos I know I'll break my promise. You see, I like watching the ladies and gentlemen at their games.'

Again Mary put her hand across her mouth. Then the sound of a door closing brought her to her feet and all she could say to Barbara was, 'Oh miss! miss!' before the governess entered the room.

Miss Brigmore was of medium height. She would have been termed very pretty if she hadn't looked so prim. Her hair was brown, her eyes

13

were brown, and her mouth was well shaped. She had a good skin and a well-developed figure, in fact her bust was over developed for her height.

Miss Brigmore was thirty years old. She had come from a good middle class family, and up till the age of sixteen had had her own governess. The fact that her governess's wages, together with those of the eight other staff her father kept in his house on the outskirts of York, and the establishment of his mistress in the heart of that city, were being supplemented by the clients of his bank, wasn't made public until Anna Brigmore was almost seventeen.

Her mother did not sustain the shock of her husband's imprisonment but Anna did. When she buried her mother she also buried her father. When she applied for her first post of governess she said she was an orphan; and she actually was an orphan when, at twenty-four, she entered the service of Mr Thomas Mallen of High Banks Hall in the County of Northumberland, there to take charge of his two nieces.

On her first encounter with Thomas Mallen she had not thought, what a gross pompous individual! for her heart had jerked in her breast. She was not aware that most women's hearts jerked in their breasts when Thomas Mallen looked at them. He had a particular way of looking at a woman; through long practice his look would convince them that they were beautiful, and interesting, and above all they were to be desired.

During her six years in the Hall Miss Brigmore had made no friends. She had been brought up to look upon servants as menials, and the fact that she was now earning her own living did not, in her mind, bring her down to their level.

Miss Brigmore now looked at the children's embroidery and her brief comment was, 'You have been idling; go and get ready for bed,' and turning towards Mary Peel she added, 'See to them.' Then she went through the day nursery and so into the schoolroom. Taking from the shelves three books, she sat down at the oblong table and began to prepare the lessons for the following day, but after a moment or two she pushed the books aside and rose to her feet, then went to the window where she stood looking out into the darkness. Yet through the darkness she pictured the lake as she had seen it earlier in the day. She could see them all in pairs, with hands crossed, weaving in and out; she could see the children tumbling about; she could hear the laughter in which she did not join.

She, like the children, preserved a vivid memory of the skating party because the master had looked at her from the ice. He had not only looked at her, he had laughed at her. But he had never asked her to skate. No one had thought to ask her to skate. And she could skate; at one time she had been an excellent skater . . . at one time she had

14

been young. But now she was thirty. Yet the master had looked at her as if she were still young. . . . Slowly she left the window and returned to the table.

It was around eleven o'clock when the first squeals of delight floated faintly up from the far hall to the nursery and brought Barbara sitting upright in bed. Hugging her knees, she strained her ears to listen. What games were they playing tonight? Would Uncle Dick be chasing Miss Fanny along the gallery, and when he caught her would he pull her behind the curtains like she did with Connie when they were playing hide-and-seek with Mary? Or would one of the ladies slide down the banister again? She had actually seen one start at the top but she had been unable to see what happened when she reached the bottom; but she had heard the squeals of laughter. Then there was the time she had seen three gentlemen in their night-shirts carrying someone shoulder high down the main staircase. She hadn't been able to see if it was a lady or a gentleman they were carrying, only that the person's feet and legs were bare up to the knees.

If Mr Armstrong and his family were leaving tomorrow then Uncle Dick and his friends would leave shortly afterwards, and Uncle Thomas, too, would go about his business. From then onwards the house would become quiet again, except for the laughter of the servants, and there would only be Miss Brigmore, with Mary for light relief.

At this moment the future appeared very dull to Barbara. She looked through the dim glow of the night-light towards the other bed and saw that Connie was fast asleep. Connie had promised Mary not to go down, but she hadn't promised, had she?

Quietly she pushed back the bedclothes and got out of bed; then getting into her slippers and dressing gown she tip-toed quietly to the bedroom door which opened into the day nursery. Having groped her way across the dark room, she now gently turned the handle of the door leading on to the landing.

The landing was lit by one candle standing in a three-branch candelabrum. She peered first one way and then the other and she was tip-toeing gently to the head of the stairs when she heard the little sound. She stopped, and looked back towards the end of the landing to the door opposite where their bedroom door would have been if it had opened onto the landing instead of into the day nursery. The sound could have been a laugh, or a moan, and it had come from Miss Brigmore's bedroom which was next to her sitting room.

There it was again, a soft moaning sound not unlike the sound she herself made when she had toothache and hid her head under the bedclothes. Was Miss Brigmore ill? She did not care for Miss

Brigmore but she must remember that the governess was always kind to them when they felt ill, and now she might be in need of assistance; perhaps she required some mixture out of the white bottle in the medicine cupboard, the same as she gave to them when they had stomach trouble.

She turned and tip-toed down the length of the landing until she was opposite Miss Brigmore's door. The sound was louder now but still soft. She noted that Miss Brigmore's door was just the slightest bit ajar. Slowly her hand lifted and she pressed it open, but only wide enough to take the shape of her face and allow her to see into the room.

What she saw caused her to hold her breath for so long that she imagined she had stopped breathing altogether. Miss Brigmore was in her bed; the bed-clothes were rumpled down to her waist, and the top of her body was bare, and lying by her side leaning over her was her Uncle Thomas. He was supporting himself on his elbow and gazing down into Miss Brigmore's face while his hand caressed her breast. She noticed that Miss Brigmore had her eyes closed, but her mouth was open and from it were coming the soft moans that weren't really moans.

As she went to take in a deep gulp of air she became conscious of a movement behind her and she turned quickly to see Connie coming down the landing. With swift silent steps she reached her sister and, grabbing her hand, she dragged her back into the nursery, and there in the dark she turned and closed the door, but softly. Then pushing Connie before her, she went towards the dim light coming from the night nursery.

'What is it?' Connie turned to her. 'I woke up; you weren't in bed. What ... what is wrong? Is Miss Brigmore sick?'

Barbara shook her head violently before she could say, 'No, no.'

'There was a noise.'

'She ... she was snoring.'

'Oh.' Constance giggled now. 'Does Miss Brigmore snore? I didn't know. Perhaps Mary doesn't know either. You must tell Mary. Does she do it like the pigs on the farm, like this?'

The snort brought a hasty 'Ssh!' from Barbara, and she pushed Constance forward as she said, 'Get back into bed.'

'Aren't you going down to the gallery?'

'No, no, I'm not. Get back into bed.'

'What's the matter, Barbie?'

'Nothing, nothing; just go to bed. Come on.' She pulled her onto the bed, then tucked the clothes round her.

'You're vexed, Barbie.'

'I'm not, I'm not. Go to sleep.'

'Good night, Barbie.'

16

'Good night.'

She herself now climbed into bed and lay rigid staring up at the rose-coloured patterns on the ceiling created by the red glass vase which held the night-light. Her Uncle Thomas doing that to Miss Brigmore and Miss Brigmore not stopping him. It was wicked. Miss Brigmore herself would have said it was wicked. But she had lain quite still with her eyes closed. Suddenly her body bounced in the bed and she turned onto her face and buried it in the pillow. But having blotted out her uncle and Miss Brigmore from her mind, they were now replaced by the ladies' and gentlemen's games she had watched from the gallery and the balcony, and she knew there was a connection between them and the scene she had just witnessed. Her uncle was bad; Miss Brigmore was bad; all the ladies and gentlemen were bad; the only people who weren't bad were Mary Peel, Connie and herself. She wished the ice had cracked today and she had fallen through and been drowned.

3

'LOOK, BOY, what the hell do you want, waking me at this ungodly hour?' Thomas Mallen heaved himself round in the bed, then pulled his night-cap from the back of his head down onto his brow as he screwed up his bleary eyes at the clock. 'Ten minutes to seven. God sakes! What's up with you?'

'I've got to talk with you, Father.' Dick Mallen hoisted himself up on to the side of the four-poster bed and, leaning forward, he said in a tense undertone, 'I'm in a fix. I . . . I need two thousand straight away. It's imperative I have two thousand straight away.'

'Ah!' Thomas fell back into the billowing soft pillows with a flop and, raising his arms towards the ceiling, he waved his hands at it as he addressed it, saying, 'It's imperative he has two thousand straight away.' Then twisting on to his side he looked at his son with an alert gaze now and said soberly, 'What's come over you? What's happened?'

'I lost.'

'But you're always losing.'

'That isn't true.'

'Well, what I mean is, you've lost before and it wasn't . . . imperative you had two thousand right away.' He glanced at the clock again. 'Ten to seven in the morning and demanding two thousand! There's something more besides this.' He pulled himself upwards, very wide awake now, and stared at his son. 'Out with it.'

'I made a mistake.'

'You what?'

'I said I made a mistake.'

'You mean you cheated?'

'No, I tell you I . . .'

'You bloody well cheated! Playin' against fellows like Lennox and Weir, you had the bloody nerve to cheat. You must be mad.'

18

'I . . . I didn't cheat; there was a slight mistake.'

'Look. Look.' Thomas shook his fist menacingly at him. 'I'm an old bull; don't try to put the blinkers on me, boy. If you want two thousand straightaway you cheated. Who's pressing you?'

'Weir.'

'It would be, that bastard! . . . Well, what's the alternative?'

Dick hung his head. 'He'll finish me in town . . . and everywhere else for that matter.'

'Has he any proof?'

'Lennox'll stand by his word.'

'By God! boy, you do pick your friends. How much do you owe them altogether?'

'Four, four thousand. But Lennox'll wait.'

'They'll both bloody well wait. Get by and let me up out of this; I'll deal with them.'

'No! No, you won't.' Dick had his hands on his father's shoulders now, pressing him back. 'See me through this and I'll promise it'll be the last. Honest to God, I promise.'

'I've heard that before. Take your hands off me.' There was a threat in the tone, and when his son quickly withdrew his hold Thomas slowly sat up and, thrusting his feet over the side of the high bed, he sat for a moment and held his face in his hand pressing one cheek in with his thumb and the other with his fingers before he said soberly, 'And now I'm going to tell you something. I've kept it from you for some time, didn't want to spoil your fun and wanted Bessie settled, but I, too, am in it up to the neck. At this present moment I couldn't raise four hundred let alone four thousand.'

The father and son stared at each other. It was Thomas who eventually broke the silence. Nodding slowly, he said, 'I've been banking on you fixing it up with Fanny. That settled, I gathered Frank would see me through, but not otherwise. I know she's a bit long in the tooth, but it won't be the first time a man's married a woman five years older than himself. I haven't pressed you, I thought I could see how things were going on their own. You asked her to stay on. . . .'

Dick's voice, almost like a groan, cut him off. 'Aye, I did, but for God's sake! not because I wanted to marry her, she's been laid more times than an old sow.'

Ignoring the scornful vehemence of his son's tone Thomas said quietly, 'That might be, but beggars can't be choosers. She's your only hope, and not only yours but mine an' all. I'm going to tell you something else, boy, and listen carefully, very carefully, for it means more to you in a way than it does to me, an' it's just this. If you don't marry her it'll be the end of the House.' He now lifted his hand and moved it slowly backwards and forwards in a wide sweep. 'Everything, every damned thing.'

There was a long pause. Then, his voice a mere whisper, Dick said, 'You can't mean it ... everything?' His face was screwed up against the incredibility of the statement.

'That's what I said, everything. I've survived on borrowed money for the past ten years. It's only by keeping up appearances that I've swum this far. Let them think you've still got it and they'll give you credit. But now, boy' – he sighed deeply – 'I'm tired of swimming against the tide. Mind you, I never thought I'd confess to that, but there it is.' He now gently patted the great mound of his stomach. 'It's beginning to tell here an' all. I haven't the taste for life I used to have.'

'You don't do so badly.' There was deep bitterness in the remark, and Thomas replied slowly, 'No, I don't do so badly, true, an' I'm not grumbling. I've had a great deal of experience of all kinds of things. But you know, I've learned very little, except one thing, boy, one thing, and that is, everything has to be paid for; sooner or later everything has to be paid for. ...'

'Oh, for God's sake, shut up! Shut up!' Dick had sprung from the bed now and was holding his hand to his brow. 'Don't you start preaching, you above all people, and at this time. Philosophy coming from you is a joke. It isn't philosophy I want. Don't you understand what they can do to me, those two? I won't dare show my face in any club, can't you see that?'

His arms were now hugging himself. His fists dug into his armpits, like a youth with frozen mitts trying to regain warmth, his body swayed backwards and forwards, and the action so lacking in dignity made Thomas turn his head away from the sight. After a moment he said quietly, 'If I ask Frank for it, will you promise to put the question to Fanny before they leave?'

When there was no answer he rose to his feet, saying, 'Well it's up to you. That's the only way. If I lose everything I'm still not losing as much as you, so think on it.'

When he next looked at his son, Dick was standing with his head drooped on his chest, his hands hanging limp at his sides, and Thomas said, softly, 'They'll be leaving about twelve. When you see me going into the library with Frank you corner Fanny, that's if you haven't done it before. If Weir's as mean as he sounds your best policy is to get it settled as soon as possible. I don't expect there'll be any hesitation on her part, she's past the choosing stage.'

Thomas now watched his son flounce about as a woman might have done and stalk down the length of the long room and out into the corridor. Then he bent his head and his eyes came to rest on his bare stomach visible through his open nightshirt, and as if the sight sickened him he turned his head and spat into the spittoon at the side of the bed.

Thomas did not take Frank Armstrong into the study, nor did Dick at the first opportunity ask Fanny to be his wife. These arrangements were cancelled by the arrival on the drive at ten o'clock that morning of a shabby cab, from which three men slowly descended. Having mounted the steps one after the other, the first of them pulled the handle that was hanging below the boar's head to the side of the great door. When the bell clanged within, the man turned and looked at his two companions, and they all waited.

The door was opened by Ord, the first footman. His gaze flicked haughtily over what he immediately stamped as the lower type of business men, and his voice portraying his feelings he said briefly, 'There is a back door.'

The first man, stepping abruptly forward, almost pushed the footman on to his back with a swift jab of his forearm, and when the three of them had entered the hall they stopped in some slight amazement, looking around them for a moment, before the first man, addressing Ord again, said, 'I wish to see your master.'

'My master is engaged. What is your business?'

'I'll tell that to your master. Now go and tell him that a representative of the Dulwich Bank would like a word with him.'

The Dulwich Bank. The very name seemed to convey trouble, and Ord, his manner no less haughty now but his feelings definitely uncertain, made his stately way towards the morning room where his master was breakfasting. There he motioned to Waite, the second footman who was assisting in carrying the heavy silver dishes from the kitchen, to pause a minute and he whispered in his ear, 'Tell Mr Dunn I want him, it's very important. There's fellas here from the Bank.'

A moment later Dunn appeared outside the morning-room door and he glanced across the hall towards the dark trio; then looking at Ord he said, 'What do they want?'

'The master; they're from the Bank.'

The butler looked at the men again, paused a moment, then turned and with unruffled step went back into the morning room.

It was a full five minutes later when Thomas put in an appearance. His head still maintained its jaunty angle, his shoulders were still back, his stomach still protruding, his step still firm, the only difference about him at this moment was that his colour was not as ruddy as usual, but that could have been put down to a series of late nights.

'Well, gentlemen!' He looked from one to the other of the men.

It was the tallest of them who again spoke. 'Mr Thomas Richard Mallen?'

'At your service.'

'I would like a word with you, in private if I may.'

'Certainly, certainly.'

The politeness seemed to disconcert the three men and they glanced at each other as they followed the portly figure across the magnificently carpeted and furnished hall. Their eyes, like those of weasels, darted around the room into which they followed the master of the house; moving from the row of chandeliers down to the furniture and furnishings.

In the middle of the room Thomas turned and, facing the men now, said, 'Well now, gentlemen, your business?'

His casual manner caused a moment's pause; then the tall man said, with some deference in his tone now, 'I represent the Dulwich Bank, sir. I understand that a representative from there called on you some three months gone when your situation was made clear, since when they have had no further word from you.'

'Oh, that isn't right. I said I would see into the matter.'

'But you haven't done so, sir.'

'Not yet . . . no.'

'Then I'm afraid, sir, it is my duty to hand you this.' Whereupon the man drew a long envelope from the inside pocket of his coat and held it out towards Thomas.

For a matter of seconds Thomas's arm remained by his side; then slowly he lifted it and took the envelope, and he stared down at it before opening it. Then still slowly, he withdrew and unfolded the double official paper. After his eyes had scanned the top of the first page he folded it again and replaced it in the envelope, and walking to the mantelpiece he placed the envelope on the marble shelf before turning to the men again saying, 'Well what now?'

'We take possession, sir.'

'Possession?' There was a crack in the coolness of Thomas's manner.

'That is the procedure, sir. Nothing must be moved, nothing. And it . . . it tells you there –' the man motioned to the envelope on the mantelpiece '– when you'll have to appear afore the Justices. Being a private debtor, of course, you'll not be put to the indignity of going inside, sir, as long as you're covered.'

'Oh, thank you.'

The sarcasm was not lost on the man and his chin nobbled before he said, 'I'm just explainin', sir. Anyway if you'd taken action two years gone when you had the chance. . . .'

'That's enough, my man!' Thomas's whole manner had changed

22

completely. 'Do your business but oblige me by not offering me your advice.'

The man's jaw moved from side to side now and his eyes narrowed and it was some seconds before he spoke again, saying, 'This is Mr Connor, and Mr Byers, they will make an inventory. It will take some days. We will board here, you understand . . . sir?'

Apparently Thomas hadn't understood the full significance of the presence of the three men until now, and he exclaimed stiffly, 'Board here!'

'Yes, sir, board here, until the debts are paid or the equivalent is made in the sale. I thought you'd be aware of the procedure, sir.'

There was a definite note of insolence in the man's voice now, and under other circumstances, and if he'd had a whip in his hand, Thomas would have brought it across the fellow's face. But he was wise enough to realize that for the next few hours he would need this man's co-operation, for he was now in a hell of a fix. It would happen that Kate Armstrong would get a belly pain in the night and was now unfit to travel until the afternoon or perhaps tomorrow.

He looked at the man again and forced a conciliatory note into his voice as he said, 'Yes, I understand. And you will be boarded and well, for as long as there is food . . . and –' he gave a weak laugh '– I should say the stocks are pretty ample. But one thing I would ask of you and that is to delay the taking of your inventory until later in the day when, I hope I'm right in saying, there will be no need for it.'

He turned now to the mantelpiece and took down the envelope again and, opening it, he read for some minutes before he said, 'I understand a sum of thirty thousand would assuage the Bank for the moment. Well, it is more than possible I shall be able to give you a note to this effect before this afternoon . . . Will you comply, gentlemen?'

The three men looked at one another. It wasn't every day that their business settled them in a house like this where they might remain for two to three weeks. It was just as well to keep on the right side of those who were providing the victuals, and – who knew? – there might be some extra pickings. The place was breaking down with finery: the china and trinkets in those cabinets lining the far wall looked as if they might be worth a mint in themselves. And then there were the pictures in this one room alone. Yet, would all the stuff in the house and the estate itself clear him? They said he was up to the neck and over. He had mortgaged, and re-mortgaged for years past now, and that wasn't counting the money owing the trades folk. Why, they said, only three years ago he had carpeted and curtained the place out afresh. Ten thousand it had cost him. Well, it should have cost him that if he had paid for it. Three thousand the firm had got and that, they understood, was all. The only tradesman who hadn't put in a claim

23

apparently was the coal supplier, but then he got his coal straight from Armstrong's pit. Would it be from Armstrong he was hoping to get the loan? It would have to be some butty who would stump up thirty thousand by this afternoon.

The tall man nodded now before he said, 'Very well, sir. But there's one thing: you'd better tell them, the servants, who we are; we want to be treated with respect, not like dirt, 'cos we have a job to do. An' tell them an' all not to try to lift anything; it's a punishable offence to lift anything, prison it is for lifting anything.'

Thomas's face had regained its colour for temper was now boiling in him, so much so that he was unable to speak. He made a motion with his head; then turning to the bell rope at the side of the fireplace he pulled it twice.

When Ord entered the room Thomas looked at him and swallowed deeply before saying, 'Take these men to the kitchen, see that they are fed. They . . . they are to be treated with courtesy. They will remain there, in those quarters, until this afternoon.'

'Yes, sir.'

Ord looked at the men and the men looked at him, then they all went out.

After staring at the closed door for some seconds, Thomas gazed slowly round the room as if he had found himself in a strange place. What was really happening was that now, on the point of losing his home, he was recognizing its full splendour for the first time. His eyes finally came to rest on the portrait over the mantelpiece. It was not a portrait of his father but of his grandfather, the man who had built this house. It had been painted while he was in the prime of his life; his hair was still black and the streak flowed like molten silver from the crown of his head down to his left temple. The face below it was a good face, and yet they said it was with him the ill luck had started; yet it was with him also that the Mallen fortunes had flourished, because although they could trace their family back to the sixteenth century it was only in the Industrial Revolution that the Mallens had come up from among the ordinary merchants.

Through wool, and various other activities, Wigmore Mallen had amassed a fortune. He'd had four sons and each one he provided with an education that could only be purchased with money. One of them gave him cause for great pride for he was sent to Oxford and became a scholar. But not one of his sons died in his bed, all had violent deaths.

Thomas's own father had been shot while deer-stalking in Scotland. It was an accident they said. No one could tell how the accident had really happened. The shot could have come from any one of the dozen guests out that day, or any one of the keepers. Thomas had often wondered how he himself would die. At times he had been a little afraid but now, having passed the fifty mark and having lived vitally every day of his life since he was sixteen, the final incident that would end his existence no longer troubled him. But what was troubling him at this moment, and greatly, was that the end, when it came, might be so undignified as to take place in drastically reduced circumstances and without causing much concern among those who mattered. Such was his make-up that this thought was foremost in his mind, for being a Mallen he must not only be a man of consequence, but be seen to be such. Even the fact that he had confessed to his son that he was weary of the struggle did not alter the fact that he had no desire to end the struggle in penury.

He laid his head on his arm on the mantelshelf and ground out through clenched teeth, 'Damn and blast everything to hell's flames!' He lifted his head and his eyes focussed on the massive gilt frame of the picture. What would become of them if Frank didn't give a hand? Frank Armstrong he knew to be a close man, a canny man. He had clawed himself up from nothing, and had thrust aside his class on the way. He had kicked many a good man down, pressed faces in the mud, and stood on shoulders here and there, all to get where he was today. Frank, he knew, had a heart as soft as the stones he charged his miners for, should they send any up from the depths in their skips of coal. Oh, he had no illusions about his friend. But there was one crack in Frank's stony heart, and it wasn't made by his wife, but by his daughter. Frank would do anything to get Fanny settled, happily settled. Fanny had flown high and fallen a number of times. Now she had pinned her sights on Dick and her father would be willing to pay a good price to secure for her, if not happiness, then respectability. But would he go as far as thirty thousand now and the same again when the knot was tied? He doubted it. And yet he just might, for he had an eye on this house and would be tempted to go to the limit in order to see his daughter mistress of it.

He straightened up, adjusted his cravat, sniffed loudly, ran his hand over his thick grey hair, then went out of the drawing room in search of Frank Armstrong.

4

BY DINNER-TIME everyone in the house, with the exception of the guests, knew that the bums were in. Even the children in the nursery knew the bums were in. They had heard Mary talking to Miss Brigmore in a way they had never heard Mary talk before, nor had they witnessed such reaction from Miss Brigmore, because Miss Brigmore could only repeat, 'Oh, no! Oh no!' to everything that Mary said.

Earlier, Barbara had been unable to look at Miss Brigmore, at least not at her face, for her eyes were drawn to her bust, now tightly covered. There were ten buttons on her bodice, all close together like iron locks defending her bosom against attack, but Barbara could see past the locks and through the taffeta bodice to the bare flesh as she had seen it last night.

Miss Brigmore had asked her if she wasn't well and she had just shaken her head; Connie had asked if she wasn't well, and Mary had asked her if she wasn't well. Then of a sudden they had forgotten about her for Mary came rushing up the stairs and did the most unheard-of thing, she took Miss Brigmore by the hand and almost pulled her out of the schoolroom and into the day nursery.

She and Connie had tip-toed to the door and listened. 'It's the bums, miss,' Mary had said, and Miss Brigmore had repeated, 'The bums?'

'Yes, duns. You know, miss, duns, bailiffs. They're in the kitchen, they're stayin' put until s'afternoon; then they'll start tabbing everything in the house. It's the end, it's the end, miss. What's goin' to happen? What about the bairns?'

'Be quiet! Be quiet, Mary.' Miss Brigmore often told Mary to be quiet, but she very rarely used her name; and now when she did it wasn't like a reprimand, because she added, 'Go more slowly; tell me what's happened. Has ... has the master seen them?'

26

'Oh yes, miss, yes, miss. An' they're all nearly frantic in the kitchen. It means the end. They'll all get the push, miss. But what about the bairns? An' where'll we all go? They say he owes a fortune, the master, thousands, tens of thousands. All the stuff in the house and the farms won't pay for it, that's what they say. Eeh! and the money that's been spent, like water it's been spent. . . .'

'Be quiet, Mary!'

In the silence that followed the children stood looking at each other, their eyes stretched, their mouths wide, until Mary's voice came to them again, saying, 'Will they be able to take the bairns' cottage, miss?'

'The cottage? Oh no, no. Well, I don't think they can touch that. It was left to the children, together with the legacy. They can't touch that. No, they can't touch that.'

There was another silence before Miss Brigmore asked, 'The master, how does he appear?'

'Putting a face on it they say, miss.'

There was a movement in the next room and Barbara and Constance scrambled to the window seat and sat down. But when no one came in Constance whispered, 'What does it mean, Barbie?'

'I . . . I don't rightly know except we may have to leave here.'

'Will we go and live in our cottage?'

'I . . . I don't know.'

'I'd like to live in our cottage, it's nice.'

Barbara looked out of the window. The view from this side of the house took in the kitchen gardens and the orchards and the big farm. The cottage lay beyond the big farm on the other side of the road, nearly a mile along it, and situated, almost like the Hall, with its front to the moors and hills and its back to a beautiful dale. It had eight rooms, a loft and a little courtyard, which was bordered by a barn, two loose boxes and a number of outhouses, and the whole stood in one acre of land.

The cottage had been the home of Gladys Armorer who had been a second cousin to the children's mother. She had objected strongly to Thomas Mallen being given charge of the children for, as she said, she wouldn't trust him to rear a pig correctly; and she would have fought him for their guardianship had it not been she was crippled with arthritis. Yet up to a year ago when she died she had shown little interest in the children themselves, never remembering their birth-days, and only twice inviting them to take tea with her.

So it came as something of a surprise when she left to them her house and her small fortune, in trust, a hundred pounds a year to be allotted to each during their lifetime, with further stipulations which took into account their marriages, also their deaths.

The house stood today as when Gladys Armorer had left it, plainly but comfortably furnished. Two servants from the Hall were sent down now and again to air and clean it, and a gardener to see to the ground.

Gladys Armorer had not made Thomas Mallen a trustee, for despite his evident wealth she still had no faith in him, but had left the business in the hands of a Newcastle solicitor, which, as things had turned out, was just as well.

'Barbie!' Constance was shaking Barbara's arm now. 'But wouldn't you really like to live in the cottage? I'd love to live there, just you and Mary and Uncle and cook, and . . . and Waite, I like Waite.'

'It's a very small cottage. There are only eight rooms, it would only house three people at the most, well perhaps four.'

'Yes.' Constance nodded her head sagely as if to say, 'You're quite right.'

It was at this point that Miss Brigmore and Mary came into the room. They came in like friends might, and Mary, after looking at the children, lowered her head and bit on her lip and began to cry, then turned hastily about and ran from the room.

Miss Brigmore now went to the table and began moving the books about as if she were dealing out cards. 'Come along children, come along,' she said gently. And they came to the table, and Barbara looked fully at Miss Brigmore for the first time that day and was most surprised to see that she actually had tears in her eyes.

The gallery of the Hall had always caused controversial comment, some saying it was in Italian style, some saying it was after the French. The knowledgeable ones stated it was a hideous mixture of neither. But Thomas always had the last word on the period the gallery represented, saying it was pure pretentious Mallen, for he knew that, even among his best friends, not only the gallery, but the whole Hall was considered too pretentious by far.

The gallery was the place Dick Mallen chose in which to propose marriage to Fanny Armstrong. However distasteful the union with her might appear to him, and the thought of it brought his stomach muscles tensing, he knew that life was a game that had to be played, and with a certain amount of panache, and he needed all the help he could get at the moment, so he picked on the romantic atmosphere prevalent in the gallery.

He opened the arched doorway into the long green and gold room and, bowing slightly, waited for her to pass; then together they walked slowly down the broad strip of red carpet that was laid on the mosaic floor.

There were six windows along each side of the gallery and each had at its base a deep cushioned window seat wide enough to seat two comfortably. The walls between the windows were papered or rather clothed with an embossed green velvet covering, and each afforded room for two large gilt-framed pictures placed one above the other. In the centre of the gallery ceiling was a great star, and from it gold rays extended in all directions.

It was in the middle of the gallery that Fanny Armstrong stopped, and after looking to where two servants were entering by the far door, she turned her small green eyes to the side where another was in the act of opening or closing a window and she said, 'Is anything amiss?'

'Amiss? What do you mean?'

'I seem to detect an uneasiness in the house . . . in the servants. When I came out of my room a short while ago two maids had their heads together and they scurried away on sight of me as if in alarm.'

He swallowed deeply before he said, 'You're imagining things.'

'I may be' – she was walking on again – 'but I also have a keen perception for the unusual, for the out of pattern, and when servants step out of pattern . . . well! Servants are barometers you know!' She smiled coyly at him now, but he didn't look at her, he was looking ahead as he said, 'Fanny, I would like to ask you something.'

'You would? Well, I'm listening.' Again the coy glance.

He still kept his eyes from her face as he went on, 'What I have to ask you needs a time and a place. This is the place I had chosen, but the time, because of the' – he paused now and smiled weakly at her as he repeated her words – 'scurry of the servants is inappropriate. Do you think you could brave the weather with me?'

Her coyness was replaced now by an amused, cynical look which made him uneasy. He knew well enough that once married to her life would become a battle of wills; for underneath her skittish exterior was a woman who would have her own way, and if thwarted all hell would be let loose.

'Why so ceremonious all of a sudden?' She was looking him full in the face. 'If I could follow the dogs and your father through slush and mud for hours then I can risk the slightly inclement weather of today, don't you think?' She made a slight moue with her lips.

'Good! We'll go to the summer-house then.' With well-simulated eagerness he caught hold of her hand and drew it through his arm. 'We'll go down the back way; I'll get you a cloak from the gun room.' There was a conspiratorial note in his voice now.

Like two children in step they ran through the door that a servant held open for them; then across a landing towards a green-baized door, and so into a passage where to the right the stairs led up to the nursery and to the left down to the gun room.

29

The gun room was at the end of a long wide passage, from which doors led to the housekeeper's sitting room and the upper staff dining room, the servants' hall, the butler's pantry; also the door to the cellars, and, at the extreme end, the door to the kitchen.

At the foot of the stairs a maid was kneeling on the flagstone passage with a wooden bucket by her side, and the expanse of stone from wall to wall in front of her was covered in soapy suds.

It was as Dick held out his hand to Fanny, with exaggerated courtesy, in order to assist her to jump prettily over the wet flags while she, with skirts slightly raised, was coyly desisting, that the voice from the butler's pantry came clearly into the corridor, saying, 'I'm sorry for the master, but not for that young skit. Now he'll likely have to do some graft and know what it is to earn his livin', but he won't have the guts for that. By! it's made me stomach sick these last few days to see the carry-on here, the Delavals of Seaton Sluice were nothin' to it. It was them he was trying to ape with his practical jokes, and show off afore his London friends. The Delavals might have been mad with their pranks but at bottom they were class, not a get-up like him.'

The girl had risen from her knees, her face showing her fear, but when furtively she made to go towards the open door Dick Mallen's hand gripped her arm fiercely and held her back. Fanny was still standing at the far side of the soapy patch and he had apparently forgotten her presence for the moment, for his infuriated gaze was fixed on the open door a little to the side of him. The voice coming from there was saying now, 'Those three in the kitchen, bums or bailiffs, call them what you like, they won't wait any longer than s'afternoon, an' they must have had their palms well greased to wait that long. But the old man thinks that by then the young upstart'll have popped the question, 'cos old Armstrong won't stump up any other way. And oh, by God! I hope he gets her. By God! I do, I hope he does, for she'll sort his canister for him, will Miss Fanny Armstrong, if I know anything. Mr Brown tells me that the old man had to kick his arse this morning to get him up to scratch, 'cos he played up like hell. She was all right for a roll in the feather tick, but marriage no. Still, beggars can't be choosers, not when the bums are in, and it means the end of Master Big Head Dick if she doesn't . . .'

When Waite was dragged by the collar of his tight-necked, braided uniform coat and flung against the wall of the corridor he was dazed for a moment, but only for a moment, because the next thing he knew was that he was struggling with the young master, and fighting as if for his life.

When he again hit the wall it was Ord's arm this time that had thrust him there, and he slumped for a moment until he heard Dick Mallen yell at him, 'Out! Out! you swine. Do you hear? Out! You're dismissed. If you're not out of the grounds within half an hour . . .'

Waite pulled himself upright from the wall, but he didn't slink away under the fury of the young master as many another servant would have done, for there was in him a stubbornness born of a long line of protesting peasants. His grandparents and great-grandparents had originally worked on the land, but his father had been forced into the pit at the age of seven and when his first child was born he had stated bitterly and firmly, 'This is one who won't have chains atween his legs an' be pulling a bogie when he's seven. My God! no, I'll see to that.' And he had seen to it, for he had put the boy into service.

Harry Waite had started first as a stable lad but soon, the ambitions of his father prompting him, he had turned his eyes towards the house, for promotion was quicker there and the work was easier and you weren't out in all weathers. He had been in two situations before coming to the Hall five years ago, and since then he had married and his wife had given him two children and was on the point of being delivered of a third.

This morning the fortunes of the house had worried him almost as much as it was worrying his master. Positions were difficult to get, particularly if you had to house a wife and three children; but being turned off because of the fortunes of the house was one thing, being thrown out without a reference was entirely another, and something to be fought against. And now the resilience of his father, and his father's father, against injustice came spurting up in protest, and he dared to face the young upstart, as he thought of him, and say in no deferential terms, 'Oh no, I don't; I don't go out of here by your orders, sir, 'cos I wasn't bonded by you; if anybody's tellin' me to go it'll be the master, not you.'

Even Ord was aghast; as for Mr Dunn, who had just come through the green-baized door and was staring with an incredulous expression at the scene, he was too overcome by the enormity of what he was witnessing to utter a word. Then, his training coming to the fore, he regained his composure and was about to step forward when he was startled by the young master leaping past him and almost overbalancing him as he rushed towards the gun room door.

His intention was so plain to everyone that pandemonium, or something near to it, took place, for now Dunn and Ord almost leapt on Waite and dragged him along the passage and into the kitchen, there to be confronted by the startled staff and three sombre-faced men.

As the butler, releasing Waite, pushed him forward, hissing, 'Get yourself away out, man,' Fanny Armstrong's voice came from the corridor, crying, 'No! no!' Then the kitchen door burst open again

31

and Dick Mallen stood there with a long-barrelled gun in his hand. Lifting it to his shoulder, he pointed it to where Waite, who was actually on his way to the far door, had stopped and turned, scarcely believing that the young master could mean to shoot him, yet at the same time knowing that he would.

'Ten seconds . . . I give you ten seconds!'

Whether it was that Waite couldn't quite take in the situation as real, or that his innate stubbornness was preventing him from obeying the command, he did not turn towards the door and run; not even when the kitchen maids screamed and huddled into a corner with the cook, while Dunn and Ord protested loudly, 'Master Dick! Master Dick!' but keeping their distance the while.

The three bailiffs too stood where they were; that is, until Dick Mallen, narrowing his eyes, looked along the barrel of the gun. Then the one who had done the talking so far said in a voice that held authority, 'Put that gun down, sir, or else you'll do somebody an injury.'

Dick Mallen's eyes flickered for a moment from the gun to the bailiff, and now his hatred of him and all his breed came over in his words as he growled. 'Mind it isn't you.'

When the bailiff sprang forward and gripped the gun there was a moment's struggle in which no one interfered. Then, as Dick Mallen had thrust Waite against the wall only a few minutes previously, now he found himself pushed backwards against the long dresser with the gun across his chest. The indignity was not to be borne. Lifting his knee up he thrust it into the bailiff's belly, then rotating the gun, he brought the butt across the side of the man's head. The bailiff heeled over and hit the stone floor with a dull thud.

There followed a moment of concerted stunned silence, then the women's screams not only filled the kitchen but vibrated through the house.

Only one woman hadn't screamed. Fanny Armstrong had just gasped before turning and fleeing along the corridor, through the green-baized door into the hall, calling, 'Father! Father! Father! Father!'

Like the rest of the household, Frank Armstrong was making his way into the hall, Thomas by his side. They had both been in the library, where Thomas had tactfully touched on the subject of a substantial loan, and Frank Armstrong after humming and ha-ing had then come into the open and said, 'Well, it's up to the youngsters, Turk. You know what I want in that direction; if my girl's happy, I'm happy and I'm willin' to pay for it.' It was at the exact moment when Thomas was exhaling one long-drawn breath of relief that the screams rang through the house. Now as he watched Fanny Armstrong throw herself into her father's arms, he cried, 'What is it? what is it?' But he received no answer, until Dunn, bursting through the door into the hall, came to his side; then was unable to get his words out.

'What is it, man? What is it, those women screaming?'

'Sir ... sir, an ... an accident.' The imperturbable butler was visibly shaking. 'M ... Master Dick, the bailiff, he ... the bailiff, he's injured. Master Dick used his gun on him.'

Thomas glared at the man as if he were about to accuse him of being drunk which he knew he could have done any night after the man's duties were over. Then he bounded across the hall, banging wide the green-baized door, down the corridor and into the kitchen. But he stopped dead just within the doorway. The expression on his face was much the same as had been on his butler's when he had come upon the scene in the corridor not more than five minutes earlier.

Thomas now walked slowly towards the man lying on the floor and looked down at him. His companions had opened his coat, his vest, and his shirt, and one of them had placed his hand on the man's heart, the other was attempting to staunch the blood pouring from the side of his head and face.

'Is ... is he bad?' Thomas's words were thin and scarcely audible. One of the two men turned a sickly white face up to him and said, 'Seems so, sir; but he's still breathin'.'

Thomas now swept his glance around the kitchen. Everyone, including his son, seemed fixed as in a tableau. The screaming had stopped; the only sounds came from the girls huddled in the corner of the room.

Thomas's gaze turned on his son. Dick was standing by a side table, on which the gun now lay. He had one hand still on the barrel, the other was hanging limply by his side; his face, which had been red with fury, now looked ashen. He gazed at his father, wetted his lips, then muttered low, ''Twas an accident. An accident ... I was out to frighten that –' he lifted a trembling finger and pointed to where Waite was standing utterly immobile looking like a mummy which had been taken from its long rest. No muscle of his face moved; he was not even blinking.

Thomas now let out a bellow and, turning to the doorway where Frank Armstrong was standing side by side with the butler, he yelled at Dunn, 'Send the coach! Get a doctor, quick! Clear those women out.' He swept his arm towards the corner of the kitchen. 'Get them to bring a door and bring the man upstairs. . . . See to it, Ord. You!' – he was pointing at the cook now – 'Get hot water. Move! Move yourself.'

The kitchen came to life, scurrying, frightened, apprehensive life.

Frank Armstrong now moved slowly forward and stood at Thomas's side and looked down at the man for a moment before

33

slanting his narrowed gaze towards where Dick was standing, his hand still on the gun. Then without a word, he turned and walked out of the kitchen and back into the hall, where Fanny was supporting herself against the balustrade at the bottom of the stairs. Without a word he took her arm and together they went up the stairs and into her room, and there, facing her, he said, 'How did it come about?'

Fanny Armstrong stared at her father. She was not an emotional type of woman, she was not given to tears. Frank Armstrong couldn't remember when he last saw her cry, but now as he watched the tears slowly well into her eyes and fall down her cheeks he put his arm about her and, leading her to a chair, said, 'Tell me.'

And she told him.

She began by saying, 'It was because he heard a servant, the footman, speaking the truth about him,' and, her lips trembling, she ended with deep bitterness, 'The whole house knows he was being forced into asking me and that he hated the very idea of it. You know something? I hope the man dies, and he dies too for what he's done because I hate him. I hate him. I hate him. Oh Father, let us get out of here, now, now.' The next minute her face was buried against his waistcoat and he had to press her tight into him to stifle the sound of her sobbing.

5

THERE WERE FOUR PEOPLE in the house who weren't aware of what had taken place during the last hour. They were Miss Brigmore, Mary Peel and the children.

Miss Brigmore, Mary thought, had turned almost human over the last few hours. She told herself that never in her life had she seen anyone change so quickly, and when Miss Brigmore, taking her aside, told her of what she planned to do that very day, well, she couldn't believe her ears, she just couldn't.

And this is what Miss Brigmore had worked out. She, Mary, was to go down into the drawing room, or the dining room, whichever room she found empty, and unbeknown to anyone she was to pick up small pieces of silver, such as silver napkin rings and a Georgian cruet. One wouldn't be missed as there were three of them on the table most days. Then there was the small Georgian silver tea service that was in the cabinet in the drawing room, there were six pieces and a tray. She was to take large pins and pin anything with handles to her petticoats – did you ever hear anything like it? And Miss Brigmore had even demonstrated how she was to do it. Then, when she had got as much small silver as possible, she was to take from here and there in the display cabinets cameos and snuff boxes. She had really gaped at Miss Brigmore when she had told her the exact positions of the pieces; she herself had been in this house almost three times as long as Miss Brigmore and she couldn't have told what was in the cabinets, let alone just where each piece was placed. When she had got her breath back she had asked, 'But what'll we do with all that stuff? They'll take account of up here an' all.'

'Don't be stupid, Mary,' Miss Brigmore had said, reverting to her usual tone. 'They won't remain long up here.'

'But how will we get them out, an' where will we put them?'

'Mary' – Miss Brigmore's voice had been slow and patient – 'the children will be going to live at the cottage, won't they? I shall most

35

certainly be accompanying them, very likely you too, and I should not be surprised if the master doesn't reside there for a time. ....'

'The master at the cottage!'

'Yes,' said Miss Brigmore, 'the master at the cottage, Mary. Now these men start taking an inventory the moment they enter a room, they take mental stock of almost everything they see, bailiffs have eyes like lynxes, nothing escapes them, so it would be foolish, very foolish don't you think, if after collecting the articles we were to leave them up here, or that we should leave the collecting until later for that matter?'

'Yes, miss,' Mary had answered.

'So you will take the children for their airing as you do every day, but today I shall accompany you, and we shall carry as many things as possible on our persons. What can't be pinned or sewn on we must insert in our bodices. The children will help. We can fasten their cloaks with cameos. ... Now, listen carefully. ....'

Miss Brigmore then told Mary where the articles in question were placed, and she ended, 'Go to the drawing room first and if you find it empty, collect the miniatures and snuff boxes, and should anyone ask you what you are about refer them to me; just tell them to come to the nursery and see Miss Brigmore.'

And Mary did exactly as she was told. She had even enjoyed doing it, getting one over on them bums, who were spoiling everything, finishing the Hall off, an' the master an' all. But eeh! wasn't that Miss Brigmore a surprise? Who would have thought it? She was acting like she was almost human.

Mary made four journeys from the nursery to the ground floor and only one person had asked her what she was about. This was Waite. 'What you up to there, Mary?' he said. 'You can't get away with that. You want to end up along the line?'

'I'm doin' what I'm told, Harry,' she answered tartly. 'You go and see Miss Brigmore.'

'So that's it,' he said.

'That's it,' she answered.

'That one knows what she's about. What's she going to do with them?' said Waite.

'Take them to the cottage for the master.'

'Well, he's likely to need what they'll bring afore he's finished, I suppose. Here, I'll give you a hand,' he said.

But to his proposal she answered, 'No, I know what I'm to get, but you could keep the coast clear outside and if anybody makes for here or the dining room, cough.'

So Miss Brigmore and her charges and Mary Peel went out for a walk before noon. They walked slowly until they were out of sight of the house and then they walked more quickly through the gardens. But their pace was controlled by the weight of their petticoats. They went out through the main gates and along the coach road to the cottage, where, there being no cellar, Miss Brigmore ordered Mary to look in the outhouses for a hammer and chisel. When these were found Miss Brigmore pushed the dining room carpet back until it touched the stout, claw-footed leg of the table, then using the hammer and chisel as if so doing were an everyday occurrence to her, she prised up the nine-inch floor board.

After thrusting her hand down into the dark depths, she said, 'This'll do nicely; there's a draught of air passing through and the bottom is rough stone. Now Mary, and you, children, hand me the pieces, carefully, one after the other. There is no need to wrap them as they won't rest here long.'

Constance giggled as she passed her pieces to Miss Brigmore. She was finding the business exciting, whereas Barbara on the other hand showed no outward sign of feeling at all.

Although Miss Brigmore had tried to turn the whole episode into a game Barbara knew it had a very serious side. She was overwhelmed by a sense of insecurity and she remembered this feeling from as far back as the time when her Uncle Thomas had first brought her to the Hall.

Miss Brigmore sensed the feeling in her charge, and after she had replaced the floor board and the carpet was rolled back and the house door closed, she took Barbara's hand and said, 'Come, you and I shall race Mary and Constance to the main road.'

Barbara, too, saw that Miss Brigmore had changed, but in spite of this and the new softness in her, she was still seeing her as she had done the previous night lying on the bed moaning, and she knew she was wicked.

It was with a certain sense of triumph that Miss Brigmore finally marshalled her pirate company through the main gates after their second visit to the cottage. The day was closing in, it was bitterly cold and raining, but the weather didn't trouble her. The last time she had been engaged in such a manoeuvre she had failed, at least her mother had, and it was only the timely assistance of a friend that had prevented her mother being taken before the Justices. But this time she had succeeded. At a rough estimate she guessed they had retrieved some thousand pounds' worth of objects, the miniatures being the most valuable. Of course, she admitted to herself, she might have been precipitate in her action for the master had a good friend in Mr Armstrong. Moreover, if the match between Miss Fanny and Master Dick were to be arranged then the problem would be solved, and indeed her action might be frowned upon – or laughed at, which would be harder to bear. But as Mr Brown had confided in her only yesterday, he had his grave doubts concerning Master Dick's intentions. To quote his own words, Master Dick was a bit of an unruly stallion, and he couldn't see Miss Fanny Armstrong breaking him in. In Mr Brown's opinion, apart from her being much too old for him, she wasn't his type; some stallions, for all their temper and show of strength, had tender mouths, and his guess was that Miss Fanny would pull too hard on the bit.

Mr Brown's similes always favoured the stables. She sometimes wondered how he had chosen the profession of valet, seeing his knowledge, and apparently his sympathies, lay so much with the four-footed creatures. Nevertheless she was inclined to take Mr Brown's opinion with some seriousness for he had proved himself to be right on other occasions with regards both to the master and Master Dick.

It was as she was crossing the drive, ushering the children and Mary quickly before her out of the rain, that she had a mental picture of herself explaining her actions to the master, at the opportune moment of course, and the opportune moment, as seen in her mind, brought a warm, exciting glow to her body, for now she could see no end to the opportune moments. If the master's affairs were in order such moments would continue at intervals; if he were forced through circumstances to retire to the cottage they would most certainly continue and more frequently. Whichever way things went she felt that for once she couldn't lose. Her cloistered, nun-like days were over. She had never been cut out for celibate life. Yet her early upbringing had made it impossible for her to find bodily expression with those males who, in the hierarchy of the staff, were classed as fitting mates for a governess; such were valets and house stewards.

She did not guide her charges towards the front door, nor yet round the corner into the courtyard to the back door, but going in the opposite direction she marshalled them round the side of the house and along the whole length of the back terrace until she entered the courtyard from the stable end. Then, opening a narrow door, she pushed the children into the passage, followed them and was in turn followed by Mary.

Mr Tweedy, the steward, Mr Dunn, the butler, and the housekeeper, Mrs Brydon, who had all been in deep conversation, turned startled faces towards her, and such were their expressions that she was brought to a halt and enquired, 'What has happened?'

It was Mrs Brydon who spoke. 'A dreadful thing, a dreadful thing, Miss Brigmore. You wouldn't believe it; none of us can believe it. Master Dick ... Master Dick attacked one of the bailiffs, the head one. He was going to shoot Waite, I mean Master Dick was, and the bailiff went to stop him. It's all through Waite, he started the trouble. They've sent for the doctor. He's bad the bailiff, very bad. He could go like that, just like that.' She made a soundless snap with her fingers.

It was Mr Dunn who said in a very low voice, 'If he does, Master Dick could swing for it seeing it's a bailiff.'

'Quiet! That is enough.' Miss Brigmore's voice thundered over them, then she turned from them and pushed the gasping children along the passage and up the stairs, leaving Mary behind.

Mary stood and gaped at her superiors, then she muttered, 'Waite? What's happened to him?'

The steward's voice was the voice of authority now, head of the household under the master. 'He is packing his belongings and going this very hour . . . now.'

'But . . . but Daisy; she's on her time, they can't . . .'

'Peel!' Mrs Brydon checked Mary's further protest. 'Enough. It's none of your business. What is your business is to see to the nursery, and get you gone there this instant.'

After a moment's hesitation Mary went, but slowly, not thinking now of the Master or of Master Dick, or even of the bailiff, but of Daisy Waite and her trouble. The bairn could come any day, she was over her time; and look at the weather. She paused at a window on the first landing and looked out. Through the blur of rain she could see the family cottages, as they were called. They were allotted to those of the staff who had children yet were in indoor service. The three houses were attached to the end of the stables. As she stared, the door of the middle cottage opened and a man came out and although she couldn't identify the figure through the rain she knew it was Harry Waite, for he was lifting a box on to a flat hand-cart that stood outside the door.

The hand-cart, which was nothing but a glorified barrow, had caused a great deal of laughter when he had arrived with his belongings on it five years ago. No one had ever heard of a footman coming to take up a position pushing a hand-cart. But he had withstood the laughter, for apparently his father had made the hand-cart for him when he first went into service, with the words 'When you've got enough luggage to cover that, lad, you'll be all right.' And now, thought Mary tearfully, he had more than enough luggage, he had two children and a wife ready for her bed. What would happen to them? Where would they go? She wanted to run out and say good-bye to them because Daisy was her friend. But Mrs Brydon was still in the passage, she could hear her voice.

She went heavily up the remaining stairs shaking her head as she said to herself, 'Eeh! the things that have happened this day; it's like the end of the world, it is that.'

6

THE HOUSE was quiet. It was like the quiet that follows a hurricane; it was so peaceful that if it wasn't for the debris no one would believe that a storm had recently passed that way.

The quiet hit Thomas with the force of deep resonant sound as he entered the Hall. Dunn had not met him at the outer door as was usual – Dunn hadn't time these days to listen for the carriage and be there to take his hat, coat and stick, for Dunn was now doing the work of a number of men – and so as he came hurrying from the direction of the study and towards Thomas he said, 'I'm sorry, sir.'

Thomas waved his hand. He had helped himself off with his coat, which he now handed to Dunn, saying, 'Has anyone called?'

'Mr Ferrier's man brought a letter, sir; it's in the study.'

Thomas walked quickly across the hall and into the study. The letter was propped against a paper-weight on the only clear space on his desk. He did not take up the slender hoof-handled paper-knife to open it, but inserted his finger under the flap and whipped it across the top.

He stood while reading the letter. It was short; it said: 'Dear Thomas. You know without my saying that I sympathize deeply with you in your trouble, and if it were possible for me to help you to any great extent you know I would do so, but things are at a critical stage in the works at present. As I told you when I saw you last I'm having to close down the factory at Shields. However, if a couple of hundred would be of any use you're very welcome, but I'm sorry I can't rise to a thousand. Drop in any time you feel like it, you'll always be welcome, you know that.' It was signed simply, 'John.'

'You'll always be welcome.' The words came like grit through his teeth. He couldn't believe it. He just couldn't believe it. He crushed the letter in his hand and, putting it on the desk, he beat it flat with his fist. After a moment he sat down in the high-backed leather chair behind the desk and drooped his head on to his chest. Armstrong, Headley, and now Ferrier, men he'd have sworn would have stood by him to the death, for they were his three best friends; moreover they were men on whom he had lavished the best of his house. Why, when John Ferrier's eldest son, Patrick, was married he bought the pair silver plate to the value of more than six hundred pounds; and when their first child was born his christening mug, plate and spoon had cost something, and now here was John, his very good friend, saying he could manage a couple of hundred. It would have been better if he had done what Frank Armstrong had done and ignored his plea altogether. His appeal to Frank had been returned, saying that Mr Armstrong, his wife and daughter had gone to London, and their stay would be indefinite. . . . And Ralph Headley? He had pushed business his way when he was a struggling nobody, he could almost say he had made him. What was more, for years he had supplemented his income with money he had lost to him in gambling. In his young days he would bet on a fly crawling up the window, and he had done just that, a hundred pounds at a time, and had paid up smiling because it was to Ralph, and Ralph needed a hand.

And because he knew just how much he had helped Ralph he had asked him for the loan of three thousand: enough to cover Dick's bail and to clear the servants' wages and see him over the next few months. But what had Ralph sent? a cheque for three hundred pounds. Margaret's wedding was going to cost him something, he said, and the young devil, George, had been spending money like water. Later on perhaps, when he knew how he stood after the wedding, he'd likely be able to help him further.

The condescension that had emanated from that particular letter, and something more, something that had come over in the refusal of his friends to stand by him in this terrible moment of his life, had hit him like a blow between the eyes and blurred for a time the knowledge that was pressing against his pride and self-esteem. But now that knowledge had forced its way into the open and could be described by one word, dislike. At one time he would have put the term, 'jealousy', to it, but not anymore. He knew now what he had really known for years; he had no friends. These men had really disliked him, as many such had disliked his father before him. He was a Mallen; Turk Mallen his supposed friends called him because his misdeeds had left their mark on the heads of his fly-blows. All men whored, but the results of his whoring had a brand on them. He was Turk Mallen, 'the man with a harem in the hills,' as one wit had said. All right, he had made cuckolds out of many men, but he had never let a friend down, nor taken a liberty with his wife, nor shied a gambling debt, and no child born of him had ever gone hungry; not to his knowledge.

A knock came on the door and Dunn entered bearing a tray.

'I thought you might like something hot, sir.'

'Oh, yes, yes, Dunn.' Thomas looked down into the steaming mug that held hot rum, and he sniffed and gave a wry smile as he said, 'This must be running short by now.'

'I've managed to secure a certain number of bottles, sir.'

'Ah! Well now, that was good thinking.' Again the wry smile. 'They'll be a comfort, in more ways than one.'

'Is there anything more you need, sir?'

Thomas sipped at the rum, then said, 'How many of you are left?'

Dunn moved one lip over the other before he replied, 'Besides Mr Brown and Mr Tweedy, there is Mrs Brydon and, of course, Miss Brigmore and Mary Peel.'

'Six.'

'Yes, six, sir, indoors, but there are two still in the stables. They . . . they will have to remain there until . . .' His voice trailed off.

'Yes, yes, of course. Where is Mr Tweedy now?'

'Visiting the farms, sir. As you ordered, leaving just the bare staff.'

Thomas now looked down at the desk, his eyes sweeping over the mass of papers and bills arrayed there. Then he took another sip from the tankard before looking up at Dunn again and saying, 'You'll be all right, Dunn; I'll give you a good reference. Just . . . just tell me when you want to go. There are a number of houses that'll jump at you.'

'There's no hurry, sir, none whatever.'

'Well, you can't live on air, Dunn, no more than any of us. I won't be able to pay you after this week.'

'I'm fully aware of that, sir. Still, there's no hurry. Mrs Brydon is of the same opinion; as is Mr Tweedy; and I'm sure you can rely on Mr Brown.'

Thomas now lowered his head. Forty staff he'd employed in the house and the farms and six were quite willing to stay with him until such times as they were all turfed out. You could say it was a good percentage. Strange where one found one's friends. He looked up at Dunn and said, 'Thank them for me, will you? I'll . . . I'll see them personally later.'

'Yes, sir.'

As Dunn was about to turn away he stopped and said, 'May I enquire how Master Dick is, sir?'

Thomas stretched his thick neck up out of his collar before saying, 'Putting as good a face on it as he can, Dunn. I . . . I had hopes of being able to bail him out but –' he tapped the crumpled letter that was lying to his hand now and said, 'I'm afraid I haven't succeeded.' Strange how one could talk like this to one's butler, and in an ordinary tone, without any command or condescension on the one hand or false hee-hawing on the other, as one was apt to do with one's friends.

'I'm sorry, sir.'

'So am I, Dunn, so am I. By the way, where are the men?' He did not call them bailiffs.

'Two are in the library, sir, cataloguing the books, the other is up in the west wing doing the bedrooms.'

'How much longer are they likely to take do you think?'

'Two days, three at the most I should say, sir.'

Thomas now narrowed his eyes and thought for a moment before he said, 'By the way, cook went three days ago didn't she? Who's doing the cooking now?'

'Well, sir –' Dunn inclined his head slightly towards him ' –Mrs Brydon and myself are managing quite well, and Miss Brigmore has been of some assistance. She has seen to the children's meals and to her own and Peel's.'

'Thank you, Dunn.'

'Thank you, sir.'

Alone once more, Thomas sat back in the chair and, stretching one hand, he pressed his first finger and thumb tightly on to his eyeballs. He had forgotten about the children because he hadn't seen them for days, she had kept them out of his way. Funny, he thought of her as she. Why? It was much too personal a tag to attach to her prim little packet of flesh. Yet she had thawed. Yes, she had indeed. Anyway, he was glad the children had her, and that they had a home to go to, and two hundred a year between them. But could they exist on two hundred a year? Well, they would have to. What did she get? He opened a drawer to the side of him and took out a long ledger and, turning the pages, he brought his finger down to the name. Brigmore ... Brigmore, Anna, employed as governess from the first of September, 1844, at a salary of forty-five pounds per annum. He noted that there was no mention against this of an allowance of beer, tea or sugar.

Forty-five pounds, that would make a big hole in the two hundred. Then there must be someone to do the work. The Peel girl, how much was she getting? He turned back the pages. Mary Peel, bonded, third kitchen maid, two pounds twelve shillings per annum, extra beer, sugar and tea allowed; promoted second kitchen maid at five pounds per annum; promoted nursery maid 1844 at twelve pounds per annum, extra beer, tea and sugar allowed.

Well, that was another twelve pounds. That would hardly leave three pounds a week to feed them all. Could it be done. He doubted it.

What could one get for three pounds a week? What could four people get for three pounds a week?

. . . And what are you going to do?

It was as if someone were asking the question of him and he shook his head slowly from side to side. If it wasn't for Dick he knew what he would do and this very night, for here he was without a penny to his name and no prospect of having one in the future. Even if the estate sold well, and the contents of the house also, he knew it would not give his creditors twenty shillings in the pound.

But damn his creditors, damn them to hell's flames, each and every one of them, for almost without exception they had overcharged him for years. Why, he asked himself now as he stared at the row of sporting prints hanging above the mantelpiece opposite to him, why hadn't he been like others under similar circumstances and made a haul while the going was good? Even Dunn had had the foresight to look to himself and secure some bottles, and he would like to bet that there wasn't a servant in the house but had helped himself to something. But he, what had he done? Well, what had he done? Could he, when the house was in an uproar, when his son had gone to pieces, when the place was swarming with officers of the law, deliberating whether it might be manslaughter or excusable homicide if the man were to die, and seeming to infer that the eventual penalty would be severe because the victim happened to be a law man, could he then have gone round surreptitiously acquiring his own valuables? Yet there was not one of his so-called friends who would believe that he hadn't done so, either before or after the bailiff incident. No one but a fool, they would say, would let bums have it all their own way, and Turk Mallen was no fool. . . . Yet Thomas Mallen, the Thomas Mallen he knew himself to be, was a fool and always had been.

But now it was Dick he must think about; he must get him bailed out of there or by the time the trial came up he would be a gibbering idiot. Thank God it looked as if the man was going to survive, otherwise there would have been no question of bail. As it was, they had made it stiff, a thousand pounds.

He had never expected Dick to break as he had done. He had imagined, up till recently, there was a tough side to him, or had he just hoped there was? His own father used to say, a man can be fearless when cornered by a rutting stag as long as he's on a horse and has a gun to hand. But meet up with the stag when on his feet and empty-handed, and who do you think will run first?

Dick had met the stag in the form of the law and he had neither gun nor horse. As he had looked on him today in that stark, bare room he had felt both pity and scorn for him, aye, yes, and a touch of loathing, because it was he, this son of his, and he alone, who had brought them

44

all to such a pass. But for the false pride that had made him turn on that bloody ingrate of a footman, everything would have been settled between him and Fanny Armstrong and no doubt at this very moment the whole Hall would have been in a frenzy of preparations for the engagement banquet, whereas he would now be lucky to have one course for a meal tonight.

He sat with his head bowed until his thoughts touched on the children again; he must see to them, get them out of this and to the cottage, the atmosphere of the house wasn't good for anyone anymore. Slowly he reached out and rang the bell, thinking as he did so what it would be like to ring a bell and have no one answer it – well, he would soon know, that was certain.

It was some minutes before Dunn made his appearance and then, deferential as ever, he stood just within the door and said, 'Yes, sir?'

'Tell Miss Brigmore I'd like to see her for a moment . . . please.' Again he felt a tightness in his collar and he ran his finger around the edge of it. That was the first time he could ever remember saying please to his butler. Sometimes he had given him a perfunctory thanks, but that was all. Had one to be destitute before becoming aware of good manners? Strange that he should learn something at this time of trial. . . .

When Miss Brigmore knocked on the study door she was immediately bidden to enter. After closing the door quietly behind her, she walked slowly up to the desk and looked at her master. Her look was open and held no trace of embarrassment. She was grateful to him for ending her years of virginity, her years of personal torment. She had never been able to see any virtue in chastity, and had questioned the right of a piece of paper which legalized a natural desire, a desire which, indulged in before the signing of the paper, earned for the female the title of wanton, or whore, while it was considered the natural procedure for a male, even making him into a dashing fellow, a real man, and a character. She had strong secret views on the rights of the individual – the female individual in particular, and it was only the necessity to earn her livelihood that had kept them secret, and herself untouched, this far.

Still she knew that had Thomas Mallen never taken her she would still have cared for him, looked up to him, and feared him a little. Now she no longer looked up to him nor feared him, but she loved him.

'Sit down –' he paused '– Anna.'

'Thank you.' She did not add 'sir'. He had used her Christian name, there was no need now for titles.

'It's about the children. I . . . I don't know whether you are aware –'

he knew she was aware all right, every servant in the house was aware of everything appertaining to his business '– but the children jointly own the cottage and have an income of two hundred pounds a year between them. Now –' he paused and ran his tongue round his lips '– if you'll still consent to take charge of them they could afford to pay you your salary, also perhaps Peel's too, though it would not leave much for living. I'm afraid your fare would be rather scanty, as would other amenities, so I . . . I shall not take it amiss if you decide to terminate your agreement.'

Anna Brigmore would have liked to retort at this moment 'Don't be silly!' What she said was, 'I have already arranged to go to the cottage with the children; everything is in order, the rooms are ready . . . yours too.' She paused here, then added, 'sir', for it seemed at this point a title was called for. 'That is, if you wish for a temporary dwelling before you make other arrangements. The house appears small at first, but it is really quite roomy. I've had the furniture rearranged and fresh drapes hung; the place is quite comfortable. What is more, I took the liberty of transferring some of your belongings . . . objects, of the smaller type, to the cottage. Certain pieces which I think are of some considerable value, and which . . .'

'You what?' He had jerked himself forward in his chair and now, with his forearms on the desk, he was leaning towards her and he repeated, 'You what?'

'I arranged for some objects from the cases in the drawing room to be transferred and . . . and with the assistance of Mary Peel and the children they are now safely hidden in the cottage.'

'An-na.' A smile was spreading over his face and he shook his head as he looked at the prim figure sitting before him, prim but pretty. He had noticed her prettiness six years ago when he had first met her, and had remarked laughingly to himself, 'This one's chastity belt's secured all right.' It was strange, he thought now, that she should be the first indoor servant he had taken. He had made a rule never to tamper with indoor servants. His father had put him up to this. 'It's always embarrassing,' he had said, 'to see bellies swelling inside the house and you having to deny claim for your own handiwork. Keep your sporting well outside; your own farms if you must, but further afield is always safer.' But there had been something about Miss Anna Brigmore, something that appealed to him; not only had he wanted to end her virginity but he'd had the desire to strip the primness from her and expose the prettiness. Well, he had taken her virginity, but he hadn't managed to strip the primness from her. She was still Miss Brigmore, softer in a way, yes, but nevertheless Miss Brigmore, even when he addressed her as Anna.

But Miss Brigmore had had the sense to do what he should have done or at least have ordered someone to do on the side. He could have said to Brown, 'See that my personal belongings are put in a safe place.' How many sets of gold cuff links and odds and ends had Brown tucked away in his own valise? He wasn't blaming Brown, he wasn't blaming any of them, let them get what they could while the going was good. But Miss Brigmore hadn't thought of herself, she had thought of him, and his future needs. Strange ... strange the quarters from which help came.

'What did you take?' he asked quietly.

'I should imagine about fifty pieces in all.'

'*Fifty pieces!*' He grimaced in disbelief.

'Some I should imagine more valuable than others, such as the pair of Swiss snuff boxes and the Louis XVI enamelled one.'

His eyes crinkled at the corner and he said softly, 'Fifty! and the Louis snuff box among them?'

'Yes.'

'How did you know what to take?'

Her chin moved slightly upwards before she said, 'I read a great deal about such things. What is more, my parents found themselves in a similar situation to yourself when I was sixteen.'

His mouth was open, and his head nodded twice before he said, 'They did?'

'Yes.'

'And ... and you managed to secure some trinkets of your own before ...?'

'No; we weren't successful. The articles were discovered for the simple reason that there were in no way as many pieces to choose from. The result was very trying.'

He nodded again, saying, 'Yes, it would be.' Then going on, he added, 'Yet knowing it could be very trying here too, you transferred fifty pieces to the cottage? How did you do it?'

'I ... I selected certain things, and ordered Mary Peel to bring them up to the nursery; then I pinned or sewed what could be pinned or sewed to ... to our undergarments; the other pieces we managed to secrete on our persons.'

In blank silence he stared at her ... 'You must have done all this before ... before the accident, and made several journeys, it's some distance to the cottage.'

'Only two journeys, and the children looked upon it as a game. If ... if you would care to come to the cottage you will be able to judge for yourself as to the value of what is there. I would have informed you sooner but there has not been the opportunity.'

Slowly he rose from the chair and came round the desk and, standing over her, he put out his hand and when she had placed hers in

47

it he pressed it tightly, saying, 'Whatever they're worth, tuppence or ten thousand, Anna, thank you, thank you.'

Her eyes blinked, her mouth pursed; then, her face suddenly relaxing, she smiled up at him softly as she said, 'I only wish I'd had more time.'

Drawing her to her feet he gazed at her for a moment before saying, 'We will go now to the cottage. Bring the children. It will appear as if we are taking a stroll.'

She looked at him as if he were proposing just that, a stroll with him along a country lane. . . .

Half an hour later they walked down the long drive and through the lodge gates, which Thomas opened himself and found it a strange experience for he hadn't realized how heavy they were. They walked briskly for it was a cold, raw day. The sky was lying low and heavy on the hills and promised snow. After a short while Thomas's step slowed considerably for he found he was out of breath, and he lightly chided the children, saying, 'If you want to gallop, you gallop, but let me trot.' And the children ran on ahead; but Miss Brigmore suited her step to his.

When at last they reached the gate of the cottage he leaned on it and stood looking at the house before him. It was built of grey granite; it had been built to withstand wind and weather, and no softness had been incorporated into its design. He followed Miss Brigmore up the narrow winding path and watched her insert the key in the lock, then they all went inside.

'Well, well!' Thomas stood in the small hall and looked about him. It wasn't the first time he had been in the cottage but he remembered it as a dull characterless place; now, even this little hall looked different.

There were five doors leading out of the hall and they were all open. He walked towards the first one to the left of him; it led into a sitting room, tiny by the standards of the Hall, being only fifteen by twenty feet in length he imagined. Yet it looked a comfortable room, solidly comfortable, although at a glance he would say there wasn't one piece of furniture of any value in it.

He turned and smiled at Miss Brigmore, and when Constance grabbed his hand and cried, 'Come on and see the dining room, Uncle,' he allowed himself to be tugged into the next room. Here he stood nodding his head as he looked about him, saying, 'Very, very nice, very nice. You should be quite happy here.' He looked down at Constance and then at Barbara. Barbara wasn't smiling. That was the difference in these two little sisters, Constance always appeared happy, whereas you could never tell whether Barbara was happy or not. He said to her now, 'Do you like the cottage, Barbara?'

'Yes, Uncle.'

'You'd like living here?'

She paused for a moment before saying again, 'Yes, Uncle.'

'I'll love living here, Uncle.' Constance was tugging at his hand again, crying now, 'Come and see your study.'

'My . . .?' He did not look at the child but turned and looked towards where Miss Brigmore was walking into the hall, and again he allowed himself to be tugged out of the room and through the third doorway and into a smaller room. He looked at the long narrow table that served as a desk, at the leather chair, the leather couch, and at the end of the room the two glass doors opening out on to a small terrace.

'This is your room, Uncle, your study.'

He turned to face Miss Brigmore, but Miss Brigmore was not in the room. He could see her now ascending the bare oak staircase.

'Come and see your bedroom, Uncle.' As Constance led him towards the stairs she pointed to the other two doors leading from the hall, saying, 'That one is the morning room and that one leads to the kitchen,' and she added to this, 'The kitchen requires a lot of seeing to; the stove smokes.'

He was on the landing now and being tugged towards a second door that led off from it. 'This is your bedroom, Uncle.'

The room was of a fair size, almost as large as the sitting room. It held a four-poster bed, a stout wardrobe and dressing table, but its most significant feature was the unusually large window that gave a view of the foothills and the mountains beyond.

Thomas turned now to where Miss Brigmore was standing in the doorway. Constance was still hanging on to his hand, and the look in his eyes spoke a different language from his words as he said, 'You have transformed the place; I remember it as a very dismal dwelling.'

'There is a toilet room, Uncle, next door too and you won't have to go out in the . . .'

'Constance!'

'Yes, Miss Brigmore.' Constance hung her head knowing that she had touched on a delicate and unmentionable subject.

Miss Brigmore now said hastily as she pushed open another door, 'This is . . . is a spare room for anyone you might wish to stay –' she did not say 'Master Dick' '– and this –' she opened yet another door '– is the children's room.'

'Isn't it pretty, Uncle? and the desk-bed in the corner is for Mary, she doesn't want to sleep in the attic. But isn't it pretty, Uncle?'

'Yes, my dear, it's very pretty.' He patted Constance's head.

Miss Brigmore did not open the fourth door, she merely said, 'That is my room.' Then leading the way down the stairs again, she added, 'If we can dispense with the morning room I would like to turn it into a schoolroom.'

'Do as you wish, Miss Brigmore, do as you wish.' He was nodding down to the back of her head.

In the hall Miss Brigmore looked at Barbara and said, 'Would you like to gather some wood for the fire? It would be nice if we had a fire, wouldn't it? And then we could have a cup of tea.'

'Yes, Miss Brigmore. Come, Connie.' Barbara held out her hand and took Constance's and forced her now to walk out of the room, not run as she was inclined to.

Miss Brigmore looked at Thomas and said quietly, 'They're in here.'

He followed her into the dining room, and watched with amazement as she knelt down and rolled back the carpet and prised up the floor boards with a chisel. When she put her arm down into the hole and began handing him articles of silver, cameos, and trinket boxes he did not utter a word, he just kept shaking his head.

At last the collection was arrayed on the top of the sideboard and the round table, and he stood gazing at it in amazement. Picking up a small Chelsea porcelain figure of a mandarin he fingered it gently, almost lovingly; when he looked at her he found he was still unable to speak. This one piece alone would be worth five hundred, if not more, and then there were the snuff boxes; three of them, no, four. He put out his hand and stroked the Louis XVI gold enamelled box, his fingers tracing the minute necklace that graced the slender neck of the lady depicted in the middle of it.

One after the other he handled the pieces: a pair of George I sugar dredgers; a set of three George I casters; and when he came to the chinoiserie tankard he cupped it in both hands, then, as if it were a child he had lost and found again, he held it tight against his waistcoat while he looked at her. And now he asked quietly, 'What can I say to you, Anna?'

She stared back into his eyes but did not answer.

'An hour ago I was a desperate man; now I'm no longer desperate, you have given me new life.'

There was another silence before she asked in a practical manner, 'Will you be able to sell them immediately?'

He looked away from her for a moment, bit on his lower lip as he nodded his head, and said, 'Yes, yes, Anna, I'll be able to sell them immediately. I know of a gentleman in Newcastle who is of great assistance to people like us.'

Her eyes were unblinking as she kept them fixed on him. He had said 'us'.

'Not that he'll give me half what they're worth; but as long as it's enough to get Dick out of that place. ...'

Miss Brigmore suddenly gasped as she felt herself almost lifted from the ground and pulled into his embrace. He kissed her, his mouth big, warm and soft, covering hers entirely. When at last he let her go she experienced a strange feeling; for the first time in her life she knew what it was to feel like a woman, a mature fulfilled woman. She hadn't experienced this when he came to her room because then he had merely given her his body. Now he had given her something from his heart.

7

FOR FIVE WEEKS now Thomas had been living in the cottage and he had taken his change of circumstances with good grace, hiding the feeling of claustrophobia that the rooms gave him, hiding the feeling of despair when he thought of the future, and hiding the disturbing feeling of disdain whenever he looked at his son, for Dick Mallen had not taken the change with good grace.

To Dick Mallen the cottage appeared merely as an extension of prison. As for thanking the governess for being the means of his temporary liberation, when his father had suggested that he afford Miss Brigmore this courtesy he had looked at him as if he were mad.

Thank the governess for giving them what was theirs! Very likely they had only received half of what she had taken.

Thomas, who up to that moment had kept his temper, had sworn at his son, saying, 'You're an ungrateful sod, Dick, that's what you are, an ungrateful sod.'

After his release Dick Mallen had visited the Hall, but had returned empty-handed. He had been informed, and in no subservient manner, by the bailiff that his strictly personal belongings, which meant his clothes only, had been sent to the cottage; as for the remainder, they had been tabulated against the day of the sale.

He knew that his man Taylor would surely have lined his pockets with cuff links, scarf pins, cravat rings and the like, and he wished he could get his hands on him but the beggar had gone long since, and he couldn't find out if he had become established in another position.

When he thought of the attitudes of their various friends he just couldn't believe it. He could understand Armstrong's reaction but not that of old Headley and Ferrier. Yet he had to admit that Pat Ferrier had turned up trumps. Then, of course, he should, he would have been damn well amazed if he hadn't, for Pat had cleaned him out time and again over the past three years; and after all, what was a few hundred compared to what he had lost to him.

He had said nothing to his father about Pat Ferrier's help. He said little to his father at all these days; the old man, he considered, had gone soft in the head. The way he treated that governess made him sick, for he constantly deferred to her as if she were an equal. One thing he was certain of, her stay would be short once the trial was over. . . . The trial! It was that word that had the power to take the bombast out of him. He was fearing the trial for although the man had recovered they said he was badly scarred; moreover he knew that public opinion would be against him. If only there were some way out. . . .

Thomas too kept thinking, if only there were some way out, but his thoughts did not run along the same channels as his son's. His idea of a way out was to beat the law by engaging one of the finest barristers and to do this he needed money, big money, and all he could call upon was the refund of the bail money and the little that was left over from the sale of Anna's haul, as he came to think of the pieces she had retrieved.

With the exception of two miniatures and a snuff box he had disposed of all the pieces to the certain gentleman in Newcastle. With regard to these three pieces he had private thoughts concerning them, but had decided he would do nothing about them until the sale was over. . . .

It was on Monday the fourteenth of April that the sale of the contents of the ground floor of High Banks Hall began. It was well attended, and the auctioneer was more than pleased with the result at the end of the day.

On Tuesday, the fifteenth, the contents of the first floor were sold; again the result was favourable. On the morning of Wednesday, the sixteenth, the auctioneer dealt with the contents of the nursery floor, the attics and the kitchens. In the afternoon he sold off the contents of the coach-house, the harness rooms, and the servants' quarters. The livestock, such as the coach horses and the four hunters, had been sent to the West Farm, where the sale of all livestock would take place on the Tuesday following Easter Monday.

But it was Thursday, the seventeenth, the day before Good Friday, that was the important day of the sale, for on this day the Hall and the estate, together with its two farms, was put up for auction. The carriages came from County Durham, Cumberland, Westmorland and Yorkshire. There were gathered in the library quite a number of men bearing names that spelt money. Then there were those who held themselves apart. These men had names that didn't only spell money but distinction of class. Yet at the end of the day the Hall had gone neither to a self-made man nor yet to one of title.

The Bank had put a reserve price on the estate and no bidder had touched anywhere near it. The auctioneer had at one time become impatient and as he looked at the men he would have liked, very much, to say, 'Gentlemen, I know why you hesitate, as on such occasions of distraint on property, beggars can't be choosers, you're thinking. But you are mistaken in this case. The Bank wants its money and it means to have it, and is prepared to wait. Oh, I know you gentlemen of old, you think if the estate doesn't go today you will tomorrow put in an offer and we will gladly take it. Oh, I know you of old, Gentlemen.'

What he did say was, 'Gentlemen, this is a very fine estate and I've no need to remind you what it contains, you have it all there in your catalogues; five hundred acres of land containing two productive farms, and then this house, this beautiful and, I will add, grand house. You could not build this house for sixty thousand today, and Gentlemen, what are you offering? Twenty thousand below the asking price. We're wasting each other's time, gentlemen. I'll ask you again: what am I bid over the last bidder of thirty thousand? . . . Well now, well, come, come, Gentlemen. . . . No? Then, I'm afraid that today's business is at an end, Gentlemen.' . . .

Thomas Mallen took the news with a deep sigh, but Dick stormed and ranted until his father turned on him angrily, saying, 'Stop it! stop it! Anyway, what good would it do you if they had bid twenty thousand over the asking price?'

'None. I'm well aware of that, none, but it riles me to think they're harping over a few bloody thousand. Pat tells me the Hamiltons were there from Edinburgh; also the Rosses from Glasgow; they're weighed down with it but both as mean as skilly bowls . . . And God Almighty, how you can sit there and take it calmly! . . .'

'Blast you to hell's flames, boy. Stop your stupid ranting, and don't say again I'm taking it calmly. Let me tell you this, I'm neither taking the loss of my house calmly, nor yet the way my son has conducted himself in this predicament. And I will say it, although I told myself I never would, but for your trying to play the injured master we wouldn't be in this position today. You're weak gutted, underneath all your bombast, boy, you're weak gutted. Only the thought of penury prodded you, but too late as it turned out, to ask Fanny Armstrong, whereas if you'd had any spunk you'd have clinched the matter a year gone, for you were up to your neck then. . . .'

The altercation had taken place in the study on Thursday evening, and Thomas's roar had easily penetrated into the children's bedroom above, where Anna was putting them to bed.

'Uncle's vexed,' said Constance; 'perhaps he didn't like his supper, I didn't like it much. We don't have nice meals now, do we, Miss Brigmore?'

'You have good plain food, that is all you require. Now lie down and go to sleep and no more talking. Good night.'

'Good night, Miss Brigmore.'

Anna turned and looked down at Barbara; then she put her hand out and pulled the sheets over the child's shoulder. 'Good night, Barbara,' she said softly.

'Good night, Miss Brigmore.'

Anna looked down for a moment longer on the child. There was something on her mind; she had changed of late, perhaps she was missing the house. She had never been gay like Constance, she was of a more serious turn of mind, but lately there had been an extra restraint in her manner. She must give her more attention; one was apt to talk more to Constance because Constance was more responsive. Yes, she must pay her more attention.

She left the night light burning and, lifting up the lamp, went out and into her own room, and there, taking the coverlet from the bed, she put it around her and sat down in a chair.

Things had not turned out as she had imagined they would. There had been no cosy nights sitting before the fire in the drawing room, Thomas Mallen on one side of the hearth, herself on the other, she doing her embroidery, he reading; or she had seen them talking; or again laughing down on the children playing on the hearth rug before the fire.

The hour that held the picture would always be the hour between six and seven o'clock in the evening. It was an hour that in most cases was lost in those preceding it and those following it, an hour before dinner or supper according to the household; or yet again the hour after the main meal of the day as in some poorer establishments; the hour before children retired, the hour when the day was not yet ended, and the night not yet begun.

But she had never visualized herself sitting huddled in a bed cover in a cold room during any part of that hour. Yet that is what had happened night after night. However, she made use of this time to collect her thoughts, trying to see the outcome of this terrible business. One outcome that didn't please her at all was the possibility that Master Dick might be found guiltless at his trial, for this would mean that he would take up his abode here permanently, until such time when he should perhaps find something better. She had asked herself if she could put up with such a situation, for Master Dick's manner to her was most uncivil. But she never answered this question because she knew that as long as Thomas Mallen needed her she would stay, and she had the firm conviction inside herself that she was the one person he would need most from now on.

Life could be so pleasant here, so happy, so homely. The children would thrive better here than they had at the Hall. They had lived as much in the open air these past weeks as they had done indoors and it hadn't troubled them, much the reverse. And the food, as Constance had so recently complained, was very plain, which in a way was all to the good of one's health. It had already shown to good effect on the master, for he had laughingly said his breeches were slack. Also he walked without coughing so much. But no doubt this had been aided by his drinking less wine.

It was strange, she thought, how wine was considered a natural necessity in the lives of some people. The master had had two visitors over the past weeks who had brought him a case of wine; one was the young Mr Ferrier, the other was Mr Cardbridge. The Cardbridges came from Hexham. They weren't monied people, more poor upper class, she would say, and Mr Cardbridge was merely an acquaintance of the master, but she knew that his visit had given the master pleasure solely because he had brought with him a case of wine. In her estimation the money that the wine had cost would have been much more acceptable; but that, of course, was out of the question. The master would have taken a small gift of money as an insult, but the equivalent in wine he had accepted with outstretched hands.

The question of values, she considered, would make a very interesting topic of conversation one of these nights when she conversed with him; if she were able to converse with him, for this would only come about if Master Dick got his deserts, and she prayed he would. . . .

After supper Thomas went to bed with a glass of hot rum and sugar. He had courteously excused himself to her, saying his head was aching, but she knew that it wasn't his head that was troubling him but his temper. During supper his face had retained a purple hue. He had not spoken to her, nor had Master Dick, but then Master Dick never addressed himself to her at the table, or anywhere else unless it was to give an order.

She was relieved when Master Dick too retired early to bed. While Mary washed the dishes and tidied the kitchen, she herself put the dining room to rights and laid the breakfast for the following morning. She also put the covers straight in the sitting room, adjusted the rugs and damped down the fire.

She was still in the sitting room when Mary opened the door and said, 'I'm away up then, Miss Brigmore.'

'Very well, Mary. Good night.'

'Good night, Miss Brigmore.'

As Mary went to close the door she stopped and added, 'Is it me or is it getting colder?'

'I think it's getting colder, Mary.'

'You know I had the feeling the night I could smell snow.'

56

'I shouldn't be surprised, Mary.'

'Nor me. I remember me mam tellin' me that one Easter they were snowed up right to the window sill; they didn't roll any of their paste eggs down the hill that year.'

Anna smiled slightly before she said, 'Put another blanket on.'

'I will. Yes, I will, miss. I was froze last night. Will I put one out for you an' all?'

'Yes, yes, you could do, thank you. Good night.'

'Good night, miss.'

When Mary had closed the door Anna looked down at the fire. The top of it was black where she had covered it with the slack coal, but in between the bars it still showed red. Slowly she lowered herself down on to the rug and, her feet half tucked under her, she sat staring at the glow. Mary had said would she put another blanket on her bed. Another blanket wouldn't warm her; once you had been warmed by a man there was no substitute.

This was a cold house. It was still an old maid's house. Strangely, up till a few weeks ago this title could have been applied to herself but she no longer considered she qualified for it. Given a chance she could make this house warm, happy and warm. She could act as a salve to Thomas Mallen's wounds. She could fill his later years with contentment. If never given a child herself, and oh, how she longed for a child of her own, she could find satisfaction playing mother to the children and turning them into young ladies; and who knew, some friend might present them at Court, as Miss Bessie had been, and they would make good matches. Yet under the present circumstances it was all too much like a fairy tale, something from Mr Hans Christian Andersen or the Grimm Brothers.

She leant sideways and supported herself on her elbow and drooped her head on to her hand. Still staring at the red bars she felt her body relaxing. She knew that she was in a most un-Miss Brigmore pose; she hadn't sat on a rug like this since she was a very young girl, because since she was a very young girl she hadn't known what it was to have a fire in her room – part of a governess's training was austerity and fresh air.

When her elbow became cramped she put her forearm on the floor and laid her head on it. What did it matter? Everyone in the house was asleep. If she wasn't careful she'd fall asleep here herself, it was so warm, so comfortable, even although the floor was hard. Should she lie on the couch? She could pull it up to the fire and sleep here all night, no one would know; and she was usually up as early as Mary in the mornings.

She didn't know how long she had been asleep, but being a light sleeper the opening of the door had roused her. She lay still, blinking towards the faint glow between the bars which told her that her dozing hadn't been a matter of minutes but an hour or more.

She felt the pressure of the footsteps on the carpet rather than heard their tread. The person who had entered the room was either the master or Master Dick. Her mind told her that if she were discovered she must pretend to be asleep, it would be most embarrassing to explain her position to either of them; especially as she realized she was lying flat on her back.

When a light spread over the ceiling her eyes opened wide; then turning her head to the side, she saw a pair of booted feet walking on the other side of the couch towards the davenport in the corner of the room near the window. She did not hear the lid of the davenport being lifted, but she did hear the slight squeak of a drawer being opened and something scraping against the wood. The feet now came down the room again; they didn't pause, but went straight to the door.

She counted up to sixty before she moved; then rising, she silently groped her way up the room to the davenport. And now she lifted the lid and opened the drawer. It was empty; the Louis miniatures and the snuff box were gone. She stood for a moment, a hand gripping her throat. If she were to call out instantly she could raise the master. Master Dick would have a horse and carriage waiting, but it would likely be some distance away and he would have to get it. There was still time to stop him.

Of all the pieces she had brought from the house she knew that Thomas Mallen treasured most the three articles he had placed in that drawer. He hadn't locked them away, or hidden them underneath the floor boards again, there was no need; if the bailiffs had suspected anything was missing they would have searched the cottage long before this. The three pieces, she knew, would have brought another thousand pounds, enough to ease his way of living for a year or two until he became quite used to the change; enough to get him a case of wine now and again, a few choice cigars and some delicacies for high days and holidays. She had seen those three pieces as an insurance against his despair.

But she did not shout and raise the house; instead, she groped her way back to the couch and, sitting on it, she stared at the dim embers as she thought, this is the answer to my prayers. By the time Thomas gets up tomorrow morning – in this moment she thought of him quite naturally as Thomas – his son will be miles away, and by the time the authorities find he is missing he will no doubt be across some water, either to France or to Norway.

To get to France he would have to ride the length of the country southwards; on the other hand he would have no distance to go in order to catch a boat to Norway. And yet the sea-ways to Norway might still be too rough and dangerous. Anyway, whichever way he had chosen, and he must have had it well planned and had help, he was gone, and at last now there would come the time when she would sit on one side of this fire and Thomas on the other. And better still, she would be warm at nights.

If he had raved and shouted she knew that in time he would recover from the blow, but on the discovery that his son had gone, and that the miniatures and snuff box had gone with him, he did not even raise his voice.

He had been cheery at breakfast. 'Good Friday, Anna,' he said, 'And a sprinkling of snow.' He always addressed her as Anna when they were alone together. 'I remember one year when they had to dig a pathway up the drive on an Easter Monday for the carriages.'

'Really!' she said, as she wondered if it was the same time as Mary's mother had been snowed up to the window sill.

'You look tired,' he said.

'I am not at all,' she replied.

'You are,' he said; 'it's all too much, teaching, housekeeping and playing housemaid, butler and nursemaid to a doddery old man.'

When she did not deny any of this jocular remark, and in particular did not contradict his last statement, he stopped eating and asked quietly, 'What is the matter? Something is wrong with you. It's odd, but I'm more aware of your feelings than of anyone else's whom I can remember. Sit down and stop fidgeting,' he commanded her now.

She now sat down opposite to him at the table, and her hands folded in her lap, her back very straight, she looked at him as she said, 'Master Dick has gone.'

He did not say 'What!' He made no comment at all. All he did was sit back in his chair, jerk his chin upwards, and wipe the grease from it with a napkin.

After he had placed the napkin on the table he asked quietly, 'When?'

'Last night.'

'Why ... why didn't you let me know?'

'Because –' now her lids veiled her eyes for a moment and she directed her gaze towards the table as she replied, 'You couldn't have stopped him; he must have had a horse or carriage waiting.'

'What time was this?'

'I ... I don't know, not rightly. I ... I had been asleep, I was awakened. I heard a movement on the stairs. I thought it was Mary going down because of something connected with the children. Then I saw him leave stealthily. He had a valise with him.'

How easily one lied, but she could not admit to the fact that she had seen his son stealing from him and had done nothing about it. He might have understood the reason for her silence because he was very much a man of the world, and of the flesh; but at the same time he might have considered the price he was being called upon to pay for their companionship together as much too costly.

At least this is what she thought until, rising from the chair, he walked slowly out of the room. It was some seconds before she followed him into the sitting room. He was standing at the davenport. The drawer was open and he was staring down into it, and when he turned and looked at her she felt the urge to run to him and fling her arms about him. But all she did was to walk sedately up to him and say, 'I'm sorry. So very sorry.'

'I too am sorry, very sorry.'

He suddenly sat down on a chair near the window and she knew a moment of anguish as she thought he was going to weep; his head was bowed, his lips were trembling. She watched him pass a hand over his face, drawing the loose skin downwards, then nip the jowl below his left cheek until the surrounding skin was drained of its blood.

It was a full minute before he looked up at her, and then his voice had a croaking, throaty sound as he said, 'I'm sorry for many things at this moment but mostly for the loss of the miniatures. I had the idea that one day, in the near future, I would hand them to you as a token of my thanks for all you have done for me and mine during this very trying time. The snuff box I intended to keep for myself, merely as a matter of pride. But now, well now –' He spread his hands outwards and in this moment he looked old, helpless and beaten.

He had meant her to have the miniatures! Really, really. The kindness of him, the thoughtfulness of him! He was a self-indulgent man, she knew this only too well; he was flamboyant, bombastic, and few people had a good word for him. Even his friends had proved to be his worst critics in this time of trial, yet there was another side to him. This she had sensed right from their first meeting. A few others knew of this side too. Dunn, she suspected, had been one of them, and Brown, his valet. Yet she wasn't sure about Brown. Brown should have stayed with him, put up with the inconveniences; he could have slept on a makeshift bed in the loft. She'd had it in her mind to contrive something like this when he had informed her that he had a new position. She had been vexed and disappointed with him, but her common sense had told her it would be one less to feed – and anyway, how would he have been paid? Her mind was galloping about irrelevant items. She felt upset, so upset.

'Don't cry, don't cry.' He took her hand and gently drew her towards his side.

After a time he said, 'Another scandal to be faced. They won't believe that I was ignorant of this, will they?'

She shook her head.

' ... Was ... was there anything in his room, a letter?'

'No; I ... I searched.'

He now released her hand and running his finger through his grey hair he muttered thickly, 'God Almighty!' It did not, as usual, sound like blasphemy but more like a prayer. Then looking up at her he asked, 'How am I going to get through these coming weeks?'

For answer she moved closer to him and, holding his head in her hands, she brought it to her breast and pressed it there, and said, 'You'll come through them, and then you'll forget them. I'll see to it that you forget them.'

8

IT WAS A WEDNESDAY, June the eighteenth, the day on which
the Battle of Waterloo had been fought thirty-six years earlier.
Constance had got the date wrong in her exercise that morning and
Miss Brigmore had chastised her firmly. But then Constance thought
she understood the reason for Miss Brigmore's harshness; she was
always short-tempered when Uncle was out of sorts, and he had been
out of sorts for some days now. That was the term Mary used. Miss
Brigmore's term was lackadaisical. So, between out of sorts and
lackadaisical, Constance reasoned it meant that Uncle Thomas
couldn't be bothered to take his daily walk any longer. Uncle Thomas
sat in the study for hours by himself, and now even his glass of wine at
dinner didn't cheer him up. Of course, she supposed, one glass of
wine wasn't very much for a man like Uncle Thomas because his big
stomach was made to hold so much more.

The wine from the house was finished long ago, and when Mary and
Miss Brigmore went into town for the shopping they only brought one
bottle back with them. She had asked Mary why they didn't bring
Uncle Thomas more wine and Mary said it was because they couldn't
carry any more. Constance knew this was not the right answer, the
right answer was they didn't want to spend money on wine. And this
seemed rather mean, especially as she and Barbara had two hundred
pounds every year to spend. She had put this to Barbara and to her
surprise Barbara had snapped at her, saying, 'Don't be so silly, two
hundred pounds is nothing to keep a household on. We're very poor,
very, very poor. We are lucky we eat as we do. If it wasn't for Miss
Brigmore's management we wouldn't fare so well.'

Constance accepted the rebuff. She supposed she was stupid. She
supposed the reason for her stupidity was because she was three years
younger than Barbara. When she was Barbara's age she supposed
she'd be very wise, but already she was finding that as one grew older
one became more puzzled by people. She was puzzled by Barbara's

attitude to Miss Brigmore, for sometimes Barbara's manner towards Miss Brigmore wasn't courteous, yet she always spoke well of her behind her back. And then there was that odd time when she found Barbara crying and Miss Brigmore kneeling on the floor in front of her holding her hands and talking rapidly. Since then she had noticed that Barbara had defended Miss Brigmore on a number of occasions, as about the wine.

She was walking by Barbara's side now along the road towards the old house, as she thought of the Hall. Miss Brigmore was walking behind her with Mary. They were all carrying baskets. She turned impulsively and asked, 'May we run, Miss Brigmore?' and Miss Brigmore said, 'Yes, you may. But don't go out of sight for there might be a carriage on the road. If you should meet one on a corner, jump straight into the ditch.'

Before Miss Brigmore had finished speaking Constance had grabbed Barbara's hand and they were running along the road until, hot and panting, they stopped within sight of the iron gates of the Hall.

The Hall still remained unsold. No one as yet had come forward with a suitable offer. The Bank had kept on a skeleton staff to see to the crops on the farms and the fruit and vegetables in the Hall gardens and greenhouses.

Twice a week, for some time now, Miss Brigmore had taken her party through the gardens and there, Grayson, who had been head gardener, filled their baskets with vegetables and fruit in season. Over the past two weeks she and Mary, between them, had made over forty pounds of strawberry preserve. There was an ample supply of spring onions and new carrots in the cottage stable and they had a barrel ready in the washhouse in which to salt the beans.

As Miss Brigmore remarked to Mary, Grayson was being very co-operative, and she calculated that by the time the potatoes were up they'd have enough fruit and vegetables stored to last them the entire winter, by which time they'd have their own plot of land under cultivation. This was if she could induce some boy from the village to till the ground. In the long nights ahead a boy could do three hours of an evening and earn threepence, and there was many a one would be glad of it. . . . But the village was three miles away.

There was no need to go near the house. When they entered the gates, they could turn to the right and cut through the shrubbery, along the cypress drive, skirt the lake and the rose walk and so come to the domestic gardens; but the children always wanted to see the house. It was strange, she thought, that they saw more of the lower rooms now than they had ever done when they lived in the house. Their favourite game was to run along the terrace peering through one window after another, and today was no exception.

63

She followed them at some distance, having left Mary sitting on the house steps. Mary was having trouble with her right leg, her veins were enlarged and very painful. Barbara called to her now, saying, 'Look, Miss Brigmore, there's more soot down in the dining room, it's spilled over on to the floor boards.'

'Yes, indeed there is, Barbara.' She stood looking over the child's head, her face close to the glass. 'The climbing boys didn't do their work thoroughly there; all the chimneys were cleaned at the beginning of the year following the big Christmas fires; of course it could be the damp. There must be big pockets of soot in the bends which the boys couldn't get at, and these have come away with the damp. Some boys are not so particular as others.' She gave this information as if it were a lesson, and it was a lesson; everything she said to them, except at very rare moments, was in the form of a lesson.

'Let's go round to the stables!' Constance was running to the end of the terrace. She had reached the corner when she stopped and exclaimed loudly, 'Oh!' then she turned her head in the direction of Barbara and Miss Brigmore, while at the same time thrusting her arm out and pointing her finger.

Barbara reached her first, but she did not make any exclamation, she just stared in the direction that Constance was pointing. Nor did Miss Brigmore make any exclamation when she reached the corner and looked at the boy standing not three yards from them.

The boy seemed vaguely familiar yet she knew she hadn't seen him before, at least not closely. Then, her gaze moving from his dark black-lashed eyes to his tousled black hair, she saw the disordered fair streak, and then she recognized him. This was the boy who came over the hills and stood on the rock to view the house. She had caught a glimpse of him once when out walking, a matter of two years ago. He had looked very small then but now he looked tall, over five feet she would say.

'Who are you, boy?'

The boy did not answer but looked at the little girl.

'Are you from the farm?'

Miss Brigmore shook Constance gently by the shoulder saying, 'Be quiet.' Then, looking at the boy she said, 'You know you are on private ground.'

'Whose?' The voice was thick, the word was thick with the Northumbrian burr, and had a demand about it; whatever home he was from, he wasn't, Miss Brigmore decided, in servitude there. She would have said by the tilt of his head and the look in his eyes that he was of an arrogant nature, as arrogant as a Mallen, or as the Mallens had once been. She gave to her own tone a like arrogance as she answered, 'This estate is the property of Mr Thomas Mallen.'

'Until it's sold . . . You are the gov'ness, aren't you?'

'Yes, I am the governess.'

'And your name is Brigmore. You see, I know.'

'I hope your knowledge affords you some comfort.'

She saw that he was slightly nonplussed by her answer and she took advantage of it, saying, 'Now tell me what you're doing here?'

'Walking round . . . lookin' . . . It's a mess isn't it? It'll soon go to rack an' ruin; all ill-gotten gains return to rack an' ruin.'

'You are a very rude boy. This house was not ill-gotten, it was Uncle Thomas's. . . .'

'Barbara.' Miss Brigmore now put her hand on Barbara's arm and patted it three times, not in addition to the reprimand that her tone might have implied but rather as an indication that she was agreeing with her statement.

The boy was staring at Barbara now and she at him, and after a moment he said, 'You live in the cottage at the foot of the tor, and he lives there an' all now . . . Mallen.'

'Mr Mallen, boy.'

The eyes, like black marbles, flashed towards her and the tone again was aggressive as he said, 'There's some must mister him but not me.'

'You really are very rude.' Constance's face had slid into a smile as she endorsed Barbara's words, and when the boy's attention came on her again she asked playfully, 'How old are you?'

'Thirteen.'

'Oh, you are very old. I'm only seven and Barbara –' she nodded now towards her sister '– she's ten. What do you do, do you work?'

Miss Brigmore was for sternly checking Constance but Constance had asked a question, the answer to which would likely give the boy's background, and so she remained silent while the boy, looking down at Constance, said, 'Aye, of course I work. All men should work; if you want to eat you should work.'

'What do you work at?'

'I farm; me da has a farm.'

'Oh.'

'And it's a fine farm, better'n any on here.' He flung his arms sideways and the gesture took in the whole estate.

'Come along.' Miss Brigmore now ushered the girls forward and, looking over her shoulder at the boy, said, 'And you get about your business and don't let me catch you here again.'

'I'll come when I think fit.'

Her back stiffened but she did not turn round.

'What a strange boy. He was very rude but . . . but he was nice, wasn't he?'

65

Barbara turned her head quickly in Constance's direction, saying, 'Don't be silly; how can you be rude and nice at the same time? He was just rude, very uncouth, wasn't he, Miss Brigmore?'

Miss Brigmore didn't look at either of the girls as she replied to the first part of the question. 'Yes, he was very rude. But now let us forget about him and get to the gardens.'

It was an hour later when the children, carrying baskets of strawberries, and Miss Brigmore and Mary Peel the heavier vegetables, were making their way to the lodge gates that they heard the voice calling, 'Matthew! Matthew!'

'It's that boy again.' Constance's eyes were wide, her face bright with expectation, and Mary Peel said, 'And another along of him by the sound of it. He didn't go when you told him then.' She cast a glance towards Miss Brigmore, then added, 'He wants his face skelped; afore you know it he'll have the place cleared. I've heard of him afore, as ready with his fists as he is with his tongue, I hear. Thinks he's as good as the next. Huh!'

They walked on until they came onto the drive, and there a short distance along it, stood the boy, his two hands to his mouth, calling again 'Matthew! You, Matthew!'

They all turned as one now, slightly startled by the sound of running feet approaching along the path they had just left, and the next minute there came towards them another boy. His hair was very fair, his face pale; he was shorter and younger than the boy on the drive who, ignoring the four of them completely, addressed him by demanding, 'Where d'you think you've been? Didn't you hear me callin'? By lad! you'll do that once too often, you will.'

The fair-haired boy too, ignoring the presence of the others and the fact that he was trespassing, answered as if they were alone together. 'I was sittin' by the river,' he said. 'It's lovely down there, man; you should have come. There was a tree hangin' over and I could see the fish in the shad. . . .'

'Shut up!' The dark boy now turned to the group who were staring at him, and by way of explanation said, 'This is me brother . . . I mean me . . .'

Miss Brigmore interrupted him, saying, 'I told you some time ago to leave the grounds, didn't I?'

'Aye, you did, an' I gave you your answer, didn't I?'

Extraordinary boy, really extraordinary. Miss Brigmore was lost for words. There was something in him that – she wouldn't say frightened her, rather annoyed her. The next minute she started as if she had been stung by the younger boy addressing the girls in the most casual and undeferential manner. 'Hello,' he said; 'it's lovely here, isn't it?'

66

Both Barbara and Constance had their mouths open to reply when she shut them with, 'Come along immediately.'

As they moved away the fair boy ran before them and tugged at the iron gate, but he could open it only sufficiently for them to pass through in single file.

'Thank you.' The words coming from Miss Brigmore were a dismissal, and the boy stood still until he was pushed forward by his brother. Then they followed within a few yards of the party until the most surprising thing happened. The dark boy was suddenly at Miss Brigmore's side and, grabbing her basket, said, 'Here let's take it.' And she let him take it while staring at him the while.

'Matthew, take t'other.' He was nodding towards Mary Peel now. Mary smiled at the fair boy as he took the basket from her, and said, 'Ta. Thanks, lad, thanks.'

Miss Brigmore, now turning to Constance and putting out her hand, said, 'Let me have yours, Constance; it's too heavy for you.' Whereupon she was checked by the voice coming at her roughly now, stating, 'She's big enough to carry it hersel'. Let her be.'

'You are a funny boy.' Constance had her head back, her mouth wide with laughter, and Miss Brigmore was too perturbed at this moment to check her, even when she went on, 'Would you like a strawberry? You can, we have plenty.'

When she held out the basket towards him he shook his head, saying roughly, 'We grow bigger'n that, and them's been left wet, they'll mould if you cook 'em no matter how much sugar you put with 'em.'

Miss Brigmore was indeed nonplussed. What were things coming to? The boy had no sense of place or class. She was all for fraternizing within limits, the boundaries of which were educational, and this boy, although he undoubtedly had good stock in him as his white quiff signified, still remained a rough farm boy, and the quicker he was made aware of his position the better. So now she turned her head and said sharply, 'We do not wish to discuss the merits or demerits of strawberries, so if you will kindly give me my basket you can get on your way.'

The boy stared at her, his black eyes looking deep into hers; then he almost caused her to choke when he said, 'We are all goin' the same road, so get along; the lasses don't mind.'

The girls were staring at her, Mary Peel was staring at her; only by a struggle could she take the basket from him, and then she doubted if she would gain anything but ridicule by such an effort. Her chin high, she said, 'Are you aware that these young ladies are Mr Mallen's nieces?'

'Aye, I know that; who doesn't?'

67

Really! Really! What could one say to such a person. It was evident that he took pride in his bastardy and because of it considered himself an equal of everyone. It was a good thing, she thought wryly, that all the master's dubious offspring weren't of like character and determination or else the Hall would have been invaded before now. And she thought too it was strange that the boy, being as he was, should have kept his distance all these years, viewing the house only from the rock. Not until the house and its master had fallen had he put in an appearance, and then to gloat apparently. Well, there was one thing she must see to, and right away, he must on no account come in contact with his . . . with Thomas, for his manner would undoubtedly enrage him to the extent of giving him palpitations; and so when they rounded the next corner she would be most firm and would relieve him and his brother of the baskets and take the path across the fells to the cottage. It would be much longer this way but it would be a means of parting company with this troublesome boy.

But Miss Brigmore's plan was shattered and her mind set in turmoil when, rounding the bend, she saw coming towards them none other than Thomas himself.

It was to her Thomas spoke when still some distance away, saying 'I needed to stretch my legs, the house is as lonely as a lighthouse when you are gone. Well now, what have we here?' He had stopped before them, but was now looking past them to the two boys, and as Miss Brigmore watched him she saw his lower jaw slowly drop. The boy was staring back at him, his dark eyes half shaded by his lids, which gave a deeper concentration to his gaze.

She felt herself gabbling, 'We . . . we met these children on the road; they were kind enough to help us with the baskets. I'll, I'll take them now. . . .' She thrust her hand out but it did not reach the boy, for Thomas's voice checked it, saying, 'It's all right, it's all right.' He gently flapped his hand in her direction but didn't take his eyes from the boy's face. Then, addressing him quietly, he said, 'You've come down off your rock at last then?'

The boy made no answer, but his eyes, holding an indefinable look, continued to pierce the heavy jowled countenance before him.

'What is your name?'

Still the boy made no answer until the younger one nudged him with his elbow while saying to Thomas, 'They call him Donald, and I'm . . .'

'I'm big enough to speak for mesel'.' The younger boy was thrust angrily aside, and he would have toppled had not the hand that thrust him grabbed at him and brought him up straight again. The boy kept tight hold of the younger one now while he spoke from deep in his throat with a man's voice, 'I'm known as Donald Radlet, I'm from

68

Wolfbur Farm an' this –' he jerked the arm in his hand '– is me brother
. . . half-brother, Matthew.' There was a pause before he ended, 'An'
you are Thomas Mallen.'

There was a suspicion of a smile around Thomas's lips as he
answered, 'True, boy, true, I am Thomas Mallen. But tell me, why
have you taken this long to introduce yourself?'

''Cos I do things in me own time.'

Thomas now stared at the lad long and hard, and his eyes had a
steely glint to them. Then, as if considering the matter, he said, 'Yes, I
suppose you would. I suppose you would.' Again he was silent, until
on a somewnat lighter note he added, 'Well, don't let us stand here
talking like hill farmers meeting in the market, let us go. . . .'

'Don't say nowt against hill farmers, they're the best uns. We're hill
farmers.'

Thomas's head jerked to the side, his jaws were tight. Six months
earlier he would have taken his hand and skelped the mouth that dared
to speak to him in that tone, but now, after a pause, he adroitly pressed
the gaping children and Miss Brigmore and Mary Peel before him,
and he walked in front of the two boys for quite some way before he
said, 'You've got to be a good farmer to make a hill farm pay.'

'We are good farmers.'

'I'm glad to hear it.'

'Our cattle are good an' all.'

'You have cattle on a hill farm?'

'Of course we have cattle. Anyway some; we have three flat
meadows. We bought two of your stock a while gone an' they were
poor things; your byre man should've been shot. Their udders were
sick, full of garget; the shorthorn was half dry, only two teats workin';
an' if t'other ever gets in calf she'll be lucky. Doubt if she'll weather a
service; the look of the bull'll scare her. We were done. . . .'

'I'm surprised, and you so knowledgeable. You must have got the
rakings, and very cheap at that. . . .'

Miss Brigmore did not hear the boy's answer; she was hurrying the
girls forward now. Such talk. Teats and calving, and bulls. And she
failed to understand Thomas's attitude towards the boy. He had
shown no sign of palpitation at the unexpected meeting. The boy's
aggressiveness seemed almost to amuse him; could it be possible he
was seeing him as his son, because when all was said and done that's
what he was, his son. She cast a quick backward glance. Thomas was
now walking alongside the boys; he seemed amused, and more alert
than she had seen him for weeks. A thought entering her mind, she
asked herself would she object to anything that would give him an
interest in life? She was fully aware that she herself could only fill his
needs in one way; or perhaps two; she saw to his comfort during the

day as well as at night. But a man had to have something else, particularly a man of Thomas Mallen's stamp. Would this boy supply it? She again glanced over her shoulder, at the same time pushing the girls further forward out of earshot. Catching her glance, Thomas made a motion with his head towards her it was as if he were confirming her thoughts.

Thomas had guessed what his Miss Brigmore, as he playfully called her in the night, was thinking and he was wondering at this very moment if this young, raw, vibrant, brusque individual who bore his mark on his head might not be the answer to a prayer that he hadn't known he was praying, for he was certainly no praying man.

There had, during these past weeks, been a deep void in him, a loneliness, that even Anna hadn't been able to fill. It wasn't, he knew, so much the loss of his home and wordly goods and a way of living, or even the loss of his son; it was the way in which he had lost him, that had left on him the taint of cowardice and shame. He doubted he would ever see Dick again. And this thought brought him no great sorrow but what did sear him, even now, was the knowledge that he had no real friends.

When the hunt for Dick was at its height no one had come near him, at least no friend, but he had had enough company of officials. It wasn't until the newspapers announced that Dick Mallen must by now be well away over the sea – in what direction wasn't stated, for it wasn't known – that Pat Ferrier had paid him a call and told him that Dick was in France. A mutual friend had taken him there on his private boat. But Pat Ferrier had brought no letter from Dick, no word of regret. Nothing. The irony of it struck Thomas when he thought that even his son could produce two good friends at least, while he himself went barren of all but Anna.

He glanced towards the boy walking by his side. There was a resemblance between them, a definite resemblance and not only in the streak. He could see himself again as a young boy; perhaps his hair had not been so black, or his eyes so dark, and definitely his manner had not been so arrogant, although his upbringing could have warranted it, for the proverbial silver spoon had certainly been in his mouth all his days. Yet here was this lad, brought up on a farm, and whether good, bad or indifferent, it was still a farm, assuming the manner one might expect from someone of breeding and authority.

When the boy turned his dark, fierce gaze on him he was put at a disadvantage, until, aiming to make casual conversation, he said, 'How large is your father's farm?'

'A hundred and twenty acres, and he's not me father. I call him Da; but he's his father.' He jerked his thumb towards the smaller boy while his gaze rested on Thomas's face. And neither of them spoke

70

during the further twenty steps they took, but the boy's eyes were saying plainly, 'Let's have no more fiddle-faddle, you known the position as well as I do.'

It was Thomas who broke the trance-like stare calling in a voice that was much too loud, 'What are we having for supper, Miss Brigmore?'

Miss Brigmore stopped abruptly, as did the girls and Mary, and stared at him. Then she said, 'Cold soup, ham and salad, and a strawberry pastry.'

'Have we enough for two extra?'

She could not prevent her eyes from widening and her mouth opening and shutting once more before looking towards the boys and saying, 'They will want to get home; they have a long way to walk over the hills. Their people may be wondering.'

'They won't be wonderin'.' The boy's voice had that definite, hard, determined ring to it that seemed to be the very essence of his nature. 'Da allows us half-day a week for roamin'; we can go back anytime so long's we're up at five.'

Miss Brigmore was silenced. She seemed to have to drag her eyes from the boy, and when she looked at Thomas he smiled broadly at her and said, 'Well there, you've got your answer. We have two guests for supper.'

She turned, and they all walked on again. She should be happy that he had found a new interest but that boy disturbed her. He was too strong, too dominant for his age. She had never encountered anyone like him before. Now if it had been the younger one, she could have taken to him, for he was much more likable, gentler, better mannered. But then he wasn't Thomas Mallen's son.

PART TWO

Donald Radlet of Wolfbur Farm

I

D ONALD RADLET was born in the winter of 1838 when his eighteen-year-old mother, Jane Radlet, had been married about five months.

Jane Radlet had been born on the West Farm of High Banks Hall. Her father was the byre-man, her mother the dairymaid. From the time Jane was born her mother hardly left her bed until the day she died; the midwife's dirty hands had set up an internal trouble, for which there appeared no cure. Constant evacuation wore her body away, yet she lived on for twenty years.

Jane was the only child of the marriage and she could remember back to when she was three years old, when she first visited the cesspool on her own to empty the bucket. She was about four when she began to soss the dirty sheets, and this she did every day of her life, until she was eighteen years and two months old when she left the farm and went over the hills with Michael Radlet.

On that day Michael Radlet took her past his farm without even stopping to look in, and to the church near Nine Banks, and there he married her, with the gravedigger and the parson's wife for witnesses. She cried all the way back to the farm; she cried on her wedding night because she lay alone; and she cried at intervals during the following days, because she knew that for the first time in her life she was going to be happy.

Michael Radlet was eighteen years her senior and he was known as a good, God-fearing, hard-working man, and a man who had rightly prospered through his hard work, for his farm, although small, was well stocked, and his land, although on hilly ground, was utilized to the last foot by his cattle. He worked daylight and moonlight for six days a week, but on the Sabbath he did only what was necessary for the animals; the rest of the day he read his Bible, as his father had taught him to do, and he allowed his one helper the day off to visit his people.

He first noticed Jane Collins when he took his only two Ayrshires

75

over the hills to be serviced by the High Banks bull. He could have taken them to Pearson's Farm, which was only three miles away, but Pearson's bull was of poor stock. Jane had been barely sixteen then, and for the next year he pondered whether he should speak to her father in case she should be snapped up. Yet he doubted if her father would allow her to be snapped up because, he understood, she was the only support in his house, where she looked after his sick wife and cooked the meals and generally did the work of an adult woman, and had, so he had heard, done so since she was a child. But he was quick to note that the long years of labour had not marred her beauty, for her face was round and smooth and her eyes gentle, and her hair a shining brown. Her body was good; her hips wide and her breasts promising high.

It was on the day following the Sunday when he had read and dwelt on the birth of Benjamin that he went over the hills to speak to her father, the words of the good book drifting through his mind: 'And they journeyed from Bethel; and there was but a little way to come to Ephrath: and Rachel travailed, and she had hard labour. And it came to pass, when she was in hard labour, that the midwife said unto her, Fear not; thou shalt have this son also.'

He wanted a son, badly he wanted a son. His first wife had been barren; that was God's will, but Jane Collins would not be barren. He had a feeling about Jane, a strong, urging feeling to hold her, to love her. Some of his love was threaded with pity for her plight, for it was evident she'd had a hard life.

John Collins was about his work in the cow-shed when he confronted him, and when he put the proposal to him he was surprised that the man should bow his head deeply on his chest. It caused him to ask, 'What is it? Is she already spoken?' And John Collins had turned his head away before nodding; then looking him straight in the face he said. 'You have come too late, she's been taken down.'

Taken down! He had not spoken the words aloud but they had yelled at him in his mind. He had come too late, she had been taken down. Well, it was as he thought, she could bear children. But he had imagined they would be his children, the children he needed, the son he needed. He experienced a hurt that went beyond anything he had felt before; even when his wife had died the sense of loss hadn't been so great as now.

His voice was hollow as he asked, 'She is to be married then?'

John Collins shook his head before he raised his eyes and said, 'No, no, she is not to be married.'

There was a silence between them, broken only by the jangle of the cows' chains and their splattering.

'You know the man?'

76

There was another silence before John Collins, looking into Michael Radlet's eyes, said, 'No.'

As they continued to stare at each other they both knew the answer was a lie, and John Collins knew that Michael Radlet knew it was a lie, and the denial told Michael Radlet immediately who the father of Jane's child was, and why this man couldn't speak the truth. There was only one man around these parts he would keep silent about, and that was his master, the whoring rake, Thomas Mallen. John Collins was handicapped. Should he protest to the Justices that his daughter had been raped, for raped she would have been by that sinning devil, then he would be out of a job with no roof over his head and a wife that needed a bed more than she needed anything else. And where would he get it for her but in the workhouse? He was sorry for the man, he was sorry for the girl; and he was sorry for himself also.

When he had crossed the hills back to his farm the loneliness of the vast spaces entered into him as never before. He had lived among the hills and the mountains all his life, as had his forbears for eight generations before him. Space was in his blood, the space of the fell lands, the space of the ever-rolling hills; the awe-inspiring space viewed from the peaks; the space of the sky reaching into infinity. He had always felt at home in space until that day, and on that day he had walked with his head down across the hills. . . .

It was six weeks later when he crossed the hills again, but with his head up now and his mind firm, one purpose in it: he would take Jane Collins in the condition she was. For five Sundays he had prayed and asked guidance of God and yesterday he had received his answer. The Good Book falling open in his lap, his eyes saw the words, 'For I was an hungered, and ye gave me meat: I was thirsty, and ye gave me drink: I was a stranger, and ye took me in: Naked and ye clothed me: I was sick and ye visited me: I was in prison, and ye came unto me.

'Then shall the righteous answer him, saying, Lord, when saw we thee an hungered, and fed thee? or thirsty, and gave thee drink? When saw we thee a stranger, and took thee in? or naked, and clothed thee?

'Or when saw we thee sick, or in prison, and came unto thee?

'And the King shall answer and say unto them, Verily I say unto you, Inasmuch as ye have done it unto one of the least of these my brethren, ye have done it unto me.'

He had wanted a sign, and he took it as a sign, and so the following day when he reached the West Farm he said to John Collins, 'I will marry her,' and the tears had run down the man's face and he said, 'She's a good girl.'

A week later, when Michael Radlet brought the girl over the hill and

77

to the church, she hadn't looked at him until he put the ring on her finger, and it was from then she had begun to cry. . . .

Jane Radlet had been surrounded by people all her life. The four men on Mallen's West Farm were old, their families grown up and scattered; her father was old. There were two young men on the East Farm, but they were both spoken for by maids in the house. It was on her journey to the East Farm that she had met the other old man, at least he had seemed old to her for he was in his forties, but he was different.

Her only break in the week was on Sunday afternoon when her father took over the household chores and she went to visit his cousin, who was wife to the shepherd on the East Farm. She did not care for her father's cousin but it was somewhere to go and someone to talk to. Sometimes on the road, too, she met people, who gave her a word. It was on the road she had met the man on horseback. He appeared a very hearty man and he had stopped and talked with her, and told her that she was pretty.

It was impossible for her to believe now that she hadn't recognized the man as the master of the Hall. Yet there was an excuse for her for she had never seen him on his visits to the farm. Their cottage stood alone and well back from the farm buildings, and such was its situation that she needn't go near the farm unless she wanted to take her father a message; yet even so she had told herself that anyone but a fool would have recognized the master because her father had talked of him, and her mother had talked of him. Big, dark, pot-bellied with high eating and drinking, but then he was no worse than the rest of the gentry and much better than some, being generous to his staff at harvest and Christmas.

Came the Sunday they had met, he had got down from his horse and walked with her through the wood, and there he had tied his horse to a tree and had laughingly pulled her down beside him on the sward. At first he just talked and made her laugh; at first she hadn't realized what was happening; when she did she had struggled, but he was a big man, and heavy. When it was over and she sat numbed and dazed with her back against the bole of a tree, he dropped a gold piece down the front of her bodice, and patted her cheek before he left her.

Weeks later, when her mother found enough strength to upbraid her, she had retorted with anger, 'Who was there to tell me? I've seen no one but you an' me da for years except for that hour once a week when I've talked with Cousin Nellie. And what does she talk about? Only the doings of her son in faraway America, and how to grow pot herbs and the like. Who was there to put me wise? Who? I had only me instinct to go by, and it didn't come to me aid, 'cos I judged him to be an old man.'

78

'Old!' her mother had said. 'And him only mid-forty. You're stupid, girl, men are bulls until they die, be they eighteen or eighty.... Instinct!'

When her father had told her that she was to be saved from disgrace and that Michael Radlet was going to marry her, her only reaction had been, he's old an' all, besides which he was short and thick-set and with no looks to speak of. She had felt she was merely going from one servitude to another, until she finally reached his farm when he told her in simple words that he would not treat her as his wife until after her child was born. She had looked at him fully for the first time and seen that he was not really old, and moreover, that he was kind; and her crying had increased.

The strange thing about her crying was that she couldn't remember having cried at any time in her life before; and afterwards she realized that the constant flow of tears was a form of relief, relief from her years of servitude. Her whole life seemed to have been spent amid human excrement, washing it from linen, smelling it, emptying it. The smell had permeated the very food she ate. She had left her mother with no regret whatever. Her mother had cried at her going, not so much, she knew, at the loss of her daughter, but because now she would be at the mercy of an old crone from the village. She was sorry though to have left her father; she liked her father, for he was of a kindly nature.

So it was that after a few days at Wolfbur Farm she knew that she was going to be happy, that Michael Radlet was a good man and, the most surprising thing, he was going to teach her to read the Bible.

Donald Radlet came into the world protesting loudly, and Jane felt he had never stopped since. As his mother, she should have loved him, but she couldn't; he had been a separate being from the moment he left her womb. She would have said that the boy himself did not know what love was if it wasn't for the protective affection he showed for his half-brother.

He was two years old when Matthew was born, and instead of being jealous, as she thought he might become, of a new baby taking his place, he was, from the very beginning, protective towards the boy, who in colouring and character was the antithesis of himself.

Donald was nine years old when he discovered that Mike Radlet was not his father. It happened on a fair day in Hexham.

They had talked about the fair day for weeks. This day was the highlight of the year; it was the day on which the hirings took place, when farm labourer and maid were bonded into service, and there were such delights as the fair ground, inside which there was every kind of entertainment from the shuggy boats to the boxing booths. Last year they had seen a Chinese lady with stumps for feet, a child whose head was so big it had to be supported in a framework, and a fat woman with a beard down to her breasts, which you could pull – if you had the nerve, for she looked as if she would eat you whole.

As soon as they entered the town Michael let the boys go off on their own for he knew that Donald, although only nine, was to be trusted to look after both himself and Matthew as well.

The boys knew where to contact their parents. The horse and flat cart was stabled in the blacksmith's yard and their mother would be drinking tea with the blacksmith's wife, and while they were exchanging their news their husbands would be out and about in the cattle market and recalling the days of their youth together, for Michael Radlet and the blacksmith were cousins.

But it so happened that the two men and the two women were in the house around three o'clock that day when Matthew came flying in to them, the tears streaming down his face and his words incoherent.

When at last he had quietened down somewhat they understood from gasping words that Donald had been fighting a boy in the fair ground, and another two boys had also set about him.

When Michael demanded to know why Donald was fighting, Matthew looked up at him through streaming eyes and said, "Cos of you, Da.'

'Me? Why me?' Michael frowned down on his son, and Matthew, after shaking his head from side to side, muttered, 'They said you weren't, they said you weren't his da; they said because of his white streak you weren't his da. But you are, aren't you, Da? You are his da, aren't you?'

Michael looked at Jane, and she bowed her head; the blacksmith and his wife bowed theirs also.

It was as Michael stormed towards the door that Donald entered, and as they all looked at him they voiced a long concerted 'Aw!' His lip was split, one eye was rapidly closing, there was blood running from a cut on the side of his temple. His clothes were torn and begrimed, and his hands, which he held palm outwards and close to his sides, gave evidence that he had been pulled over rough ash ground for the thin rivulets of blood were streaked with the cinder dust.

'Oh! boy. Oh! boy.' Jane put her hand to her face as she approached him, then said pityingly, 'Come, let me clean you up.'

He made no move either towards or away from her but stared at her fixedly, and for the first time she knew what it was to suffer his scorn and his condemnation. She had noticed before that when he was angry or deeply troubled, like the time Matthew took the fever and they thought he would die, there came into the bright blackness of his eyes a glow as if from an inner fire. You couldn't say it was a film of pink or red because his pupils still remained black, but there was this change in their gleaming that gave the impression of a light behind them, a red ominous light.

He looked past her at Michael, and he said, 'I want to go home.'

Without a word Michael went out and harnessed the horse to the cart, and five minutes later they set off. Donald, unrelieved of dirt or blood, did not, as was usual, mount the front seat and sit beside Michael; instead, he clambered up into the back of the cart. His feet stretched out before him, his palms still upturned resting on his thighs, his head not bowed but level, his gaze directed unseeing through the side rails of the cart; thus he sat, and didn't move except when the wheels going into a rut or jolting over a stone jerked his body, until they came to the farm.

There, Michael got down from the cart and went to the back of it and, looking at the boy, to whom he had been father in every way possible, said, 'Go and wash yourself and then we will talk. And you, Matthew –' he waved the younger boy towards his brother '– go with him and handle the pump.'

Slowly Donald let himself down onto the yard, and as slowly walked to the pump.

In the kitchen Michael, putting his hand on Jane's shoulder, said kindly, 'Now don't fret yourself, it had to come. Sooner or later we knew it had to come. Perhaps we've been at fault; we should've told him and not waited for some scallywag to throw it at him.'

'He hates me.'

'Don't talk nonsense, woman.'

'I'm not talkin' nonsense, Michael, I saw it in the look he gave me back there.'

'It's the shock; he'll get over that. You are his mother and he should be grateful for it.'

He smiled at her but she didn't smile back. In some strange way she knew that her days of happiness were past. Just as she had been aware of the time they were beginning for her in this house, now she knew that that time had ended as abruptly as it had begun. . . .

Michael led the way into the parlour, which in itself proved that this was a very exceptional occasion, for the parlour was used only on Sundays and Christmas Day. 'Sit down, boy,' he said.

For the first time the boy disobeyed an order given him by the man he had thought of as his father and, speaking through swollen lips, he said, 'You are not me father then?' He had never used the father before; father and da meant the same thing, yet now he was, by his very tone, inferring a difference.

Michael swallowed deeply before answering, 'No, I am not your father in that I didn't beget you, but in every other way I am your father. I have brought you up an' I have cared for you. You are to me as me eldest son.'

'But I'm not your son! I'm nobody's son, I'm what they said I am, the fly-blow. The fly-blow of a man called Mallen. One of dozens they said; he's fathered half the county, they said.'

Michael didn't speak for a moment; then he was forced to say, 'I wouldn't know anything about that, an' people always make mountains out of molehills. There's only one thing I do know, an' I want you to know it too, your mother was not at fault; she was but a girl, an innocent, ignorant girl, when she was taken down.'

Ignoring completely the reference to his mother, Donald said now, 'Matthew, he's not me real brother.'

'He's your half-brother.'

'He's your real son; you're his father, not just his da.'

'They both mean the same thing, father an' da.'

'Not any more they don't. Not any more.'

It was as Michael stared at the boy, who was at that time almost as tall as himself, that there came into him a feeling of deep compassion, for he saw the lad was no longer a lad or a boy. True, he had never really been childish, always appearing older than his years, both in his actions and his talk, but now the very look of him had changed. He had the look of an adult man about him; it came over in the expression of his eyes. His eyes had always been his most startling feature. At odd times when some pleasant incident had softened them he had thought them beautiful, but he wondered if he would ever think them beautiful again. He said now, 'Nothing has changed; whether you think of me as your da, or your father, or whatever, I remain the same. Go on now and have your meal, an' be respectful to your mother. And hold your head up wherever you go, for no blame lies on you.'

Donald turned about and walked to the door, but before opening it he stopped and, looking back at Michael, he answered his last statement by saying, 'They called me a bastard.'

When the following Sunday, Matthew came into the house, his head hanging, and stated, 'Our Donald's gone over the hills an' he wouldn't let me go with him,' Jane closed her eyes and muttered to herself, 'Oh my God!' And Michael laid down the Book and said, 'When was this? How long ago?'

'Just a while back. I thought he was going over to Whitfield Law but he changed his mind and went towards the Peel, and then wouldn't let me come on.'

Jane, bringing out her words between gasps, said, 'He must have started asking. What if he should go . . . I mean right . . . right to the Hall? Oh Michael, Michael, do something, stop him.'

Michael wasn't given to running. If you want to walk a long way you don't run, had always been his maxim, but on this day he ran, thinking as he did that it had been one of his mistakes not to have brought the boy over these hills before. It was six years since he had been this way himself, for now that both Jane's parents were dead there was no need to take this road. Yet, he thought now that in denying this route to the boy when on his Sunday jaunts he must have eventually raised some suspicion in his mind.

He was blowing like a bellows before he had gone very far. He thought the boy, too, must have run for when he reached the peak and looked down into the next valley there was no sign of him.

Michael had been on the road over an hour when at last he saw him. He stopped and stared. The boy, about a quarter of a mile distant from him, was standing on the summit of the last hill. It was the one that towered over the foothills where they spread out into the valley in which was set High Banks Hall. In the winter and the spring when the trees of the estate were bare you could get a view of the entire Hall and the terraces and sunken gardens from that point, but for the rest of the year only a gable end and the windows of the upper floor were visible.

As if he knew he was being watched Donald had turned about and looked in his direction and then waited while Michael walked slowly towards him. When he came up with the boy he said loudly and sternly, 'You're not to go near that place, do you hear me? Anyway, you'd be thrown out on your backside an' made to look a fool.'

The boy stared at him. His face, still discoloured from the blows he had received in the fight, was tinged a deep red as he answered, 'I'm no fool.'

'I'm glad to hear it. Now come away back home.'

From then on Donald went over the hills every Sunday, and on special holidays, the weather permitting, and no one could do anything about it. But he went no further than the last hill until one day in 1851 when he heard that Thomas Mallen had gone bust and that Dick Mallen had nearly committed murder. That Sunday he walked along the road and stood outside the gates for the first time; but he did not venture inside until after the auction had taken place. Then he walked round the house peering in the windows, not like the children had done, more in the manner of someone returning to his rightful home after a long absence.

The rooms were almost as he had pictured them in his mind's eye over the years. They were big and high and had coloured ceilings. Some were panelled up to the ceiling, and even in those with only skirting boards the wood was moulded three feet high from the floor. He had run his hands over the great front door, then counted the iron studs; there were ten rows of eight.

He walked through the empty stables and saw fittings that he couldn't believe any man would waste on a place where a horse was stabled. The hooks were of ornamental brass, the harness-horse was covered with leather like doe-skin, and four of the stalls each had a silver plate bearing a horse's name.

When he stood back from the house and looked up at it the most strange sensation filled his breast. It began in some region hitherto unknown to him; he felt it rising upwards and upwards until it reached his throat, and there it stuck and grew to a great hard painful thing that was all set to choke him. Even when he was shaken by a violent fit of coughing it didn't entirely dissolve.

He had visited the house a number of times alone before the day on which he took Matthew with him, the day when he encountered Miss Brigmore and the girls, and later his father.

When they had returned home that night he had not stopped Matthew from pouring out the exciting news that they had been to supper with Mr Mallen.

This news had actually shocked Michael, and it had not only stunned Jane but increased her fear of this son of hers, while she asked herself what he expected to get out of it now, for Thomas Mallen, they said, was utterly destitute, living on the charity of his nieces.

That night, when Michael said to her, 'I suppose it's only natural that he should want to see his father' she shook her head violently and answered, 'Nothing he does is natural, and never has been.'

From that time on Jane lived in fear of the years ahead. There was a dread on her that she couldn't explain. Yet as one season passed into another and the two boys grew from youth into young men and nothing untoward happened, she looked back and felt like many another woman, in saying to herself that she had been foolish in wasting her time worrying about someone over whom she knew she had no control, for she was fully aware that she meant less to her son than did the cattle in the byres. Indeed, she had watched him show affection for them, especially when a cow was in labour. He had lost sleep to make sure that a cow was delivered of her calf and that both should survive in good fettle; but for herself, she felt that if she were to drop down dead at his feet he would show very little concern, except to make sure that she was put away decently. This was one trait that was prominent in him, he was very concerned with doing the right thing, and this in turn warranted that he should be well put on in his dress. His taste in dress, she considered, was above that suitable to a farmer; but then she had gleaned one secret thought of his: he considered himself a cut above the ordinary run of farmer. Inside, she knew he was proud to be Thomas Mallen's son, while at the same time despising her for her part in it.

She also knew that he would never admit to this. His thoughts were locked deep within him. He never spoke his real thoughts, not even to Matthew, and if he cared for anyone it was Matthew. Not until the time came for him to act on any plan he had devised in his mind concerning the farm did he even speak of it to Michael. He rarely if ever informed her of what he was about to do.

So it was on this bright autumn Sunday morning in 1861 when the four of them were seated round the breakfast table in the kitchen, and only a second after Michael had finished the grace, saying, 'We thank you, Lord, for our food which has come to us through your charity, Amen,' that Donald said, 'I'm going straight over this morning.' They all looked at him, and each face registered reserved surprise, for they recognized by the tone of his voice and the fact that he'd altered his routine that he was about to impart something of importance.

'I'm going to ask Constance to marry me ... it's time,' he said.

Now the reserve slipped from their faces and they gaped at him, in a mixture of amazement, disapproval and even horror. On any other occasion they would have been more wary, for they never showed their true feelings to him. This attitude, which had been born of a desire never to hurt him, had developed in varying degrees in the three of them. He had to be humoured as one might a sick person in order that he would not upset himself with bouts of temper or withdraw into a continued silence. There was a similarity in their attitudes towards him that was strange for they all viewed him in different ways. But now Michael blurted out, 'You can't do that, she's near blood to you.'

'She's not near blood to me.'

'She's Mallen's niece.'

'She's not. Her mother was his step-sister, there's no blood tie atween them at all.'

Still Michael's face was grim now. 'It doesn't seem right.'

'And why not?'

'Don't shout at me, boy. Don't shout at me.'

'I'm not shoutin'. And don't forget, I'm no boy.'

'You'll always be a boy to me.' Michael thrust his chair back and stumped – for his left leg was stiff with rheumatism – from the table into the sitting room where, as usual on a Sunday morning, he would read for half an hour from the Book before attending to his Sunday duties on the farm. And even on this morning he did not depart from his usual pattern.

Now Jane spoke. Quietly she asked, 'Does she know?'

'Know what?' He looked at her coldly.

'That ...' She was about to say, 'That you want her,' but she changed it to, 'What to expect. I mean, have you given her any inkling?'

85

'Enough.'

She stared at him for a moment longer as she thought. That girl in this house with him for life, he'll suffocate her. Now she rose from the table and walked slowly across the stone-flagged kitchen and out through the low door that just took her height, and into the dairy. It was cool and restful in the dairy and she could ponder there, and she had much to ponder on this day, she knew.

Donald now looked at Matthew, waiting for him to speak, and as he waited his face took on a softness that slipped into a smile. After a time he asked quietly, 'Surprised?'

Matthew didn't answer, he couldn't as yet. Surprised? He was staggered; shocked, dismayed; yes, that was the word, dismayed, utterly dismayed. Dear, dear God, that this should happen, that it should be Constance he wanted. He had always thought it was Barbara, and he had the idea that Barbara thought along the same lines. Why, whenever they had been over there it wasn't to Constance he had talked but to Barbara, and when he had seen them together he had thought, they're much alike in some ways those two, given to silences. There were depths in both of them that were soundless, and their silences were heavy with brooding, secret brooding, lonely brooding. As his thoughts were apt to do, he had dwelt on their brooding because he knew that their brooding coloured their lives. He knew that each in his way was lonely and craved something. When the craving became intense it showed, in Donald's case at least, in bursts of temper.

It was as recently as last summer that Donald had shown this side of himself when, entering the cottage on their Sunday visit, they had found company there. There were two young men, one called Ferrier, scarcely more than a boy, and the other by the name of Will Headley about his own age, which was twenty then. It wasn't the first time he had encountered these two young men; at different times over the years they had met up. He understood them to be the grandsons of Thomas Mallen's old friends and so it was natural that they should visit him.

On this particular Sunday when they entered the sitting room they were engulfed in a burst of laughter. Constance was laughing gaily; but then Constance always laughed gaily, her beauty of face and figure was enhanced by a joyous soul which contrasted sharply with Barbara's looks and temperament. But on this day Barbara, too, was laughing unrestrainedly, and he thought that it was this that had annoyed Donald, for he scarcely spoke during the whole of their visit; in fact his presence put a damper on the gathering. They had hardly left the cottage on their return journey when he burst out, 'That old witch of a Brigmore is planning to marry them off.'

Matthew did not contradict the statement but it overwhelmed him with sickness. He'd be very sorry for Donald if Barbara did marry Will Headley; but rather that than it should be Constance. He did not take into account the Ferrier boy; he was much too young and, as he gathered from the conversation, his mind was on nothing but this Oxford place to which he was going in the autumn.

Matthew now shook his head slowly from side to side. He was shaking it at himself, at his blindness, at his lack of knowledge of this half-brother of his. He should have known that Donald never did anything the way other men did, for he wasn't like other men, he had a canker inside him that gnawed at him continuously. He had been born and brought up on this farm, but from that day when he was nine years old he had disowned it while at the same time attempting to run it, even of late be master of it.

But there was one thing sure, if he didn't belong here, then he certainly didn't belong over the hills in the house where his real father lived, for always when in the company of Thomas Mallen Donald appeared gauche and out of place, and this caused him to assume an air of condescension, as if it was only out of the goodness of his heart that he visited this old man. The butter, cheese and eggs he took over every week only emphasized this attitude. But Thomas Mallen showed plainly that he liked this son; and Donald's attitude seemed to amuse him. And the girls liked him; they, too, had been amused in those early years by his bombast; and when the bombast had, with time, turned into a cautious reticence they had tried to tease him out of it, at least Constance had.

There was only one person in that household who didn't like him and who showed it, and that was Miss Brigmore, and Donald, on his part, hated her. Years ago Matthew had felt he should hate her too because Donald did, but secretly he had liked her, and whenever he could he drew her into conversation because he learned from her. He knew that Miss Brigmore had things that he wanted, she had knowledge, knowledge to give him the power to talk about things that he understood in his mind but couldn't get off his tongue; things that came into his head when he looked down into water, or watched the afterglow, or when his thoughts deprived him of his much needed sleep and he crept quietly from the pallet bed and knelt at the attic window and raced with the moon across the wild sky – Miss Brigmore had once said it wasn't the moon that raced but the clouds, and he just couldn't take that in for a long time. It was she, he knew, who could have made these things more clear to him, could have brought his feelings glowing into words; but he did not talk with her much because it would have annoyed Donald, and he was, and had always been, secretly afraid of annoying Donald.

87

But oh dear, dear God! Matthew's thoughts jumped back to the present. Donald had just said he was going to ask Constance to marry him. Constance in this house every day. He wouldn't be able to bear it. He had loved Constance from the moment he saw her offering Donald a strawberry; he knew it had happened at that very moment. He also knew that it was a hopeless love, for he considered her as far above him as the princesses up there in the palace. So much did he consider her out of his reach that he had never even thought of her and marriage in the same breath; what he had thought was, I'll never marry anyone, never. And when he thought this he always added, anyway it wouldn't be fair, not with this cough. They hadn't said he had the consumption, but he'd got the cough all right, and as time went on he became more and more tired, so much so that often he thought that it would be a poor look-out for the farm if Donald weren't as strong as two horses. And Donald delighted in being strong. Give him his due, never had he balked at the extra work. Many a day, aye, many a week he had done the work for both of them, and he had been grateful to him. But now as he stared into the dark face, whose attraction was emphasized with a rare smile, he experienced a moment of intense hate. Then he began to cough, and the cough brought the sweat pouring out of him.

'Don't let me news choke you.' Donald came round the table and thumped him on the back. 'Here, take a spoonful of honey.' He reached out for the jar, but Matthew shook his head and thrust the jar away.

When he had regained his breath, Donald asked him, 'Well now, are you going to say something?' and Matthew, after a deep gulp in his throat, muttered, 'Have . . . have you thought that she mightn't fit in here, in the house I mean?'

'The house? What's wrong with the house? It's as good as the one she's in now.'

'But . . . but it's different.'

'How do you mean, different? It's got as many rooms, counting the loft, an' the countryside around is bonnier.'

Matthew again shook his head. What could he say? Could he say, Yes, but it's an old house, and it's a cold bare house because it hasn't got in it the draperies and the knick-knacks, nor yet the furniture that's in the cottage? Yet, of its kind, he knew it was a substantial house, a house that many a farmer's daughter would be glad to be mistress of. But Constance was no farmer's daughter, and although she had been brought up in the cottage she had also been brought up in an atmosphere provided by Miss Brigmore, an atmosphere of refinement and learning, Constance was a lady. They were all ladies over there, in spite of their poverty. Then again, their poverty was relative. He understood that they had two hundred pounds a year between them, and that to him, and thousands like him, was far from poverty. He said now, 'I thought it was Barbara.'

'Barbara! Good God, no! Never Barbara. Barbara's all right, mind, she's got a sensible head on her shoulders, but she's as far removed from Constance as night from day; sometimes I wonder at them being sisters. No, never Barbara.' He walked down the length of the kitchen now and stood looking out of the window and into the yard. A line of ducks were waddling down the central drain on their way to the pond. His eyes ranged from the stables, over the grain store and the barn, to the side wall where the cow byres began, and next to them the dairy. He now pictured Constance in the dairy. She would take it all as fun. She mightn't take to the work as quickly as another brought up on a farm, but that didn't matter. There would be no need for her to do all that much, his mother would do the rough as usual. But Constance would transform the house; transform him, she would bring gaiety into his life. He had never experienced gaiety, only as an observer when he went on his Sunday visit across the hills. Although he rarely allowed himself to laugh he liked laughter, he liked brightness in another, and she was all laughter and brightness. She would rejuvenate the whole atmosphere of this place; she'd bring to it a quality it had never known. It was a sombre house, and he admitted to himself that he was responsible for a great part of the feeling. It all stemmed from something in him he couldn't get rid of. Yet even before the knowledge of his parentage had been kicked into him on that day at the fair he could not recall being any different. But once Constance was here, once he was married, he would feel different.

He thought wryly it was as if he were a female bastard and marriage would give him a name, a legal name. He couldn't explain the feeling even to himself; it was mixed up with his children; he knew that as each one was born his isolation would lessen. What was more he intended to give them the name that should rightly be his. He would call his first son after Matthew because he liked Matthew – he did not use the term love – but following the name Matthew he would add the name Mallen. Matthew Mallen Radlet; and as time went on he could see the Radlet fading away and his children being known as Mallens; and if they bore the streak as he did, all the better.

One thing only troubled him and then but slightly, what would be the old man's reaction to him wanting Constance? He knew that the old man liked him, and he took credit for bringing a certain spice to his life. Without his weekly visits he guessed that Thomas Mallen would, over the years, have been very bored indeed with his existence, for he had grown sluggish in his mind if not in his body; the latter had been kept active, no doubt, by that shrew of an old cow, who not only acted as if she were mistress of the house but to all intents and purposes

89

was mistress of the house. He had no doubt whatever about her re-actions to his wanting Constance because she would not want to lose Constance, nor the hundred pounds a year that went with her.

He himself wasn't unconscious of the hundred pounds that Constance would bring with her. He could make a lot of improvements on the farm with an extra hundred pounds a year. Oh, quite a lot.

When he turned from the window Matthew was gone, and he pursed his thin lips and pushed aside the feelings of irritation that the empty kitchen aroused in him. But he could excuse Matthew for not being enthusiastic at his news; Matthew was sick, and he'd be more sick before he died. He jerked one shoulder, he didn't want to think about Matthew dying. Anyway, the consumption could linger on for years; if he was well cared for he might live till he was thirty.

He walked smartly out of the room; he must away and get changed. This was one day he'd look his best, his Mallen best.

2

MISS BRIGMORE set the bowl of porridge, the jug of hot milk and the basin of soft brown sugar at one side of the tray, and a cup and saucer and silver coffee jug at the other, and in the middle of the tray she placed a small covered dish of hot buttered toast. As she lifted up the tray from the kitchen table she looked to where Barbara was attending to her own breakfast, as she always did, and she asked, 'Did she cry in the night, do you know?'

'I didn't hear her.'

'She's taken it much better than I expected.'

'You can't tell; beneath her laughter you don't know what she is thinking; her laughter is often a cover.'

Miss Brigmore raised her eyebrows as she went towards the door which Mary was holding open for her, and she thought to herself that she was better acquainted with what went on inside Constance's head than was her sister. In fact, she was well acquainted with what went on in both their heads. It would have surprised them how much she knew of their inner thoughts.

She went slowly up the narrow stairs on to the landing, turned her back to the bedroom door and pushed it open with her buttocks, then went towards the bed where Thomas Mallen was still sleeping.

'Wake up! wake up!' Her voice had a chirpy note to it. 'Your breakfast is here.'

'What! Oh! Oh yes.' Thomas pulled himself slowly up among the pillows, and when she had placed the tray on his knee he blew out his cheeks and let the air slowly pass through his pursed lips, then said, 'It looks a grand morning.'

'It's fine . . . I think you should take a walk today.'

'Aw, Anna,' He flapped his hand at her. 'You and your walks, you'll walk me to death.'

'You'll find yourself nearer to it if you don't walk.'

He looked towards the window, then said, 'It's Sunday,' and she repeated, 'Yes, it's Sunday.'

They both viewed Sundays with different feelings. He looked forward to Sundays; she hated them for this was the day when that upstart came over the hills and acted like the lord of the manor himself. Talk about putting a beggar on horseback and him riding to hell; if ever he got the chance there was one who would gallop all the way.

She had never liked Donald Radlet from when he was a boy; as he grew into manhood her dislike had at times touched on loathing. She, who could explain everyone else's feelings to herself, couldn't give a rational explanation for her own with regard to Thomas's natural son. It wasn't jealousy; no, because if his son had been Matthew not only would she have liked him but she might also have come to love him. But in Donald she saw only a big-headed, dour, bumptious upstart, who made claims on this house because of his bastardy.

But perhaps, she admitted to herself, there was a touch of jealousy in her feelings towards Donald, because although the matter had never been discussed openly she guessed that Thomas not only liked the man but strangely even felt a pride in him. In a way she could understand this, for not having had a sign or a word from Dick all these years he had come to think of him as dead, and had replaced him in his affections with his fly-blow, because that's all Donald Radlet was, a fly-blow. She did not chastise herself for the common appellation for she considered it a true description. But for the tragedy that had befallen the Hall and its occupants those ten years ago, Donald Radlet would not have been allowed past the outer gates and Thomas, although he might have been amused by the persistency of the boy who viewed the Hall from the top of the crag, would no more have publicly recognized him than would any of his other numerous illegitimate offspring.

Thomas said now, 'How is Constance?'

'I haven't seen her this morning, but Barbara tells me she passed a good night; at least she didn't hear her crying.'

'She was disappointed.'

'More than a little I think. It was dastardly of him to call as often as he did when all the while he was planning his engagement to another.'

'As many a man before him he was likely astraddle two stools. If things had been as they used to be he would, I'm sure, have chosen Constance, but which man in the position the Headleys are in now could take a young woman with a hundred a year? They are almost where I was ten years ago, an' I should crow. But no; having tasted such bitterness, I wouldn't wish it on anyone.'

'He had no right to pay her attention.'

'He didn't pay her attention as such, he's called here for years.'

'You didn't see what I saw.'

He put his hand out towards her now and caught her arm and, gazing into her face, he said softly, 'No one sees what you see, Anna. Have I ever told you you're a wonderful woman?'

'Eat your breakfast.' Her eyes were blinking rapidly.

'Anna.'

'Yes, what is it?' She stood perfectly still returning his look now.

'I should marry you.'

The start she gave was almost imperceptible. There was a silence between them as their eyes held; then in a matter-of-fact way she said, 'Yes, you should, but you won't.'

'If I had put a child into you I would have.'

'It's a pity you didn't then, isn't it?'

'Yes, indeed it is; but you can't say it wasn't for trying, can you?' His voice had dropped to a low whisper and the corner of his mouth was tucked in. She now smacked at his hand playfully before saying, 'Eat your breakfast, the toast will be cold, the coffee too. And then don't linger, get up; we're going for a brisk walk through the fields.'

'We're doing no such thing.'

She had reached the door and was half through it when she repeated, 'We're going for a brisk walk through the fields.' And as she closed the door she heard him laugh.

She now paused a moment before going across the narrow landing and to the door opposite, and in the pause she thought, Men are cruel. All men are cruel. Thomas was cruel; he would have married her if he had put a child into her, and how she had longed that he should. She needed children. There was a great want in her for children. That the time was almost past for her having any of her own hadn't eased the longing, and she assuaged it at times with the thought that once Barbara and Constance were married there would be children again who would need her care; she would not recognize that marriage might move them out of her orbit.

As for Thomas not giving her a child, she knew that the fault did not lie with him – the proof of this came across the hills every Sunday. But over the past ten years he had not strayed for she had served him better than any wife would have done. In serving him she had sullied her name over the county. Not that that mattered; she cared naught for people's opinion. Or did she? She held her head high now but if she had been Mrs Mallen it would have needed no effort to keep upright.

And now here was her beloved Constance suffering at the hands of another man. Will Headley had courted Constance since she was sixteen; there was no other word for it. Before that, on his visits he had

93

romped with her and teased her, but during the past year his manner had changed; it had been a courting manner. Then yesterday when she was expecting a visit from him, what did she receive? A beautifully worded letter to the effect that he had gone to London where his engagement to Miss Catherine Freeman was to be announced. He had thanked her for the happy days they had spent together and stressed that he would never forget them, or her.

After Constance had read the letter, the bright gaiety that shone from her face, even when in repose, had seeped away. She had looked stricken, but she hadn't cried; she had folded the letter in two and, when about to return it to its envelope, she had paused and said, 'Anna,' for now she called her Anna, 'read that.'

When she had read it she, too, was stricken; but her training helped her to keep calm and say, 'I am very disappointed in Mr Headley.' Then she had taken Constance's hand and looked into her face and said, 'These things happen, they are part of your education, what matters is how you react to them. If you must cry, cry in the night, but put a brave face on during the day. You're only seventeen; the same could happen to you again before you marry.'

At this Constance had turned on her, and in the most unusual tone cried, 'It won't! It won't ever happen to me again.'

She had dismissed the outburst by saying, 'Well, we'll see, we'll see.'

Now she went across the landing and gently opened the door. She did not knock, she entered as a mother might and said, 'Oh, there your are; you're up, dear.'

It was evident that Constance was very much up. She was dressed and putting the last touches to her toilet as she sat before the small dressing table; and she looked through the mirror at Miss Brigmore while she continued to take the comb through the top of her brown hair. She did not, as usual, speak first, remarking on the weather or some other triviality; it was Miss Brigmore who, coming to her side, and smoothing an imaginary crease out of the back of her lace collar, said, 'Did you sleep well, dear?'

Constance stared at Miss Brigmore, still through the mirror, and she addressed her through the mirror as she said, flatly, 'I'm supposed to say, yes, Anna, aren't I? Well, I can't, because I didn't sleep well.' She now swung round and, gripping Miss Brigmore's hands, she whispered, 'Do you think I'll ever marry, Anna?'

'Of course you will, child. Of course you will.' Miss Brigmore released one hand and gently stroked the delicate tinted cheek, but her eyebrows moved up sharply as Constance jerked her head away from the embrace, saying, 'Of course you will, of course you will. . . . Of course I won't! Where are the men around here who will come flocking for my hand? Whom do we see? Let us face it, Anna, Will was my only chance.'

'Don't be silly, child.'

'I'm not silly, and don't try to hoodwink me, Anna. And I'm no longer a child. Will led me to believe ... Oh, you don't know ... anyway, what does it matter? As you're always saying, these are the things that make life and must be faced up to. But –' her head drooping suddenly, she ended, 'but I don't want to face up to them. I ... I don't want to end up like Barbara, resigned. I'm ... I'm not made like Barbara, Anna.' Once again she was gripping Miss Brigmore's hands. 'I want a home of my own, Anna; I want ... I want to be married. Do you understand that, Anna? I want to be married.'

Miss Brigmore looked down into the soft brown eyes with pity. She was saying she wanted to be married and she was asking did she understand. Oh, she understood only too well; she could write volumes on the bodily torments she had endured, not only during the developing years, but in those years between twenty and thirty. She had even taken to reading the lives of the saints and martyrs in the hope of finding some way to ease her bodily cravings.

When Constance turned away from her, saying helplessly, 'Oh, you really don't understand what I mean,' she gripped her shoulders tightly and twisted her none too gently back towards her, and bending until their faces were level, she hissed at her, 'I understand. Only too well I understand. I've been through it all, only much more than you'll ever realize. Now listen to me. You'll marry; I'll see to it you'll marry. We'll make arrangements to do more visiting. We'll go over to the Browns in Hexham; there's always company coming and going there. And the Harpers in Allendale; they've invited you twice and you've never accepted.'

'Oh, the Harpers.' Constance shook her head. 'They're so vulgar; they talk nothing but horses.'

'They may be vulgar, horsey people are nearly always vulgar, but they keep an open house. We'll be going that way next week; we'll call in.'

Constance shook her head slowly from side to side. 'It all seems so ... so mercenary, so cheap, con ... conniving.'

'You have to connive in order to exist. Come on now.' Miss Brigmore straightened her back and again smoothed out the imaginary crease in Constance's lace collar. 'It's a beautiful day, and Sunday, and we're going for our walk. Now come along and put a brave face on things, and who knows, it may all have happened for the best. You know what I've always said, every step we take in life has already been planned for us. We are not free agents in spite of all this talk about free will. Have your breakfast so that Mary can get cleared away and I will get your uncle ready.' She always gave the title of uncle to Thomas when speaking of him to them. 'And don't worry, dear.' Her voice dropping to a muted tone, she now looked lovingly at Constance. 'Everything will work out to your advantage, you'll see, you'll see. Don't my prophecies nearly always come true?' She lifted her chin upwards and looked down her nose in a comical fashion, and Constance smiled weakly as she said, 'Yes, Anna; yes, they do.'

'Well now, believe me when I say everything will work out for the best. Come along.'

She turned briskly about and walked out of the room, leaving the door open, and Constance rose from the dressing table and followed her, thinking with a slight touch of amusement, When Anna speaks it's like the voice of God.

3

IT WAS AT ELEVEN O'CLOCK when they were on the point of going for their ritual walk that Donald came up the path and entered the house by the front way, and without knocking. Whereas Miss Brigmore didn't knock when she entered Constance's bedroom because she felt that she had the right of a mother, Donald didn't knock at the cottage door because he felt he had the right of a son.

The girls were standing in the small hallway. Miss Brigmore was coming out of the sitting room buttoning her gloves, and behind her, protesting, as he always did on these occasions, came Thomas. When the front door opened and they saw Donald, they all exclaimed in their different ways, 'Why! we didn't expect you till this afternoon.' That is, all except Miss Brigmore, and she fumbled the last button into the buttonhole of her glove while she thought, What brings him at this time? She turned and looked at Thomas, who made a quick effort to hide his pleasure, which she knew at this time was twofold for he would see Donald Radlet's arrival as the means of getting out of taking exercise.

'Well, well! my boy, what have we? Something untoward happened? Have you closed up the farm ... or sold it?' Thomas's deep-bellied laugh caused his flesh to shake.

'Neither.' Donald never addressed Thomas with any title, either of sir or mister. 'As to something untoward, well it all depends upon how you look at it.' He turned now and smiled at the two young women, who were smiling at him, and he said to them, 'Are you off for your walk?'

'Yes, yes.' It was Barbara who spoke and Constance who nodded.

'Well, do you mind being delayed for a few minutes?'

They looked back at him and both of them said together, 'No, no,' and Barbara added, 'Of course not.'

Donald now turned to Thomas and in a manner that set Miss

Brigmore's teeth grating slightly he said, 'I want to talk to you for a minute . . . all right?'

'Yes, yes, all right, all right.' Thomas was always amused by his natural son's manner, for he thought he knew the true feelings that his bumptiousness and pomposity covered. He had been a little like that himself in his young days when at times he wasn't sure of his footing or was out to show that he was not only as good as the rest, but better. He turned to Miss Brigmore now, saying, 'You and the girls go along, go along; we'll catch up on you.'

Looking Thomas straight in the eyes, Miss Brigmore said, 'We'll wait.' Upon this she turned round and went back into the sitting room, and Constance went with her. Thomas now lumbered along the corridor towards his study, and Donald, after casting a half-amused glance in Barbara's direction where she remained standing looking at him, followed Thomas.

Standing by the sitting-room window, and looking towards Barbara as she entered the room, Constance said, 'I wonder what's brought him at this time, and what he wants with Uncle? Did you notice he was wearing a new suit? He can look very smart when he likes.'

Barbara didn't answer, but sitting down, she folded her hands on her lap. Yes, he could look very smart when he liked; to her he had always looked smart. But what had brought him at this time of the morning and all dressed up, and asking to speak to Uncle privately? What? Her heart suddenly jerked beneath her ribs. That look he had given her before he had gone along the corridor. Could it be possible, could it just be possible? He had always paid her attention; but really not sufficient to warrant any hope that his thoughts were other than brotherly. Yet, had some of her own feelings seeped through her façade and had he recognized them, and this had made him bold, and he was in there now asking for her hand? . . . Oh, if it were only so. She had loved him for years, in spite of what she knew to be his failings. His weekly visits had been the only bright spot in an otherwise drab and formal existence. She had, however, kept her secret locked tight within her; the one person she would have confided in she couldn't, because Anna disliked Donald and always had done. But she didn't care who disliked him, she loved him, and if she became his wife she'd ask nothing more from life. . . .

In the study Thomas sat stiffly in the big leather chair staring at Donald. He had been utterly taken aback by the young fellow's request. Now he could have understood it if he had asked for Barbara's hand, because, over the years, it was to Barbara he had talked, and she to him. Sometimes on a Sunday afternoon after they'd had dinner and he was dozing in his chair they had put him to sleep with their talking, she explaining about books and answering his questions, much as a teacher would do. She was in that way very like Anna. But he didn't want Barbara, it was Constance he was after. Well, well now, this was a strange state of affairs. And he had to ask himself a question: did he want his natural son to marry either of these girls, even if they would have him? Well, why not, why not? He had just said he would own the farm when old Radlet died. Apparently Radlet had told him this. . . . He said to him now, 'You say the farm will be yours, have you it in writing?'

'No, but I know for certain it will be.'

'What about his own son?'

'He has the consumption, he won't last for very long.'

'You never know, you never know, creaking doors. Anyway, should Radlet die, Matthew, were he alive, would inherit, and then he in turn could leave the farm to anyone he liked.'

'He wouldn't; he can't run the place, he has no strength. Anyway, I'm not worried about that side of the situation. I'm putting money on the place every year with buildings and stock, and will go on doing so. It's a prosperous farm an' I'm thinking of buying more land an' all.'

The self-assurance silenced Thomas for a time. He was buying more land, he was putting in more stock, putting up more buildings, and hadn't a thing in writing. It was wonderful to have such self-confidence. This son of his knew where he was going, and Constance might do a lot worse, for now that Will Headley had failed her, he couldn't see anyone else in the running, not for the time being at any rate. Most of the young fellows today were on the look-out for wives who would bring with them a good dowry. It was as it had always been, if a man had to choose between his heart and hard cash, the hard cash always won. If it didn't, it was a proven fact in most cases that the heart pact soon led to disaster.

'Have you any objections?'

'Well –' Thomas let his head rest against the back of the chair, and his eyes ranged around the room before he answered, 'I don't know whether I have or not; your request has come as a surprise, and if I'm not mistaken I think it will surprise Constance too.'

'It shouldn't, she knows I like her.'

'Like her! Huh! liking and loving are two different things. Of course she knows you like her, everybody likes her.'

Thomas now got to his feet and walked with heavy tread back and forth from the desk to the door a number of times before he said, 'This'll cause talk you know, because folk don't realize that the girls have no blood connection with me. It'll be said I'm letting my niece marry my son.'

He stopped in his striding and the two stared at each other. It was the first time the relationship had been brought into the open, and the fact caused Donald to rise slowly to his feet. Eye held eye until Thomas, chewing on his lip, swung his heavy body around, saying, 'Well, you have my consent, but knowing you, you'd go ahead with or without it.'

When he looked at Donald over his shoulder he saw that he was smiling, and his own lips spreading slowly apart, he said on a laugh, 'You're a strange fellow, a strange fellow, and I should understand you, if anybody should, I should understand you, shouldn't I? But I don't, and I doubt if anybody ever will.'

'I don't see why not; if they understand you they should understand me.'

'No, boy, no; because you know you don't take after me, not really; you take after my father's youngest brother, Rod. He too went after what he wanted and took no side roads.'

'Did he always get what he wanted?'

'I don't know; I don't know whether he wanted to be drowned at sea or not but he was drowned at sea. I don't know if he got what he wanted, but by all accounts he got what he deserved.'

The smile had left Donald's face as if it had been wiped off and, his voice stiff now, he said, 'I've been handicapped for years, an' I've risen above it. I've worked hard all me life, I've worked like two men, many a time like three; I hope I get what I deserve.'

'I meant no offence, boy, I was merely making a statement. And I say with you, I hope you get what you deserve. But . . . but' – Thomas now rolled his head from side to side – 'we're getting very serious and deep all of a sudden; come, we were talking of a proposal of marriage, weren't we?' He poked his head forward. 'That was the idea, wasn't it?'

'Along those lines.' The cold look still remained in Donald's eyes.

'Well then, go ahead, you have my consent; I won't say blessing because' – he now laughed a deep rumbling laugh – 'a blessing from me might have little to recommend it, eh?' He thrust out his heavy arm and dug Donald in the shoulder with his fist, and they were both aware that the blow did not even stagger the thin frame.

Thomas now turned abruptly and went out of the room and made straight for the sitting room. He opened the door and said, 'Anna, spare me a minute will you?' And before she could move or answer he had turned away and gone into the dining room.

When Miss Brigmore entered the dining room she closed the door behind her, then walked slowly towards him. He did not take her hand, nor was there any placating note in his voice when he said, 'I have news for you, news that will surprise you and certainly not please you. He has asked that he may marry Constance.'

As he watched her face screw up until her eyes were almost lost from view, he waved his hand at her and turned from her, and when still she didn't speak he turned towards her again and said, 'Now it's no use, don't create a scene. I have given him my consent and that's that. After all, he is my son, and who has a better right I ask you? And –' his voice and manner arrogant now, he went on, '– they're no blood relations, the girls, you know they're not, there's nothing against it. Except that you don't like him. All right, you don't like him, you've never liked him, but I repeat, he is my son, he is part of me.'

When she suddenly sat down in a chair he went to her, and now he did take her hands and, his voice soft, he said, 'What have you against him really? He's hard working, and as he himself has just said, he's lived under a handicap for years. You don't like his manner, he's full of the great I am. Well, in his position I likely would have been the same; I would have had to put on a front. In a way he's to be admired, not scorned.'

'You can't let it happen, Thomas, you can't.'

'Well I have, I have.' He was standing up now, his voice arrogant once again. 'And that's that. It's up to her now, and nobody's going to force her. Oh no, nobody's going to force her. It's ten to one she'll laugh at him an' that'll be the end of it.'

'It's come at the wrong time.'

'What do you mean?'

'She has been rejected. She may take him as a means of escape.'

'Don't be silly, don't be silly, woman. She has no need to escape. Escape from what?'

'You don't understand.'

'I don't see what there's to understand. She either takes him or she doesn't. If she takes him I'll be happy for her.'

'And I will be sad to my dying day.'

'What?'

'I said, and I shall be sad to my dying day.'

'Why, Anna, why?'

'It would be no use trying to explain to you, only time can do that.'

She rose from the chair and went out and towards the sitting room. The door was open and she stood on the threshold and, ignoring Constance and Donald, she looked at Barbara and said, 'Will you come with me for a moment, Barbara.'

'What is it, Anna?' Barbara came hurrying from the room.

'Let us go for our walk.'

They were at the front door now and Barbara turned and looked across the hall and said, 'But ... but the others.'

'We will go alone this morning.'

'Are you ill?'

'I am not ill, but I am not well.'

They had gone down the path and reached the garden gate before Miss Brigmore said, 'He has come this morning to ask Constance to be his wife, and your uncle has consented.'

She had taken three steps into the road before she stopped and looked back to where Barbara was clutching the top of the gate-post, and for a moment she thought that the stricken expression on her face had been brought about by the shock of the news, but when Barbara put her hand tightly across her mouth and closed her eyes in order to suppress the tears that were attempting to gush from them she clutched at her, whispering, 'Oh no, no! Oh my dear, my dear . . . you didn't expect him . . . not you? You're so sensible, if only you could see through him; he cares for nobody but himself, he's a ruthless creature. Oh not you, not you, Barbara.'

When she was pushed aside she made no complaint, but walked slowly after the hurrying figure. And she had thought she knew what went on in both their minds.

From the sitting-room window Constance saw Barbara going down the road with Miss Brigmore following, and she turned to Donald saying, 'They've gone, what's the matter? Where's Uncle?' She was making for the door when Donald said, 'He's in his study. Don't go for a minute, I've got something I want to say to you.'

'Oh.' She turned and looked towards him, her face straight.

He had noticed that she wasn't her merry self this morning, it was as if she'd had a quarrel with someone, but with whom he couldn't imagine, for they all adored her and she them. Even that stiff-necked old cow held her in affection.

He went past her now and closed the door. Then having walked slowly towards her again, he stood in front of her, his back very straight, his head held high, and he said, 'Your uncle has given me permission to speak to you.'

She had asked, 'What? what about?' before the meaning of the phrase struck her, and then she wanted to laugh; long, loud, and hysterically she wanted to laugh. For months she had been imagining how she would respond to Will Headley when he came from the study and said, 'Your uncle has given me permission to speak to you.' Those words could only have one meaning, and here was Donald saying them to her. It was funny, very, very funny; Donald was saying 'Your uncle has given me permission to speak to you;' he would next say, 'Will you be my wife, Constance?' But she was wrong, at least in the form of the proposal, for he did not make it as a request but as a statement. 'I want to marry you,' he said.

'Marry? Marry me? You ... you want to marry me?'

'That's what I said.' His face was straight now.

She was laughing at him; he couldn't bear to be laughed at. 'Is there anything funny about it?'

'No, no.' She closed her eyes and bowed her head and she wagged it as she murmured, 'No, no, Donald, there's nothing funny about it, only –' she was looking at him again '– I'm ... I'm surprised, amazed. Why ... why you can't really be serious?'

'Why not? why shouldn't I be serious?'

'Well –' she put her fingers to her lips now and patted them. 'Well, what I mean is ... oh!' As Miss Brigmore had done a few minutes earlier, she sat down abruptly on a chair, but her manner was quite unlike that of Miss Brigmore's, for she was laughing again. 'Well, for one thing I would never make a farmer's wife, I'd be useless at milking and making butter and such, I wouldn't know how.'

'You could learn if you wanted to; but there would be no necessity for you to make butter and such.' He did not say his mother saw to that but added, 'That's already seen to. You'd be asked to do nothing you didn't want to do.'

Of a sudden she stopped laughing, she even stopped smiling, and she looked down at her hands which were now joined tightly on her lap. Yesterday the man she loved and had thought one day to marry had written her a letter, which by its very charm had seared the delicate vulnerable feelings of her first love as if she had been held over the blacksmith's fire, and definitely the letter had forged her whole conception of life into a different pattern.

'Well!'

She rose to her feet, her arms thrust out now to each side of her as if pushing away invisible objects, and, her body swaying slightly, she walked from him to the farthest corner of the room, saying, 'I ... I can't take it in, Donald. Why ... why you've never given any sign. You've always talked to Barbara more than to me. Why should you want me?' She now turned swiftly and, all animation gone from her body, she stood still, her arms hanging by her sides, staring at him.

He didn't move from where he was, nor did he speak for a time, his words seemed wedged in his throat, and when finally he uttered them they came like an echo from deep within him. 'I love you,' he said.

There was a long pause before either of them moved. During it she looked at him as if she had never seen him before. He was a man, a good-looking, stern-faced young man; he was thin and tall, with jet-black hair that had a white streak running down the side of it; his eyes were dark, bluey-black; he was her uncle's natural son, and because of this he had an opinion of himself. She did not blame him for that; he was hard working and had gained the title of respectability even with the stigma that lay on him. She had heard her uncle say that his judgment was respected in the cattle markets and that men did not speak lightly of him. He would, she felt, make someone a good husband – would he make her a good husband? He had said he loved her. She didn't love him, she had never thought about him in that connection; she liked him, she was amused by him. Oh yes, he amused her. His austere and bumptious manner had always amused her; she had teased him because of it. But love; could she ever grow to love anyone again? She looked him over from head to foot. He was very presentable; in a way he was much more presentable than Will Headley. Change their stations and what would have been her reactions then?

She said, 'But I don't love you, Donald. I ... I've never thought of you in that way.'

'That will come, I'll see it comes.' He moved towards her now and he reached out and took her hand. 'Give me the chance and I'll see that it comes. You will love me, I know you will.'

She gave a small laugh as she said, 'You are as you ever were, so confident, Donald; nothing can shake your confidence in yourself and your ability, can it?'

'I know my own value.'

'And you think you can make me love you?'

'I don't think, I know I can. It may sound like bragging, and I suppose it is when I say I could have married five times over these last few years, and that's not heightening or lessening the number; five times over I say, and to one the daughter of a man who has nearly enough cash stacked away here and there to buy the Hall. I'd just to lift me finger, but no, I knew who I wanted, there was only one for me, and that was you.'

'Oh Donald!' She didn't know now whether she wanted to laugh at his cock sureness, or to cry at his devotion.

When he lifted her hand and rubbed it against his cheek she detected a new softness in him and she said haltingly, 'Will ... will you give me time, time to think it over?'

'All the time in the world ... a year.'

'But you said all the time in the ...'

'I know, but a year is all the time in the world that I'm going to give you. At the end of a year we'll be married, you'll see.' When he put his arms about her she remained still and stiff and something recoiled in her while she thought, Is this in the plan for me? and her mind gabbled rapidly, No, no. Yet when his mouth touched hers she did not resist him, she even experienced a shiver of excitement as she felt the strength of him and smelt the strange odour that emanated from the mixture of soap, rough tweed, and the farm smell that she always associated with him. He was a man, and he wanted her – and Will Headley didn't.

PART THREE

Constance

I

THERE WERE PERIODS during the following year when Miss Brigmore's feelings towards Constance's suitor softened and she was forced, even if grudgingly, to show her admiration for him. These were the times when although the hills and mountains were impassable with snow, he would appear as usual for his Sunday visit; that he accompanied these feats with an element of bravado was visible to all, but that he accomplished them at all she was forced to admit was due not only to his physical strength but also to his sheer tenacity.

Of course there were other times when he had to admit defeat. On these Sundays – once there had been three in succession – she had observed Constance's reactions closely. The first Sunday she had taken as a matter of course and even shown some relief, but when he hadn't appeared on the second and third Sundays, she had shown concern, and when the day came that he finally arrived she had greeted him warmly.

Constance had been three times over the hills to the farm. Her first visit had not turned out to be a complete success. Its failure had nothing to do with the farm or its inhabitants; she had spoken highly of his parents and their reception of her, stating only that the farmhouse seemed a little bare after the cluttered homeliness of the cottage. What had actually spoilt the visit for her was the storm; she had a horror of storms. Thunder and lightning terrified her. Since she was a child she had always sought the darkest corner during a storm, and its approach always made her nervy and apprehensive. On this occasion she was actually sick and had to delay her return until quite late in the evening; and Donald, although he couldn't understand her fear, had been concerned for her.

Constance could not herself pinpoint the time when she had specifically said to Donald that she would marry him, but the date had been fixed within six months of the particular Sunday when he amazed her with his declaration of love.

As the weeks passed her reactions had varied from excitement to fear bred of doubt. But the latter she always tried to laugh off, even as she laughed at the man who was the cause of it. The questions 'What is there to fear from Donald?' and 'And if I don't marry him who then?' would nearly always dispel the fear.

For the past two days the weather had been sultry owing to the unusual heat that had continued daily for over a week now, and Constance had been on edge as she often was with an impending storm. Added to this, Miss Brigmore did not discount the nerves that frequently attended marriage preparations, not that the preparations for this wedding were anything elaborate, but nevertheless there were the usual things to be seen to, such as the clothes she would take with her, the linen, and what was more important and what had been causing a great deal of discussion, the amount of money she would retain.

At first Constance had insisted that she transfer her hundred pounds a year income to Barbara; for, as she stated plainly, were the house deprived of it they would find great difficulty in managing. What was more, she had insisted that Donald would confirm her opinion on the matter.

But Donald hadn't confirmed her opinion; when the question was put to him he had remained silent for a time before saying, 'It's a good thing for everyone to have a little money of their own, it makes them sort of independent.'

Thomas had wholeheartedly endorsed this, while at the same time Miss Brigmore knew that he was only too well aware that the household strings were already pulled as tight as it was possible for them to be without actual discomfort. She, herself, had taken no salary from the day they had come to the cottage in order that he might have the little luxuries of cigars and wine that made life more bearable for him. As for Mary, she was on a mere pittance; it was only her devotion to the girls that had made her suffer it all these years.

The question of the money had not, as yet, been resolved. Constance had said only that morning she would have none of it. She had got into a tantrum, which was unusual for her, and said that unless she could do as she pleased with her allowance she wouldn't marry at all. She had made quite a scene in front not only of Donald but of Matthew too.

It wasn't often that Matthew came to visit them now. He hadn't been more than half a dozen times during the past year. Matthew always aroused a feeling of sorrow in Miss Brigmore. Why was it, she asked herself, that a person with such a nice nature as Matthew's should suffer such a crippling disease, while Donald, with his arrogance, be given enough health for two men?

Matthew's speech and manner had always pleased her, and she had thought secretly that if the half-brothers could have exchanged places she would have welcomed the match without reservation.

She looked at the young man now sitting opposite her. They had the room to themselves. Thomas had retired to the study for his after-dinner nap; Barbara was in the garden reading. Barbara read a lot these days, but now she didn't discuss what she read. Instead, she had become very withdrawn over the past year. Deep in her heart she was sorry for Barbara; and here again she wished that the roles could be changed, for she would have been less unhappy about the situation if Barbara had been marrying Donald, because there was a firm adultness in Barbara that was, as yet, lacking in her sister. Yet she felt that perhaps she was not quite right in this surmise, for Constance too had changed during the past year: only at intervals now did her gay girlish self appear; for most of the time she wore a thoughtful expression.

She brought her whole attention to Matthew as she said, 'I have not had time to ask you yet, but how have you been feeling of late? We haven't seen you for such a long time.'

'Oh, about as usual, Miss Brigmore, thank you. No worse, no better.' He shrugged his thin shoulders. 'I'll be quite content if I continue like this. And I could' – he now nodded at her as he smiled – 'if we had this weather through the winter.'

'Yes, indeed,' she laughed with him, 'if we had this weather through the winter. It really has been remarkably warm of late, too warm some days I would have said. Yet in another month or so we shall have forgotten about it, and be shivering once again.'

He said now, 'It's very cold this side in the winter, I think we're more fortunate over our side.'

'I'm sure you are. And Constance tells me it's very pleasant in your valley.'

'You must come over and see it. Don ... Father is going to get a horse and trap or some such, he's going into Hexham for the sales next Friday. My mother suggested, as we were using the horses we come over by the waggon today, but Donald would have none of it.' He now pulled a face at her and they both exchanged smiles. 'Besides the fact it would have to be cleaned up for the journey, it's a bit big and lumbering and has no style about it whatever.'

There was a slight mocking note to his last words, and Miss Brigmore brought her lips together tightly while her eyes smiled back at him with a knowing smile.

There followed a companionable silence between them now, as if each were waiting for the other to speak, and Miss Brigmore wanted to speak, she wanted to ask him so many questions: How did his mother

III

and father view the alliance, particularly his mother? How did Donald act in his own home? Did he still keep up his authoritative manner amidst his own people? Was he kind? Of course he had shown kindness for years in bringing the commodities of the farm on his Sunday visits. But that wasn't the kindness she meant. There appeared no softness in him, no gentleness. A man could appear arrogant and bumptious in public, she knew only too well, but in private he could become a different creature. It was strange but she couldn't imagine Donald becoming a different creature in private. But there was only one person who would ever know if he changed character, and that was Constance. She had often wondered how he acted towards her when they were alone for his manner in public gave off the impression that he already possessed her. She turned her gaze towards the window from where she knew, if she rose, she'd be able to see them going towards the curve in the road, taking the same walk they did every Sunday, because Donald liked that walk, for at the end of it were the gates of the Hall. . . .

It would have surprised Miss Brigmore at this moment if she could have overheard the conversation between the two people who were deep in her thoughts, for the subject was the same as that in her own mind, kindness.

Walking with a slow, almost prim step, Constance was saying, 'He appears to have such a kindly nature.'

'He has.'

'You're very fond of him.'

'Aye, I'm very fond of him. There's nobody I like better except –' he turned his head towards her and paused before he said, 'you. If I were speaking the truth there are only two people I care about in the world, the rest could sink, burn or blow up for me.'

His words brought no change in her attitude, but she asked, 'What about Uncle?'

'Oh.' He nodded his head once or twice, then repeated, 'Uncle? Funny, but I can't explain what I think about him. Pride, hate, grudging admiration, loathing, oh, I could put a name to all the vices and very few of the virtues that go to make up my feelings with regard to him.'

She had paused for a moment in her walking and stared at him as she said, 'But I thought you liked him?'

'I do, an' I don't. I don't and I do.' His head wagged from side to side with each word. 'Aw, don't let's talk about – Uncle, for I wouldn't be able to speak the truth about my feelings for him if I tried, 'cos I don't know them myself. There's only two things I'm sure of, as I've told you, and the main one is I love you.' His voice dropped to a mere whisper as he stopped and turned towards her. 'I love you so much that I'm afraid at times, and that's proved to me the strength of my feelings, for fear and me have been strangers up till now. Now, every time I leave you I fear something'll happen to you. But once I have you safe over the hills, it'll be different. I'll know peace, an' I'll be whole. You know, that's something I've never really felt – whole; but once we're married you'll make me whole – won't you? ... Aw Constance, Constance.'

Her lips fell slightly apart and she looked at him in something of surprise, for in this moment she was seeing him as never before, and she felt stirring in her an emotion she hadn't experienced before. It wasn't love – or was it? She couldn't tell, for it had no connection with the feeling she had felt towards Will Headley. Was it pity? But how could she pity him, he was the last person one could pity; if he were dressed in rags and begging on the road he would not evoke pity. And yet, when she came to consider it, she could not give to this feeling any other name. She realized that he had allowed her to see beneath the surface of his arrogance wherein she had glimpsed a depth of loneliness. She herself had no understanding of loneliness, never once having been lonely. There came into her mind the fact that she had never been alone in her life except in the privacy of the water closet; sleeping or waking there had always been someone, Barbara, Anna, Mary, or her uncle.

When his arms went about her and pulled her fiercely to him she gasped and whispered, 'We're on the main road.'

'What of that! Have we ever met anyone on the main road at this time on a Sunday?'

His mouth was on hers, hard, searching. After a moment her stiff body relaxed against him and her lips answered his.

When he released her he stood gazing down into her face; then he cupped her chin in his hand as he said, 'A fortnight today we will have been married for twenty-four hours.'

She gave a nervous laugh, drew herself from his embrace and walked on, and he walked close beside her now, his bent arm pressing hers tight against his side.

A fortnight today at this time they would have been married for twenty-four hours.

A fortnight ago she had all but decided to tell him she could not go through with the marriage, and then she had asked herself if she did that, what would life hold for her, what prospects had she of marrying if she refused this opportunity? She could see herself ending up, not only like Barbara, but like Anna, and she couldn't bear the thought. She wanted a husband and a home of her own and children, lots of children. She had read in a Ladies' Journal only recently an article that explained that the bearing of children, and the doing of good works within one's ability and the contents of one's pocket, brought to women great compensation, and contributed towards a better and longer-lasting happiness than did the early experience of so-called love marriages, wherein the young bride saw life through rosy-tinted glasses.

There was another thing that was worrying her, she did not know whether she would like living in the farmhouse; it wasn't that she disliked his mother and father, nor that they disliked her, but there was a restraint in their manner towards her. They acted more like servants might be expected to do and this made her uneasy. The one comforting thought was that Matthew would be there. She got on well with Matthew, she liked Matthew, she had always liked him, he seemed to belong to another world altogether from that which had bred Donald. He was more refined, gentle. She had never teased Matthew as she had teased Donald, which was strange when she came to think of it; perhaps because Matthew had talked little and had been rather shy. He was still shy.

They had walked in silence for some time, and she didn't like long silences; she always felt bound to break silences, and now she reverted to their previous topic and said, 'I thought Matthew was looking very well today.'

'He's well enough considering, an' if he sticks to the horse and doesn't walk too much he'll be better. If I don't keep my eye on him he's off up the hills with a book; he'll be blind afore he dies, I've told him that. Had things been different from what they are with him he would have made a good school teacher; he's learned, you know.' He had turned his head towards her and there was a note of pride in his voice as if he were speaking of a son, and she nodded and said, 'Yes, yes; I think he is.'

'Think!' he repeated. 'Be sure of it; he never goes into Hexham òr Allendale but he borrows a book. That reminds me. I've got to go to the sale next Friday an' that's when you were coming over to meet Uncle and Aunt, so Matthew'll come for you early on. He'll bring Ned along; Ned's back's as broad as an ingle-nook, and you couldn't fall off him if you tried.'

She laughed now as she said, 'I could, even without trying, you know I'm no horsewoman. It isn't that I dislike horses, I just can't ride them. Now Barbara, she sits a horse as good as any man. I always think it's a pity we weren't able to keep one; she would have loved it.'

He said abruptly, 'Barbara's grown sullen.'

'You think so?'

'I know it. It's because she doesn't want to lose you. And that's understandable.' He was nodding at her. 'They all don't want to lose you, but their loss is my gain.' He pressed her arm tighter into his side.

Then, his voice unusually soft, he said, 'You know, I determined years ago to get everything I set me heart on, and I set me heart on you from the beginning. But even so there were days and nights, long nights when I doubted me own ability, an' now it's come about, well' – he gazed sideways at her and, his voice just above a whisper, he said, 'Have you any idea how I feel about you, Constance?' Without waiting for an answer he made a small motion with his head and went on, 'No, you never could have, for I can't explain the sense of . . . what is the word?' Again he made a motion with his head. 'Elation, aye, that's it, the sense of elation I feel every time I look at you.'

'Oh Donald! don't, don't; you make me feel embarrassed, as if I were someone of importance.'

'You are. Look at me.' He jerked her arm and when, half-smiling, she looked at him, he said 'You are, you are someone of great importance. Get that into your head. There's nobody more important than you, and there's only one thing I regret.'

When he paused she asked, 'And what's that?'

And now he pointed along the road towards the iron gates. 'Them,' he said.

'Them?'

'Aye, them. If I could perform a miracle I'd have them opened as we get near. The lodge-keeper would hold them wide, and we'd go up the drive sitting in a carriage behind prancing horses, an' the lackeys would run down the steps and open the house door. They'd put a footstool out for you, and they'd bow their heads to me, and the head lackey would say, "I hope you had a pleasant journey, sir?" And we'd go through that hall and up the staircase and into our apartments – not rooms mind, apartments, an' I'd see you take off your hat and cloak; I'd see you change into a fine gown; then down the stairs we'd go together and into the dining room an' . . .'

They had reached the gates now and she gripped the rusty iron railings, and leaning her head against them she laughed until her body shook, and when she turned to look at him her face was wet with her laughter; but his was straight and stiff and he said, 'You think it funny?'

'Yes, yes, Donald, I do, for it would take a miracle, wouldn't it?'

He stared at her for a long moment before saying, 'If I had been brought up in that house as I should have been, as his son, we would be there the day, I know it, I feel it inside.'

'Don't be silly.' Her voice held an imperious note. 'You were a boy then only thirteen; you could no more have made a miracle then than you could now; the miracle that was needed then was the sum of thirty thousand pounds, I understand, and that would only have acted as a stopgap.' Her own face was straight now, and what she said next was a statement rather than a question, 'You have always hated the fact, haven't you, that you weren't recognized as his son.'

When she saw his chin go into hard nodules and his cheek-bones press out against the skin she said hastily, 'Oh I'm sorry, Donald, I . . . I didn't mean it in a nasty way. I'm sure you with your forethought and tenacity would have tried to do something, I'm sure you would, even as young as you were. Believe me –' she put out her hand and touched his '– I wasn't intending to hurt you in any way. You do believe me?'

He drew in a deep breath, then let it out slowly before answering, 'Aye . . . aye, I believe you. And what you say is true.' He turned from her, and now he gripped the iron bars and looked through them and up the weed covered drive and into the dark tunnel where the trees were now meeting overhead, and he said, 'It's a blasted shame.' He turned his head and glanced at her. 'I don't mean about me, but about the place. Why didn't they stay, they paid enough for it? Only three years in it and then they cleared out and didn't leave even one man to see to the grounds.'

She, too, was looking up the drive as she said, 'This part of the country accepts or rejects as it pleases. They were from Hampshire, this was another world to them; what was more they were new to money and thought it could buy anything. If they had been disliked I think they could have understood it, but not being ignored. Uncle was disliked. Oh yes.' She nodded at him. 'He was hated by many people; but he was someone they couldn't ignore – not even now.' She chuckled, and he smiled as he muttered, 'No, I'll give him that, you can't ignore him.'

Once again she was looking up the drive and her voice had a sad note to it as she said, 'They'll never get the gardens back in order; it took two years before, but now the place has been deserted for almost four years. The house must be mouldering. This lock always annoys me.' She now rattled the chain attached to the huge lock. 'And that glass they had put all along the top of the walls.' She looked first to the right and then to the left of her. 'It seems an act of spite to me. And when I think of all that fruit going rotten inside. Oh, I feel like knocking a hole in the wall, I do.' She nodded at him, her face straight, but when he said playfully, 'I'll do it for you if you like. Wait till I go and get a pick', and pretended to dash away, she laughed again.

They turned from the gate, walked a little way along the road, then mounted the fells to take the roundabout way back to the cottage, and when with an impulsive movement she slipped her hand through his arm he gripped it tightly; then swiftly he caught her under the armpits and lifted her into the air and swung her round as if she were a child; and when at last he stopped whirling her and put her feet on the ground she leant against him gasping and laughing and he pressed her to him as he looked away over her head towards the high mountains, and the feeling that he termed elation rose in him and burst from him and formed itself into a galloping creature, and he saw it clear the peaks one after the other until it reached the farm.

2

THEY WERE ALL STANDING in the roadway outside the gate seeing her off, Matthew at the head of the two horses. Mary was giggling, saying, 'I don't blame you, Miss Constance; you wouldn't get me up on that, not for a thousand pounds you wouldn't.'

'If I offered you one gold sovereign you wouldn't only be on it, but you'd jump over it this minute, woman.'

It spoke plainly for the change in the social pattern that Thomas could joke with his one and only servant and Mary answer, 'Oh, Master. Master, I'd as soon jump over the moon, I would so, as get on that animal. I don't envy you, Miss Constance, I don't that, I . . .'

'Be quiet, Mary!' At times Miss Brigmore's manner reverted to that of the Miss Brigmore that Mary remembered from years back, and on these occasions she obeyed her without murmur.

Miss Brigmore now stepped towards Constance where she was standing near the big flat-backed horse and she said, 'You have nothing to fear, he'll just amble.'

'He won't gallop?' Constance divided the question by a look between Miss Brigmore and Matthew, and Matthew, smiling, said, 'His galloping days are over, long since.'

'It's so close; you don't think there'll be a storm?'

Constance was now looking at Barbara who, her face unsmiling but her expression pleasant and her voice consoling, said, 'No, I'm sure there'll be no storm, it's passed over. Look –' she turned and pointed '– it's passing to the south of us. By the time you get on to the hills the sun will be out.'

The two sisters looked at each other. It was a long probing look as if each had the desire to fall into the other's arms.

'It'll be tomorrow you'll get there if you don't make a start; hoist her up, Matthew, and get going.'

Matthew bent down, cupped his hands and Constance put her foot on them; the next moment she was sitting in the saddle. Then without a word Matthew mounted the brown mare, and after inclining his head towards those on the road he said, 'Get up there!' and the two horses moved off simultaneously.

No one called any farewell greetings, but when Constance turned her head and looked back at them Miss Brigmore raised her hand in a final salute.

It was almost ten minutes later, after they had left the road and were beginning to mount upwards, that Matthew spoke. Looking towards her, he said, 'You all right?'

'Yes, Matthew, yes. He's ... he's quite comfortable really.'

'Yes, he's a steady old boy, reliable.'

They exchanged glances and smiled.

A few more minutes elapsed before she said, 'It's looking dark over there; you don't think we'll ride into the storm do you, Matthew?'

Matthew did not answer immediately because he was thinking that that was exactly what they were likely to do. Barbara's statement that the storm was passing south was quite wrong; it was coming from the south-west if he knew anything, and it would likely hit them long before they reached home. He said, 'Don't worry; if it does come we'll take shelter. There's the old house on the peak, you remember it?'

'That derelict place?'

'Yes, it's derelict, but it's been a haven to many in a storm these past years, and even before that when the Rutledges lived there.'

'I can't imagine why anyone would want to live in such an isolated spot.'

'Needs must in most cases; they had their sheep and a few galloways; and some people want to be alone.'

'Yes, I suppose so.' She nodded towards him. His face looked grave, serious. On each of the few occasions she had met him over the past year his expression had been the same; grave, serious. At one time, even in spite of his shyness, he had appeared jolly. When he smiled she thought he looked beautiful, in a delicate sort of way. She had wondered often of late whether he was displeased at the prospect of her coming to live on the farm. If that was the case it would be a great pity for she had imagined him lightening the evenings in the long winter ahead. She had visualized them conversing about books, as he did with Anna. She knew she wouldn't be able to converse with Donald about books; she had remarked to Anna recently it was a pity that Donald wasn't a reader, and Anna had replied tersely that she had to face up to the fact that her husband-to-be was a doer rather than a dreamer. That was a very good definition of Donald, a doer rather than a dreamer. Matthew here was the opposite, he was a dreamer rather than a doer, but it was his health she supposed that made the latter impossible. She felt a deep pity for Matthew and a tenderness towards him. She had realized of late that she had been somewhat hurt by his restrained attitude towards her.

The path was getting steeper. The land on one side of them fell sharply away to a valley bottom before rising again, but more gradually, to form distant peaks. On the other side of them it spread upwards in a curving sweep to form what, from this distance, looked like a plateau.

Matthew, glancing towards this height, calculated that before they covered the mile that would bring them to the top, and within a few minutes' ride of the old house, the storm would break. Even as he stared upwards the first deep roll of thunder vibrated over the hills, bringing a startled exclamation from Constance, and he came closer to her side, saying, 'It's all right. If it comes this way we'll take shelter.'

She was gripping the reins tightly; her face had gone pale. She looked at him and murmured hesitantly, 'I'm . . . I'm sorry but . . . but I'm really afraid of storms. I've tried to overcome the feeling but I can't. It . . . it seems so childish. . . .'

'Not a bit, not a bit. There are plenty of men who are afraid of storms an' all.'

'Really?'

'Aw aye, yes. I know . . . I know two.'

'Men?'

'Yes, men. There's a fellow who lives over by Slaggyford, a farmer he is.'

'And he's afraid of storms?'

'Yes; dives for the cow byre every time the sky darkens.' He hoped she never repeated this to Donald for he would laugh his head off.

'Is . . . is he a grown man?'

'Yes, he's a good age. But it's got nothing to do with age. There's a young boy in the market. I see him at times, that's when there's not a storm about, for he makes for shelter when there's the first sign of thunder, mostly under a cart. So you're not the only one, you see.'

She smiled at him, and he smiled back while he congratulated himself on his ability to tell the tale.

'Get up there! Get up there!' He urged the horses forward, but Ned, having maintained one pace for many years now, refused to alter it; and the coming of a storm didn't make him uneasy, he had weathered too many. But the younger horse was uneasy. She tossed her head and neighed, and Matthew tried to calm her, saying, 'Steady now, steady,' while at the same time thinking whimsically it was no good lying to a horse.

As the first flash of lightning streaked the sky above them Constance bowed her head and smothered a scream, and Matthew, bringing his horse close to hers again, put out his hand and caught her arm, saying, 'It's all right now, it's all right. Look, we're nearly at the top; another five minutes and we'll be in shelter.'

She lifted her head and looked at him and gasped, 'Can . . . can you make it hurry, the horse?'

'No, I'm afraid he'll go his own gait, come flood, storm or tempest. But don't worry, don't worry, everything'll be all right; just sit tight.'

'It's getting dark.'

Yes, it was getting dark; the valley to the left of them was blotted out; the sky in front seemed to be resting on the hills. Her face appeared whiter in the dimness, there were beads of perspiration round her mouth. He looked at her mouth and shivered. Then moving his horse forward, he gripped Ned's rein and yelled, 'Come on! Come on, Ned! Get up with you! Get up!'

The quickening of the horse's stride was not perceivable, but he kept urging him.

When the next roll of thunder came he was startled himself for he thought for a moment that Constance had fallen from the horse. He moved back to her side where she was doubled almost in two, her face resting against the horse's mane, and he leant towards her and put his hand on her shoulder and soothed her, saying, 'There now, there now, it's passed. Look, it's passed.'

As he spoke, the first big drops of rain descended on them and before they had moved a hundred yards they were enveloped in a downpour, so heavy that his body too was now doubled against it.

It was more by instinct than sight that he left the road at the spot where the derelict house stood. Dismounting, he made his way round to her side and, her body still bent, she fell into his arms and he guided her at a run into the dark, dank shelter. Then leaving her to support herself against the wall, he said, 'I won't be a minute, not a minute; I'll just put them under cover,' and dashing out, he led the horses into a ramshackle lean-to that had once served as a stable, where he tied them before running back to the house.

Groping his way towards her, he found that her body was no longer bent; she was standing with her back pressed tight against the wall, her hands cupping her face, and he said to her, 'Come over here, there's a bench and rough table of sorts. The road travellers use this place as a shelter; there might be some dry wood, we'll make a fire.'

When he had seated her on the form she clutched at his arm and muttered through chattering teeth, 'You're soaked. You . . . you shouldn't be soaked.' Anna had told her that people with consumption should never get their feet wet, in fact should never be out in the rain; people with consumption should, if they could afford it, go and live in a different climate. 'Take your coat off,' she said; 'it may not have got through.'

He made a small laughing sound at her solicitude, and it held some relief with the knowledge that she had for the moment got over her fear of the storm.

'I'm all right, don't worry about me,' he said. 'You're like a wet rabbit yourself.' He pointed to her hat, where the brim was drooping down each side of her face, and he added, 'A very wet rabbit, its ears in the doldrums.'

When she lifted her hands and took her hat off he said, 'I would take off your coat an' all.'

'No,' she said as she shivered, 'I'm cold.'

He turned from her and made his way through the dimness to the far corner of the room where there was a rough open fireplace, and from there he called, 'We're in luck, there's dry wood here, quite a bit, and kindling. You'll be warm in no time.'

'Have you any matches?'

'No; but if I know anything the roadsters will have left a flint around somewhere; they look out for each other, the roadsters do. That is, the regular ones.'

There was a long pause, and then his voice came again, on an excited note now, 'What did I tell you! In this niche, a box with a flint in it. Here we go.'

As Constance watched the sparks flying from the flint her agitation eased; they would soon have a fire and their clothes would dry. She wished she could stop shivering. Why did storms petrify her? She had tried, oh, she had tried to overcome her fear, but it was hopeless, she seemed to lose control the moment she heard thunder.

'There you are; look, it's alight. Come over here and get your coat dried.'

She rose from the form and was making her way towards the flickering light of the tinder when an earsplitting burst of thunder appeared to explode over the house. When its rumblings died away she was huddled on the floor to the side of the fire, her face buried hard against Matthew's shoulder; his arms were about her holding her close. When at last the only sound they could hear was the hard pinging of the rain on the slate roof and an occasional hiss as it came down the chimney and hit the burning wood, they still remained close pressed together.

The wood was well alight and sending the flames leaping upwards before she raised her head and looked into his face and whispered, 'I ... I'm sorry, Matthew.'

He made no answer, he was half kneeling, half sitting, as she was. Their positions were awkward and cramped but neither of them seemed to notice it. She did not withdraw from his hold but she stared into his eyes and could not help but recognize the look they held, and read there the reason for the change in him these past months.

As she watched the firelight passing shadows over his corn-coloured hair she had the greatest desire to run her fingers through it, bury her face in it, and she told herself she was a fool, a fool of a girl, not to have recognized what was in his heart, and, what was more terrifying still, in her own. She had known she held a certain special feeling for Matthew; even when she was in love with Will Headley she had still retained this feeling for Matthew, but she had looked upon it as sympathy and compassion for his ill health. And perhaps that is how it had begun; but what it had nurtured was something much deeper.

When he whispered, 'Oh, Constance! Constance!' she answered simply, 'Matthew! Oh, Matthew!'

Still with their arms about each other they slid into a sitting position now, and again they gazed at each other in silence while the fire blazed merrily to its height.

After a period he asked softly, 'Didn't you know how I felt about you?'

She shook her head. 'No; not ... not until this moment.'

'And you, Constance, you, what do you feel for me? Look at me, please ... please. Tell me.'

He had to bend his head towards her to hear what she was saying above the noise of the rain which had increased in force. 'I ... I don't know, Matthew, I really don't know. It, it can't be true, I feel it's unreal. Can one suddenly know in a moment? Things ... things like this have to grow.'

'It's been growing for years.'

She was looking at him again. 'But you never gave any sign; why?'

'How could I? And I shouldn't now, no, not at this late stage, when I'm getting ready for my grave.'

'Oh don't, don't!' She put her hand over her mouth now and her head drooped deeply on to her chest.

'Oh, don't worry, dear; don't worry. I shouldn't have said that. It sounded as if I'm sorry for meself, but nevertheless it's a fact that's got to be faced. But ... but I'm not sorry you know how I feel; no, I'm not sorry.'

'You ... you could live for years and years.'

He shook his head slowly. 'Not years and years; another winter like last and ...'

'No, no.' She was holding his hands now. 'Don't say that.'

'But Constance' – he shook his head at her – 'it's the truth. Yet you know something? I feel happier at this moment than I've ever done in me life before. I've died a number of deaths already, thinking of you marrying Donald. But now it doesn't seem to matter so much, and . . . and I don't feel I'm betraying him by . . . by telling you how I feel. When you're married. . . .

'I could never marry Donald now.'

'What! Oh!' He was kneeling in front of her now, gripping her hands. 'Oh, but you must, you must. You're his life; there's no one in the world for him but you. I know him, I know him inside out. He's a strange fellow, possessive, pig-headed, and big-headed, but his feelin's are as deep as a drawn well, and all his feelin's are for you.'

As she stared up at him a flash of lightning illuminated the bizarre room and once again she flung herself against him and the impact overbalanced him. When there came the sound as if a thunderbolt had been thrown in through the open doorway she almost buried herself in him, and before the last peal of thunder had died away the inevitable was beginning.

On the bare floor they lay, the fire crackling to the side of them, the rain beating on the tiles and blowing through the paneless windows and the open doorway, and strangely it was he who protested, but silently, yelling at himself, 'No, no!' He could never commit this outrage against Donald. Even while his hands moved over her submissive body his mind begged him to stop before it was too late.

But it was too late, and when the lightning once again lit up the room, her crying out was not against it alone but against the ecstasy and the pain that was rending her body.

When it was over he rolled away from her for a moment and hid his face in his hands and groaned, and she lay inert, her eyes closed, her heaving breath stilled like someone who had died in her sleep.

When of a sudden she drew the breath back into her body again he turned swiftly to her and, enfolding her in his arms, cried, 'Oh Constance! Constance, me darling; me darling, me darling.'

She made no move now to put her arms about him, not even when the thunder broke over the house again did she press herself against him; she was spent and her body was no longer her own; she was in it, but not of it. A short while ago she had been a young girl, a prospective bride who was terrified of storms, now she was no longer a young girl, so different was she that she could listen to the thunder unmoved.

It was as if Matthew had read her thoughts, for now he was looking down into her face and talking rapidly, saying, 'I'm sorry. Oh God above, I'm sorry, Constance. Try to forget it, will you? Try to forget it. If Donald knew he would kill me. Oh aye, he would.' He was nodding his head at her as if refuting her denial of this. 'He would slit my throat like he does a pig's. God! If only it wasn't Donald. I don't want to hurt Donald, I wouldn't hurt him for the world.'

Gently she pressed him away from her, and as if she had performed the function a dozen times before she adjusted her clothes, her manner almost prim; then she said, 'I could never marry Donald now, but . . . But I could marry you, Matthew. And . . And I could look after you. You . . . you could take your share of the farm and we could go away perhaps to a new climate.'

For answer he sat back on his hunkers and covered his face with his hands. When he looked at her again he said slowly, 'I . . I could claim no share of the farm, I have put nothing into it. What me father would give me would be of his generosity. But then, then again, were I to leave an' take you with me, Donald would leave an' all. I know this; I know it in me heart, he wouldn't be able to stand a second disgrace, a second rejection. You see, that's what he's been suffering from all his life, being rejected. He was a bastard, and all bastards know rejection. Strangely, I know how he feels, and should I take you away the second rejection would hit him worse than the first, he wouldn't be able to bear it. And what's more, it would mean the end of the farm, for me father's a sick man; you've seen yourself he's crippled with rheumatism, he depends on Donald for everything. Donald runs the farm, he is the farm.'

Slowly she rose to her feet, dusting down the back of her skirt as she did so. Then as slowly she walked towards the form and, sitting on it, she put her joined hands on the table and bowed her head over them. And when he came and sat opposite to her and gripped her hands between his she looked at him and asked, 'Could you bear to see me married to Donald?'

He gulped in his throat twice before answering, 'I'll have to, won't I? There's nothing else for it. But now it won't be so bad, for I have part of you that I'll hold tight to until my last breath. Nothing seems to matter now, although I know it shouldn't have happened. It's my fault . . . my fault. . . .'

As she looked now at his bowed head, she knew that she was seeing not only a sick man but a weak one; he was as weak as Donald was strong. Yet the blame for what had happened was not only his. She knew in her heart that if blame, as such, was to be apportioned then more than half of it should be put to her credit, for without her mute consent he would have got no further than kissing her. Even if he had forced himself upon her she could have resisted him, for in physical strength she was the stronger; but she hadn't resisted him.

Did she love him? She stared into his flushed face, into the soft tender gaze of his eyes. She didn't know now, she thought she had before . . . before that had happened, but now she felt empty, quite empty of all physical feeling. When she returned to normal, would she know then? Only one thing she was sure of at this moment, and that was she couldn't marry Donald. Nor could she go to the farm now.

It would be impossible to look Donald in the face with Matthew there.

She turned her head slowly towards the doorway. The rain was easing now; the thunder was still rumbling, but in the distance. She looked back at Matthew and said, 'I'll return home.'

'No, no' – his tone held fear – 'you can't do that; he's ... he's expecting you. If you're not there when he gets back tonight he'll be over first light in the morning.'

'Well, that's tomorrow. It'll ... it'll give me time to think. But Matthew, can't you see, I couldn't possibly meet him today and, and spend the night at the farm. I couldn't. I couldn't.'

'Oh Constance.' He was gripping her forearms now, his voice trembling as he gabbled. 'Let things be as they were. What's happened atween us, let it be like a dream, a beautiful dream. If things were different I'd run off with you this minute; but as I can't support you I won't live on you, so it's no use you bringin' up your hundred a year. Anyway we both know you'd be a widow in no time.'

'Oh Matthew! Matthew!' She screwed up her face. 'Don't keep saying that.'

'I must 'cos you've got to believe it's the truth. If it wasn't I wouldn't be sittin' here persuading you to go ahead and marry Donald.'

They were both quiet now, their heads bowed, until he began to mumble as if talking to himself, 'I feel I've done the dirty on him though, and it isn't right, for he's treated me well over the years; another one in his place, a half-brother with no claim on me father, would have taken it out on me, especially one as strong in body and mind as he is. And ... and there's another thing. I'm goin' to feel very bad about this later on, but it'll be nothing compared with my feelings if you turn from him. Do you know something, Constance? Look at me. Look at me.' He shook her arms, and when she looked at him he said, 'He's much more in need of you than I am, and God knows I need you, but his need goes deeper than mine.'

She stared at him. He was making excuses. He was a weakling in more ways than one. She turned her gaze towards the fire. The bright glow had dimmed, the thin sticks had dropped to ash leaving red stumps supporting each other. Gradually like one awakening from a dream, she looked about the room. She could see it as a whole now, for the light was lifting outside. It was a filthy place. She noticed now that there was a smell of excrement coming from some part of it. She looked down at the floor. It was criss-crossed with filth, dried mud, pieces of straw and broken sticks. . . . Yet she had lain down there and given herself to a man. How could she! *How could she!* What had come over her? Had her terror of the storm deprived her of her wits? No, no.

She had given herself to Matthew because she'd wanted to; with or without a storm she had been ready to give herself to someone. Then why hadn't she waited for just one more week. She had acted like a wanton, a street woman, giving way to the impulses inside her without thought of the consequences.

It was the thought of the consequences that brought her to her feet, and she gasped, 'I must, I mean I can't go on with you, I must go back. You . . . you can tell him that I was very frightened – and I was, I was, that is the truth – and you had to turn back. . . . I must return home, I must, I must.'

'Constance.' He had come to her side now. His hands outstretched appealingly, he said, 'Please, please.' But she shook her head and turned away from him and went towards the door, saying loudly, 'It's no use, I won't go on. I can walk back; it will be downhill all the way. That's it, I'll walk back.'

'Don't be silly.' He caught her hand, and held her still as he stared hopelessly at her. Then saying gently, 'Come on,' he led her outside.

The rain had become a mere drizzle. He brought the horses from their shelter and helped her up on to Ned's back, and there were no more words between them. . . .

They were going down the last slope and were in sight of the cottage when she drew her horse to a standstill and, looking at him, she said, quietly, 'Don't come any further, Matthew. I know your clothes should be dried and you need some refreshment, but I couldn't bear to give them my explanation in front of you, as . . . as I'll have to lie, you understand? I'm . . . I'm sorry.'

He nodded at her, then got down from his horse and helped her to the ground. His hands still under her armpits, he gazed at her and asked softly, 'Can I kiss you once more?'

She said to him neither yes nor nay, and she did not respond when his lips touched hers gently; but when he looked at her again her eyes were full of tears and he said brokenly, 'Aw, Constance, Constance. Aw God! if only –' Then turning round abruptly, he grabbed at the horses' reins, turned them about, hoisted himself up in Daisy's saddle, and tugging at her he muttered, 'Get up there! get up!' and Daisy and her companion moved off, their steps slow, steady and unruffled.

She stood on the rough road for a moment watching him, then she swung about and ran. Her skirts held above her ankles, her coat billowing, she ran until she arrived breathless on the road leading to the cottage, and not until she had reached the gate did she pause; and then, gripping it in both hands, she leant over it.

It was like this that Miss Brigmore saw her from the bedroom window. With a smothered exclamation she hurried out of the room, down the stairs, and so out onto the pathway, saying as she met her, 'Why! Constance, my dear, my dear; what has happened?'

During the journey Constance had rehearsed what she was going to say. 'I just couldn't go on, the storm was terrifying. I made Matthew bring me back some of the way. He was very wet, so I wouldn't let him come any further than the boar rock.' But she said none of this, she just flung herself against Miss Brigmore, crying, 'Anna. Oh! Anna.'

'Ssh! Ssh! What is it? Something's happened?'

They were now in the hall and Miss Brigmore looked about her. Thomas was in his study reading or dozing, Barbara was in the outhouse with Mary pickling onions and red cabbage.

Sensing that something more than ordinary was afoot, Miss Brigmore said again, 'Ssh! Ssh! Now come upstairs. Come.' Soft-footed, she led the way hurriedly up the narrow stairs, and when they were in the bedroom she closed the door and, untying the strings of Constance's hat, she asked, 'What is it? what has happened? Oh my goodness!' She looked down at her skirt. 'Look at the condition of you; your dress is filthy, and your cloak too. Constance.' She backed from her just the slightest, her brow furrowed; then said sharply, 'Come, get those things off and into a clean dress. Come now, stop crying and change, and then tell me.'

A few minutes later, when she'd buttoned the dress up the back, she turned Constance about and sat her down, and sitting opposite to her she took her hands and said firmly, 'Now.'

It was an order, but Constance couldn't obey it. How could one say to the person who had been teacher, and then friend, since one could remember anything, how could one say, 'I have given myself to a man. The act took place on the filthy floor of a derelict house. So much for all your training ... Miss Brigmore.'

'Something's happened to you, what is it? Tell me.' Miss Brigmore had leant forward now and was shaking Constance by the shoulders. Then as a thought came into her mind, she suddenly straightened her body, sat back in her chair, and clasping her hands tightly against her breast, murmured, 'You ... were attacked?'

'No, no.'

Miss Brigmore heaved a short sigh, then demanded, 'Then what?'

'... I can't marry Donald, Anna.'

'You can't marry Donald, what do you mean?'

'Some ... something's happened.'

Again Miss Brigmore joined her hands and pressed them to her breast. 'Then you were attacked ... ?'

'No, I wasn't attacked. . . . But Matthew, he, he loves me. It was in the storm. We were sheltering in that old house. Something

128

happened, happened to us both. He . . . he isn't to blame.' Her head drooped now on to her breast, and then she repeated in a whisper, 'He isn't to blame.'

'Oh my God!'

Not only the words but how they were expressed brought Constance's head up. She had never heard Miss Brigmore speak in such a way; it was as a mother might, fearful for her daughter's chastity; it was too much. She flung herself forward onto her knees and buried her face in Miss Brigmore's lap.

It was a second before Miss Brigmore laid her hands on Constance's head. The consequences of the situation were looming before her, racing towards her. She was demanding that her mind think clearly but all her mind kept saying was, she must have gone insane, she must have gone insane. And with Matthew of all people!

She said it aloud, 'You must have been insane, girl, and with Matthew of all people! He . . . Donald will kill him when he knows.'

'He . . . he needn't know. He'll never know.' Constance had lifted her tear-drenched face upwards. 'I can't marry him.'

Miss Brigmore stared down at her for a long moment, and then she repeated, 'You can't marry him? Are you going to marry Matthew then?'

'No, no. Matthew. . . .' She couldn't say 'Matthew won't marry me;' what she said was, 'Matthew can't marry me; he wants to but he can't. He's a sick man as you know, and . . . and as you said, Donald would kill him if he knew, and I believe that.' She nodded her head now. 'He's capable of killing him even though he loves him.'

Once more Miss Brigmore took hold of Constance's shoulders; and now she was hissing at her, 'And you say you are not going to marry Donald? What of the consequences of your act today then? What if you have a child?'

For the second time that day the breath became stilled in Constance's body, and when her lips did fall apart it was to emit it in a thin whisper as she asked the question, 'It could happen after just . . . just that once?'

'Yes, yes, of course, girl, after just that once.' Miss Brigmore's voice was still a hiss.

They stared at each other in wide-eyed silence as if watching the consequence taking on actual shape.

It was Miss Brigmore who broke the silence, her voice weighed with sorrow now as she said, 'This morning if you had said you weren't going to marry Donald I would literally have jumped for joy, but now I'm forced to say you must marry him, and I also must add, thank God that the ceremony is but a week ahead. . . . Oh dear! Oh dear!' She put her hand to her brow now and closed her eyes and groaned.

'Constance! Constance! what possessed you? What in the name of God possessed you?'

For answer Constance turned her head slowly towards her shoulder and gazed out of the window, and when she saw that the sun was shining now she almost said, 'It was the weather, you could put it down to the weather.' And in a way that was true because if she had not been afraid of the storm and had not taken shelter in the derelict house it certainly, certainly would never have happened. Who made the weather, God? Well, if He did He had certainly laid it as a trap for her.

She now looked towards Miss Brigmore where she was bustling about the bed, turning down the counterpane, adjusting the pillows; and when she said, 'Get your clothes off,' Constance did not say, 'But I've just changed,' but she did say, 'Why?'

'You're going to bed. Your uncle and Barbara must be given a reason for your return, and they will accept the fact that you're upset by the storm. Moreover, you must be in bed when . . . when he comes, as come he will. This will save you having to talk at length with him.'

Without a murmur she began to undress.

When at last she was in bed, Miss Brigmore said, 'Don't sit up on your pillows like that, lie down, and say little or nothing to anyone except that the storm made you ill, that you just couldn't go on, and Matthew had to bring you back. . . . Oh, and it's fortunate in a way that Pat Ferrier is calling this afternoon with a friend. Your uncle received a letter just after you left; he is going back to college at the weekend. His presence will divert Barbara's attention from you, for whatever you do you must not tell her about this. Barbara could never look lightly upon such a matter, she'd be shocked.'

She was tucking the sheet under Constance's chin when Constance, staring wide-eyed up at her, asked in a whisper, 'Are you shocked, Anna?'

In response Miss Brigmore sat down quickly on the side of the bed and, enfolding the girl in her arms, murmured, 'No, child, no; for I did the same myself, didn't I? There's only one difference between us, you have the chance to cover up your mistake, and in this way you are lucky, very lucky. You can have your cake and eat it. It falls to too few of us to have our cake and eat it.'

3

IT WAS OVER. The wedding party had been driven to the church in Donald's new acquisition; it wasn't a trap but what he called a brake, a sturdy, square vehicle on two large wheels. It seated three people at each side and another beside the driver. It looked more suited to utility than pleasure for the seats were plain unpadded wood and the back rests afforded little comfort, being but two low iron rails. Donald had explained that it wasn't exactly what he wanted, but it was the only one going at the sale and it would do in the meantime.

He had driven over the hills alone. He should have been accompanied by Matthew as his best man, but Matthew, unfortunately, as he explained, had had a bad bout of coughing last night and had shown blood for the first time. It was understood without saying that neither his mother nor his step-father would attend the wedding.

It had been anything but a merry wedding party. The only one who had shown any sign of gaiety was Thomas, and, as he commented to himself, it was getting harder going as the day wore on. What was the matter with everybody? He said this to Miss Brigmore immediately on their return. They were alone in his room. He was loosening his cravat to give himself more air, and he exclaimed impatiently, 'Wedding! I've seen happier people at a funeral. Look,' he turned to her, 'is there something going on that I should know of? I've had a feeling on me these past days. She wanted to marry him, didn't she?'

'Yes, yes, she wanted to marry him.'

'Well then, why does she look as she does? In that church it could have been a funeral and she a lily on the coffin, I've never seen her looking so pale . . . And Barbara, I can't get over Barbara, not a word out of her these days. As for you . . . now Anna,' he came towards her wagging his finger, 'I know when something's amiss in your head, so come on,' his voice dropped to a whisper, 'tell me. Is there something I should know?'

She stared at him for a moment while her nostrils twitched and her

131

lips moved one over the other in an agitated fashion, and then she said, 'If there was something you should know, do you think I could keep it from you. It's your imagination. It's Constance's wedding day; wedding days I'm told are a strain. Though of course I wouldn't know anything about that.'

'Aw An-na, An-na, that's hitting below the belt. Tell me' – he took her chin in his hand – 'do you mind so very much, for if you did. . . .'

'If I did, you would still do nothing about it so it's well that I don't mind, isn't it?'

'You're a wonderful woman.'

'I'm a fool of a woman.' There was a deep sadness in the depths of her eyes as she smiled at him. Then taking his hand, she said, 'Come, we must join them now, and please me by being your entertaining self.'

At the wedding breakfast Thomas did his best to please her but as much for his own sake as for hers, for he was susceptible to atmosphere. He could never tolerate company where there was a feeling of strain. If he found it impossible to lighten it, he parted with it at the earliest opportunity. He would have liked nothing better now than to retire to his study, but as that was impossible he spread his congeniality as wide as possible, extending it to the meal and to Mary. When she almost tripped as she was carrying a dish to the table he cried at her, 'You're drunk, woman! Couldn't you wait?'

As Mary placed the dish in front of him she spluttered, 'Oh, Master, the things you say. I've never even had a drop yet; I've not even had a chance to drink Miss Constance's health.' She smiled at Constance and Constance smiled back at her, a white, thin smile.

No one seemed to notice that Mary had excluded the bridegroom. Although she would have said she had nothing against him, and she would have gone further and said there were things about him that she admired, the way he had got on for instance, and the way he presented himself; but she would have also said that in her opinion he wasn't the man for Miss Constance. Miss Constance should have married a gentleman, and although Donald Radlet was the master's son he was in her opinion far from being a gentleman. But anyway, it was done, and there she was, poor lamb, looking as white as a bleached sheet. Yet she supposed that was nothing to go by, most girls looked white on their wedding day. Now that was funny; Miss Constance had never wanted to be married in white. Months ago she had made up her mind to be married in yellow, and she had bought the material, yellow taffeta with a mauve sprig on it, and together she and Miss Barbara and Miss Brigmore had made it; and they had made a good job of it because she looked lovely, really lovely.

Barbara, too, thought that Constance looked lovely, and she knew in this moment that the soreness in her heart was concerned not only with the loss of Donald, because, as she had told herself, how could you lose something you had never had, but with the real loss of Constance herself, for she hadn't been separated from Constance since the very day she was born. In those early days she had cared for her like a little mother, and in this moment the pain of losing her was obliterating every other feeling. She could see the winter days ahead; for her the inside of the house would be as barren as the outside. There would still be Anna and her uncle, but she must face it, they had each other. Even Mary; Mary had someone she went to see on her day off once a fortnight; they lived over near Catton. She said it was an old aunt of hers but she also mentioned that the aunt had a nephew. She had never said how old the nephew was, but it was noted by all of them that Mary always came back from Auntie's very bright-eyed and somewhat gay. For years past Mary's Auntie had been a private joke between Constance and herself. Well, whoever he was, Mary had someone. They all had someone, except herself. And in another few years she'd be twenty-five. Then she would be old, and being plain, past the attractive stage, unless it was to some old man who needed nursing.

But even an old man who needed nursing would be better than reading her life away in this isolated spot where a visit from an outsider was a red-letter day. And she knew now that even the red-letter days would be few and far between once Constance was gone; not even young Ferrier would come any more.

Barbara was startled as a hand gripped her knee tightly and she turned her head to look into Miss Brigmore's eyes. Miss Brigmore was smiling and her eyes were telling her what to do. Miss Brigmore's eyes were very expressive. She remembered the time when she had first realized that Miss Brigmore was two people; it was on the day she had told her she thought she was wicked. She had dared to tell her what she had seen, and Miss Brigmore had knelt before her and held her hands and she had talked as if she were speaking to an adult. Strangely, she had understood all Miss Brigmore had said, and when she had finished she had realized that servants, even governesses, had few privileges compared with people such as herself; and in her old, young mind she had come to the conclusion that Miss Brigmore was someone she should be sorry for. Now, Miss Brigmore – dear, dear Anna – was someone whom she envied.

The meal was almost at an end. When it was over Constance would change her dress and leave immediately. Would she be able to talk to her before she left? She had become very distant this past week, almost as reticent as she herself was; reticence was part of her own nature but it never had had any place in Constance's character.

Constance was open, uninhibited, but these past few days she had scarcely opened her lips. This attitude had caused a secret hope to rise in her that perhaps Constance was going to change her mind and not marry Donald. Yet at the same time she was well aware that if this should happen it would avail her nothing because to Donald Radlet she was merely someone who read books and newspapers which gave her a knowledge of everyday matters, on which he could draw for his own information without taking the trouble or time to garner it himself.

Cynically she thought that he had used her as a form of abbreviated news-sheet, and she could imagine him repeating the information he had gathered on his sundry visits to his associates or at the cattle shows, or in the market. She imagined him throwing off bits of world news with an authoritative air, which gave him the name for being a knowledgeable fellow. Oh, in spite of her feelings regarding him she knew him, indeed she thought she knew him better than Constance ever would.

She looked at him now and found that he was surveying her. There was a smile on his lips, a possessive, quiet, controlled smile. He looked so sure of himself, proud, as he should be for he had gained a prize in Constance; much more so than if he had married her, for she had nothing but her brains to recommend her. . . .

Donald, looking back at Barbara, thought, she really hates the idea of me having Constance. She feels as bad in a way about it as that crab across there. He turned his set smile on Miss Brigmore and let it rest there. Well, he had beaten her, well and truly he had beaten her, and she knew it. When he entered the door this morning there had been a look on her face he had never seen before; it was there still. He took it to mean defeat.

He now turned his gaze on the man who was his father and wondered how he really felt about it all. He was the only merry one present; except Mary of course. He didn't seem to mind Constance going. But then you could never tell with the old man really; behind that boisterous laugh and his joking tongue there was a keen awareness, a cunningness that was the shield of his class and which covered his real feelings. Well, let them all react as they might; he had won Constance, she was his. In one hour or less they'd be setting out over the hills. She was his wife, she was his for life. At last he had something of his own! And he would love her as a woman had never been loved before. And each year she'd give him a child, sons first, daughters later. He'd bring the colour back to her cheeks, conquer her fear of storms. By God! yes, he meant to do that after what Matthew had told him about the effect the weather had on her. He wasn't going to allow her to be fear-ridden for the rest of her life; he'd conquer her fear or he'd know the reason why.

They were drinking to them now. There they stood, the old man, and – her, and Barbara. As he gazed at them he quietly groped under the table-cloth for Constance's hand and when he found it he squeezed it tightly; but she did not turn and look at him, for she was looking up at the three beloved faces that were gazing down on her. And they were beloved faces, each and every one of them was beloved. She had never imagined that leaving them would be such a wrench. She knew that she loved them all, but in different ways. She felt like flinging herself forward and embracing them all at once and crying to them, 'Don't let me go. Don't let me go.' She could not believe that she was now a married woman, that the short ceremony in the bare and quiet church had given her over to Donald for life. Yet she recalled that the moment the ceremony was finished she had known a surge of relief, for now should a child be born through her madness there would be no disgrace. No life isolated in this cottage and burdened with the stigma of an unwanted child. No, the short ceremony had made her safe – but at what a price.

Donald did not stand and respond to the toast, he knew nothing of such ceremony, but he drank deeply, one, two, three glasses of wine, and all to his wife, while she still sipped at her first glass.

When Constance left the table and went upstairs both Miss Brigmore and Barbara accompanied her. Miss Brigmore did not want to leave the two sisters alone, so that there could be no private, tear-filled farewell between them. Constance's luggage was already packed, she had only to change her dress. This was quickly done, and when she was arrayed in a brown corded costume and wearing a biscuit-coloured straw hat, she stood for a moment and looked around the room. Then her eyes came to rest, first on Miss Brigmore and then on Barbara, and the next moment they were all enfolded together. But only for a moment, for Miss Brigmore, her voice breaking as she turned hastily away, said as she picked up the pair of gloves from the dressing table, 'No more now; what's done's done; it's over. Come, come.' She turned again and, spreading her arms wide, ushered them like two children through the door, and when they were on the landing she called, 'Mary! Mary! Come and help with the luggage.'

But instead of Mary appearing on the stairs it was Donald who bounded up to them, saying, 'You leave that to me. What is there? Where are they?' Miss Brigmore, pointing back into the room, said, 'There are three cases and four packages.'

'Three cases and four packages.' He imitated her voice, then let out a deep laugh and, going into the room, he picked up two cases in one hand and tucked a bulky package under his other arm before picking up the third case and, as Mary entered the room, he cried at her, 'I've left three for you.' Then in very much the manner that Thomas might have used, he poked his head forward and uttered in a stage whisper, 'How would you like to come over the hills and work for me, eh?'

'Go on with you. Go on with you.' She laughed shrilly. 'You're a funny fellow you are; you're taking enough away when you're takin' Miss Constance. Go on, get off and don't let the master hear you sayin' you want me an' all; they're losing enough the day, they are that.'

Mimicking her now, he said, 'And you've had more than a drop the day, Mary, you have that. You like your duckie, don't you?'

He was at the top of the stairs now, she behind him, and she giggled as she said, 'Eeh! the things you say. Go on with you.' He wasn't so bad after all, she thought to herself, she liked him she did; yes, she did.

The women were outside now; only Thomas was in the hall. He was no longer smiling, his expression was sad and there was a tightness to his jaws, and when Mary, still laughing, said, 'He's a funny fellow this, Master,' he admonished her as the master of the Hall might have done at one time, saying, 'Be quiet, woman;' and she became quiet, subdued. Not until she had put the packages among the others in the back of the brake and Constance had come towards her and, putting her arms about her, had kissed her did she speak again; and then her words came out on a flood of tears and she cried, 'Oh Miss Constance! Miss Constance!' and putting her white apron to her face she turned about and ran back into the house.

When Constance stood in the circle of Thomas's arms and felt his big body quiver with emotion, it was too much, and she leant against him and cried, 'Uncle! Dear Uncle!' and Thomas, his own cheeks wet, looked over her head to where his son was standing near the horse, waiting, and he said, 'There now, there now. Go on, over the hills with you.' Then he took her face in his hands and added, 'Don't forget us, my dear. Come and see us often, eh?'

She nodded at him helplessly. The next moment she was lifted bodily in Donald's arms and placed in the seat at the front of the brake, and not until he had taken his seat beside her and picked up the reins did she lift her head and look at them again. They were standing close together gazing up at her, and she spoke to them as if they were one, saying, 'Good-bye, good-bye' and they all nodded their heads at her, but not one of them spoke.

Before the brake rounded the bend in the road she turned right round in her seat and waved to them, and now they waved back.

As soon as they were out of sight, Donald gathered the reins into one hand, thrust out his other arm and pulled her to his side with a jerk that caught at her breath and made her gasp, and his eyes covering her with their dark gleaming light, he muttered thickly, 'At last, at long last,' and the words brought home to her more than anything else the depths and the fierceness of his passion for her; and if it had aroused only fear in her there might have been some hope for him, but not when it also created revulsion.

4

THEY GREETED HER KINDLY, most warmly. Both Michael and Jane came from the house into the yard as the brake drew up. It was as if they had been waiting together.

'Well, here we are then,' said Michael with a smile, and when Donald had lifted her to the ground Jane held out her two hands and Constance took them gladly. But when Jane said, 'Welcome home, my dear,' all Constance could reply, and in a stiffly polite tone, was, 'Thank you.'

Although the day was warm they had lit a fire in the sitting room. The horsehair suite had been lightened with crotchet arm and head rests, a large new, hand-done proggy mat lay the length of the long stone fireplace, and the round table in the centre of the room was set for tea. On the snowy cloth lay the tea-set that had not been out of the cabinet since Matthew was christened, and the rest of the table was covered with a variety of home-baked cakes and plates of cold ham and beef, and pickles.

'Would you like to go upstairs or would you have a cup of tea first?' Jane's voice was warm, even comforting.

'I should love a cup of tea, please.' And not only one, she thought, but two, three, four, anything to delay going upstairs and being alone with him. It was no use telling herself that she had to be alone with him for the rest of her days; all she could think of at the moment was, she wanted a little breathing space.

She watched Jane bustle from the room to the kitchen back and forth several times, while Michael sat in the high-backed armchair opposite to her and nodded at her at intervals. At last he endeavoured to open a conversation.

'You've got it over then?' He still nodded at her.

'Yes, thank you.'

'How did it go?'

At this she glanced at Donald, where he was standing with his back to the fire; and he answered for her. On a laugh, he said, 'Well, it's done, signed, sealed, and I've put me brand on her.' He leant sideways and lifted up her hand showing to Michael the ring on her finger.

'I'm sorry that Matthew couldn't get along.' Michael was still nodding.

'Yes.' She swallowed, then said again, 'Yes,' before forcing herself to ask, 'Is he any better?'

'Better than he was yesterday, but still rather poorly. We're thinkin' of sending for a doctor come Monday. He won't hear of it, as usual, can't stand doctors; but I'll have me way if he's no better come Monday.'

Jane said now, 'Will you sit up, my dear?' and Constance came to the table, and the four of them sat down. One after the other they handed her the plates, and in order not to seem impolite and ungrateful to this kind little woman she forced herself to eat, and as she ate she thought, Thank God I shall like her. That at least is one good thing. And the father too; they're good people. And she prayed, 'Please God, take this feeling that I have against Donald from me; let me at least like him, don't let me hurt him, for . . . for he means well, and he cares for me.'

That was the trouble, he cared too much for her. She had not realized to the full extent the intensity of his passion; before, it had been somewhat veiled, but during the journey over the hills he had expressed his feelings, not only in words, but in looks, and touch.

She now tried to delude herself into thinking that once tonight was over the fire in him would be damped a little; his intensity would relax, and they would fall into a pattern like other married couples. But what other married couples? Whom did she know who was married? She had come in contact with no young married couples, all she knew about marriage was what she had read, and most of the stories ended up with the couple getting married and living happily ever after. Those that didn't were tragedies, where the husband took a mistress or the wife took a lover. Her husband would never take a mistress, she felt sure of this. Although he was a Mallen in part, he wasn't made like that. In an odd way he was much too proper. But she had already had a lover.

She glanced at Donald. He was sitting straight; he looked arrogant, utterly pleased with himself. He turned and looked her full in the face and jerked his chin upwards at her, and the action expressed more than any words the confidence he had in himself; and rightly, for was she not his wife and sitting, to all intents and purposes, at his table. The air of possession that emanated from him was frightening and she

139

recalled, on a deep wave of sickness, Matthew's words, 'He would slit my throat like he does a pig's.'

It was about a quarter past seven when Jane lit the lamps. Constance stood by the table and watched her fitting on the coloured glass shades, the plain white one for the kitchen and a blue one, patterned with gold spots, for the sitting room. She remarked that the blue one was pretty and Jane replied, 'Aye, it belonged to the father's' – she always referred to her husband as the father – 'it belonged to the father's grandmother and the globe hasn't got a crack in it. I get scared out of me wits every time I light it.'

Jane turned her head to the side and smiled at the girl who was to share her home, and she was surprised that her presence was creating in her a feeling of shy happiness. She told herself that if the girl settled it would be like having a daughter in the house, and somebody to talk to. That is if Donald wasn't about. But of course it all depended on her settling, and at the moment she looked as if she could take flight. She couldn't explain to herself the look on the girl's face; she didn't want to put the word fear to it because she couldn't see what she had to fear; she had taken Donald with her eyes open, she'd had time to think about it, and then gone through with it, so she couldn't see that it was Donald who was making her uneasy. But uneasy she was. And there was another strange thing. When they rose from the table she hadn't gone with Donald but had followed her round the house asking questions about this and that, saying she wanted to be of assistance. Only a minute ago she had smiled at her kindly and said, 'There's plenty of time. Now don't worry, I'll find you all the work you feel inclined to do; you never can be idle on a farm you know.' And now here she was wanting to help with the lamps.

She had seen immediately the difference the girl's presence was going to make to Donald; he was like a dog with two tails, she had never seen him so amenable. He had spoken to her as he had never done before, had even made a request of her. He had come into the larder, and standing at her side, had said, 'If she wants to learn the dairy show her, will you, but don't press her. I don't want her to do anything she doesn't want to do.' And she had turned and looked at him. His expression had been soft, and for the first time in his life he looked really happy, and she had answered, 'I'll tell her anything she wants to know.'

He had nodded, and stared at her silently for a moment before turning away, and leaving her standing with her hands pressed flat on the cold marble slab and thinking, it's going to work out all right after all. This is what he needs, a wife such as this one, someone he can be proud of and show off, someone he could have married if he'd had his birthright. And at that moment she had understood a lot about her son she had never understood before.

When she carried the lamp in both hands held well in front of her into the sitting room she did not speak until she had placed it on the table, and then, standing back from it, she looked at Constance and said, 'You'll find life here strange at first because we mostly work to the light, up with the dawn, to bed with the dusk, or pretty near it. At the end of a long day we're ready for our beds, especially in the winter, 'cos that's the warmest place, bed. Of course when I say that' – she now nodded her head and smiled broadly at Constance – 'I'm forgettin' about our Matthew. He'd burn oil to the dawn readin' his books. But not Donald.' She put out her hand now and indicated that Constance should sit on the couch, and as she sat down opposite to her she finished, 'Donald works very hard, very hard indeed. Since the father's had rheumatics it's been extra heavy for him. And there are times, as now, when Matthew can't do anything at all.'

Constance stared back through the lamplight into the round, homely face of this ordinary woman who in a way was on a par with Mary, but who nevertheless was her mother-in-law, and all she could do was nod. She knew already that she liked this woman. She also knew that she was going to need her in the days ahead. What she had the urge to do now was to sit close to her and hold her hands, cling to her hands. She thought too that her liking was returned. Yet what would this woman do if she knew that her new daughter-in-law had lain with one son before marrying the other? Just as Matthew had said of Donald, she would want to slit her throat. That terrible phrase was recurring in her mind more and more.

When she spoke again her question must have appeared as if she were anxious for Donald's return, for what she said was, 'Does it take long. . . . I mean the last round at night?'

Jane smiled quietly as she said, 'Well, it all depends. You see the cattle are still out, and he goes round the fields. Then sometimes the hens won't take to their roost. There's a couple in particular go clucking round in the dark; they're deranged, an' one of these mornings they'll wake up and find themselves inside the fox and that'll give them a gliff.'

She laughed, a soft gay laugh, and was herself surprised to hear it; then in a more sober tone she went on, 'Of course, in the lambing time he can be up all hours that God sends; an' then with the calfing an' all. He's very careful of the animals, very careful.' She nodded at Constance, her expression quite serious now, then added, 'He's well thought of as a farmer, oh very well thought of. They take his word for lots of things roundabout.'

All Constance could say to this was 'Yes.' . . .

An hour later Jane thought to herself that she had never talked so much at one go in her life. Michael was no talker; Matthew was always in his books; and when you got a word out of Donald it was usually a comment on the animals, or a definite statement of what he was about to do. She had talked as she had done because the girl was nervous; she was all eyes. She looked a child, too young to be married, yet she was the same age as herself when she was married. She recalled her own first night in this house, her fear of having to go to bed with Michael, and then her overwhelming feeling of happiness when she realized the goodness in the man she had married. But there was a great difference between Michael and Donald, and there was a greater difference between herself at that age and this girl; yet it was the first night of marriage and she was in a strange house, and they were all comparative strangers to her. She must be filled with a great unease.

She leant forward now and said gently, 'Would you like to go upstairs and see to your things and such? You must be tired; it's been a trying day for you.'

Before she had finished speaking Constance was on her feet, saying, 'Yes, I would, thank you. Thank you very much.'

'I'll light your lamp, it's up there already. I'll take the kitchen one to see us up the stairs. I'd better not take that one.' She smiled and nodded towards the blue-shaded light, and Constance said, 'No, no, of course not.'

Constance had been in the bedroom earlier. She had opened one case and hung some of her things in the old dutch wardrobe that stood against one white wall, but she had not attempted to unpack the rest of the luggage. All she had wanted to do was to get away from the sight of the high bed covered by the patchwork quilt. Jane had pointed out to her that she had spent the winter making the quilt, and she had duly admired it; she had also thanked her for decorating the room, which decoration consisted of lime-washing in between the black beams that strutted the walls at uneven angles and those that supported the low ceiling in three massive beetle-pierced lengths, and which gleamed dully where the linseed oil that Jane had applied so generously to them had failed to soak in.

Setting the lamp down on the round oak table to the side of the bed, Jane now turned to Constance and, her hands folded in front of her waist, she said, 'There you are then, dear. I'll leave you now and wish you good night.' But she didn't move immediately, she stood staring at Constance and Constance at her; then, as if motivated by the same thought, they moved towards each other and their hands held and their cheeks touched. Then muttering something like, 'May your life be good, God bless you, dear,' Jane hurried from the room. And Constance was alone.

She looked about the room as she had done earlier in the day, and now, although she was still filled with panic, she knew she could run no farther; she had come up against a rock face as it were, and from now on she'd have to steel herself and climb.

The room was cold, there was a dankness about it. She knelt by one of the cases on the floor and, having opened it, she took out a warm nightdress, a dressing gown and a pair of slippers from where Anna had placed them to be ready to her hand. As she laid them on the bed she hesitated whether to wash her face and hands now or to wait until she was undressed; deciding she'd be less cold doing it now, she went to the corner washhand stand at the far side of the room. The basin was set in a hole in the middle of the stand; the jug in the basin was full to the top with water – and icy cold; the towel she dried on was clean and white but rough; but all these were minor inconveniences and would, she thought, have been endured with something of amusement if only the man with whom she was to share that bed behind her was anyone but Donald. If only it had been Matthew, even a sick Matthew, she would have been happy; or at least she wouldn't have been filled with fear as she was at this moment. But let her get this one night over and she would cope. Oh yes, just let her get this one night over and she would cope.

As she was about to undress she looked at the picture that was hanging above the bed. It was one of three religious prints that Jane had hung in the room; it showed colourful even in the lamplight, the picture itself was a travesty created by an artist who had undoubtedly taken liberties with the book of Esther, for not only did it show King Ahasuerus seated in his marble-pillared palace surrounded by his seven chamberlains, with Vashti, the wife he had put away, standing at a distance from him but it also showed Esther, whom he had taken to be his Queen, seated to his side, and at her feet seven maidens, undoubtedly virgins all.

Quickly now she began to unbutton her dress. Having stepped out of it, she folded it lengthwise and laid it over the back of a chair, as of habit; then she undid the strings of her first waist petticoat and stepped out of that; and she did the same with her under petticoat. It was as she stood in her bloomers, soft, lawn, lace-trimmed bloomers, a new innovation created by an American lady – the daring pattern of which she had copied from a ladies' journal – that the door opened. She did not turn her head to look towards it, but with one swift movement she gathered up her two petticoats and holding them against her neck she dropped down on to the edge of the bed and drew up her knees under their trailing cover.

Slowly and with a look of amusement on his face, Donald came towards her and, standing above her, he shook his head as he put out his hand and gently but firmly made to relieve her of her undergarments. When she resisted he closed his eyes for a moment, then said softly and as if reasoning with a child, 'Constance. Constance, you remember what happened today?' He now stretched his face at her in amused enquiry. 'Eh? You were married, remember? . . . Look' – he now caught her hand and, holding the wedding ring between his finger and thumb, he shook it vigorously – 'you were married . . . we were married. Come.' With a twist of his body he was sitting beside her, one arm about her, the other forcing her joined hands down over her chest.

When her protesting hands touched her lap he released them, and his fingers now moved upwards to the buttons lying between her breasts. As if she had been stung she sprang away from him and, grabbing up her nightdress, pulled it over her head, and now, half shielded by the foot of the bed and with rapid contortions, she undressed under it as she had done as a child when she shared her room with Barbara.

Miss Brigmore had early on introduced them to this pattern, reciting a little poem that went: 'Modesty becomes maidens making ready for the night.' And when alone, they had mimicked her but altered the words to: 'Modesty becomes maidens who are little mealy-mouthed mites.'

Still seated on the bed, Donald surveyed her. He was no longer smiling, no longer amused. From a deep recess in his mind a thought was oozing, like the matter from a suppurating sore. As it gained force it brought him up from the bed, and the action seemed to stem its flow; but he was still aware of it as he gripped her by the shoulders and said from low in his throat, 'Constance, you are me wife, you're no longer in the cottage with them, you've started on a different sort of life. And you're not a child, so stop acting like one.'

When he thrust her from him she fell backwards and leant against the brass rail at the foot of the bed. Her eyes were wide, her mouth open. She watched him for a moment as he turned from her and walked across the room and pulled open the top drawer of the chest; then like the child he had denied she was, she scrambled up the side of the bed, tore back the clothes and climbed in.

When she next looked at him he was undressed down to his trousers. At this point she closed her eyes. She did not open them again until she felt him moving by the side of the bed; and what she saw would, under happier circumstances, have made her laugh, for he was dressed in a night-shirt that barely reached his knees. It wasn't the first time she had seen a man dressed in a night-shirt, she had often glimpsed her uncle on his journeys back and forth to the water closet in the early morning. But then her uncle's night-shirt reached his ankles. But Donald's night-shirt exposed his lower limbs and she saw that they were hairy, as also was his chest that she glimpsed through the open shirt; and for a reason she couldn't explain she became more fearful.

Her body stiff, she waited for him to put out the lamp; but when he clambered into the bed the lamp was still burning. Now, leaning on his elbow, he was hanging over her, looking down into her face, saying nothing, just staring at her; and as she stared back at him she saw his whole countenance alter. There came over it the softness that she had glimpsed now and again, and her thoughts, racing madly, gabbled at her. It might have been all right if that storm hadn't overtaken them. Yes, yes, it might. If only she could forget what had happened in the storm, put it out of her mind, at least for tonight. But she couldn't because Matthew was there, somewhere across the landing, coughing – and knowing, and thinking.

He still did not speak when he drew her into his arms and held her body close to his. But he did not bring his face close to hers; he kept his head well back from her and peered at her, and his whisper bore out the expression in his eyes: 'I just want to look at you,' he said; 'look and look. I've dreamt of this moment for years. Do you understand that, Constance?'

As the muscles of his arms suddenly contracted her body jerked against his, yet remained stiff. For the moment he seemed unaware of it, lost in the wonder of his own emotions and not a little blinded by his own achievement. But when his mouth dropped to hers and there was no response from her lips he brought his head up again, and now he asked, almost as a plea, 'What is it? What is it, Constance? Don't be afraid, please. Don't be afraid, I love you. I told you I love you, and I'll love you as no one has ever been loved afore. I need to love you, and I need you to love me. Do you understand that?'

'. . . Say something.' Again her body jerked within his hold.

When she did not speak, the softness seeped from his face and he said thickly, 'That damned old cow has filled your head with bloody nonsense about marriage, hasn't she?'

At this she managed to gulp and mutter, 'No, no.'

'Then what is it?'

If she had replied, 'I'm afraid, Donald; it's all so strange, everything,' he undoubtedly would have thought he understood and might even have given himself another explanation for what he was to discover within the next few minutes; but she could not put on an act for him, she was not subtle enough, sly enough, and she was aware of this.

'No, no! not yet, please, please, not yet.' Her voice was strangled in her throat, his mouth was eating her. His hands seemed to have multiplied like the snakes on Medusa's head and were attacking her body from all angles. . . .

It was a full three minutes after she ceased to struggle that he raised himself from her. In part she had known the man Donald Radlet five minutes earlier, but she knew nothing of the man who was gazing down at her now. The face that she was staring into had about it a stricken look; then like wind-driven clouds that changed the face of the sky, the expression turned into one of wild black ferocity. She held her breath and tried to press her body deeper into the feather tick in order to ward off the violence threatened by his expression, but to her relief and surprise his body moved away from hers until there was a foot of space between them, and he was sitting upright, half turned from her, but with his eyes still on her.

As if obeying a warning voice within himself, Donald moved still further towards the edge of the bed, but continued to look at her. And as he looked he knew that the pus from the secret sore in his mind was flooding his brain, and that if he didn't control it he would put out his hands and throttle the thing he loved, and wanted to go on loving. But now there was a question about that for he knew that he had been duped; he, Donald Radlet, who was no man's fool, who was as smart as they came, who allowed no one to take the rise out of him without paying for it, who knew, who had always known, that if you followed the principle of wanting a thing badly enough you would surely get it, had been made a monkey out of.

This then was the reason for her attitude. He could see it all plainly now; it was as clear as the white light that occasionally covered the hills, the light that took your gaze away into infinity. Her manner this past week, her being afraid to face him a week gone. She had taken to her bed when he had dashed over the hills to find out what the trouble was.

It was as he was leaving the cottage that he had met the Ferrier boy, because that's all he was, a smooth-chinned, weak-kneed boy. But he was just going back to Oxford he'd said, and it was doubtful if that old cow would have left him alone in the bedroom with Constance for a moment. But if not he, then who else?

There was that family in Allendale, with the two sons. Both were a deal older than her, but what did that matter? Yes, what did that matter? Look at the old man for example. Yet it must have been a month since she had visited Allendale and what had taken place had taken place within the last fortnight.

He looked into her face, beautiful, even angelic looking . . . but fear-filled. Had he made a mistake? Hell's flames, no! he had made no mistake. He was no amateur coming to bed for the first time; he had been but fifteen when he took his first woman. And that was the correct term, took her; she hadn't taken him, although she had been long at the game. She had laughed at him, and liked him, and every market day in Hexham he had managed to slip up the alley. She had supplied him until he was eighteen.

One particular time when he went up the alley the door was opened by a young girl. Bella had died the previous week she said, but would he like to come in. Her name was Nancy; she was fourteen and she was the one and only virgin he'd ever had. But if he'd never had that experience he would have known that she, lying there, his wife, on this the first night of their marriage was no virgin.

His pride was under his feet, his head was dragged down, his arrogance was broken, his self-esteem was as something he had never heard of for his mind was utterly deprived of it. He was no longer a Mallen flaunting his streak, finding pride in his bastardy, and through it feeling he had the right to confer condescension on even those who considered themselves his superiors – he was nothing. He was now as he had been that day in the market place when the Scolley brothers had laughed at him and called him a bastard. Yet he was not even as he had been on that day, he was less, much less, for on that day he had become aware that there was high blood in him, gentleman's blood. On that day he found out that he was the son of a man who owned a grand Hall over the hills, a man of property and substance; and on that day he had sworn that he would grow so big in all ways that nobody would dare turn a disdainful look in his direction without paying for it, and that whatever he desired from life he would get. . . .

And he had got it. She was lying there, and she was no better than any whore.

She smothered a scream as he pounced on her, his hands round her throat, his nose almost touching hers, his words like grit spitting into her face. 'Who was it? tell me! Who was it?'

When her body became limp under his hands he released the pressure of his thumbs; but now he had her by the shoulders, lifting her bodily upwards, and in a whispered hiss he demanded, 'Tell me! else I'll throttle it out of you.'

When she moved her head from side to side and gasped he shook her like a dog shaking a rat, and when the tears spurted from her eyes and a cry escaped her lips he turned his head quickly and looked towards the door before thrusting her back into the mattress.

He remained still, listening. Then satisfying himself that if her cry had carried beyond the room they would likely take it as the result of a marriage bed caper, he moved up to her again. And now leaning over her, his hands one on each side of her, he said slowly, 'You've been with somebody, haven't you?'

Her hands were holding her throat as she shook her head; then she stammered, 'N ... n ... no.'

'You're lying. You can't hoodwink me, not on this anyway. Who was he? I'll not keep askin' you, I'll shake it out of you. I'll beat it out of you. Do you hear, my dear Constance? I'll beat it out of you. Who was it?'

'I tell you, I tell you ... nobody.'

He screwed up his eyes until they became mere slits, then repeated, 'Nobody? nobody you say? Then why didn't you come over as you intended last week? It must have taken some storm to have put you to bed.'

'It ... it was ... it was the storm.'

'You're lying.'

'I'm not.'

As she gazed into his face she realized that not only would she have to lie, but lie convincingly, for she knew that this man was capable, as Matthew had predicted, of slitting her throat as he did the pigs'.

Like an actress taking her cue she obeyed the inner voice in her and, hoisting herself away from him, she tried to assume indignation, and in no small tone she cried at him, 'You are mad. I don't know what you mean, what you suspect, and ... and I won't stay with you to be treated in such a manner, I'll go home. ...'

Immediately she knew she had overdone her part for he turned on her now, growling low, 'You what! you what!' His lean face was purple with his anger; the fact that she could even voice such a thing showed him a new aspect of his humiliation, a public aspect, something to be avoided at all costs, especially in his case, for were she even to attempt to go back over the hills he could never outlive the humiliation. But being who he was he knew that he would never allow it to get that far, and he told her so. In a thick whisper now, leaning towards her but not touching her, he said, 'You'll go home, as you call it, when they carry you over in a box to the cemetery but not afore, not if I know it.'

When she closed her eyes and the tears washed down her face his teeth ground into his lip, and he bowed his head for a moment and, in real agony now, he groaned, 'Oh Constance! Constance! why? why? How could you do it?'

'I didn't, I didn't. I tell you you must be mad. I don't know what you're talking about.'

He was looking at her as he said, 'Well, if you don't know what I'm talking about why do you say you didn't?'

Her head wagged on her shoulders in a desperate fashion now as she muttered, 'Because you are suggesting that I ... I ...'

She suddenly turned from him and rolled onto her face and pressed it into the pillow to stifle the sound of her sobbing, and he straightened his back and turned from the bed. Having crossed the room to where his clothes lay, he slowly got back into them, all except his shoes, and these he carried in his hand.

Without a backward glance towards the bed, he went to the door and, gripping it firmly so that it shouldn't creak, he opened it and closed it after him. Cautiously he crossed the landing and went down the stairs. There was no light; he didn't need one, he knew every inch of this house. Unbolting the back door, he went into the yard.

He looked up at the sky for a moment. It was high and star-studded; the air was sharp with frost, there would be rime on the walls in the morning. He crossed the yard and went through a door next to the cow byres and into the warm atmosphere that came from the boiler where the pig mash was simmering. The room was part harness room, part store-room. He pulled down a bundle of hay and brought it near to the boiler and, sitting on it, he dropped his head into his hands and for the first time in his life Donald Radlet cried.

Towards morning he must have dozed; but he became wide awake at the sound of the cockerel giving answer to the faint echo coming from another of his breed across the valley. He rose from the hay on which he had been lying and dusted himself down, then went out into the yard. He did not look up into the sky to see the light lifting, for his attention was caught by the gleam of the lamp coming from the kitchen. His mother must be up but it was early for her.

When he entered the kitchen and Matthew, a teapot in his hand, swung round from the fireplace, he stopped and stared at him before saying, 'Why are you up?'

Steadying the teapot in both hands. Matthew went to the table and placed the teapot on it before he muttered, 'I . . . I needed a drink; I . . . I had the shivers.'

Donald was standing at the other side of the table now and he said, 'Why didn't you knock for Mam?'

When Matthew gave no answer but reached out and drew a mug towards him Donald's eyes focused on his hand which was trembling; then they lifted to his face. His skin had not the usual transparent glow about it this morning except for the two high spots of red on his cheekbones; it looked yellow, as if it had taken the tint from his hair. His gaze was held by the odd expression in his eyes; it was a startled expression holding fear. Well, he would be fearful, wouldn't he? When a man knew he was going to die it would make him fearful.

'How . . . how is Constance?'

'Look out, you're spilling the tea all over the place. Here! give it to me . . . She's all right, tired, exciting day yesterday.' He actually forced his lips into a smile; it was the first effort in the pattern he had worked out for himself last night. He would act before the others as if everything were normal, and he would see that she did the same. By God! he would. One thing he wouldn't tolerate and that was pity; even from those in this house who were near to him, for he knew that, being human, they could not help but think, And how are the mighty fallen! His da had a saying: If the eagle dies in the air it still has to fall to earth. Well, he had been an eagle and last night a vital part of him had died and he had fallen to the earth; but no one would know of his fall.

'Here, here! hold on a minute.' He could not get round the table quickly enough to save Matthew from falling backwards. When he reached him he was lying on the floor, his face now no longer yellow but deathly white.

'Matthew! Matthew!' He raised his head, then put his hand on his heart; it was still beating and quite rapidly. Bending now, he picked the inert figure from the floor as if it were a child and carried it upstairs, and as he passed the first door on the landing he put out his foot and kicked it as he yelled, 'Matthew's bad, get up.'

He was lifting his foot again to thrust it out towards Matthew's bedroom door when he saw Constance standing in the open doorway of their bedroom. Her face looked almost as white as the one hanging over his arm, and he cried at her, 'Come and make yourself useful.' It was his second move in the new game and it seemed to have an immediate effect on her for she sprang from the doorway to his side and as he made his way towards the bed she muttered, 'What . . . what have you done? What have you done?'

He didn't answer until he had laid Matthew down and was taking off his shoes, then he looked at her from the side and said, 'What do you mean, what have I done?' His eyes followed her to Matthew's face where the lips and chin were now covered with blood, and he thought he saw the reason for her question.

'It's his lungs, he's fainted.' Then his voice harsh, he growled at her under his breath, 'And don't you do the same, 'cos you'll witness more than a spot of blood afore you're finished.'

The words were like a threat, yet they steadied her for she, too, had actually been on the point of fainting, and for much the same reason that had tumbled Matthew into unconsciousness, relief.

PART FOUR

Barbara

I

NOVEMBER AND DECEMBER 1862 had been cruel months. Miss Brigmore had caught a severe cold through sitting on the carrier's cart exposed to a biting wind as it travelled the hills between the cottage and the farm.

The newly married couple had visited the cottage only once, and then she'd hardly been able to have a word alone with Constance for that man had hovered over them like a hawk. But during the short conversation she had gauged enough to gather that life was bearable during the day-time but that at night it became a special kind of purgatory, because Donald was aware of her lapse; he had seemingly been aware of it from the first night of their marriage. Constance had stared at her while waiting for a clearer explanation of this, and she might have been able to satisfy her except that they had been interrupted by Donald.

Repeatedly since that visit Miss Brigmore had blamed herself for having neglected a very important part of the girls' education, yet at the same time excusing herself: should she under any circumstances have had to explain to them that they were virgins but once?

It was when the weather was about to break and there had been no further visit from the farm, that Thomas said, 'You know, I've got a feeling that everything isn't right across there; why doesn't he come like he used to? Hail, rain or snow didn't stop him this time last year, except when the roads were absolutely impassable, and they'll soon be like that again. If it wouldn't be the means of embarrassing both myself and those people across there' – he was referring now to Jane and Michael – 'I would order a carriage and go over, I would indeed.'

He had looked at her as he finished and then had stood waiting for her response, which she knew should have been, 'And where do you think the money is coming from to provide you with a carriage?' But what she said was, 'I will go across myself; the carrier's cart will be running for a while yet.'

So, on a day when six layers of clothes were no protection against the icy wind she crossed over the mountains to the farm, and there, at the sight of her dear Constance, she had wanted to cover her face with her hands and weep. Three months of marriage had put almost twice as many years on her. There was no spark of joy left in her; in fact the mother, who was, Miss Brigmore thought, about her own age, was much more lively than the young wife. Only one consolation did she bring back with her across the hills. The mother was kind to Constance; she evidently had a liking for her, and was glad to have her at the farm. What little she saw of the father, too, she liked. He had welcomed her quite warmly. But she had found it almost impossible to look at, much less sympathize with, Matthew where he sat huddled in blankets to the side of the roaring fire. Indeed, when their eyes had met she knew that there was no secret between them.

What she had found strange too, was that Constance no longer wanted to be alone with her. She had not suggested taking her to her room, and when Jane had said, 'Wouldn't you like to take Miss Brigmore round the farm? Go on, wrap up well, it will do you good to get some air,' she had answered, 'Can you spare the time to come too, you can explain things better than me?' And she had turned her head in Miss Brigmore's direction but had not looked at her directly as she ended, 'I'm new to all this, you understand?'

In fact the whole being that Constance now presented to her was new to Miss Brigmore; the old Constance might never have existed, her spirit had been crushed. This wasn't altogether unexpected; for she had imagined it might happen. Nevertheless she had thought it would take a number of years to come about; yet Donald had accomplished the change in the course of a few weeks.

When she had at last returned to the cottage she was cold to the very core of her being, even her mind seemed numbed, and she had not hidden all the truth from them when they asked how she had found Constance. 'She's changed,' she had said.

'Changed?' Thomas had demanded. 'Changed, what do you mean?'

'She's much more quiet, sort of subdued.'

'Connie subdued? I'll never believe that, I'll have to see it first. When is she coming over?'

'I ... I don't think she'll be over yet awhile; she's been having a rather distressing time with sickness and such.'

'Oh. Oh.' Thomas had risen from his chair, his head bobbing. He had turned and looked at her and said, 'I don't mind telling you I miss her, I miss her chatter. Do you know something?' He had poked his head forward. 'I realize I've hardly laughed since she left. Funny now that, isn't it? Barbara's different, too quiet. You could always get a laugh out of Constance.'

'No, no, it isn't funny,' she had replied evenly. 'As you say, Barbara is sedate, and I cannot claim that any part of my nature tends towards provoking hilarity either.'

At this he put his head back and let out a bellow of a laugh before saying, 'I take it all back. I take it all back because there are times, my dear Anna, when you appear very, very funny.'

'Thank you.'

'Aw' – he flapped his hand at her as he turned away – 'you can't put me in my place, mentally or otherwise. Go on with you.' And he flapped his hand again as he went out, still chuckling.

Barbara had asked, 'How did you find her?' and she had answered again, 'Very changed.'

'She's not happy?'

She had stared at Barbara. Would it make her happy to know that her sister was unhappy, human nature being what it was? She didn't know.

Barbara now said, 'She's not settling?' and to this she answered, 'Yes, she's settling. But regarding happiness, no, I'd be telling a lie if I said she was happy.'

'Then why did she marry him?' The words were brought out with deep bitterness, and Miss Brigmore answered, 'There was a reason, a special reason. She had changed her mind and wasn't going to marry him. Yes' – she nodded at Barbara's surprised look – 'and something happened and she was forced to marry him.'

Barbara's thin face had crinkled into deep lines of disgust as she whispered, 'She had misbehaved?'

'Yes.' Miss Brigmore nodded her head. She had decided during these last few minutes to tell Barbara the truth. Whether she would sympathize or even understand she didn't know but she felt compelled to tell her the real reason why her sister had married Donald Radlet, and so she repeated 'Yes, she had misbehaved . . . but not with Donald.'

'Not with . . . ?' Barbara's mouth had fallen into an amazed gape.

'It happened in the storm when Matthew was taking her to the farm. You know how fearful she becomes in a storm. They took shelter in a deserted house on top of the hills. He comforted her and that was that. He told her that he had loved her as long as Donald had and she realized in that moment that she loved him too. From what little she told me I gather that she begged him to marry her but for obvious reasons he couldn't, or wouldn't. I think the main reason was he was afraid of Donald and what might happen to him if the truth were ever known.'

Barbara stood with her two hands pressed tightly over the lower part of her face; and after a time she whispered, 'And Donald, he . . . he doesn't know?'

'Yes and no. He knows that she did not come to him as a wife should but . . . but he doesn't know who was responsible.'

'Oh dear Lord! dear Lord!' Still holding her face, Barbara had paced the floor; and then much to Miss Brigmore's surprise she said with deep feeling, 'Poor Connie! poor Connie!' And she had endorsed it, saying, 'Yes, indeed Barbara, poor Connie.'

When, the day following her visit to the farm, Miss Brigmore had developed a cold she had treated it as an ordinary snifter – Mary's term for streaming eyes and a red nose – but on the third day when she went into a fever there was great concern in the house; and the following week when the cold developed into pneumonia and the doctor rode six miles from the town every day for four days a pall of fear descended on them all. What, Thomas had asked himself, would he do with his life if he lost Anna?

And what, Barbara has asked herself, would become of her if she lost Anna? She'd be left here with Uncle and Mary, Uncle who only thought of his stomach and – that unmentionable thing – and Mary, who had appeared to her as a wonderful person during her childhood, but whom she now saw as a faithful but very ordinary, even ignorant, woman. What she needed above everything now was mental companionship, so she went on her knees nightly, or whenever she gave herself time to rest, and beseeched God to spare Anna.

And Mary too – as she rushed between the cooking and the cleaning and the washing and the ironing, and lugging the coal upstairs to see that the room was kept at an even temperature twenty-four hours of the day – had also asked what would she do if anything happened to the Miss? There had been a time when she hadn't liked Miss Brigmore, when she hadn't a good word in her mouth for her; but that was many years ago. But since they had all come to live in this house she had come to look upon her not merely as a woman of spirit, but as a sort of miracle worker. If anything went wrong Miss Brigmore would put it right; moreover she had a way of spreading out the money so that it seemed to go twice as far as it would have done in anyone else's hands; and she never went for her now as she had done in those far-off days back in the nursery. Mind you, aye, she wasn't lavish with her praises, but you always knew when she was pleased. 'You've done very well, Mary,' she would say. 'I don't think you've made a better pie than that, Mary,' she would say. 'Put your feet up, Mary, and rest that leg,' she would say. The only times she showed any displeasure was when she was foolish enough to take more than three glasses of her Aunt Sarah's brew on her days off, for when she came back she couldn't stop her tongue from wagging, or herself from giggling. The girls used to laugh at her, and with her; but not Miss Brigmore. And a telling off would always come the next morning.

She often brought a bottle back with her. At one time, she kept it in her room, but she had more sense now. Now she left it in a rabbit hole beyond the hedge – you couldn't see the hole from this side, and all she had to do was to go on to her knees, put her hand through the privet and pull the bottle out. She generally waited until it was dark and they'd all gone to bed, and then just before she locked up she'd slip down the garden and have a little nip. It was a great comfort, her Aunt Sarah's bottle, on cold nights.

Once, when she had taken more than the three nips and Miss Brigmore had gone for her, she had nearly turned on her and said, 'Well, I haven't got the master to keep me warm, have I!' Eeh! she was glad she hadn't let that slip out, she would never have forgiven herself. And she knew that if it would be any help to Miss Brigmore at this moment she would promise her she would never touch a drop again as long as she lived. But all she could do was to ask God to see to it.

And God saw to it, but He took His time. Miss Brigmore survived pneumonia but it left her with an infection that the doctor could put no name to, but which, he said, could be cured with time. The infection took the form of making Miss Brigmore unable to assimilate her food. Within half-an-hour of eating a meal her bowel would evacuate it. Patience, said the doctor, patience. He had seen cases like this before. It might take two, or four, or six months, but it could be cured.

Up to date, Miss Brigmore had suffered the infection for four months. She was not confined wholly to bed but she was still unable to do anything other than sit in a chair by the side of the window, near enough to it to see the road, but far away enough from it to avoid a draught. . . .

It was now a March day in 1863, the sky high and clear blue. The snow had gone for the present, except from the hilltops. If you gave your imagination licence you could see spring not very far ahead. At least, this is what Barbara was saying as she bustled about the room. 'In a fortnight's time,' she said, 'three weeks at the most, we'll see the bulbs out, and the rowans too . . . and with the carrier's cart tomorrow we should have a letter from Constance. I must write one tonight and have it ready for him. Do you think you can do a note to her, Anna?'

'Yes, yes, of course I'll write a note.' Miss Brigmore's tone was absent-minded. 'By the way, who is that person talking to your uncle on the road?'

Barbara came to the window and, looking over the garden, she said, 'Oh, I understand her name is Moorhead, a Mrs Moorhead. Mary refers to her as that Aggie Moorhead. She comes from somewhere near

157

Studdon; she's working daily at the Hall doing the rough, I understand. Mary tells me they have engaged half-a-dozen such to get the place to rights before the staff arrive; but as she says, and I agree with her, it'll take six months not six weeks, and that's the time they have allowed them to clean the place down.'

'Why is your uncle talking to her?'

Barbara gave a little hunch to one shoulder as she turned from the window, saying, 'I don't suppose Uncle's talking to her, she's talking to him; to quote Mary again, she's got a loose lip.' She smiled now at Miss Brigmore, but Miss Brigmore was still looking in the direction of the road and she said, 'Your uncle's laughing.'

Barbara had been about to turn away, but she stopped and looked down at Miss Brigmore. Anna was jealous of Uncle. Well, well! It was strange, she thought, that a person could maintain jealousy into middle years. What was she now? Forty-two? No; forty-three? forty-four? Anna never talked about her age, but nevertheless she was a settled woman. She sighed heavily within herself. She wished she was over forty, for then she, too, would be settled, and she was sure that by then she'd be past all feelings of jealousy and discontent – and desire. She glanced out of the window again. The Moorhead person was walking away. She was passing the lower gate and she saw that she had a jaunty walk or, what would be more expressive, a common walk; her buttocks swayed from one side to the other. As Mary had suggested, she was a very common person, low even in the working class stratum. . . .

Down on the road Thomas was thinking much the same thing. She had a lilt to her walk, that piece; she swung her hips like a cow did its udders. And she was a little cow all right; if ever he had met one, there she went.

He had spoken to her on several occasions during the past few weeks. In fact it was she who had told him that his former home had been sold at last. After being confined to the house for days during the rough weather he had been taking the air on the road – he liked to walk on the level, he was past bobbing about on the rough fell land – and on one particular day it was she who had stopped, and smiled at him as she said, 'You're Mr Mallen, aren't you? Your old house's been sold again then.' And he had raised his brows at her and pursed his lips as he said, 'Has it indeed! Has it?'

'He's a man from Manchester way they say has took it.'

'Manchester? Oh, well, if he comes from there he won't stay long here.'

'They say he was born this way, at least his grandparents were. Bensham they called them. He's payin' well, shillin' a day an' your grub.'

She had jerked her head at him. But her familiarity had not annoyed him, he was long past taking offence at not being given his due, because, as he so often asked himself, what, after all, was his due these days? And so with a laugh he had said, 'You are lucky then.'

'Aye,' she replied. 'Aye, I'm always lucky. Never wanted, me. Live and let live I say, an' live it well as long as you've got it 'cos you're a long time dead.'

'You've got the correct philosophy.'

'Eh?'

'You're quite right, you're a long time dead.'

'That's what I said.' She had looked at him with round, bright, unblinking eyes, and her lips had slowly fallen apart showing her strong white teeth, and as they, in turn, widened he had watched her tongue wobbling in her mouth. Then she gave a laugh as her head went back and in a slow movement she turned from him, saying, 'Ta-rah, then, mister.'

He hadn't answered for a moment, but had watched her take four steps before saying, 'Good-bye.'

And she had turned her head over her shoulder and cried at him 'An' to you.'

He had walked on down the road smiling to himself. There went a character. 'And to you,' she had said. It appertained to no part of the farewell that had passed between them, but it had sounded amusing, and meaningful. 'And to you,' she had said. She was no chicken, but what vitality. God! how he wished he were younger. No, no – he shook his head at himself – those days were gone; that past was dead and long since buried. All he wanted now was to end the time left to him quietly, with Anna herself once again. Yes, that was the important thing, Anna to be herself once again.

When he allowed himself to dwell on his past he owned that Anna was the only woman in his life who had satisfied all his needs together, for she played the roles of mistress, wife and mother to him . . . aye, and teacher, for over the past twelve years he had learned much from her, and so realized he owed her much. And at these times he asked himself why he hadn't married her. There was nothing standing in the way.

Deep within himself he knew the answer; he had been afraid that the band of marriage would change her and he would lose the mistress and mother, and there would remain only the wife and teacher. He'd had experience of this state with his two previous wives, for they had been wives and nothing more; not that he had wanted anything more from his first marriage. It was in his second marriage that he had realized he needed something more than a bed partner, because a bed partner could be picked up any time of the night or day. Love, he had learned of recent years, had little to do with the needs of the body, yet the needs of the body were such that they couldn't be put aside. In his own case he had never been able to ignore them. He considered that celibates must be a different species of man, for man, as he understood him, was born with a hunger running through his veins from the moment he felt the breast in his mouth. Here he was in his sixty-eighth year and that hunger was still on him, and of late it had become an irritation because Anna had not been strong enough to feed it. It was months since he had taken her, and it looked as though it might be as many again before she was able to come to his bed.

Of a sudden life had become full of irritations. He didn't like to admit to himself that he missed the weekly visits of his natural son, although he could admit openly that he missed the company of Constance. Yet he had never said this in Barbara's hearing, knowing that it would hurt her because Barbara was a good girl, a good woman. But she had never been a girl in the sense that Constance had been a girl. Still, she was good and kind, and Anna owed her life to her care during these past weeks.

There was another irritation he had to suffer, and this came through Mary. Mary was a pest. He had known for a long time that the wine she drank when on her visits to her aunt was no wine at all but came from some hidden still, and although he had hinted at first, then asked her openly but on the quiet, to bring him a bottle, she had steadfastly refused. 'Eeh! no,' she had said. 'What would Miss say?' Miss would have her head. He had wanted to say, 'I'll have your head if you don't obey me,' but the days were past when he could take such a line with his one servant, for he knew that he was in her debt, and had been for years.

There was something else he had discovered about Mary that had heightened his irritation towards her. She didn't come back from her aunt's empty-handed. Coming down to the study one night not so long ago to replenish his pipe, he saw the lamp was still burning in the kitchen, and, looking in, there she was, sitting in the rocking chair before the fire, her skirts well above her knees, warming her legs. Her head was lolling and she was dozing. To the side of her on the table was an empty glass. As he had lifted it from the table and smelt it she had woken up, crying, 'Eeh Master! Eeh Master!' And he had nodded at her slowly as he repeated, 'Eeh Master! Eeh Master! Come on, where's the bottle? where've you got it hidden? Go and fetch it.'

She had stammered and spluttered, 'Eeh! no, Master, I wouldn't. And I haven't got none hidden. I wouldn't dare bring any into the house, not a bottle I wouldn't, the Miss would be upset. I had the sniffles, I just had a drop.'

'You've got a bottle somewhere, Mary,' he said slowly. 'Come on now, where is it?'

Mary had looked at him for a moment and what she saw was a big, fat old man, with heavy jowls and a completely white head of hair, but with eyes that were still young and showing a vitality that only death would quench. With innate understanding she recognized what it must be costing this one-time proud man to beg for a drink, for since Miss Brigmore had been ill there had been no hard stuff brought from the town; every spare penny was needed for extra coal to keep the house warm and a few delicacies to tempt the invalid's appetite. And all this had to be done on an income that had been cut by a quarter since Miss Constance had got married. And so she had said, as if speaking to one of her own kind, 'Well, sit you down there. Now mind, don't move, I'll be back in a minute.'

It was five minutes before she returned, and she brought him half a tumblerful of the stuff, that was all, no more, and so raw and strong it was that it seemed to rip his throat open as it went down. But it put him to sleep and gave him an easy night's rest.

And that's all she would ever give him, half a tumblerful now and again. He would go down on odd nights hoping to find her in the kitchen warming her legs, but she was crafty now, for the others would hardly retire before she went up to the attic.

And so he got into the habit of watching her whenever possible, trying to find out where she had the stuff hidden. He knew it wasn't in the house, and he had searched the outbuildings from floor to ceiling. He had an idea it was somewhere in the barn. He poked among the potatoes, the onions, the carrots and such-like in the pretence of tidying up; he poked around looking for a hole in the top of the turnip pit. There were times when his body was aching from so many needs that he pleaded with her, 'Come on, Mary, come on, just a drop.' And she would say, and truthfully, 'Master, it's all gone. Honest to God it's all gone, and there's another four days afore me leave.'

Yes, indeed, Mary was an irritation.

But over the past four weeks he had found a little diversion from the daily monotony, because when the weather was fine he'd had an exchange of words with the woman, Moorhead. That she was a trollop of the first water simply amused him; he never thought he'd have the opportunity of chatting with any of her kind ever again. Such a woman had a particular kind of dialogue, stilted, double-edged, and suggestive. He knew that this piece and himself had one thing in common, the needs of the body, and in her case she wasn't particular about who satisfied her.

When years ago he'd been able to pick and choose he would doubtless have passed her over, but now he wasn't able to pick and choose she appeared in a way as a gift from the gods, the mountain gods, in whose fortress he was being forced to end his days. He would not allow himself to think that his thoughts were in any way disloyal to Anna. Anna was a being apart, Anna was a woman who held his life in her hands, who nourished him in all ways; at least she had up till her illness. In any case Anna had a key to his thoughts; she would have understood, for she had known what kind of man he was from the beginning; had he been made in any other but the Mallen pattern he would never have gone up to her room in the first place and, of course, she understood this.

So gradually, over the past weeks he had enjoyed the exchanges with the Moorhead woman, knowing exactly what they were leading to. All he needed now was a time and place. His body was too heavy to allow him to walk far; the length of the road before it bent towards the hills one way and turned towards the Hall the other was the limit of his daily exercise, so a hollow on the fells was out of the question. The only place with cover that would suit his purpose was either the stable or the barn, and both were risky; yet not so much once darkness had fallen, for neither Barbara nor Mary ventured out often in the dark, except when Mary was after her bottle. But wherever the bottle was it was certainly not in the stable or the barn, of that he had made certain.

As he now watched the buttocks wobbling away into the distance he felt his blood infusing new life into him. By God! get her on the floor and he would take some of the wobble out of her. And he could at any time from now on. She had indicated as much by the simple action of heaving up her breasts with her forearm while she looked at him with a look that did not need to be interpreted in words.

He turned about and, squaring his shoulders, walked back up the road to the house, and he did not find it incongruous that he should immediately go upstairs to Anna.

'Ah! ah! there you are.' He almost bustled into the room. 'It's a wonderful day; pity we couldn't have got you out.'

'Did you enjoy your walk?'

'Yes and no. You know I don't like walking, but the air's good, sharp; cleans you as it goes down.'

'The woman you were talking to, who is she?'

He turned his head sharply and looked at her. 'Oh. Oh, her. You saw us? Oh, she's one of the sluts that are cleaning out the Hall; right pigsty she says it is.'

'But I understood the new people are due in shortly.'

'Yes, yes, they are. Well' – he now nodded towards her, saying slowly, 'A right pigsty she said it was when she first went there.' He walked to the window and looked out, and there was a silence between them for a moment until he said, 'Funny, you know, Anna, but it doesn't hurt me to know that someone is going to live there again; in fact I think I'm rather pleased. It was sad to see it dropping into decay. It's the kind of house that needs people. Some houses don't, they seem to have a self-sufficiency built into them from the beginning, but High Banks never had that quality; it was a mongrel of a house, crossed by periods and giving allegiance to none, so it needed people by way of comfort.'

'You sound quite poetical, Thomas.'

He turned to her, his face bright. 'Poetical? I sound poetical? Oh, that's good coming from the teacher.' He bent over her and put his lips to her brow, then ran his forefinger through her hair, following its line behind her ears.

As she looked up at him she caught hold of his hand and pressed it against her cheek and murmured softly, 'I'll soon be myself again, have patience.'

He was now sitting in front of her, having dragged a chair quickly forward. 'Patience? Have patience? What do you mean? I've never been impatient with you.'

'I know, my dear, I know.' She bowed her head. 'But you need comfort and I'm unable to give it to you.'

'Nonsense! nonsense!' He thrust the chair back now and was on his feet again, his tone stern, even angry sounding. 'What's put such ideas into your head? You give me everything I need. Haven't I told you' – he was now bending over her – 'haven't I told you that you are the only person I've really cared for in the whole of my life? God above! woman, if I've told it to you once I've told it to you a thousand times over the past years. Comfort.' His voice suddenly softened to a whisper, 'Oh, Anna, you're all the comfort I want, all the comfort I need.'

When again she brought his hand to her cheek he said in a hearty manner now, 'Another week; give yourself another week and you'll be coming down those stairs dressed in your best finery and I will have a carriage at the door and we shall drive into Hexham. Now, now, no protests.' He waved his hand before his face. 'And don't ask where the money's coming from. I've already thought up an idea that will pay for the trip. We'll take those three first editions in with us. If Barbara is right they'll be worth, twenty, thirty pounds . . . who knows, more. Anyway, I'm positive they'll cover our jaunt. Now what do you say?'

'I say that will be a wonderful treat, Thomas, I should like that. And it was very thoughtful of you to think up the means whereby you could carry it out.'

He stood looking at her, his head on one side, a gentle smile on his face; and then very quietly, he said, 'You know something, Anna. You are two entirely different people; Miss Brigmore who talks like a book during the day, and Anna, the lovable woman of the night; but I love you both . . . Good, good, you're blushing. Go on blushing, you look pretty when you blush.' He wagged his finger as he stepped back from her; then turning away, he went out of the room laughing.

Thomas fully intended to carry out his suggestion of taking his Anna for an outing, as also he fully intended to give the Moorhead woman a time when she could come to the barn or stable.

The following day the carrier cart brought a letter from Constance which afforded him the opportunity of bringing at least one plan to fruition.

2

BARBARA sat next to the driver of the carrier's cart, this being the most comfortable seat. Ben Taggert had been most solicitous for her comfort; he had not only tucked a rug around her legs but had asked Mary to bring another shawl that would go over her bonnet and round her shoulders, for, as he said, you couldn't go by the weather at the foot of the hills; up there on the peaks it didn't ask any questions, it just cut you in two.

And Ben Taggert's words were proved right, for as they mounted higher her breath came out of her mouth like smoke from a chimney and mingled with the steam rising from the bodies of the horses.

When they reached the edge of the plateau Ben Taggert pointed his whip, saying, 'That always amazes me, miss, that yonder; from Lands End to John o' Groats you'll never see anything like it, nor, from what travellers tell me, in any other part of the world either. Bonnier, they'll say, prettier, but not grander. There's majesty there. Don't you think that, miss? Majesty, that's the word. Of course there's higher ones than them hills, I admit, but it's the way they're set. And that bowl down there. One fellow I brought across here described it like this. "God," he said, "must have looked at it and thought He'd made it a little bit too rough, craggy like. And so He took His hand and smoothed out the hollow." And it was a mighty hand that did it for it's a mighty hollow. It was a good description, don't you think, miss?'

'Very, very good, Mr Taggert. It's a very impressive sight; but I must admit I find it rather awe inspiring. And I shouldn't like to walk these hills alone, there's a great feeling of loneliness here.'

'Aye, there is, miss, I'll admit that. But many do, you know. Oh aye, I see them every day. Look yonder, there's one of them.' He pointed now to the derelict house where a man was standing in the doorway, his body mis-shapen by his odd assortment of clothes. 'That's one of 'em.'

'What-cher there. Fine day it is.' The man's voice came to them, each word separate, sharp-edged as if it had been filed in its passage through the air.

'Aye, it's a lovely day, Charlie. But look out, it won't last; weather's changin', I saw the signs this mornin'.'

'That right?'

'Aye, that's right, Charlie.'

Ben Taggert had not slowed the horses, the cart was still rumbling on. The man and house passed out of Barbara's vision but the memory it evoked did not leave her for some time. That was the place where it had happened. And the child that had been born last week, was it the result of that escapade or was it Donald's child? Would Constance know? She doubted it. Not until the child grew up and showed some resemblance to its male parent would the answer be given.

The letter they had received yesterday from Constance had informed them that her child had come prematurely; it had been born at three o'clock on Saturday morning. She thought that this was the result of the shock she had received when she discovered Mr Radlet dead in the kitchen. She had come down in the night to make herself a comforting drink and she'd found him lying on the floor. The day after he was buried the child was born, a boy. She had ended her letter by saying, 'I am longing to see you, all of you, or any one of you.'

It was the 'any one of you' that was the telling phrase and had made Miss Brigmore insist that Barbara go over the hills at the first opportunity.

She saw the farm when they were quite a distance from it; it was lying in the valley and she looked down on it. It looked like any other farm, the solid stone house, the numerous outbuildings, the walled fields surrounding it, some level over quite an area but others sloping upwards to the hills beyond.

As Ben Taggert helped her down on to the road she said to him, 'What time will you be returning?' and he replied, 'Well, I'm usually at this spot around three, but I could be a bit later the day as I've got a number of messages to do an' things to pick up. In any case it'll be well afore four o'clock 'cos I like to get clear of the hills afore dusk sets in, and home afore dark. Anyhow, miss, I'll give you a "hello", and I won't go back without you, never fear.'

'Thank you, Mr Taggert.'

'You're welcome, miss.'

She took the valise from him, then turned away and walked over the rough ground to where a gateless aperture in a grey stone wall led into the farmyard. She walked slowly, looking from right to left. There was no one about. The front door to the house was away to the side; she made for the door that she guessed was most used and would lead into the kitchen. As she approached, it opened and Jane Radlet gaped at her. Then, a smile stretching her sad-looking face, she said, 'Well! well! I don't need to ask who you are, you're Barbara, aren't you?'

'Yes; and you Mrs Radlet?'

'Yes. Come in, come in. Oh, she'll be pleased to see you. She's just gone back up the stairs this minute.'

Barbara stopped herself in the act of speaking. Constance gone back up the stairs? Constance up from her bed when the child was only seven days old? She asked hastily now, 'Is she all right?'

'Yes, yes. Weakly a bit you know, but that's to be understood; but she's all right, an' the bairn's fine. That's what she went up for, to bring him down. She'll be here in a minute. Give me your hat and coat; I'm sure you could do with a drink, it's sharp outside.'

As Barbara unpinned her bonnet and handed it to Jane she thought, What a nice woman; so thoughtful yet she must still be feeling her own sorrow.

She offered her condolences, saying, 'I was deeply sorry to hear of your loss, Mrs Radlet.'

'Thank you. Thank you. An' it was a loss, for he was a good man. But as he would have said himself, God giveth and God taketh away.' She paused before adding softly, 'I miss him.'

'I'm sure you do.'

They looked at each other for a moment; then Jane, turning abruptly away, began to bustle, saying, 'Come, sit down here, sit down by the fire.' She touched the back of the high wooden chair, and Barbara sat down. Then again they looked at each other without speaking, until Jane repeated, 'Oh, she will be pleased to see you,' and added, 'If I'd known you were comin' I would've had the fire on in the parlour.' Then looking towards the door she said, 'Where is she? Where is she? I'll go an' call her.' She nodded, smiling at Barbara, then bustled across the room and out through a door at the far end.

Barbara looked about her. Everything her eye touched on was clean and shining, showing that it had either been scoured or polished; but like the outside of the house there was a bleakness about the room. It wasn't only that the floor was made entirely of stone slabs and was sparsely covered with two clippy mats, one which lay in front of the hearth, the other placed by the side of the long wooden table that took up most of the space in the middle of the room, or that the walls were lime-washed; it was something to do with the lack of colour. The curtains on the windows flanking the door were of white Nottingham lace, and the chairs were devoid of pads or cushions; the whole room seemed dominated by a big black stove. Her eyes were brought sharply from it and towards the door as it was thrust open, and there stood Constance.

They met at the top of the table and fell into each other's arms and they held tightly, not speaking, the while Constance's body shook with her inner sobbing.

They drew apart as Jane, rocking the child gently in her arms, said, 'Here he is then. Here he is,' and Barbara turned and looked down at the swathed bundle. She stared at it for almost a minute without speaking. The child was different from what she had expected. It looked all fair; it had an unusual amount of hair on its head for such a young baby, and it was fair hair. The eyes were blue, but then she understood most babies' eyes were blue to begin with, and a baby's hair often changed colour.

'He takes after his mother, he's going to be as fair as her.'

Barbara felt a little quiver inside her and she brought her eyes from the child and looked at her sister. Could it be the child of a different fairness from Constance, a golden corn fairness such as the fairness of Matthew which would become evident later?

'How is Anna, and Uncle?'

'Oh, she's improving daily but she's still somewhat weak. But you know Anna' – she smiled – 'she's made up her mind to get well, so she'll get well.'

'And Uncle?'

'Oh, Uncle is still Uncle. He's had a new lease of life lately, he appears quite frisky. He's even taking exercise on his own, without being browbeaten.'

'I don't believe it.'

'Well, it has to be seen to be believed, I admit.' They both gave a little laugh together then looked towards Jane, where she was placing the child in a basket cradle, set in an alcove to the side of the fireplace, and saying as she did so, 'You must be famished, coming all this way and the wind so raw. The kettle's on the boil; I'll make you a cup of tea first and then get you a meal.'

'Oh, that's very kind of you, but a cup of tea is all I need. I'm not at all hungry, I could wait until you have your meal. Please don't put yourself out.'

'Well, you can have a griddle to put you over. But sit down, sit down and make yourself at home.' Again she motioned to a chair, and again Barbara sat down, with Constance now close to her, and like two lovers they held hands and looked at each other while Jane bustled back and forth between the table and the stove. Their silence must have told on her for she broke it by saying on a high note, 'Shall I go and tell Donald?'

'No, no.' The quick reply brought her to a standstill and she looked at Constance, adding, 'It'll be no bother, he's up on the top field doing the wall.'

'No, no, thank you, Mam. I'll . . . we'll, we'll take a walk up there, won't we?' She turned and glanced at Barbara. 'You'd like to see round the farm, wouldn't you?'

'Yes, indeed I would.'

'That's what we'll do then, Mam. When Barbara's had her drink I'll show her round, and then we'll walk to the top field.'

'Shall I call Matthew down then?'

'I . . . I wouldn't bother. He . . . he was very tired yesterday and. . . .' Her voice trailed away as the door opened and Matthew entered.

Matthew stood looking across the kitchen to where Barbara was sitting, her head turned towards him, and the high spots of colour on his cheekbones spread outwards and up on to his brow. When he came slowly across the room Barbara rose to meet him and endeavoured not to give evidence of the shock his changed appearance had on her. He had always been thin but now his body looked devoid of flesh; he had always been pale but now his skin looked transparent; his eyes had always been large but now they seemed to fill the entire bone sockets and had sunk back into his head and appeared as dark in colour as Donald's.

She was the first to speak. 'Hello, Matthew,' she said. She did not add, 'How are you?'

He did not repeat her greeting but in a throaty voice said, 'This is a surprise.'

'Yes, yes; I thought I would like to come over and see the . . . the baby.' She motioned her head towards the cradle, and he turned and looked in the same direction and it was a moment before he said, 'Yes, yes.' Then he sat down on a chair near the side of the table although she was still standing; he did not now, as he had been wont to do, show his manners to be those above Donald's and his own class in general, but then, of course, she thought, he was a very sick man.

'Would you like a cup of tea, Matthew?' His mother spoke to him in a gentle voice, her body bent towards him as if she were coaxing a child, and he looked at her for a moment without answering, he looked at her as if he wasn't seeing her, and then on a quick intake of breath, he said, 'Yes, yes, I'd like a cup.'

Jane poured out the tea for them all; she handed round the griddles, but only Barbara accepted one, and this out of courtesy; and it was between herself and Jane that the conversation ranged, and mostly about the weather.

'We're not finished with it yet,' Jane said, nodding her head sagely, 'not by a long chalk; there'll be another big fall you'll see. And the wind's come up in the last hour, it's a wonder you weren't cut in two comin' over the top.'

'It was very keen.'

'Yes, I should say it was. It's years since I was up there in the winter, an' I have no desire to go, it's breezy enough in the summer. You going out now?' She turned to where Constance had risen from the chair, and Constance replied, 'I'm ... I'm just going to get my cloak.'

'Perhaps your sister might like to go upstairs with you, she might like to see the house, would you?'

It was evident to Barbara that this kindly woman was very proud of her house. It was all a matter of values she thought; but then, the other rooms might show some comfort. She said quite brightly, 'Yes, yes, I would; I'm very interested in old houses.'

'There now, there now. Then take her up with you, Constance.'

The sisters looked at each other for a moment before going out of the room together like children obeying a bidding.

The hall they went into was dark, having only one small window next to the door. The oak staircase mounted steeply from opposite the door, and Constance took hold of Barbara's hand and guided her up it and on to the landing. Here it was lighter, being illuminated by a long window at the far end. She noted that there was no article of furniture on the landing, not even a table on which to place a lamp. Then Constance was opening a door, and she was in her bedroom.

She had often imagined Constance's bedroom and in the early days the thought of it had been bitter to her mind. Now that she was in it the last shreds of jealousy she had felt towards Constance seeped from her, for here, and reflected deeply, she saw the same starkness as in the kitchen, and part of her mind was wondering why it should be so because Constance had an artistic sense; it was she who had gone a long way towards making the rooms in the cottage not only comfortable but pretty.

Alone together now, they did not throw themselves into each other's arms once more but stood somewhat apart, each gazing at the other, waiting.

It was Barbara who spoke first. When Constance lowered her head and extended her hands towards her she gripped them, saying, 'What is it? you don't look well. What possessed you to get up so early? Shouldn't you be in bed for some days yet?'

Constance now drew Barbara to a wooden seat that was placed beneath the window and they sat down before she answered, 'One is not pampered on this side of the hills. A cow walks about immediately after calving, so what's the difference between us?'

Barbara was startled, not only by the bitterness in Constance's voice but by the context of her reply. She moved nearer to her and, putting her arms about her, she asked gently, 'Aren't you happy?'

'Oh Barbie!' Constance was now pressing herself tightly against her, her hands clutching at her as if she were drowning, and Barbara whispered, in concern, 'What is it, what is it? Oh my dear, tell me, what is it? Tell me.'

And Constance might have told her if at that moment a voice had not risen from the yard calling loudly to a dog, saying, 'Leave it, Prince. Leave it. Here! Here, I tell you.' It caused her to raise her head and look sharply towards the window. Then withdrawing herself from Barbara's hold, she got to her feet and began smoothing down her hair, then the front of her bodice, then the folds of her skirt over her slender hips; finally, she brought her hands to her waist where her fingers plucked at each other as she said, 'We'd ... we'd better go down, that's him – I mean Donald. He must have finished in the top field. It'll save us walking and ... and you've seen the room.' She now flung one arm wide, then stopped abruptly and turned and faced Barbara again and, her voice dropping low in her throat, she repeated, 'You've seen the room. She ... I mean Mam, she thinks it's nice, and it is to her. She's ... she's very good to me; I don't know what I would have done without her.'

Constance was at the door, the latch in her hand, but Barbara, after standing up, hadn't moved from the window seat. She said now in a whisper, 'You're not happy, what is it?'

Constance bit on her lip, swallowed deeply, and her chin gave a nervous jerk before she said, 'Is anyone happy? Do you know of anyone who is really happy?'

'We were happy at one time.'

'At one time, yes.' Constance now nodded slowly. 'The only trouble is we never recognize real happiness when we have it.'

'But ... but Donald, Donald loves you.' She found it surprising that it didn't pain her to say this aloud, and when she saw Constance close her eyes tightly she said again, 'What is it?' and now she moved swiftly towards her. But before she reached her Constance had opened the door; then they were on the landing, then going down the stairs, silent again.

Donald was in the kitchen when they entered and he greeted her heartily as if he were pleased to see her. 'Well, well! Look what the wind's blown in,' he said, coming towards her with hand out-stretched. 'What's brought you to this neck of the woods, eh, on a day like this with the wind enough to stiffen you?'

'Oh, I wanted to see the baby and find out how Constance was.'

'Oh!' The exclamation was high. 'You knew about the baby then?' He turned and glanced in Constance's direction, and Barbara noticed that she didn't look at him and say, 'Yes, I wrote,' so it was left to her to explain, and she did as casually as possible, saying, 'Yes, Constance sent me a note. And oh, by the way' – she turned to Constance now who was at the table laying it for a meal 'I brought some things for the baby. Not knowing if it were going to be a boy or a girl we knitted white.' She went towards the valise where it lay just as she had left it by the side of the chair and, opening it, she drew out first a white shawl, then a variety of socks, bonnets and coats.

'Oh!' Jane exclaimed delightedly as she fingered the shawl. 'Oh, it's beautiful and so soft. This was knitted with fine wool; indeed it was. And look at the wee boots. Aw! did you ever see anything so dainty, did you now, Constance?'

'No, they are lovely. Thank you, thank you, Barbara. And thank Anna for me too. What a lot of work it must have taken.'

'It was a pleasure.' Their eyes held for a moment longer; then Jane put in, 'Well, you came with a full bag an' you'll go with a full bag. You must take some butter, an' cheese, and eggs back with you.'

'Thank you. . . .'

During the next hour Barbara noticed a number of things. Matthew never uttered a word, Constance only spoke when necessary, and Jane never stopped chattering. But it was a nervous chattering. Her face sad, she kept up a constant conversation as if with herself.

When they sat down to the meal no one sat at the head of the table. Donald sat to the side with Constance opposite him; Jane sat at the bottom of the table with Matthew to her left; but although the chair at the top was empty Barbara had no doubt who was master of this house. Not only had Donald been served first but Jane ministered to him with a deference that she might have extended towards her husband, except that this deference held a nervous quality.

Barbara wondered how the farm had been divided. There would surely have been a will; she must ask Constance.

The food itself was rather tasteless. It was a stew that had been well stewed and, surprisingly, without herbs. But that didn't trouble her; what did was the atmosphere at the table. To say it was strained was not adequate, tense would have been a better description.

One other thing she noticed. Although Donald brought a smile to his face now and again it never touched his eyes. When she had loved him – she noted with relief that she was using the past tense with regard to her affection towards him – she had never seen him look as he did now. His eyes were like pieces of slaty coal, their blackness was a dull blackness. She wondered now how she had allowed herself to become so attached to him. Perhaps because he had flattered her by appealing to her mind. Yes, that was it. Pride, pride.

Before the meal was over she was thinking, I could not have endured this any more than Connie is doing. Poor Connie. Poor, poor Connie.

Rising from the table, Jane said, 'I'll light a fire in the parlour.' She did not look towards Donald as she spoke yet it was as if it were a question directed towards him, a question that required an answer, an answer giving permission, and when the answer was not forthcoming immediately Barbara put in quickly, 'Please don't trouble on my account; Mr Taggert will be here with the cart around three he told me, and it is near two o'clock now.'

'Oh well then, well then.' Jane nodded at her, then bustled around the table gathering up the dishes.

It was at this point that Constance went to the cradle and lifted up the baby and was moving towards the kitchen door leading into the hall when she was stopped by Donald saying, 'Where you going?'

Constance turned slowly and for the first time since coming into the room she looked straight at him, and her voice had a note of defiance in it as she answered, 'I am going to feed the child.'

'There's plenty of room here, isn't there?' He jerked his head in the direction of the empty chairs bordering the fireplace.

Their eyes held, the silence in the kitchen emphasised the sound of the wind buffeting the house, and as Constance turned about and walked out of the room Jane exclaimed loudly, 'Do you hear that? It's gettin' worse.'

Ignoring his mother's remark, Donald looked now at Barbara and said on a thin laugh, 'You can carry modesty too far; what's more natural than feedin' a bairn, I've told her.'

Matthew seemed to have risen clumsily from the table for his chair toppled backwards and hit the stone floor, but as he went to right it Donald was there before him and, swinging it up with one hand, he stood it on its feet, saying on another thin laugh, 'You want to take more water with it, lad.'

Matthew now looked up under his lids at Barbara; then in a voice as tight as the smile on his face he said, 'I'll say good-bye. I'm glad to have seen you. Give my regards to Miss Brigmore, will you, and to your uncle?'

'I will, Matthew, I will.' She held out her hand, and he took it. It felt like a piece of damp dough in her grasp and she was glad to relinquish it.

Donald was now standing with his back to the fire, his coat tails divided, letting the heat fan his buttocks. She often saw her Uncle Thomas stand like that. It was the stance of the master of the house, and it was as if Donald were acting out his part for her. After a moment he asked, 'How are things across there?'

'Oh, very well. Mary and I have re-decorated the sitting room for when Anna comes downstairs. We've had a boy come all last summer in the evenings to do the garden; it's in very good shape. We had two cartloads of wood brought, and he has sawn it up. We're all prepared for an extended cold spell, should it come.'

Her answer did not seem to please him, he made no reply to it; and when there came the sound of a bucket being tumbled across the yard by the wind he made it an excuse to take his leave, saying, 'Well, somebody's got to work round here, so I'll say good-bye to you.'

'Good-bye, Donald.' She nodded politely towards him, then added, 'Will you be bringing Constance across soon? Uncle would like to see the child.'

He had his back to her, walking towards the kitchen door as he said, 'I doubt it; she's afraid of storms, as you know.'

'But the fine weather's coming, there are periods when there won't be any sign of a storm.' She had risen to her feet.

'She's also afraid of the heights. Didn't you know?' At the door he turned and looked towards her.

'The heights?'

'Yes, the heights; terrified of heights, she tells me. Apparently there are lots of things about her you didn't know if you didn't know that.'

As she stared at him across the dim kitchen she thought, He's cruel.

'Good-bye, Barbara.'

She didn't answer, and he went out, having to pull the door closed behind him against the force of the wind.

When she sat down, Jane began to chatter again. She chattered about the cattle, the butter-making, the cheese-making; she referred to her husband as if he were still alive; and every now and again she looked towards the window and said, 'Eeh! that wind.'

It was almost twenty minutes later when Constance returned. Putting the baby once again into the cradle, she smiled at Barbara before saying to Jane, 'What will I do, the dishes, or go in the dairy?'

'You'll do neither, my dear, just you sit here with your sister and have a nice talk, you don't see each other that often. Now sit yourself down.'

Constance sat down at the opposite side of the fireplace to where Barbara was sitting, and they looked towards Jane, who was now standing over the shallow brown stone sink which was full of dishes; then they looked at each other again, and their eyes said, 'What shall we talk about?'

For the next half-hour they talked small talk. Barbara learned that the child was to be named Michael, after his step-grandfather. Constance learned that the Hall had been sold again, and that it was being cleaned up by a small regiment of workers, one of whom was named Aggie Moorhead, a very forward piece who wasn't above stopping Uncle and chatting with him.

By three o'clock Barbara was ready and waiting to hear Ben Taggert's call, and when a quarter of an hour had passed she said anxiously, 'I wonder if he's gone on? Perhaps we didn't hear him call because of the wind.'

'Oh, no.' Jane shook her head. 'Ben would come over an' knock you up. Ben would never go on without a passenger once he had made arrangements. Oh no, that's not Ben. . . . Listen, do you hear? There he is.'

Barbara strained her ears and heard a faint, 'Hello there. Hello there.'

Jane now grabbed up the valise and went out and for a moment Barbara and Constance were alone again. As they had done on first meeting they enfolded each other tightly, and once again Barbara felt her sister's body tremble, and she heard her murmur as if in agony of mind, 'Oh Barbie! Barbie!.'

Hand in hand now they went out, their bodies bent against the wind, and when they reached the road Jane had already handed Ben Taggert the valise and he had put it in the back of the cart where there was an assortment of bundles and boxes and a bird in a cage.

'If you would like it better I could push them all aside' – Ben nodded to the back of the cart – 'you'd be more sheltered there.'

'Oh, I'll be all right riding with you, Mr Taggert.'

'It's going to be rough, miss, the higher we get, you know that. Still, if you change your mind we can always stop. Come on then.'

Quickly now Barbara turned again to Constance and, taking her face between her hands, she stared at her for a moment before kissing her on the lips; then she shook Jane by the hand and thanked her once more for the dairy produce she had put into the valise, and also for her hospitality.

Sitting high up in the front of the cart she looked down on Constance's upturned face. With an impulsive movement she reached down holding out her hand, and when her sister's hand gripped hers she felt such pain in her heart as she never thought to experience again. It was a more intense pain than she had known a year ago, a different pain, it could have been a pain of farewell. She made herself smile, but it was a smile weighed with sadness, it was as if she knew she would never smile again.

The return journey was eventful with moments that created terror in her, such as the one when the wind seemed to lift the whole cart and the animals from the road and to tip them into a shallow hollow to the side of the rising hill. That they all landed the right way up seemed nothing short of a miracle to her. What had happened was that the horses and cart were blown to the side and left contact with the ground in going over the shallow ditch.

Once on the road again, Barbara, still shaking from her experience, realized that perhaps she was lucky to be able to feel the trembling of her body at all, for if they had been blown the other way then surely they would have rolled down the steeply wooded hillside to the valley below. The snow posts that were spaced at intervals along this stretch of the road and threaded by a wire would not have prevented them from being hurled over the edge to be bounded from one tree trunk to another until they reached the bottom.

Another time she found herself clinging to Mr Taggert's arm. It was most embarrassing, at least to her. She saw his head nodding in assurance, and knew that he was yelling something at her, but she could not distinguish anything he was saying, for his words were carried away on the wind.

When, for a few minutes, there was a lull, he shouted at her, 'I've known some trips but this one'll take a beatin'. Give me snow any time. But don't worry, don't you worry, miss, Jake'n Fred'll make it; they're as surefooted as mountain goats.' It was a pity, she thought, that she hadn't his faith in Jake and Fred.

If anything, the storm increased in violence as they descended to lower ground, and it was almost as dark as night when finally Ben Taggert helped her down from the cart and handed her the valise. She thanked him warmly and said she would never forget the journey and he laughed at her and said, 'You must try it in a blizzard, miss; that's what you must do, try it in a blizzard. Go on now, get yersel' inside quick. Good night to you.'

Her reply was lost to him. The cart moved past her, and holding down the shawl that covered her bonnet with one hand and carrying the valise in the other, she fought her way to the gate. But when she went to push it open she found it was held fast. In peering forward she realized that the obstacle holding it closed was a branch of the rowan tree that had stood in the front garden for years. The whole tree had been blown down.

Her body bent, she made her way to the lower gate which led into the yard. The noise of the wind was beating on her eardrums with a force almost equal to that on the heights; in fact, the wind seemed to have increased in fury, which she would have thought impossible a short while ago.

When some object rattled across the path in front of her she fell forward and would have gone on her face had not the end wall of the outbuilding saved her. She stood leaning against it for a moment, thankful that she had it as a guide for it was like black night now. She decided to keep near the wall and to skirt the yard until she reached the kitchen door, for if she crossed the yard her feet would likely be whipped from beneath her.

On this side of the yard facing the house was the woodshed, stables,

176

and lastly the barn. There was a narrow passage between the corner of the barn and the wall of the wash-house which led into the vegetable garden. The wash-house itself was connected to the scullery and larder, which were single-storey buildings, and going off at right angles from the end of these was the house proper.

She had groped her way as far as the barn when her passage was stopped abruptly by two hands grabbing her, and after the first moment of shock she sighed with relief and leant against the bulky figure of her Uncle Thomas. He held her close, protectingly, he held her so close that she dropped the valise onto the ground.

Protecting her further, he pulled her inside the barn, where the noise seemed intensified for the old timbers were rattling like castanets. She went to shout to him, 'Isn't it dreadful?' but he hugged her with a compulsive movement and her breath was taken from her body by a force even stronger than the wind. What was the matter with Uncle? Was he having convulsions? Was he ill? And why . . . why was he out in the storm? It was madness for him to be out, for anyone to be out on a night like this, unless they were compelled.

'Oh, Uncle! Uncle!' She heard herself screaming, but only in her head for her breath had been knocked out of her again as she was borne backwards. What was happening? what was the matter? It . . . it was her uncle? Of course it was her uncle. She knew by the size of his body it was her uncle. She knew by the odour of him it was her uncle. That particular odour of tobacco and rough tweed and stale wine, a not unpleasant odour and definitely peculiar to him, for no other of her acquaintances smelt like this. But he also smelt strongly of spirits – *Oh my god! My God! She must be going insane, it couldn't be*. She began to fight him, to struggle madly, and it appeared to her that of a sudden the wind had transported her into a lunatic asylum because her uncle was also struggling with her, tearing at her undergarments, actually tearing them from her. *No! No! No! Oh Jesus, Lord of all the earth, what was happening to her*. The weight on her body – She couldn't breathe – She could struggle no longer – She had gone mad, for this thing could not be happening to her. She made one more effort. She dug her nails deep into the flesh of his neck, she couldn't get near his face for it was covering hers.

At the moment her body was shot through with torture, and her mind, standing apart as it were from her, told her that this was death, the death of decency, of self-respect, of love of family life – of life itself.

When the pressure on her body was released she lay still in what seemed comparative silence for the storm seemed to have held its breath for a moment. Then as it released another blast she let out an ear-splitting scream; then another; then another; on and on and no hand came over her mouth to check her; not until a lantern swung above her did she stop. Her eyes wide, she stared up into the light. She could not see the face above it, or who else was present; not until the lamp swung to the side did she see the grey dishevelled bulk of her Uncle Thomas. His body seemed to fill the barn. He looked like a deranged giant. Then the lantern swinging again, she saw the figure of a woman running through the light and towards the open door; then she heard Mary screaming. 'God Almighty!' was what she was screaming. She screamed it a number of times.

Then Mary, dropping onto her knees, lifted Barbara's stiff head and shoulders from the ground and, cradling her, she repeated her cry, 'Oh, God Almighty! Oh God Almighty!' After a moment, her voice breaking with her sobbing, she cried, 'Come on, get up out of this, me bairn. Get up out of this. Come on, come on.' And Barbara got up and allowed herself to be led from the barn and into the house. . . .

Thomas watched them go. He was leaning against a beam to the side of the door. The lantern was still on the ground. He looked towards it. His eyes stretched wide, his mouth agape, he seemed to see himself reflected in it, an obese, dirty old man, a filthy old man. He was so repulsive in his own sight that his stomach revolted and he turned his head to the side and retched, bringing up the entire meal he had eaten only an hour before at the same table as Anna.

Anna! Anna! Anna! . . . Barbara! Oh, Christ Almighty!

His mind now went completely blank for a moment and shut off from his consciousness the act he had perpetrated. When it moved again it pulled him from the support of the beam and turned him about and he staggered from the barn out into the wind.

When he reached the kitchen door the blast almost drove him through it. There was no one in the room; he crossed it, holding on first to the table and to the chairs for support; then he was in the hall, and in the lamplight he saw Anna coming down the stairs. She stopped and he stopped; they looked at each other for a long moment and the misery their eyes exchanged was untranslatable.

When he could no longer face the pain in her eyes he bowed his head and stumbled towards his study. Once inside he locked the door. Going to the wall above the fireplace he took down his gun and, placing it on the desk with the barrel pointing towards the chair, he released the safety catch; then sitting himself in the chair he leant forward, and as he did so the handle of the door was gently turned. He did not look towards it but put his finger on the trigger and pulled.

PART FIVE

Matthew

I

THE SCANDAL surrounding Thomas Mallen's death would, the self-righteous in the countryside said, not die down for many a year, seeing he had left living proof of it in a young woman whom he had brought up like a daughter.

It was Aggie Moorhead who had made it impossible to put any version but the true one on Thomas's death. She had looked upon the mix-up between his niece and herself as the best joke in the world, until the girl had begun to scream. Then, when the news spread that old Mallen had shot himself the story made her the centre of attraction, not only locally but with those men who came from the newspapers.

And the newspapers didn't just deal with the incident either; they delved into Thomas Mallen's whole past and it made quite exciting reading. Even though he had been living in retirement for the past twelve years, being a Mallen, he hadn't lived alone but had taken for his mistress the governess of his two nieces, and what made things more interesting still, they stated that one of his nieces had married his natural son.

Yet even with all this, the nine-days' wonder might have died a natural death if the gardener boy hadn't observed the rising globe of Miss Barbara's stomach, and this on the first occasion he had caught sight of her in five months. This latter fact did not appear in the papers but the hill telegraph was as efficient in spreading it around the countryside.

This particular piece of news came to Donald's ears in the market place and he couldn't get back quickly enough to the farm to throw it at Constance.

It was three months since he had allowed her over the hills, and then he had escorted her himself as on the former occasion when that old cow of a Brigmore had sent him the news that Mallen was dead. He hadn't found out how he died until he had entered the cottage. He hadn't seen Barbara at all, not then, and not since.

And now he had learned that she had her belly full of the old man. The Mallen image died hard. By God! it did. And that lot in the market laughing up their sleeve at him. By Christ! he'd let them see who they were laughing at afore he was finished. He'd show them. He'd get land, and more land; he'd drag the respect out of them, then spit in their eyes.

And there was another thing he'd tell his lady wife when he got in: she was bringing that fifty pounds a year over the hills; there wasn't the old man to keep now, and he could do with another fifty a year. Yes, by God! he could. She had stood out against him on this, openly defied him in fact. She was getting brave over certain things, but she'd better be careful. He hadn't lifted his hand to her yet but there was plenty of time for it.

Sometimes he thought he could have forgiven her the other business if she had been good to him, shown a little affection, but what she had shown him from that very first night couldn't be given any other name but scorn; at times it even overrode her fear of him. Inside her, she looked down her nose at him, and the farm and the house. She got on with his mother because she saw it as policy to keep on the right side of her. And yet that wasn't all there was to it. He suspected, and had for some time now, that there was something between them, a sort of understanding. Whatever it was, the relationship irritated him, for if there was anybody she should look down upon it was his mother who, in her turn, had been a slut. But as they said, birds of a feather, no matter from what class, recognized each other. She even turned her nose up at Matthew; she hardly opened her mouth to Matthew.

Matthew'd had a new lease of life these past few months. Perhaps it was due to the unusually dry warm weather. Nevertheless his time was fast running out for he was no thicker than two laths, and though his cough had eased a bit, the blood came more often. His manner too had changed in the last year or so. He supposed it was his illness, for he could get hardly a word out of him nowadays. There was a sullenness about him; perhaps because he knew that death was galloping on him; it wasn't good for a man to see death before it actually came.

He flapped the reins briskly and put the horse into a trot. The cart bumped over the rough road and the dust rose in clouds about him.

When he came to the junction of two roads he took the left-hand one. This would mean a longer run to the farm, but it might save an axle; on the outward journey he'd had to take the cart through a new subsidence in the road and this had strained it. He'd made a note in his mind to bring a load of stone and fill in the hole.

The road he was on now was a prettier one, it wound its way through woodland and shady lanes, and the open ground was moulded into small hills where the sheep grazed, a burn ran down the valley and there was a rocky outcrop over which the water tumbled so that you could fairly give it the name of a waterfall.

He rarely came by this road, he hadn't time for scenery. All the scenery that interested him was within the stone walls of his farm.... And it was *his* farm.

Michael had left no will. By law the place was Matthew's, but by right of work it was his, and let anyone try to say it wasn't. It had never been a bad farm, but it was he who had made a good one into a better one, and from now on he meant to turn it into a rich farm . . . and a rich man's farm.

He passed by the side of a small copse that threw the path into shadow and when he emerged he blinked into the sun for a moment, then screwed up his gaze to take in two figures sitting some distance away in the shade of a mound. With a soft word of command and a tug on the reins he drew the horse to a halt, and his eyes narrowed to slits as he peered into the distance.

If he had failed to recognize the couple the sound that now came to his ears would have identified at least one of them. Not once since they were married had he heard Constance laugh, and the reason for hearing her laugh now was that the child's hands were pulling at her nose. He had seen the child doing this before, but it certainly hadn't brought any laughter from her. He had caught her smiling at it, but this would be when he happened on her unawares.

Then he witnessed something that caused a pain to rip through him, as if his body had been licked by a fierce flame. She had passed the child to Matthew and Matthew was holding him up in the air above his head and shaking him from side to side; then lowering him down, he folded him against his chest and rocked him backwards and forwards, as only a mother, or a father might do.

What he next saw was Constance hitching herself forward and smoothing the child's hair back while Matthew still held it. What he was looking at was the cameo of a family.

He was numb. The pain seared all the nerves in his body. It now passed the bearing point, and for a moment he felt nothing; there followed a blessed period of time when all emotion was dead in him.

But the numbness melted, the space filled, and now there swept into him and over him with the force of a mighty wave a feeling of such hatred that if they had been within arm's length of him at that moment he would have murdered them both.

It was a gentle neigh from the horse that caused them to turn their heads in his direction, but they could not see either him or the cart. In the shadow of the trees he watched them remain still for a moment peering towards the road; then there was a quick exchange of words before they got to their feet, she carrying the child now, and they went down the field and made for the gate that led into the extreme corner of the farmland.

Not until they were out of sight did he lead the horse forward, and then he took it from the road and tied the bridle to a tree, after which he walked a short distance and lay down in some long grass. There, at full length, he stared unblinking into the soil while he tore up handfuls of grasses and snapped them into small pieces. After a while, as if his body had suddenly been dropped from a height, he slumped into the earth and with his hand under his mouth he bit on the pad of his thumb until the blood came. . . .

Fifteen minutes later when he entered the house, the baby was in the pen outside the dairy and Jane was in the kitchen, her arms in a bowl of flour. She looked at him as if in surprise, saying, 'You're back early.'

'Where's Matthew?'

'Matthew! Oh, he's in bed. You know he always goes to bed in the afternoon.' She dusted the flour from her hands and turned her back on him and went towards the oven.

He had the urge to pick up the heavy rolling pin from the table and batter her on the head with it. She knew, she knew. They must all have been laughing up their sleeves at him all this time, the three of them. Why? Why hadn't he twigged anything before? He was seeing things now as plainly as a blind man who had been given his sight. That day Matthew had gone over the hills for her and the storm was supposed to have frightened her and he had taken her back; it had happened then. But Matthew had changed towards him long before that. And he could pinpoint the date. It was from the Sunday morning, in this very room, when he had told them he was going to ask her to marry him. God above! Christ Almighty! Why had he been so blind?

The answer was simple. He had trusted Matthew, because he had loved Matthew. Matthew was the only other person in the world besides her he had loved, and they had both fooled him, right up to this very day they had fooled him. If God Himself had come and told him before he had seen them together he wouldn't have believed it, because they never spoke to each other. . . . Not when he was about. . . . No, that was it, not when he was about.

And his mother, that old bitch there. No wonder they were all thick. He could murder the three of them. He could take a knife and go from one to the other and slit their throats. But where would that get him? The gallows. No, there'd be no gallows for him, he had paid enough for being who he was; but by God! somebody was going to pay for this. He would play them at their own game. Christ! how he would play them. The cat and the mouse wouldn't be in it. He would make

184

them think he knew, then make them think he didn't. He'd give them such hell on earth they'd wish they were dead, all of them. Well, one of them soon would be, but he'd make a vow this minute he wouldn't let him go until he had told him that he hadn't been so bloody clever after all. He'd see he tasted hell afore he died; he'd play him like a tiddler on a pin; he'd play them all like tiddlers on a pin, and he'd begin right now.

As if answering an order, he turned and stamped out of the kitchen, across the yard and into the dairy. She was standing at the far end with her back to him, and even at this moment the sight of her slender form made him ache. She had half turned as the door opened and then turned away again, and he came up behind her and stood close and did not speak until, pressing herself against the stone slab, she slid away from him before turning to face him, her face stiff as always when she confronted him.

'It's a grand day,' he said. 'You should be out in the sunshine with the child.'

She continued to stare at him before she answered quietly, 'You have allotted me duties; you would doubtless have something to say if I didn't carry them out.'

'Yes, yes, doubtless I would.' He nodded his head at her; then went on in a casual tone, 'I heard a bit of news in the market, caused some belly laughs it did. That's funny, belly laughs. Barbara is five months' gone. The old man worked well up to the last. What do you say?'

He watched the colour drain from her cheeks, her mouth opened and shut in a fish-like gape; then he turned from her and was near the door of the dairy before he looked towards her again and added, 'By the way, I was talkin' to a young doctor in the market, I was tellin' him I had a son and about my half-brother being a consumptive. I said there was none of the disease on my side, not that I knew of, and could it be caught like, and he said, aye, it was better not to let the child come in contact with anybody who has the disease, so if I was you I'd break it to Matthew, eh? You can do it better than me, put it more gently like.'

He watched her for a moment as she leaned back against the slab for support; then he went out well satisfied with the result of his new tactics. He would get something out of this, something that would be more satisfying than sticking a knife in their necks. Although one of these days, when he had her on his own, he mightn't be able to prevent himself from doing just that.

185

2

WHEN MARY OPENED THE DOOR and saw a small, neatly dressed man standing there and, beyond him, on the road a hired cab with the driver slapping his arm about himself as he stamped his feet, she thought, Another of them. What's this one after now? And that is what she said to him, 'What are you after now?' She did not add, 'There's nothing new happened for you to put in your papers.'

'Is this Mr Mallen's home, I mean the late Mr Mallen?'

'Yes, it is; you know quite well it is.'

The small man raised his eyebrows slightly before saying, 'I should like to speak with your mistress.'

'She's not seein' nobody, neither of them.'

There was a slight look of bewilderment on the man's face and he didn't speak for a moment, but surveyed Mary; then, he said quietly, 'My name is Stevens, I am Chief Clerk to Maser, Boulter & Pierce, Solicitors, of Newcastle. I have some business I would like to discuss with your mistress. Please give her this.' He held out a square of card, and she took it, glanced at it, then back at him, before saying in a more moderate tone, 'Well, come in then.'

In the hall she hesitated whether to leave him standing there or to show him into the breakfast room, the room that had once been the schoolroom. She decided to leave him standing there. Then giving him a look as much as to say, don't you move, she went towards a door, tapped on it, then opened it immediately.

In the room she tiptoed almost at a run across it and, coming to Miss Brigmore, where she was sitting by the fire unpicking the skirt of the last of Barbara's dresses in order to make it fit her during the late months, she whispered, 'There's a man here – not a gentleman, yet he's not one of them – he's from a solicitor's. Look.' She thrust the card at Miss Brigmore and noticed that she hesitated before taking it. She had been like that ever since . . . the business, hesitant about any contact with those outside. Well, she was like that herself; she hadn't got over the shock yet and her conscience still worried her, especially at night. She still wondered if it all would have happened if the master hadn't found her hidey-hole. He must have drunk a whole bottle, for that very night she had found it empty. Nothing worse could have happened if he had drunk the two bottles, but being the man he was he had taken only one and left her the other. Oh, the master, the poor, poor master. She was still sorry for him, she couldn't help but be sorry for him. And she was sorry for herself an' all because the business had put her off the stuff and there was no comfort anywhere, no, not anywhere, for this house that had once been merry and full of laughter, in spite of having to stretch every farthing to its utmost, was now as quiet as a cemetery.

'Show him in, Mary.'

Miss Brigmore slowly rolled up the dress and laid it in the corner of the couch and she was rising as slowly to her feet when the man entered.

From his manner and appearance she, too, knew that he wasn't 'one of them'. She looked at the card and said, 'Will you take a seat, Mr Stevens?'

'Thank you, ma'am.' He motioned with a gentle movement of his hand that she should be seated first.

When they were seated facing each other she said, 'It's a very raw day;' and he answered, 'Yes, it is indeed, ma'am.' Then coughing twice, he went on, 'I won't intrude on your time more than is necessary. My firm is wishful to trace the next-of-kin of the late Mr Thomas Mallen and thought perhaps coming directly to his home would be the surest way of getting in touch with his relatives.'

'For what purpose?' Her back was straight, her voice was almost that of the old Miss Brigmore, and he, sensing her distrust, was quick to put her mind at ease, saying, 'Oh it would be something to their advantage, I should explain. Mr Mallen had a son, Richard, that is so?'

'Yes.'

'Well, apparently Mr Richard Mallen has sojourned in France for some years, but under an assumed name. This was the difficulty the French lawyers encountered when dealing with his estate. They eventually gleaned that he had left the country under troubled circumstances, and so their enquiries were slow and cautious, but recently they contacted us through a French associate we have in Paris, and asked us to ascertain the whereabouts of Monsieur le Brett's relatives.' Mr Stevens again coughed twice before continuing, 'We became acquainted with the fact that Mr Thomas Mallen had died intestate, unfortunately only a fortnight after his son's death.'

187

Miss Brigmore now said, 'He has two nieces, one is married and one still lives here.'

'No close relatives? He was married twice I understand.'

'Yes, his two sons by his first wife died. He has a daughter, she's in Italy.'

'Ah, a daughter in Italy. May I ask if you have her address?'

'Yes, yes, I have her address.'

Yes, she had Bessie's address. She had written to her telling her briefly of the tragedy, and what had she received in return, a letter full of bitterness. They had scarcely got over the '51 affair. Did she know that it had even got into the Italian papers? Alfo was angry, his people were angry, she had barely lived down the disgrace of her father being turned out of his home for debts, and her brother almost killing a man of the law, and now this – well, they said there was a curse on the Mallens. . . .

There was indeed a curse on the Mallens, and all connected with them. If the last Mallen had married her, if Thomas had married her this man would not be searching for his nearest relative at this moment. She asked quietly, 'Did he leave a large fortune?'

'No, when the beneficiary eventually receives it, it will amount to about two thousand five hundred pounds, somewhere in that region. There has been a great deal of expense incurred – you can understand. . . .'

No muscle of her face moved; not a considerable fortune, two thousand five hundred pounds! And they were now reduced to living on a hundred pounds a year. Their menu had been frugal for a long time, for she had seen to it that Thomas always had the pick of what was to be had, and when she became ill Barbara had continued along the same lines. . . . Poor Barbara, poor Barbara. She dared not think too much of Barbara's plight or her whole being would disintegrate in pity.

She thought in justifiable bitterness now that if anyone had earned Dick Mallen's legacy it was herself. Her cheating of the bailiffs had not only helped to get him out of prison but had likely afforded him the basis, through the selling of the snuff box and cameos, of some nefarious business. But there, that was life, and life was bitter, like alum on the tongue, and she couldn't see time washing it away.

She rose saying, 'I will get you the address,' then she added, courteously, 'Can I offer you some refreshment?' As she watched his head move to the side and a thin smile appear on his face she added hastily, 'A cup of tea maybe?'

The smile slid away, his head shook. 'It's very kind of you,' he said, 'but I shan't trouble you; I had breakfast late and my dinner is awaiting me at the hotel, as also is the cab man.' He smiled again, and she went out of the room to see Mary scurrying towards the kitchen door.

In the study she took Bessie's letter from the desk drawer, copied the name and address onto a piece of paper. Then, going back into the sitting room, she handed it to Mr Stevens.

'Thank you, ma'am; I'm much obliged.' He looked down at the address written on the paper. Then, his eyebrows jerking upwards, he repeated, 'Countess. Well, well! I don't suppose two thousand five hundred will mean much to her.'

He walked past her now as she held the front door open, and he doffed his hat and bowed to her, and he noted she did not close the door until he had entered the cab.

The door closed, she did not return to the sitting room but went into the study, and Mary coming into the hall and hearing the study door click shut stopped for a moment, looked towards it, then returned to the kitchen. That was one room she never barged into. When Miss went in there she wasn't to be disturbed. It had become a sort of unwritten law. She sat down by the kitchen table and, laying her hands on it, she joined them tightly together and, bending her head over them, she shook it from side to side. Two thousand five hundred pounds going to that Miss Bessie, and her an upstart if ever there was one, never written to her father for years. Eeh! things weren't right.

She started visibly when the kitchen door opened and Barbara entered. She was wearing a long coat and had a shawl over her head.

Rising quickly, Mary went towards her, saying, 'Eeh! Miss Barbara, you'll get your death, I thought you were never coming back. Here, come and get warm.' She drew her towards the fire, pulling off her gloves as she did so; then taking the shawl from her head as if she were undressing a child she pressed her into a chair and, kneeling beside her, began to chafe her hands, talking all the while. 'You're froze. Aw, you're froze, lass; you'll do yourself an injury, an' – she stopped herself from adding 'the one you're carrying' and went on, 'You can't walk quick enough to keep yourself warm. You shouldn't go out, not on a day like this; wait till the sun comes out.'

'Who was that, Mary?'

'Oh. Oh, you saw him. Well, you won't believe it, you won't believe it even when I tell you. It was the solicitor's man. He came to find the nearest kin to ... to the master.' She never said 'your uncle' as she used to do, in fact no one spoke of the master to her in any way; but now, having mentioned his name, she gabbled on, 'Master Dick, you know, well, well he's died and left some money and it goes to the next-of-kin. An' you know who the next-of-kin is? Miss Bessie. You wouldn't believe it, two thousand five hundred pounds. Imagine two thousand five hundred pounds an' going to Miss Bessie. Eeh! if anybody should have that it should be her, meanin' no offence, Miss Barbara, you know that don't you, but the way she's worked, what she's done. . . .'

'And still doing.'

'Aye, and still doing.' Mary now smiled into Barbara's face. It was the first time she had heard her make a remark off her own bat so to speak since 'that business'. She rarely spoke unless to say yes or no; she moved around most of the time like someone hypnotised. She remembered seeing a man hypnotise a girl at the fair some years ago and the girl's mother went hysterical 'cos the man couldn't get the girl to come back to herself and stop doin' daft things and there was nearly a riot. Miss Barbara put her in mind of that girl, only she didn't do daft things, except to walk; she walked in all weathers, storms held no fear for her. Since that night of the great storm when 'that business' happened there had only to be the sign of a storm and out she went.

She rubbed the thin white hands vigorously between her own now, saying again, 'You shouldn't do it, you're froze to the marrow. Look; an' your skirt's all mud. Go upstairs and change your frock. Go on, that's a good lass.'

When Barbara rose from the chair she pushed her gently towards the door, then across the hall and up the first three stairs.

Once in her room, Barbara didn't immediately change her dress, but walked slowly to the window and stood looking out. It was late October. The day was bleak, the hills looked cold and lonely as if they had never felt the warmth of the sun or borne the tread of a human foot; the wind that was blowing was a straight wind, bending the long grass and the dead flowers in the garden all one way; the garden was no longer neat and tidy, for the boy came no more, not since Constance had been forced to deprive them of the second fifty pounds a year. She thought, as she often thought, that they had been cursed, that both of them had been cursed; the tragedy of the Mallens had fallen on them. But they weren't Mallens; there was no Mallen blood in them. He who touches pitch is defiled; perhaps that was the reason. It was like contracting a disease. She and Constance had been in close contact with the Mallens all their lives and they had caught the disease. Her stomach was full of it. She looked down at the mound pushing out her dress below the waistband. The disease was growing in her and she loathed it, hated, hated and loathed it. Given the choice she would have accepted leprosy.

She heaved a deep sigh. All life was a disease and she was tired of it. She would have made an end of it months ago if it hadn't been for Anna. She could not add to Anna's sorrow, she loved Anna, she was the only one left to love. Anna had given unselfishly all her life and what had she got? Nothing. Yet she knew that Anna would refute this.

And now this latest injustice, two thousand five hundred pounds going to Bessie. Bessie was just a vague memory to her: a round laughing face and a white train which she and Constance held; it was connected with the memory of people saying, 'Isn't she pretty, isn't she pretty?' But they weren't referring to the bride but to Constance. Poor Connie! Connie, who was now virtually a prisoner on that farm.

Again she asked herself why this should happen to them. Three people who had done no harm to anyone. Her mind checked her at this point. Constance had done harm to Donald before she married him, and she also harmed him by marrying him; but nevertheless she did not deserve the treatment being allotted her. She had not seen Constance since her visit to the farm, but every now and again she had a letter from her, smuggled to the carrier no doubt, for in each letter were the same words 'Please write to me, Barbie, but don't refer to anything I have said.'

She had only once replied to the letters, and that was as recently as a fortnight ago when Constance had desperately beseeched a word from her. The letter was short and terse and held nothing personal, except to hope that she and the baby were well. Her own plight was bad but she considered that her sister's was worse.

She turned from the window and took off her dress and, standing with it in her hand, she said to herself, But what of Anna's plight should anything happen to me when the child is born?

It was the next morning at the breakfast table that Barbara said suddenly, 'Do you think we could afford to ask our solicitor to visit us out here?'

'Our solicitor? . . . why? Why do you want a solicitor, Barbara?'

Barbara lowered her head, rested the spoon against the side of her porridge bowl, then said slowly, 'Should anything happen to me, I . . . I want you to be provided for.'

'Oh, my dear, my dear.' Miss Brigmore rose from her seat and came round the table and put her arms around Barbara and, pressing her head against her breast, whispered, 'Oh child, my dear child, don't think about such things, please, please, for what would I do without you?'

'One must think about such things. If they had been thought of before, you would be two thousand five hundred pounds richer at this moment.'

Miss Brigmore made no answer to this for she was surprised that Barbara had for the moment forgotten her own tragic condition and was concerned for her. It was the first time in seven months that she had made voluntary conversation. And she was right in what she said, if Thomas had thought of her. . . . Oh, she must not start that again.

191

She had wrestled for most of the night with the bitterness in her, not against Thomas, she could never feel bitter against Thomas, but against the quirk of fate that would now further enrich the comfortably off Italian countess by two thousand five hundred pounds, for although the count had been classed as a poor man, his poverty was comparative. Patting Barbara's head now, she said softly, 'We will talk no more about it; nothing is going to happen to you, my dear.'

Barbara withdrew herself from Miss Brigmore's arms and, looking up at her, she said, 'I don't want to go into the town but if I'm forced to I shall.'

'But . . . but Barbara, my dear, the money is in trust, Constance and you only receive the interest. It is something that couldn't be transferred. If . . . if what you say did happen, and God forbid, unless you left . . . issue, the money would go back into the estate.'

'I . . . I don't think so. I've been looking into *Everyman's Own Lawyer*, and there's such a thing as a Deed of Gift. Anyway, this is what I want to find out, and make it legal, that if and when I die my allotment and share in the house will pass to you.' She paused here and, staring fixedly into Miss Brigmore's eyes, she ended, 'Whether I have issue or not.'

'But Barbara dear, you're . . . you're not going to die, you're so young and. . . .' Her voice trailed away before she added, 'healthy,' for that would have been, if not a falsehood, a grave exaggeration.

'I shall write to Mr Hawkins today.'

Miss Brigmore sighed a deep sigh, went around the table and sat down. She was not thinking of what Barbara's gesture might mean to her in the long run, but of the fact that they could not really afford the ruinous fees the solicitor would ask for coming all this way from Newcastle. If it had been from Allendale or Hexham it would have been expensive enough, but all the way from Newcastle. . . . She wondered what they could do without in order to meet this further expense. . . .

When half an hour later she saw Barbara going down the garden path towards the gate at the bottom which led on to the fells, she opened the windows in the study and called, 'Barbara! Barbara dear! don't go too far, please, please.'

She knew Barbara had heard her although she didn't turn round. She looked up at the sky. It was high and blue and the sun was shining. It was much warmer than yesterday, in fact it was a nice day, an enjoyable Indian summer day. Not that the weather had any effect on her now, except that she worried about the extended cold days when they used more wood and coal than they could afford.

She closed the windows and sat down in the leather chair behind the desk. It did not pain her to sit in this chair, the chair in which Thomas had paid the price for his crime, the crime he had in all ignorance committed, for she knew he would have suffered crucifixion rather than knowingly perpetrate such a sin against Barbara, whom he had loved as a daughter.

She leant her head back against the top of the chair. She was feeling tired, weary, but strangely she was no longer enduring the physical weakness that had plagued her for so long following the pneumonia. Perhaps it was the shock of that night, and the call made on her inner resources, but since she had heard the gun shot she had ceased to be an invalid; necessity had made her strong enough to cope with the terrible circumstances.

'Miss! Miss! Miss! Come quickly.'

As she pulled the door open she ran into Mary.

'Oh miss! miss. . . .'

'What is it?'

'Miss Barbara, she's, she's in the kitchen with pains.'

'But she's just gone out.'

'No, she's back; like a ghost she is an' doubled up. . . . Oh! Miss! . . .

When she burst into the kitchen Barbara was sitting by the table, gripping its edge; her eyes were tight closed and she was gasping for breath.

'You have pains?'

She nodded, then muttered, 'Something . . . something seized me. I turned back, and then a moment ago it came again.'

Miss Brigmore now turned to Mary, saying sharply, 'Get an oven shelf, two, she's freezing, and more blankets. . . . Come along, dear, come along.' She put her arm around Barbara's shoulders and eased her to her feet. 'We must get you to bed.' . . .

After putting Barbara to bed with a blanket-covered oven shelf at her feet and one to her side she and Mary had a quick consultation in the kitchen. 'It would be safer to get the doctor,' Mary said. 'It might just be a flash in the pan but on the other hand it mightn't.'

Miss Brigmore did not think it was a flash in the pan. She agreed with Mary that it would be wise to get the doctor; but the carrier had passed and how were they going to get a message to him?

'I could run down to Jim Pollitt's,' said Mary. 'He generally drops in for his dinner around one o'clock. He might be takin' the sheep over that way or going to the farm, an' Mr Stanhope might let him run in for he's not a kick in the backside from Allendale.'

Miss Brigmore did not check Mary for her coarse saying for she knew it was only when she was anxious that she made such slips of the tongue in her presence. She said, 'Get into your coat; wrap up well, for the sun's gone in and there's a mist falling. How long do you think it will take you to get there . . . I mean to Mr Pollitt's?'

'I could do it in half-an-hour if I cut through the bottom of the Hall grounds, an' I will. An' if they catch me I'll explain; they can't hang me.'

As she talked she was winding a long woollen scarf around her head and neck. A few minutes later Miss Brigmore, opening the door for her, said, 'Tell them how urgent it is, Mary,' and Mary nodded at her and answered, 'Yes, miss, I'll do that, never you fear.' . . .

It was two hours later when Mary returned. She had come back much slower than she had gone for the mist had come down thick. After taking off her things she went upstairs and before she reached Miss Barbara's door she heard the groaning.

The doctor arrived when the dusk was falling into dark, and he confirmed what all three knew; the child was struggling to be born.

It struggled for the next ten hours, and when at last it thrust itself into the world it seemed to have little life in it, hardly enough to make it cry.

As Mary took the child from the doctor then hurried out, Miss Brigmore held Barbara's two hands close to her breast and whispered in a choked voice, 'It's all right, my dear, it's all right.' But how, she asked herself, could she say it was all right? Half the time words were stupid, language was stupid for it did not convey what the mind was saying and at this moment her mind was saying that no one should have to suffer as this poor girl had done in order to give birth. For what seemed an eternity she had sweated with her and her own stomach had heaved in sympathy; but even so she had not experienced the excruciating pain of the convulsions, although she would gladly have suffered them for her had it been possible.

The tears were spilling down her face as she murmured, 'It's all over, dear, it's all over.' But even as she spoke she experienced a new terror as she realized that for Barbara it was all over, for she was letting go of life.

Barbara had lifted her hand towards her and her lips were mouthing the name 'Anna, Anna' but without sound; then on a deep sigh her head fell to one side.

'Oh no! No! Barbara, Barbara my love, Barbara.'

Miss Brigmore's cry brought the doctor from the foot of the bed. He took hold of Barbara's shoulders as if to shake her while saying, 'No, no! Everything's all right. Come along now, come along now.'

There was a long silence in the room before he gently laid her back on the pillow. Then straightening his back, he looked across the bed at Miss Brigmore and shook his head as if in perplexity as he said, 'It was all right. Everything was quite normal. The child is small but . . . but everything was all right.'

Miss Brigmore brought her agonized gaze from his and looked

down on her beloved Barbara, Barbara who had been like her own daughter. Of the two girls, it was Barbara who had needed her most although she would never admit it; she herself had had to make all the advances. And now she was dead, as she had planned. If anyone had arranged her death she had. She had walked herself to death, she had starved herself to death, but more than anything she had willed herself to death. 'Oh Barbara. Oh, my dearest, my dearest.' She fell on her knees and buried her head to the side of the limp body.

A few moments later the doctor raised her up, saying gently, 'Go and see if the child is all right.'

When she shook her bowed head he insisted, 'Go now, and send Mary to me.'

As if she were walking in a dream she went out of the room and down the stairs.

In the kitchen Mary was kneeling on the mat, a bowl of water at her side. She was wrapping the child in a blanket and she didn't look at Miss Brigmore but said, on a light note, 'It's small but bonny.' She placed the child on a pillow in a clothes basket in front of the fire, then turning her head to the side, she looked up at Miss Brigmore and slowly her mouth fell into a gape. She sat back on her heels and shook her head, and when she saw Miss Brigmore drop down into a chair and bury her face in her hands she exclaimed softly, 'In the name of God, no. Aw no, not Miss Barbara now. Aw no.'

When, rocking herself, Mary began to wail, Miss Brigmore got to her feet and, putting her hands on her shoulders, she drew her upwards, and then she held her in her arms, an unprecedented gesture, and Mary clung to her, crying, 'Oh Miss Barbie! oh poor Miss Barbie!'

After a time Miss Brigmore pressed her gently away and in choked tones said, 'Go up. Go up, Mary, will you, the doctor needs you.'

Rubbing her face with her apron, while the tears still poured from her eyes, Mary asked helplessly, 'What'll we do? what'll we do, miss? what'll we do without them?' and Miss Brigmore answered, 'I don't know, I don't know, Mary.'

A moment later she knelt down by the wash basket and looked on the child, the child that was the outcome of lust and terror, Thomas's child; Thomas's son or Thomas's daughter, she hadn't up till this moment thought about its sex. As if loath to touch it she took the end of the blanket in her finger and thumb and slowly unfolded it.

It was a girl child.

3

IT WAS TOWARDS the end of November, the dreary month, but as if to give the lie to the defaming tag the morning was bright; there was no wind and the earth sparkled with a thick rime of frost. But the morning had no pleasing effect on Constance, she was numbed to the bone. She felt as if she were standing on the edge of a precipice trying to work up the courage to jump, and she knew she would jump if something didn't happen soon to alter the situation.

Last week when they had returned from burying Barbara she had almost gone mad with grief, and at one moment had almost screamed at him, 'It's Matthew's! Do you hear? It's Matthew's! Do what you like. Do you hear? Do what you like!' Such an outburst would have taken the implement of torture out of his hands, but it was his mother who had prevented her. As if she knew what was in her mind she had said, 'Be patient, lass, be patient, it can't go on for ever;' and she had looked at her and said, 'It can, it can;' and Jane had shaken her head and answered, 'God's ways are strange, they are slow but they're sure.' And in that moment she knew that Jane was not only afraid of her son, but she hated him as much as she herself did, and the bond between them was strengthened.

The dairy door opened, and now Jane's voice came to her softly, saying, 'Come on, lass, there's a drink ready, and he's bawling his head off.'

Constance left what she was doing, rubbed her hands on a coarse towel hanging on a nail in the wall, and went towards Jane who was holding the door open for her. Then on the threshold they both stopped at the sight of Donald crossing the yard with a man and boy by his side.

They themselves crossed the yard and met up with the men at the kitchen door. Donald went in first, but the man and boy stood aside until they entered; then followed and stood just inside the room.

'Give them a drink of tea.' Donald jerked his head towards the pair as if they were beggars; but they were dressed decently if poorly, and didn't look like beggars.

When Jane had poured out two mugs of tea, she motioned the man and boy to sit down on the form, then asked, 'Would you like a bite?' and the man said, 'Thank you, Missis, we would that; we've been walking since shortly after five. The others are outside.'

'My! my!' she nodded at him. 'Where you from?'

'Near Haydon Bridge, ma'am.'

'Haydon Bridge? My! that's a way. You must have found the hills cold this mornin'.'

'Aye, an' slippery underfoot; the rime's thick up there.'

'It would be, it would be.'

'Who told you I wanted a man?' Donald was standing with his back to the fire in his master attitude, and the man answered, 'Mr Tyler who I worked for, at least did, afore he was bought out. He said he heard in the market you were goin' to set somebody on.'

'Aye, I was; but one man, not two of you and a family. You say you've got a family?'

'Only two, I mean a wife and a daughter; we lost the others. But Jim here, he's fourteen gone and can hold his own with any man. And the girl, she's thirteen, an' she's been the last four years in the farm kitchen an' the dairy. She's very handy, me wife an' all.'

'Huh! I daresay, but I'm not asking for your family. Anyway, I've got no cottage to offer you; the only place habitable, and then not much so, are two rooms above the stables.'

'We'd make do with anything.' There was a deep anxiety in the man's voice. 'As long as it's a shelter we'd make do. And you wouldn't lose by it, sir. I'll promise you you wouldn't lose by it. We'd give you more than your money's worth.'

'What are you asking?'

'Well, well' – the man shook his head – 'it'll be up to you, sir. But I can tell you we wouldn't press as long as we had a habitation.'

'Aye, yes.' Donald walked from the fire towards the table and, lifting up a mug, he took a long drink of the hot tea before he said, 'Habitations are necessary in the winter. How long were you at Tyler's?'

'Over ten years, sir.'

'Always been in farming?'

'No ... no.' The man's voice was hesitant now and he said on a weak smile, 'I was a footman at one time in the Hall, High Banks Hall, over the hills.' He now jerked his head to the side and looked at the young woman sitting at the table. She had spilled her mug of tea and the liquid was running between the plates. She did not seem to notice this but she stared at him and he at her. He knew who she was. But that was by hearsay, for he would never have recognized her from the child he remembered, and should she remember him that might be the end of his chances.

'What's your name?'

He brought his eyes back to the master of the house and said slowly, 'Waite, sir. Harry Waite.'

Waite . . . Waite. The name sounded like a bell in Donald's mind awakening the memories of twelve years ago. Hadn't Waite been the man who had started all the hubbub? the man Dick Mallen wanted to shoot? He glanced from him to Constance and at the sight of her face a mirthless laugh rose in him. He had the power to engage a footman, the footman who at one time had waited on her. Well, well! the irony of it. All round, it was going to be a very exceptional day. He had a surprise for her but this bit was added interest.

'Drink up and I'll show you those rooms. If you're as handy as you say you are you should be able to make them habitable.'

Before he had reached the kitchen door the man and boy were on their feet, and the man, nodding first to Jane, and then to Constance, and awkwardly muttering his thanks, followed him.

Waite. The footman who had lifted the lid of the armour box and got them out. The man who had tapped her on the bottom, had tapped them both on the bottom, saying, 'By! you're a couple of scamps.' The nice footman, as she had thought of him, but also the man who was the cause of her sitting in this kitchen at this moment. Without him having expressed his opinion of his young master it was doubtful if anything that had happened since would have taken place; but for that meek-looking man they might all still be in the Hall, Uncle Thomas, Barbara, herself. . . . Yet how could she blame the man. As Anna so often said, lives were cut to a pattern, all one did was sew them up. The man looked desperate for work and shelter for his family, and he would get it. Oh yes. She had seen the look in Donald's eyes; he thought that by engaging him he would be cutting another sinew of her pride.

The child began to cry and she picked it up and started to feed it. The clock ticked the minutes away. Jane bustled about the kitchen washing up the mugs, sweeping up the hearth, doing a lot of necessary and unnecessary things, and neither of them spoke.

When the door leading from the hall opened and Matthew entered they both looked towards him. He coughed all the way across the room, short, sharp coughs. When he reached Constance's side she did not raise her head and look at him but went on feeding the child as she said below her breath, 'He's engaging a new man, with . . . with a family. He was Waite, the second footman at the Hall.'

Matthew looked from the top of her head across the table to his mother, and she nodded silently at him.

His coughing became harsher. Sitting down slowly by the side of the table, he said in a low husky tone, 'Well, he was going to hire a man anyway; but where will he put a family?'

'In the rooms above the stables.' It was his mother who spoke.

'They're not fit.'

'The man's desperate.'

'There's no place for a fire or anything else.'

'They'll likely cook in the store-room. . . .'

'In the boiler with the pig meat!'

Whatever response his mother would have made to this was cut off by the door opening and Donald entering, alone now. He did not walk towards the fire and stand with his back to it as was usual when he had anything special to say, but standing just within the doorway and looking at his mother, he said, 'You'd better set the dinner for one more, there'll be a visitor.'

'The man and . . . and boy?'

'No; what would I be doing with the man and boy at our table . . . Miss Brigmore.'

In one swift movement Constance returned the child to the crib and was on her feet.

'Why?' The word was so laden with apprehension that he laughed before saying, 'Because she's bringing the child across.'

'Bringing the child here?'

They all moved a step forward, and it brought them into a rough line facing him. His eyes swept over them as he said, 'Aye, bringing the child here. Where should it be but with its nearest relations; and we are that, aren't we?' He was looking directly at Constance. 'You're its only relation; apart from meself, that is, because what hasn't appeared to strike any of you afore apparently' – he now nodded first at his mother and then at Matthew – 'is that the child is as much me half-sister as you, Matthew, are me half-brother, and so, therefore, I want her under my care.'

Constance's words seemed to spray from her twitching mouth as she spluttered, 'What . . . what do you mean? What are you doing? What's going to happen to Anna and Mary? There's the house.'

'I've been into all that.' His voice was calm. 'I saw the solicitor at the beginning of the week. Barbara's share of the property and her income naturally fall to the child; and as the child's coming here we would have no further use for the cottage. I have ordered it to be put up for sale.'

'No!' She moved towards him until she was within touching distance of him. 'No, you won't! You won't do this. You're a fiend, that's what you are, a fiend. You're mad. I won't allow it; I have some say, some rights.'

He looked down into her face. The hatred in his eyes rising from deep in their black unfathomable depths struck her like a physical force yet it wasn't so frightening as his voice when he said quietly, 'You have no rights; you are me wife, what is yours is mine and' – he paused – 'what is mine is me own.'

Seconds passed and no words came; as was usual he had frozen them within her. It was Matthew, after a fit of coughing, who said, 'But Anna, she worked for Mallen for years and brought them up.'

Donald took his eyes from Constance and looked at Matthew. He looked at him for a long moment before he said, 'She was paid for her services.'

'She was never paid, you know that, she . . . she's worked for years . . . without pay. . . .' He was coughing again.

'There are more ways than one of receiving payment. *She was a whore.*'

His calmness had dropped from him like a cloak; every word was a bark; his face was contorted with passion. 'And she wasn't the only one, was she? You're all whores, every one of you.' His arm swung before him with such force that had Constance been a few inches nearer it would have felled her to the ground. Then he turned and stamped from the kitchen.

They all stood still for a full minute, then they looked at each other and their eyes said, He's come into the open, what now?

It was eleven o'clock when Miss Brigmore got off the cart and walked into the farmyard, but she had no child in her arms.

Constance met her at the gate and they enfolded each other in a close embrace, and when Constance muttered, 'Oh! Anna, what can I say?' Miss Brigmore answered, 'I didn't bring her; I've . . . I've come to appeal to him. I'll go on my knees to him, anything as long as he doesn't take her from me. She's all I have; there's no other purpose in my life, nothing to live for.' Constance said again in an agonized tone, 'Oh! Anna'; then added, 'I'm helpless.'

As they crossed the yard still clinging to each other, Miss Brigmore murmured, 'I couldn't believe it when I got his letter; he had given no indication of it when I last saw him. I thought, well, naturally I thought I would stay in the cottage with Mary and bring up the child. I . . . I never dreamed for one moment' – she paused and came to a halt and, turning her face to Constance, said, 'Yes, I did dream. I have been in terror for months now in case he should do something to force you to persuade Barbara to fall in with his plans and sell the house, because . . . because, Constance, it is a plan. It is a plan of vengeance.

His letter was so cold, so ruthless, it was as if he had been waiting all these years to do this to me. In between the lines I could read that he blames me for everything that has happened.'

Constance could say nothing to this for she knew it was true. He had a hate of Anna that was beyond all reason. He had always disliked her, in the first place because she had not liked him, but the main reason was because she had been close to Uncle Thomas.

'Is ... is he in the house?'

Constance shook her head. 'No, no, he's out walking *his* land. He walks it every morning. Legally he doesn't own a foot of it but no one would dare to resist his claim to it, he is the farm. He works it, or has done up till now, almost by himself, but now he has engaged a man and his family. You will never guess who that man is.'

'Who?'

'Waite, the footman.'

'Waite! the footman?'

'Yes.'

'And he has engaged him?'

'Yes. Oh, I don't mind the man being engaged; strangely I remember him as a very kindly man. It's the reason he did it. He has no compassion for the man or his plight. He has a family and needed a home for them. Tyler's farm, where he worked, has been sold and the new owner has his own men. Anyway, the man heard that there might be an opening here. It ... it was the first I knew of it, or, or Mam either. But then' – she shook her head – 'he's determined to expand. He has bought another fifty acres. Most of the dairy produce is sold now. We have an allowance in the house, so much and no more. Oh! Anna, Anna' – she shook her head – 'life is unbearable. Why did I do this? Why?'

Miss Brigmore now drooped her head as she said, 'You didn't do it; you wouldn't have done it, I forced you. On this at least I accept the guilt. You wouldn't have married him if I hadn't pressed you. But any shame you might have had to bear would have been better than your present state.'

'Oh, you mustn't blame yourself, Anna; you did what you thought was best for me. There's one culprit in this business and that is myself. When I look back and see myself distressed at the thought of not being married before I was twenty I think I must have been insane. . . . But come inside, you're cold, and you look ill.'

They had just entered the kitchen, and Miss Brigmore, after greeting Jane, was turning to Matthew where he sat crouched over the fire when the sound of hurrying, almost running steps across the cobbled yard froze them all.

Constance, turning to see Donald coming over the threshold, his face red and sweating, knew that he must have run at high speed from the far fields where he would have seen the carrier pass. The cart was well before its time this morning, the fine weather doubtless having set the pace.

No one spoke for a moment. Then, the colour in Donald's face deepening to a purple hue, he demanded of Miss Brigmore, 'Where is it?'

'I . . . I didn't bring her. I wanted to talk to you.'

'You can talk till you're black in the face, and it'll be useless. What I said in that letter holds; as I've told you already I have the law behind me.'

'I . . . I know you have.' The placating sound of her own voice made Miss Brigmore sick at herself, but she continued in it as she said, 'You . . . you are quite within your rights to want Constance to bring up the baby, but . . . but I have come to beg of you to be lenient and to leave her with me. You know I'll do all in my power to educate her and . . .'

'Aye and teach her to lie and cheat and whore.'

Miss Brigmore put her hand to her throat and her body swayed slightly before she said, 'You do me a terrible injustice.'

'I do you no injustice; they took their pattern from you. Well, now you've come without her so there's nothing for it but for me to go back and fetch her.'

'You'll not, you'll not do this, I'll never let you.'

He moved slowly about until he was facing Constance and asked, quietly now, 'How are you going to stop me? You haven't a leg to stand on and you know it, so what I say to you now is, get yourself ready because you'll be carrying your niece back with you.'

'I won't! I shan't, and I'll fight you. Do you hear? I'll fight you.'

Still gazing at her, his lip curled in scorn as he said, 'Don't be stupid.'

He had turned from her and had put his foot over the step before his mother's voice stopped him. 'Don't do this, Donald,' she said.

He glared at her, his eyes narrowing; and then, his voice low, he said, 'I'll advise you to keep out of it.'

'I've kept out of it long enough. When you're talking about legal rights you forget that Matthew was my husband's only son.'

Donald didn't speak for some seconds, and then he said, slowly, 'I forget nothing. To all intents and purposes I am Michael Radlet's eldest son; it's only hearsay that this' – he tugged at the white tuft of hair to the left side of his brow – 'makes me a Mallen, and it would be hard to prove in law. There are a number round about with white streaks; it wouldn't be possible they are all the result of frolics in the wood.' Their eyes held for some seconds before he finished, 'You're wasting your breath if you think you're going to achieve anything by that. Now' – he cast his glance over them all – 'as far as I'm concerned the talkin's finished. In ten minutes' time I'll have the brake in the yard, an' you' – he nodded towards Constance – 'be ready.'

The kitchen was weighed in a silence like that which follows an announcement of the plague. The three women stood where they were, and Matthew sat where he was, all immobile, until the child in the cradle gurgled; then Matthew turned his head and looked towards it. He kept his eyes on it for some minutes before pulling himself up from the chair, and the almost imperceivable motion of his head he made towards Constance told her that he wanted to speak to her.

As if awakening from a dream she looked first at Miss Brigmore, then at Jane, then back to Miss Brigmore again before, bowing her head deeply on to her chest, she went out of the kitchen and into the hall.

Matthew was waiting for her just outside the door. He put out his hand and drew her to the far end of the hall and into a clothes closet that was near the front door, and there in the dimness he held her face as he said softly, 'Listen now; listen, dear. You . . . you are not to go over there. You must make on you have taken bad, you must faint or something, and I'll . . . I'll go with . . .' He pressed his hand tightly over his mouth as he began to cough, and Constance whispered desperately, 'But . . . but you couldn't stand the journey, Matthew; it'll be dark before you get back, and the cold will set in and . . .'

'Don't, don't worry about that, just listen to me. Listen to me, dear. Pay attention, don't cry. Now listen. I want you to go into the front room and lie on the couch; just say you feel bad. . . .'

'But . . . but he won't believe me. And he'll never take you. . . . And why . . . why do you want to go with him?'

'It doesn't matter why, only do what I ask.'

She shook her head slowly. 'He won't take you, he'll bring her himself.'

'He can't, there's only a chain to the back of the brake and a basket could slip through.'

'Oh, Matthew, don't be silly, you know him, he'll think of some way. He'll tie it on. But why, why? what are you going to do if you go?'

'Listen to me, dearest, please. Now you and I know that I've had much longer time than was due to me. I might go the night, I might go in the mornin', but one thing's certain, I won't get through the winter. It was a miracle I got through the last. Now listen, listen. Look at me. We haven't much time.' He stared at her in silence for a moment, then whispered, 'Aw Constance, I love you. Aw, how I love you. It's this that has kept me alive, but now I'm suffering the torments of hell 'cos I know I'll be leaving you here alone to suffer him. 'Cos Mother's no match for him, no more than I am meself. He's turned into a devil, and to think that I once loved him, and he me. I know I wronged him but ... but ... Oh! my love, my love, I would wrong him again for you.' He touched her face with his fingers and his voice was scarcely audible as he said, 'I've ... I've never kissed you but that once.'

Slowly his face moved towards hers and his lips touched her brow and her eyelids, then traced her cheek, but before they reached her mouth a fit of coughing seized him and he turned his head away and held a piece of white linen to his lips, then screwed it up tightly before he looked at her again.

The tears were raining down her face and when she went to speak he put his finger on her lips and muttered, 'No questions, nothing, no more; as he said, the time for talking's past. Come on, my dear; just do what I ask, go and lie down on the sofa.'

'No, Matthew, no.'

'Please, please, do this for me, make me happy Constance, make me happy. Let me think there's been some meaning in me being alive. . . .'

'Oh, Matthew, Matthew, what are you going . . .?'

He had opened the door and drawn her into the hall again, and now pressing her towards the sitting room he said quickly, 'Don't speak to him when he comes in, not a word, be prostrate.' He bent quickly forward and kissed her on the mouth, then whispering, 'Good-bye, my love.' He opened the door and pressed her inside, then closed it quickly as she went to protest. The next minute he was in the kitchen and, with a briskness in his voice that his mother hadn't heard for years, he said, 'Constance has fainted, she's lying down in the sitting room.' Then, putting his two hands out one towards Miss Brigmore and the other towards his mother as they made to move towards the far door, he said, 'Leave her alone, please. . . . Leave her alone. I'm . . . I'm going over with Donald.'

'You? you're not!'

'I am. It's a nice day an' the drive will do me good.' As he stared into his mother's eyes, she put her hand to her mouth and whispered, 'What, what have you in mind, boy? what are you . . .?'

'Nothing, nothing, Mother; I'm just going over in Constance's place to bring the baby back.' He turned now and looked at Miss Brigmore. She was staring at him, her eyes wide and questioning, and he smiled weakly at her and nodded reassuringly before saying, 'Don't worry.'

'No! Matthew, no!' Jane pulled him round to her. 'There's nothin' you can do, nothin'. What chance have you against him, or ever had for that matter? Things have got to take their course.'

'Be quiet.'

204

The door opened and Donald entered. He stood for a moment looking at them, and then he said, 'Where is she?'

It was Jane who answered, 'She's had a turn, she's lying down.'

'Huh!' His laugh was pitying. 'She's had a turn, she's down is she?' He stalked across the room and they heard him going up the stairs, taking them two at a time; then his steps running down again and the sitting-room door opening. In a few minutes he was back in the kitchen. Walking slowly to the middle of the room he looked from one to the other and said, 'Well, whatever you've planned it won't work. I'll bring it back if I've got to nail the basket to the cart or lay her in a bundle under my feet.'

'There won't be any need for that, I'll come along of you.' Matthew's voice was quiet, tired sounding; it was like someone saying, Anything for peace.

Donald turned his head sharply and looked at him. He looked at him for a full minute before he smiled grimly and said, 'Well, that mightn't be a bad idea after all. We could stay overnight and I'll load the brake up with the bits and pieces I want to bring across.' He had turned his gaze on Miss Brigmore, and she closed her eyes against the look in his; then swinging round he went outside.

Jane now ran into the hall and returned with a heavy coat, scarf and cap, and as she helped Matthew into them she kept whispering, 'What is it? Tell me, what is it? what are you up to?'

When he stood muffled up to the eyes he looked into her face and said gently, 'Nothing, Mother, nothing; what could I be up to? Now I ask you, what could I be up to? You go and see to Constance, she needs you. Good-bye.' All he did now was to touch her shoulder with his fingers. Then he turned to Miss Brigmore and, addressing her as he always had done, he said, 'Come on, Miss Brigmore, come along.'

'Can't . . . can't I see Constance just for a moment?'

He went close to her now before he spoke. 'It would be better if you didn't. You'll see her again. Don't worry, you'll see her again.'

She shook her head before letting it fall forward, and like someone in whom all hope had died she went out of the kitchen, without a word to Jane, and across the yard to the brake.

Donald was standing to the side of it. He did not speak to her but pointed into the back of it, and it was left to Matthew to help her up.

Slowly she covered her ankles with her skirts and sat, for once in her life, without any signs of dignity while the cart rumbled out of the yard and began the journey over the hills.

As they drove higher Matthew's coughing became harsher, but only once did Donald turn his head and glance at him and noted there was more blood than usual staining the piece of linen. It would be odd, he thought, if he died on this journey. He wanted him to die, and yet he didn't want him to die. There were still grains of love left in him that at times would cry out and ask, Why had he to do it to me? I could have suffered it from anybody else in the world except him. But such times were few and far between and his hate soon stamped on the grains.

They were nearing the narrow curve in the road where the guard or snow posts stuck up from the edge above the steep partly wooded hillside. It was the place where Barbara had experienced the terrifying fierceness of the gale as it lifted the carrier's cart over the ditch. The line of posts curved upwards for some forty yards and it was at the beginning of them that Matthew, putting his hand tightly over his mouth, muttered, 'I'm . . . I'm going to be sick.'

Donald made no comment but kept on driving.

A few seconds later he repeated, 'I'm, I'm going to be sick, stop, stop a minute. I'll . . . I'll have to get down.' His body was bent almost double now.

The horse had taken a dozen more steps before Donald brought it to a halt, and Matthew, the piece of linen held tightly across his mouth, got awkwardly down from the cart and hurried to the edge of the road, and there, gripping one of the posts, he leaned against the wire and heaved.

Miss Brigmore watched him for a moment from the side of the cart and as she slid along the seat with the intention of getting down, Donald's voice checked her, saying, 'Stay where you are.' Then he called to Matthew, 'Come on, come on.' But Matthew heaved again and bent further over the wire. After a short while he slowly turned around and, leaning against the post, he gasped, 'I'm . . . I'm bad.'

Donald looked down at him. There was blood running from the corner of his mouth, his head was on his chest. He hooked the reins to the iron framework, then jumped down from the cart and went towards him, and as he did so he slipped slightly on the frosted rime of the road, which as yet the sun hadn't touched. When he reached Matthew's side he said sharply, 'Get into the back and lie down.'

'I . . . I can't.' Matthew turned from him and again leant over the wire and heaved.

Donald, bending forward now, looked down. There was a sheer drop below them before the trees branched out. He said harshly, 'Come back from there, you'll be over in a minute.' It was at this moment that Matthew turned and with a swiftness and strength it was impossible to imagine in his weak state he threw both his arms around Donald's shoulders and pulled him forward. Almost too late Donald realized his intention, and now he tore at the arms as if trying to free himself from a wild cat while they both seemed to hang suspended in mid-air against the wire. Donald's side was pressed tight against it; he had one foot still on the top of the bank, the other was wedged sideways against the slope. With a desperate effort he thrust out one hand to grab the post, and as he did so he heard the Brigmore woman scream. Then Matthew's body was jerked from him and he was free, but still leaning outwards at an extreme angle over the drop. As he went to heave himself upwards his foot on top of the bank slipped on the frost-rimed grass verge, and the weight of his body drew him between the wire and the top of the bank, and with a heart-chilling cry of protest he went hurtling through the air. When he hit the ground he rolled helplessly downwards, stotting like a child's ball from one tree trunk to another. . . .

They lay on the bank where they had fallen, Miss Brigmore, spread-eagled, one hand still gripping a spoke of the cart wheel, the other clutching the bottom of Matthew's overcoat.

When, getting to her knees, she pulled him away from the edge of the drop and turned him over she thought he was already dead, for the parts of his face that weren't covered in blood were ashen.

'Oh, Matthew! Matthew!' She lifted his head from the ground, and he opened his eyes and looked at her. Then his lips moving slowly, he said, 'You should have let me go.'

She pressed his head to her and rocked him for a moment, then murmured, 'Try to stand. Try to stand.' Half dragging him, half carrying him, she got him to the back of the brake, and pulled him up, and he lay on the floor in a huddled heap.

Before she got up into the driver's seat to take the reins she walked a few tentative steps towards the edge of the road and looked downwards. Far, far below a dark object was lying, but it could have been a tree stump, anything. If it was Donald he might still be alive.

She urged the horse upwards to where the road widened and, having turned it about, she drove back to the farm.

It was five hours later when the men lifted Donald from the flat cart and carried him into the farm kitchen, where they laid him on the wooden settle to the side of the fireplace.

Miss Brigmore, Constance and Jane stood together near the dresser; one might have thought they had their arms around each other, so close were their bodies.

Matthew was lying back in the wooden chair near the kitchen table. If his eyes had not been wide open and moving he too could have been taken for dead, such was the look and colour of his skin.

The four of them watched the men as they straightened their backs after laying Donald down but no one of them spoke, or moved.

It was Willy Nesbitt from Allendale, a man who had been on many winter rescue expeditions, who broke the silence. Looking at Constance, he said, 'He's fought hard; don't know how he's done it, Missis. He's smashed up pretty bad; he should have been dead twice

207

over, but he's fought to keep alive. I thought he was gone two or three times, but even now there's still breath in him.'

The man's eyes seemed to draw Constance from the protection of Miss Brigmore and Jane, and like a sleep-walker she went around the end of the table, past Matthew, and to the settle, and there she stood looking down on Donald. He looked twisted, all of him looked twisted. His face was bruised and shapelessly swollen, all that is except his eyes, and these were open.

His eyes had always been dark, black when he gave way to emotion, but now they were like pieces of jet on which a red light was playing, and the feeling that emanated from them struck her with a force that was almost physical, for she fell back from it. She even flung out her arm as if to protect herself; and then she cried out as it beat on her and bore her down. When she fainted away the room became alive with movement.

She recovered lying on the mat in front of the fire, Miss Brigmore was kneeling by her side. Donald was no longer on the couch; under Jane's direction the men had carried him into the front parlour.

Miss Brigmore, stroking the damp hair back from Constance's brow, whispered, 'It's all right, my dear, it's all right, he's gone.'

Constance's breast was heaving as if she had raced up a hill. She did not need to be told he was gone, she knew, for with his last look he had tried to take her with him. The strength of his mind, the intensity of his hate, the futility of his life had all been in that last look and he had kept himself alive to level it on her. If ever a man had wished death on another he had, and as she had slipped into the black depths she thought he had succeeded.

When she went to rise Miss Brigmore helped her to her feet, saying, 'Sit quiet for a while, sit quiet.'

Matthew was still in the same position in the chair. It seemed that he hadn't moved and when she looked towards him and whimpered, 'Oh Matthew! Matthew!' he answered through blood-stained lips and in a voice that had a thin, flatness about it, 'It's all right, it's all over.'

Constance leaned her head against the high back of the chair and closed her eyes. It might be over, but it wasn't all right, and it might never be all right. Matthew had killed Donald; as surely as if he had stuck a knife between his ribs he had killed him but the guilt was hers. She had known, as had his mother, when he set out in the cart to go over the hills that it wasn't in order to bring Barbara's child back, but to put an end to Donald. . . . Yet there had had to be an end, it had to come in some way for she could not have stood this way of life much longer. Donald had not been a sane man; his jealousy had turned his brain. . . . But there again, was she not to blame for that? Oh God! God! At this moment she wouldn't have minded if he had taken her with him for then she would not have had to face the prospect of living with this feeling of guilt.

She opened her eyes to look at Anna who was again stroking her brow. But here was something she could be thankful for: Anna's future, however long or short it might last, was secure, and Barbara's child would not be brought up in hatred. And that was another thing, neither would her own. She took in a deep breath. Some good could come out of this deed other than her own release. She'd have to think along these lines.

Matthew now moved in his chair and muttered, 'Get my mother,' and as Constance went to rise Miss Brigmore said, 'I'll go, sit quiet.'

Constance sat quiet and she and Matthew looked at each other, until Matthew closed his eyes to shut out the pain that the sight of her always brought to him. . . .

Miss Brigmore went from the kitchen and into the sitting room where the new woman Daisy Waite was helping Jane to lay out the body of her son.

Donald was lying on the table, the stairs having been too narrow for the men to carry him up. The two women had him undressed down to his long pants and vest, and Daisy Waite was unbuttoning the pants that were stained red around the hips, while she cried as she talked. 'God Almighty! To end like this. Did you ever see anything like it? Aw, the poor man, the poor man. An' no matter what, let everybody have their due, it was him who gave us shelter when nobody else would. And to come to this. Aw, dear God. Where's the sense in anything?'

Miss Brigmore turned her gaze away from the now partly naked body for she too felt on the point of fainting. She touched Jane on the shoulder and said softly, 'Matthew needs you.'

Jane nodded but did not turn and follow her or look at her, but she kept her gaze fixed on the face of her son. He was gone, he was dead, they were rid of him, they were all rid of him, they were free and she was glad. Then why was there this pain in her? She had never wanted him. When she was carrying him she had never wanted him, and when he was born she had never wanted him for she had seen him as something that had been thrust on her – into her, and since the day he had first breathed he had brought strife with him. He in his turn had never liked her, had even hated her. Yet she was feeling an over-whelming pity for him, as if she had sustained the loss of a loved one. She couldn't understand it. If it had been Matthew she could have. And she would be feeling like this again soon, for Matthew wouldn't be long in going now.

What would happen to Matthew when he died? Would he be brought before the Judgment? His father had instilled the Good Book

209

into her, so she must believe in the Judgment, but surely the dear God would take everything into account. But she didn't know, she didn't know. He was a fearsome God at times. Her poor Matthew! her poor Matthew! And Donald? At this moment she could say, if not 'My poor Donald', at least 'Poor Donald', for he had never been hers nor she his, but yes, she could say, 'Poor Donald.'

She turned her dry eyes on Daisy Waite and said, 'I'll be back in a minute.'

'Don't worry, Missis, don't worry, I can manage. He isn't the first, and he won't be the last I've put ready for a journey.'

Miss Brigmore took Jane's arm and led her from the room, but they did not go immediately into the kitchen. In the dim hallway they instinctively turned and looked at each other, and the look was deep. Neither of them said a word but their hands gripped tight for a moment before they moved on again into the kitchen.

When Jane stood beside Matthew's chair and he said, 'I want to go to bed, Mother,' she replied, 'Come away then, lad.' And tenderly she helped him to his feet and with her arm around him led him from the room.

Constance had not moved, and now Miss Brigmore went to her and, bending over her, said softly, 'Try to think no more of it, what's done is done. It ... it had to be this way, you couldn't have gone on, something would have happened, perhaps something more terrible.'

'But ... but what will happen to Matthew?'

'Nothing will happen to Matthew. I've told you, I mean to explain it all as I saw it, and nothing will happen to Matthew.'

'Oh! Anna.' Constance jerked to her feet, her hands gripping her neck. She seemed to be on the point of choking, until the tears, rushing from her eyes and nose, relieved the pressure. Miss Brigmore put her arms tightly about her and they both swayed as if they were drunk.

When the paroxysm passed, Miss Brigmore, her own face showing her distress, murmured, 'There, there, my dear. You must forget it, all the past, all of it, all of it. Just ... just thank God that you've been saved and you're still young and, and beautiful. There's a life before you yet, you'll see. There's a life before you yet.' And to this Constance made a deep dissenting sound.

At the inquest a week later Miss Brigmore explained to the Coroner exactly what had happened. Mr Matthew Radlet, who had the disease of consumption, had been in distress, and because he was feeling sick had got down and stood at the side of the road. His brother, Donald, had gone to his assistance. She could not explain how it had happened because she was sitting in the back of the cart at the time, but she surmised he must have slipped on the frost-rimed verge; the frost had been very heavy the night before; all she knew was Mr Matthew Radlet had made an effort to grab his brother, but without success.

It was an awful tragedy, everyone said so, for Donald Radlet was the most up and coming farmer in the district. They said this aloud, but among themselves in the drawing rooms, the parlours, and the select ends of the inns they reminded each other that, after all, he was a Mallen and did anyone know of any Mallen who had died in his bed?

AFTERMATH

IT WAS THE END of the harvest supper. The barn had never witnessed such gaiety for it was the first time such a function had been held there. Michael Radlet had not countenanced harvest suppers nor had his father before him, nor, of course, had Donald Radlet, and they would all have stood amazed, not believing their eyes at the changes that had taken place during three short years. In Donald's case, he would surely have experienced chagrin that his farm, as he had always considered it, was now being managed by a woman, a young woman, his wife in fact.

Matthew Radlet had survived his half-brother by only six weeks, and his going had drawn Jane and Constance even closer together. Their guilt, their remorse and their relief were mingled and shared.

For months after Matthew's going they had lived a cheerless, guilt-ridden existence, until one day Jane, as if throwing off a mental illness, had stood in the kitchen and actually cried aloud, 'Look, girl, let us put an end to this. If we're going to live in misery then it's a pity he ever went the way he did. That's how I'm seeing it now, and you must see it the same way. Oh yes, more so than me, you must see it like that, for you are young, and healthy. And you have a child to bring up, and he should be brought up amid cheerfulness, not the gloom that's been hanging over us these months past.'

It was from that time that, as Daisy Waite expressed it, the missis and the young mistress came out of their sorrow.

It would not have been considered unusual had Constance left the running of the entire farm to Harry Waite. Harry was quite knowledgeable on farming matters, and more, more than willing to do all in his power to assist her, as were his wife, son and daughter; but no, from the day Jane lifted the curtain of guilt, as it were, from their shoulders, there had risen in her a determination to manage the farm herself.

And so she went to market, driven by Harry Waite, and stood by his side as he bargained in both the buying and the selling. She said little or nothing on these first visits but kept her head held high and her gaze straight, and her look defied the neighbouring farmers to laugh at her, at least in public. That in the inns it was a different matter she had no doubt, for on one occasion Harry Waite drove her home having only the sight of one eye, the other being closed and fast discolouring, besides which his knuckles were bleeding. She did not ask him if he had been drinking, for Harry Waite, she had discovered, was a moderate man; his main concern in life being the welfare of his family and, since being in her service, protecting her.

His loyalty had been well repaid, for two months ago he moved his family into the three-roomed cottage she'd had built for them in a small enclosure about a hundred yards from the farmhouse proper.

Harry Waite's son, Jim, who was now seventeen was, among other things, a shepherd on the farm, and his daughter, Lily, now sixteen, divided her time between the dairy and the house.

The house had changed beyond all recognition, for the horsehair suite no longer adorned the sitting room, nor was there linoleum on the floor, but a new chesterfield suite now stood on a patterned carpet, and there was never a day in the winter but a fire was lit in this room. Jane no longer sat in front of the kitchen fire warming her feet and knees before going up into the freezing bedroom, but she and Constance usually ended the day sitting side by side on the couch, slippers on their feet, and a hot drink to their hands. On extremely cold nights there was the welcome glow of a fire in their bedrooms, an extravagant innovation this, and there was always a fire, except on days that were really warm, in the room that was now called the nursery.

So in the late summer of 1866 when Constance did her books and found that the profit for the year was well up on the previous one, and this in spite of having to engage extra labour for the threshing and the hay making, which crops were the first results from the land that Donald had so proudly acquired, she decided, with a little glow of excitement, to give a harvest supper. She would bring Anna, Mary, and the child over; they would enjoy it. Then besides the Waite family there would be the Twiggs, the father, mother, and three children – they had been very helpful. Then there were Bob and Peter Armstrong, two brothers who had a farm in the next valley. They had been most kind from the beginning, going as far as to come over and offer her advice; and it hadn't stopped there, for their help had also been practical. She liked the Armstrongs, Bob in particular, he had a merry twinkle in his eye.

The supper had not been lavish as some harvest suppers tended to be. She had provided plenty of wholesome food, and a certain amount to drink; and no one had overstepped the mark in this direction, except perhaps Mary. Two glasses of ale always led to three with Mary, and three to four, and then she became very merry; but she had caused a great deal of laughter tonight and she had got everyone dancing. Constance herself had danced for the first time in years. It had been strange feeling a man's arms around her once again. At first she had felt stiff, resisting both touch and movement in such close proximity; then Bob's merriment, and young Jim's fiddle playing, seemed to melt the aloof encasement within which she had remained for the last three years, and she had ended the dance with her head back and laughing as she used to do years ago when life had spread out before her like a never-ending series of bright paintings.

But now the visitors had gone. Peter Armstrong, shaking her hand as if he would never let it go, had told her in fuddled tones that she was – a grand lass, which had caused great hilarity. Bob had not taken her hand, he had just stood before her and had said simply, 'We'll have to have a night like this again, but not wait till next harvest supper, eh?'

In reply she had said formally, 'I'm so glad you enjoyed it,' and his eyes had laughed at her, but in a kindly way.

And now she and Anna were seated before the fire, to use Mary's term, taking five minutes off, and they were alone, for Jane always tactfully gave place to Miss Brigmore during her visits.

Turning her head from where it rested on the back of the couch, Constance looked at Miss Brigmore and asked quietly, 'Did you enjoy it, Anna?'

'Enormously, enormously, my dear. Now I can understand why there's so much fuss made about them. And to think that years ago when I used to hear of the excitement surrounding them on the Hall farms I used to turn my nose up.'

Constance looked towards the fire again as she said softly, 'We turned our noses up at so many things in those days, didn't we? Life is strange; you've always said that it's a pattern that is already cut. I wonder what shape mine's going to take from now on?'

'A good shape I should think, dear.'

'I'd like it to remain exactly as it is now; I'd like to keep everything and everybody static, Michael for ever small, Jane happy and content, and all the Waites so loyal and good, and myself at rest.'

'You are too young to be at rest, you'll marry again.'

'No, Anna, no.' Constance's voice, although low, held a definite ring.

They were both looking straight ahead into the fire when Miss Brigmore said, 'I like that Mr Armstrong, the younger one; I should say he's an honest man and he has a great sense of humour.'

Constance did not move as she replied, 'I like him too, Anna. He is as you say an honest man, and his company is enjoyable . . . but that's as far as it will go; I wouldn't risk a repeat of what I've been through.'

'Well, time will tell. You are so young yet and life, in spite of the pattern being already cut' – she slanted her eyes towards Constance – 'no doubt has some surprises in store for you . . . as it's had for me. Now who would have thought that I'd ever sit in the Hall schoolroom again! In your wildest stretch of imagination, would you have said that was in my pattern?'

'No.' Constance shook her head as she laughed, then added, 'And you know, I still don't like the idea of you being there. I've always considered you belonged to Barbara and me exclusively, I mean with regards to education. But it would appear that he was determined to have you in the end, and his motto seemed to be: If at first you don't succeed.'

Miss Brigmore laughed gently and nodded towards the fire. 'Indeed, indeed, that is his motto, which he applies to everything, I should say. He's a strange man, Mr Bensham; you dislike him, yet at the same time you admire him, except that is when he's speaking to his wife, for he not only considers her a numskull but tells her to her face she is one, using that very hard word. Poor Mrs Bensham. Yet it's odd but I find no need to pity her, she's a woman who can hold her own in her own way. As I told you she's such a common type, it's almost impossible to imagine her in the Hall as one of the staff, let alone its mistress, yet it's very strange you know' – she turned her head now and looked at Constance – 'the staff don't seem to take advantage of her. She bustles, shouts, fumbles her way through each day, but there at the end of it she sits in the drawing room quietly knitting. I think she must do this every evening after dinner; and he, when he is at home, sits there too, smoking and reading his newspaper. . . .'

'Smoking in the drawing room?'

'Yes, smoking in the drawing room, and not cigars but a long, smelly old pipe.'

'Have you been to dinner? You didn't tell me.'

'Well, there hasn't been much time. But yes, I went to dinner to discuss the new arrangement. And you know, Constance' – Miss Brigmore's voice had a touch of sadness in it now – 'it was the first time I had sat down to dinner in the dining room of the Hall. It was a strange experience; I felt most odd.'

'Oh, Anna, it is unfair when you think of it, isn't it?'

'No, no.' Her tone became airy. 'Yet it did strike me as peculiar at the time. It was a very good meal, by the way, and well served. The butler had not the dignity of Dunn of course; apparently at one time he had worked in Mr Bensham's mill and ill-health had prevented him from continuing, which doesn't speak well for the conditions there, yet such is the make-up of our Mr Bensham that he took him into his house service when they were in Manchester. Mrs Bensham addresses him as . . . 'Arry as she does her husband. Oh, I shouldn't make fun of them, because they have been, and are still, very good to me.'

'It is to their own advantage.'

'Perhaps, but to mine also because I am using them for my advantage, or at least for little Barbara's. I was adamant at first against going every day; I said I had my ward to see to and couldn't possibly think of leaving her except in the mornings for three hours as the arrangement stood, and then it was he who said, as I hoped he would, "Bring her with you, woman, bring her with you".'

'Does he call you woman?' Constance was laughing.

'Yes, very often. The only time he gave me my title was when he came to see me, and then that was only after he had said, "You're harder to get at, woman, than the Queen herself. I've written you three times. What is it you want, more money? A pound for six mornings a week, you'll not get an offer like that again." It was then I said, "My name is Miss Brigmore. Won't you sit down?" and for the first and only time he gave me my title, "Aye, well, Miss Brigmore," he said; "now let's be sensible. I hear you're a good teacher an' I want you to teach my young 'uns. Three of them I have; a boy of seven, another six and a girl coming five. Three so-called governesses the missus's had for them in a year, an' what've they learned, nowt. The boys will be going off to school in a year or so, private like, but I don't want them to go with nothing in their heads, you understand?"'

Miss Brigmore now stopped her mimicking and leant her head against Constance, and as they laughed together she recalled, but only to herself, how Mr Bensham had ended that introduction by saying, 'I've heard all kinds of things about you but it makes no matter to me; I've always said, a man's reference is in his hands or his head. They say you're a good teacher, and ladylike at bottom, and that's what I want, someone ladylike.'

Strangely she had not taken offence at the man. He was a common man who had made money – there were many such these days – but she saw it was to his credit that he was wanting to educate his children above his own standards. Moreover, as he said, a pound a week for morning work was a very good offer indeed. She now knew security in so far as she owned half the cottage, Constance having transferred to her her own share by deed of gift together with fifty pounds a year, and this with the child's income of a hundred pounds enabled them to live better than they had done since she had left the Hall. Even so this new addition to her income would be a means of carrying out the vague plans that had been formulating in her mind with regard to Barbara's future.

A young lady's education could not be accomplished without money. She regretted that there was no musical instrument in the cottage; Barbara must have music lessons. Then there were languages; she herself unfortunately had only French to her credit. Moreover, a young lady needed dancing lessons if she was to fit into any civilized society; added to this, riding lessons were necessary; and there were so many, many more things her child – as she secretly thought of Barbara's offspring – would need before she could take her rightful place in society, and this she was determined she should do. God sparing her, she would see to it that Thomas's daughter was educated to fit into the life that was rightly hers.

She was recalled to the present when Constance, chuckling, said, 'So you cornered him.'

'Just that, just that.'

'Does he know that she isn't yet three?'

'Yes; he's seen her.'

'And when do you start to take her?'

'She's already been there. I took her along on Thursday and I must say that the first meeting didn't augur well for the future.' Miss Brigmore pursed her mouth and her eyes twinkled as she added, 'Barbara ended her visit by attacking the daughter of the house.'

'No! ... What happened?'

'Well, she had never seen so many toys in her life before. She has three dolls, you know, Betsy and Golly and Fluffy, but the nursery at the Hall is now stacked with toys and dolls of all shapes and sizes. Barbara became fascinated by a Dutch doll. It was neither big, nor small, nor outstanding, it was just a Dutch doll, but apparently it was Katie's favourite. She went to take it from Barbara, but Barbara refused to let it go. When Miss Katie forcibly took possession of her own Barbara gave way to one of her tempers, and oh dear, before we knew what had happened she had slapped Katie and pushed her onto her back, and Katie yelled as she is apt to do when she can't get her own way. Then ...' Miss Brigmore now stopped and bit on her lip and, her expression serious, she looked at Constance before adding, 'Something strange happened. There had been no surnames used between the children, just Christian names: "This is Barbara, Katie," and "Katie, this is Barbara." But when I lifted Katie to her feet she ran from the room crying, "Ma! Ma! the Mallen girl has hit me. The Mallen girl has hit me, Ma".'

They looked at each other in silence now; then Constance said quietly, 'You never told them her name's Farrington?'

'There was no need, the occasion hadn't arisen when I was required to give her full name, but it proved one thing to me, she's known already as a Mallen. Mrs Bensham must have spoken of her in front of

Katie as the "Mallen child", and Mrs Bensham would have heard it from someone else. I think it's going to be difficult to get people to realize that her name is Farrington, and it's going to be awkward as she grows older. It'll have to be explained to her.'

Constance sighed now and, pulling herself to the edge of the couch, she dropped onto her knees and, having taken up a shovel, scooped from a scuttle some small coal and sprinkled it onto the dying embers; then she patted it down before saying, 'There's a lot of things that'll have to be explained to her. But in the meantime, let her be happy . . . And she will be happy' – she turned and nodded her head – 'because she'll have her own way or die in the attempt. Look how she dominates Michael already, and he's willing to let her. Oh' – she put out her hand and covered Miss Brigmore's – 'she'll be all right. She has you, so she'll be all right. Come, let's go up; we'll look in on them before we go to bed.'

A few minutes later they stood in the nursery between the cot and the bed. The candle glowed softly in its red glass bowl, showing to one side the boy lying on his back, his fair hair curling over his brow and around his ears; the bed-clothes were under his chin, and his body was lying straight; he looked in deep relaxed sleep. But on the other side the small girl lay curled up into a ball; her forearms were crossed above her head and her black straight hair half covered her face; the bed-clothes were rumpled down to her waist; she looked as if she were pulling herself up out of some dream depth.

As Miss Brigmore gently brought the clothes up around the small shoulders she thought that, even in sleep, the children looked poles apart. They were full cousins yet showed no apparent blood link in either looks or character.

The two women turned and tiptoed quietly from the room, and on the landing they kissed each other good night.

Constance went into the bedroom which now held no resemblance to the one she had shared with Donald, and Miss Brigmore went into the room that had been Matthew's.

Strangely, their thoughts were running along the same channel now, for they were both thinking they would be glad when tomorrow came, Constance so that she could fall back into the daily routine when she and Jane would be alone together and the older woman would become her relaxed and motherly self again. Anna's intellectual presence always put something of a damper on Jane, indeed her whole outlook was foreign to the farm atmosphere. It was lovely to have her for a short time but it was, and Constance hated to admit this, a relief when she went.

She did not probe this feeling too far for it seemed to be linked up with the day of Donald's death and Matthew's act. Would Matthew have taken the step he did if Anna hadn't come to the farm begging to keep the child? If? If? If?

But there was another reason why she was always glad when Anna departed. It concerned little Barbara, for the child, as young as she was, dominated Michael and in a way that annoyed her. The little girl had an attraction that was unusual, to say the least, in one so young. Yet she herself had never been able to take to the child, and this seemed strange because she had loved her mother dearly. Anyway, she told herself, she'd be glad when tomorrow came.

Miss Brigmore too thought she'd be glad when tomorrow came for then she'd be home where she was mistress, really mistress now, and in the cottage she would have the child all to herself.

It was very nice visiting the farm but the atmosphere was – well, how could she put it, a little raw. And Constance was changing, changing all the time. She noticed it on each visit. She wouldn't be surprised if Constance did marry that Mr Armstrong, and it wouldn't be a case now of marrying beneath her for, of late, she had become very farm-minded. She wasn't being disloyal to Constance, oh no, no, she loved her, and would always love her, she was just facing facts.

Almost the last thing Miss Brigmore told herself before dropping off to sleep was, I go to the Hall on Monday. It was exciting being back at the Hall. There were moments when in the schoolroom she thought she had never left it. Already she had a status in the house, and it would grow; oh yes, it would grow, for she was needed there. She had sensed this from the beginning. Mr Bensham needed her. 'What's the best way to tackle an invitation like that?' he had said to her on one occasion as he handed her a gilt-edged card; and then on another, 'Who do you think's best for running a house, a housekeeper or a steward?' Yes, Mr Bensham needed her.

And Mrs Bensham needed her. 'Do you think this is too flashy-like to go to tea in? What happened in the old days when you lived here and they gave parties? How did they go about it, were they flashy-like or selectish?' Yes, Mrs Bensham needed her very badly.

And Katie needed her. Oh yes, Katie needed her to discipline and train her, and in the coming years to stand as a buffer between the young lady she would become and the parents she would undoubtedly look down on, as was usual in such situations.

And the boys needed her, but their need would only be for a short time. Her influence on them would be felt mostly during their holidays; yet they were very important in the future she was mapping out.

As the necessity for her presence at the Hall grew with the years so would Barbara's future become more and more assured, for 'the Mallen girl' would always have one asset the young Benshams lacked, breeding; but they, in their turn, would have one thing the Mallen girl lacked, money.

Who knew, who knew but Thomas would reign in the Hall once again – through his daughter.

Happy, she went to sleep, forgetting as she did so the adage she so often quoted, that the pattern of life was already cut.

THE MALLEN
GIRL

PART ONE

Young Barbara

I

THE TRAP had hardly stopped opposite the cottage gate before the lithe figure of the young girl sprang down from it, ran up the back path, across the small courtyard, thrust open the door of the kitchen and slammed her beaded handbag and the book she was carrying down on the table, which action caused Mary Peel, who was standing at the far end of the table, to space her lips widely apart and mouth her words in a loud voice, crying, 'Now Miss Bar-bara you! Now don't you start the minute you're in; keep your tantrums for those who caused them.'

The young girl's hand went to the book again, and as she grabbed it up and threw it, the door leading from the hall opened and Miss Anna Brigmore entered. The book had missed its target, skimming by Mary Peel's face, but it hit Miss Brigmore's shoulder, bounded off and on to the dresser, knocking a jug on to the stone floor.

After the resounding crash of the jug splintering there was quiet in the kitchen for a moment. Miss Brigmore, staring in pained silence at the young girl who was known as her ward, but whom she thought of as her daughter, cried from her heart, 'Oh Barbara! Barbara, my dear.' But Mary Peel, looking at the girl, thought, By! if I had me way I'd skelp your backside for you, I would that. Your neck's been broken, that's your trouble, miss.

And apparently her thinking was endorsed by Jim Waite as he held the door open when Miss Brigmore took hold of Barbara's hand and led her out of the room, for as soon as she closed it he said, 'That one wants her ears scudded.'

'Aw, don't say that, Jim,' said Mary Peel now; 'I know she deserved her hammers, but it's her ears an' not being able to hear right that makes her as she is. Sit yourself down, the kettle's just on the boil. How's things been?'

Jim Waite lowered his long length on to the wooden kitchen chair and stretched out his hands towards the fire before saying, 'Oh, much

225

as usual. I suppose I'm sayin' it as shouldn't, but I tell you everybody on the farm breathes a sigh of relief when that young monkey steps up into the trap. They do, they do.' He nodded at her. 'She makes the young master's life hell. She never lets him out of her sight; he can't go to the netty for her, an' that's a fact. And I'm not just usin' that as a sayin', 'cos only this mornin' he was in the closet and there she was standin' in the middle of the yard looking at the doorway, waitin' for him coming out. It isn't decent. You would think Miss Brigmore would be able to do something about it, now wouldn't you? If anybody could you'd think she could. And yet on the other hand, as me da was sayin' just the other night, it's her who's partly to blame for the way Miss Barbara is now. Oh, not her ears, no, but the way she carries on, 'cos she's given into her all along the line.'

'Here, drink this.' Mary handed him a mug of tea and asked, 'Would you like a bit of new fadge, it's just out of the oven?'

'Aye, ta, it'll fill a corner.'

'An' you've got some corners to fill.' Mary pushed him in the shoulder with the flat of her hand. 'You would've thought you'd stopped growin' years ago.... How's your ma and da?'

'Oh fine, fine.'

'And Lily?'

'Oh, Lily. You'll never believe it but I think she's got Bill Twigg up to scratch at last.'

Mary sat down abruptly now and, clasping her hands, she bounced them on her lap as she leaned towards him and said, 'No! What's brought it on?'

'Well, Harry Brown's wife died over Allendale way. He's got a bit of a farm, not much to brag about but enough to keep the wolf from the door. Well, he's been over three times in the last three months, an' each time stood chattin' and laughing with our Lily. It's made Bill think.' He jerked his head as he ended, 'An' so he should, he's been courtin' her for seven years. But it was his mother to blame there, at least up till three years ago when she died, 'cos she always used to tell him that it was unlucky to marry a woman older than himself. Two years, I ask you! Eeh! the things people say an' believe in.... This is a nice bit of fadge, Mary.' He took another huge bite out of the buttered bread, then ended, 'Folks in the main are ignorant you know, ignorant....'

In the sitting room Miss Brigmore was using the same words. 'It is ignorance, my dear,' she was saying, 'just ignorance.' Miss Brigmore did not speak as loudly as Mary Peel, but her voice was a pitch above normal, and she moved her lips in a slightly exaggerated fashion.

'She is horrible, and I hate her.'

'You mustn't say that, Barbara. Sarah is only a little girl, but she is about twelve years old.'

Miss Brigmore did not think that the girl standing before her at this moment was also twelve years old for she considered Barbara older than her years. Knowledge, she thought, had made her so, the knowledge that she herself had imparted to her. The child, although having the terrible disadvantage of being almost completely deaf, nevertheless had the balancing advantage of being as well informed on a great many subjects as any young lady of twenty.

She gazed at the child, who was over-thin, and over-tall for her age . . . and over-beautiful too. Her straight black hair was shining with the sheen of a wet seal. The skin that covered her long face was creamy and thick of texture and without tint. Her eyes were a dark brown and the look in them now, as at other times, made Miss Brigmore uneasy, for it reminded her of the look in Donald Radlet's eyes, Donald Radlet who had been the husband of Barbara's aunt, Constance, but who was much closer to her than an uncle, did she but know it. This fact often kept Miss Brigmore awake at nights as she searched for a way to break to her beloved child the truth of her beginnings. She was fully aware that but for the girl's deafness her origin would have been made clear to her long before now, and, if by no one else, by one of the Waite family over at Wolfbur Farm, for she had aroused the animosity not only of Harry and Daisy Waite, but also of Jim and Lily, their son and daughter, and all because she had taken a dislike to Harry Waite's niece, Sarah.

Harry Waite had brought Sarah to the farm when she was two years old, when her parents had both died of the fever. Sarah had grown into a pretty and lively little girl and she was popular not only with the Waite family, but with the mistress, Constance Radlet, and her mother-in-law, Jane Radlet, too.

All this would have been quite in order and accepted by Barbara had the attention to Sarah stopped there, but her cousin Michael had championed the little girl from the day she arrived on the farm, for Sarah, although so much smaller than himself, was someone with whom he could play and at the same time protect. Previous to Sarah's coming the only time Michael had anyone of his own age to play with was when Barbara visited the farm. In the summer the visits could be frequent, but during the winter months the children were lucky if they saw each other twice.

The first time the rift between the children came into the open was one exceptionally mild Christmas. Miss Brigmore herself had driven Mary and the child over expecting to be able to return home within the week, but their stay on the farm had lengthened into almost three weeks, and although Michael, then eight years old, had played with

Barbara and tolerated her domination, he had continued to take notice of young Sarah.

It happened during the evening of the yearly event when Constance had the Waite family in for supper and, as Jane Radlet termed it, a bit of jollification. Little Sarah, after entertaining the company with a clog dance, taught her by her cousin Jim, was receiving the loud applause of all those present when she found herself suddenly sitting on her bottom on the farm kitchen floor. Although the floor was covered with drugget it was made up of slabs of stone, and the impact caused the little girl to howl aloud. The only one who dared voice her disapproval was Constance, who said, 'You're a naughty girl, Barbara,' accompanying her words with slapping Barbara's hands.

Miss Brigmore was very annoyed and she expressed her annoyance to Constance. Didn't she understand the situation? she asked. Wasn't it natural that Barbara should be jealous when she saw Michael making a fuss of the Waite child? Didn't she understand that in her little mind she imagined Michael belonged to her, like a brother? It was merely a childish reaction and she would grow out of it.

Miss Brigmore remembered for a long time afterwards that Constance had made no reply whatever; she had just stood staring at her before turning about and walking out of the room.

Her prediction that Barbara would, with the years, change her attitude towards Michael had not, however, proved correct; if anything Barbara's possessiveness had increased, until now Miss Brigmore found herself longing for the winter so that their visits would be controlled by the weather. In the summer Barbara insisted on trailing over the hills at least once a week. Lately, she had broached the subject of having a horse; if she had a horse she would not need to trouble anyone, was her argument now.

Among other fears also assailing Miss Brigmore was the fact that the childish infatuation Barbara had for her cousin Michael might not die away during her adolescence, but might mature into love, and such an outcome as this was definitely not in her plans for her child. As prosperous a farm as Wolfbur was, she did not see Thomas Mallen's daughter acting the farmer's wife. No, the route she had mapped out for her lay in the opposite direction, just a mile or so down the road where stood the Hall, High Banks Hall, in which Barbara's mother had spent her young days, and over which Miss Brigmore was determined her spiritual daughter should reign in the future. And everything would work out splendidly she felt, for already John Bensham, at sixteen, was showing a marked interest in Barbara. If only the child would get over this obsession for Michael and also her equally strong hate for young Sarah Waite, for the two were linked together.

She would like, at this moment, to be able to reassure Barbara that she had nothing to fear from a girl like Sarah Waite, because after all what was she but a maid, and the niece of a farm labourer. True, she was not actually treated like a maid, and so therefore did not act like one, for Constance had made the mistake of teaching the girl to read and write. She could have been happy to reassure her that her Aunt Constance did not prefer a little working class maid to herself. But she knew this was not true. Constance had no feeling for Barbara, and this was strange because she had loved Barbara's mother. The sisters had been inseparable. Yet Constance, she suspected, would prefer that her son stepped out of his class and took someone like the Waite child to wife rather than her own niece.

It was a most strange state of affairs, Miss Brigmore thought; yet it suited her book, because were it otherwise the second stage of her life's work would go for nought.

She now sat down on a chair and, drawing Barbara to her, she held the child's hands between her own, and, looking up at her, she said slowly, but in loud tones, 'Don't you understand, my dear, that when you quarrel with Sarah you are bringing yourself down to her level?'

'Don't shout at me, I can hear you.'

Miss Brigmore stared up into Barbara's eyes, which had now turned as black as her hair, and she dragged her lower lip slowly between her teeth before saying in a normal voice, 'What did I say?'

'You said that when I quarrel with her I reduce myself to her level.' The answer was correct and the words were as precise as Miss Brigmore would have wished; she sometimes forgot that this child could read most of what she was saying by the movement of her lips, and so she said, 'Well then, you understand what I mean, only inferior people quarrel openly. You mustn't forget that you are a young lady. . . .'

'And I mustn't forget that I am deaf. I'll soon be stone deaf, won't I?'

'No, no, my dear.' Miss Brigmore's head was moving slowly, and her words were merely a whisper and full of compassion. 'No, no,' she repeated. 'No, no; something will be done. Mr Bensham promised to see a certain gentleman in Manchester; he's heard of a man who's very clever with ears. . . .'

'Yes, he'll give me a big horn to stick in it, like the caricatures in. . . .'

'No! No! No!' Miss Brigmore's voice was loud again and with each word she shook Barbara's hands up and down. When she stopped they stared at each other, both in deep sadness. Then the girl, her thin body seeming to crumple, fell on to her knees and buried her face in Miss

229

Brigmore's lap, and her voice high and tear-broken now, she gasped, 'Why am I deaf? Why, why?' She lifted her face and appealed, 'Brigie, why? Why should I be deaf? Is it because Michael tipped me out of the barrow?'

Miss Brigmore did not answer immediately because this was always a question in her own mind. It had seemed that there had been no ear defect at all until the child was five years old; yet of late she had recalled having before this chastised her for disobedience, whenever she appeared to take no notice either of some question or of being called.

The accident appeared a minor one at the time. Michael had been wheeling her in the farm barrow when it capsized and she fell head over heels and suffered a slight concussion. Was it from that time that her deafness became noticeable? Or was it really from the time of her first nightmare?

As if the girl were picking up her thoughts she said, 'I told Michael today that he was to blame for my deafness.'

'You shouldn't have done that, my dear; it ... it isn't true.'

'It could be.'

'Your hearing was slightly defective before that.'

'Throwing me on my head didn't help.'

'That was an accident.'

'The doctor said it didn't help, didn't he?'

'Who told you that?'

'I saw you talking to Mrs Bensham one day.'

'Oh, my dear.' Miss Brigmore closed her eyes; then slowly she said, 'It may not have helped but ... but you would have become deaf in any case, so I understand. Yet as I have said, there are remedies; I refuse to believe there are not. And I want you to believe that too, you understand? Now dry your eyes.' She dried them for her. Then taking the child's face gently between her two palms she looked down into it and said slowly, 'It doesn't matter so much about your impediment, just remember you are very beautiful and highly intelligent.'

A sad smile slowly spread over Barbara's face, but there was a glint of mischief in it now as she said, 'I haven't got a bust, not a sign of one, and you can't be beautiful without a bust.'

'Oh Barbara! Barbara!' Miss Brigmore was trying to suppress her laughter. 'You shouldn't say things like that, one doesn't, they're not....'

'Ladylike?'

'Yes, if you put it that way.'

'That doesn't alter the fact that I haven't one. And look at yours; you're old and you've got an enormous bust.'

'Really! Barbara.' Miss Brigmore rose to her feet and her voice

230

lost a little of its controlled calmness as she retorted, 'I'm not, I haven't.'

Jumping up now, Barbara placed her hand over her mouth to stifle her laughter; then she fell against Miss Brigmore as she giggled, 'Well, you have; and it's a lovely bust, a lovely bust.'

When she went to put her hand on the tightly laced breasts Miss Brigmore slapped at it hard and, bringing her upright, said, 'Barbara ... Barbara, behave yourself.' Her lips moved widely now. 'One does not mention these things. I have told you before, there are certain parts of the anatomy to which one does not make reference. Nor does one refer to another's age. You're old enough to have learned these things, they are elementary.'

'Oh, Brigie!' Barbara flounced away; only to be pulled sharply round to face Miss Brigmore again.

'Never mind taking that attitude. Come, sit down, I want to talk to you.'

Seated once again, they looked at each other and Miss Brigmore's mind was distracted from her theme as her protesting thoughts said, Old, indeed! She felt younger now than she had when Thomas was alive. Her body was straight and firm; she had as yet no grey hairs, and but for some lines under her eyes her skin was smooth; as for her mind, it had never been more active than during these last few years. Old indeed! She swallowed deeply; then folding her hands on her lap, her head slightly tilted to the side, she said, 'Tell me exactly what caused the rum. . . .' She had almost said, rumpus – Mary's speech had a way of infiltrating. 'What caused the altercation at the farm?'

'Need you ask? It was Sarah, as usual.'

Miss Brigmore did not say, 'Sarah is not always to blame'; instead she asked, 'What did she do?'

'She said I was deaf.'

'Did she say it spitefully?'

Barbara heaved a deep sigh, closed her eyes and slumped back in her chair before saying, 'Spitefully or not, she said it.'

'Sit up straight; put your buttocks well back ... straighter. Don't have to be told so often.'

'Will sitting straight make me hear better?'

'Don't ask ridiculous questions, Barbara. You shall hear; I've told you, you shall hear; everything is being done. What you must understand is that you're not the only one who has this impediment.' She now tapped her ear; then dropped her hand away as if it had been stung, remembering too late that nothing angered the child more than sign language. Yet if only she'd admit to her deafness the sign language would be of untold help to her. She herself had been reading at great length recently about the different methods of sign language; it

231

was amazing what one learned through tribulation. She would never have dreamed there had been methods of trying to make the deaf and dumb speak as far back as the seventeenth century. She had also learned that deafness could be brought about by shock. This new knowledge, gleaned only during the past week, had brought the nightmares into question again and opened up another possibility for the child's deafness. For she had received a shock; as she herself had the first night Barbara's screams had awakened her. When she had reached the child's bed it was to see her sitting stiffly upright, her arms stretched out, her fingers pointing to the corner of the room, and screaming hysterically, 'The man! The man! The big man! send him away.'

Even after she took Barbara into her own bed and soothed her by telling her that she had been dreaming, the child still insisted that there had been a big man in her room, a big man with a fat stomach and white hair all over his head and face. The description had been like the painting of Thomas over the mantelpiece, and for nights afterwards she had hardly slept and she had talked to the unseen figure, begging him to go and rest in peace and not to frighten the child.

She had never before associated this, and further incidents of the same nature, with Barbara's deafness, being of the opinion that deafness was congenital and could slumber for years in a child, except in cases of malnutrition which supplied bad blood to the brain and resulted in bad eyesight, deafness and rickets. Nor did she associate deafness such as Barbara had with that of the deaf and dumb. The latter she considered a malady quite apart, and associated with mental defects; at least she had done until she'd had cause to go more fully into the matter.

She said now, 'Your deafness is different; it's a deafness that could go like that.' She snapped her fingers. . . .

'Or get worse like that!' Barbara imitated her.

'Barbara!' Miss Brigmore's voice was stern again. 'You've got to believe what I say; and you've also got to help yourself.'

'By talking on my hands?' She now made wild exaggerated gestures, then said, 'I won't, I won't. It makes you look mad; people think you're mad, daft. That's what Mary said when I did it. "Don't act daft," she said.'

Oh! Mary. Miss Brigmore said sharply, 'Mary wasn't inferring that you were. . . .' She stopped, and now she closed her eyes in irritation and flicked her hand as if dismissing Mary before saying, 'I have been reading about a Mr Pestalozzi and a Mr Froebel. Mr Pestalozzi was from Switzerland; he had a school there. He was a great educationist and he advises. . . .'

'That you should take your earwort medicine. Oh you! You! You're silly; with your Mr Froebel and Mr Pestalozzi, and all your ideas. Pestalozzi! Psst! Psst! . . .'

When Miss Brigmore's hand came out and struck Barbara's with two resounding blows the girl was really startled for she couldn't ever remember Brigie striking her, not for insolence or anything else. Then her pale face went a shade paler as she read Miss Brigmore saying, 'All right, all right, I'm silly, as is Mr Pestalozzi, so we will have it the way you want it. I shall no longer pester you with my theories, I shall no longer continue to probe into ways and means of helping you. But one thing I shall do, I shall see that you are helped, I'll send you away to a school for the deaf. Yes, yes; that's what I'll do.'

Miss Brigmore stood up. Her body was as straight as a ramrod, her neck was stretched and her head pushed back on her shoulders.

For the first time in her life Barbara now felt real fear. Brigie was wild; she . . . she could mean what she said. She was so determined that she should hear that she could really mean what she said and send her away. Oh no! She would die. . . . Like a young animal, she sprang on Miss Brigmore, clutching her, crying, pleading, 'Brigie! Brigie! no. Please, don't be angry, don't be angry. I'm sorry, I'm sorry. I'll do what you say, I'll do all that you say, only don't, don't send me away to school. I'd die. Yes, I'd die, or do something. You know I would, because I get so angry inside, and I can't help it, and should you send me away I'll get worse. Please, please, Brigie, please. . . . Look, I'll go over, straight back tomorrow, to the farm and tell Sarah I'm sorry, because I know she didn't mean it, I know she didn't. It was Bill Twigg really. I couldn't make out what he was saying, he mumbles; and it was then that Sarah said to him, "She's deaf. Don't you know she's deaf? Make your mouth go more." It was that . . . when she said make your mouth go more. It was awful. It was as if they were talking to one of the animals; I felt like an animal I did, I did. Brigie, I felt like an animal and I went wild. I couldn't hit him so I hit her. I'll apologize, I will, next time, or tomorrow. I tell you I'll go over tomorrow.' Her voice broke on a high sob.

'There, there.' Miss Brigmore was breathing deeply. Her body slowly relaxing, she put her arms around the girl and drew her close and stroked her hair, murmuring now, 'There, there; don't cry, don't cry.'

After a moment Barbara raised her tear-stained face and said, 'You'll never say that again will you, Brigie? Never say you'll send me away to one of those schools.'

'Then you'll have to co-operate.'

'I'll . . . I'll co-operate.'

233

As Miss Brigmore stared into the beloved face and saw the fear still on it, she realized, perhaps for the first time, the full extent of the child's agony of mind caused by her affliction, but she also realized that the very fear of being sent away had given to herself a handle, a handle which she meant to use.

2

THE FOLLOWING DAY being Monday they arrived at High Banks Hall at nine-thirty sharp. With the exception of holidays, this had been the daily procedure since Miss Brigmore had taken over the education of Mr Bensham's daughter, Katie, nine years ago in 1866. Unless they were returning late in the evening or the weather was stormy Miss Brigmore insisted on them walking. The distance from the cottage to the Hall was well over a mile along the main road before they entered the gates, but unless she had been battling against the wind she always mounted the steps leading to the front door of the Hall without any show of exertion.

Brooks, the butler, invariably opened the door to her. He was no longer called, 'Arry, for Miss Brigmore had pointed out, very tactfully, to the mistress of the house, the fact that two 'Arrys in her household might cause some confusion, one being her husband, so 'Arry became Brooks to all except the master of the house. Miss Brigmore had found that there was very little she could do concerning certain matters when dealing with the master of the house. In some things he was quite pliable, in others most obdurate.

'Good morning, miss.'

'Good morning, Brooks.'

Miss Brigmore led the way across the hall, up the main staircase, turned to her right across a wide landing and made her way towards the gallery. As she pushed open one of the double doors she almost knocked over a bucket of water from which Alice Dunn, the third housemaid, was wringing out a cloth.

'I'm sorry. Did I hurt you?'

'No, miss. No, miss.' Alice Dunn smiled as she shook her head vigorously, then she sat back on her heels and watched the pair go down the long gallery before she dried up the soap from the mosaic tiles of the floor. It was as they said, she gave folks their place. Yet some resented her, saying they didn't know who was mistress of the

Hall, her or Mrs Bensham. Still, as everybody knew, Mrs Bensham couldn't run a place like this, not really, not cut out for it. And The Brigadier, give her her due, had done a good job on the bairns, there was no doubt about that; they behaved themsel's, at least when she was about. They could be devils, oh aye, but they weren't upstarts of devils like some she had seen in other houses; spit on you some of the young ones would, and did. Talking about spittin'; they were sayin' in the kitchen The Brigadier's next battle was to get the master to take the spittoon out of the bedroom. By! aye, that would be the day. She hoped she lived to see it.

Miss Brigmore continued through the gallery, through another set of double doors, across another landing at the end of which were two sets of stairs, one mounting to the second floor, the other descending to the corridor that led to the kitchen quarters.

The nursery floor, as it was called, had changed little over the years except that the room which had once been Miss Brigmore's bedroom was now a sitting room. When she had first taken up her duties she'd had her meals and Barbara's served in her sitting room; but this hadn't lasted for long. At the repeated requests of both the master and mistress she had joined them at their table, while Barbara had hers with the children. It is true to say that because of this arrangement Miss Brigmore's own education was advanced if not improved, for in the early days she learned the type of conversation that went on between two ordinary people, and she found it anything but edifying.

Having taken her outer clothes off in her room she smoothed her hair from its centre parting over her temples and her ears to where it was fastened in a knot at the nape of her neck. Then she looked Barbara over, puffed up the shoulder frills of her pinafore, and smiled at her before she said, 'Come.'

When they entered the schoolroom Katie Bensham, who had been reclining, not sitting, in the old leather chair near the fire, sprang to her feet, pulled her pinafore straight, smiled brightly and said, 'Good morning, Miss Brigmore.'

'Good morning, Katie.'

The two girls now exchanged a glance that had a conspiratorial quality about it before they gave each other greeting.

'Good morning, Barbara.'

'Good morning, Katie.'

After which they both walked sedately down the long room and to a bookcase on the far wall, where from her own particular shelf each of them extracted a book, returned to the table and stood behind her chair.

Miss Brigmore was already standing behind hers. She bowed

her head, joined her hands together and began to recite the Lord's Prayer.

'Amen.'

'Amen – Amen.'

They sat down. The girls, with their backs tight against the rails of the chairs, looked towards Miss Brigmore, waiting for her instructions, for they both knew it was no use their turning to the last lesson they'd had in English Literature, for she jumped about like a frog from one period to another; it was nothing for her to spring on you when you were in the middle of George III and demand to know where Boccaccio came in the Renaissance; if you hadn't linked him up with Dante and Petrarch you were lost; or she would throw Erasmus at you, and that was usually only the beginning. When she was in one of her memory moods she'd run the gamut of the Renaissance, finishing up with Marlowe and Shakespeare.

Katie Bensham had long ceased to wonder how Miss Brigmore came by such knowledge. She didn't believe what John had said last holidays that she was like the masters at his boarding school, she read it up the night before. No one, she imagined, could read up Miss Brigmore's knowledge, it seemed as innate in her as if she had been born with it and never had to learn it. She admired Miss Brigmore, but could laugh at her, and did, because she wasn't afraid of her. Funny that; everybody else seemed afraid of her in some degree, except perhaps her father. She prided herself that she was like her father, afraid of nothing or no one. But Brigie was speaking.

'We shall waive our lesson on the poets this morning and touch on the subject of educationists. Of course, as you already know, Katie' – she cast her glance towards Katie while keeping her face in full view of Barbara – 'in your home town of Manchester there was founded in 1515 a Grammar School which has grown into a very large school. But who founded it? And *why* was it founded? That is a much more important question. . . . Why? Eton College was founded by Henry VI.' She seemed to be speaking pointedly to Barbara now, her lips moving wider. 'Why was it founded?' Although she paused they did not answer for they knew from experience that she was far from finished. She now looked from one girl to the other as she went on: 'The Sunday School movement was started by Robert Raikes, why? And only five years ago there was formed a compulsory system for education for all children; why? That is the question, *why*! The answer is because of a need. . . . This morning we are going to deal with this question of need, and we're going to begin in France. Yes' – she nodded from one to the other – 'in France, and with a priest, whose name was the Abbé de L'Épée, who lived in the eighteenth century. He began a particular kind of school; again why?' She

237

divided her glance once more between them, and they stared back at her, their interest aroused, their faces holding a keen look, until she said slowly, while looking now straight at Barbara, 'Because he felt compassion for the numerous deaf children, deaf and dumb children ... *really* deaf and dumb children, children without hope, children who were tied up like animals, hidden away in dark rooms, put into asylums because they could neither hear nor speak.'

Barbara was staring back into Miss Brigmore's eyes. She seemed in this moment completely unmoved. But not so Katie; her face had gone red with indignation. Brigie was really playing The Brigadier with a vengeance, she was being cruel.

At this point there was a sharp knock on the door and Armstrong, the first footman, entered, and looking towards Miss Brigmore he said, 'The master would like to see you, miss, if you can spare the time.'

Miss Brigmore drew in a deep breath that clamped down on her impatience, then paused a moment before saying, 'I shall be down'; then repeating to herself, If you can spare the time! Mr Harry Bensham would never have added those last words, not if she knew anything about him.

As she rose from the table Katie's glance caught hers. The child looked angry, and she understood why. Katie had a big heart, and she considered that she was being cruel to Barbara. In her ignorance, like that which pervaded her family, she, and by far the majority of the population were, in fact, of the opinion that the afflictions of deafness, dumbness, and even blindness, should be ignored out of kindness; and as for any malformation of the body or defectiveness of the mind, that should be locked tightly behind barred doors.

She now picked up the book that had been to her hand on the table and said, 'This book is in French; it tells of the struggle that the Abbé had to establish his system of teaching of the deaf, the teaching which, I may say, has been reviled and is questionable to this day. Nevertheless he was a good man, with good intentions; as also in a way was his successor Sicard. You will note' – she again spoke pointedly to Barbara – 'the Abbé advocates sign language. Bring your chairs together and read this book diligently until my return. I shall expect to hear what you know of these men, and others you come across, all bent on the same purpose, that of assisting the deaf to hear and the dumb to speak in their own language.'

When the door closed behind Miss Brigmore, Katie sat back in her chair and on a long, slow letting out of breath, she said, 'We-ll! we-ll!' then putting her hand over Barbara's, she added, 'She's cruel, she is. I can't understand her; she's supposed to love you and yet she's....'

238

'I understand her.'

'You do?'

'Yes; and she's right. I should know about myself, about my disease.'

'It's not a disease.' Katie poked her face forward. 'And don't start washing yourself in self-pity.'

'I'm not.' Barbara's denial was harsh. 'And it is a disease. Do you know' – she stopped and her lips trembled slightly before she went on, 'I . . . I can barely hear my own voice, even when I shout.'

'You said you heard the bells ringing last week.'

'Yes, but I was near them.'

'And when I scraped the knife over the glass you heard that.'

'They're unusual sounds. Just a short while ago I could hear the cry of a bird when it was startled, I can't now.'

They looked at each other. Then Katie, her face sad, murmured softly, 'Oh, Barbara. Mightn't it just be your imagination?'

'Now, now.' Barbara leant back in her chair and, her voice high and strident, said, 'Who's talking of pity? Don't do it, because you know I can't stand it, it makes me feel like a cripple. And don't suggest, either, it's my imagination.'

They stared at each other in silence for a time until Barbara asked flatly, 'What happened this week-end, did the boys come? I looked for them downstairs but didn't see anyone.'

Katie nodded. 'Yes, they came; but they went back last night. They missed you. They told me to tell you they missed you.'

'Did they?' Barbara smiled slowly.

'Dan said it was awful having no one to fight with.'

They both laughed; then leaning forward, Katie said, 'Do you know who's here?'

'No.'

'Willy.'

Barbara screwed up her face and her lips formed the word slowly, '*Woolly*.'

'Willy. Willy Brooks, you know. Of course you do.'

'Oh, you mean Brooks's son?'

'Yes' – Katie drew back – 'Brooks's son, Willy.'

For the moment there was a look on Barbara's face very like that one would expect to have seen on Miss Brigmore's had she been told that the daughter of the Hall was excited because the butler's son had arrived. Quick to notice this, Katie pushed Barbara none too gently with the flat of her hand, saying, 'Don't be so priggish; Willy's nice, and Dad thinks a lot of him. He's promoted him, and he's got the idea of making him manager later on. . . . And don't you think he's good looking, handsome?'

'Not very.'

'Not very! You must be. . . .' She almost said 'blind' but that would have been awful; you had to be careful in a way what you said to Barbara; so she reverted to her mother's idiom and said, 'You must be daft; he's the best-looking fellow I've ever seen; he's better-looking than either our John or Dan.'

'He isn't; John's very good-looking.'

'Do you think so?'

'Yes, of course.'

'But not so good-looking as Michael Radlet.' Now Katie's tongue was hanging well down over her lower lip, the teasing light was deep in her eyes, and it was Barbara's turn to push at her; then they both sat with their heads together for a moment as they laughed, before turning in a concerted movement to the book on the table.

Miss Brigmore heard the master of the house before she was half-way down the main staircase. His loud bellow was coming from the library, which room he also used for his office, not because he wanted the proximity of books, for she had never seen him read one, but because, he would have her understand, he liked the light from the tall windows. But her own opinion of why he preferred to work there when he was at home was because it was the one room in the house free from falderals, as he termed the over-ornate furnishings and decorations chosen by his wife. If a room had any dignity about it, Mrs Bensham had the unfortunate knack of making it homely by adding bobbled and scalloped mantel-borders, antimacassars, and numerous 'nice' pictures and hideous ornaments.

As she approached the library door Harry Bensham was yelling, 'Why the hell didn't you bring this matter up afore, lad? On the point of leavin' and then you tell me this. 'Tisn't my business, 'tis the missus's by rights. . . . Come in. Come in.' This was in answer to Miss Brigmore's knock on the door.

When she entered the room she saw that the lad in question was Willy Brooks, the butler's son, a tall young man, and she wondered what he was doing here at this time on a Monday morning. Her attention was brought from him, where he was standing at the side of the long table that served as a desk, to Harry Bensham, who was seated in a leather chair behind the table. His bullet head thrust forward, each of his short unruly grey hairs, that never showed a parting, seemed to be standing up in protest from his head; his face had a blotchy grey look, a sure sign that his temper was reaching its highest peak, for temper, in Harry Bensham's case, did not heighten his colour but usually drained the natural redness from his face. In his hand he had a letter, and as she came to a stop before the desk he thrust it out at her, saying, 'Have a look at that; go on, have a look at that. Tell me what you think on't.'

She took the letter from his hand and she read:

'To Mabel Docherty: In reference to your application for the post of kitchen maid in High Banks Hall the mistress has consented to engage you. You will present yourself at twelve o'clock on Saturday, the fifteenth day of May, bringing with you two print dresses for weekday work, and one extra and of superior quality for Sunday, when you'll attend service; one pair of light boots, one pair of heavy boots; four pairs of black stockings, three changes of underclothing with two pairs of extra drawers, preferably woollen. Your duties will commence at six in the morning and will end at seven in the evening, except on Tuesdays when you will have a half-day free starting at one o'clock and finishing at eight o'clock. You will have one Sunday off in three and you will receive three pounds eighteen shillings per year together with an allowance of extra tea or beer. Signed Hannah Fairweather (Mrs), Housekeeper.'

Miss Brigmore's mouth was slightly open when she looked back at Harry Bensham.

'Well?'

'What do you expect me to say?'

'What do I expect you to say!' He was on his feet now, his two hands flat on the desk, leaning towards her. 'I expect you to say, the woman's a bloody fool. I expect you to say, how did she come to write that? I expect you to say, who gave her authority?'

Miss Brigmore's mouth was tightly closed. She could not stand to hear the man swear; not that she was unused to a man swearing. When Thomas Mallen had been master here he had done his share of it, but then Thomas had sworn in a different way altogether from Mr Harry Bensham. When she opened her lips she said stiffly, 'Shouldn't you be putting these questions to Mrs Bensham?'

'No, I should not. Anyway' – he jerked his head to the side – 'she's off colour, she's bad this mornin'. But it was you who picked this one.' He now grabbed the letter from her hand. 'Housekeeper? Huh! bloody upstart. Fancy writing a letter like that to the Dochertys an' not a bloody one of them can read. They took it to Willy here.' He thumbed towards the young man. Then he turned his furious gaze on the letter again and read, 'Two pairs of extra woollen drawers. God! I don't suppose the lass has had a pair of drawers on her in her life. As for two pairs of boots, the whole lot of them's run barefoot since they were born.' He now banged the letter down on the desk, ending, 'I'll break that buggerin' woman's neck, I will that. An' you're damn well to blame.'

'I'll thank you, Mr Bensham, not to swear at me, and also to get your facts right.'

Harry Bensham now bowed his head, gnawed hard on his lower lip, banged his doubled fist once on the table before looking up at her and saying in a more moderate tone, 'Aw, woman, I'm sorry. But I'm. . . . I'm real narked, I am that.' He put out his hand as if appealing to her now for understanding. 'The Dochertys. All right, they're Irish an' they're feckless like all their kin in Manchester, but Shane Docherty's worked for me for years, and Pat, his father, worked for mine. All right' – he now flapped his hand at her as if checking her protest – 'they drank nearly all they earned and lived on taties and oatmeal for the rest of the week, but what they did with their money was their business, what they did for me was another. They were good workers, an' still are, but Shane's worried about young Mabel, she has the cough. He wants her out of the mills an' the place altogether, an' I left word with Tilda last week to tell that Fairweather woman to write a note to the priest to tell him to what kind of place the child was comin'. Priests!' He again bit on his lip and banged his fist on the table. 'It's fantastic; they rule the bloody lot of them. As I said at the merchants' meeting last week, if we had half the power of the priests we'd. . . .' He stopped suddenly and looked towards the young man. 'I'm sorry, lad, I forgot.'

'Oh, that's all right, Mr Bensham, it's all right by me; you couldn't say nothin' that I haven't said meself about 'em.'

'That so, lad?' Harry's face slowly relaxed, his eyes crinkled into a deep twinkle; then he said softly, 'Well I never! We've never got down to religion, have we? We'll have to think on't, eh? 'Cos it's always riled me, the power they've got. Some of the poor buggers are frightened to breathe without the priests say so.'

'Aye, Mr Bensham, you're right there. By! you are; you're right there.'

Miss Brigmore drew in an audible breath that brought their attention sharply back to her and she said stiffly, 'Are you finished with me, Mr Bensham?'

Harry Bensham looked at her, then he sat down slowly before he said, 'No, I'm not.'

'Then may I ask that our further business be discussed in private?'

Harry Bensham now stared at her under lowered brows. Then looking towards Willy Brooks, he said, 'I'll give you a shout when I'm ready, Willy.'

'Aye, Mr Bensham.'

As the young man moved from the table he turned his head and looked straight into Miss Brigmore's face; it was a bold look, the look of someone who had never known subservience.

Not until the door was closed did Miss Brigmore speak, and then coldly she said, 'If you wish to reprimand me in the future, Mr Bensham, I'll be obliged if you'll refrain from doing it before subordinates.'

'Subordinates! Willy's no subordinate, not to nobody. And he's a good lad into the bargain, is Willy.'

'I must take it then that you consider him my equal?'

Harry Bensham now screwed up his eyes and wagged his hand towards her, saying, 'Aw, sit down, woman, and ease out of your starch; for God's sake let it crack for once.'

It was some seconds before Miss Brigmore allowed herself to sit down, and when she did her back showed no indication of her starch having cracked.

'Now look –' his voice was quiet now, even placating, as, with his forearms on the table, he poked his head towards her and said, 'We've got to get rid of her, Fairweather.'

'You wanted a housekeeper. After Foster died you insisted on having a housekeeper. I told you another steward would be preferable.'

'Aye, I know you did. You're always right, you're always' – he omitted the 'bloody well' and ended lamely, 'right. It was for the missus you see; she thought a housekeeper would be better, more homely. She was a bit frightened of Foster, could never give him an order. You know how she is. It was different with you, you could manage him. Even me; I sometimes felt awkward when asking him for anything. It was like asking a grand duke to take your boots off.'

'He was very competent; things ran very smoothly under his charge.'

'Aye, they might have, but there's a difference between things being smooth and things being happy.'

'You mean happy-go-lucky.'

He leant back in his chair now and let out a laugh, 'Aye, that's it, happy-go-lucky. You can't change us you know. You know that, don't you? You can't change us.'

'I don't think I've tried.'

He turned his head to the side while still keeping his eyes on her. 'You've given us plenty of examples.'

'My work was to inform the children.'

'Aw well' – he nodded his head now, slowly – 'I'll grant you, you've done a good job there; even the bits you did on the lads afore they went to school shows. Why, when I listen to them talkin' I don't feel they're mine. But' – he screwed up his nose now – 'I'm proud of them. An' Katie. Aw Katie.' His expression changed. He leant forward again but drooped his head, and, his voice deep in his throat, he said, 'I love to

243

hear her talkin' French. I don't understand a word she says but I just love to hear the sound of it comin' from her mouth. Oh, an' by the way.' He lifted his head. 'When we're on about talkin', which leads to hearin', I made some enquiries as I said I would. You know' – his eyes stretched wide now – 'it's amazing what you learn 'bout different things. There I've been in Manchester, man and boy, all me life an' knew nothin' about the deaf school. An' started by a merchant man like meself, I understand. Phillips was his name. He got a committee together of bankers and manufacturers and such, chaired by Sir Oswald Mosley, an' they formed this school along Old Trafford. Amazing really when I come to think of it. I saw the place often enough, passed it for years, but took no interest. Well, when your own are all right you don't bother, do you? You should, but you don't. Anyway, they tell me they do a lot of good for deaf bairns there. Now I was just wondering this, how would you like to send her along? She could be boarded and I would see to it that. . . .'

'No, Mr Bensham, no. . . .'

'What! You want her better, don't you? I mean you want all the assistance you can get for her?'

'Yes, yes, I do, but . . . but only yesterday morning when we were having a small altercation and I became annoyed with her, I told her I would do just that, what you have proposed, send her away to a school, and –' now the starch appeared to crack, for her back sagged and she looked down at her hands folded in her lap and her head drooped before she said softly, 'The anguish and fear on her face at such a proposal was as unbearable to me as the idea was to her. And I am not casting aspersions on the Manchester school, Mr Bensham, but the conditions under which some of the children live in such schools are deplorable. I understand that some of these establishments demand long hours of religious instruction. To be made to sit in church for three hours at a time on a Sunday is not unusual for the children, and in winter time too.'

'Aye, well,' he sighed. 'That's that, isn't it? Still' – he pulled his chin upwards – 'never say die, that's my motto, you know. What about tryin' some of the old cures? I'd lay me life some of them's a damn sight better than the newfangled medicines. I mentioned it to Ted Spencer; you know, Spencer, he's got the mill over the other side, I told you afore, an' he said he'd heard of a dumb bairn whose tongue was loosened by big doses of cod liver oil. You could try it. If it could loosen the tongue it could loosen the eardrums.'

Miss Brigmore looked across at him and her glance could not conceal a certain amount of pity for his ignorance. It was years ago, during the last century, that they had used cod liver oil for deafness, attacking the trouble as if it were one connected with the bowels, pouring the obnoxious unrefined oil down poor children's throats, ignoring their vomiting, all with the best intentions in the world, as those before them had used hot irons on the neck in order to create suppuration in the belief that pus could be drawn from the ears, being of the opinion that deafness was caused by a blockage. The agonies that some children had undergone, and to this very day were still undergoing, at the hands of those who wished them nothing but well was to her an agonizing thought in itself, as was the controversy that raged between the exponents of one method and those of another.

If she had spoken the truth to him she would have cast aspersions on the Manchester school for she abhorred the practice, started there in bygone times, of putting their children on exhibition in order to raise money. True, it was out of great necessity to keep the school going that the practice was first begun, but in her opinion it had put the children on a level with caged animals in a travelling zoo.

She had read exhaustively about the predicament of the deaf, and what she had hoped from Mr Bensham's interest was that his influence, in such a place as Manchester, would have brought forth someone, some specialist whose methods were new and that, if the treatment was expensive, he himself would act as patron. But what had he proffered? An ordinary school that dealt with children from all walks of life, and although she wanted all deaf children to receive the best of treatment she wanted her darling Barbara to receive specialized treatment; and now, before her ailment became worse. But could it become much worse than it was, for she was almost totally deaf, being able to hear only high and unusual sounds?

'You worry too much.' The words were sharp and they startled her. 'You're miles away. You're always thinkin' of that child; you want to think a bit more of yourself, for I'm gona tell you something. She'll get by. I know people; she'll get what she wants out of life or die in the attempt; deaf or not, she'll have her way. She was a little monkey when she was young, she still is. Anyway, her looks 'll get her where she wants to go, that's if she fills out a bit. Her deafness won't be all that of a drawback. Any road, we can talk more on this later; the point now is, what are we going to do about Fairweather? You can't get over the fact she took it upon herself to tell the bairn she had to buy her own uniform. When did any of my lot buy their own uniform?'

'She was likely intending to start a new rule in order to economize. You do not hide the fact that you consider too much money is being spent on household expenses.'

'Aw, well, that's just to keep them in mind that I know what's what. I'm away half me time, an' I don't want them to take advantage of Tilda. ... So what's to be done?'

'What do you want to do?'

245

'Sack her.'

'Then you must sack her.'

'You picked her.'

'I helped to choose her on her references. I recommended her because she was the best of the ten applicants, and I still think she's a good housekeeper. But perhaps. . . .'

'Aye, perhaps what?'

'I will be as candid as you, Mr Bensham. Perhaps not for this establishment.'

'An' what do you mean by that?'

'Just what I said, not for this establishment. She has been used to managing a different kind of house and staff.'

'What's the matter with me staff?'

'As regards work, nothing; as regards manners, some of them leave a lot to be desired.'

'You mean the ones I brought from Manchester?'

'Yes, that is what I mean.'

'Aye, well, it's my house and I want it run in my way. Everybody's got too much starch in this life.'

When a silence fell between them he pursed his lips and stared at her fixedly, then said, 'Go on, say somethin'. Why don't you say things aren't what they were in the old days? You've looked it for years, so you might as well say it, like the rest. They say, "Common as muck, those Benshams are. Don't go huntin' or shootin'. Never have the hounds billeted on him," they say. That's what they say, isn't it?'

'I don't know what they say, Mr Bensham, my time is mostly taken up in the nursery.'

Again there was silence between them, until he said grimly, 'Aye, broken with trips across the hills to the lady farmer an' visits from Old Master an' Mistress Ferrier. They're glass people aren't they, the Ferriers, big pots in glass? An' they move among the top notchers, don't they? Hobnob with the Percys and such, I'm told. You see I've got me Indian runners an' all; there's little goes on around here that I don't know. Not that I'm interested; but I can sit back and laugh.'

'And do you?'

'What do you mean, do I?'

'Do you sit back and laugh?'

He did not answer her, he just sat staring at her; and then he said, 'You know there's times I get so bloody annoyed with you that I could take me hand and skelp you across the mouth.'

She was on her feet, her body rigid. He was on his feet too. Beads of sweat were showing on his forehead and he wiped them off with the side of his forefinger before he moved slowly around the table and stopped within a yard of her. Then, his voice thick, he said, 'I'm

246

sorry, I really am; that was uncalled for. You've done nothin' but service to me and Tilda, an' then for me to go and say a thing like that. I don't know what got into me. Aye, yes I do, yes I do. Let's face it' – he put his hand to his brow again and pushed his fingers through his hair – 'you never unbend, you're stiff, starchy, as I said. Admitted, you've learned Tilda a lot of things, you've carried her along through difficult times; and I'm not sayin' you haven't learned me something now and then; but you've never unbent. You should be one of the family by now, like a friend, but you're still Miss Brigmore. The bairns call you Brigie, but you know what the staff call you? The Brigadier. . . . Aw.' He scratched his head in a number of places, then walked sharply away from her up the room to the fireplace, and standing with his hand outstretched gripping the mantelpiece, he said, 'Here I am talkin' about trifles an' household bits and pieces when I should be on me way back to the mill. Why do you think Willy's here at this time?' He now turned and looked at her, but she was still facing the window, and he addressed her back as he said, 'Strikes. He's found out that Pearson's bloody agitators are plannin' a strike. A strike mind you, and in my factory! After what I've done for them; cut half an hour off their time these last two years, and an hour for those under twelve. There's not a bairn in my place works after six at night. An extra shilling in their Christmas packet; then bread and coal for those who are sick. An' then they'd harbour the thought of strikin' on me. But as Willy says, it's Pearson's lot; he's got a right rabble has Ted Pearson. Well, I'm going back there an' I'm going to remind them of what happened the last time the looms stopped spinning, an' by God I won't put a tooth in it.' His voice suddenly changing, he asked softly, 'Are you listening to me?'

She turned and walked slowly towards him, and when she stopped, he said, 'No hard feelings?'

She did not answer for a moment, but when she did she was still Miss Brigmore. 'I am what I am, Mr Bensham. If I irritate you I would advise you to dispense with my services.' Even as she said this she knew it would be a major disaster for her if he were to take her at her word; but he wouldn't, and he didn't.

'Aw, dispense with your services? Don't be daft, woman!' He half turned from her. 'How do you think we'd go on here without you? Why, if I even gave it a thought Tilda would have me skinned alive. She thinks very highly of you . . . Tilda. And that's another thing I wanted to ask you. Would you look in on her a bit more than usual these next few days, until I get back? She's got a pain. . . .'

'A pain?'

'Aye; here.' He put his hand on his flat stomach. 'I've told her she's got to see the doctor, but, you know, although she's so easy goin' in

247

some ways she can be as tough and stubborn as dried hide in others, won't be pulled or pushed. She doesn't like doctors, frightened of 'em, so if you'd have a talk with her, ask her what it's like, the pain, I mean. That's all she says when I get at her, she's got a pain. And you know me, I've got no patience, I'm like a bull at a gap. Oh, aye! Oh, aye!' – his voice had a laughing note to it now – 'I'm like you there, I am what I am, an' I know meself, nobody knows Harry Bensham like Harry Bensham, except perhaps' – his tone dropped to a lower key – 'Tilda. I told you, didn't I, we were brought up next door to each other? Aye.' He shook his head now. 'That was in the early days when we were small; but when me dad got on we moved away and we lost touch for years. Until I saw her on the looms; but I was married then. Aye' – he turned and looked towards the fire and repeated, 'I was married then, I'd married a factory.' His head came round sharply and he stared at her.

'I knew what I wanted so I married a factory. Now you would have been interested in that kind of household.' He nodded at her. 'Aye, you would an' all. Upstarts. God Almighty! there's nothing makes me sick like an upstart; and embarrassed into the bargain. Now you wouldn't think that a fellow like me could be embarrassed, but upstarts embarrass me, get me hot under the collar trying to be what they're not.... Anyway, that period passed and I married Tilda. Funny, but she'd been waitin' for me all those years; she had, she said she had. Women are queer cattle, queer cattle.... But here I go again, yammering like Bessie Bullock in the pea shop.' His voice was rising again, and he turned from the fire, buttoned his coat briskly while looking at her and said, 'That's something I can't understand. Every time I'm along of you I start to yammer; I'm not a yammering man; and the funny thing about it is, you don't give a body any encouragement. Now do you?' A slow smile spread over his face and transformed it so that now Miss Brigmore, as she had at odd times before, saw someone other than the bigoted, ignorant, raw factory owner who took pride in keeping his image unchanged; she saw the man Tilda must have seen years ago, the man who, in spite of his shortcomings, was at bottom just and kind.

He ended now, saying, 'I can't even get a smile out of you, an' yet when you're with the bairns I often hear you laughin'. What makes you laugh? Aw' – he dismissed his own question – 'I've got to get away. But you'll do what I ask, won't you? You'll look in on her?'

'Yes, I'll look in on her.'

'Thanks. Ta-rah; ta-rah then; I'm off.'

'Good-bye, Mr Bensham.'

After he had left the room Miss Brigmore sat down suddenly on the nearest chair. That man! She closed her eyes and said again to herself,

248

That man! He was impossible, quite impossible. She had never encountered anyone like him. Daring to say to her he would skelp her across the mouth! She shouldn't be sitting here, she should be upstairs ordering Barbara to get her books and her belongings, for they were going to leave this house never to come back into it again. Skelp her across the mouth, really! really!

She let out a long-drawn breath, then sat perfectly still for a time until she told herself, she must be fair, did her manner aggravate the man? It must do, for he had spoken to her in much the same manner as he spoke to his wife. In the early days here his manner of addressing his wife had shocked her; he used to go for her as if she were some kind of lower servant, rarely addressing her without using a swear word of some kind. Really! really! he was the most amazing man. No, that wasn't the correct term for him.... Then what was?

She rose from the chair and made sure that the buttons on her bodice were intact, smoothed down the front of her dress, then went slowly from the room, across the hall and up the stairs and knocked on Mrs Bensham's bedroom door.

When she entered the room she saw Matilda Bensham sitting propped up in bed. She was dressed in a bright pink flannelette nightdress which had a large collar trimmed with white lace; the sleeves, too, ended in large frills trimmed with white lace, and the whiteness was in sharp contrast to the greyness of her face and the mottled red-veined skin of her hands. 'Hello there, dear,' she said.

'Good morning, Mrs Bensham. I hear that you are not feeling too well.'

'It's me stomach.' The words were hissed in a whisper and Matilda tapped the coverlet where it rested across her waist.

'Is it upset?'

'Well, not in the usual way, dear; but I've had a sort of constant nagging for some time now.... But mind, don't tell him. Now promise you won't tell him, 'cos he's got enough on his plate. By! he has that; I'd never have believed it. Willy came yesterday you know. Set off on Saturda' night he did; had the devil of a time gettin' here an' all. Those trains aren't what they're cracked up to be. Like the manager 'Arry's got in, they go when they're pushed. A strike's afoot and him not supposed to know! There's something fishy there, 'cos we don't have strikes, not us. 'Arry gives them the earth, even thinkin' of letting the women finish at three on a Saturda' to save them having to do everything on a Sunday, you know like washing an' cleaning an' cooking, 'cos Sunday is the only day in the week they've got. And then a strike. So you understand, dear, I don't want him worried. So anything I tell you, you'll keep it to yourself now, won't you?'

'Yes, of course, Mrs Bensham.'

'Well, lass, it's like this.... Pull up your chair and sit down.' She indicated a chair with a sweep of her arm. 'I've had this pain on and off for over a year now; oh, more than that. Wind, I used to think it was, 'cos of the way I eat. You know I eat twice as much as our 'Arry. I don't know how he can resist some of the things that's put afore him, but he does. He takes pride in his stomach being all muscle an' not looking his age. He's vain, you know.' She smiled widely now as she nodded towards Miss Brigmore. 'And of course he's got every right to be, 'cos you'd never think he was fifty-six, would you? A man in his middle forties you could take him for any day in the week, and he knows it. Oh aye, he knows it. So you see, I thought it was what I was eatin'. But I've cut that down a lot and I've still got the pain, worse at times. It's gettin' so that I can't hide it.'

'You must see a doctor, Mrs Bensham.'

'Do you think so, lass?'

'Oh yes, very definitely, if you've had the pain all this time. I think it was very unwise of you not to have it attended to before now. It might be some simple thing.'

'Such as what, lass?'

The question was quiet, it even conveyed a hint of calm resignation.

'Well –' Miss Brigmore rubbed the tips of her fingers together and paused as if thinking, then said, 'It could be colic, caused by the bowel twisting.'

'The bowels can get twisted?'

'Oh yes, yes. If for instance there has been any undue strain owing to ... to constipation.'

'Oh. Oh, I see.' Tilda looked over the foot of the bed and nodded, then said, 'Well, you might be right, lass, you might be at that.... Twisted bowel.' She brought her eyes to Miss Brigmore again. 'They could cure that?'

'Oh yes, yes, I'm sure they could cure that.'

'Would that cause bleedin'?'

'Bleeding?'

'Aye, from inside like.'

Miss Brigmore wetted her lips and said, 'Well, yes; through ... through inner haemorrhoids.'

'Piles, you mean?'

'Yes.'

'Inside?'

'Yes.'

'Well, that puts a different complexion on it, doesn't it as they say in upper circles?' She was laughing widely now, showing a mouthful of strong, short teeth, with two overlapping at each side of her mouth.

'You've cheered me up, lass; it's true what our 'Arry always says, you're the only sensible bug . . . sensible one in the house. You always know the right answer, the right thing to do, you always have. Aye, I've often thought of how handicapped I'd have been right from the start in this place if it hadn't been for you. You were a god-send, a real god-send. You know something?' She leant towards Miss Brigmore now, her voice low. ' 'Arry's got plans for you.' She nodded her head once. 'Now mind, don't let on about this either, else he'll leave me black and blue from head to foot, but he's going to see that you're all right when you finish here, you'll be able to live better'n you've lived afore, apart from with us.'

Miss Brigmore felt the colour rising to her hairline. What could she say? She felt so ill at ease, yet she must not take this offer amiss; these people were kind, embarrassingly so. Reluctantly, she had to admit that they were far kinder than the previous owners of this establishment, far kinder.

It was in a surprisingly broken tone that she voiced her thanks. 'You are very kind, Mrs Bensham, very kind.'

'Aw, lass, it's not me, it's him. He's always been a kind man, always, not only just now. By! no. Oh, the things he's done for people; even the bloomin' Irish. Eeh! mind they're a dirty lot, them Irish. Him and me were brought up next to each other. You know that, but did I tell you there were eleven of us in two rooms, while in 'Arry's house there was only five of them? They were lucky. But both our houses were as clean as new pins. Me mam would be up at five o'clock in the mornin' gettin' us and herself off to the mill. In the beginnin' we were there until nine at night, but if it had been twelve o'clock she would have done her fireplace, and shook her mats. The fireplace was black-leaded once a week until she died. . . . But the Irish! When 'Arry and his people left from next door we got a family in. Eeh! by, you never saw anythin' like it. They brought a pig with them, they did.' She made a deep obeisance with her head and began to laugh. 'That's the Irishman's bank in Manchester, a pig; soon as they got a bit o' money in those days, if they didn't drink it, that is, they bought a pig. There were two families of them in those two rooms, seventeen there were; they didn't only sleep head to tail, they had to stand up against the walls.' She was doubled forward with laughing now, and Miss Brigmore found herself laughing with her, while at the same time her mind was appalled at the conditions described.

'Eeh!' – Matilda dried her eyes – 'me mother did work hard. Her only pleasure was her pipe. Twelve o'clock at night she would take it out and have a draw. You know, lass' – she lay back on her pillows – 'I've been in bed since Friday. Just after you went I came up to bed, and it seemed a long week-end 'cos I've done nowt but think. I've gone back over all those early days, an' you know I just cannot believe I'm sittin' here in this house with umpteen servants to wait on me. I . . . just . . . cannot . . . believe . . . it. And how many years have I been here now? Nearly twelve. Aye, well, they say a leopard cannot change its spots, an' I suppose they're right 'cos I'm still not at ease. You know that, lass, don't you? I'm still not at ease.'

'Oh, Mrs Bensham, you must feel at ease; this is your home and . . . and every one of your staff respects you, and your family love you.'

'Aye, aye, I suppose they do, I mean the family lovin' me, 'cos they haven't turned into upstarts yet. But still, there's plenty of time, they're still young. What'll they think though when they start courtin' and bringin' their lasses home, an' Katie her lad . . . or should I say finnances? Will they love me then, d'you think? Aw' – now she tossed her head – 'why am I worryin', we could all be dead the morrow, couldn't we?' She stared at Miss Brigmore and Miss Brigmore, looking back at her, said, 'That's very unlikely; you'll live to see your grandchildren, and very likely their offspring, too, running around the house.'

There was a short silence before Matilda said softly, 'No, lass; no, I won't.'

As they continued to stare at each other Miss Brigmore swallowed deeply, then she whispered, 'Oh, Mrs Bensham.'

'Don't you think you could call me Tilda just for once.'

'It . . . it would be very difficult.' Miss Brigmore's voice was still soft. 'And . . . and it would be out of place. But . . . but I want you to know that I regard you very highly and . . . and I will think of you as Matilda even if I don't allow myself to call you by your christian name.'

'You're a funny lass.'

'Yes, I realize I am, in the way you infer. My manner must be very irritating to you at times, as it is to Mr Bensham.'

'*What!* Oh, you don't irritate him. An' you don't irritate me. Now, don't get that into your head 'cos I've said you're a funny lass. What I should have said was you're a grand lass.'

Miss Brigmore felt at this moment that she could not stand much more of the emotional stress being forced upon her this morning. Here she was at the age of fifty-four, nearing fifty-five, and being termed a lass, but in the most complimentary fashion, and from this woman, this dear woman, and she could think of her as dear in spite of her ignorance and uncouth manner, for she was bravely facing the fact that she was carrying a disease inside her which was likely to terminate her life within a short period of time. As she went to rise to her feet Matilda said, 'There's something you can do for me, lass.'

'Anything.'

'Willy was up, an' he told me about Mrs Fairweather sending a letter off to the Dochertys. Do you know about it?'

'Yes.'

'That's all right then. Well, I told him to show it to the boss and let him deal with it, but not let on that I knew anything about it, for I knew that once 'Arry saw that letter he'd want to get rid of her, and I want to an' all but I've never had the pluck to tell her. Do . . . do you think you could see to it for me, lass?'

Miss Brigmore did not pause a moment to consider the unpleasantness of the task before she answered, 'Yes, I'll deal with it. Don't worry yourself; I'll deal with it.'

'Aw, ta, thanks. Did you see the letter? Did you ever see anything like it in your life? The Dochertys live in a warren. The men are good workers but the mother is hopeless. The last time I saw them the lice was carryin' them around, an' Mabel, the one that 'Arry wants to take on, she was just a bairn crawlin' in the filth of the gutter, and when I say filth I mean filth. Everything was thrown out of the door; it was piled up back and front. They died like flies around there. They tell me they've pulled Cods' Row down, an' not afore time I say, not afore time. Anyway, you tell her, lass, eh? You tell her.'

'Yes, I'll tell her. Now rest quietly; don't attempt to get up; I'm going to send for the doctor.'

'Aw. . . .'

'No aw's.' Miss Brigmore shook her head, and there was a reprimand in it; it was as if she were speaking to the girls. 'You're going to see the doctor, and as soon as possible.'

'It'll worry 'Arry if I have the doctor.'

'It'll worry 'Ar . . . Mr Bensham . . . if you don't have the doctor.'

The room was filled with a great guffaw of laughter now as Matilda, holding her head, lay back among the pillows, saying, 'Eeh! Eeh! you nearly said 'Arry. You did now, you did; you nearly said 'Arry.'

Miss Brigmore tried to suppress a smile but she failed. She turned quickly about and went out of the room, but once on the landing she stopped and pressed her hand over her lips, for now she was on the point of weeping. Really, really, such courage. But she must not give way like this. She had two things to attend to immediately; first, she must send the coachman into the town for the doctor, then she must go into the library and from there she must send for the housekeeper and inform her that she had been given permission to dismiss her. What a morning!

3

'WHAT ARE THESE Bensham fellows like, Mother?'
'Now you know as much about them as I do.'
Constance Radlet turned out a great mould of brawn
on to a side dish before she went on, 'I only know what your Aunt
Anna tells me. John is sixteen, Dan fifteen and the girl, Katie, is
fourteen.'

'And you've never seen any of them?'

'No, of course not.' Constance turned and looked at her son, where
he was sitting at the end of the long white scrubbed kitchen table, and
as always when she gazed on him a smile came to her lips, for as his
grandmother, Jane Radlet, was fond of saying in her Biblical way, he
was good to look upon. His hair was a corn yellow, his eyes were a clear
grey, the lids inclining to be overlong, giving him a slightly oriental
look; his nose was large and his mouth full, but it was a firm fullness;
and the firmness was expressed in his chin which had a squareness to
it; yet his overall nature gave the impression that he was an easy-going,
indolent type of boy; his movements were slow, his laughter came
slow and deep, but when it reached its full pitch it was an infectious
bellow. He was nearing thirteen years old and was tall for his age, but
he had bulk with it; he was going to be a big man. Yes, he was good to
look upon.

'Why do they want to come over, they've never been before?'

'Likely that's the reason, because they've never been before.'
Constance's smile widened.

'They go to a boarding school, so you say?'

'Yes, and so do you.'

'But likely theirs is a very stylish affair; the father's rich, isn't he?'

'Yes, and common and ignorant from what I gather.'

'They say he's good to his staff.'

Constance turned to where her mother-in-law Jane Radlet was
sitting peeling potatoes near the fire. She had her feet on a cracket and

254

a large tin dish on her knees, and from it she kept dropping the peeled potatoes into a black kale pot on the floor at her side. She nodded at Constance as she smiled, and Constance returned her smile with cocked head now, saying, 'Well, he's not the only one, so are we.'

They both laughed and it was a harmonious sound as between friends.

Turning back to the table and pushing the plate of brawn away from her, Constance called across the room to a plump little girl standing over the sink washing pots, 'Bring me a clean side dish, Sarah, please.'

The girl came hurrying to the table, drying the dish on the way, and she placed it before Constance; then looking up at her, she said, 'They don't hunt; they say they don't hunt, not even the hares, or partridge, not like the gentry.'

'Who said they didn't hunt, Sarah?'

'Me . . . my dad.' Sarah always called her uncle Dad.

'Well, that doesn't make them any better, or worse, than the next. Bring me the ham from the pantry.'

The girl turned immediately to do Constance's bidding. But she did not, as would be expected, say, 'Yes, ma'am.' A stranger would have found the situation very curious that this orphan girl should be allowed to speak without first being spoken to unless she wished to convey something absolutely necessary, but in this instance she had casually joined in the conversation with her mistress and young master and the young man's grandmother.

And Sarah Waite's position was unusual in that the mistress of the house, besides teaching her to read and write, had shown her all the big towns in England on a map, and made her learn what they produced, and for a full year she had allowed her to sit by the young master's side when doing her lessons, until at seven years old he went away to the school in Hexham, only returning at the weekends, and during his absence she had continued to teach her head man's niece.

If anyone had dared to tell Constance that her philanthropy had a selfish motive she would have denied it while admitting its truth to herself, for although most of her time was taken up with farm affairs, there were long hours in the evening, especially in the winter, when her mind craved for some other outlet besides those of making clothes, darning and tapestry. She was slow to admit that she had imbibed some of Miss Brigmore's character while being taught by her, for she also had the desire to impart knowledge. When she reluctantly decided on the course of sending her son to a boarding school where he would come under influences other than those of the farm labourers, there was left in her a gap that could be filled only by the moulding of another character. Then indeed, she knew that she had imbibed more than general knowledge from Miss Brigmore.

And there was also the necessity at that particular time of covering up her disappointment – she refused to acknowledge it as a dashing of her hopes. Although she had said more than once that she would never marry again, she had not rejected the advances of Bob Armstrong, the younger of the two farming brothers who lived but three miles away. From the night of that first harvest supper she had given in sixty-six he had openly shown his admiration for her. He had called in when passing, and when not passing he had made a point of visiting her, giving her advice, joking with her, letting his eyes tell her what was in his mind. And this silent courtship had gone on for three years.

It was when she had almost decided to give him enough encouragement to speak that his visits ceased abruptly. He even avoided her on market day. It was from Peter, his honest but shambling brother, that she learned he was going to marry a Miss Fanny Winters, a farmer's daughter. The farmer had died, and his wife was oldish, and Miss Fanny Winters, a bit long in the tooth, as the forthright Peter had put it, had in a way offered. It was a big farm, and Bob had always hankered after a big farm. He would miss him, Peter said, 'cos he was good company was Bob. But twenty-five miles was twenty-five miles and you couldn't keep running back and forward all that way, now could you?

Constance hadn't cried at the news, she had been too angry, too humiliated; although she hadn't a doubt that he had desired her, nevertheless his need for a big farm had been greater. Wolfbur hadn't apparently been a large enough attraction.

So this was another reason why it was desirable for her to have a pastime, and Sarah Waite filled the need. It also deepened the gratitude of the entire Waite family towards her.

Sometimes when Constance looked in her mirror, her reflection showed the inner panic that filled her, a panic created by the mounting years, for was she not thirty-two? and the question of age would engender in her the special terror that one day when Michael took a wife she might be brushed aside, discounted. That she was all-in-all to him now she was fully aware, but she knew that this emotional state couldn't last; another few years and he could marry.

When her mind touched on him marrying her nerves almost jangled into hysteria. What if he should choose Barbara? As things stood Barbara's father and Michael's grandfather were one and the same man, at least in the eyes of the world, and she would gladly have left the situation like this in order to prevent Michael bringing her niece into this house as his wife; but there were two others who knew the true situation, Anna and Jane, and Anna, she knew, would move hell and earth to make that girl happy; and Jane would do the same for her grandson. She could, in times of such panic, see their combined efforts forcing her to reveal to her son the real truth of his beginnings.

And Michael, where did he stand in all this? The fact that Barbara was deaf would be no impediment to him taking her; rather the reverse, he would be drawn to her out of compassion. She was well aware that he had, since a small child, maintained a fondness for her. Although he teased her and called her Madam, and grumbled about her following him around, nevertheless she sensed that deep within him he had strong emotional leanings towards his cousin. What she constantly hoped and prayed for was that with the years he would grow out of this feeling, for there was bad blood in Barbara, she being part Mallen.

'How will they get back if there's no moon?' Michael asked.

'What do you say?'

'I say how will they all get back if there's no moon?'

'Oh, there'll be a moon.' It wasn't Constance who had answered but Sarah. She had turned from the sink and, her face bright and smiling, she nodded at them and repeated, 'There'll be a moon tonight, sure there'll be a moon.'

'Ah! The oracle has spoken.' Michael raised his hand and his voice was solemn as he went on, 'Listen . . . listen all ye present, listen to the voice of the sage . . . and onions.'

As he and his grandmother laughed Constance asked, 'How can you be sure, Sarah, there was mist last night?'

'The sky this mornin', the way the sun came up while the moon was still showing.'

'Is that a sign?' asked Constance.

It was Jane Radlet now who replied as she threw a potato into the pan with a plop. 'Oh aye, it's a sign; she's right.' She exchanged a smile with Sarah. 'Of course, it's to do with the way the moon was lying at the beginning of the month, it had to be lying on its back if there were to be three full nights clear at the end.'

Constance did not question the truth or otherwise of the forecast, for she had been proved wrong on similar points so many times before.

Michael rose from the table, saying, 'Well, I'm off.'

'Where?'

'I'm going with Jim to the top fields.'

'Oh no, you're not!' Constance checked him with lifted hand. 'They'll be here within half an hour.'

'Well, I'll see them coming even before you do, and I'll scamper back.'

'But you should be dressed . . . changed.'

'Why? we're going to see the hill racing, aren't we? We'll all be up to our eyes in mud after the rain these last few days, if I know anything.'

257

'That doesn't matter; you should be dressed to meet them, especially as you haven't met them before.'

'Are you going to change?'

'Of course.'

'And you, Grannie?' He lifted his head in Jane Radlet's direction, and Jane, laughing loudly, said, 'Not me, lad, not me; they take me as they find me.'

'And what about Sarah, has she got to change?' He looked towards the small girl, and she turned her head over her shoulder and laughed at him, while Constance answered for her, 'Sarah's going with Jim to the games.'

Michael gave an exaggerated sigh and was about to resume his seat when Constance said, 'Now don't sit down again, there's no time to dawdle. Come, I'm going up too.' She stretched out her hand and caught him by the ear, and he pretended to cringe and yelled, 'Oh! . . . oh! . . . oh!' and they all laughed.

When Constance and Michael had left the room, Jane beckoned Sarah to her and in a conspiratorial whisper said, 'Go on . . . over home, hinny, and make yourself tidy. Put your best hair ribbons on, and your clean pinny, and show the gentry what a bonny lass you are.'

The bright smile left Sarah's face and she said quietly, 'Dad says I've to keep out of the way once they come, and Uncle Jimmy's takin' me straight off to the games.'

The old woman and the child looked at each other and knowledge of the situation was exchanged in their glance. 'Aw well then,' said Jane; 'go on then and enjoy yourself.'

'Yes, yes I will.' Sarah turned away, her face still unsmiling, and made to go to the sink, but Jane said, 'Leave them be, I'll finish them; go on now,' and the child went out.

The kitchen to herself, Jane stopped peeling the potatoes and through the window she watched the small girl dashing across the yard, and when she was gone from her sight she muttered, 'All because that one's coming;' and as if picking up Constance's thoughts, hers said, 'Everything old Mallen bred was tainted.' Hadn't she herself proof of it? The result of Mallen's raping her when she was a girl had been her son Donald, and what had he turned out to be? A devil, yes a devil if ever there was one, and he had proved it when he wed the lass just gone upstairs there, for he had led her a hell of a life before he was. . . . her mind shied away from the word murdered and substituted destroyed, which seemed less terrible to her.

And what of Mallen's last raping? That Barbara too had the devil in her, and a temper like a fiend, and she hated young Sarah because

258

Michael made much of her. It was a great pity she hadn't been struck dumb as well as deaf.

It was at this point that her thinking proved Constance wrong, for she muttered aloud, 'I'd sooner see him alone to the end of his days than take up with that one across the hills.'

The trap driven by Miss Brigmore was first to come through the gateless gap in the stone wall. Seated opposite her was Mary Peel; they had the vehicle to themselves. Close behind came the wagonette; it was driven by Yates, the coachman, and seated behind him were John and Daniel Bensham, Katie Bensham and Barbara.

As they alighted they were each greeted by Constance and Michael, who were standing outside the front door of the farmhouse.

'How nice to see you. How are you, dear?' Constance and Miss Brigmore exchanged kisses.

'And you, Barbara?' Constance and Barbara exchanged kisses, light touches on the cheek these. And then the introductions were made.

'Miss Katie Bensham . . . Mrs Radlet.'

'How-do-you-do, ma'am?'

'How-do-you-do?'

'Mr John Bensham . . . Mrs Radlet.'

'How-do-you-do, ma'am?'

'How-do-you-do?'

'Mr Dan Bensham . . . Mrs Radlet.'

'How-do-you-do, ma'am?'

'How-do-you-do?'

The same process was repeated but with Michael this time; then Constance led the way into the house, through the hall, not so dark now because of another window that had been added to it, and into the drawing room.

'Do please be seated.' Constance spread her arm wide, and when they had taken chairs there fell on them an awkward silence, until it was broken by a high laugh from Barbara, which both startled and annoyed Miss Brigmore but which brought answering smiles from the younger folk when she said, 'It's funny, we all look ridiculous, everybody sitting like waxworks.'

Katie began to laugh and the boys to grin widely; then Michael, who had been standing near Barbara, leant towards her and, mouthing his words, he said, 'Trust you, Madam, to break eggs with a mallet,' and as her hand went out to slap him Miss Brigmore said sharply, 'Barbara!' But Barbara was not looking at Miss Brigmore and didn't see her speak, and so she slapped Michael and went on, 'We had a wonderful time coming across; we laughed all the way, didn't we, Dan?'

259

Daniel Bensham, fifteen years old, was of small stature but inclined to be thick set. His hair was sandy; his eyes, a deep blue, had a keenness to them; his nose was rather broad at the nostrils and his mouth was large. He had no claim whatever to good looks yet there was something arresting about his face. He did not answer Barbara except by making a moue with his mouth, for his attention was taken up by the company, by the lady of the house in particular; the lady who had once lived in the Hall and who, he imagined, had expected to go on living there for ever. How had she felt when she was turfed out? Barbara said she was seven at the time; she must still remember. And then there was the son. This was the one that Barbara was always talking about, and he could see the reason, a mythological god here, a son of Olympus. Yet he didn't look as if he had much spunk; he had the look of Ripon about him. Ripon was in the Upper House; he looked in a daze most of the time, and was always spouting poetry; he had been up before the Head this term for wearing fancy collars; he had copied Byron's dress from a picture hanging in his room. And yet for all his dreaminess they said he was a flogger, and because of him some of the boys were afraid to be sent up. He, himself wasn't afraid; let him start any of his flogging antics on him and he'd kick him in the teeth. By God! yes; then he'd walk out. And his dad would support him. He already felt a deep animosity towards Ripon, and he could towards this fair fellow too.

'Dan, what are you staring at, you look all eyes and teeth?'

Dan turned his gaze from Michael on to Barbara, and he laughed with her as he said, 'Well, I am all eyes and teeth.' Then turning, he smiled at his hostess; and she smiled back at him as she thought, What a nice boy! And such a nice voice. They appeared to be nice children, and all well spoken. As usual, Anna had done a good job on the girl, and the public school had certainly left its stamp on the boys and erased the vernacular inheritance of their parents, which, from what she could gather from Anna, remained deplorable.

She looked from the sandy-haired boy to the taller red-headed one and said, 'I see you have come suitably dressed for the walk. It's a good three miles across the moors and very rough terrain in parts. Have you been to the hill races before?'

'No, ma'am.' John shook his head. 'It may seem strange, but we've never been this side of the range before. It was lovely coming over, wonderful scenery. And you're in a beautiful valley here. The country appears much softer this side. Over home it's harsh ...' he finished lamely, colouring a little as he too remembered that this woman had once lived 'over home'. It was all rather embarrassing. He was sorry that he had let Barbara persuade them to come; but then once Barbara got her teeth into anything you might as well give up. He looked now from this beautiful woman to Barbara. There wasn't a vestige of resemblance between them, yet there was a strong blood tie. He again concentrated his gaze on Constance. She'd kept her elegance and style even if she had been running a farm for years. This, he supposed, was what they meant by breeding.

Katie was also looking at Constance, and she was thinking, She keeps smiling all the time, but she looks sad.

'Excuse me a moment.' Constance cast her glance over the visitors, adding, 'You must have a little refreshment before you start on your . . . arduous journey, and I would also like you to meet my mother-in-law, Mrs Radlet.'

As she turned towards the door it opened and Jane entered. She glanced quickly at the assembled company; then putting her face close to Constance, she whispered, 'There's a gentleman called. He wants to see you; he's in the yard on horseback.'

Constance almost repeated aloud, 'A gentleman on horseback?' Traps, carts, brakes, her visitors usually used one or the other of these vehicles, and if one came on horseback he was likely a farmer. She knew Jane well enough to know that she would not give this title to any of the farmers from hereabouts, she would have announced them with 'It's Armstrong' or, 'Him over from Alston way,' or 'Bradley from Nenthead,' but she had said, 'A gentleman.'

When she reached the kitchen door she stopped and stared at the man standing at the horse's head, and before she had time to prevent it her mouth dropped into a wide gape. Pat Ferrier – her heart lifted – Pat Ferrier who had at one time been a regular visitor to the cottage along with Will Headley, Will, who had courted her then discarded her practically overnight for a young lady of wealth. It was on the day after she had learned of Will's desertion that Donald Radlet had proposed to her – How fate took advantage of the emotions.

And young Pat, he'd had an affection for her too, but she had laughed at him and treated him like a young boy. But here he was, and no longer young Pat, but a man, a handsome man.

'Pat! Pat!'

Pat Ferrier turned sharply towards her, then came forward with outstretched hands, and gripped hers. 'Constance! Ah! Constance. How good to see you!'

'Come; come in.' She was hanging on to his hand. 'What are you doing here? I thought you had gone to live abroad, permanently; the last I heard of you, you were in Austria.'

'Oh, that was three years ago. I've been in London for the past year.'

'You have? Oh! Come through.' She led the way out of the kitchen; then stopped in the hallway. Her hand to her cheek now, she laughed as she said, 'This is a day of surprises; I have three visitors from the Hall.'

'The Hall. . . . You mean?'

She nodded quickly, 'Yes, High Banks; the children of the present owner. Barbara brought them.'

'Barbara? I thought. . . .'

'Her daughter.'

'Oh, her daughter. I see.'

'You're not in a hurry, are you? Would you care to come and meet them? They'll be leaving shortly, they're going to see the games, and then we can talk. . . . Oh! Pat.' She grabbed at his hands again. 'It's lovely to see you; it just makes me happy to look at you.'

'I should have said that.'

'Yes, yes, of course.' She lowered her eyes in a mock-modest fashion. 'I forgot myself, sir.'

At this they both laughed and as they walked towards the drawing room door, he said, 'But I can endorse it a thousandfold.' Then after a pause he added, 'You've changed, Connie.'

'Yes, time doesn't stand still.'

'You're more beautiful.'

'If I remember rightly, Pat, you always did say the correct thing.' She opened the door and ushered him in, and the whole company turned and looked towards him.

Miss Brigmore recognized him instantly, although he had been but a boy when she had last seen him. She remembered he had married quite young, but it had turned out to be a tragic affair, his bride having died within three months of the ceremony. This had driven him abroad, and there he had remained for years. They had heard of him now and again through Mr Patrick Ferrier senior when on the rare occasions he called at the cottage. And now here he was. Had he married again? Or was he still a widower? Why should he have sought out Constance? But why not? They were old friends. Dear, dear; her mind was in a whirl. Now wouldn't it be wonderful if. . . .

She was shaking his outstretched hand, saying, 'I recognized you immediately.'

'And me you. You're like Constance, you haven't altered one iota.'

'I've told him,' Constance put in now, 'that he always did say the right thing. You remember, Anna, you used to say, "That young man is correct in everything." But isn't it lovely? And what a surprising day! Now let me introduce you.'

As Miss Brigmore watched Constance, her face alight, making the introductions she thought, Indeed! Indeed, what a surprising day!

· · · · ·

Everyone was in accord; it had been an exciting, happy, wonderful day. If anyone had enjoyed it more than another it was Barbara, for she'd had Michael to herself most of the time, at least whilst they were out. He had taken her hand and pulled her up gullies, he had caught her when she jumped from high banks, and she had felt so proud of him as she showed off his knowledge of country lore to the others: pointing out a badger's set, taking them to see an otter's slide, showing them the tracks of a weasel. She had noted that John got on very well with Michael, but that Dan had talked to him hardly at all. But then Dan had moods; and when he did talk he was inclined to be argumentative.

She herself had been charming to everyone; it was so easy when there was no one to irritate her. She hadn't set eyes on Sarah Waite since they had come into the farmyard. She didn't know where she was or what had happened to her and she didn't care; she only knew that life on the farm was wonderful when that girl wasn't there.

And the day wasn't quite over yet; but she knew it would end for her once she stepped up into the trap, or the wagonette; it would likely be the trap, but that didn't matter, she had no great longing to ride with the boys. But she had a longing, amounting to a craving, to dance with Michael once again, and alone, dance with him with no one else there, feeling him whirling her around in a polka. They'd all been dancing a Roger de Coverley in the drawing room. Katie had played the piano and her Aunt Constance had danced with Mr Ferrier and she had looked quite gay, acting almost as though she were a girl again, skittish was the term Brigie would use when describing someone old acting like someone young. Yet Brigie, too, had danced. At first she had thought she would die laughing when she saw Brigie dancing, yet she guided Dan through all the steps and was light on her feet.

But oh, she wanted to dance with Michael alone. Oh! she did, she did.

The room was full of chatter noise and laughter. Mrs Radlet was handing round bowls of hot broth to support them on the journey for it was already turning chilly and the full moon tonight would likely shine on an early frost. Her eyes strayed for a moment from Michael to where Katie was laughing with Mr Ferrier. He was moving his hands and describing something to her; it looked as if he were showing her how he toppled from a horse. She thought she could hear the high note of Katie's laughter. She turned her eyes back to Michael, or to the spot where Michael had been; but now he was going into the hall.

Her thoughts galloped as she searched for an excuse to follow him. . . . Her handkerchief, there was mud on it, where she had wiped some spots from her face splashed up by a horse's hooves. She went hastily

263

towards Constance where she was talking with John and said, 'Do you think you could loan me a clean handkerchief, Aunt Constance? Look' – she drew the dirty handkerchief from her pocket and explained laughingly how it had come to be soiled.

'Of course, of course, I'll get you one.'

'No, no, let me.'

Constance was about to affirm that she would go and get the handkerchief when Pat Ferrier came to her side, bringing Katie with him and saying, 'This young lady tells me she doesn't ride, she hasn't a horse; now can you understand that?'

Constance looked at him and laughed; then turning fully to Barbara again, she said slowly, 'You'll find some in the right-hand top drawer of the dressing table in my room, the small drawer.'

'Thank you, Aunt Constance.' Before she finished speaking she turned and was about to rush away when Miss Brigmore's hand came out and stopped her. 'Where are you going?'

'To get a handkerchief; Aunt Constance said I may go up to her room and get a handkerchief.'

'Oh, very well. But don't be long because we're almost ready to go. And when you come down collect your cloak and bonnet from the other room.'

'Yes, Brigie. Yes.'

Once in the hall, she looked towards the stairs, then ran to the front door, and down the steps, along by the side of the house and into the farmyard. In the far corner of the yard she saw Michael talking to Mr Waite; then she watched Mr Waite turn and go into the stables, and when Michael was about to follow him she whispered loudly, 'Michael! Michael!'

When he looked towards her it seemed almost as if he had no hair on his head, a fading shaft of light had caught it as in a single beam. She gazed so entranced she wasn't aware that he had moved towards her.

'What is it?'

She looked into his face that was just above the level of her own and she said slowly, 'It looked as if you hadn't any hair, your head had turned to gold.'

'Don't be silly. Is that what you want to tell me?'

'No.' She shook her head. 'Michael' – she leant further towards him and her voice dropped to a whisper now – 'dance with me.'

'*What!*'

'Dance with me.'

'Out here? Are you *mad*? They'll lock us up.'

She was laughing widely now. 'There's no one to see; he's gone, Waite has gone.' She pointed towards the stable.

'Don't be stupid.' He shook his head as he stepped back from her.

264

Her face now dropping into solemn lines and her mouth into a petulant droop, she muttered, 'You danced with Katie.'

'Yes, because' – he stopped himself only just in time from saying 'because she can hear the music.' What he said was, 'You danced in the de Coverley.'

'That's not the same.'

'But . . . but there's no music.' He spread his arms wide.

'I don't need to hear music, I'll feel the motions through you.'

'You're barmy.' He accompanied the words with a soft smile; then said, 'I'm no dancer anyway; Mother's found me hopeless. She said I glide as smoothly as Sandy, and I have six legs to his four.'

'I saw you waltzing with her.'

'She dragged me around; I tell you I'm club-footed when it comes to dancing. Come on, come on in.' He held out his hand and she took it; then she pulled him to a stop, saying quickly, 'I'll take you, I can waltz. Katie and I often waltz together. Come round here.' She now dragged him out of the yard and along past the kitchen to the corner of the house and then, stopping, she held her arms out to him. Clumsily he put one arm around her waist and took hold of her right hand; and now she commanded, 'Sing! Go on, sing! I can follow you if you sing.'

At this he threw his head backwards and forwards as if in despair; then sighing deeply, he began to hum a tune.

They danced in a small space at first, their bodies apart; then without being conscious of it, they moved round the corner and on to the drive fronting the house.

'Haven't you had enough?' He was panting with his effort to sing and dance at the same time.

'No! No!' She had lessened the space between them and consequently his arm had moved further around her waist. 'I could go on like this all night; it's lovely, lovely. Do you think I'm beautiful?'

'*What!*' When he went to stop she tugged him back into the step saying, 'Don't bawl at me, I can read you. Brigie says I am.'

'Well, if Brigie says you are, then you are; who dare dispute Brigie?' He was laughing down into her face now.

She went to shake him, and their bodies pressed close, and when like this she demanded, 'But am I? Do you think I am?' He said haltingly, 'Aw Barbara. . . . Well, you're all right.'

'Oh Michael! Michael! Tell me, say it.'

'*Michael! Michael!*'

The boy sprang round so quickly that he almost threw Barbara from him; but he still had hold of her hand as he looked towards his mother and Mr Ferrier standing at the front door.

'Michael!' Constance came towards him. 'What is this?' she demanded.

He didn't speak, he just stared at her, his face scarlet.

'I thought you were seeing Mr Yates about the carriage lights.'

'I . . . I . . . w . . . was,' he stammered in his confusion, 'but . . . but Waite, he . . . he was talking w . . . with Mr Yates.'

'I should go and see if the traps are ready.'

The boy hadn't been aware that he was still holding Barbara's hand; and now he dropped it like a hot coal and ran from them.

Constance stared at her niece, and Barbara stared back at her aunt, until the man in the doorway laughed and began to speak. He articulated well and Barbara read his lips. 'She doesn't carry the Mallen streak, but she's a Mallen all right; I saw that instantly, deaf or not. You mustn't blame the boy, Constance. Anyway, what is a waltz? But it would have been better if they'd waited till the moon was up.' He laughed softly.

Glancing at him for a moment, Constance repeated the words to herself; What is a waltz? Nothing, nothing in the ordinary way. But they were holding each other close, entwined. Really! that girl.

'You said that she couldn't hear at all, are you sure?' Pat Ferrier muttered as he turned towards Constance, now slightly concerned. 'She looks as if she understood.'

'She can read your lips.'

'Oh Lord! I'm sorry. Still, she knows she's a Mallen; and I suppose she knows all about the streak by now.' His voice dropped even further. 'I was always glad that you weren't one, Constance.'

She wanted to say, 'Were you, Pat?' She wanted to look at him, linger with him, because she had the feeling that this could be the beginning of a new lease of life for her. He had been in love with her at one time; true it was a boyish love but it had nevertheless been ardent. But, but that must wait; there was this girl, this disturbing girl. She turned to Barbara where she was still standing staring at them and she said, 'I thought you were going to get a handkerchief?'

'Yes, I am.' There was nothing subdued about the tone, no shame in it that she had been caught showing an utter lack of decorum, waltzing with a young boy in the farmyard like any common serving maid might do at a wedding or harvest supper.

She passed between them as they stood on the steps, glancing quickly first at one and then at the other, defiance showing in her back as she walked across the hall and up the stairs and into Constance's bedroom.

She had opened the door before she realized she could hardly see, for now the twilight had deepened and the room had but one small window, so she returned to the top of the landing and picked up the two-branched candelabrum which Jane had just lit and carried it into the room. She placed it on the dressing table and tugged open the drawer to the right of her; then stared down into it, thinking as she looked at the sets of lace collars and cuffs and bodice frills, 'She said the drawer to the right.' Well, this was the drawer to the right. She pulled it out a little further and thrust her hand to the back of it. She could feel no pile of neatly stacked handkerchiefs, nor yet a handkerchief satchel, but what she did feel was something hard beneath a bodice flounce.

Pulling the drawer open further still, she impatiently thrust the flounce to one side and saw that the hard thing it covered was a small framed picture. There was no immediate curiosity in her manner, she did not even think, Why has Aunt Constance hidden this photograph under the flounce? Not until she drew it out and held it to the light and saw that she was looking at a face like Michael's did excitement rise in her.

The face in the round frame was an exact replica of Michael's except that it looked older. The eyes, the nose, everything, especially the hair, were the same. There was only one difference, the face didn't show Michael's strength, it was a pale, sick face. She knew who this was; it was Matthew Radlet. She had seen another portrait of this man when he was a young boy. It had been taken with his elder brother, Michael's father. They were both wearing knickerbocker suits and caps. The picture was now hanging in Grandma Radlet's room, as was another picture of the brothers, taken when they were grown up. But this latter one was indistinct; it had been taken in the cattle market, and it merely showed a dark man and a fair one standing one on each side of a cow.

The sound of laughter coming from below caused her to thrust the picture back into the drawer and close it. Then she stood biting on her little finger for a moment before shaking her head and murmuring, 'Aye, Aunt Constance.'

As if she had just experienced a revelation she turned and looked towards the door, and her gaze carried her beyond it down the stairs and on to the drive, and she saw her Aunt Constance standing there, as she had a moment ago, looking at her as if she had committed some crime.

Quickly she turned to the dressing table again and her darting gaze now alighted on a set of small drawers flanking the mirror. When she pulled the top one open she found it full of handkerchiefs, and she took one out and held it to her nose. It smelt strongly of lavender.

She stood now tucking the handkerchief into the cuff of her dress, her eyes were bright, her face alight as if it were going to burst into laughter. She looked about her. This was her Aunt Constance's room. She had never really seen it before although she had been in it many times; it was comfortable, colourful. It was almost as smart as the bedrooms in the Hall. Her Aunt Constance didn't like her; her Aunt Constance had never liked her; but now she had found something out about her Aunt Constance. She didn't really know the full extent of her discovery, but one thing was certain, she'd never be afraid of her Aunt Constance again.

She had always assumed an attitude to give the impression she was afraid of no one, but secretly she had stood in awe of her Aunt Constance; perhaps because she had such power over Michael, and it had been policy that she herself should remain in her Aunt's good books. But now. . . . Now.

She pressed her lips tightly together as if to prevent the excitement that was filling her from spilling over. . . . She knew about things – the forbidden things that happened between men and women. When they were alone Katie and she talked, and their talk hinted at these secret things. And now her Aunt Constance. Really! She could scarcely believe it, but it was true. Oh yes, the photograph was proof enough for her. She remembered her Aunt Constance saying, 'Michael takes after his grandmother Radlet's side.' And of course he did, but his father hadn't been Mr Donald Radlet. Really! Really!

When she went out of the room there was a slight swagger to her walk.

Fifteen minutes later they were all ready for the road. Barbara had known that she would not be allowed to ride in the brake, not now it was coming on dark, even if the moon were to shine ever so brightly. But it didn't matter; it had been a wonderful day and she had danced alone with Michael. Her Aunt Constance could never take that from her. She could still feel him holding her close. She could still feel the pumping of his heart through her dress. If her Aunt Constance hadn't come on the scene at that moment he might have kissed her; he might, he just might. He had looked down on her and his eyes had been big and round and soft, and his hands had been hot with perspiration. Her Aunt Constance had made them lose something, but it would come again, that moment would come again. In the secret depths of her where her desires ranged wildly she felt old and full of knowledge, strange knowledge.

From her seat in the trap she looked towards where Mr Ferrier was saying good-bye to Katie; and oh my! he was kissing her hand and Katie was dropping him a deep curtsey; everybody was laughing. . . . Now he was coming towards them.

'Good-bye, Miss Brigmore.' Brigie and he were shaking hands.

Then he was talking to Mary. 'Hello, Mary,' he said. 'I hope you are well. Do you remember me?'

'Indeed I do, sir. You haven't changed much.' It was the first time on this occasion Mary had seen him, for she had been spending the day with her friend, Nancy Waite.

'That is very kind of you, Mary. If I remember rightly you were forever tactful; Miss Brigmore's influence, no doubt.' He cast a glance towards Miss Brigmore. 'Good-bye.'

'Good-bye, sir. Good-bye.'

Now he had hold of her own hand and, leaning forward, he put his lips to it; but his eyes were raised to hers, and they held a mischievous glint as if they shared a secret. 'Good-bye, Miss Mallen.' He stressed the Miss. 'I trust you've had an enjoyable day.'

She read only the latter end of his words because he had bowed his head, and she said, 'Good-bye, sir, and thank you.' It was a suitable retort covering all occasions.

When he stepped back, Yates cried 'Gee-up!' and the brake went from the yard first; then Miss Brigmore shook the reins of the pony trap and the pony moved forward; and now those who had free hands began to wave. She waved to Michael where he was standing between his mother and his grandmother, with Mr Ferrier behind him. He did not run beside the trap as he usually did and call a last farewell from the road; but somehow it didn't matter for she knew if it lay with him he would have done so. She felt strong, powerful, important, her deafness didn't matter. Was she only twelve, near thirteen? But she felt so much older, and so full of knowledge. One thing she was determined on; she wouldn't cease pestering Brigie until she got her a pony, and then she could ride over the hills whenever she liked, and no one could stop her. . . . No one.

They had gone about a quarter of a mile along the road when two figures, one very tall and one very small, jumped a ditch and mounted the high bank that edged the road in order to let them pass; then the two figures waved to them and they waved back. Even when she saw it was Jim Waite and Sarah she waved back, for as she looked at the small figure of Sarah Waite, dressed in a common coat and heavy boots and straw bonnet, she felt she had been silly to be jealous of her, for what had she to fear from a little thing like that. She knew that Jim Waite had taken Sarah to the games, doubtless at the suggestion of Aunt Constance and Brigie, because the Benshams had been coming. If that hadn't been the case Sarah Waite would have been allowed to tag along with them; and as Brigie herself had said on other occasions, it wasn't right to allow the girl such licence. But it didn't matter any more, nothing mattered any more; she had danced with Michael alone and he had almost kissed her.

The following morning at breakfast Barbara caused Miss Brigmore to choke on her food and drop her fork on to her plate when she was asked the question, 'What is the Mallen streak? Should I have it? Oh, don't choke.' Barbara rose hastily from her chair and came round the table and patted Miss Brigmore between the shoulders as she asked, 'Was it the bacon, or what I said?'

'Don't, don't!' Miss Brigmore shrugged herself away from Barbara's hand; then wiping her mouth with her napkin, she muttered, 'It was the bacon; Mary does it much too well. I've told her. What . . . what did you say about the Mallen streak?' She picked up her fork and proceeded with her breakfast, and as Barbara resumed her seat she said, 'I asked you what it was and should I have it.'

'What makes you ask such a question? Where did you hear this?'

'Mr Ferrier talking to Aunt Constance last night. He said I hadn't got it, nevertheless I was a Mallen all right, or words to that effect.'

Dear, dear Lord! It was a silent exclamation but Miss Brigmore had closed her eyes and it took on the form of a prayer. She could not stand another tussle with the child and the truth would be disastrous at the present time for she was getting on so well with her sign language. She looked across the table and said slowly now, 'Most of the Mallen men who are born with black hair have a paler streak of hair running down from the crown' – she demonstrated – 'usually on the left side.'

'Did Mother's Uncle Thomas have it? His hair is white in his picture in the drawing room.'

Miss Brigmore lowered her eyes before she said, 'In his young days, yes, it was very prominent.'

'Did my father have it?'

Again Miss Brigmore said silently, 'Dear Lord! Oh dear Lord!' Now she must repeat the tale of Thomas Mallen's fictitious younger brother who had been drowned at sea before Barbara was born. She had invented the story when the child had first enquired about her father, and she had regretted it ever since, for it had further complicated an already very complicated situation.

When she spoke she mumbled her words and Barbara asked loudly, 'What did you say?'

Miss Brigmore lifted her head sharply and her voice, too, was loud as she replied, 'I said he had it slightly.'

'Why haven't I got one then?' Barbara put her hand up to her hair.

'The women in the family don't carry the mark.'

'Carry the mark?' The words were repeated slowly. 'Why do you call it a mark?'

'Oh child!' Miss Brigmore jerked her head to the side. 'No reason. It . . . it was merely to describe the pigmentation of the hair.'

'My uncle, Constance's husband, he was Uncle Thomas's son, wasn't he, the fat man?'

'Don't say, the fat man; your . . . your mother's Uncle Thomas was stout, stout, that's all.'

'He was fat; in his picture he is fat.'

'Barbara! you're being annoying, and acting like a small child.'

'I'm sorry. But Brigie, listen to me, because I want to know. If Aunt Constance's husband Donald was Uncle Thomas's son why did he live on the farm? Why didn't he live at the Hall before it was sold, or here with you? Why? And why was he called Radlet and not Mallen?'

'Be . . . because, because, his, his mother married again.'

'What!' Barbara screwed up her eyes. 'But she couldn't marry again if Uncle Thomas was alive, and he'd only just died when I was born, you said so yourself, when he had his heart attack. And Uncle Donald's mother is Mrs Radlet, isn't she, and she's still on the. . . .'

Miss Brigmore sprang up from her seat and she did an unusual thing for Miss Brigmore, she doubled her fist and thumped the table, much in the fashion that Mr Bensham would have done, and she shouted at Barbara even as she mouthed each word separately: 'I am not going to go into the entire history of the family at this moment to please you or anyone else, do you hear? When I think the time is ripe I will give you the full story, I shall even write it down for you, but the time is not ripe, and I would thank you not to raise the subject again until I give you leave to. Is that understood?'

Barbara stared up at Miss Brigmore but she did not answer her; she could see that Brigie was furious and all because she was trying to keep something from her, and she imagined it concerned her Aunt Constance and the man called Donald Radlet who had been her husband, but who was Uncle Thomas Mallen's son.

She had the strong urge at this moment to say to Brigie, 'Aunt Constance is a bad woman; she has a picture of her husband's brother secreted in her collar drawer, and his face looks exactly like Michael's.' But no, this was her secret. Unlike this other business however she would not wait until she was given leave to speak about it. When she herself thought the time was ripe she would startle a number of people by asking questions, but most of all she would startle Aunt Constance, that's if Aunt Constance tried to thwart her.

'If you've finished your breakfast go and get ready for the Hall.'

When Barbara reached her room she walked immediately to her dressing table and, sitting before it, she peered into the glass; and as she looked at her reflection she thought, I know a lot of things other people don't know; perhaps it's because of being deaf I notice more. When I am sixteen I shall be very knowledgeable in all ways. I shall know as much as . . . she was going to say Brigie, but she changed it to Aunt Constance, for she felt that her Aunt Constance knew much more of the world than Brigie did.

271

Of a sudden her mood altered. She leant further towards the mirror and, the lines of her face drooping into sadness, she said to her reflection, 'Parts of me are not nice and I want every bit of me to be nice so that Michael will love all of me. I want to be kind like Katie, and gentle like' – she actually started back from the mirror as she checked her mind forming the name 'Sarah'; then, her body slumping, she asked herself, 'Is that why I hate her – not only because Michael makes a fuss of her but because she is so different from myself, being of a gentle nature?' Leaning slightly forward again she peered at herself, then asked in a whisper, 'Why am I not gentle and kind and loving? But . . . but I am loving. Oh yes' – she shook her head as if in denial to a voice accusing her unjustly – 'I am loving, I love Michael; I've always loved Michael, I don't know a time when I didn't love Michael; and I love Brigie; yes, I love Brigie, but in a different way; and I love Katie, because it would be hard not to love one so generous as Katie; and I like the boys, particularly John. I . . . I really like everyone, everybody except that Waite family and . . . and Aunt Constance.'

Well – her spine straightened itself – if ever she hoped to have Michael she would have to learn to love Aunt Constance, wouldn't she, because when she and Michael married they'd all have to live in the same house, wouldn't they? Not necessarily. In her mind's eye she saw the picture of her Aunt Constance standing looking at Mr Ferrier.

She was able to recognize love when she saw it.

So you see, she nodded at herself, she really did know a lot, much more than anyone else of her age. Perhaps it wasn't only because she was deaf, perhaps it was because she was a Mallen. Mallens seemed to be different, special, because of that streak.

But Mr Ferrier had recognized her as a Mallen without the streak.

Wouldn't it be strange if Mr Ferrier proved to be the solution to her main problem.

PART TWO

Matilda Bensham

I

'NOW LOOK HERE, LAD; I'm going to put some straight questions to you and want some straight answers; you've buggered me about enough over the last year or so. Why, in the name of God, can't you be like John there?'

'I can't be like him because I'm not him, I'm me.' Dan Bensham leant over the table towards his father and paused before he finished, 'And it's like you to expect people to be of a pattern.'

'Now look here, lad; I'll have none of that.' Harry rose from his chair and came round the desk, his arm outstretched, his finger pointing towards his younger son. 'You can act the man and the big fellow as much as you like among your fancy friends, but just you remember this is my house an' to me you're still a nipper, nowt more, just a nipper.'

'Oh, I'm glad to hear that. Yesterday you said I was of an age to know my own mind.'

'Well, so you are. An' that's what all this is about. I've slaved for years, an' me father afore me, to build up one of the best mills in Manchester, an' I've got two sons who should be damned glad they've got the chance to carry on after me. But here you are nineteen, an' not knowin' which bloody end of you's up. If you had stuck to the idea of goin' to one of those universities I'd 've been with you; aye, I would, but now you come home and tell me you don't know what you want to do, except you want to travel about until you find out. Well, I'm gona tell you something, lad; you're not bloody well travelling about on my money.'

'I can travel without money.'

'Huh! huh! listen to him. I'd like to see you.' Harry now stalked down the room, his arms spread wide; then he turned and came back and faced his son before he continued, 'Just tell me this. What's wrong in you goin' into the mill for a year? It'll be half yours one day so you should know where your money's comin' from an' how it's got.'

275

Dan didn't answer for a moment, but stood grinding one fist into the palm of his other hand and he closed his eyes and his chin dug deep into his chest as he growled out, 'That's just it, I've told you; if I've told you once, I've told you a dozen times I can't bear to see them from Monday morning till Saturday night working, working, never stopping....'

'Now look you here, lad, let's get this straight; my ... my people are better cared for than any others in the town. Shaftesbury himself couldn't do more.'

'*No?*'

'*No!* An' don't you insinuate otherwise with that tone of voice. God Almighty! you couldn't treat me worse if I was a John Bright and opposed nearly every damn reform along the line. Look what I've done over the last few years, aye, an' long afore that, long afore seventy-four. I was ahead of me time for I never took a workhouse apprentice in if they were under ten, lass or lad, and then I raised it to twelve.'

'Because it became law.'

'Bugger you for an aggravating young snot. I could have kept it to ten an' been better thought of by other owners. I've been blacklisted by some of them, do you know that? Blacklisted, me! Now I'm tellin' you, lad, you'd better watch out else you'll find yourself lying on your back, as cocky as you are.'

As father and son, similar in build and appearance, only different in age and not all that different in temperament, glared at each other, John's voice broke in on them quietly now, addressing Dan and saying, 'If you're so troubled by the conditions why don't you do as Father suggests and give it a trial, find out where improvements are necessary and put them forward?'

Harry cast his enraged glance now towards his elder son as he cried, 'Now there's sense, there's sense; see for yourself what goes on afore you start condemnin' wholesale out of hand.' He looked at Dan again, stared at him, then letting out a long slow breath that deflated his body he said in a slightly calmer tone, 'And if you go off now what effect do you think it's goin' to have on your mother, and her bad as she is? And you know she's bad, don't you?' His voice sank lower still as he ended, 'Real bad.'

Dan's head was level now, and he asked tersely, 'What do you mean, real bad?'

'Just what I say.'

'But the operation, it was a success.'

'For the time being, for the time being; but you might as well know, both of you' – he cast a glance towards John before lowering his head – 'her days are numbered, they're fast runnin' out.'

John rose hastily from where he had been sitting near the end window of the library, and he came and stood near Dan, and they both stared at their father, and he at them; and then he nodded slowly.

After a moment the two brothers glanced at each other, then Dan went to the fireplace and, putting his forearm on the mantelshelf, he leant his head on it, and he did not lift it until he heard his father say, 'That's why I've stayed back here more than usual of late, an' that's why I wanted the both of you at the mill; not just one, it takes more than one to run a place like that. I wanted you both to get the hang of it under Rington afore he retires, an' believe me that won't be soon enough to please my book. I've never relied on him, not fully, since he almost let that strike sweep our place. If it hadn't been for young Willy havin' his wits about him it would have an' all. Willy could take over the morrow 'cos he could buy and sell Rington in lots of ways, but then don't forget he was one of themsel's, and even the best of them 'll take advantage if there's not a bit of class at the top; aye, class' – he nodded his head slowly before he went on – 'like you would provide.' He held their gaze, then said lamely, 'It was different in my case an' that of me dad. We grew with it, we were part of the machinery you could say; but we made something. It mightn't be the biggest mill but it's always been my ambition to make it the best in the town, an' not only in turning out the cloth but for the conditions in which it's turned out, an' so it hurts me, lad, when I'm accused of neglecting me own folk.' Harry now nodded sharply towards Dan, and on this emotional and strategic point he left the room.

After a moment the two brothers turned and looked squarely at each other; then John said quietly, ' 'Tisn't too bad, not too bad at all, you get used to it.'

'I'll never get used to it. The place itself, the town, the muck. Oh God, the muck!'

'Well, you've got no need to go where the muck is, that's up to you. We live almost two miles away from the muck, as you call it.'

'They live like . . . I was going to say cattle but cattle are clean. Have you seen how they live?'

'Yes, of course I have.'

'And didn't it affect you?'

'It's awful, but what can you do? I mean you can't reform the whole town, not at one go. They've pulled a lot of places down and are rebuilding.'

'Yes, and what? I saw some of the rebuildings, streets and streets of houses no bigger than huts.'

'They're clean, new, and some of them have water laid on in the back yards.'

The scathing expression on Dan's face caused John to wet his lips and flush slightly, and when Dan repeated, 'Some of them have water laid on in their back yards,' then added, 'and some of them haven't; and some of them still throw their filth into the street,' he cried angrily, 'They're not all like that, you've only seen half the picture. There's lots of our folks whose places are as clean as it is possible for them to be.'

'You've said it' – Dan's voice had risen too – 'as it's possible for them to be. And look, you're blaming me as much as he is, but I ask you this, why did he move us here in the first place, miles away from grime of any kind, right into the heart of the country, this wild country, fresh air, hills and rivers all about us, and then expect us to go back into Manchester? All right, all right, we've got a house on the outskirts – like all the rest of the wise merchants – but even there you can't get away from the filth, their fancy buildings, their churches, their assembly rooms, the lot; to me they still reek of the filth, for they were built out of filth.'

John stared at this brother whom he cared for dearly. Dan was almost a head shorter than himself in height but thicker in stature, and he had a spark, a vitality that he himself lacked; he also had the power to express himself on all subjects whether taboo or not. Yet in a way he was indolent, and of course too he was idealistic. This last trait created the Manchester conflict. He said quietly, 'It's because of Blake's "Dark Satanic Mills" that we've been able to enjoy the fresh air, and the hills and the streams; you mustn't forget that.'

A slow smile now spread over Dan's face for, as usual, he had regained his temper quickly, and he said on a laugh, 'Trust you to bring everything down to earth and plain facts.'

'Well, isn't it better so?'

It was a moment before Dan asked flatly, 'What am I going to do?'

'Well, if you'll take my advice you'll do as he says and give it a chance, and . . . and also, if as he says Mother's so ill, well you couldn't possibly go away now even if he gave you the money.'

Dan turned and looked into the fire again, and then he muttered, 'What'll we do if Mother goes?'

'I don't know; we'll have to wait and see.'

For a time they were both silent, then John glanced at his watch and said, 'I'll have to be going.'

'Where to?' Dan looked to where John was walking slowly towards the door.

'I promised to ride over to the farm with Barbara.'

'Since when have you taken to accompanying Madam when she goes a visiting the lord of the hills?'

'It appears that Brigie won't let her go over on her own since she was lost in the mist that time. . . .'

'And so she's making use of you?'

'And so she's making use of me.'

'How do you feel playing second fiddle to the farmer?'

'I didn't know I was playing the fiddle at all.'

Dan went towards John now and he did not put the question until he was level with him. 'You serious about Barbara?' he asked quietly.

'No.'

The answer was firm and definite, and caused Dan's face to stretch as he repeated, 'No? Then Brigie's going to have a surprise, isn't she?'

'Brigie's not such a fool.'

'Brigie is a fool where Madam is concerned. Brigie's determined you'll marry her long lovely child and you'll all live here happy ever after.' He waved his hand above his head.

'Don't talk rubbish. Brigie hasn't been with Barbara all these years not to know there's one person and one person only on her horizon, and that's the farmer.'

'Oh, Brigie knows that, and Barbara knows that, and I know that, and you know that; there's only one person who doesn't know it and that's the fair farmer himself.'

'What do you mean? He ... he's devoted to her.'

'Yes, in a brotherly fashion, like we all are, but I'll lay a hundred to one now that he doesn't marry her, and you do. I'd bet my last penny on Brigie.'

At this John put his head back and laughed quietly as he said, 'Make it two hundred.'

'Done! What about a time limit?'

'A year today.'

'A year today it is.'

They were smiling as they walked out into the hall; then they both looked slightly embarrassed when their eyes alighted on the objects of their discussion. Barbara had just come in from the front porch and Armstrong was already helping Miss Brigmore off with her coat.

After greetings had been exchanged Miss Brigmore looked at John and said, 'It's a beautiful day, I'm sure you'll enjoy your ride; but bring her back early mind, well before dusk sets in.'

'Never fear; I'm too careful of my own skin to come across those hills in the dark.'

'What did you say?' It was Barbara looking at John now, but it was Dan who answered for him. Rapidly on his fingers he repeated what John had said, and Barbara answered with her fingers. Then speaking verbally to John in a throaty muffled voice, she said, 'Don't worry, I'll look after you.'

John laughed as he turned away saying to Miss Brigmore, 'Excuse me a moment, I'll just say good-bye to Mother.'

279

Now looking Barbara straight in the face, Miss Brigmore said, 'Give your Aunt Constance my warm regards, won't you?'

'Yes, Brigie.'

'And tell her I shall try to get across next week, weather permitting of course.' She turned to Dan with a smile, saying, 'It's always weather permitting here. Isn't it strange how our lives are ruled by the weather? How's your mother this morning?'

'She seemed a little better, quite lively.' And he had thought she was. But he felt slightly sick now with the weight of his present knowledge.

'Oh, I'm glad.' Miss Brigmore nodded and smiled. She had no doubt but at the moment of death Matilda would appear quite lively. Of late years she had come to admire Matilda Bensham more and more, and there had grown in her a deep affection for the woman who was, after all, her mistress.

She spoke to Barbara again, saying, 'Now take care, won't you?' then turned and went towards the stairs.

Dan, left alone with Barbara, looked at her quizzically for a moment before saying on his fingers, 'Come and wait in the drawing room.'

'He won't be a minute,' she answered verbally.

'You never know with John. Anyway, you can come and sit down.'

When they entered the room Barbara sat down on an occasional chair not far from the door, which caused Dan, still speaking to her on his fingers to say, 'That's it, don't come right in, you'll have farther to run.'

Before answering him she tossed her head to one side; then said, 'Don't be silly,' and made to rise, but he checked her with an exaggerated movement, saying, 'Oh, don't get up; you make me less embarrassed when you're sitting; we're of a height then.' He surveyed her teasingly, his head on one side; then stretching out his arm, he spaced his thumb and finger as he said, 'I suppose you are about two inches taller than me now, and if you keep on growing until you're twenty-one, just imagine what you'll be like then, a beanstalk!'

'And if you don't grow any more, just imagine what you'll be like then.'

This brisk sparring was always the tone of the conversation between them, whether with gesture or lips, and seemed at times to border on open hostility.

'You going to see the farmer?'

'Who else?'

'You're making a convenience of John.'

'I'm making a convenience of no one. John proposed coming with me.'

'You wouldn't have been allowed over if he hadn't.'

She pressed her lips tightly together as she stared at him, and then she said verbally, 'Your advanced education was intended to give you the cloak of a gentleman....'

When his head went back and he burst out laughing she jumped to her feet, and he now looked straight into her face and answered her, also verbally, saying, 'You sounded just like Brigie; and you know, you are like Brigie; under the skin you're just like her.'

'I'm like no one but myself.'

The light in his eyes changed, his face took on a stiff look for a moment as he stared at her: that is just what he had said a short while ago to his father. The mischievous glint returned, and now he nodded at her as he said, 'You're right, you're like no one but yourself, you're very leggy.' He looked down her length, over her slight bust and narrow waist, to the long flow of her riding skirt, and he said, 'You'll soon have to have a bigger mount than the cob, else your feet will be trailing on the ground, like the picture of Christ in the nursery where He's riding the donkey....'

Now she was shocked, he had really roused her. 'You're being blasphemous, and it isn't amusing. You never succeed in being amusing, only aggravating, and now you have to resort to blasphemy.'

His whole attitude changing, he said contritely, 'I'm sorry; I am, I'm really sorry.' But when he put out his hand to touch her arm she slapped it away, saying, 'One of these days you'll be sorrier still;' and on this she turned and marched out of the room.

He stood staring at the closed door. One of these days he'd be sorrier still. He couldn't be sorrier than he was at this moment, and about a number of things: Manchester, the mill, his mother, the frustrated desire to roam, and then this other thing, this other hopeless thing, this thing he had mismanaged for years, this thing without hope. This thing that was perhaps the main reason for his wanting to get away.

Once again he went to the fireplace and put his arm on the mantel-shelf and rested his head on it.

Miss Brigmore automatically smoothed down each side of her hair and straightened the skirt of her grey cotton dress before tapping on the bedroom door and entering. It was many years now since she had waited to be bidden to enter.

'Aw, hello there.' Matilda's voice greeted her from the window. 'You see I'm up; she's got me up afore me clothes are on.' She jerked her head towards where the nurse was making the bed; then added, 'Come and sit down. Come and sit down.'

As Miss Brigmore took a seat opposite to her she asked, 'And how do you feel this morning?'

'Oh fine, fine; can't you see? I was just sayin' to 'Arry there, that if this weather keeps up he's goin' to drive me into Newcastle and I'm goin' to buy a complete rig-out, maybe two, and stay in one of them big hotels. Didn't I? Didn't I, 'Arry?'

'Aye, you did, lass; and just you say the word and we'll be off any minute now.'

'There, what did I tell you. And how are you yourself?'

'Oh, I'm very well, thank you.'

'Well, you couldn't help be otherwise could you on a mornin' like this. Just look out there, isn't it grand? Look at those hills. Eeh! you know, the times I've promised meself I'd climb those hills. Just one of them, I've said to meself, go on just climb one, just to say you've done it; but the most climbing I've done is to get into the carriage. Laziness it is; that's what it is, nothing but laziness. Isn't it, 'Arry?'

'Aye, you're right there, Tilda. As lazy as you're long, you are. Never done a hand's turn in your life as far back as I can remember.'

As their laughter joined, Miss Brigmore looked from one to the other. They could laugh about it. Never done a hand's turn in her life, this woman, who started to work when she was six years old, walking the dark muddy streets, her eyes gummed with sleep, the only guide her mother's skirt. Six o'clock in the morning till seven or eight at night. As lazy as she was long! This woman had told her tales that had actually brought the tears to her eyes, of how her sister had lost her hand when she was nine years old. Running between the machines, she had been so overcome with sleep that she had fallen forward and put her hand out to save herself, and, as Tilda had said, it was God's blessing she hadn't put both out. It hadn't come off right away, she said, it was just mangled at first, but when they got her to the Infirmary they had chopped it off.

Over the years Miss Brigmore had come to realize that her wisdom gained from the reading of books had not increased half as much as had her knowledge of human nature which she had gained from listening to Matilda Bensham.

'John's just been in to tell me he's ridin' over to the farm with Barbara. If we keep our weather eye open we'll see them passin' the end of the drive there. By! she looks a picture on a horse, does Barbara. Not like our Katie; a real bundle of duds, our Katie looks on a horse. Did he tell you about the visitor we had yesterday?' She nodded again towards Harry, and he replied, 'No, I didn't. What time have I had; she's just come in, hasn't she? And anyway, I've spent the mornin' talking to those two numskulls of yours, tryin' to knock some sense into them, at least into that Dan.'

'Oh, Dan's all right, he'll get by.' A warm smile spread over

Matilda's pale bloated face. 'But about our Katie and the visitor' – she nodded to Miss Brigmore – 'that Mr Ferrier called yesterday.'

'Really! I didn't know he was home.'

'Oh, he's home all right. He took her for a short dander as he calls it on the horses, and he's callin' for her the day again. He's bringing the coach this time an' takin' her into Hexham. Now what do you make of that? I ask you, what do you make of it? I thought nothin' of it last year when he went to the school in Hexham and picked her up, but now he comes a callin', and this is the second year runnin' you know. Oh, what am I talkin' about? more than that; he's called every year since he's come back from abroad, since the first time he met her on the farm. Now what do you make of it?'

What did she make of it? And what would Constance make of it when her secret hopes – that weren't so secret – were dashed yet again?

When Pat Ferrier first returned to England from abroad he stayed only a matter of a few weeks, but during that time he was very attentive to Constance, and she regained her youth, hope acting like an elixir on her, but when he told her of his departure through a letter, as Will Headley had once done, the elixir lost its effect and she reverted to the farmer's wife, and the loving mother, and the very, very irritable aunt. When the following year he reappeared on the scene he again paid attention to her, if not court, and so it had gone on for nearly five years, until now she felt that the hope that lingered in Constance was but a dim spark, yet nevertheless was lying waiting to be kindled. But if she were to hear that he was visiting the Hall with the precise intention of seeking the company of Katie, then the spark would be finally quenched, and what would the dead embers do to her character? A marriage such as she had made, and then to be spurned by two would-be suitors, because spurned was the correct word. Oh! it wasn't to be thought of.

'He's all of fifteen years older than her, but it would be a good match, grand. Don't you think it would be a good match? Imagine our Katie with a house in London, and one in Paris, France, and a manor in Northumberland. My! My!'

'That means nowt.'

They both turned and looked towards Harry. 'We've got a house here in Northumberland, we've got one in Manchester. I could take one in London the morrow and another in Paris and it wouldn't make a dent in what we've got. It isn't the property a body wants to consider, it's the man.'

'But you like him?'

'He's all right, aye, I like him; he hasn't acted like the rest of them, too big for his boots. But still who's to know whether we would've seen hilt or hair of him if he hadn't been after something, and that something Katie? Aye, let's face up to it; he wouldn't have come knockin' at our front door if it hadn't been for our Katie.'

'Well, that's the way of things with any lad, isn't it? Anyroad, he seems set on her.'

'Now don't get ideas, Tilda. Two visits an' you say he's set on her. Why, I know some folks who've courted ten years and then it's fallen through. Set on her!' The sound he made was a definite pig snort.

'Look, there they go, Barbara and John. And look, they've stopped; our Katie's runnin' up to them, likely giving Barbara her news. Oh, they're a pair, those two; been like sisters, haven't they?' She turned to Miss Brigmore, and Miss Brigmore nodded and said, 'Yes, indeed, like sisters.'

'An' they're very fond of each other; different as chalk from cheese but very fond of each other, you can see it.'

'Yes, they're very fond of each other.'

'By! as I said, she looks well on a horse, does Barbara. An' so does our John; he's well set up is our John. Don't you think he's well set up, Brigie?'

'Yes, indeed, he's a very smart young man.'

'They make a nice-looking pair.'

'Yes, they do.' Oh yes, indeed, they made a nice-looking pair, and they were suited. Miss Brigmore endorsed this firmly to herself. John was kind, gentle and thoughtful, and he could handle Barbara. He had the knack of talking her out of her tantrums. But such exhibitions had been replaced of late by moods. In the beginning, she had called them thoughtful periods, but now she thought of them as black spasms, for when Barbara was in them she would neither speak verbally nor communicate on her fingers but would go out and walk the hills, very like her mother had done when she was carrying her. Sometimes Miss Brigmore would find her staring fixedly at her, a question deep in her eyes, many questions deep in her eyes, but as yet she hadn't asked them with her lips, nor with her fingers; but increasingly Miss Brigmore felt that the day was not far off when she would be confronted by a young woman who would want to know the whole truth.

She started slightly when Matilda shouted across the room, 'Would you go and get us a glass of wine, nurse?' That was one thing she had never been able to do, instil into Matilda the fitness of things, the manner in which to address a servant. The nurse was a new addition to the household and was looking slightly indignant when Harry said, 'Don't worry her, I'll ring for Brooks.'

'No, 'Arry; she'll go and get it, won't you, dear?'

The nurse looked from Matilda to Miss Brigmore and when Miss

Brigmore made an almost imperceivable movement with her head she turned away and went out of the room.

'That's it; I just want to get rid of her for a minute, we can't talk in front of her. It's not policy to let everybody know your business, now is it? Sit down, 'Arry, and stop gallopin' about, you're actin' like a dray horse that's been let loose in the cellars. Tell her what we were talkin' about last night, go on.' She looked at her husband but pointed at Miss Brigmore, and Harry, seating himself with unusual obedience, said, 'Oh, there's plenty of time for that, Tilda.'

'There's no time like the present, that's what you're always sayin'; you said that to me years ago, remember? There's no time like the present, you said; get your hat and coat on and we'll go an' get married.' She threw her head back and her sagging cheeks wobbled with her laughter, and Harry smiled as he looked down and nodded his head, then said, 'Aye, aye, I remember, there's no time like the present. Although mind' – he nodded and glanced towards Miss Brigmore – 'it wasn't done nearly as quick as that, it took us almost a week.'

Again Tilda's laughter filled the room; and then ceasing abruptly, she put out her hand towards Miss Brigmore and, gripping her wrist, she said, 'We want to do that something for you, lass, we talked about ages ago. Something permanent like, something that'll put you over in the meantime until the next lot's ready for you to have a go on.'

Looking her bewilderment, Miss Brigmore turned her face towards Harry and as her eyes questioned him he said with a grin, 'She's meaning when they get married an' their bairns start comin' up and you take them on.'

'Oh! Oh!' The syllables came out on a shaky laugh. 'Oh, I doubt if I will ever take on any more children, not in my lifetime.'

'Why not? why not? you could have another thirty years afore you, and twenty of them workable ones.' It was Harry speaking directly to her now. 'You don't look anything near your age, not by a long chalk, does she, Tilda?'

'No, not by a long chalk; an' I've always said it, haven't I? I have, I have.'

'Well, let's get down to brass tacks.' Harry's manner was brisk now. 'It's like this; let's put our side of it first. We want you to come along here every day, as usual, but not any settled hours, just please yourself, but just pop in and give Tilda a hand here and there with the running, as you've always done. But, if there's days when you don't feel up to it an' don't want to bother, well, that'll be all right with us. And so's you can feel independent like we thought about settling a sum on you.'

'Oh no! No!' The movement Miss Brigmore made caused a chair leg to slip over the edge of the carpet and to scrape against the polished boards. 'I have been well paid, very well paid, you have been over generous. Look what you have done for Barbara, and the horse and trap; and caring for the horse too. I could never repay your generosity. Oh no! No! I couldn't accept anything more.'

'It isn't what you could accept or what you couldn't accept.' Harry Bensham was on his feet again, his usual manner to the fore. 'A hundred and fifty pounds a year you've got to live on, oh I know, I know; an' the three of you were cheeseparing out of that afore you came here.' He swept his hand in a wide motion towards her as if wiping away her denial and went on, 'And if Barbara gets married, who knows but that she'll want that hundred of hers; it all depends on who she takes. Aye' – he nodded – 'it all depends on who she takes.' He was not so cruel as to add 'or who takes her,' but instead said, 'There's many a slip, an' then where will you be? You'd have a house over your head and a pound a week for two of you to live on.'

As she looked at him she thought, The incongruity; he was pitying her for living on an income of a pound a week, yet that was almost three times as much as he paid some of his hands. He was an odd man, an intractable man, but a generous one, and she knew in her heart that no matter what protestations she made, as courtesy demanded, she should be glad to accept his offer, for even now finance was a constant problem to her because Barbara had tastes that went far beyond their income.

But when she heard him say, 'Three thousand, that's what we thought, Tilda and me, three thousand; and I'll invest it for you. That'll bring you in nearly as much as you're getting now, if not more,' she did protest. But he silenced her with, 'Now don't start.' Pointing his finger at her as she rose hastily to her feet, he went on, 'I'm not going to hear one word from you for, knowin' you, if you open your mouth you'll come out with something that'll floor me. So it's settled. I'll be away downstairs. And you sit still.' He nodded towards his wife, and she nodded back at him, a quiet smile on her face as she said, 'Aye, 'Arry, aye, I'll sit still.' 'As for you' – he was again looking at Miss Brigmore, but now as if she were a culprit – 'if you can spare me a minute in a while or so, I'd like to have a word with you about something.'

'Yes, very well.' Her voice was small.

'Well then' – he nodded from one to the other – 'that's that.'

'Won't ... won't you stay for a glass of wine?'

He turned from the door and looked towards Miss Brigmore. 'Aw, there's plenty of time for that; wine never troubles me. Nobody's going to accuse me of having a belly.' He patted the front of his trousers, jerked his head, then went out.

286

Uncouthness, kindness, love: this house was a mixture of all three.

Sitting down again, she now put out her hands and gently took hold of those of Matilda and murmured softly, 'What can I say?'

'Nowt, lass, nowt; about that anyway. About other things, do as you always do, give it straight from the shoulder an' in your proper English, an' without fear or favour. That's what 'Arry says about you, you speak without fear or favour. He thinks you're a lady, 'Arry does, and he's right. By aye! he's right, and I'm glad to have known you. So, talkin' of getting things straight, tell me, lass . . . how much longer do you think I've got?'

'Oh, Matilda.'

'Now, now, don't you give way. You see I know me time's short, but I don't know if it's a week or a month, an' there's things I want to do, set right.'

Miss Brigmore bit deeply down into her lower lip and for once words failed her.

'Do you think he knows?'

'No, no,' she lied firmly.

'He's been quiet lately, an' soft like, you know. I thought he might have a glimmer.'

'No, no; he's kind because he's concerned for you. He thinks of you very, very dearly.'

'Aye, aye, he does. But an outsider wouldn't think it 'cos of the way he used to go for me. But it was like water off a duck's back, 'cos that was his way. And I aggravated him for I was always a bit of a numskull where learnin' was concerned. He wanted me to learn 'cos his first wife was learned but as I said to him once' – she was smiling faintly again – 'she didn't do much bloody good for you with her learnin', did she? Eeh! there I go; I shouldn't swear afore you, but that's what I said to him, an' he laughed and slapped me on the backside, and he said, "No, you're right there"; and that's the last time he tried to learn me. And you know, lass, I've thought to meself over these past years, if you couldn't learn me nobody could 'cos you're marvellous at learnin' people . . . I . . . I don't want to die, Brigie.'

Miss Brigmore looked helplessly at the woman gazing at her now with tears in her eyes and found it impossible to make a reply. Her throat was full, her heart was full. People who followed no rules with regard to the course that conversation, even of the most personal kind, should take, disturbed you; flummoxed you, Mary would have said. She gulped audibly as Matilda went on, her voice thick now with emotion. 'It's not because I don't want to leave all this, 'cos this hasn't meant more than a pennorth of drippin' to me; I'd have been just as happy in a two-up, two-down, an' I've missed Manchester, I have, I have, but I wouldn't let on to him. No, no. But why I don't want to go is 'cos of him. You see, I don't know what he'll do, lass; I only hope to God Florrie Talbot doesn't get her hooks into him. I would hate to see her in me place here. By God! I don't think I could stand it, just the thought. . . .'

Miss Brigmore again swallowed audibly, then asked on a cough, 'Flor-Florrie Talbot? I haven't heard of her.'

'No; we don't speak of her very much, it's his cousin. When his first wife died she made a dead set at him, an' she was younger than me by over six years. She's just in her late forties now, but she's a blowzy bitch. An' she's no better than she should be; when she was young her father had to go an' bring her from the yards more than once.'

Miss Brigmore's eyes narrowed questioningly and Matilda said, 'You know, I told you about them, where the whores hung out; daylight, starlight, midnight, made no difference to that lot. Eeh! they were brazen; an' she was among them. Her father hammered her black and blue from head to foot an' kept her for three days in a room without a stitch on to cure her. But I doubt if she was ever cured. Still, she married respectable after that, a gaffer in the Liverpool docks. When he died she came back to Manchester. She's there still, an' the minute I'm gone she'll be on my 'Arry like a blood-thirsty leech.'

'Oh, no! no! Don't worry, Matilda, Mr Bensham would never dream of putting anyone in your place.'

'No, not for a while he wouldn't. An' I'll always have a corner of his heart, I'm sure of that, but human nature's human nature all the world over as you an' I know, lass, an' when needs must the devil drives. It was that I wanted to ask you about. If she should turn up here – and I wouldn't put it past her, I'd hardly have time to settle in me grave afore she'll be comin' up that drive, I bet what you like – Well, if she should, you have a talk with him, will you, and tell him to wait; wait for a year, say, eh? He'll listen to you. He's got great respect for you, you've no idea.'

'I'll do what I can, don't worry; don't worry about anything. Oh' – she turned towards the door with relief – 'here's the wine. A glass of wine will make you feel better.'

'Aye, lass, aye; there's nothin' like a glass of wine for puttin' new life into you.' Matilda now blew her nose while managing to wipe her eyes at the same time and she smiled at the stiff-faced nurse as she placed the tray on the bedside table.

2

'**Y**OU KNEW I WAS COMING.'
　　　'I didn't.'
　　　'You got my letter?'
'Yes, but only yesterday, and it was too late, the arrangements were already made.' Michael spoke quietly and slowly.

'The arrangements!' Barbara tossed her head scornfully. 'To go into the town with the Waites! Arrangements! Who are the Waites anyway? You'd think they were royalty. They're servants.'

'Now stop it, Barbara.' He mouthed the words widely.

'What do you mean, stop it? I said they're servants and they are servants; you know they're servants.'

'We're all servants.'

'Don't start on that philosophical tack, you know what I mean.'

'I know what you mean and it can't be done; Jim and I have business to do.'

'And Sarah makes three.'

'Yes, and Sarah makes three, as you say.'

As she stood looking at him, her eyes wide and glistening with unshed tears, his tone, as always, immediately softened and he took her hand and said slowly, 'Oh Barbara, Barbara, don't be silly, there'll be other times. And look; you've brought John over with you.'

'Simply because Brigie wouldn't let me come alone.'

'All right then, I'll come over next Saturday and fetch you.'

'You will?' Her face brightened.

'Yes; that's a promise.'

The prospect of spending hours alone with him caused her face to shine with uninhibited pleasure and love, until she thought that that was a week ahead and if Brigie could stop her being alone with Michael she would, even going as far as to accompany them herself. She was back with today's problem.

'Michael.'

'Yes, what is it?'

'Do something for me.'

'Anything, anything, Madam.' It was strange that he should use the same title for her as Dan Bensham did. He didn't know if he had copied Dan or Dan him.

'Don't, don't take Sarah with you.'

'Now, now.' He turned half from her, then slowly back towards her again. 'You're being ridiculous. Sarah goes into town with us every week. Why should I stop her today?'

'Every week! Always?'

'Yes, every week, always.'

'I . . . I didn't know.'

'Well, you know now. Look, Barbara, this is all nonsense. You've got to get over this.'

'Get over what?'

The question nonplussed him. He did not say, 'Your jealousy of Sarah,' but neither did he say, 'There is no reason for you to feel like this.' Perhaps last year or the year before he might have said that, but as he had grown older his feelings had changed; not entirely, oh no, he still had a deep affection for her, and sometimes he thought it was more than affection, for she fascinated him, and she was beautiful. Her handicap did not mar her in any way. She was full of life, vital, and she was so attractive and pleasing, when she was in a good mood. But she had this obsession about Sarah that marred her, and it had grown so strong of late that it raised some disquiet in him; he would not term it fear.

'I hate that girl.'

'You mustn't say that, Barbara; she's never done anything to you to deserve it.'

'She inveigled herself into the household and into Aunt Constance's good books.'

'She's done nothing of the sort; she's worked hard and made herself pleasant, she's naturally pleasant.'

'Oh, is she? I'm glad you find her so. And you intend to take her with you?'

'Yes, I intend to take her with me. . . . Oh no I don't, I mean I'm not, I'm not taking her with me, she's coming along with Jim as she always does. And look' – his face became stiff – 'when you're acting like this I could get on my high horse about him.' He pointed towards the dining-room door and in the direction of the sitting-room where John was talking to Constance.

'Why don't you then?'

'Because. . . .' Could he say, 'It doesn't bother me who you ride with,' because in an odd way it did? He was concerned for her, concerned about her; it could not be otherwise with the association they'd had since they were children. And it wasn't only that, his feelings went further. Oh, he just didn't know what he felt. But he knew how his mother felt; she didn't like Barbara – would it have made any difference to his feelings if she had liked her? He ended lamely, 'Because I don't like rows. We don't row, except when. . . .'

'Except when I visit. I suppose Aunt Constance says that, and I suppose she hasn't objected to you associating with a maid?'

His tone matching her own now, he answered. 'No, She hasn't voiced any objection because I'm sure she doesn't feel any. She's got no feeling about class. Anyway, who are we to be uppish, we're simply farmers? You're the only one who's got ideas about class.'

'And rightly so –' She drew herself up as she ended childishly – 'as I'm from class on both sides.'

This was too much; he'd have to get away from her before he said something that would set her thinking. He was aware of his father's parentage – his mother had told him last year that his father had been the natural son of Thomas Mallen. She had not told him this until after his grandmother had died so that he would not think less of his grandmother. He thought it was from this time too that his feelings towards Barbara had changed; he had had to change them when he realized that he must be just once removed from being her half-brother. He also knew that she was not aware of her real parentage but had been given some fairy-tale version by Brigie.

'Where are you? Michael! Michael!' It was with relief he heard his mother's voice, and going to the door, he called, 'Here we are.'

Constance came and stood within the threshold and looked to where Barbara was standing, her face stiff and white and as always appealingly beautiful, and as always she thought, Oh that girl! Then turning to Michael she said, 'They're waiting.'

'Oh! Well, I'm ready.' He glanced back at Barbara. 'I'll be over next Saturday,' he said, then hurried away.

Constance now went towards John, saying, 'They're off to the market, usual routine;' and together they walked across the hall and through the kitchen; and it wasn't until they had been in the yard for a few minutes that Barbara joined them.

Standing apart, she looked to where Michael was sitting at the front of the waggon with the reins in his hand, and from the ground Jim Waite with one sweep and heave was lifting Sarah on to the seat beside him. Then he himself mounted the cart.

When Constance waved Sarah waved back. Then John raised his hand while he said quietly, 'I hardly recognized her; she's grown so tall in the past year, and pretty with it. She still seemed a child last year at the harvest supper. Does she still dance?'

'Like a linty; she's so light on her feet.'

Constance had turned in Barbara's direction and so she caught the last words. Light on her feet, like a linty!

Constance was still facing her but, addressing John, she said, 'I don't know what I would have done without her over the years. I have played Brigie to her; you know what I mean?'

'Yes, yes, indeed.' He nodded as he laughed.

'Did you know Mr Ferrier was home?' Barbara's voice was low, her speech blurred.

The question obviously startled Constance, and caught her off her guard; she looked straight at Barbara and it was some seconds before she made a slight movement with her head and said, 'No.'

'Oh, I thought he would have called; he's been home for some days. He went riding with Katie yesterday and he's bringing the coach for her today to drive her into Hexham. . . . It is Hexham, isn't it, they're going to?' She appealed to John, but he made no answer, he just stared fixedly at her.

'Shall I give him your regards if I see him?'

Again there was a moment's pause before Constance said, 'Yes, do that. Please do that.'

'Well, we must be off.' She moved a step forward, then stopped. 'Oh, I did tell you that Brigie sent her warm regards and says she'll be over some time next week?'

'You did tell me.' Constance's face was expressionless.

'Michael's coming over for me next Saturday; we're going for a run.'

Constance made no reply.

'Well, we really must be off.' She went towards where the horses were tethered to a standing post, calling over her shoulder, 'Help me up, John.'

Unsmiling, John performed the task of putting her in the saddle; then he mounted his own horse, and they were about to move off when Barbara reined her horse sharply in again, and now looking down on Constance, she said, 'Oh, I knew there was something I meant to tell you. It was odd, but I saw a man in Hexham when I was last there. He was dark but had a fair streak down the side of his hair.' She demonstrated by running her finger down her riding hat. 'Brigie says it's called the Mallen streak; Michael's father had one, hadn't he? Mary tells me his hair was as black as mine except for this white piece; she tells me it's always passed on to the male offspring; isn't it odd that Michael should be so fair?'

The young face looked down into the older one; their eyes poured their animosity each into the other. The years of polite courtesy were swept away and what was revealed was hatred.

It was John who urged the horses forward, saying hastily, 'Good-bye. Good-bye, Mrs Radlet.' He knew that he had just witnessed an asp using its barbed fang. What poison was in the venom he could only guess at, but from the look on Mrs Radlet's face it might mean death. She was a young devil, Barbara, she was vicious.... And they imagined he might marry her. Not him! ...

Constance, back in the house and alone in it, felt so overcome by her emotions that she thought for a moment she would collapse. Going into the dining room, she went to the sideboard and took up a bottle of brandy from which she poured out a good measure and sipped at it as she left the room and hurried up the stairs and into her bedroom. Dropping into a chair, she took a longer drink from the glass, then leant back and closed her eyes.

That girl! that vixen, for she was a vixen. There was something in her that was bad, equally as bad as that which had been in Donald. Both sired by the same father, they may not have inherited their wickedness from him for, as she remembered, he was not a bad man, but somewhere in his lineage there was evil. How did she know about Michael? How had she found out? Not through Anna. No. No. Anna would never have told her. Oh God! If Michael should ever find out how would he then act towards her? He loved her. You could say he adored her; and more, he reverenced her as an ideal woman. She put down the glass then turned and buried her face in the wing of the chair.

Sometime later, after dabbing her face with cold water, she stood before her mirror and her mind touched on the other humiliation. Pat in England; to be near and not to call, but to visit the Hall two days running and to see that young girl. But then she was no young girl, she was a woman; she was older than she herself had been when she had married. Katie Bensham was nineteen, or almost, old enough to marry and to consider a man fifteen years her senior quite suitable. Will Headley, and Bob Armstrong, and now Pat. Why, why was she treated so? She seemed fated to be spurned by the men who attracted her, and desired by those she couldn't stand. But she must not forget Matthew Radlet. She had loved Matthew Radlet. She had loved Matthew, and he her. But the need in her, the loneliness in her, was nothing compared to the new threat hanging over her. That girl! That girl! How had she come by the knowledge of Michael's real parentage? No one had ever questioned it before, either by hint or look: Michael took after his grandmother's side of the family, and his grandmother's side were fair. That had been all there was about it until now. She felt almost physically sick as she realized the girl's knowledge had wiped away the last defence she had against her and Michael coming together. If the worst had come to the worst and Michael had declared his love for her than she would have felt forced to beg Anna to explain to the girl the close relationship between them, even knowing she was asking her to countenance a lie. But as it stood now Barbara was aware that there was no blood tie between her and Michael. That scene in the yard had in a way been a declaration of war.

There swept over her the feeling that had been constantly with her while Donald was alive, the feeling that he had her trapped and that she could never escape him. Yet she had escaped him. But in the present case there was no one willing enough to free her from Barbara as to do murder. It wouldn't be the case of Donald and Matthew over again.

3

'YOU ARE LATE IN GETTING BACK.'

'Am I?'

'Barbara, please don't answer me in that manner.' Miss Brigmore's mouth went into a tight line; and when Barbara remained silent she asked, 'Did you have an enjoyable ride?'

'No.'

'Then I assume the fault was yours?'

'Yes, you would assume that, wouldn't you? you're lining up on the other side.'

'Barbara, don't talk in that fashion to me; I've told you. Come, tell me, what has happened.'

'Nothing has happened, what could happen?'

'Don't raise your voice, Barbara.' Miss Brigmore now spoke rapidly on her fingers, and looked to where Brooks was mounting the main staircase. Then she turned about and walked quickly towards the gallery, through it and up the flight of stairs that led to the nursery floor, and she did not look round until she'd actually entered her sitting room. Here she stood stiffly in the middle of the room awaiting Barbara's approach.

Barbara entered the room slowly and when she did not turn and close the door behind her, Miss Brigmore, forming her words with extra precision, which was a definite sign of her annoyance, said, 'Be good enough to close the door behind you. . . . Now then.' She looked at the tall, thin figure clothed in the green cord riding habit, her jet hair lifted high from her pale face, a brown velvet stiff-brimmed hat perched on top of her hair, and even in her annoyance and irritation she could not help but be aware of the girl's beauty. Her tone a little gentler now, she asked, 'What is all this about? What has put you in a temper? Have you quarrelled with John?'

'Quarrelled with John?' Barbara's eyes widened in mock surprise. 'Whoever quarrels with John? I left him at the cottage and galloped across the fells; gave him a run for his money, as Mary would say; and when he caught up with me all he could pant was, "Barbara! Barbara! You! You!"'

'It's to his credit that he kept his temper. Remember what happened the last time you decided to take a run over the fells?'

'I knew he would follow me. Anyway, the sun was shining.' She pulled off her hat and threw it aside.

If it were someone other than her beloved child who was talking and acting in this manner Miss Brigmore knew that she would dislike her intensely, but because it was her beloved Barbara she laid the blame for her attitude against her affliction; that one so beautifully endowed should be so cursed could create nothing but conflict inside. She took a step towards her now, saying gently, 'John is very fond of you, you know that.'

'I don't want John to be very fond of me and you know that.'

'Barbara! come.' Miss Brigmore now caught hold of her hand and pulled her towards the couch, and when they were both seated she looked straight into her face for a moment before she said, 'You're no longer a child, not even a young girl, you are on the threshold of womanhood. . . .'

'Oh, Brigie, Brigie, please!' The words were drawn out, and now Barbara covered her face with her hands and she kept them there for a moment before slowly dragging them downwards to her neck and gripping it while her eyes remained closed. When she opened her eyes and looked into Miss Brigmore's startled face she said flatly, 'I'm not going to marry John, so get that plan out of your mind. Anyway, he doesn't want me.'

Miss Brigmore's tightly bound bust stretched. She swallowed twice before saying, 'Of course he wants you.'

'What makes you think so? Because he's kind to me? John's kind to everybody, polite and kind . . . and wary. Nobody really knows what John's thinking. But I know what he isn't thinking; he isn't thinking of asking me to marry him. At the present moment he doesn't even like me. And he's like all the rest, always has been, he's sorry for me. Anyway, can you imagine me in Manchester mouthing my way among his friends? How . . . are . . . you . . . Mrs . . . Money-bags? How's-ta-mill?'

'Stop it! Stop it this moment.' Miss Brigmore, reverting to nursery days, slapped out at Barbara's hands; and as if she had been struck a blow on the face, Barbara sprang to her feet and her voice was muffled now as she said, 'Don't do that, Brigie! You said I was no longer a child, so don't treat me as one. And let us put this matter straight once and for all. There's only one person I want to marry and you know who that is. You've always known, as I have; and if I can't have him I'll have no one.'

Miss Brigmore's lips were trembling, and her fingers could do nothing to still their trembling. She kept patting them as if trying to stop herself from speaking, but the words came out slowly and sadly as she said, 'You can't marry Michael.'

'Why not?'

'Because . . . well, there are so many things against it.'

'You mean Aunt Constance?'

'Perhaps.'

'She hates me. Do you know that? Aunt Constance hates me. You know something else? I hate her.'

'Barbara! Barbara!' Miss Brigmore bowed her head now and held her brow in her hand; then her head was jerked up as if someone had given her a blow under the chin and she was staring at Barbara as the girl said rapidly, 'But she'd better be careful and not try me too far else I'll explode her nice comfortable little world. I know something about her, I've known it for years but I've kept it to myself. But if she stops me having Michael I'll see she won't have him either.'

Miss Brigmore felt very sick. When she spoke her lips were widely articulating but her voice was a mere whisper. 'What do you mean? What can you possibly do to separate Constance and Michael?' But even as she asked the question she was already aware of the answer that Barbara was going to give her.

'I could tell him that the Mama whom he idolizes and imagines is a queen among women is nothing more than a slut, and he nothing more than a bastard.'

Miss Brigmore felt she was going to faint. She put out her hand and gripped the head of the couch, all the while staring into Barbara's passion-swept face; and when Barbara, now bending towards her, her voice low and heavy with excitement, said, 'I am right? I am right then?' Miss Brigmore closed her eyes and shook her head while Barbara went on, 'I knew I was, I knew I was, for I found proof of it. Why else would she have his picture hidden in her collar drawer? I found it years ago when she sent me up to her room for a handkerchief. Why should she keep her brother-in-law's picture hidden away in her drawer and not her husband's, I ask you? And they weren't real brothers either, only half-brothers, for her husband was the son of Uncle Thomas. He was a bastard too because Mrs Radlet was never married to Uncle Thomas. You were his housekeeper, you should have known she was a. . . .'

Miss Brigmore was on her feet now and she was crying, 'Don't you dare use that word again in my presence! What has come over you, girl? you're acting like a fiend. All these years of training and this is the result; you are talking like some low kitchen slut.'

'I am merely speaking the truth.'

'Truth!' Miss Brigmore barked the word. Then her head moved slowly from side to side before she said, 'Girl, you know nothing about the truth,' and a voice inside her added, 'I hope to God you never do,' while at the same time she knew that this was the opportune moment in which to tell her all the truth, the complicated, bitter truth of her own beginnings. But she warned herself against taking such action for the result might be disastrous, coming as it would on top of this distressing scene.

As Barbara glared back into Miss Brigmore's face that for once was showing neither understanding, nor love, nor compassion, there was in her the craving to probe into something that she felt was being withheld from her. But there was also that in her, the fear that made her shy away from the knowledge; the fear was like a mist that was pursuing her and would one day catch up with her and envelop her, and she'd become lost in it.

They were staring at each other in as near enmity as they had ever been when Katie's voice came from the landing, calling, 'Are you there, Barbara? Barbara!' There was a sound of a door opening and closing, then another, and a tap came on Miss Brigmore's door. Before she could speak it opened and Katie bounced in. Her round face was alight, her eyes shining; she was swinging her bonnet widely by the strings, but as she looked from one to the other she brought the swinging bonnet to a stop and, taking in the tense situation, she said, 'I'm sorry; I didn't know you were. . . .' She paused for a word to substitute for arguing, because she knew from experience that when Barbara got on her high horse a discussion could quickly turn into an argument, and an argument into open battle, and so, lamely, she substituted, 'busy.'

'No, no, we're not busy, Katie. Do come in.' It looked to Katie as if Miss Brigmore were openly welcoming the intrusion, and when adopting her usually polite manner she asked, 'Have you had an enjoyable day?' Katie answered on a high laugh, 'Oh wonderful! it's been fun. He's great fun is Mr Ferrier, so very entertaining. You wouldn't have approved a bit, Brigie, because he made me laugh out loud in public in the tea room.'

'You had tea?'

'Yes. In a sort of club, a gentlemen's club. The seats were plush and there were waiters. It was all so very grand.' She ended her words in mock solemnity; then burst out laughing. Now, turning fully to Barbara, she asked, 'Did you have a good day?'

'Very good.'

'So we've all had a good day.'

There was a slight pause in the conversation as she and Barbara looked at each other; then swinging the bonnet once more, Katie addressed herself in mocking tones to Miss Brigmore but in such a way that Barbara could read her. 'I have to inform you, Brigie, that I am going to dinner at Burndale Manor. Evening dinner, not a three o'clock do, with entertainment to follow. I'm going to get an evening dress cut low, right down to –' she was pointing to the middle of her breasts when Miss Brigmore said stiffly, 'And you accepted without consulting your parents?'

'Oh, Brigie!' Katie swung the bonnet in Miss Brigmore's direction. 'Mother's tickled to death; I've just told her, and she said–' now she adopted an attitude very like that of her mother. Holding out her arms and wagging her head, her voice took on the unmistakable Manchester accent: 'Well lass, what d'you think of that! You're going up in the world, eh?'

'Don't make mock of your mother, Katie.' Miss Brigmore's voice was stern, and Katie, now standing still and her bonnet held between her hands, looked straight at Miss Brigmore. 'I am not making mock of my mother, not in the way you imply; and if I may mimic her to her face and she doesn't object I cannot see why. . . .'

Miss Brigmore, her voice still stern, now checked her with, 'If you cannot see why there is a difference in what you do in the privacy of your family and with its members, and what you do outside, I'm afraid all my years of teaching have been for nought.'

Katie continued to look into Miss Brigmore's face before she said slowly and in the diction of which Miss Brigmore would have approved, 'I have been labouring under a false impression then; in fact, I think I may be correct in saying our entire family have been labouring under a false impression; and that impression has been created by you, because we, for our part, considered you were of our family. But I know now that we have presumed, and you are still Miss Brigmore and we are still the Benshams and that the gulf between us is very wide.'

Miss Brigmore again had her fingers across her lips and was about to speak when Katie swung round and made for the door. But when she pulled it open with a jerk she was brought to a stop; confronting her was the upper housemaid, Jenny Dring. Her hand raised as if about to knock, she gabbled, 'Oh! Miss, miss; the master wants you in the bedroom. It's the mistress; she's, she's. . . .'

'But . . . but I was . . . I've just left her.'

'It's happened suddenly.'

As Katie ran from the girl Miss Brigmore hurried to the door. 'What has happened?' she asked softly.

'I don't know, miss, only that everybody's in a panic down there all of a sudden. The mistress was asking for them, and Mr Brooks sent Armstrong post haste to the stables to get Mr John and find Mr Dan.'

With Barbara behind her, Miss Brigmore now hurried down the stairs and through the gallery, and when they reached the main landing she turned to Barbara and said, 'Go downstairs and wait.' When Barbara hesitated, she added firmly, 'Please.' Then she went towards the door, knocked gently and entered the bedroom.

Matilda was lying deep in her pillows; her face was drawn and grey, even her lips looked colourless. They were moving slowly as if mouthing words but making no sound, and Harry Bensham's voice, gentle and his tone unlike any Miss Brigmore had heard, was saying, 'Yes, lass; it's all right, everything'll be done as you want.' Then, his words dropping into muttered thickness, he said, 'Here's Katie.' He moved slightly aside but still retained hold of the fat podgy hand.

The door behind Miss Brigmore opened and John and Dan entered, and when they went hastily to the bed she could no longer see Matilda's face, not only because she was surrounded by her family, but because she was allowing herself to cry audibly in public for the first time in her life. She knew in this moment that she was losing a friend, a friend who had considered her one of the family. Yet Katie's accusation was true, because on her part she had been in the family, but not of it. The feeling of superiority that was a natural part of her nature and which had been engendered still further by the association with Thomas Mallen had created a gulf too wide for her to step across and embrace the Benshams, but she had been willing that they should cross it and benefit from the standards she set. She wasn't, however, entirely to blame for this situation because from the beginning they themselves had set her apart by deferring to her for advice on problems appertaining to the correct procedure to be taken, not only in the running of the household, but in personal matters also.

She looked towards the wash-hand-stand by the side of which the day nurse was standing, her hands idly folded one on top of the other at her waist; and the fact that she was making no move towards the bed seemed to add a touch of absolute finality to Matilda Bensham's life. Blindly Miss Brigmore turned about and went silently from the room.

Three maids were standing close together at the top of the stairs. They looked at Miss Brigmore's face and they bowed their heads and began to cry.

She went on down the stairs and was met at the bottom by Brooks. Brooks had never been the imperturbable butler; he had remained very much a working man; he had not acquired the subservience necessary for a good servant. There was an aggression, not only in his way of addressing one, but even in his stance that would have made him absolutely unemployable in the capacity of butler in any household other than this.

Now she looked at him through a tear-misted gaze and saw his chin going into a hard knobbled flatness as his lips pressed tightly against one another, and when he said, 'It won't be the same; nothing will be the same,' she moved her head once as she replied, 'As you say, Brooks, nothing will be the same.' She passed him and Armstrong, the first footman, and Alice Conway, the still-room maid, where they were standing with their heads slightly bent, and she went into the drawing room.

Barbara, sitting on the couch, was not aware of her presence until she stepped in front of her, and when she looked into her face she stammered, saying, 'Sh– . . . She's not, she's not?'

'She soon will be.'

'Oh. Oh.' Barbara's face now crumpled; and then she whispered, 'I'm sorry; I am sorry; you know that, don't you?'

'Yes, I know that, because you, like me, are losing a very good friend.' She now lowered herself slowly down on to the couch. Her head bowed and, aloud but to herself, she said, 'Things will never be the same again. He's right, so right.'

It was strange, she thought, that a woman as common as Matilda Bensham had maintained the love of her family through their years of transition from the level on which she herself stood, to the present one, where they could class themselves as equals, at least in manner and speech, with any family in the county.

On looking back she remembered seeing herself in the position of buffer between Katie, the young lady, who would emerge from her teaching and example, and the young lady's parents, for she had imagined the newly made young lady would undoubtedly look down upon them. How wrong she had been; Matilda Bensham had evoked a love in her family that could not be marred by education and the trappings of society.

If only Barbara showed half the love for her that Katie showed towards her mother, then she would have had no need of late to stamp down on the comparisons she was frequently making between them, because these comparisons were creating a deep hollow within her, a hollow wherein she felt she would be forced to spend the remainder of her life.

4

MATILDA WOULD HAVE BEEN PROUD of her funeral for she had twelve coaches following her coffin, and all the horses wore bouncing black plumes. The drivers of the coaches were encased in deep black with tall shiny hats and bows of black ribbons on their long whips.

In the first coach sat Harry, John, Dan and Katie; the next three coaches were taken up with Matilda's closest relatives. The fifth, sixth, seventh and eighth coaches held those nearest in relationship to Harry, and in the ninth coach sat Miss Brigmore, Barbara, and Mr Pat Ferrier.

Three neighbouring families were also represented. The Eldens had come, father and son, both having taken a day's leave from their chain of haberdashery businesses in Newcastle and district; the Fairbairns, too, he being of much more note than the Eldens in that he was a mine owner, at least in partnership with Jonathan Pearce; and Mr Pearce was also represented by his son and his son-in-law. That these six gentlemen had been regular visitors at Burndale Manor for many years, being friends of Mr Patrick Ferrier senior until his death, and afterwards continued to visit whenever young Mr Pat was in residence may have had some bearing on their showing their last respects to a woman at whom they had scoffed, and to whom their wives, after meeting her but once, had resolutely refused to proffer further invitations.

Following the last carriage came the male servants of the household, then the gardeners; lastly, the farm manager and his men. There were no female servants at the funeral; in fact, it had been a debated question whether any of the female relatives should attend, for it wasn't really etiquette; but as Harry's cousin, Florrie Talbot, had pointed out, who was there to notice or talk in this empty neck of the woods; now, if it had been in Manchester then things would have been different; you had to keep up a certain style there if you didn't want to get talked about.

And for once the female members of the family had agreed with Mrs Talbot.

The sun was shining brightly, the birds were singing; they seemed to have assembled from the whole countryside in the trees bordering the small cemetery, and their song seemed to mute the sound of the first shovelful of earth being dropped on to the coffin, making it seem as if there were nothing in the highly polished, ornately decorated box. But there was something in it, and Katie, standing between her father and Dan, whimpered, 'Oh! Mam. Mam.' Her mother had liked to be called Mam, and so she had often used the term when Brigie wasn't about. She wondered why she wasn't crying. Dan was crying silently; she could feel the shudders that were passing through his body. It was odd, she thought, that Dan should be the one to cry. Dan, of course, had had a special love for their mother; it was undemonstrative but deep; but she, too, had borne a special love towards her. So why wasn't she crying? She had hardly shed a tear since her mother had died; she had felt over the past days that because she couldn't cry she'd never smile again, never love again. All the heart-lifting joy that had been part of her nature had, as it were, sought another course, and was flowing in another direction, a direction that was going to change her life.

It was just five days ago she was in Hexham with Pat. He had said she must call him Pat, and before the carriage had reached the Hall he had taken her hand and told her he would like her to see his home; and would she come to dinner? Up till that moment she had looked upon it all as a game; as her mother might have put it, she was tickled to death that a man like Mr Ferrier should be seeking her out, while at the same time she kept her eyes shut to the consequences of his attention. But looking into his face that night, she had been unable any longer to close her eyes and her ears to the question he would be putting to her sooner or later; and also in that moment she was human enough to think, He is next in line to a title. . . . Sir Patrick and Lady Ferrier! She had almost giggled at the picture in her mind. She had giggled too, a short while later, as she bent over her mother and asked in a whisper, 'How would you like your daughter to have a title?'

Her mother had smiled and touched her cheek and said slowly, and now she remembered how slowly her words had come, 'All I would like for you, lass, is to know that you'll marry somebody who can keep you happy always . . . always.'

Why hadn't she stayed with her then instead of dancing out of the room? Why hadn't she known that she was fading away before her eyes? And now she was down there and the sun was shining and the birds were singing and Dan's body was shuddering with his weeping,

303

and her father was crying; all the family were crying now, everybody except her.

When she turned from the grave she took hold of Dan's arm; it looked as if he were supporting her and not she him.

There was a gigantic meal set in the dining room but only relatives were seated round the table. The seven gentlemen, including Mr Ferrier, had taken wine in the breakfast room; then, after offering their condolences to Harry, they had departed in their carriages.

Katie did not take a seat at the table but slipped quietly away upstairs to the nursery. She hoped to find Dan there, for she hadn't seen him since their return. Instead, she found Barbara.

Barbara was standing looking out of the window, and she had to touch her arm to attract her attention, and when they looked at each other Katie saw that Barbara too was crying.

Barbara now put out her hands and caught hers and said, 'I'm ... I'm sorry Katie, so sorry. I ... I was very fond of her.'

For a moment Katie stared into the beautiful face, the face that at times she envied, the face that had often aroused her keen jealousy, which she would sublimate into compassion because of the infliction behind it, and she was surprised at herself as she said, 'Were you?' for this wasn't a statement but a question, a question asked flatly, even accusingly.

'Yes, yes.' Barbara had interpreted the tone of the words from the look on Katie's face and she added, 'You know I was.'

'You thought she was common.'

'Oh! Katie; how ... how could you say such a thing! And on a day like this too.'

'Because it's true. You did, didn't you? You thought she was common, so common, not a bit like Brigie. You laughed at her at times.'

'I never did.'

'No, not to me you didn't, but with Brigie years ago when you first came. I heard you.'

Such memories don't die and the colour rushed over Barbara's pale skin. She said now in her own defence and quietly, 'You ... you must admit it is not a week since you were mimicking her yourself.'

'I explained all that. It's a family licence; you're allowed to mimic those you love.'

'I ... I loved her. You ... you can't understand; I can't explain myself, but deep inside I ... I did love your mother because ... and not only because she was kind to me, more than kind, getting your father to give me the horse and clothes and so many other things, but oh' – she put her hand to her head now and screwed up her eyes – 'how

304

can I explain? I . . . I am not a nice person, I know I'm not, I say awful things, and I do awful things, and I put it down to my deafness, but it stems from something more than that. But I want you to believe I was more than fond of your mother, because I . . . I envied you having her. When she used to put her arms around you and call you love or lass, I lost something; every time she did it I lost something. Oh, I can't explain, I can only tell you that many and many a time I wished she was my mother.'

'What about Brigie?' Katie's voice was soft now, the stiffness had gone from her face. She sat down on the wooden nursery chair near the table and her body slumped but she still looked up at Barbara waiting for her answer.

Not until Barbara was seated opposite her, her hands joined, her forearms on the table, did she say, 'It's different, Brigie is not my mother, she's . . . she's not even a relation. I love her, but in a different way; it's . . . it's gratitude I think, yes, out of gratitude.'

They stared at each other. Then Katie said quietly, 'It seems to be a moment of truth, doesn't it?'

'Yes, yes, you could say something like that.'

'Life's never going to be the same again.'

'I know that.'

'What are you going to do?'

'Marry Michael.'

'What if you can't?'

'I will. If I can't have Michael there is no meaning to anything, nothing to life.'

'Brigie's against it.'

'I know.'

'She wants you to have John.'

'John doesn't want me.'

'I wouldn't be too sure. I used to think he did. Yet at the same time you never know what John's thinking, not really.'

'Anyway, I wouldn't have John; I want no one but Michael. And you? What are you going to do?'

'I don't know, I can't think. It's very odd; it's just as if I have changed to someone else over these past few days.'

'Do you think Mr Ferrier might ask you to marry him?'

'Perhaps; or perhaps not. He may just be amusing himself, as I was.'

'Do you like him?'

'Yes, I like him, but liking isn't loving. The last time I spoke to Mother I said to her, "How would you like me to marry a title?" and she said to me, "All I would like for you, lass, is to know that you'll marry somebody who can keep you happy always . . . always." And I think that is what one has got to find out. But how can you know if a man is going to care for you always? I think the best thing to do is to ask yourself if you can put up with him when he's not his charming self, when he's not laughing and joking and paying you attention. Dad used to yell at Mam' – Katie gave a cynical smile here. 'You see how quickly one reverts, not Father and Mother as Brigie would have it, but Dad and Mam. At times they fought like cat and dog; he used to call her such awful names. When I was young I thought her second name was numskull.' She smiled again, but the smile was tender now. 'But all through it she loved him, and she knew that he loved her. She may have been a numskull – she was in lots of ways, she wasn't intelligent – but she was wise in her own way and she was full of heart, and I wouldn't have changed her for anyone. Do you hear that, Barbara? I wouldn't have changed her for anyone, not for all your Brigies, or your Aunt Constances, or any of the big-pots you're so proud of being connected with, because at bottom they weren't fit to wipe her boots! Do you hear me?'

She was shouting. The blocked reservoir inside her was spilling over. The tears were flooding up through her chest and blocking her throat; with an explosive sound they gushed out of her eyes, down her nose and out of her mouth, and she jumped up from the table and ran from the room.

Barbara made no effort to follow her, but she rose from the chair and tried to steady the trembling of her body by going to the window and gripping the high sill. She gazed out over the gardens and into the far distance where the moorland joined the hills, and she thought that they had indeed experienced a moment of truth, a moment of truth in which she had been made to face what she had always known deep within her, that you could love only one person, really love that is, and you could really like only a few people. She liked Katie, but she thought that Katie would never really like her again, and it wasn't only because she imagined she had looked down on her mother, it was something that went deeper, some change that had taken place in Katie.

And then there was John. She liked John, because John had always been kind to her.

And Dan? No, she didn't really like Dan; Dan annoyed her; Dan had never treated her with sympathy, but had acted towards her as if she were of no account. . . . And Brigie?

She had said that she had wished at times Mrs Bensham had been her mother, yet hadn't Brigie played mother to her since she was born, and she should be grateful for that alone. She was, she was; then when had she stopped loving her? Gradually, she supposed as she realized that she did not want her to have Michael; and also when she realized that she was withholding something from her, something that she should know, that it was her right to know; something that even Mary knew, because whenever she tried to get Mary to talk about the Mallen family, she would become too busy or would have a sudden toothache, or her leg would hurt her, always something to put one off.

Because of her deafness she had acquired a subtle sense that probed people's attitudes towards her even when she could not read their lips; but this did not overcome the handicap of being unable to hear snatches of conversation that might have helped her to piece things together.

There was no means of finding out what she should know other than through another moment of truth, and she was aware that that moment would only come when she herself forced it; and this she knew she was afraid of doing, for truth was cruel, it changed the pattern of one's life. But didn't she want the pattern of her life changed? Didn't she want to fly from the cottage to the farm across the hills and spend her life by Michael's side? In his arms? In his bed? She bowed her head and bit tightly on her lip. Oh yes, in his bed. Nights were becoming nightmarish because she could think of nothing now but being beside Michael in his bed. Her thoughts on this subject, she imagined, would have shocked Brigie to the core of her being, for in that no-man's land before sleep finally takes over she saw herself standing naked before Michael; and not only that, Michael standing naked before her.

In the light of day she realized she was wicked, not so much because of what she imagined about herself and Michael, but because of the thoughts that always accompanied this image, the realization of which could alone turn her desires of the night into reality, and when, as today, the thoughts had dared to creep into the light as she watched the coffin being borne to the hearse, she had become physically sick with the force of the wish that it were bearing her Aunt Constance to the grave and not Mrs Bensham.

Harry Bensham rarely called Miss Brigmore to his presence; if he wanted to talk to her he went up to the nursery floor where she was usually to be found, but this morning he sent for her.

Brooks informed Armstrong that the master wanted to see Miss Brigmore. Armstrong gave the message to Emerson, the second footman, who carried the message to the first floor, where he met Jenny Dring, the upper housemaid, and he passed it on to her.

Miss Brigmore was in her sitting room. She had just taken off her cloak and bonnet and sat down to review, calmly if possible, the situation.

It was a week since the funeral and not during all the years she had spent in this house had she experienced such irritation. Matilda's prophecy had certainly come true. Mrs Talbot was indeed attaching herself to Mr Bensham like a blood-starved leech. The woman was an impossible creature, common – in such a way that Miss Brigmore regretted ever having applied the appellation to Matilda – while at the same time adopting a pseudo-veneer of refinement; her accent and her idea of correctness both in manner and conversation would have been laughable if they hadn't aroused her disdain for the woman. To use Matilda's expression, Mrs Talbot was scavenger material, and what was more distressing still he, Mr Bensham, did not seem to be adversely affected by her; in fact, at times appearing to be grateful for her solicitude.

One thing was certain, she herself could not remain in this house in any capacity were that woman to become its mistress. Although she had promised Matilda she would try to influence her husband against a close association with her she knew that this would be impossible; Harry Bensham was a headstrong self-opinionated man, and even softened as he was now by his bereavement, she couldn't see him accepting any advice from her with regard to his personal behaviour.

Having received the message, she obeyed it. The expression on her face matched the stiffness of her back as she went down the main staircase, across the hall, and into the library. She opened the door and Florrie Talbot's shrill voice greeted her: 'Oh, there you are! Thought you were never comin', dear. I was just saying to 'Arry here, he should close it up, for the winter like, like they do, 'cos he's got his house in the town. Haven't you, 'Arry?' She turned her big, fresh-coloured face towards Harry, where he stood before the fire, one elbow resting on the mantelshelf. He did not reply, and she went on, 'I just said to him, as good as you are, it's too much to manage on your own, 'tisn't fair, 'tisn't fair now, dear, is it? 'Tisn't like as if you were young any more, and sprightly. What's more. . . .'

'Florrie!' Harry's voice was quiet, but although the tone conveyed a command for her to be quiet it held no impatience; he might have been addressing Matilda when in one of his good moods.

'Well, I was just sayin'. I've been working it out, 'Arry. You've got enough on your plate with the mill and all that lot without having to bother about 'ouses, big, little or middling.'

Again Harry said, 'Florrie!' this time adding, 'Go and see if Katie's near ready.'

When, however, Mrs Talbot showed no sign of rising from her chair and when the oily smile slid from her puffed features and her round blue eyes took on a steely glint Harry's tone altered. There was a touch of the old harshness in it now as he said bluntly, 'I want a word alone with Brigie. Now get on your way, Florrie; no more of it.'

Mrs Talbot lifted her heavy body from the chair; she did it slowly as if to add to her show of indignation, and she paused to adjust the bows of black ribbons on the six-inch wired platform of material that circled her already ample waist, and her departure from the room matched her dress, for she flounced out.

When the door closed behind her none too quietly, Harry looked at Miss Brigmore and, shaking his head, said, 'She means well; and you know, I've been thinking these last few days she might be right. What do I want two houses for now? But as I've asked meself, if I had to give one up which would be the easiest for me to part with? And I've got to admit, the Manchester one.' His lips bared from his teeth but not into a smile, it was more of a self-derisive gesture.

He stood now with his back to the big well of the empty fireplace and he rubbed his hands down the seat of his trousers, as he often did when the fire was blazing. He lowered his head for a moment before slowly turning his gaze round the room and saying, 'It's funny how a place like this grows on you. You don't belong, you're an intruder, an outsider, yet you've got the upper hand, 'cos you've got the money, and you think you can buy yourself in ... but you can't, 'cos money isn't what it wants, not a house like this.' He brought his gaze on to Miss Brigmore now and said, 'It was only me that wanted to stay put here, Matilda would have gone back to the town years ago if I'd said the word. But what I said was, it's the best place to bring up the bairns. And I was right, at least I think I was. What do you say?'

'Yes, I think you were right.'

'Aye, you would say that, of course you would, and I think I was. But then again, it might've proved that we were both wrong, for in the first place there's our Danny. He can't bear to look on muck or poverty, it upsets him; he's got the make-up of a reformer or, worse still, an agitator; perhaps it was a damn good job he wasn't in the mill from a lad. Still, he's promised to give it a try for the next year; and he'll be along of John, and John's steady. Aye, I've got one rock at least.'

He moved from the fireplace and, pointing to a chair, said, 'You might as well get off your feet.'

When she was seated he walked from her towards the desk at the end of the room, and stood to the side of it idly pushing papers here and there until she said, 'Katie; she is going with you to Manchester?'

'Aye.' He turned in her direction. 'She made up her mind at the last minute; that's what I wanted to see you about really.' He came slowly towards her again and, stopping within an arm's length of her, he asked, 'Has she said anything to you on the side about this fellow Ferrier?'

A moment passed before she answered, 'No, she hasn't given me her confidence.'

'So you don't know if anything happened atween them?'

'No.'

'He came late on yesterday and she wouldn't see him, said she had a headache; that's one thing she's learned, the ladies' excuse, a headache; meaning no offence to you.' He gave her a sharp nod. 'Well, he came in here, and from what he said, not right out like, but as they put it he implied his intentions were honourable, and I told her as much when I went up to see her. It was after that she decided to come along of me the day. Her mother going has hit her hard, she hasn't taken it like the rest, no crying that I've seen. But with regard to the Ferrier chap, I can't understand it. She seemed all for him up to a week or so ago, and I don't mind telling you on the quiet I thought it would have been a damn good match. What is more, I like the fellow. He's almost twice her age, admitted, but that's not a bad thing. What do you say?'

'No, it isn't a bad thing.'

'I don't mean about age, I mean about the man himself and the match.'

'It would be very good on both sides; she'd make him an excellent wife.'

'Aye, but you're thinking along the lines that she could pass herself, and there's all credit due to you for fittin' her for that kind of life. Aw well' – he pulled from his waistcoat pocket a heavy gold watch and, clicking the case open, looked at the bold lettered face and said, 'Time's running on, we want to make the town afore dark, I'd better be putting a move on. I just wanted to say one thing further; will you keep an eye on the place while I'm away? It may be a fortnight or more afore I'm back; I've already told Brooks to refer to you for anything he might want. And I think you could give an eye to the household accounts if you've a minute, they're getting staggerin'. The amount of tea that's used in the kitchen, they must be washin' in it. I've an idea there's quite a bit of stuff going out on the side. They get their perks, and I'm generous with them at that, but I won't stand being done; I can't bear to be made a monkey out of; so will you look into it?'

She had risen from the chair, and she said quietly, 'I'll attend to the accounts, but you'll understand that I cannot go over Brooks's head and investigate unless I have your authority. If you remember, I warned you that this situation might arise when you decided not to engage another housekeeper or steward after Mrs Fairweather left.'

'Aye, you did, I know you did.' He was walking away from her now. 'And you needn't rub it in. Yes, you have my authority to investigate all you like, and I'll tell him that afore I go. And if you think it will help

310

matters' – he half turned towards her now – 'you can see about engaging a housekeeper because I can't expect to keep putting the load on you. But for how long she'll be here God knows, with the state me mind's in.'

He turned more fully towards her now and finished quietly, 'What I meant to say straightaway was, thanks for all you've done this past week, seeing to the crowd of them and everything. You impressed them, you did that, although I think they were a bit frightened of you.' Again his lips moved from his teeth. 'You know something?' His voice dropped low in his throat as he ended, 'They're my folks but I was glad to see the back of them. Funny how your ideas change. But a little of them goes a long way now. And yet I'm ashamed of meself, thinking along those lines. Money's a curse you know. You know that? It is' – he nodded slowly at her – 'it's a curse, it makes you so that you're neither flesh, fish, nor fowl. . . . So long for the present, I'll be seeing you.'

Flesh, fish, nor fowl. She turned and moved slowly back up the room towards the desk and, seating herself in a leather chair, she drew the scattered accounts towards her.

He had left her with the unenviable job of curbing extravagance and putting a stop to pilfering, and of choosing a suitable housekeeper, one capable of keeping Brooks in his place. And why would she be doing this? Merely to set the house in order for a new mistress after a suitable lapse of time. And most likely it would be that obnoxious creature who, because of their common ancestry and her past experience of men, would, as Matilda had prophesied, hook him on the rebound.

Well, there was one thing certain, the day that woman came permanently into the Hall would be the last time she herself would set foot in it.

PART THREE

Daniel

IT WAS NOW OVER THREE MONTHS since Matilda had died
and during that time Harry had spent only four week-ends at the
Hall, on two of which he was accompanied by Mrs Talbot; John's
visits, too, had been fewer; only Dan had come every other week-end.

As for Katie, she had stayed five weeks in Manchester before paying
a visit to the Hall, and after only one week she had returned to
Manchester because, she gave Miss Brigmore to understand, she had
taken up various interests there; one of which she was sure would gain
her approval in that it had to do with education. She was, she said,
teaching girls and women to write their names and addresses, as she
considered it demeaning that any human being should be identified by
an unidentifiable cross.

Of all the people and things affected by Matilda's death, and many
were, Katie and her reaction were to Miss Brigmore the most mystifying. More mystifying still was the very fact that a person of such lowly
birth, and one so utterly devoid of education or culture of any kind as
Matilda had been, should now be influencing a number of people, in
such a way as to alter their lives.

That she herself had come under this influence was more than she
cared to admit, but it added to the unexplainable situation when she
posed herself the question, Was education so necessary after all for
human happiness?

One thing Miss Brigmore was extremely grateful for during these
trying weeks of being in sole charge of the Hall was that Barbara
seemed to be making an effort to co-operate, in that her temper was
more even and that they had on several occasions talked like two
amicable companions.

On one special occasion when Barbara had re-opened the delicate
subject surrounding Michael's birth, she had thought it wise to tell her
the truth so that she might view Constance in a more friendly and
understanding light. It was true, she said, as Barbara had discovered,

315

that Michael was not the son of Donald Radlet but of his brother Matthew. Constance and Matthew had discovered that they loved each other when they were forced to take shelter from a storm in the old ruined house on the fell. Barbara had sat enraptured during the telling, only breaking in to ask that things might be explained more fully on her fingers. One such point she had to make clear to her was that Michael had not been born in the ruined house up in the hills, Barbara had misunderstood her on this. She had not gone on to explain that he was merely conceived there. She had ended by saying, 'You must never, never voice this. Promise me, now promise me, Barbara, that under no circumstances will you ever speak of this again. You discovered the truth by accident, and it is a secret you must keep to yourself.'

Barbara had not promised immediately, but said, 'Michael's no relation to the Mallens at all then? If Aunt Constance's husband was not Michael's father then Thomas Mallen was not his grandfather, then we are not even distantly related through my father being Thomas's brother – we're just cousins on our mothers' side?'

Miss Brigmore had taken some time to answer, stooping first to attend to her shoe lace before she had said slowly, 'No, he is no relation.' She had surrendered her last defence, at least in this sector of her private war, and she sighed deeply before she said again, 'But now I ask you once more to promise me, Barbara.'

Barbara had promised, and life had run very smoothly in the cottage since that night.

But Michael's own attitude towards Barbara puzzled Miss Brigmore at times for although he always appeared pleased to see her wherever they met, whether at the farm or the cottage, it seemed that he was merely humouring her and that his show of affection was drawn from him because of her affliction. Yet at other times when she watched them walking together and she could not overhear what they were saying, she imagined she could detect an affinity between them expressed merely by their proximity to each other. But what gave her hope that his affection was nothing more than brotherly was that he was in his twentieth year and if he were going to speak surely he would have done it before now.

And John? She was disappointed in John; she had pinned her hopes on John for his manner towards Barbara had always been very affectionate. But he had scarcely been home since his mother died. Yet, perhaps it was the pressure of business that was keeping him away at the moment, rather than his recent bereavement. In any case, under the circumstances it would not have been correct to make a fuss of Barbara, and he always made a fuss of her when they met. But let her ask herself a straight question; did he pay her more attention than he did others? She couldn't answer this because everyone was considerate for her; her looks plus her affliction seemed to draw men to her; all except Dan.

But there, she herself had never understood Dan; he had been one apart even as a child. Dan had been an obstinate, rebellious boy and had grown into an obstinate, rebellious young man, as his father only too well knew. She was finding his presence, when he visited home, more and more annoying, for he had developed the habit of drawing her into arguments with regard to class and social conditions. . . . Why should there be three classes of travel on the railway he demanded to know. Some of the compartments weren't fit for pigs to travel in, and he knew because he had travelled by all three. Eight hours from Manchester on wooden seats in a freezing box, would she like it? And why should one human being have to raise his hat and address another as 'sir' just because the 'sir' was driving in the carriage and the man was pulling down the steps for him to alight, or holding his horse's head. Things weren't right, wealth was badly distributed.

She had the idea that if Master Dan did not curb his tongue he would find himself in trouble before many years had passed over his head. Yet looking back, she recalled the time when she had found him interesting because of his lively mind. But minds needed to be kept under control, especially when they tended to be influenced by radical ideas.

There were times since Matilda's death when Miss Brigmore thought that she would gladly sever her connections with the family and retire to the cottage and live out her life quietly. Yet this thought would always be attacked by another; to do so would be dire ingratitude. Anyway, it would not be possible as the arrangement stood now, for Harry Bensham, in his generosity to her, had in a way elicited from her an unwritten agreement that she would help in the administration of the house for as long as she were needed.

It was not unusual for any member of the family to turn up unexpectedly, so on this particular Saturday morning in late September when Miss Brigmore entered the Hall she was not altogether surprised to see Katie descending the stairs, and she greeted her warmly, even forgetting to thank Armstrong when he relieved her of her cloak; hurrying forward, she said, 'When did you arrive, you must have got in very late? I did not leave until about seven last evening.'

'Oh, we arrived about nine. How are you?' They were walking towards the breakfast room now.

'I'm very well. And you?'

'Oh, I'm fine.'

Miss Brigmore looked at Katie, and confirmed in her mind that she did look fine. Her cheeks were red, her complexion clear, her eyes bright, her abundant hair glossy. She looked as she used to look; it was only her manner that had changed. There was a covert defiance in it, as if they were at loggerheads but being polite about it. But this was not so, for she was very fond of Katie.

'Is your father with you?'

'No.'

They had entered the breakfast room where Brooks was placing a large covered dish on the sideboard. He turned towards them and said, 'Good-mornin', Miss Katie . . . Good-mornin', miss.' The last was addressed to Miss Brigmore and she answered, politely, 'Good-morning, Brooks.'

Katie hadn't answered the butler's greeting which Miss Brigmore thought was very remiss of her but was in keeping with her new attitude.

'Would you like some breakfast an' all, miss?'

'No thank you, Brooks.' Miss Brigmore sat in the big chair at the head of the table and Katie sat to the right of her.

'Are the boys with you?'

'No, no they're not with me, you know Saturday's a working day.' Katie made the latter statement as if she were pointing out the fact that most people had to work on a Saturday and Miss Brigmore should be old enough to understand this.

'You didn't travel alone?' Miss Brigmore left her lips apart as she waited for the answer. But it did not come immediately for Brooks was now placing before Katie a plate on which reposed two slices of crisp bacon, an egg and a kidney, and when he said, 'Will that do, Miss Katie?' she answered, 'Yes, thanks, Brooks; just what I want.'

As the man returned to the sideboard and lifted the covered dish Miss Brigmore asked again, 'But you didn't, you didn't travel alone?'

'No, I didn't travel alone, Brigie; I came down with Willy.'

The butler was walking down the room now and Miss Brigmore, glancing at his back, waited until the door had closed behind him; then she said one word, 'Really!'

'Yes, really, Brigie, I really travelled down with Willy.' Katie swallowed a mouthful of bacon, then glanced sideways at Miss Brigmore. 'Terrible, isn't it? I spent eight hours with the butler's son; no, nearer ten by the time we got here.'

Miss Brigmore swallowed, then swallowed again before she said stiffly, 'I don't know what you're trying to prove, Katie, but I can only tell you that if you're not embarrassing yourself, you are embarrassing others, and not least of all Brooks.'

'Brooks?' Katie brought out the word on a high laugh. 'Me embarrass Brooks because I travelled with his son? You don't know Brooks, Brigie; you never have.'

Miss Brigmore eased herself back into the chair and sat stiffly upright, and she allowed a period of time to pass before she said, 'And I'm beginning to think that I don't know you and never have.'

'That could be.' The words were flat, ordinary sounding. Then the tone changed as if a sharp gust of wind had blown open a door, and Katie's voice now was harsh, Miss Brigmore would have said commonly strident, as she said rapidly, 'You've lived in a cocoon all your life, Brigie, and like all the people who've lived in this house before us you're half dead, you don't know what is going on in the world. I was saved, we were all saved, all our family, because we were born in Manchester and our threads – and that's a big pun – the cotton threads drew us back there. It seems impossible to believe that you're shocked because I travelled in a train with a man whose father is a butler; you wouldn't have minded in the least if it had been Mr Pat Ferrier, would you? Before Mother died I spent a full day with him and that didn't turn anyone's hair white, but because it's Willy, whom I've known all my life, it comes under the heading of lack of decorum. . . .'

As suddenly as her tirade had begun so it stopped, and her whole manner changing, she put out her hand and grasped Miss Brigmore's arm and, her voice soft now, she said, 'Oh, I'm sorry; I'm sorry, Brigie. Don't look like that, please. I . . . I owe you so much, I know I do, we all do. It's just that well' – she shook her head from side to side – 'they're two different worlds, this and . . . and the house in Manchester. There's only four servants there altogether and it's more like home. I can't explain.'

The room became quiet. Miss Brigmore stared straight before her while Katie rested her head on her hand.

After a while Katie began to speak. Her voice low, her words hesitant, she said, 'Before Mother died I used to have bouts when I thought I wasn't happy, and, and then I would tell myself I was, because I had everything to make me happy, and I'd laugh at everything and work up an excitement about clothes and horses; and finally when Mr Pat Ferrier started paying me attention, and not just this year but last, I told myself that this was what I wanted. Then from Mother dying it all changed; it was just as if a curtain had come down on a play and I had to step back from the stage into real life. I . . . I know I've been horrible to you lately. You see. . . . How can I explain?'

'I shouldn't try, Katie.' There was a deep hurt in Miss Brigmore's voice as she rose from the table, and Katie, grabbing at her hands, said, 'But I must. I must. You see, you represent the, the other side of me, the refined side, and there is a refined side, and a taste for gracious living, and good books, and art, and all the things a young lady is supposed to want, all the things a young lady is supposed to need. But, Brigie, you were dealing with very raw material. We were already formed before you had us, and even when you had us there was still Mam and Dad on the side pointing out to us from where we had sprung. Don't you understand, Brigie? You know, as Danny said the other night, John's the only one you've succeeded with. John acts the gentleman, and he feels a gentleman, he's the same in whatever company he finds himself. I'm not; neither is Danny. But ... but we don't blame you, we love you none the less; it's just that you don't know the outer world, the rough and tumble of living. You ignore it as something not quite nice, you do, Brigie, you do.'

Miss Brigmore slowly withdrew her hands from those of Katie, and she flicked imaginary specks from each side of her bodice below her breasts before she joined her hands together at her waist and said quietly, 'You are under the mistaken impression, as many another, that only the poor suffer, that you've got to be cold, or hungry, or ill-housed before your heart breaks. Well let me tell you that the poor have a great advantage over their superiors, for they can cry out loud when hurt, they can afford the relief of tears, they can wail in unison over bereavement, and when they are scorned they can, as they often do, stick their tongues out. Some male members of the upper class allow themselves certain relief to their feelings, but the female members rarely, and' – she paused long here before finishing, 'governesses never,' and on this she walked out of the room.

Turning to the table, Katie pushed her breakfast to one side and, covering her face with her hands, ground out, 'Oh, Brigie, damn you! Damn you!'

Miss Brigmore was greatly disturbed but she showed no sign of it as she took the morning's report from the new housekeeper.

Mrs Kenley was an efficient, sensible woman, who was slowly winning the war against Brooks. Mrs Kenley had been in good service and, as Mary would have said, she knew how many beans made five. Privately, Mrs Kenley considered Miss Brigmore to be the only person in the household superior to herself, and this included members of the family, and so, therefore, she gave her the respect that was due to her. The term the other members of the staff gave to her loyalty towards The Brigadier was, sucking up; even so the majority were glad that she had quickly put a stop to old Brooks feathering his nest, the privilege which he had, over the years, claimed to be his, and his alone.

At this particular meeting Miss Brigmore informed Mrs Kenley that she would not be staying to either lunch or dinner, nor would she be in tomorrow, but she could be expected on Monday morning. She trusted that Mrs Kenley would see to the comfort of Miss Bensham.

Mrs Kenley said she would indeed, and she assured her she would find everything to her satisfaction when she returned on Monday and that she hoped she would enjoy her rest.

Miss Brigmore thanked Mrs Kenley, and Mrs Kenley thanked Miss Brigmore, then departed, accompanied by the rustle of her black alpaca skirt.

The library to herself, Miss Brigmore sat for a moment stiffly upright in her chair; then rising, she went up to the nursery, where she stayed for an hour before going downstairs again, collecting her hat and cloak and leaving the Hall.

Her departure looked unhurried, as she intended it should.

She knew that Katie, when she discovered that she had gone to the cottage without leaving any verbal message, would go up to the nursery expecting to find a letter; and she would not be disappointed. The letter was merely a note saying that under the circumstances she felt that Katie was quite capable of looking after herself and in no way required a chaperone over the week-end.

Miss Brigmore defended her attitude as she walked briskly along the road to the cottage, for the brief, one-sided conversation in the breakfast room had put to nought almost fifteen years' work. Granted she had been well paid – when she counted their kindness and indulgence towards Barbara, she would concede, more than well paid – but money did not pay for everything; there were such things as loyalty and respect, and both had been denied her.

Why was it, she asked herself, that her life had been made up of frustrated endeavour? Putting aside personal desire, she had gained little or no satisfaction from those on whom she had spent her life's work.

When she entered the cottage Mary's first words to her were, 'By! you look off colour.' Then she added, 'You're back early.'

'I have a headache,' said Miss Brigmore; 'I excused myself. Do you think I could have a cup of strong tea?'

'Why yes, certainly, this minute. But if you ask me, you want more than a strong cup of tea. And I've said it for weeks, you want a break, a holiday, a long one.'

Ignoring this comment, Miss Brigmore said, 'Did they get away all right?'

'Oh aye; but not without an argument.'

'An argument, what about?'

'Oh, Michael said he couldn't stay all that long, he had promised to be back by two o'clock or something like that. And you know she'd expected him to take her into Allendale! Still, don't you worry about her, go and sit down and I'll bring you that tea.'

Miss Brigmore went upstairs and took off her outdoor clothes; then she sat down on the cradle stool in front of the dressing table and quietly and thoughtfully she looked into the mirror. It was right what Mary said, she needed a change, she needed a rest; she wasn't as young as she was, almost in her sixtieth year. Of course no one would guess it to look at her. The few grey hairs that appeared she treated success-fully with cold tea, and now they were hardly distinguishable from the natural brown. Her skin was still clear and although her cheeks had lost a little of their roundness there were few lines on her face except those at the corners of her eyes, and two vertical ones on her upper lip. Moreover, her figure was still very trim and firm. No; no one would ever guess that she was almost sixty. She could pass for fifty or less. . . . That was outwardly, but inwardly at this moment she felt every day of her age – and, moreover, she felt so alone, so very much alone. . . . She hadn't experienced this feeling so acutely since the day the shot had rung out in Thomas's study and she had rushed in to find him slumped over the desk. Then she had known what it was to be alone, for no one had understood her like Thomas, no one but he had known Anna Brigmore. It was only at night in his arms that she had become Anna Brigmore; in the daytime she had remained Miss Brigmore even with him, and it had been a joke between them. But now she was Miss Brigmore to everyone; Miss Brigmore, Brigie, The Brigadier – and a person who lived in a cocoon. Such sweeping statements were forgiv-able because they came from youth, yet they nevertheless pierced you and thrust you deeper into isolation.

She had her cup of tea but did not follow Mary's advice of putting her feet up; instead, years of discipline coming to her aid, she decided to read; but something light, diverting. Yet when she went to the bookcase her fingers hesitated on picking up *Vanity Fair*, which she had read at least six times before, and hesitated over Mrs Gaskell's *Mary Barton*; then returned to *Vanity Fair* and almost snatched it from the shelf. The last thing she wanted to read about this morning was the problems of life facing Manchester mills and factory hands.

Yet it was at the precise moment when her mind rejected delving into this social problem that a 'factory hand' knocked on the cottage door.

Mary entered the room almost on tip-toe and made her announce-ment in an undertone as if the visitor were a personage of high importance. 'It's young Brooks, Willy, Brooks's son; he says he wants to see you.'

Miss Brigmore put her head to the side as if thinking before she said, 'Show him in, Mary.'

Young Brooks was twenty-four years old, but the appellation 'young' did not apply to him, he looked a man, a stiff-faced, arrogant man. He was above average build for a mill worker, for malnutrition and excessively long hours of labour when the bones were still soft did not usually tend towards natural growth. He was over five foot ten in height and broadly built with it. His eyes were deep set and did not show their colour at first glance, appearing to be black instead of blue. His mouth was full-lipped and wide, but his face was thin and would tend later to be lantern-jawed. His hair was brown and had a deep ridge in it like a wave running over the top of his head. He held his hard hat in one hand that hung down by his side, not as was usual with a man in his position, in both hands and in front of his chest. But what was his position? She was soon to know.

'Good morning, Miss Brigmore,' he said.

'Good morning, Willy.' The tone was the polite one she kept for the family servants, not stiff but without any touch of familiarity. She did not ask him to be seated but added, 'What can I do for you?'

'Give me the key to the safe.'

His request and the manner in which he made it nonplussed her for a moment; then, her back stiffening, she definitely became Miss Brigmore. 'By whose authority are you asking for the keys?'

'Mr Bensham's.'

They stared at each other before she said, 'I have received no letter from Mr Bensham to the effect that I must hand you the keys to the safe.'

'Look' – he gnawed on his lip for a moment, then looked towards the carpet as if something had attracted his attention before returning his gaze to her and continuing, 'Mr Bensham wants a certain paper out of the safe and as I was comin' down to see me father he said it would save him a trip, he said you would give me the key.'

'Mr Bensham usually informs me by letter if there is anything out of the usual that he requires to be done.'

'Well, apparently this time he didn't; he's a busy man. And anyway he likely saw no need for it when I was comin' down.'

'What is so important about the paper that it cannot wait until he comes down himself?'

She watched the rough tweed of his waistcoat swell, then deflate again, before he said, 'It's a deed.'

'Mr Bensham has a bank; I understand he keeps his deeds there.'

He stared at her for what must have been a full minute, during which the point of his tongue came out between his teeth and traced his bottom lip several times. Then he said, 'Well, apparently you don't know everything, Miss Brigmore. The boss – Mr Bensham – told me there's a deed in the safe with the name of Pollard and

Bensham on the envelope in the left-hand corner. He must have forgotten to mention it to you.'

'I want none of your sarcasm, Mr Brooks.'

'Fair enough, Miss Brigmore. And I want none of your suspicion, or condescension.'

Really! Really! what were things coming to! She was, to put it mildly, flabbergasted.

'And I don't happen to be one of the servants at the Hall, Miss Brigmore, I'll have you bear that in mind. I'm under-manager in the firm of Bensham & Sons; I have a standin', whether you like to recognize it or not; and what's more I've worked for that standin' from I was six years old. I'll shortly be made manager of the factory under Mr John. I bend me knee to nobody, miss, nobody.'

Dreadful man, awful person, and yet she felt she could be listening to his master, Harry Bensham, when he would have been the same age, for this undoubtedly would have been his attitude. Then at his next words she found herself gripping the front of her bodice.

'While I'm on, I'll take advantage of the opportunity to tell you that although I might travel in a train with Katie, it doesn't mean I'm going to take her down, or that 'cos she sits next to me she'll get the smit. I might as well make it plain to you now, I've got a great concern for Katie, always have had, 'cos one day I'm going to marry her.'

She did not feel faint as might have been expected on hearing the fate of a young lady whom she had trained to take her place as mistress of at least an upper-middle-class establishment, but she felt anger rising in her at the thought of all her efforts, all her work wasted on a man such as this.

Her words were cold and pointed like icicles as she said, 'Have you made Miss Bensham aware of your intentions?'

'Not in so many words but she knows which way the wind's blowin', she's no fool; which she proved lately when she turned down the moneyed geyser you'd set up for her.'

'You are being offensive, Mr Brooks.'

'Perhaps I am, but it's the only way to get through to you and your like; you live your lives on the side as it were, cosily shut off from the rest, and you never call a spade a spade.' His tone softened, and again he looked down at the carpet before saying, 'I suppose it's not your fault you are how you are, no more than it's mine that I was born with nowt; the thing is, as I said, it isn't our faults, but it's up to us to change things if we don't like them. Apparently you've got nothin' to grumble about in your way of life, so you remain what you are; me, I don't change much in meself, but I'm determined, and always have been, to change the place and conditions in which this self has got to live, if you follow me.'

She followed him all right, and she asked herself a question, were all the men in Manchester like this, uncouth, raw, brash individuals? Was he really the cause of the change in Katie? No; as hard as it was to accept, she recognized that Katie was in essence made up of the same material as this man, he represented the other side she had spoken of.

The ice still in her tone, she asked, 'Is Mr Bensham aware of your intentions?'

'Not so far; I didn't want to say anythin' so soon after Mrs Bensham going, but I mean to tell him as soon as I get back. It'll save you breaking the news to him.'

'And you're already sure in your mind that he will approve.'

'Well, almost you could say, 'cos he values me, not only because he knows that I could run the mill blindfold, but because he likes me for what I am; I'm a pusher just the same as he was.'

What could one say to a man who openly exposed his less creditable traits in such a fashion, almost as if he were proud of them, as undoubtedly he was. Oh, she was tired of it all, worn out by the futility of trying to shape people who were already set in strong moulds.

Again they were staring at each other; then turning stiffly from him, she said, 'If you will kindly wait I will get my cloak.'

'There's no need for that, just give me the key and I'll bring it back to you, or leave it on the desk.'

Facing him fully, she said slowly, 'Mr Bensham left the keys in my charge; I will open the safe and allow you to take out the paper he requires.'

She walked from him, her back like a ramrod, and whilst passing from the sitting room into the hall, she only just prevented herself from turning around and showing her indignation when his words, delivered on a deep laugh, came at her back, saying, 'How did they stick it all them years!'

The week-end was over. Katie and that individual, as she now thought of Brooks's son, had left the house that morning together to return to Manchester.

During the farewells Katie had returned to her old self for a moment, saying softly, 'Aw, Brigie, try to understand. I wouldn't have you hurt for the world, I wouldn't really. I'll never shame you, because there's part of me cannot forget that I am *Miss Bensham*.'

The farewell had done little to soothe Miss Brigmore's feelings. During the remainder of the morning she went about her duties, most of them self-imposed. Everything seemed to be as usual except there was that in Brooks's expression that annoyed her. He did not actually wear a half-smile on his face, nor were his eyes laughing, but when he happened to address her she imagined she could hear him thinking in

Mary's vernacular, 'You've had one in the eye this week-end, miss, haven't you?'

Brooks, to say the least, irritated her and always had done. However, in his case one avenue of relief was in sight; he was past sixty-six and he was no longer oversteady on his feet, there could be a possibility of him retiring shortly. But then, it wasn't her concern. If that dreadful woman became mistress of the house, which seemed more than likely, then there would be two of a kind controlling affairs, and it would be no longer any of her business, and so she need not trouble herself about it; but until such time she intended to keep Brooks in his place, and also to make him aware of the fact.

So it was that after lunch she provided herself with the opportunity by sending for Mrs Kenley and informing her that the stewed carp had not been sufficiently cooked, nor yet had enough salt to flavour it; moreover, the last time she had ordered it, she had precisely asked that there should be quin's sauce served with the carp, not parsley. Would she inform the cook of this and she herself ensure that the error did not occur again?

Under ordinary circumstances she would have shown no such finickiness, but she wished for a confrontation with Brooks, and for it to be sought by him; he would undoubtedly mount his high horse when he found that she had ignored his superior position and made her complaints to the housekeeper concerning things appertaining to the table, for he considered the dining room and all therein his special domain.

She waited all afternoon for him to approach her; when he at last did, it was to announce in his most polite tone, 'Mr Patrick Ferrier, miss.'

She was slightly startled by this announcement and she had to collect her wits from trifling mundane things to meet the questions she knew Pat Ferrier had come to ask.

'How nice to see you!' She extended her hand towards him, and he took it and bowed over it, saying, 'And to see you. And I hope I find you well?'

'Yes, I'm very well, thank you; one could hardly be otherwise, the weather has been so good.'

'Yes, indeed; most unusual for England, and especially for this part of it.'

'Do sit down.'

When they were both seated she bent her head towards him and smiled as she said, 'I had the idea that you had returned to France.' She'd had no such idea, and she wondered herself why she'd said it.

'Oh, someone has been precipitate in forecasting my future plans. . . . Is everyone well in the family?'

'Yes, as far as I know they are all well.'

Mr Ferrier now gently stroked each side of his small moustache, which was immaculately cut leaving about an eighth of an inch of bare lip below its even line, and each hair looked as if it had been individually set into place. His clothes were also immaculately cut, the tails of his long cord riding coat hanging down each side of the chair like panniers, their colour matching to perfection the soft shining brown leather of his high boots.

There was a certain asceticism about his thin face, yet his eyes had a merry glint to them, which was prominent now as he looked at her and said, 'I'm happy to hear that Katie has returned home.'

'Oh, I'm afraid her visit was very short; she left for Manchester this morning.'

His chin moved to the side; his glance now shaded by his eyelids was cast towards the long windows as if he had just noticed someone passing, and when he looked at her again the merry gleam was no longer to be seen. As Willy Brooks had done, so he now stared at her for almost a minute without speaking; but unlike the reaction that other period of silence had had on her, she now felt a deep sympathy going out towards this man. She did not know what kind of a life he had led when abroad, she only knew that he had loved his first wife and lost her so early in their marriage, and he must have seen in Katie a chance of reviving that brief happiness. She did not think of Constance in connection with him at the moment.

'Brigie – I may call you that, may I not?'

'Yes, Pat, of course you may.'

'May I also ask you a very straightforward question?'

Unblinking, she stared at him before answering, 'Yes, yes, of course.'

'And expect a straightforward answer?' His voice was very low now.

Again she paused before saying, 'Yes, if ... if I consider it expedient.'

'Only that?'

'Please ask me the question.'

The leather reinforcing the inside legs of his riding breeches squeaked slightly as it moved against the silk tapestry of the chair before he said, 'Is Katie purposely avoiding me?'

Expediency; there were many ways this word could be adapted; using expediency she could hedge, she could lie tactfully, or she could lie outright saying she knew nothing of Katie's intentions. What she did say was, 'I think so.'

He moved his head twice in small nods before he said, 'Can you give me the reason for it?'

'No, not really; except that after her mother died her attitude to life

327

seemed to change; she considered this' – she spread out her hands to indicate the drawing room – 'and what the house stood for as too great a contrast to the lives that some people are forced to live. I . . . I think with her mother's passing she may have recalled much too vividly her early beginnings.'

'She hasn't gone back to live under those conditions?' His face was stretched in enquiry now, and she shook her head and said, 'Oh no, no; but she is busying herself with what is usually' – she gave a slight shrug of her shoulders now – 'termed good works.'

'Well, she must not be criticized for that. But I cannot see her changed opinions in that direction as an entire reason for avoiding me. Do you not know of any other, a new interest perhaps?'

She picked up the inference in his voice and replied, 'Yes, a new interest perhaps.'

'Oh.' Again his finger went to his moustache, but now he stroked it thoughtfully from the middle of his lip to the end, first one side and then the other, before he said, 'Don't you think she might have told me? We had become rather good friends you know.'

'As far as I can gather the new interest has only been recently acquired. The first reason I gave you I think was the main one. She is very young, and sees everything at present in black and white; there is only good and bad.'

'Well' – he smoothed down the front of his coat, his fingers pausing as they came to each button, and when he came to the last one he rose to his feet, saying, 'I mustn't detain you; I have a great deal to attend to before I leave.'

'You are going away again then?'

'Yes, yes; your precipitate guess was correct.'

As she looked at him she knew that her guess had been just that, merely a guess, and that his intention of leaving suddenly had been kept in abeyance, a reserve defence to counter what might be disappointment. As she walked into the hall with him she asked, 'Have you seen Constance lately?'

'Yes, we met about a fortnight ago in Hexham; she was on a shopping spree, we had tea together.'

On the terrace they stood for a moment in the late afternoon sunshine looking over the garden, and as he raised his hand towards the groom on the drive below, which was an order for his horse to be brought round, Miss Brigmore said gently, 'Constance is very fond of you, Pat; I believe you know that.'

She hadn't looked at him as she spoke and she heard him sigh before replying, 'Constance and I understand each other, Brigie; we always have done. I had a very youthful passion for her at one time; when she married it died. It would have died in any case, I think, because first loves are based on pure idealism and idealism is never strong enough to hold up life, married life. Yes, Constance and I understand each other.'

She was looking at him now and she thought sadly, very sadly, how blind some men were, especially if they happened to be moral men. Thomas had never been blind to a woman's needs; but then Thomas had never been a moral man.

He was bowing over her hand again and saying, 'When you next see Constance give her my warmest regards, won't you? Good-bye, Brigie; and . . . and thank you for your candour, you have been very helpful.'

She said nothing. She watched him running down the steps on to the drive; he was still a young man, his step was light, his bearing and everything about him was what any sensible girl would admire. But were girls ever sensible?

A few minutes later, after he had mounted, he raised his hand to her in farewell, then urged his horse forward into a trot, and as she watched him disappearing down the avenue of trees she thought, Constance and I understand each other. Poor Constance. She did not think, Poor Pat, deprived of love for the second time, because a man such as he could find consolation if he so desired; nor did she think, Poor Katie, for although it went against the grain to admit it, Katie as she had become would be much happier with Brooks's son than ever she would have been as Mrs Ferrier, perhaps someday Lady Ferrier. There remained Constance, and again she thought, Poor Constance.

DAN ARRIVED AT THE HALL unexpectedly in the middle of the week, but it was not unusual for him to arrive at odd times for apparently his absence from the mill in no way affected the workings of the establishment. Since the staff had been given no notice of his arrival the carriage wasn't at the station to meet him, so he had taken a lift on the carrier's cart, he informed Brooks, then asked, 'Miss Brigmore about?'

'No, she's not in today, Mr Dan; Miss Barbara came along a while back to say she'd caught a bit of a chill an' was staying indoors.'

'Oh.' He walked across the hall to the foot of the stairs, and there he turned and said, 'I'm going to have a wash. Have a drink sent up to my room, will you? Whisky.'

Not being an imperturbable butler, Brooks showed his surprise on his face. He hadn't known Mr Dan to drink whisky; a glass of wine with his dinner perhaps, and then he didn't seem over fond of that either.

When, a few minutes later, he handed the tray to Armstrong he said confidentially, 'I've made it a double, he needs it by the look of him. Peaked he is; hard work doesn't seem to agree with him.'

When Dan came downstairs again he ordered a meal. 'Something light,' he said; 'I'll have it on a tray by the fire, and I'll have it now.'

The young master's attitude huffed Brooks; he considered that the six months Mr Dan had spent in the factory had not only taken some of the flesh off his bones and the colour from his cheeks, but also it had altered his manner; there was a grittiness about it that hadn't been there before. He would have said he had turned from a boy into a man, even more so than Mr John had, and Mr John was older by more than a year. He didn't approve of the change; once upon a time Mr Dan's manner had been almost chummy; now, the name he would put to it was bossy.

Brooks would have been very surprised indeed had he been able to read Dan's mind as he placed the tray on a small table before him.

It was hardly believable to Dan now that at one time all his sympathy had lain with the staff, when he had seen them as the poor under-dogs; but, after having spent six months in Manchester, he had become not only appalled with the conditions in his father's mill, which were considered good by the standards of the times, but also more incensed with conditions in mills known to be behind the times. The whole scene horrified him and aroused in him an anger which he knew to be fruitless, for he could do nothing to alleviate the conditions he saw, or, more to the point, he was going to do nothing to alleviate the conditions, for once his year of probation was up he was getting out and as far away as possible from the grime, poverty and sordidness that hurt him.

Time and again over the past months he had asked himself why he didn't do something, but he was honest in that he knew his efforts would be futile, for he wasn't the crusading type. There was in him, he knew, a soft core; how it had come to be there he didn't know, being the offspring of Harry and Matilda Bensham. He only knew that the sight of bare-footed women, their bodies stripped of all but garments that looked like shifts, working like clockwork bees in an overheated hive, caused in him a pain for which there was no salve but beauty.

Yet when he talked to the clockwork bees the majority of them would laugh and joke with him, especially the spinners whose ambitions or dreams he understood from them were simply of becoming weavers.

But there were those who didn't laugh and joke at their lot, for they were too old, too worn, too pain-racked, yet had to continue to work in order to die slowly.

Like Engels before him, he, too, drove through the streets of the poor on his way from his home on the outskirts of the town to the mill in an earnest endeavour to enable him to realize the real position of the workers. Idealistically, at first he had scorned the carriage, but a week of plodding through narrow alleys, battling his way through the stench which surrounded everything like a curtain of gas, of finding his boots covered with excrement, and more than once missing by inches an indescribable deluge from a bucket heaved out of an upper window, locked out for good and all his feeble ardour in that direction.

When he tackled his father about the conditions, suggesting that many of their own workers had to suffer them, Harry's caustic answer to his son's tirade had been short and telling: 'Put a paddy in a palace and he'll fetch in a pig.'

As time went on he had to admit that his father was right. They were a feckless crew the Irish; yet strangely, these were the ones who, besides the stench, gave off the aroma of cheerfulness. They were also, he soon found out, no respecters of class for they didn't recognize the barriers. Within a couple of days of his being in the factory they were addressing him as if they had known him all their lives. 'Begod! you're looking well this morning, Mr Dan. Now isn't that a fine piece of cloth you've got on you, as good as they'd make in any cottage in the old country. Tweed that is, isn't it? And every thread crossed with love. And you're the man to carry it, Mr Dan. Christ Jesus! but you're an attractive-looking fellow, you are that.'

What could you say? What could you do?

What he could do and now, was to tell Brooks that he was having it soft. But then Brooks had not always had it soft; wouldn't this be the life he, too, would like to give all of them, every man Jack of them back there in the mill? There were seven of the indoor staff here from Manchester, his father had done that at least.

Oh. . . . He lay back in the chair, his meal untouched. This was Wednesday; he had up till next Monday to fill his body with fresh air and feast his eyes on the endless hills – and to see Barbara.

'Why hello, Mr Dan,' said Mary; 'you dropped out of the sky?'

'Yes, Mary, just this very minute.' Dan laughed down into her round, rosy face. 'I'm the second fallen angel; I was on my way to join Lucifer, but I thought I'd just pop in.'

'Aw you! Mr Dan.' Mary pushed him in the back as she had done since he was a small boy, then added, 'Miss is in bed. She's got a cold on her chest an' I wouldn't let her up. You go in the sitting room there and I'll tell Miss Barbara you're here.'

As he crossed the hall he cast a glance towards the stairs which Mary was now mounting stiffly, for her leg was troubling her. Then he saw her stop, and he too stopped and looked upwards to where Barbara was standing at the head of the stairs, one minute looking down at him, the next running down towards him, her face alight as if she were glad to see him. He stared at her as she came forward, her hand outstretched, and when he grasped it he did not speak but just continued to look at her.

'Why have you come? Anything wrong? It's only Wednesday.' Her voice was high, her words clipped.

'Is it? I wouldn't know, I never count days.' Automatically he mouthed the words.

'Oh.' She shook her head at him the while she continued to smile. 'Well how did you get here? Did they know you were coming? Brigie didn't say.'

'I arrived on the carrier cart; no one knew I was coming, not even Brigie.'

They were in the sitting room now and as they seated themselves at opposite ends of the small couch, he said rapidly on his fingers, 'Are you very bored?'

'Bored?' She spoke the word.

'Yes, bored.' He, too, now spoke the word.

'No. Why? Why do you ask that?'

'Oh' – he shrugged his shoulders – 'I imagined you must be because you were so pleased to see me. The women have a saying in the mill, Better the divil for company than be alone with your mind.'

The smile slid from her face, her chin went up and her lips fell tightly together for a moment before she said, 'The same old Dan.'

'Yes' – he was smiling now – 'the same old Dan, irritating, annoying, always saying the wrong thing. Anyway, how is Brigie, not really ill I hope?'

'No.' She shook her head. 'It's just a cold and . . . and she's tired. I've been worried of late; she seems listless, not her brisk self, you know?' She shook her body, stretched up her neck and put her head to one side in a good imitation of Brigie, and he laughed and said, 'Yes, I know.'

'But what's brought you here, I mean in the middle of the week? How is the mill managing without you?'

'Oh the mill.' He pursed his lips. 'It's closed down until I go back; everybody's out of work, but' – his lips pouted further – 'what do I care? Let them starve.' He waved his hand airily, and she, joining in his mood, waved hers too and repeated, 'Yes, let them starve.' Then they both laughed together.

'Are you getting used to it there?' she now asked.

'No.'

'Why?'

'That would take a long time to answer. Come and see the mill and then you'll know. Yes that's what you should do' – he was nodding deeply at her as he spoke on his fingers – 'you should come and see the mill, it would do you good.'

'It doesn't seem to have done you much good, you look thinner, much thinner.'

'Yes.' His face took on a mock sad expression. 'I know, I've shrunk still further; I should say I'm almost three inches shorter than you now.'

'Yes' – she too assumed a mock attitude and her manner became matronly as she said, 'I should say you are. Yet when I saw you standing at the bottom of the stairs I imagined you had grown taller. It was a mistake.'

'Undoubtedly.'

They were sparring but sparring amicably, which was a change.

'But tell me,' she insisted, 'what's brought you in the middle of the week?'

'Oh' – he made a dramatic gesture – 'Dad thought it advisable to get rid of me for a time. You see' – he leant towards her – 'I'd fallen in love with one of the mill girls, handsome' – he spread his two arms in an embracing curve – 'jet black hair' – he waved his hand around his head – 'flashing black eyes.' He now took his eyebrows between his middle finger and thumb and pushed them up and down. 'Really, really attractive. He had the idea I was going to run off with her, so he separated us.'

She gave him a scornful look before closing her eyes and turning her head to the side, and when she looked at him again he said solemnly, 'It's a fact.'

And in a way it was a fact; his father had separated him from young Mary McBride, for twice in two days she had made him sick. The first time she affected his stomach was when he was crossing the yard from the mill to the office. It was bait time. He saw her running to a bench in order to be first to get a seat when she slipped in a thick puddle near the closets. She had managed to save herself from falling but her bait had burst from the hanky, the slices of bread spattering into the filth. He had paused for a moment, thinking to go to her aid if she fell, and he still paused as he watched her pick up the bread and rub it on her skirt, then bite into it as she sat down.

His breakfast had been well digested when he witnessed this, and so the nausea had no result; but the following day when by his father's side he saw her running between looms, then stop for a moment to scratch her head vigorously, take something from it, examine it for another second as she held it between her finger and thumb, then squash it under her nail against the side of the machine, he had put his hand over his mouth. Only fifteen minutes before he had returned from the club after eating a very heavy meal, and the sight of the girl ridding herself of head lice had the effect upon his stomach as a storm at sea might.

Looking at him in some alarm, Harry had shouted, 'What in Christ's name! lad, you're not going to bilk, are you? My God! because you saw her killing a dicky? Don't you know all their heads are walkin'?'

No, he hadn't known all their heads were walking. He knew that the body smell of some of them was nauseating, he knew that their lives were crude and their language cruder still, but what he remembered at that moment was what this girl had eaten yesterday, and the combination of the two was too much.

When his father joined him in the office a short while later he had looked at him somewhat sadly and said, 'Look lad, I've been noticing you've been peaked for days now. I was going to write to Brigie and tell her about the week-end, but you can take the message down instead. Get yersel' off first thing in the mornin'.'

He had made no protest, it was like a reprieve; as he had told himself, the only antidote against it was beauty.

Now he was feasting his eyes on it. She grew more beautiful every time he saw her. Some day when some man told her she was beautiful she wouldn't be able to appreciate it, for soundless words and fingers, no matter how expressive, had unfortunately no inflexion.

When he saw that she was not going to meet his bantering mood much longer he said, 'What I really came down for was to tell Brigie that the family will be arriving en masse on Friday afternoon, together with one extra guest.'

'Katie too?'

'Yes, Katie too.'

'And who is the guest?'

'Ah! Ah! that's a secret, I haven't to let on.' He dropped into the vernacular.

'Don't be silly.'

'I'm not being silly. I was told I hadn't to say anything about the extra guest until they arrived.'

She looked intrigued now. 'Is it someone that's been before?'

'Ah! you're trying to catch me. I cannot tell you.'

She again assumed Miss Brigmore's attitude but quite unconsciously now as she said, 'You are reverting to your irritating self. Why did you mention the extra guest if you weren't going to tell me who it is?'

'Because my orders were to ask Brigie to tell Mrs Kenley to prepare an extra room.'

'Male or female?'

'It doesn't matter as long as the room is habitable, the roof doesn't leak, the bed has sheets on it and there's a fire in the grate.'

She looked at him in annoyance for a moment; then, her manner changing, she asked, 'Is . . . is the guest someone important, I mean is there something connected with him or her, some event?'

'Yes; yes, you could say that, there's something connected with him or her, some event.'

'Oh, Danny!' She moved her head in two wide sweeps before going on, 'No one in this world has been able to irritate me like you have. I . . . I was really pleased to see you, I haven't seen anyone for nearly a fortnight, and . . .'

'What's happened to the blond farmer?'

'The blond farmer as you call him has been very busy, it's the end of the harvest; they're preparing for the winter.'

'Did they have a harvest supper this year?'

'No, no, they didn't have one.' Her face was straight; her expression told him nothing.

'But they always have a harvest supper.'

'Not always. Apparently Aunt Constance didn't feel up to it.'

'Oh.'

'Satisfied?'

'No. Do you still go over there a lot?'

'Yes, frequently.'

'How frequently?'

'What a silly question! Whenever I can.'

He was staring into her face as he told himself not to ask the question, but he did. 'When are you going to be married?' he said.

'Married? Who said I was going to be married?'

'Well ... well, aren't you? You're getting on you know. You're seventeen and as Mary would put it' – he nodded towards the door – 'you've been courtin' for years.'

She was on her feet now, her expression almost ferocious and her voice high and shrill as she cried, 'You're ... you're impossible, Danny Bensham! You always have been. You are tactless, uncouth. . . .'

'Look, look.' He rose slowly to his feet, but his hands came out quickly and grabbed her by the shoulders as she went to turn away, and he held her in a grip that hurt her as he mouthed, 'It's no insult to ask if you are going to be married when you've been stark staring mad over the fellow for years. Hasn't he asked you?'

She went to wrench herself away but he still held her as he repeated, 'Hasn't he?'

When her lips showed a slight tremble his own voice dropped and the mouthing of his words became less exaggerated as he said, 'Well, if he hasn't it's about time he did, don't you think so?'

He watched her throat swell, he watched her gulping before she could get out the words, 'Why don't you mind your own business!'

'Yes; why don't I. . . . Tell me, does Brigie still not allow you to go over alone?'

Her lids drooped and she made a small movement with her head. Taking his hands from her shoulders but bringing them together, he spoke on them, placing them so that she could read them from her lowered gaze: 'I'd like to take a ride, shall we go out tomorrow?'

She kept the eagerness from her voice but was unable to do anything with the light in her eyes as she said, in mock politeness now, 'Thank you, Mr Bensham, I will accept your company but as yet I cannot say if I shall enjoy it. Now would you like to come upstairs and see Brigie for a moment?'

He did not immediately follow her but remained until he heard her running up the stairs.

When he entered the bedroom, guided by her voice because it was the first time he had been upstairs in the cottage, she was saying to Miss Brigmore, 'And they're bringing a guest and he's very mysterious, he won't tell me who it is.'

'Good afternoon, Brigie.'

'Good afternoon, Dan.'

'I'm sorry to see you unwell.'

'Oh, I'm not unwell, not really; this is Mary's doing, she is coddling me. Do sit down. Barbara tells me that the family will be down at the week-end and ... and you have a guest, a surprise guest.'

'Yes, you could say that, a surprise guest.'

'It sounds very mysterious. Why haven't you to say who it is we may expect?'

'Because he wants to tell you himself. . . . Dash, now I've indicated that the guest in question is female.'

Miss Brigmore continued to keep the thin smile on her face as she looked at Dan; it hadn't been hard for her to identify the mysterious guest as female. She asked now, 'Is it to be an occasion?'

'Yes; as I said to Barbara it's to be an occasion, but not a very elaborate one under the circumstances.'

Why couldn't he have told her himself? He must have known what was in his mind a fortnight ago when he was here, but likely he was ashamed of the fact that he had chosen someone so soon to take Matilda's place. She had promised Matilda she would try to do something to prevent this very happening, but what could she do? Mrs Talbot was a woman who would bulldoze her way through a stone wall. From something John had let slip on his last visit she had gathered that the woman had almost taken over the housekeeping of the Manchester house. Never off the doorstep was the term he had used, and he had added, as his father had done, 'She means well does Auntie Florrie.' And now the mysterious guest was to be Mrs Talbot and the occasion, the announcement of their forthcoming marriage. Really! when she came to think of it it was disgraceful, disrespectful; it would never happen in organized society. Matilda had said she'd hardly be cold in her grave before that woman got to work on him, and her words had come true, for it was now just over six months since she had died. Well, two things were certain: first, the announcement would put the seal on the plans for her own future; secondly, as much as she owed Mr Harry Bensham, no amount of gratitude on her part and no persuasive talk on his would coerce her into attempting to make a silk purse out of that big gormless numskull.

Part of her mind chastised her for resorting to Mary's verbal level for words to describe the woman; pretentious ignoramus, would have been more appropriate.

'Shall I pass the order on to Brooks with regard to what you would like doing, it will save you having to bother?'

'Not at all, not at all.' She shook her head sharply. 'I shall be down tomorrow, and I shall make the preparations, as usual, with Mrs Kenley. I shall work out some menus tonight.'

'You shouldn't get up for a day or two.'

Miss Brigmore looked at Barbara and replied, 'I am perfectly all right; it's nonsense that I should be in bed at all.' She turned to Dan now. 'Will you be at home for dinner tomorrow?'

'Well, I thought about going out riding, and I've asked Barbara if she'd like to come along; that's, of course, if you can spare her.'

'Oh, yes of course.' Miss Brigmore looked at Barbara now as she answered Dan. 'That'll be nice. You can go into Hexham and get some shopping; I need some wool and tapestry threads.'

Barbara's expression did not alter but her voice was flat as she said, 'Danny said he would like to go over to the farm.'

'Oh.' Miss Brigmore blinked now; then again she said, 'Oh,' and turned her head slightly towards Dan while keeping her face in full view of Barbara's as she said, 'I'm afraid that would be inconvenient because of the wedding.'

'*What! What did you say?*'

'The wedding, dear.' She spoke directly to Barbara now. 'Lily Waite is marrying Bill Twigg.'

Barbara could not prevent her body from slumping visibly, and her hands gripping the bed rail relaxed. She smiled faintly as she said, 'Oh, Lily Waite. I didn't know.'

'Nor did I until Mary told me just a short while ago. Apparently Jim Waite called in and he mentioned they were all very busy. Constance is giving the couple a wedding breakfast in the barn.'

Barbara was staring at Miss Brigmore, repeating in her mind, a wedding breakfast in the barn. She had seen Michael a week gone Sunday. He must have known about the wedding then yet, he hadn't mentioned it. A wedding breakfast in the barn . . . there'd be dancing. Sarah Waite would dance; she'd do the clog dance and then she would waltz, she'd waltz with Michael. She felt the old fury rising in her again, then checked it. She must stop thinking this way. Michael had been wonderful to her the last time they had met; they hadn't ridden into town but had raced all over the moors; they had sat on the stone bridge over the burn, then he had guided her over the stepping stones and had caught her when she slipped, holding her close for a moment, and they had laughed into each other's face. It had been a wonderful day. She had never been so happy for a long time, and the happiness

338

had stayed with her up till now. But a moment ago she had received a shock when Brigie mentioned the words 'wedding at the farm'. This, coming on top of Dan asking her when she was going to be married, revived the question she was continually asking herself: When was she going to be married? It was time he spoke; if he didn't speak soon, she would, because she couldn't bear the uncertainty much longer. He wanted her as much as she did him, she knew this, she was positive of it. Deep within she knew that he desired her, and there was only one thing, one person, stopping him from declaring his love for her, and that was his mother.

He could not help but be aware that his mother didn't like her, and so he was torn between two loyalties; but he was young and had his needs, needs which a mother couldn't fulfil; yet her Aunt Constance had done her level best to supply them all, with the exception of the most vital one. And it was here that she herself held the winning card; for this need sooner or later would bring Michael to her and a thousand mothers, a thousand Aunt Constances couldn't prevent it.

She was unaware that Mary had entered the room until she passed her and put a tray on the bedside table to Miss Brigmore's hand and, turning to her, said, 'I've set yours downstairs, don't let it get cold.'

'You should have asked me, I would have brought it up.' Barbara's manner was now conciliatory as she looked down at Mary's swollen foot, and Mary said, 'Stop blatherin' and go and get your tea. You an' all, Mr Dan.' And she now shooed them both out of the room as if they were children; then coming back to the bed, she poured out a cup of tea for Miss Brigmore and as she handed it to her she asked, 'What's brought him then?'

'Just to say that the family are expected home for the week-end and they're bringing a guest.'

'A guest? Who's it likely to be?'

'I don't know, Mary.' Miss Brigmore and Mary exchanged straight looks. 'But it's my guess it's the future Mrs Bensham.'

'Well, well.' Mary shook her head. 'If he had galloped from the grave he couldn't have done it much quicker, could he? Disrespectful I'd say wouldn't you? Is it that woman, that Mrs Talbot who got on your wick?'

'Yes, Mary, Mrs Talbot; at least, I assume it is.'

'Well, there's one thing certain, an' I suppose you can be glad of that, being the age she is there'll be no bairns to bring up. Not that you would want to, for you've had enough. Anyway, at your time of life you're past it, and about time too, I'd say. . . . There now, drink your tea; I'll go down and see to the pair of them.'

Miss Brigmore did not seem to draw in another breath until the door had closed on Mary. Past it! She was past nothing, nothing at all, nothing that went to make up life. Inside, her emotions were still flourishing, every single one of them, and painfully. That was why she was so incensed about this woman, this Talbot woman. Thomas would surely turn in his grave at the thought of such a creature being mistress of the Hall. . . . Yet she hadn't thought of him turning in his grave when Matilda became mistress of it. Oh, Matilda was different. . . . But what had Thomas to do with it anyway; it was Mr Harry Bensham's business, his choice. The man had no taste. Of course this was no news to her. In taking the Talbot woman he was but keeping to his own standards. And could she really blame him?

Yes.

3

THE BIG BLACK IRON-STUDDED DOORS were wide open. Miss Brigmore stood some way back within the lobby while Brooks and Armstrong went down the steps to where the carriage was drawing up on the drive below.

When the carriage door was opened and the steps were pulled down Harry Bensham was the first to alight. He did not turn to assist anyone out of the carriage but spread his arms wide, took in one gulp of air, then came up onto the terrace and into the house.

'Well! here we are again. By! it's grand to smell the air. I think I'll bottle some and take it back with us. How are you? Let me look at you.' To her embarrassment he put one hand on her shoulder and pulled her round towards the light so that her eyes were taken from the carriage for a moment.

'You're lookin' washy; aren't you eating? With air like this and good food you should be as round and as comfortable as a tub.'

When she could get a word in she said, 'My health is quite all right, thank you. And yours?'

'Oh, me?' He was letting Emerson divest him of his coat. 'No need to ask about me; I'll never die from disease, they'll have to shoot me. You know the best cure against disease?' He poked his face towards her. 'Go amongst it, that's what I say, live amongst it. . . . Well, it's nice to be back again.' He cast a quick glance around the hall, then turned towards the door where Katie was entering with a strange young woman by her side.

Where was Mrs Talbot, she certainly wouldn't be coming up in the rear? Mrs Talbot was always to the fore. And who was this person?

As Katie came up and kissed her on the cheek, saying, 'Hello Brigie,' and she was about to give her a greeting, Harry Bensham shouted to John, who was entering the hall, 'Come on then, lad, come on, do the honours, it's your business.'

'Hello there, Brigie.' John was bending down to her. He also kissed her cheek; then putting his hand out towards the stranger, he drew her nearer, saying, 'May I present Miss Jenny Pearson, Miss Brigmore, Jenny.'

The young lady extended her hand and Miss Brigmore took it. This then was the surprise; not Mr Bensham going to marry the Talbot woman, but John presenting his future wife. The hopes that had become slender of late, yet which she stubbornly insisted on preserving, snapped and sank into the well among her other unfulfilled desires, taking with them the picture of Barbara ever becoming mistress of this house.

It was unfair. He had over the years shown an open affection for Barbara, at the same time giving evidence of having no interest in any other woman. . . . Yet what proof had she of this when for the past six months nearly all his time had been spent in Manchester? The name Pearson had a familiar ring. Yes, yes, of course; this was likely the daughter of the rival mill owner. She remembered first hearing the name years ago when there was talk of a strike. She could even recall the exact time; she pin-pointed it by remembering it was the first time she had seen Willy Brooks in the library.

But this girl; she was plain, tastefully and well dressed admittedly, but very plain; and he had chosen her rather than Barbara. Yet the reason, she felt, wasn't far to seek. Like his father before him he was marrying a mill, in this case another mill; very likely a bigger and wealthier mill – women always had values set on them.

'How-do-you-do?'

'How-d'you-do? I've heard so much about you, Miss Brigmore; I am very pleased that I'm able to make your acquaintance at last.'

Well, she had been educated, that was something; and her voice was pleasing, musical she could say; and now she was smiling she did not look so plain. She could imagine that she could be of a kindly nature.

'Come on, come on, what are we standing here for?' Harry was shouting across the hall now. 'You take Jenny up to her room, Katie. By the way' – he turned round and looked towards Miss Brigmore – 'where's our Dan? And for that matter, where's Barbara?'

'They're . . . they're both up in the nursery. . . .'

'What! at their age?' He put his head back and let out a great bellow of a laugh. Then noticing the expression on Miss Brigmore's face, he flapped his hand at her and said, 'All right, all right, bad joke, but what they doin' up there?'

Miss Brigmore hesitated before giving him the answer. 'Dan is doing a sketch of Barbara in an endeavour to paint her portrait.'

342

'Paint her portrait! Well! Well! And by, you've said it, endeavour's the right word, for if he's as successful at that as he is at learnin' a business. . . . Aw! what's the good of keeping on. Come in here a minute' – he jerked his head in her direction – 'I want a word with you afore I go upstairs. And as for you, Katie' – he now called towards his daughter where she was mounting the stairs with Miss Pearson – 'when you've got the dust off you, you'd better take Jenny up to the nursery an' introduce her to Barbara; better get it over.'

On this he turned and walked towards the library, and after a moment Miss Brigmore followed him. Having to pass John on the way, she stopped and, looking straight at him, she said, 'On short acquaintance I approve your choice, John.'

A flush spread over his face, and she could not say whether it was caused through embarrassment or pride; but he answered warmly, 'Thanks Brigie, thanks.'

She went into the library, and after closing the door quietly she walked down the room to where Harry was already standing in his usual position with his back to the fire, his hands on his buttocks. As she moved towards him she felt she had been doing this at intervals all her life, walking down the room towards this man whilst her body stiffened and she bristled inwardly in preparation for the attack he would undoubtedly make on her senses. And today as on other occasions, she did not find the preparation had been unnecessary, for the first thing he said to her was, 'I've just told Katie to break it to Barbara. But she'll take it all right, that one, 'cos she's got her sights set elsewhere; it's you it should have been broken to, isn't it, 'cos you thought John had his sights on her? In fact, in a way, I could say you've been working at it.'

'Really Mr Bensham!' Her indignation was evident, in her voice, her face, her back. 'You are insulting. You. . . .'

'Aw now, Brigie, you know me; a spade's a spade. And be honest. Come on, woman, be honest, you hoped to make a match of them. And you know, I'm going to tell you something, I did an' all. I was a bit put off by her deafness at first, but then I thought, He likes her, he understands her, he's got sympathy for her; and her drawback's more than made up for by how she looks, because she looks a spanker, like a thoroughbred. But over the past year or so I've realized it was just sympathy that's all, 'cos she draws it from you, you know; she draws it from everybody.'

He stared at her now in silence and when she made no effort to speak he slapped at his buttocks and the sound was like that on a horse's flank. Then, half apologetically, he said, 'I'm not saying mind I wasn't pleased about him wanting Jenny, and for more reasons than one, because I'm human. She's an only child, she'll come into the mill.

Yet with him, it was meself over again as I once told you, but in a different way, 'cos he's taken Jenny because he loves her, and that's the right reason. And you know, when he first let on to me about this I thought of you. Aye, you were my first thought. She's going to be disappointed, I thought.'

She closed her eyes, then opened them sharply to find him standing in front of her, his hand coming out to take her arm.

'Come on, come on, sit down. Get out of your stays.'

Really! Really! Why did she submit to it?

She submitted to being led to the couch and plonked down as if she were a wilful child; and there he was standing in front of her grinning; then turning abruptly away he said, 'Let's have a drink, I'm parched.'

He pulled the tasselled cord to the side of the fireplace and a moment later, when Brooks entered, he said, 'Get us a drink, Brooks. Bring the decanter.'

'No spirits for me, thank you.' Her voice was merely a stiff whisper, and he said, 'Oh aye.' Then turning to Brooks again, he added, 'Put some wine on the tray, a port.'

'Aye, sir.'

'How you gettin' on with him now?' Harry jerked his head towards the door, and Miss Brigmore jerked her chin upwards as she asked, 'Getting on with whom?'

'Brooks, of course; you know who I mean, don't play dumb; Brooks. You've never hit it off, now have you? No. Anyway, I was thinkin' about him recently. He's gettin' past it; I'll pension him off soon. And while I'm on about him I'd better tell you something else. It won't come as such a shock to you as it might have done because, as I understand it, he baited you in your den.'

'Baited me in my ... what do you mean?'

'I mean Willy. You know I do, don't you? Now mind. . . .' He now came and sat on the couch, not beside her but in the further corner away from her, and he leant his head against the back of it before he said, 'I can't say I was over the moon at his proposal, not that I've got anything against him, he's a good lad is Willy, but at the same time I'd somehow set me sights high for our Katie. I thought she had an' all, and I'm positive that she would have made a go of it with Ferrier if Matilda hadn't gone when she did. But it was something in her going that changed our Katie. She's tried to explain it to me, but I'm not one for delving into the cobwebs of the mind. She says now she wants to live out her mother's life, do the things she knew her mother wanted to do deep within her, make things better for people like her mother used to be when she was young. Well, that was all very well, and worthy, but I put my side of it to her and told her what's being done in the town. I pointed out to her there was an Education Act gone through these last few years, and a lot of my younger lasses could read. I won't say they favour the *Saturday Review*, but I've caught them pushing *Ella the Outcast* into their busts – and *Gentleman Jack* an' all. I've had a laugh about that one many's the time.' He put his head back and laughed now while she continued to stare at him, then he went on, 'Well, like I told her, Manchester hasn't just been dug up, there's dozens of bookshops all over the place if folks want to read, but like all reformers she's got the idea that they've been sitting in the mud just waitin' for her to come and clean them up, mentally like – I won't say that some of them don't want cleanin' up otherwise – but that'll come in time, but being Katie she's not content to wait, nothing's being done in the way she thinks it should be. . . . You know, her and our Danny are a pair, but with this difference, she goes in head first and does something about it, while our Danny turns and runs. It's funny isn't it, them both thinking alike, having the same things at heart, and yet it's the woman, the female, doin' the pushing. That's something that's hard for me to stomach you know. . . . Oh' – he leant towards her now and wagged his fingers at her – 'you're not the only one with worries, I've had me share these past few months. Anyroad, I found Willy's intentions more honourable than those of some of the gentlemen I could name, for he said he'd say nothing to her until a year had passed from Matilda going. By that time, too, he hoped for a rise in position.'

He laughed now, a deep rumbling laugh coming from his belly as he said, 'He told me as much. Aye, you know, he's very like meself at his age; the things he says and the things he does was just me at that age. And so I cannot help but like the lad. You understand that?

The question had been put to her softly and she answered, 'Yes, yes, I can understand that.'

He was looking into the fire as he said, 'Their concerns have kept me mind off meself these past months. You know, it's funny, but sometimes I didn't see Matilda for two to three weeks at a time, but I knew she was here waitin', and the minute I came in at the door she would say, "Oh, there you are, lad. Well, how is it?" And with that I would know I was home, because it's a woman that makes a place a home, not furniture and falderals.' He allowed his gaze to travel slowly from one side to the other of the fireplace, then said, 'I've told you, I think, that I like this place better than me house in Manchester, aye, much better; yet that's become more like home recently because they're all there you see, Katie, John, Dan. And then there's Florrie. Huh!' He jerked his chin. 'Florrie . . . Florrie's always there, she's so big and bouncin', she's there when she's not there if you know what I mean.'

He turned his head and looked at her, and she at him, and she replied stiffly, 'Yes, I know what you mean.'

Now he was leaning towards her again, his voice a humorous murmur now. 'She's another one you didn't cotton on to, isn't she?'

'I suppose you could say so; I didn't find her company compatible.'

'Eeh!' He shook his head at her while laughing loudly again. 'That's putting it mildly. By! you have a nice way of expressing yourself. But then you always had. That's your business isn't it, to express yourself nicely? Aw' – he turned round – 'here's the drink.'

After Brooks had placed the tray on a side table and Harry had poured out a glass of port, and for himself a good measure of whisky, he handed her the wine, then held his glass towards her as he said, 'Here's to a better understanding, eh, all round?'

She did not reply to the toast but inclined her head slightly towards him; then when he was seated again he almost catapulted her from the couch with his next remark.

'You know, Brigie, it's hard to believe, in fact it's almost impossible to believe you've been married in a way – being a man's mistress for over ten years is just the same as. . . . Oh God! don't choke yourself.' He took the glass from her hand. 'I . . . I haven't said anything out of place. What I mean is, I meant no offence, I was just leading up to something I was meanin' to tell you. . . . Oh blast!' The exclamation was muttered as the door opened and John entered.

Miss Brigmore had risen from the couch. She did not look at Harry but walked behind it, her hand over her mouth as she tried to restrain her coughing.

As she passed John he looked towards his father, and Harry said, 'The wine, it went down the wrong way. Aw, I'm off to change.' Yet he didn't move but brought a look of surprise to John's face and caused Miss Brigmore's chin to jerk upwards and her coughing to increase with his remark, 'There's a lot to be said for the Florrie Talbots of this world. You take my word for it, lad.'

When Miss Brigmore mounted to the nursery floor she did not pause on her way to her room, nor cast a glance towards the schoolroom from where were coming very unladylike peals of laughter, among which she recognized Barbara's; but the sound bore out Mr Harry Bensham's remark that Barbara would be unaffected by John's news.

Reaching her own room, she stood leaning with her back against the door, her hands joined tightly together at the nape of her neck. He had dared to say that to her. It was impossible to believe. . . . Married in a way, a man's mistress! She had never been Thomas's mistress, she had been his wife in all but a marriage ceremony, she had been his wife, a true wife. Laws! What did laws know about relationships? With a swift movement she buried her face in the crook of her arm against the door and she cried as she hadn't done in years.

When the door was thrust open she stumbled backwards gasping; then, her eyes blinded with tears, she looked into Barbara's startled face.

'What ... what is it, Brigie? Oh! Brigie, Brigie.' Barbara's arms were around her, leading her to a chair, sitting her down; then she was on her knees, her arms still about her waist, still saying, 'Oh! Brigie, Brigie; what is it?' And all of a sudden she was sitting back on her heels and, her fingers moving rapidly, saying, 'Oh! Brigie, don't take it like that; John wasn't meant for me, nor I for John. You must have known it for a long time. Brigie, Brigie darling.' She brought herself upwards and took Miss Brigmore's wet face between her palms and, her own eyes soft and pleading now, she gazed into the face of the woman who had been mother to her all her life, and she said, 'It's no good, Brigie, you've got to face up to it; there's only one for me, ever, and that's Michael. If I don't have Michael I don't wany anyone. I'll end my life like you, an old ma. ....' Her fingers stopped tapping, her head drooped quickly and she said, verbally, 'I'm sorry, I didn't mean that; you ... you could never be an old maid. And if I end my days like you, it ... it will be an honour. But I could never really be like you, I know that, I'm too selfish, too headstrong. But I also know that I will be a different person altogether once ... once I marry Michael. He'll make me different, he'll make me good. I don't expect you to understand my ... my need for him, but ... but I need him so much. You ... you wouldn't know how I feel, not having experienced. ....'

'*Be quiet! Be quiet!*'

'But Brigie.'

'Be quiet, girl! Say no more.'

It was too much, it was too much. Within the last few days she had been told that she was too old to experience emotions, she had been reminded only a few minutes ago that she had played mistress to a man for a great number of years, which in the ordinary way had stamped her as a whore, and now here was Barbara trying to explain to her that because she had never been married she was unable to understand the needs of the body.

But when all was said and done she was still Miss Brigmore.

Drying her face she turned to Barbara now and said, 'Leave me for a while; I'm going to wash and change. I'll see you downstairs in a short while.'

'Don't be vexed with me, Brigie.'

'I'm not vexed, dear.'

'But you're very disappointed.'

'Disappointed, yes, but not very.' She did not add that this was not the reason for her distress; but it was just as well to let her think it was.

'She's ... she's quite a nice girl and I think very suited to John.'

'Yes ... yes, I'm sure what you say is quite true.'

'You know I wouldn't hurt you wilfully, don't you, Brigie?'

'Yes, yes, dear, I do.'

In this moment Barbara meant what she said for all the old feeling of affection had rushed back into her as she had witnessed Brigie crying so passionately. She had never thought to see old Brigie give way like this, and all because John hadn't chosen her. For her part, she was relieved that the obstacle of John had been taken from her path. Of course he had never been much of an obstacle; for she had always known he had paid her attention because he was kind at heart, and it hadn't been hard for him to be nice to her because she was pretty, beautiful.

She was glad she was aware of her beauty; it was some small compensation for the silent mountain inside her, the mountain she yelled at, screamed at, hated, and which answered her by buzzing in her ears, and tapping with a hammer on the inside of her skull.

It was a happy week-end, at least for some members of the household. As John explained to Miss Brigmore, they couldn't have a formal engagement party until his mother had been dead a year and Jenny understood that, but when they should have it her father insisted that it be a big affair. John also said that he thought they could be married a year from now; that would leave eighteen months for respect, as his father put it. What did she think of that?

She thought it met the demands of decency.

She'd had little or no private conversation with Katie during their stay for Katie seemed to avoid being left alone with her.

Nor did Mr Bensham show any sign of attempting to continue the conversation so mercifully terminated by John; but she felt he was talking at her when, just before their departure on the Sunday, he complained irritably about the long and tedious journey ahead of them and, in his inimitable fashion, said, 'We want our heads lookin' at, travelling all this way for little more than a day in between. I'll get rid of the place, that's what I'll do, I'll get rid of it.'

There was only Dan and herself within earshot when he made this remark, and she could hear him saying at some future date. 'Well I did warn you, didn't I? Anyway, Florrie would never be comfortable here, she's more at home in forty-seven.'

Different members of the family had over the week-end talked of forty-seven, referring to it as home; it was as if they had been brought up there, and not in this house.

No, it wouldn't come as any surprise to her when he told her he was getting rid of the place, and she told herself she wouldn't mind if he made his final decision tomorrow because she was tired of it all, tired of them all. One way and another they had drained her dry; what was left of her she would take to the cottage and quietly let it shrivel into old age. Mary had been right after all.

4

S ARAH WAITE covered the round mould of freshly made butter
on the wooden platter with a muslin cloth, which she then carried
out of the dairy, across the yard into the farm kitchen.

As she entered the door Constance turned from the long narrow
delph rack fronting the wall opposite the fireplace and said, 'We
simply must get rid of some of this stuff or it'll go bad on us. Daisy has
just taken as much as she can carry over home, and I said I know who
wouldn't turn their noses up at a ham shank or the remainder of the
veal pie.'

'Lily and Bill.'

'You've named them.' Constance smiled over her shoulder. 'Lily
and Bill; cooking was never one of Lily's assets, was it?'

'No, it wasn't, although Ma's shown her enough times. But as she
said to her on the very morning of the wedding: "You're on your own
now, and I can tell you one thing that men don't like and that's burnt
water".'

As they laughed together Constance brought from the pantry a ham
bone, still with a large quantity of meat on it, and half of an enormous
veal pie, the last of a dozen that had graced Lily Waite's wedding table
the previous Saturday, and she said, 'I'll put one of the rice loaves in
too; you can tell Lily to tell him she's baked it.'

Again they laughed together.

Sarah now sat down on a wooden chair and placed her elbows on the
corner of the table and, cupping her chin in her hands, she said
dreamily, ''Twas a lovely wedding though, wasn't it? Do you know,
Mam, I'm still dancing.'

Neither she nor Constance could have told you now whether her
'mam' was meant to convey the title of ma'am or was taking familiar
licence and using the word in a parental way; true it was that she
addressed as Da and Ma Harry and Daisy Waite, who were actually
her uncle and aunt, so perhaps if Constance had been asked she might
have pointed out that the term after all was one that a maid naturally

used to a mistress; yet the relationship between the two was not that of mistress and maid but rather one of mother and daughter, and Constance was well aware of this. She smiled down on the girl now as she said, 'I wonder you had any legs left, you were never off the floor for one minute.'

'No, I wasn't, was I?' Sarah's round face shone with the memory, her eyes sparkled and her lips fell apart and, her voice still with a far-away quality to it, she said, 'And I could have gone on and on. Fancy dancing till five o'clock in the morning and then not going to bed until it was light. Oh, it was a wonderful wedding. As me da said, she had waited long enough to bring Bill up to scratch, but even he must have thought it was worth it with the do you gave them. Da said they were talking about it in the market in Hexham; Mr Randall met him and said, "I hear you had some do up at Wolfbur, danced over the hills with the bride and bridegroom in the small hours." Isn't it funny how people add things on, because we set them off in the cart by themselves from the yard afore twelve, didn't we?'

'Oh yes, well before twelve; but that's people, especially in the market.'

'Did you like dancing when you were young, Mam?'

Did she like dancing when she was young? To Sarah at seventeen, she must appear old. And had she liked dancing? She'd never had much opportunity to dance. The first time she had really danced was on this very farm in the barn at the harvest supper when Bob Armstrong had whirled her round the rough floor and laughed into her face and told her with his eyes that she was desirable. She was a young widow then and intoxicated with her freedom; if she hadn't been so she would have married him straightaway. Yes, yes, she would have married him straightaway. And another man she had danced with had looked into her face and told her that she was still desirable. His grip hadn't been so close as Bob Armstrong's, he had held her more as a gentleman should, and it had pleased her more, because by this time she was weary of her widowhood and her freedom, and craved to belong to someone again before it was too late; but already it was too late. She should have known that men when they are reaching middle age clutch backwards to youth in order to revitalize their masculinity and that women who have reached her age are already considered old and should expect to be spurned. Yet in this case the cavalier attitude had been dealt with justly, for he, in his turn, had been spurned. Why otherwise should he have left the country once again?

Constance knew that she'd never again see Pat Ferrier, and she also knew that she would carry bitterness against him in her heart until she died.

Last Saturday she had danced again, but mostly with Michael, that was when he wasn't dancing with Sarah. But even dancing with Michael had afforded her no pleasure for her heart had ached while she smiled, and as the night wore on and she watched the schottisches, the polkas, the de Coverleys and the clog dances, she wondered if the next time the festivities were held in the barn it would be for Michael's wedding, and when she asked herself who would then be his bride she could not put an actual face or name to her.

The fear in her that Barbara might become her daughter-in-law had lessened slightly during the past year for Michael had seen less of her; whereas he still welcomed her warmly when she came here, his visits to the cottage had become shorter and with longer intervals between them. Sometimes she thought he was more than a little attracted to Sarah; but then again, they had been brought up almost as brother and sister and his attitude to her was much the same as that which he showed towards Barbara.

That he may have acquired female interests in Hexham had not escaped her, for he had twice of late called at the McCullens' home. Mr McCullen had been his English master at school and he had first gone to his house when, as a pupil, he had been invited to dinner. Mr McCullen had three daughters and a son. James was Michael's age, but she did not think it was James that Michael went to see, for he had recently received a letter from Hexham, and when she had handed it to him she had smiled and was about to remark on the scent of perfume that emanated from the envelope, but the blank look that appeared on his face had checked any flippancy on her part.

Then there was Miss Ann Hunnetson; yet she could not see him becoming attached to Miss Hunnetson because Miss Hunnetson was very scholastic. Even in her ordinary conversation she impressed you with her scholarship, as, she supposed, was necessary in order to run a bookshop. She herself frequented Miss Hunnetson's bookshop whenever she visited Hexham, and on these occasions Michael had shown a desire to accompany her. But she dismissed Miss Hunnetson, for even in her early twenties, as she surely was, she was already too much like Brigie.

And there was no way of finding out what was in Michael's mind for during the past year he had become, what was the word she could use? Reticent? Well, at least not so open where his thoughts were concerned. He was no longer spontaneous in his opinions of this one or that one, and he no longer discussed Barbara with her. At one time, after Barbara's visits he would have said, 'Madam's on her high horse today' or perhaps 'Madam has behaved herself today', but not any more. She realized that very often now after visits from Brigie and

352

Barbara he would take himself off for a long walk, or visit the fields, or check on the sheep, anything that would take him from the house – and herself.

There was a barrier rising between them and she couldn't break it down because she didn't really know what was creating it, except that her son had left youth behind and now in his eighteenth year had become a man.

Sarah said, 'While I'm that way shall I take a can of tea to Michael and Uncle Jim, it'll be nippy up there?'

'No, I shouldn't bother; they won't be long. It isn't foot rot, so they won't be bringing any of them down.'

'What is it then?'

'Oh, one of them had got a piece of wire round its foot and another had a festered pad; they have no sense, sheep. Still I shouldn't say that, they have sense enough to keep warm in weather that would freeze us to death.'

'Yes, Da says they save themselves by all going to bed together.' She laughed gaily. 'I remember the six last year that were buried in the snow lying head to tail as if they'd been put to bed, and the lambs we brought up in the stable. Oh, poor things.' She put her head on one side. 'They didn't know what had hit them when they were pushed out on to the fells. I thought about them for days after, especially at night when the frost was still thick, because like always the ewes give them a rough time. I can never understand that part of it, pushing their own out, it's funny isn't it?'

'You mustn't get sentimental about sheep, or any other animals on the farm except the dogs and horses, the rest are just part of a business.'

Constance was no longer surprised that she could talk this way. It had been hard at first to clamp down on sentimentality but she had achieved it, as she had achieved supremacy over other weak facets of her personality.

'Well, there's the bits and pieces; put them in a basket. But first run and get your cloak, for as you say it'll be cold up there.'

A few minutes later Sarah left the farmyard carrying the basket of eatables. She wore a green cloth cloak with a hood to it which she had made during last winter, the material having been a Christmas present from Constance. She swung the basket as she walked and every now and again she hitched a step or two as a child might do.

After keeping to the cart track for some distance from the farm she mounted a bank, went through a small copse, and when she emerged she kept to a footpath that ran along a ridge. The ground to her left dropped sharply for a distance of about twenty feet to a long strip of land that didn't deserve the name of valley, for it was more like a narrow passage bordering the foothills where they mounted gradually to their larger companions.

The slope and the strip of land was known as Rotten Bottom, a name it had earned because most of it was scree-covered, and here and there large boulders stuck out of the earth. Also at one point it had become a dump for old and useless farm machinery. Like most farms Wolfbur at one time had, scattered around its corners, old ploughs, rusty scythes, broken blades, waggon wheels and often old waggons themselves, and the rubbish and litter strangely did not, in any way, detract from the farm being considered successful. No farmer was thought to be a bad manager because he did not get rid of useless tools. Who knew but that the very thing they might throw away today they might want tomorrow. So Wolfbur for years had had its assortment of useless implements, until Constance had taken over and found that the litter in the yard and surrounding buildings offended her eye, and so she'd had it all gathered up and thrown down into Rotten Bottom.

The path was a short cut to the cottage now occupied by Lily and Bill Twigg, and it ended abruptly at a roughly made gate that hung in two stone sockets between the dry-stone walls that bordered a field.

Sarah climbed the gate – nobody went to the trouble of lifting it out of the sockets, not even the men – and she crossed the field that now went sharply uphill. When she reached its summit she stopped for a moment and looked first to the right in the direction of Alston and then to the far left where Allenheads lay. The sky was high, the light was white and clear. She felt she was looking to each end of the earth; then a movement attracted her attention and she brought her gaze down to the track that she had left earlier, and there, making their way back towards the farm, she saw the small figure of her da leading Chester and Nellie, the two Clydesdales, and even from this distance she could see that they were all walking in unison. She could even see their fetlock hair bouncing with each step they made; even if she couldn't see their colour, she knew which was which because her da always walked next to Chester who was black while Nellie was bay-coloured. Her da was bringing them back from the blacksmith's where they had been shod. It was funny but Nellie didn't like being shod; Chester would stand without murmur but Nellie would do quite a bit of stamping before she could be induced to lift her foot. Nellie was all woman, her da said.

Oh, it was a beautiful day, frosty, sharp; she wanted to run, fly. She often wondered what a bird felt like. There was an old buzzard hereabouts; she always stood and watched him whenever he came in sight.

Suddenly she sprang from the top of the hill and took the steep slope to the field below at a run that gained momentum as she neared the

354

bottom. When she reached the level ground she kept on running like a spring unwinding until she came up against a wall, and she leant on it gasping, then looked down into the basket. The cloth had come off the ham bone, the crust had fallen away from the pie. Eeh! what was the matter with her? She could have joggled the lot out of the basket running like that. She placed the basket on the ground and, putting her forearms on the top of the wall, she rested her chin on them and gazed into the distance where the smoke from Lily's chimney spiralled straight upwards. She felt so happy, so light inside; she felt she was still dancing, that she had never stopped dancing since Sunday morning. Why was she feeling like this? The answer she gave herself caused her to bring her head down; and now her brow was resting on her forearms. And thus she stayed for some minutes; then, straightening, she picked up the basket, went along by the wall until she found a gap, and went through it and over the narrow footpath that led to the cottage.

On a distant slope Jim Waite turned to Michael and said, 'Did you see that? That was our Sarah coming down the hill. What was she doing, trying to fly? She could have broken her neck.'

'Not her' – Michael jerked his head upwards – 'she's as sure-footed as a mountain goat.'

'Well, I'll believe that after seeing her doin' that stunt. That was Head's Hill she came down; I mean to say, you take that carefully at any time; an' with its face to the north as it is, the frost'll still be thick on it.'

'Well, she reached the bottom all right. And there she goes across to Lily's.'

They stood looking at the distant figure for a moment before Jim said, 'Aye . . . well, I think that's about the lot. Are we for making our way back?'

'Yes, Jim, but I think I'll go the top road just to make sure there's none over there. If they get over the burn they could make for the lead workings; we've had it before.'

'Aye; but I don't think you'll find any of them over there. Still you never know; best put your mind at rest. I'll go down the bottom track. See you.'

Michael did not move away immediately from the hillside. He thought he could still see Sarah as she made her way round the side of the cottage and his mind stayed on her. Only last night he had asked himself what his true feelings were concerning her. He always liked to be with her; he missed her when she wasn't there, even the kitchen seemed bare when she left it. He felt at peace when in her company; her face was always bright, her laughter gay. Was it just sisterly affection he had for her? Was it just sisterly affection he had for Barbara? God! he didn't know. ... Well, he should know; he had reached the age when he should know. Barbara had the opposite effect on him altogether from Sarah; Barbara disturbed him, Sarah soothed. He didn't seem to worry when he was with Sarah; there were no problems to life when he was with Sarah; perhaps because Sarah's thoughts never went beyond the farm, and cooking; but life became one big problem when he was with Barbara.

He had tried the association of others. There was Beatrice McCullen; Beatrice was pretty and entertaining but she didn't affect his senses in any way. He must stop seeing her for he wasn't really being fair to her. And then Miss Hunnetson. Oh, Miss Hunnetson; now Miss Hunnetson had an effect on him, but mostly on his mind. He liked talking to Miss Hunnetson. She had stretched his view of the world had Miss Hunnetson by suggesting that he should read more books. The names of the authors she gave him he had never heard of, nor yet, he was sure, had his mother. Miss Hunnetson was what you would call one of the new women. The newspapers ridiculed them and made funny sketches of them, put them into trousers and, taking the ridicule to extremes, made the men half their size. Miss Hunnetson also believed in unions for women as well as for men, and votes too. He had to laugh at that. Why it was only a matter of thirteen years ago that they allowed the working man a vote. She was a very odd person was Miss Hunnetson, yet informative. Oh yes. She had been the means of clarifying his thinking which had made him reassess his values. He happened to say to her one day as he was looking at a book how he envied any man who could write at such length, even without taking the quality of the substance into account; it was an achievement he considered to write words to fill six hundred and seventy pages. Whereupon she had asked him if he had read any of the essays by a man called Addison. He had blushed when he admitted he had never heard of Addison.

The next time he went into the shop she said she would loan him an old book; it was called *Selections from The Spectator*, and in it she had pencilled an essay by this man. It had impressed him so much that he had re-written part of it out, and had read it so many times since that he knew most of it by heart. It ran like a piece of poetry in his mind:

'When I look upon the tombs of the great
Every emotion of envy dies in me;
When I read the epitaphs of the beautiful,
Every inordinate desire goes out;
When I meet the grief of parents upon a tombstone,
My heart melts with compassion;

When I see the tomb of the parents themselves,
I consider the vanity of grieving
For those whom we must quickly follow;
When I see kings lying by those who deposed them,
When I consider rival wits placed side by side,
Or the holy men that divided the world with
        their conquests and disputes,
I reflect with sorrow and astonishment on the little
        competitions, factions and debates of mankind.
When I read the several dates of the tombs of those
        that died yesterday,
And some six hundred years ago,
I consider that great day when we shall all of us be
        contemporaries,
And make our appearance together.'

The more he recited these words to himself the more often he knew that here was fundamental truth, here was the clarification of all the jumbled thoughts and probings of his late schooldays, and of the past few years, especially of the year just past, for during this time his mind and emotions had been taxed so much he knew that it was imperative he should soon find a solution to the things that were troubling him.

He was a farmer and he'd always be a farmer, but he had no intention of being a gormless one. As he sowed the crops, so he intended to sow knowledge. He sometimes thought it had been a mistake on his mother's part to send him away to school because there the main part of his education had been to make him think, and when this process was once begun there was no stopping it. It would have been better if, together with Jim and boys from surrounding farms, he had attended the day school, for here no depths of his mind would have been stirred, and his main thought in life would have been the concern of the farm and the people on it.

Yet wasn't that still so? Weren't the farm and the people on it his main concern? He turned abruptly now and went in the direction of the ridge, thinking, Why trouble one's mind, for as Addison said, we would all one day be contemporaries; yet his mind countered with the statement, That's all very well, but until that day you have to go on living, and he was brought back to the beginning, Barbara, Sarah ... and his mother.

As he walked briskly along the side of the hill his feet kept slipping from under him and each time he only just saved himself from falling. When he reached the brow he went along by the wall until he came to the gate where Sarah had crossed earlier and as he looked over it and upwards he saw her coming away from the cottage, and he stopped and waited.

She was some way down the sloping field before she saw him. As soon as she caught sight of him however she began to run, and he laughed as she approached and shouted and made pretence of lifting the gate off its hinges to let her through.

When she flung herself against the gate she was hardly out of breath, her uplifted heart-shaped face was rosy, the green hood had fallen back from her cloak and her brown hair looked tousled as if the wind had been blowing through it, or hands had teased it.

He laughed down into her face before he said, 'You'll break your neck one of these days; can't you walk?'

'No.'

'I don't suppose it has occurred to you, Miss Waite' – he now assumed a mock fatherly manner – 'that young ladies bordering on seventeen years of age do not run, they have reached a stage of decorum, or should have.'

'Yes, sir.'

'Don't you want to be a young lady?'

'No, sir.' Taking her cue from him, she had assumed the attitude of a child now.

'Why?'

''Cos ... 'cos I ain't cut out for it.'

'Monkey! Come on, get yourself over.'

As she climbed up the bars he put his hands under her oxters, and when he was about to lift her over the top, he stopped and set her down on the bar with a plop, saying now, as he looked up into her face, 'I'm serious though, really I am. If you had lost your footing on Head's Hill you could have broken your neck; I'm not laughing.'

'No, Mis ... ter Mich ... ael.'

He shook her and she laughed, her face hanging over his.

Slowly now he lifted her to the ground but still held her; then, as if testing her weight, he lifted her slight form lightly upwards, saying, 'By! you're going to be a fat old woman in no time. You must be all of twelve stone now.'

'Thirteen.'

His face was close to hers, and in the silence that held them it moved closer still until the silence was shattered and the moment torn from them by Jim Waite's voice shouting, 'Mr Michael! Mr Michael! here a minute.'

When Michael turned round, Jim, in the field behind them, was stubbing his finger towards the ground.

'What is it?'

'Come and have a look; this one's bad.'

'Oh Lord!' He looked back at Sarah and, putting his hand out, he gently pushed her away in the direction of the path along which she had come, saying, 'You go on home. I don't know what it is he's found, but I don't want you to be sick all over me. You know what you are.'

'I'll not, I'll. . . .'

'Go on with you.' He made to chase her, and once again she was running and laughing as she ran; and she continued to laugh until she came to the beginning of Rotten Bottom and saw a figure emerge from the copse and come swiftly towards her. . . .

Miss Brigmore and Barbara had arrived about twenty minutes previously. Barbara had remained patient long enough to drink a cup of tea in the sitting room before enquiring where Michael was, and, being told by Constance that he was attending to some sick sheep up on the high lands, she had said quietly, 'Oh I'll take a walk in that direction because we can't stay long; Brigie wants to get back before dark.'

The fact that she had said that the visit was going to be short checked the protest that Constance would otherwise have made.

Like Sarah, Barbara, too, took the short cut through the copse, and it was as she emerged that she saw the figures by the gate. She saw the girl sitting on the top bar and Michael with his arms up and about her. She saw that they were talking, their faces close. She saw him lift her to the ground, then bounce her. She saw them become still while staring at each other, and although she couldn't hear the call nor see who had made it, she knew the lover-like trance had been broken by a voice.

The feeling the picture of them evoked in her mind was unbearable; she was being consumed by a flame of jealous hatred which had been smouldering for years and now was enveloping her in a white heat that blotted out sanity. There was in her a desire to rend, to tear, to grind her heel into the face of the girl approaching her. So powerful were the emotions controlling her that Sarah's features were blotted from her sight for a moment as they came face to face.

Then words erupted from her throat. She was aware of shouting but not of how loud, or of how terrible her voice was. '*You! You!* you're trying to steal him, you horrible, low dirty creature you!'

'I'm not. I'm not.'

She read the whispered frightened words coming from between Sarah's trembling lips.

'You are! you are!' As she advanced on her, Sarah retreated. 'You common low creature you!' With the last words her hands came out like talons and would have gripped Sarah's throat only that in the last moment Sarah strained away. But as the hands clutched at the front of her cloak and flung her from side to side, the terrified girl screamed '*Michael! Michael!*' Then the scream ended in a long drawn out '*o o o oh!*' as the hands sent her flying and she felt herself falling backwards.

Like an animal deprived of its prey, Barbara stood on the brink of the slope and watched the green-enfolded figure tumbling downwards towards the bottom, and she did not hear the long blood-curdling cry that Sarah uttered as her body fell in among the rusty machinery. Nor did she see the two men racing towards her. Not until they paused at the top of the bank beside her and looked downwards was she aware of their presence. Then the look they both turned on her took the blood mist from her eyes and she staggered back as they jumped downwards and disappeared from her sight.

The sweat was running down her face and her garments were wet with it. She went back to the copse, leant against the bole of a tree and waited; she waited for an eternity that covered five minutes, and then they came into sight struggling upwards over the top of the bank, carrying the limp form between them.

They didn't look towards her, they didn't know she was there. She didn't move from the tree but she turned her head and followed them with her ears. Their arms entwined, they walked crabwise, Sarah's head hanging down between their shoulders and her legs dangling over their clasped hands. One end of her green cloak trailed on the ground, but it was green no longer, for its colour was marred with dark brown patches, as was the colour of her white apron, but here the colour was scarlet, bright scarlet.

She began to moan inside herself like a child calling for its mother. She repeated over and over again, 'Brigie. Oh! Brigie.' What had she done? Had she killed her? Well . . . well, if she had she wasn't sorry. . . . Yes she was; oh, yes she was. But he had been about to kiss her; and she had enticed him, she had held her face up to him. She hoped she would die. No! no! she didn't. Oh dear Lord! Dear God! What was the matter with her? Brigie. Oh! Brigie.

She moved from the tree and began to walk round the copse, circling the small area again and again as if she were in a dark forest trying to find a way out.

Why didn't Brigie come? Why? She wanted to feel her arms about her, to see her say she understood; she wanted someone to understand. She stumbled towards the end of the copse facing the road, and there on the sunken track coming from the farm she saw Jim Waite urging his horse forward.

He had almost passed her when some movement she made brought his head round towards her, and he reined the horse in sharply, and he stared at her for a moment before alighting from the saddle and

360

coming up the bank, even in his climb not taking his eyes from her.

As he came slowly towards her the look she saw on his face interpreted in some strange fashion the feeling she herself had experienced so short a while ago. He looked fierce, mad, no relation whatsoever to the Jim Waite she had known from childhood and had never really liked.

'*You . . . murdering . . . bitch . . . you!*' His big mouth looked cavelike as he stretched his lips in slow enunciation. '*I've . . . a . . . good . . . mind . . . to . . . kill . . . you . . . meself.*' His great arm swung up in front of her eyes and when the flat of his hand crashed against the side of her head the world exploded. As she fell against a tree all the sounds on earth reverberated through her. She heard a voice, something that she hadn't heard in years, but this was a screaming terrible voice, like the voice of God, a fearsome God. She heard the birds screeching, the branches groaning; she heard the very air breathing in on itself. The silent mountain within her was being filled with noise, indescribable hell-exploding noise. She wanted to flee from it, rush back into the silence, away from this sense she had longed for but which was now beating on her with physical force.

She pressed tight against the tree, her head thrust back on her neck, while staring into Jim Waite's mouth. Hearing and seeing his words at the same time had a double impact on her. 'You're a cruel bugger, you always have been; you're like all your breed, you've got the streak of the Mallens in you. By God! you have. White and wide it is on the men and there to see, but black in you and hidden. You're a chip off the old block, you are that. One of old Tom Mallen's bastards to a tee, an' the worst of the bunch if you ask me. You were bred of a rape. Do you hear me? You were bred of a rape.' His mouth opened so wide it seemed to envelop his face. 'They say you don't know about it; well, I'm tellin' you. Do you hear? You were bred of a rape. He raped your mother who he had brought up as his daughter. Rotten he was, fat, dirty old bastard. An' the one that brought you up wasn't much better than a whore, for she was his kept woman for years, and she stole from the house to keep him, aye she did, silver, jewellery, the lot. She should have been nabbed an' all. Oh, you've come from good stock you have and don't my family know it. Your uncle. . . . No. No, he wasn't your uncle, he was your brother, the one that ran away after he nearly murdered one of the bailiffs they put at High Banks when old Mallen went bust. An' he tried to do for me dad an' all. And now you, true to your breed, have done for our Sarah.'

His arm was lifted once again, and again he struck her. Her head bounced with a resounding crack against the trunk of the tree and for a moment she could see nothing. The current of noise made by the trees, the air, and the birds was still tearing through her. He mouthed at her, 'Did you take it in, you dirty bastard? Did you take it in? And now listen an' take this in an' all. If she pegs out I'll come and do for you, I will. That's a promise. With these very hands I'll come and do for you.'

Gripping her by the shoulders now, he shook her like a rat, and when he released her she slowly slid down to the ground. Her eyes were wide, her mouth was wide, her face in front had the pallor of death on it, but at each side it was red. She saw him go towards the bank, then he disappeared from her view, to appear again by the side of the horse. Then as he was about to swing himself up into the saddle she heard a voice shout, 'Hie! there, Jim. Wait! Wait a minute.' It was a man's voice, one she hadn't heard before, but she knew it to be Michael's.

Unblinking she stared before her until his head and shoulders came into view. She saw him speak rapidly to Jim Waite but she could not hear what he said, nor Jim Waite's answer, but a moment later they both looked in her direction. Then Jim Waite mounted the horse and put it into a gallop. She knew it was galloping because she could hear the dull thud of the hooves.

When Michael disappeared from her view too she thought he had returned up the road; but just as she pulled herself drunkenly to her feet in order to call to him he came over the top of the bank.

Her hands thrust backwards gripping the trunk for support, her breath coming in great gasps that caused her head to wobble, she watched him cover the distance between them. He stopped when about two yards from her and she saw instantly that he, like Jim Waite, had also changed. There seemed to be no recognizable feature in the face before her for it was suffused with an anger that had given the fair skin a purple hue and made it look old in contrast to the dishevelled mop of straw-coloured hair.

She watched his teeth grind against each other before his lips too moved into wide articulating movements. 'You've done it at last, haven't you? You've always meant to; you always meant to hurt her. *You!*' He drew the word out and shook his head slowly as the echo of it died away.

Michael was talking to her, she was hearing his voice and she didn' like it for it matched the man before her; it wasn't the voice she put to her Michael, her beloved Michael; it wasn't the voice that whispered to her in the night telling her that she was beautiful, beloved, adored, desired.

'You're cruel. Mother's always said there was a cruel streak in you and she's right; she's been right about everything. I must have been mad to think that I could care for you. Well now, listen to me and

362

listen well. Read my lips because what I'm going to say I would have likely said to you in any case. I'm going to marry Sarah, do you hear? I'm going to marry Sarah; that's . . . that's if she lives. If she doesn't I'll hate you, I'll curse you till the day I die. I'll curse you anyway because it's ten to one you've left her crippled. That would please you, wouldn't it, if you knew she was a cripple? You used to hate to see her dance. You! I . . . I wonder how I came up from the same branch?'

'M . . . M . . . Michael.'

'Don't Michael me.'

'Please, please, Michael, listen to me.'

'I never want to see you again, to speak to you again, do you hear, never!' His body was half bent towards her.

When he flung round from her the pain in her head, the noises beating on her brain were for the moment blotted out by a rebirth of her anger. Like lightning it flared through her and she yelled at him now, 'Who are you to feel so proud of your beginnings! And you needn't wonder any more about coming from the same branch because you didn't. He wasn't your father; Mallen's son wasn't your father.'

He had stopped at the top of the rise, his face half turned over his shoulder staring at her. She was still supporting herself against the tree trunk, but her upper body was straining forward; and now she screamed at him, 'You're like me, there's a pair of us, did you but know it. We're both bastards. And your mother's no better than a whore, for no one but a whore would go with her husband's brother in the filthy derelict house on the high fell, and that's where you were begat. Now, now, how do you like the truth, Mr Michael Radlet?'

He did not move for some seconds and their eyes held like joined firebrands across the distance; then he turned slowly from her and went down the slope.

Once again she slid to the ground, weighed down by the renewed rage still burning within her. It was churning all the strange sounds about in her head. She wished they would stop; she wanted silence, silence. Suddenly her body doubled up, she buried her face in her hands, and rocked from side to side. The great cacophony of sound was terrifying and she had no way of modifying it.

Her silent world had disintegrated when Jim Waite struck her across the ears. Brigie had said it could happen, that one day she might hear again, but it had come too late. Her life was finished, she had nothing more to live for. . . .

The sound of the trap wheels as they came over the rough road screeched through her eardrums.

When Miss Brigmore came into view sitting erect in the front seat she did not rise and go towards her but watched her lift her hand and imperiously beckon to her.

It was a full minute before she dragged herself to her feet; then slowly, as if slightly intoxicated, she walked towards the top of the bank, stumbled down it on to the road and around the back of the trap. When she pulled herself up into the seat she did not look at Miss Brigmore, nor Miss Brigmore at her; and so they began the journey.

Not a word was exchanged throughout the journey because Miss Brigmore did not turn her head towards her once, but when she murmured in an agonized fashion to herself, 'Oh girl, you have not only almost severed that child's leg, you have, did you but know it, severed a number of lives this day. What is in you? What is in you? Where have I failed? It must be me for there was no real harm in Thomas, and none whatever in your mother,' the words resounded like a bell tolling out doom in her ears.

Thomas, the big, pot-bellied man, whose picture dominated the fireplace in the cottage; that man was her father. The truth had indeed been spilled today. That horrible fat man had raped her mother, and this after having brought her up as his own child. Yet here was Brigie saying there was no real harm in him. And she had been his mistress, this prim, even sanctimonious woman had been her father's mistress, not his housekeeper as she had understood, but had slept in his bed, in the bed of that man with the big fat stomach and the fleshy jowls. . . . And he was her father! No wonder Brigie had been afraid of her knowing. *She was sick. She was sick*, she would vomit.

Was it surprising there was wickedness in her? Was it surprising there was violence in her? Was she to blame for what she did? And Jim Waite had said that her brother – she had a brother then, or a half-brother and he almost murdered two men. The Mallen streak. . . . This is what they meant by the Mallen streak. Badness. Badness of all kinds. And she was a Mallen! But was she to blame for that?

The question was as loud now in her head as was the noise and creaking of the cart, the clop-clopping of the horse's hooves, the sound of the wind, the cutting wind that was chilling her through. The wind was made up of voices; they were coming over the valley, shouting at her in Jim Waite's voice, in Michael's voice; 'You're a bastard, that's what you are, a murdering bastard! I'm going to marry her. I never want to see you again. I'll hate you all my life.'

They were passing the house where he was begot, the filthy house with the holes in the roof. Michael himself had taken her there. They had ridden their horses up to the doorless gap and it was he who had pointed out where the tramps slept. Ha! ha! ha! Ha! ha! she was laughing loudly inside. It was funny, funny. He had come into being on that filthy floor, his mother and father were no better than the tramps. Her Aunt Constance was a tramp, a road woman; and he, who was he to spurn her? He had left her with the weight of the world on her; he had burnt out her heart so that she could feel no more, but he would go on feeling, on and on, and every time he looked on his mother he would hate her. Oh, she hoped that he would hate her; she hoped that her Aunt Constance would live in misery for the rest of her life.

The wind's voice became louder as they went downwards towards the valley, and it was screaming in her ears when Brigie stopped the trap outside the cottage gate. But even before the horse had put its last foot down she had jumped from the seat and was running. She heard the voice calling, 'Barbara! Barbara! come back. Don't be silly, come back. Please! please! Barbara. Do you hear?' Brigie must have forgotten that she couldn't hear. Her mind was still sufficiently rational for her to realize the incongruity of this reaction.

The twilight was falling and she ran into it, on and on towards the time when she would feel no more.

5

'NOW LOOK HERE, lad, what you've got to understand is that a mill has a six-day working week and that you can't go jaunting off every week-end. I've been very lenient; you can't say but I haven't. I meself would like to go down every weekend. . . .'

'Then why don't you? There's nothing really stopping you.'

'Nothing stopping me!' Harry's brows gathered over the top of his nose and he flung his arm outwards indicating that beyond the office walls lay the mill that couldn't manage without him.

'Well, what's Rington there for? . . . and Willy? Willy's just waiting for the chance to run the whole concern on his own.'

'Oh, is that what you think about Willy?'

'Yes, it is. He's not satisfied with a ten-hour day, he goes to extremes and works twelve, and would make everybody else do the same if he got the chance. Oh, I've got Willy's measure; there's two distinct sides to Willy, and that you'll find out.'

'Well, that's interesting to hear; it's as much as tellin' me I've been blind all these years, and don't know men.'

'You don't know Willy. Anyway, there's our John. What do you think he's doing, if not seeing to the mill . . . and all its works?'

'John's got to spend most of his time in the office, like meself. Anyway, that's not the point; the point is you're here to learn the ropes, and if you let hands see you going jauntin' off on a Friday night week after week, they'll go slack.'

'Oh, Dad, who'll go slack under you? Anyway, no one pays much attention to me. As McClurk said only yesterday, "You, Mr Dan, are only here to make the number up."'

'McClurk wants his big mouth stopped. If he's not careful he'll get his pay stopped an' all; that'll keep him dry for a time. I would have done it long since if it hadn't been for the thirteen he's got in his squad.

Aw, go on.' He flapped his hand now towards Dan. 'Get yourself away.'

'No, I won't bother.'

'Get yourself off, I tell you. God Almighty! I don't want to spend three nights and all day Sunday lookin' at your face.'

'Is Aunt Florrie coming on Sunday?'

'Aye, I suppose so. Why d'you ask?'

'Well, you won't have to bother looking at my face.'

'Now look here, lad, your Aunt Florrie means. . . .'

'Yes, I know; I've heard it all before, my Aunt Florrie means well. But she gets on my nerves. And why do you encourage her?'

'Encourage her! What do you mean, encourage her?'

'Just that. Tell me something. Have . . . have you ideas in her direction?'

'Hell's flames! who do you think you are, lad, questioning me along those lines? Look, it doesn't matter what ideas I've got in that direction, it's got nowt to do with you.'

'You wouldn't, would you?' Dan's voice was quiet and serious now.

'Wouldn't what? What the hell are you on about?'

'You know.'

'All right I know, an' I think I'm old enough to please meself, that is when the time comes, when it's decent to talk about such things. Now get out of me sight, and if you're going over you'd better get a move on 'cos as it is you won't land there till late the-night. And by the way' – Harry checked Dan as he made for the door – 'you and The Brigadier can get talkin' and comfort each other over the same subject, your Aunt Florrie, because she sniffs every time she looks at her. Aye, that's it, you get talking to her and tell her how worried you are about me having ideas in that direction, eh. And give her my regards when you're at it. And listen a minute.' He again checked Dan. 'Bring some butter and cheese back with you from the farm; the stuff I've had the last few days has never seen a cow. An' that's an idea. Tell Brigie that if there's none of us there at the week-end to send on some farm stuff. I don't see why they should all stuff their kites with the fat of my land and us livin' here on shop ket. I must have been barmy all these years. And by! lad' – he now nodded his head sharply – 'I'm positive I'm still barmy, 'cos why do I keep the bloody place on anyway? You tell me that.'

'So as I can go down at week-ends.'

Harry didn't answer this, but leant back in his chair and said quietly, 'You know I think I'd be savin' money if I let you go your own way now, but I said a year, and you said a year, and we'll stick to it. Go on, get yourself out afore I change me mind.' His voice trailed away; then he grabbed some papers towards him and looked to where Dan

367

was still standing near the door, and now he bellowed, 'Go on with you! else I will, mind.'

'Why don't you come down? I'll wait till tomorrow morning if you'll come down. There's no need for you to stay. . . .'

'Look, lad, I see no fun in scurrying to a train, spending eight solid hours travelling, only to get a whiff of fresh air, have a meal, go to bed, and then do it all backwards again.'

'You enjoyed last week-end.'

'You think so? Well, for your information I'll tell you this, I didn't. I had a bloody miserable week-end. Once in three weeks or a month is enough for me. And there's nothing hurting down there. As long as The Brigadier's in charge things will be run accordin' to the book.' He pressed his lips together and jerked his head and ended, 'I picked a good 'un there. I've often thought that if she was at this end there wouldn't be need for half the staff. By the way, lad – I suppose I should have thought of this afore to ask you – what's your attraction down there? What makes you want to take such a journey for so little?'

'Let's say it's the air, Dad.' Dan nodded at his father, grinned, then went out, and Harry, tapping the desk, said, 'The air? Now who is there down there that would qualify for air?'

Long before Dan reached his destination he was thinking his father was right. Why make this long tedious journey by train, and a further bone-rattling one by cart or carriage from the station, twice in forty-eight hours, and for what? Yes, for what?

His only guide in the black dark as he went down the road from the little station to the cluster of cottages was the distant dim lights in the windows.

He had to knock three times on Ben Taggert's door, and the third time he banged on it to make himself heard above the din of voices coming from within. The door was opened by a boy of about ten who peered up at him and said, 'Aye, what's it?'

'Is your father in?'

'No.' The boy now turned his head on his shoulder and yelled, 'Ma! a man wants me da.'

The woman who came to the door was surrounded by a group of children that looked a series of steps and stairs, and by the roundness of her middle she was about to add to their number.

'Ben's not in, Mister,' she said.

'When is he due back?'

'Don't know; couldn't say the night.'

'But is he coming back tonight?'

'Couldn't say, Mister, not with the carry-on. Finished his journey around five, then went off again to help in the search.'

She turned to one of the children, crying now, 'Bring the lamp!' and when the child brought the lamp she held it up high and exclaimed on a laugh 'Ho! it's you, Mister, one from High Banks. Aw well, 'tis to your part he's gone an' workin' round there this minute.'

He paused for a moment before he asked her, 'Has he taken visitors?'

'No, no, not visitors; looking for the girl he is; lost yesterday on the hills. All Hall an' farm out, an' lots of others all night. Perhaps you know her, it's the Mallen girl. Ben's known her from she was a mite, an' her mother afore her, took 'em over the hills many's the time. . . .'

Incredibly he repeated the name, then added, 'Lost last night? How?'

'No tellin'; just know she went out on the hills an' the folk from your place went a-lookin' for her, and when Ben went that way this mornin' the place was an uproar. They asked him to keep on the look-out an' he did, but t'were no sign of her he says, and as soon as he got back the night off he went again. Knew her he did, and her mother afore her, like I said. But there's more in it than meets the eye, he said. Picked up something at Wolfbur Farm, he did. She'd been over, the Mallen girl. In an uproar there an' all. I couldn't get the bottom of it. He just gulped his tea an' off he went. Usually tells me the tale he does but just said "More in it than meets the eye" he said. Big trouble over at Wolfbur. You can come in and wait if you like.'

No, no. He shook his head and tried to control his thinking. Barbara gone and trouble at Wolfbur. What trouble? Had she in desperation done something to Michael? And where had she got to since last night?

'Do you know where I could get a horse?'

'A horse?' The woman spoke as if she had never heard of a horse before; then she repeated, 'A horse, this time a night?'

'Big Ned's got one in the smithy, not being collected till the day after the morrow.' It was the boy who had opened the door speaking: 'Might lend it to you, Mister. It's not his, but still he might lend it to you.'

'Whereabouts is the smithy?'

There was a chortle from the children at the ignorance of the man, and some of them chorused together, 'Why! yon end, round the corner.'

'Light a lantern and take the gentleman to Big Ned's.' The mother was commanding the tallest boy now, and the boy went back into the room and appeared within a minute with a candle lantern.

Dan thanked the woman, and the children chorused after him, 'So long, Mister! So long, Mister!' and he looked back at them where they stood huddled round the woman like a group of little demons in the dim light and he answered them in kind, saying, 'So long. So long.'

The blacksmith was on the point of retiring. 'A horse at this time of night?' he said. 'I don't know, I don't know; it isn't mine.'

'Whose ... whose is it?'

'Jim Shallbrank's.'

'Oh, the farmer on the Allendale road. I know him slightly, I'm sure he wouldn't mind. I'll recompense him well for it. Anyway, you'll have it back tomorrow.'

'You from the Hall you say?'

'Yes.'

'They don't bring their shoeing here, do they?'

'No, no, I don't suppose they do.'

'No, they don't.'

'I suppose it's because there's a smithy much nearer.'

'Not so much as all that.'

Dan took a half-sovereign from his purse. It shone like a small new moon as he held it out between his finger and thumb and the man, looking at it, said, 'Aw, well, well. You'll have to wait till I get me things on, coat and the like; it's bitter the night an' ... an' it'll be worse afore mornin'. Black frost this is.'

Fifteen minutes later the horse was saddled and Dan was mounted, the boy walking by his side from the smithy yard on to the rough road and there Dan, again putting his hand into his picket, drew forth a coin which he handed down to the boy, and the boy, his mouth agape, having taken it, stared at it as he said, 'But ... but 'tis a full golden sovereign, an' ... an' I've done nowt.'

'You got me a horse. And now you can do me another favour; you can loan me that lantern, it'll be returned to you tomorrow.'

'Aye, sir, aye, with pleasure.' The boy handed the lantern up to him and Dan, gathering the reins in one hand, took it from him and held it against the pommel. Then nodding down at the boy and saying to the horse, 'Get up! there,' he moved off; while the boy's voice came through the darkness, shouting, 'I'm your man, Mister. Any time, any job, I'm your man.'

'Good enough,' he called back, then held the lantern up over the horse's head until they were clear of the pot-holed lane and had reached the carriage road.

That he did the journey without mishap he knew was more by good luck than management, for the lantern proved of dubious benefit to both the horse and himself. Not being stabilized, the candle several times threatened to extinguish itself, and it was only by the horse's instinct and good sense that he had been saved from going over its head more than once....

When he slipped from the saddle on to the empty drive there was no one to be seen, not even in the stable yard, nothing to suggest any anxiety being present. He looped the reins over a post, then ran up the steps, but when he turned the handle of the front door and found it open he knew that this was unusual, for his parents, being town bred, never went to bed without bolting the doors and had insisted on the same habit being carried out since they had come to the Hall.

There was no one to be seen when he entered the house but making a guess where Brooks would be at this time if still up, he made for the staff room, and as he thrust open the door three startled faces turned from the table towards him, those of Mrs Kenley, Brooks and Armstrong.

Without preamble he demanded, 'What's happened, what's this they're saying? Is there any truth in it?'

'Why! Mr Dan; we didn't expect you.' Mrs Kenley was the first to rise; and Brooks, following, said, 'No, Mr Dan; we didn't expect you, we didn't think you'd get the letter till the morrow mornin'.'

'Letter! We've had no letter. But ... but tell me, what has happened?'

They now looked from one to the other. Then Brooks, assuming the debatable position as head of the house in the absence of his master and The Brigadier, said, 'If you'll just come this way, Mr Dan, I'll give you the details as far as is known.'

As they reached the door Mrs Kenley said, 'Would you like something to eat, sir?'

'Yes, please, Mrs Kenley, but just a snack. It's a hot drink I need most.'

After standing aside to let Dan enter the drawing room, Brooks closed the door, then stood just within the room because Dan too had stopped.

Showing impatience and his voice bearing this out, Dan demanded, 'What is it? What is all this about, Brooks? They say Miss Barbara's missing.'

'Yes, sir, she's missing. Been gone since yesterday afternoon. Coming on dark when she ran from the trap and on to the fells. So ... so Miss Brigmore says.'

After a moment during which Dan gulped in his throat and his hands, which had been stiff with cold, became suddenly clammy, he muttered, 'And there's been no sign of her since?'

'Neither hilt nor hair. The staff's taken it in turns all day to scour the hillsides an' the countryside, to Hexham one way, Haltwhistle t'other. But, as I said, I couldn't see her gettin' that far; she'd be dead beat long afore she reached there, it being eight to ten miles distance. ...'

'Did ... did they search the river?' He asked this question quietly.

'She didn't go that way, so Miss Brigmore said. She's convinced she went into the hills. As for meself I'm convinced that if she did, an' didn't get into shelter, there's not much use searching for her. A night up on there and her without a pick on her bones she wouldn't. . . .'

'All right, all right.' He walked slowly towards the fire, then turned to where Brooks was still standing and asked, 'Where's Miss Brigmore now?'

'The last I saw of her was around five o'clock. Mrs Kenley tried to get her to lie down 'cos she was droppin' on her feet but she wouldn't stay; she went along home; like a mad woman she is. It's been a time, I can tell you. . . .'

The door was pushed open and Armstrong entered with a tray and when he placed it on a table to the side of the fireplace and began to arrange the things on it, Dan said sharply, 'Don't fuss with that. Tell me, is there anyone in the stables?'

'Yes, Master Dan; Howard's there, but the rest are still out lookin', but they should be back anytime 'cos it's not much use. . . .'

'Tell Howard to get me the trap ready,' Dan cut him off. 'No, on second thoughts, just a horse. And have him fix me a lantern. Oh, and by the way, I've left a horse on the drive, I forgot.' He shook his head. 'Tell him to see to the animal; it's got to be returned to Shallbrank's Farm tomorrow. I'll send a note along with it. Tell him to remind me.'

After the two men had left the room he stood, his head bowed, gripping the mantelpiece while his teeth dug deep into his lower lip.

After a moment he turned and poured out a cup of black coffee which he drank almost at one go, then picking up a piece of cold pie he chewed on it as he hurried out, then ran across the hall and up the stairs to his room.

It was Mary who opened the door to him. Her face weary for want of sleep and tear-stained, she peered at him, then said, 'Oh! Mr Dan. Oh, am I pleased to see you! Oh am I! am I! Come in, come in. She's in the sittin' room. Do something with her, will you? Get her to rest. Oh! Mr Dan, for such a thing to happen to her. Is it never going to end?'

She kept talking to him as he crossed the hall and opened the sitting-room door, and when he saw Brigie sitting before the fire, her body lost in the big leather-backed chair, he groaned inwardly, for her whole appearance spoke of despair.

'Dan.' She brought herself wearily upright. 'Dan. You've heard?'

'Yes, yes, a little.'

'My Barbara's dead, Dan.'

He forced the saliva down his dry throat before asking, 'They . . . they've found her?'

'No, no; but if she were alive she would have come back.'

'She could have tripped and fallen, and be . . . be lying in some ditch, or deep gully.'

She was looking into his eyes now and she repeated, 'Or deep gully, Dan; and all night in the freezing cold. What she did was terrible, but . . . but she didn't deserve that. Poor, poor Barbara, she didn't deserve that.'

'What did she do?' he asked quietly.

'She . . . she pushed Sarah down a hill, the place where they throw the old machinery. She wasn't to know what would happen. Sarah's leg was badly hurt.' Her head moved again in small slow movements, and as if she were making a confession she said, 'More than badly hurt, broken, and the flesh torn and gashed to the bone.' She closed her eyes as if shutting out the picture, then ended 'And . . . and then she was attacked by Jim.'

'Attacked Barbara?' He screwed up his face at her.

'By his own words to Michael he struck her and . . . and if she understood one quarter of what he said he had told her, part of her must have died then; and the rest Michael killed, for his fury was as great as her own must have been as he looked into my face and repeated what Jim Waite had said to her, and then he added, "Never come back here again, do you hear?" Those were Michael's words to me Dan, "Never come back here again." Moreover, he went on, "I've told her I never want to see her as long as she lives, and if anything happens to Sarah I'll hate her until my dying day. I've told her I'm going to marry Sarah. And that's for you too, do you hear? I'm going to marry Sarah. It's finished, the plotting, the scheming, it's finished." And it was finished, Dan. When she mounted the trap on the road I knew it was finished. She was already dead inside, the only thing that was left to her then was to kill her body and. . . .'

'Stop it, Brigie.' His voice held the same note as it had done when he checked Brooks's ramblings. 'If you haven't found her there's still hope. Look, tell me, tell me exactly which way she went.'

'She mounted the bank just along the road that would take her on to the fells, and from there she could go in any of three directions, straight ahead towards Allendale, or to the left towards Catton, or towards Allenheads.'

'She would never get that far. And anyway she'd have to cross the river.'

'There are stepping stones and bridges.'

'She would never find them; it was near dark they tell me.'

'Then she's in the river.'

'If she were in the river at this end they would have found her by now. In the South Tyne it might be different, there's pools there she could be lost in, but not this end.'

'Yes, this end too, Dan, there are. . . . .'

'Stop it! For God's sake! stop it, Brigie. I'm amazed at you giving in like this.' He held his hand to his head for a moment. 'Did they look in the pits . . . . I mean the lead mines?'

'I don't know. They would most surely do so, but . . . . but most of them are near Allenheads and . . . . and she wouldn't go that way, she would never go that way again, not in that direction; no, she would never go in that direction. He said he never wanted to see her as. . . . .'

'Brigie!' His voice was gentle now. 'You must rest, you must go to bed for at least a few hours. Look, I'm . . . . I'm going out. I can't do much until daylight but nevertheless I'm going out, but only if you promise me you'll go to bed.'

She lay back in the chair again and stared up at him and said quietly, 'It's strange how the Waites have been the Jonahs of the Mallens. It was Jim's father, Harry Waite, who was the means of Thomas's downfall. If he hadn't been overheard slating the young master, Thomas wouldn't have been made bankrupt, he wouldn't have had to spend his last days in this house and . . . . and Barbara would never have been born. Now Jim Waite has killed Barbara.'

'Don't talk like that, Brigie.' He turned round and shouted 'Mary! Mary!' and when Mary came scurrying into the room, he said, 'Brigie's going to bed for a few hours.'

Miss Brigmore shook her head, 'I'll . . . . I'll rest here; I'll sleep here.'

'Then if you do. I'll stay here too, I won't go out.'

They stared at each other. 'Very well,' she said, 'I'll go presently.'

'You'll go now. Go up with her, Mary.'

'Yes, yes, I will, I will that. There'll be another one on our hands if she doesn't.'

'And I'll stay here until you come back and tell me she's in bed.'

Miss Brigmore got slowly to her feet. She looked at Dan but did not speak further, nor did she sway as she walked down the room but her step was like that of a mechanical figure.

It was almost ten minutes later when Mary came into the sitting room again, and she said, 'Well, she's in bed, but I can't promise she'll sleep.'

'She'll sleep once she's lying down.'

'Aw, Mr Dan, isn't it awful? Did you ever hear of anything like it? You know there's something in old wives' tales, by! there is, an' it's been proved again. They've always said the Mallens are fated to bring

374

death an' disaster an' this last business is proving it, for what Miss doesn't know is that that poor lass, Sarah, is handicapped for life.'

'What do you mean?'

'Ben Taggert told me on his way back the night; he dropped in for a minute to see if they'd found her, and as he said, it'd be God's blessing if she's stiff when they do, for if not she'll have to answer for her last act. He said they'd taken young Sarah's leg off; when they got her to the hospital they couldn't do anything, broken and splintered all over it was, and the flesh torn from the bone as if a wild animal had ravished her. "It's a black day for them over there," he said, "for she was a bonny lass." And she was, she was the star that shone in Waite's house she was. Harry Waite's niece she was, but they looked on her as a daughter, and Jim Waite worshipped her, he did. He was more like a father to her than a cousin. Ben said you'd have thought a plague had hit the farm and, it's understandable, isn't it, a lass like that, bonny, to be left with one leg. .... Aw! Miss Barbara. But I'm not at all surprised, Mr Dan, not at all surprised; she was a wilful child and a wilful young woman. It's all to do with Mr Michael you know. Unnatural her feelings for him between you and me' – she stooped towards him – 'it could never have come to anything, being just once removed from half-brother and sister, 'twasn't natural, was it? Her whole life's been twisted. Aye, the things I've seen in my time, and in this very house. It was me who found her mother after the master had done his work on her, and it was me who laid him out when he shot himself. Aye, aye, I tell you. And then some folks say it's the back of beyond here and nothin' happens. .... Where you going, Mr Dan?'

'I'm going to see if I can find her, Mary.'

'But you might go and get yourself lost, Mr Dan; and it's a bitter night, there's a frost formin', it's not safe for the horse. We don't want any more trouble.'

'I don't think you need worry about me, or the horse, Mary.'

She followed him to the door and as he opened it she said quietly, "Twould be better Mr Dan if you made up your mind, like her, that she's gone. Tonight's bad, but last night was worse. It would have finished a bear off if it had to lie out in it.'

'We can but see, Mary.'

There was no more said and he went around by the side of the house, across the yard to the old stable where he had left the horse in shelter, and, mounting it, he rode out into the blackness.

Yet he had only gone a few yards from the cottage when he stopped and asked himself which way should he go? Before him was the road over the hills, but to the left of him was a narrow bridle path that eventually came to an old toll-gate. There were two paths beyond the gate, and both led into the foothills. There were caves up there and an isolated stripped lead mine which he remembered exploring years ago; he also recalled to mind an old house of some kind.

He turned the horse onto the overgrown bridle path and as he went on he had at times to bring his feet forward to prevent himself being whipped out of the saddle by the entangling branches. Twice the animal stopped and refused to go on, until he used his heels on its haunches. When it stopped for a third time he saw in the faint gleam from the lantern that they had reached the turnpike gate.

Dismounting stiffly, for he was already cold, he thought of Mary's words: 'It would finish a bear off if he had to lie out in it.' And he knew it would for there would be little chance of her surviving a night on the open hills in cold such as this.

Pushing the broken gate to one side, he led the horse through; then mounting again, he took the path to the right. Half a mile on he came on the remnants of the house, shrunken now compared with his memories of it. Dismounting once more he led the horse into the questionable shelter of the ruined barn, and after tying it to a stanchion and covering it with the blanket from the back of the saddle he took the lantern and went to move away from it when the animal neighed loudly as if in fear. He went back and patted it and said, 'It's all right, it's all right; I won't be long,'

He could see nothing beyond the radius of the lantern light, but he knew that there were a number of small hills clustered closely together around this part.

When he attempted to climb up the side of the first slope he came to he slipped and fell onto his knees and only just saved the lantern from being extinguished.

When he pulled himself to his feet he stood muttering aloud. This was stupid, bloody stupid! What did he expect to find here? But within a minute he was climbing again and, slipping and sliding, he reached the top of the slope. And now he did what later he considered an odd thing, for, putting the lantern down, he cupped his hands over his mouth and called into the night, 'Barbara! Barbara!'

There was a scurrying to the right of him as if an animal had been startled; then a small, thin scream from somewhere down below which indicated that an animal not startled enough was meeting its end.

He now looked at the lantern; it was running out, he must get down or he, too, would be lost in a very short time. Without the light he'd never find his way back.

The horse neighed again as he went towards it, but it was the sound of welcome now, and as soon as he untied the reins from the post it made an effort to be off before he could mount.

When he came out onto the road near the cottage he saw that the house was itself in darkness, which he took to mean that Brigie was asleep, so he rode on to the Hall.

There was no sign of life in the house except faint gleams coming from side windows. He went into the stable yard, and here too everything was quiet. He had the desire to bawl and wake them up, but instead he unsaddled the horse, gave it a brief rub down, put it into its stall and saw it had food, then returned to the house.

The front door was unlocked and the lobby was lit with only one candelabrum, as was the hall; all the other lights had been extinguished. Again he had the desire to bawl until his reason told him that they were the sensible ones, they had gone to bed in order to meet the day, and he must do the same.

He did not undress, except to take off his two outer coats and his boots; then, lying on top of the bed with just the eiderdown over him, he lay staring at the ceiling.

The wind had come up and was buffeting the gable, but so stout were the walls and so strong the frames that supported the windows that the flame of the single candle burnt straight and steady, its edge unruffled.

Perhaps she wasn't out there; perhaps she had found shelter somewhere; perhaps she had got as far as the towm. . . . . What! in the dark, and in her state of mind? All things taken into consideration, it was more likely to be as Brigie said. *No. No.* He turned over in the bed and buried his face in the pillows. If that were so, his own life would have been senseless. For her to be dead and him never to have told her that he loved her. Risking her laughing face, he should have told her. There would have been some point, some meaning to all the years of make-believe if he had given it a climax and come out in the open and said, 'Barbara, I've been in love with you all my life, well, at least from the first time I saw you standing in the nursery with Brigie, so cocky, so sure of yourself, the little madam. You spoke and acted like no one I'd ever seen before, and because I was small, hardly any bigger than you then, you treated me as so much dirt on your shoes, and you became for me then an aim in life, something to conquer; and all I conquered were my feelings and the power to hide them from you by covering them with quips and sarcasm and teasing.'

He screwed his face into the pillow and muttered brokenly now, 'Oh, Barbara, Barbara, don't die, don't be dead. If you had married Michael I would have gone away. In any case I would have gone away, but I would still have you there in my mind, beautiful, yet maimed by your affliction; tortured by it; but if you had been blind too it would not have mattered to me. Oh, how many times have I wanted to say that to you, to take your hands and look into you eyes and say, "Blind and deaf I would still love you. But not dumb." I would have to hear your

377

voice, cracking and breaking on the words, pitching them to unnatural heights. Yes, I'd always have to hear your voice. Don't be dead, Barbara, don't be dead. For God's sake! don't be dead.'

'Oh, I'm sorry, sir; I . . . . I didn't know you'd got back. They said you were out so I brought the warming pan up for the bed.'

The girl stood at the bottom of the bed holding out the pan towards him, and he pulled himself up and muttered, 'What time it it?'

'About half six, sir.'

'Six, six o'clock?' He threw the cover back and swung his feet to the floor, saying to the girl as he did so, 'Bring me some hot water, will you, and a pot of coffee? Bring the water first; leave the coffee downstairs.'

'Yes, sir. Yes, sir. Will . . . . will I put the pan in the bed?'

'No, no, take it away. Oh, by the way.' He checked her as she was going out of the door. 'Send word to the stables to have The Colonel saddled for me right away. . . . .'

The clock above the stables struck seven as he crossed the yard. Knowles, the stable boy, sleep still in his eyes, met him almost at the stable door leading the horse. 'Mornin', sir,' he said. 'Snifter, ain't it! I've put the blanket on the back like you like it.'

'Thanks, Knowles. By the way, have . . . . have you heard anything more?'

'No sir. I was out meself with Mr Steele till right late on; the Morgans' men had coupled up with them from over Catton; they had the dogs out an' all but they couldn't make much headway in the dark, though we all had lights. The constables from Hexham are goin' to start again soon's it's daylight; they said they would give it another day but it's a poor look-out.'

Shut up! boy. Shut up! boy, his mind yelled at the boy while he said, 'I'm going in the direction of Studdon and over to Sinderhope; I'll make my way to Blanchland Moor. Should any of the men come, tell them that I've gone in that direction. It's no use us all going over the same ground. And bring me Bess.'

'Aye, sir. Aye, sir, I'll tell them. . . . . But Bess, sir, she ain't got no nose, never had, an' she's gettin' on.'

'You may be right, Knowles, but nevertheless I'll take her.'

'As you say, sir.'

The morning light was lifting rapidly and it appeared at first sight that there had been a light fall of snow, so white was the ground with frost. In the fields the grass was banded together in stiff contorted tufts and where the cattle hadn't trod each blade stood up individually encased in white rime.

The air cut a way down his throat and seared his gullet until he coughed it out again in steam. He put the horse into a trot, and before he reached the cottage he mounted the bank to the fells and went over the burn and crossed a sloping field and eventually came to the toll-gate by this shorter route.

He did not immediately dismount from his horse but sat looking around him as he asked himself why he had come back here. If she had intended to run away she would have run away much farther than this. He was wasting his time. And what did he expect Bess to do here with the ground like iron? He looked down at her. It was right what young Knowles had said, she hadn't a good nose on her and she was getting on. She looked up at him and wagged her tail and he nodded as if they were exchanging words; and when he went through the broken gate and took the path that led to the ruined farmhouse.

Having tethered the horse, he left the clearing and immediately scrambled upwards, wondering as he did so how he had avoided breaking his neck in the dark last night. Stopping at one point he called the dog to him, and then looked about him. The light was playing tricks with the valley bottoms; the green and brown of the land was moulded into gigantic waves that flowed to the foot of the far hills, whose peaks were now being teased and rolled about by low clouds, not one yard of this land remained the same for an hour at a time. He remembered vaguely standing on this spot before; it was a natural plateau. He turned his eyes away from the valley and up towards the next hill. Somewhere around here there was the old lead mine; you had to round a butte to come to it. He remembered once likening the butte to a huge scab on delicate skin. Yet who would call any part of the earth hereabouts delicate?

It was years since he had been here; and then he hadn't been alone. He had been young, they'd all been young, and had scampered over the hills shouting to one another, John, Katie, Barbara and he. His legs were short and so he was last, and they had laughed at him because he slid down a slope. The rough scree had torn the back of his legs and made them bleed. The girls had been full of contrition.

How many years ago was that? He couldn't remember. But would she have remembered and come up here and gone into the dark hole? He could see them now, all of them, standing within the bricked arch of the mine, pushing each other, urging each other to go forward; then John bringing their play to an abrupt end, saying, 'We must get back, Brigie will be wondering,' and he had thought, John's afraid; he's just said that because he's afraid to go inside.

'Come, Bess. Come.' He now hurried forward, urging the dog with him, over another hill and another, slipping and sliding; until there was the butte facing him. It stood alone, cut off from its rock fellows, as if isolated by its ugliness.

His feet giving way with every step he went crabwise down the hill; then with laboured breathing climbed halfway up the steep side of the butte until he reached a narrow rough path no wider than a goat track. Following this, he came round to the other side, and right opposite him was the entrance to the lead mine.

The hillside, like the butte, was scarred but softened here and there with patches of brush and greenery and bracken singed to winter brown.

Not more than a matter of minutes later he was standing in front of the opening, but it looked so much smaller than he remembered it, in fact he wondered if it was the right one for he guessed there were other such mines and he had but to search the hills to find them. But now as he stood in front of this one he was experiencing a strange feeling, it was as if it were yesterday when he had been here with the others; seeing that he'd only ever been here that once why should he choose to come here rather than any other place?

In his waking hours last night his mind had led him round and round these hills; yet when he rose this morning he had thought of taking the opposite direction, that was until he was out on the road; then it had seemed that his horse, not he, had taken the initiative.

Now, as all those years ago, like John, he was afraid to enter, afraid to go into the darkness. Bess was sniffing at the ground. He saw her nose go down to a small pool of water some way inside, and when her paw rippled the surface he was surprised that it was not frozen; the minute waves were crested with dull streaks of colour as on oil.

When Bess disappeared from view he called her sharply, saying, 'Here! Here, Bess! Bess!' He could see some way ahead, perhaps for a distance of four or five yards, but Bess had gone beyond the light. He heard her snuffling and called again, 'Bess! Bess!' He did not know how far the workings went into the hillside, and there could be passages or drops. He yelled again, 'Here! Bess! Here!' and she came scrambling back into view. Then coming to his feet, she sat on her haunches, looked up at him and barked twice, and he bent down to her and asked, 'What is it?' and she turned from him and ran into the darkness again, and once again he heard her snuffling.

Slowly he moved forward; then stopped abruptly, for there on the floor against the wall of rock something was lying. He could just dimly make out the shape in the diminishing light. Bess was sniffing at it, and as he sprang forward his foot caught a jutting piece of rock and he almost fell alongside the form on the ground.

He was on his knees, his hands moving over the prone figure. He gave a great gasp before he cried, 'Barbara! Barbara!'

She was lying with her face to the rock wall, her arms crossed on her breast and her hands doubled under her chin; her knees were drawn up and almost touching her elbows. He turned her over, muttering all the while, 'Barbara! Oh Barbara! Thank God!' Then when he tried to straighten her body he wondered why he was thanking God, for it was stiff and unyielding. Rapidly now he got to his feet and attempted to lift her, but found it impossible, so he put his hands under her armpits and drew her slowly over the rough floor towards the opening.

In the light of day he looked down at her. Those parts of her face that were not covered in dirt had the waxen colour of death on them. The upper garments felt dry but her skirt and the lower parts were heavy with water, and the bottom of her coat and dress and her boots were caked with wet mud, pointing to her having gone through some part of the river, for the roads were dry and hard.

Hastily now he forced her arms apart, undid the front of her coat and her dress, then put his hand inside her bodice. He could feel no movement, no beat. Frantically he undid some buttons that were evident, then thrust his hand between a lawn garment and her bare flesh. Still he could feel nothing. Now his ear was pressed against her breast bone; perhaps it was imagination but he thought that he could hear a faint beat. Plunging his hand into his overcoat pocket he brought out his flask. He unscrewed the silver top that could be used as a cup and filled it to the brim; then cradling her shoulders and upper body against his knees he brought her head upwards and gently poured the liquid between her slightly open lips.

When the cap was half empty the brandy was running out from the side of her mouth. And now he began frantically to stroke her neck with his fingers, talking all the while, pleading: 'Barbara; come on, come on; let it go down. Barbara, for God's sake! come on.' It couldn't be too late, it couldn't. Why had he to come up here if it was too late? No, no. 'Come on.' Oh God! Christ! make her swallow it.

As if his prayer had been instantly answered she gulped and he almost laughed aloud.

She gulped again, and after the third gulp she began to cough. It was a small faint sound, reluctant; following it she drew in a deep breath and her body shuddered; her knees began to tremble, then her trunk, then her arms until the whole of her was shaking violently.

Holding her tightly to him for a moment he rocked her; then laying her back on the ground he tore off his overcoat and put it around her, then again he held her, talking quietly to her now, knowing that she could not hear. 'It's all right, my love, it's all right, it's all over, you'll soon be home and warm. Oh my dear, my dear; that you should have been driven to this. I don't care what you've done, or who you've done it to, it'll make no matter to me. Oh, Barbara. Barbara.'

When her eyes slowly opened he looked down into them and said,

'You're all right, there is nothing to worry about, you'll soon be home. Do .... do you think you can get to your feet?'

She showed no sign of understanding him; her face was expressionless and still held the deathly pallor.

He now put one arm right around her shoulders and tried to raise her upwards, but her weight remained a dead weight; the stiffness had gone from her body only to leave a shivering limpness that was equally heavy. He urged her now, mouthing his words slowly, 'Try Barbara, try to stand. Come on, come on.' But there was no movement from her body, no flicker from her eyes.

He laid her back and stood up and looked down over the hills to the valley; then brought his gaze to Bess and shook his head. He should have paid heed to Knowles; all Bess was good for was wagging her tail, or licking your face. If he had brought Rory he could have given him his hat and he would have gone down there in a flash and led someone back. This is what came of being sentimental and impractical because of boyhood associations.

But it was no use ranting at the dog, he must get her down. But how? He couldn't carry her. In a moment of bitterness he thought that if he had been made like the blond farmer he could have done so; and to drag her down to the clearing was out of the question. It was either going for help or attracting it.

He looked down towards her and he kept his gaze on her for a moment before turning away and running swiftly to the butte. After climbing to its highest point he stood and, placing his hands around his mouth, bellowed over the hills, 'He .... lp! He .... lp!' then added 'Any .... body .... there? He .... lp!'

He waited some seconds before calling again. And again he waited. Then just when he had made up his mind to dash down to the clearing and ride to the cottage he saw two moving figures far away down in the valley. They came into view from behind a stone wall and stopped and looked upwards. And now he was bellowing again and waving them towards him.

After some minutes of watching them moving along the valley bottom a voice came up to him, calling, 'Hello there! .... What is it?'

Again he waved and shouted 'Help!' then pointed away to his right.

He thought for a moment that they were going back the way they had come, and they did for some distance, for they disappeared from view, but re-appeared again much nearer, mounting the hills. They did not approach him by the way he had come, but cut knowledgeably across the foot of the hills until they came out almost below the butte on a path screened by bracken. One man he recognized as one of the their farm-hands; the other man, a big broad-shouldered tousle-headed youth, he did not know.

The farm-hand shouted up, 'You found her, sir?

'Yes, over here; quick!'

Before they reached the path he was already going ahead, and by the time they had caught up with him he was kneeling by Barbara and had raised her head once again from the ground.

Looking down at her, the farm-hand said, 'Aye, God! but she's in a state. She alive, Master?'

'Yes, yes; but .... but she's ill, and very cold; we must get her down as quickly as possible. I'll .... carry her shoulders if you'll support her legs.'

'Lumbersome way that.'

Dan turned and looked up at the big face hanging over him, and the young man said, 'Twould be all right if she were on a door, but going like that she'd be jogled. Best let me carry her alone.'

'Twould be best thing, Master.' It was the farm-hand speaking now. 'Barney's very strong, he's champion wrestler round these parts, she'd be nothin' to him to carry.'

Dan rose to his feet, saying, 'Of course. Doesn't matter how we get her down so long as we get her down, and quick.'

Not without envy, he watched the young fellow stoop, place one arm under the inert figure's legs, the other under her shoulders and lift her up as if she were a child; then, sure-footed as a goat, he went before them, but again not the way he had come. Now he followed the path round the butte and down towards the clearing, while Bess ran backwards and forwards in front of him yapping and barking as if it were all a game.

When they reached the clearing the young fellow stopped and, hitching his burden higher up against his chest, he asked, 'Where am I for?'

'The cottage, Miss Brigmore's cottage. You know it?'

'Aye, I know it.'

'I'll .... I'll get my horse.'

Neither the young fellow not the farm-hand waited for him and so, once mounted, he had to put the horse into a trot to catch up with them.

As they neared the cottage he galloped ahead; then jumping from the horse he ran across the yard and burst unceremoniously into the kitchen, startling Mary so that she cried out, 'God's sake! what is it now?'

'I've .... I've found her!' He was gasping as if he had run all the way.

'Oh! no, no. Oh! Mr Dan; you haven't, have you, you haven't?'

'Yes, yes. Where's Brigie?'

'She's asleep; she didn't go off until nearly dawn, nor me neither. I

.... I just got up meself. But oh, thanks be to God! Thanks be to God! I'll tell her, I'll tell her.' She ran from the kitchen, shouting, 'Miss! Miss! come. She's here! She's here!'

He ran into the yard again where the two men were entering, and he beckoned them towards him, and the young red-headed fellow walked sideways into the kitchen while Dan, backing from him saying, 'Through here, through here,' opened the door into the little hall, then the door into the sitting room; he then pointed to the couch and the young fellow went to it and laid the now utterly limp form down on it.

When he straightened up he stood for a moment looking down at the girl; then turning away, he said, 'Well, that's done,' and marched out of the room, just as Miss Brigmore came running down the stairs. Her eyes wide, she stared at the strange man for a moment before darting into the sitting room and to the couch, where, cradling her child in her arms, she moaned over her while Mary stood to her side wringing her hands.

Dan stood just within the doorway looking at them. He could do nothing for the moment and. remembering the men, at least the stranger whom he would have to compensate, he hurried back into the kitchen. As he went in one door they were going out of the other and the young red-headed fellow was grinning as he said, 'Aggie, she'll laugh her head off when she knows 'twas me who carried the Mallen girl down from the hills. "Barney Moorhead," she'll say, '"twould have to be you." Oh, Aggie'll get a laugh over this, right sure she will.'

'A moment, a moment, please.' He was standing in front of the young red-headed fellow, having to look up to him. 'Thank you, thank you very much indeed for what you've done this morning. If .... if you will come to the Hall later I'll .... I'll see you.'

'Oh, no need for that, sir, 'twas a pleasure, an' I don't want payin' for pleasures. Ain't every morning I get the chance to carry a young lady over the mountains, or the hills, or over a hummock for that matter. It's me should be payin' gate fee. Mornin' to you, sir.' At this he turned about and stalked slowly away.

The farm-hand, looking apprehensively from the straight back towards the young master, said as if pleading the other man's cause, 'He's very strong is Barney, sir; but he holds to be no man's man, 'tis with the wrestlin' like, Master. He meant no offence.'

'And there was none taken. What is your name again?'

'Cousins, sir; I'm .... I'm on your farm.'

'Yes, yes, I've seen you. Yes, yes, I know you. Thank you, Cousins, thank you. Perhaps .... perhaps you'll be able to pass on something to .... to .... what did he say his name was?'

'Moorhead, sir, Barney Moorhead. And no, sir' – he gave a short

384

sharp laugh now as he ended, 'Not me sir; 'twouldn't be me, sir, that would pass anythin' on to Barney. No, as he said, sir, he don't want nothin', not Barney. I'm glad she's found, sir. I'll skip back to the Hall and tell 'em, an' they'll bring the men in, for some of them have been out since early on. I was out lookin' meself when I came across Barney. 'Twas fortunate-like that I did.'

'Yes, indeed it was. Thank you, Cousins.'

'Very welcome, sir. Good mornin' to you.'

'Good morning.' He went back into the kitchen, stood a moment by the table, drew in a long breath, then went slowly walking like a sick man himself towards the sitting room.

He hadn't entered the doorway before Miss Brigmore came swiftly to him saying, 'Oh! Dan, Dan, thank God. But she's ill, very ill. We must get a doctor quickly.'

'I know, I'll see to it right away.'

'How can I thank you?' She was gripping his hands.

'By getting her better.'

'Oh yes, yes; with God's help we'll get her better. But she . . . . she's so cold, her body's like a piece of ice. Where did you find her?'

'Not so far away, up in an old lead working, just . . . . just inside. But I couldn't get her down myself. That . . . . that young fellow carried her. We have him to thank really. If she had been left any longer out there she might have died.'

'Who . . . . who is he? I've never seen him before.'

'He said his name was Moorhead, Barney Moorhead.'

'Moorhead . . . . Moorhead.' She repeated the word to herself. There was only one Moorhead hereabouts and she lived over near Studdon. She was that dreadful, dreadful woman, Aggie Moorhead, the woman who had helped to clean the Hall before the Benshams took it, the woman Thomas used to meet on the road, the woman whom he chose to satisfy his need and then thought he was doing so, but in the confusion of the storm and the blackness of the barn he had raped Barbara's mother instead with the result that she lost the will to live, and on the birth of her daughter she had voluntarily released her hold on life.

In some strange way she too had lost her life then, for from the moment she took the baby Barbara into her arms, every emotion, every thought and action became centred around the child, then the young girl, and more so if that were possible around the young woman.

Life was strange, very strange in that it should fall to one of Aggie Moorhead's illegitimate offspring to carry Barbara to safety. She had the odd fancy that someone somewhere was laughing at the word illegitimate. Perhaps it was herself and she was going insane, and she

385

would not be at all surprised at that. But enough of herself for the present; her child was back. Oh! her child was back.

She almost pushed Dan towards the door, saying, 'Ride, ride yourself and bring the doctor will you, will you please?'

'Yes, yes, I'll do that, Brigie, right away.' As he reached the door she actually ran to him and gripped his hands again and said, 'Oh! Dan, I'll never be able to thank you enough for finding her; and it's because you didn't give up hope, you believed. But you look so tired, are you all right, are you fit to ride?'

'Yes, yes, I'm all right Brigie.'

He left her without any further words and she watched him for a moment as she thought, And I have never really liked him.

6

'YOU MEAN TO LEAVE THEN?' John looked at Dan with a sadness in his face.

'Yes.'

'What about if she doesn't have you?'

'Well' – Dan paused – 'I'll .... I'll go in any case, I'll have to. But I suppose I'll come back sooner than I would have done.'

'Does she know how you feel?'

'No. No, I shouldn't think so. She only sees me as someone kind and attentive; I'm the only one besides Brigie and Mary she's seen in weeks. When I asked if she'd like to see Katie she became agitated.'

'How did you make that out, when she doesn't speak?'

'Oh, just something in her face.'

'She doesn't attempt to talk on her fingers?'

'No, she just lies there.'

'But she knows what's going on?'

' I don't really know, but there's a keeness in her look as if she were talking with her eyes.'

'Does Dad know how you feel about her?'

'Not from me he doesn't, but .... but from his reactions, letting me stay down there those first two weeks, and sending me off early on a Friday, he might have guessed. On the other hand, he just might want me out of the way, my absence is less of a handicap than my presence I think.'

'Nonsense! you're getting on splendidly; and you're handling number two shop very well. They like you, all of them, and there's more than a few hard cases among that lot.'

Dan laughed gently now as he said, 'You might change your tune if I were to stay on, because then I'd likely join Katie, and you'd have a pair of agitators to contend with. It'll be funny you know if she ever marries Willy, because he's moving away from workers into management, he's aping the boss's outlook – you can hear it in the new tone he's adopted, and see it in the cock of his head – while she's going the other way, defending the down-trodden: higher wages, shorter hours, water in the houses, and closets; full-time school for all children. By! I can see the sparks flying if those two ever make a match of it.'

'Oh, I don't know.' John shook his head. 'I think they'll be well suited that way. But I might as well tell you, as much as I like Willy I wish she had set her sights on someone else, it's going to be awkward. Jenny would accept the situation but old Pearson's bristles'll rise when he hears of it, and there'll be a large family conference, no doubt of it.'

Dan laughed and repeated, 'No doubt of it.' Then as he made his way through the overcrowded furniture in the sitting room towards the door, John said, 'If I don't see you in the morning give Brigie my regards, and . . . . and convey to Barbara I'm thinking of her.'

Dan paused at the open door and looked over his shoulder, saying, 'Yes, yes, I will, John.' Then his head jerked round as his father's voice came from across the hall saying, 'Here a minute, lad.'

Harry was beckoning him from outside the room that was termed the office, and when he reached him he said, 'I've just been thinkin', I've a mind to go down with you the morrow.'

'Oh! good, good.'

'Aye, aye. Come in a minute.' He went into the room.

Dan followed him and he stood by the side of a long littered ornate ugly desk as Harry dropped heavily into the leather chair behind it, and when his father didn't immediately speak, Dan asked, 'Is anything wrong?'

'No, no.' Harry began to sort some papers in front of him; then leaning back he said, 'Well, nothing that can't be put right. It's the house, the Hall; I'm in two minds about keepin' it on. Brooks and Mrs Kenley appear to be waging their own private war down there, an' there's no arbitrator sort of to keep things on an even keel since Brigie's been so occupied, and the way things are shapin' it looks as she could be occupied for evermore. I want to ask you' – he nodded his head slowly now – 'and I want your honest opinion, do you think Barbara will ever really get her senses back?'

'She hasn't lost her senses, Dad.'

'Well, she's lost something, lad; if she won't open her mouth or talk with her hands as she used to I can see Brigie having to nurse her for the rest of her life.'

'No, no.'

'You say no, no, as if you know something different. Does she talk to you?'

'No.'

They were staring at each other very hard when Harry said quietly,

'It surprised me, you know, when I discovered you had ideas in that direction. Gave me a gliff, to say the least. I used to think you liked going down there for the air and change 'cos your nose couldn't bear the rotten stink round these quarters, and then, well quite candidly, lad, I thought you were a bit gone in the nut, even to think of her, because as far as I could see she had firmly made up her mind in another direction. And another thing, if I remember rightly, you two never did hit it off, sparring was your occupation, when you met. Now, well, I've got to thinking otherwise. Am I right?'

'Yes, yes, you're right, Dad.'

'Well, what are you going to do about it?'

'Try to get her to marry me.'

'Aw, lad! lad!' Harry pulled himself forward to the edge of the chair, leant his forearms on the desk and bowed his head over them before he went on, 'You're lashing a dead horse, aren't you, from all sides as I see it. In the first place, if she was so mad over the young farmer that she almost killed the lass because he looked at her, than she's not goin' to forget him lightly. Have you thought of that?'

'I've thought of that.'

Harry lifted his head back on his hunched shoulders and stared at his son, and his voice had a kindly note to it as he continued, 'And then apart from her being in this trance-like state, and from what I can gather from Doctor Carr – aye' – her nodded sharply now – 'I had a talk with him about it. He explained it like, to use his words, it's sort of like a safety guard on a loom, as I see it, put there so's you can't probe too far, and as he said it could go on for years. Then there's this other thing she's got to live with, her deafness. Lad, have you thought well about it 'cos you'll be taking something on your plate whichever way you look at it?'

'I'll be glad to take it on my plate, that's if I get the chance.'

'Oh, well, you know your own business best. Does it mean then you're going to settle down and stick it out here?'

'No.' The answer came sharp and definite, and Harry showed his surprise on his stretched face and he repeated, 'No? Then what do you intend to do, 'cos in any case she'll have to be kept in the style, as they say in that class, to which she has been accustomed? Brigie has given her the manners and education, and it's meself that has supplied most of the trimmimgs, so to speak. Not that I minded doing it, 'cos I was grateful for what Brigie did for you all, especially Katie. But now' – he gave a short laugh – 'it looks to me that Brigie's efforts in that quarter have been wasted an' all 'cos something 'll have to be done with our Katie. Talk about a rebel in the camp, my God! I never thought to live to see the day. But that's another story and it'll have to be dealt with later. At present we're talking about you and .... and Barbara. You say you're not staying on here, so would you mind telling me what you intend to do?'

Dan moved a step away from the end of the desk. He turned his head and looked at a glass-fronted bookcase that held few books but stacks of ledgers and papers; then he rubbed his hand hard over the lower part of his face before looking at his father again and saying, 'We .... ll, it's something I was going to bring up with you but .... but later. I was going to ask you if you'd be kind enough to give me my share that would be due. ....' he closed his eyes and gave his head a quick jerk to the side, then added rapidly, 'I didn't mean that, there's nothing due to me, you've given me everything so far and generously, but .... but you would in the end, I suppose, be sharing things out between the three of us, and .... and I wondered if you'd give me what you consider, well, the amount that .... that I might get later on, or at least some of it, enough to enable me to travel for a while with. ....' He stopped.

Harry was glaring at him now but his voice was quiet as he said, 'Aye, go on.'

'Well, with Barbara; if she'll have me.'

'And .... and how much do you think your share will be?'

'I've .... I've no idea.'

'But you've got a sum in mind?'

'Well, I thought three or four thousand.'

'Three or four thousand.' Harry pressed his lips tightly together and sucked them inward for a moment; then he said, still quietly, 'Three or four thousand, just like that; three or four thousand. And if you get it, how long do you think it's going to last you travellin' the world?'

'Quite some time the way I would spend it; I'm .... I'm not looking for the high life. I .... I just want to see places, learn, think. Oh' – again he shook his head, closed his eyes then jerked his chin upwards – 'I .... I can't explain it properly, I'm not putting it over as I should. I .... I only know that I've got this urge in me to move. And whether she comes with me or not, I've got to get away.'

Harry now dropped his chin forward and, his voice very low, he said, 'That makes me sad, lad, to hear you say that you've got to get away; it's as if we had the mange.'

'Aw! no, no, Dad. You've got me wrong, quite wrong. I .... well, how can I put it? I .... I care deeply for you and John and Katie. We're a family, we've always been happy together. How can I make you understand my need?'

'Don't try, lad, don't try; but if gettin' away's so important to you there's nothing more to be said. You know me, I keep nobody against their will. But let me put this to you, have you thought about if she'll marry you and not want to move? An' then there's the woman who's been mother and father to her, who she's clung to all these years, will Barbara want to leave her? And there's still another side to it. You take Barbara away from the cottage and what has Brigie got left? Nowt as I can see. She's built her world around that lass, she's eaten, breathed and slept her. I can look back to when she was a little bairn, Barbara, and Brigie holding her in her arms and the mother look on her face. Have you thought about that side of it?'

'No, but now that you mention it I . . . . I would be very concerned for Brigie's feelings; but it wouldn't stop me taking Barbara if she'd come.'

'Well then, that's settled.' Harry now clapped his two hands flat down on the desk. 'As I see it all you've got to do is to persuade the lass to come back to life, then woo her as the saying goes, marry her, and go off. . . . . How long do you think it's going to take you?'

'I don't know.'

'And if she doesn't have you, you say you'll still go off?'

'Yes, I'll still go off.'

'Aye, well' – Harry pulled himself to his feet – 'Now we know where we stand, at least you do, but I'm still left with that bloody house and all its bloody problems.' His voice was getting louder now. 'And I've nobody to go to but meself to ask advice, so I ask you, do you see any reason for me keeping it on? John doesn't. As soon as he's settled he'll go over to Pearson's semi-mansion 'cos Jenny doesn't want to leave old Walter. Funny that, John gone, you gone; I wonder if Katie will insist on bringing Willy here 'cos she'll think I'll be lonely. Well if she does, I'll say this to her, no bloody fear. I like Willy, I've nothin' against him, but when I leave the mill, I leave the mill, I don't bring it home to bed. The mill's becoming a mania with Willy . . . . you said something along those lines a while ago, if I remember, not that it's a bad thing mind, as long as it's kept in its place. Well, what I'm saying is, I just couldn't stand the two of them in the house: trade unions, politics, slum conditions, an' the poor for breakfast, dinner and tea. No, no, I'd rather finish the race on me own. But I can't see meself finishing it sitting in that Hall alone, nor yet here.'

There was a faint smile on Dan's face as he said, 'Aunt Florrie's doing her best.'

Harry turned his head slightly to the side while keeping his eyes fixed on Dan, and he said, 'Aye-aye. Don't think I haven't noticed. But I thought you didn't fancy her as a step-mother.'

'I don't.'

'Oh, well, whether you do or don't makes little odds, your future's yours, though of the two, mine seems more plain-sailing.

Anyway, lad, let's get to bed if we want to get up in the mornin' with the lark.'

Dan did not move for a moment, but stood looking towards Harry before he said quietly, 'Thank you, Dad, thank you for everything. And . . . . and I'd like you to know that I've always appreciated what you've done for me.'

Harry, his head nodding up and down now and a twisted smile on his face, said, 'Well, that's something to know; 'tisn't every son that thanks his father for bringing him up. But if the truth were told I've only been the provider, standin' in the margin so to speak, letting the others get on with it, while your mother and, of course, not forgetting Brigie, did the work. . . . . Aw, Brigie' – he put his hand on to Dan's shoulder and led him towards the door and out into the hall, saying now, 'Funny how that woman's been the pivot we've swung round on for years, isn't it? Brigie this, Brigie that; would Brigie like it? Would Brigie approve? And if ever there was a bloody stiff starchy bitch, she's been it; never bend an inch, would she? An' still won't.'

As they looked at each other and laughed, Harry said, 'You know, I've only seen her off her guard once, an' then it was 'cos she thought I'd insulted her, but . . . . but I was just leading up to something, something I was going to say to her when our John came in and that was that. I admitted to meself later on that I might have been a bit tactless in the way I put it, saying to her that nobody would think she'd been mistress to a man for ten years, but in my way I meant it as a compliment and. . . . .'

Dan stopped at the bottom of the stairs and his mouth remained open for a moment before he whispered, 'You . . . . you didn't, Dad! You didn't say that to her?'

'Aye. Well' – Harry looked to the side – 'I suppose saying it ice-cold like that it does sound a bit much, but, as I said, I was leadin' up to something else and I thought it was common knowledge anyway, and she knew that. And it is, it is. She was an old man's mistress, wasn't she? Talk of the countryside. I'd heard all of it afore I ever clapped eyes on her, and when I did meet her I couldn't believe it. She was so blasted ladylike, I couldn't imagine her ever taking her shift off to go to bed.'

'Oh! Dad.' Dan was laughing deep in his stomach now and as the laughter rose he again said, 'Oh! Dad.' And Harry's laugh now joined his and he gasped, 'By! it is funny isn't it when you come to think on't? I'm still a bloody ignorant bugger at bottom. It's true what they say about silk purses and sows' ears.'

They went upstairs together, step in step, their heads back, their mouths wide, and when they parted on the landing and went to their respective rooms they were still laughing.

7

D AN SAT BY THE SIDE OF THE BED and looked at
Barbara lying propped up on her pillows. Her cheeks were
hollow, her face was colourless, she could have been thirty
years old from the look of her. Her hands lay on top of the coverlet,
separate, the fingers straight out.

'Would you like to see Dad, he's downstairs with Brigie?'

Her eyelids closed, which meant no, and when her mouth opened
and her lips trembled slightly he said quickly. 'All right, all right.'
Then after the pause that followed he said, 'It was an awful journey
down, freezing, but I was better off than Dad, I was squashed between
two fat women.' He demonstrated with his hands the size of the
women. 'It was so desperately cold that I nearly cuddled up to one, the
one with the foot warmer.'

There was no flicker of amusement on Barbara's face, but her gaze
held his and he went on, 'But I'd pass through Iceland to get out of
Manchester and away from the mill and' – he smiled wryly now –
'number forty-seven. I can look back to the times when the meals used
to be jolly affairs, but not since Katie took over. Oh my! our Katie!'
He shook his head. 'You wouldn't believe the change in her, you
wouldn't, Barbara.' He nodded at her. 'The only thing I can say in her
favour is that she's taught me a lot of social history just from listening
to her. How she must have read this last year! And you know, she's
made me read too, just to be able to argue with her. I got a bit tired of
hearing the unions glorified. And there's so many of them; the Amalgamated Society of Engineers, the Amalgamated Society of Carpen-
ters and Joiners, societies of bricklayers, iron founders, iron workers,
cotton spinners, weavers' unions, and I forgot to mention black
pudding, pease pudding and rice pudding associations.'

He laughed down into her face as she stared back at him; then his
smile slowly fading, he asked softly, 'Do you feel any better, Barbara?'

Was there a slight movement of her head or did he just imagine it?

There was another pause while he looked into her eyes, then he sat back and, assuming his jocular tone, went on, 'To hear our Katie talking about the unions you would think their members had been bred in monasteries, all the men are so good, honest, upright individuals, all fighting their wicked masters. Mind, I'm not saying that some of the masters don't deserve that title and they need to be fought, but hearing it from Katie meal after meal got to be too much, so' – he now nodded his head at her – 'you can understand when I came across a certain piece of information concerning a little gunpowder plot, and nothing to do with Guy Fawkes but with a union and its members, I lapped it up, so the next time she started I said to her, in my most aggravating and superior way, you know what that's like' – he pulled a face at her – 'I said to her, "Did you ever hear of a tin of gunpowder that was placed in the house of a Sheffield non-unionist in an attempt to blow him up?" Oh, you should have heard her. Yes, she had heard of it. But that was in '66 and the men had been provoked beyond endurance, she said. And then I asked if she had heard of the Sheffield unionists and those members of the Manchester brick-makers' clubs who had done murders in the name of the unions – they had actually killed one employer whom they considered was unfair. Of course, they'd hired someone to do their dirty work and paid him twenty pounds for the job.' He laughed again as he ended, 'Believe me, Barbara, I nearly laid myself out for assassination, she became so angry. She was red in the face and bawling. This was an isolated case, she said; the unions were fighting for their lives, which meant the lives of their wives and children. . . . Do you know, it's a good job they don't allow women in Parliament else she'd be there tomorrow. If the men of the towns hadn't got the vote in '67, believe me she would have got it for them this year. She talks of a junta, of Comte's theories, you know positivism. Or perhaps you don't. I didn't. Anyway, he was some French philosopher who died over twenty years ago. He started a religion of humanity, as he called it, and this is what our Katie keeps on about, among other things of course. You wouldn't recognize her, Barbara. I tell you you wouldn't. She quotes from some fellow called Harney, who ran a newspaper, *The Red Republican*. Every proletarian who does not see and feel that he belongs to an enslaved and degraded class is a fool, was what he said, and she believes it. She talks about the death of the Chartists' Movement as if it were a family affair. There was a prominent member of it called O'Connor and the other night during the whole of dinner she gave us his life. I went to blow her up but Dad just laughed. Fifty thousand people followed his hearse she said. The poor fellow had died in the asylum, I think, and I told her that that's where she'd end up if she didn't stop all this ranting.'

He stopped suddenly; and now, his voice very soft again and his lips moving widely, he said, 'You're tired; you don't want to hear all this rubbish.' And when her eyes blinked rapidly he said, 'Oh well, then, our Katie's doing some good with her life after all.'

But he found he couldn't continue yapping about Katie and her socialistic ideas; for at this moment he had the painful, awful, gnawing desire to drop his head forward and rest it on her shoulder, on her breast, to put his arms about her, to put his lips on that still mouth, gently at first, then hard, fiercely, to bring it into life. He took up her hand and held it between his own, stroking the thin, bony fingers, and he looked into her face again, saying, 'It's beginning to snow again. Remember when we used to take the sledge over to the hills? Remember the time when I went head first into a drift and there were just my legs sticking out and nobody bothered to pull me out right away because you were all laughing your heads off? I might have died.' He shook his head slowly. 'I might at that, and you would still have gone on laughing. Do you remember?'

There was no movement from her lids and he bent forward and said softly, still mouthing the words, 'Oh! Barbara.'

He was brought upright by the door being pushed open and Mary entering carrying a tea tray. When he turned towards her she cried at him, 'Sitting on the bed again, Mr Dan! I've told you it spoils the mattress, it does.'

'I'll buy you a new one, Mary.'

'Likely have to by the time you're finished.'

'I thought you were out.'

'Well, I'm not, am I? I got back fifteen minutes or more ago. By! it's cold. It would freeze the nose of a brass monkey, and sitting on that cart I told him, I told Ben, I did. You should have a cover over this, I said, an' supply blankets. By the time I got off I didn't know whether me feet finished at me knees or not. And then in the town you couldn't get moved.'

She kept up her chattering as she poured out the tea; then taking a cup to the bed she put it to Barbara's lips saying, 'There, dear, there; just as you like it,' and as Barbara sipped at the tea, she added, 'That's a good girl. That's a good girl,' as if she were speaking to a small child. Then turning to Dan, she added, 'If you want to go downstairs, Mr Dan, I'll stay put here for a time.'

'No, thank you, Mary, I can stay put too. You brought an extra cup I see.'

'Oh aye. Knowin' you never say no to tea I came prepared.'

After she had poured out two more cups of tea she took hers and sat in a basket chair at the head of the bed, almost on a level with Barbara herself, and Dan resumed his seat on the edge of the bed, and as he spoke to Barbara, saying jocularly, 'She makes a good cup of tea, I'll say that for her, if she can do nothing else,' Mary, talking between gulping from her cup, said, 'Good cup of tea indeed! And I say what I've said afore, 'tisn't seemly you sittin' on the bed, Mr Dan, 'tisn't right, 'tisn't right or proper. Yet' – she took another gulp of tea – 'what does it matter. As I said to meself earlier on, what does it matter, what does anything matter. Aye, I felt awful in the town the day, Mr Dan. I've said nothin' to Miss about it, but eeh! I felt awful.'

Dan cast a look in Mary's direction, and he knew from the tone of her voice that what she had to say wasn't for Barbara's eyes, and as if it even might reach Barbara's ears her voice was low as she continued, 'Saw young Sarah I did, went slap into her. There she was, crutch an' all. Eeh! it was a shock seein' her like that. I knew she had lost her leg, but it was different, different seein' her with just one leg and a crutch, and he was with her, Michael, an' they looked happy enough. But . . . but I was cut to the bone, 'cos you know what, Mr Dan? They passed me as if they didn't know me. I could have touched them by just puttin' me hand out, but they both passed me as if they had never seen me afore in their life. Eeh! I was cut up. I did a bit of a cry when I got on the cart. Ben Taggert said they were married last Saturday and. . . .'

It was almost as if an explosion had thrown him off the side of the bed. The cup went spinning from his hand and Barbara's tea came on to his face and neck; then the scream that she emitted almost brought his hands from his scalded flesh to block out the sound from his ears. The next minute he was struggling with her, trying to hold her down while her screams, mixed with Mary's cries, seemed to shatter the walls of the room.

It seemed only seconds before Miss Brigmore's hands were entangled with his own, and also those of his father.

As quickly as Barbara's screaming had begun so it ended and brought them all into a huddle in the middle of the bed, and from their several contorted positions they gazed in alarm at the limp figure, thinking that now she really had died.

It was Harry at this point who took command of things, saying, 'Come on then; come on then; get her up on to her pillows. It's all right; she's just passed out; her heart's still going. What was it all about?' He turned an accusing gaze on Dan, who from the other side of the bed and still gasping said, 'You . . . you know as much about it as I do.'

Having settled Barbara more comfortably against the pillows, and covered her discreetly once more with the bedclothes, Miss Brigmore looked from Dan to Mary and asked in a murmur, 'What . . . what upset her?'

Again Dan answered, 'I don't know. No one, nobody.'

'You ... you weren't talking to her about anything in ... in particular?'

'No, I was just sitting on the bed like this' – he demonstrated – 'facing her and ... and Mary, Mary was sitting there. She ... she was telling me....' He stopped, and now Mary and he stared at each other. Then he moved his head, saying, 'But she couldn't! she couldn't have heard you from there.'

'Heard what?' Miss Brigmore's voice had the old ring to it as she confronted Mary, and Mary, with a defiant movement of her head, now said, 'She couldn't have heard; I was dead level with her, or behind her, like this.' She now demonstrated how she had been sitting when she was talking.

Miss Brigmore, still with her gaze intently bent on Mary, asked slowly, 'What were you talking about?'

Mary turned her head to the side. There was a look of defiance on her face now and she did not answer until Miss Brigmore said again, 'Well, I'm waiting.'

'I ... I just said I'd seen them, Sarah and him in the town and ... and she was using her crutch and' – her voice sank low – 'I said Ben Taggert had told me they had been married a week gone.' She faced Miss Brigmore again. 'She couldn't have read me mouth 'cos she couldn't see me, an' I talked low, right low. I ... I had to tell somebody; I couldn't tell you, so I told Mr Dan there 'cos I was upset like, 'cos they cut me dead as if they'd never seen me afore. It was natural I was upset.'

Miss Brigmore stood perfectly still as she stared back at Mary. After a moment she turned slowly about and looked at the white mask-like face sunk in the pillows; then she brought her gaze to Dan and asked quietly, 'Do you think she could have read Mary's lips?'

'No, definitely no, not from the way she was lying. And ... and she was looking at me. The only way she could have taken in what was being said was if she could hear....'

Now Miss Brigmore looked at Harry, who a moment ago had turned from the bed, and asked, 'What do you think?'

'Well' – he rubbed his hand hard over his mouth before saying – 'from what I gather she threw that fit because of what she heard Mary say, an' she could have only heard what Mary said if she had got her hearin' back. It looks as though when she lost one sense she gained the other. It seems far fetched but that's the way I see it at the moment. We'll have to see what line she takes when she comes round. Look, she's moving now....'

Barbara was moving. She was fighting her way up through layers of blackness. There was no substance to the blackness. As she grabbed at

397

it, it melted through her fingers like mist, and as she breathed it i
blocked her throat as if she were trying to swallow wool, and i
weighed on her as if blanket after blanket were piled on her body. I
was when she was feeling she could struggle no more that she saw :
glimmer of light. It became stronger, like the dawn seeping through
the curtains, and the nearer she got towards it the brighter it became
and the nearer she got towards it the more fearful she became, for now
she had a desperate urge to fall back into the blackness out of which
she was emerging, for a voice was screaming through her head, 'We
will have to see what line she takes when she comes round. We will
have to see what line she takes when she comes round. *We will have to
see what line she takes when she comes round.*'

She had heard every word that had been spoken in the room since
she had regained consciousness that long, long time ago. When at first
she had tried to tell them that she could hear and there was no longer
any necessity for them to mouth their words at her, or contort their
fingers into language, she had found she was unable to do so. But what
did it matter anyway? She was dead

When she had jumped down from the trap she had run wildly
through the dusk to meet death. Reaching the river she had determined to lie in it and bring her dying to quick finality. But when she
fell forward it was on to rock and the water just flowed gently over her.
It wasn't until she dragged herself up and went towards the middle
and found the mud sucking her down that, in spite of what her mind
was telling her, her body automatically struggled until she freed
herself.

She ran no more after that, she just walked and stumbled and fell
and rose again, and repeated this as she mounted the hills. The
twilight had almost gone when she came across the workings and,
falling into its shelter, she lay down and began the process of dying.
But it was long in coming, as sleep was, and she lay shivering well into
the night.

When she awoke the daylight was streaming through the entrance
and her body felt hot and she wanted a drink, above all things she
wanted a drink. She slept fitfully all day and the last time her eyes
opened it was into terrifying blackness and to the sound of someone
calling her name. The voice came from a great distance, 'Bar . . . bara!
Bar . . . bara!' it said, and she answered, 'I'm coming,' and as she
closed her eyes she knew it was for the last time.

The memories after that were dim and confused. A man was
holding her in his arms as a lover would hold her, but it wasn't
Michael. Then she seemed to sleep for an eternity, and when at last
she awoke she knew that in a way she had got her wish and she had
died, for there was no desire in her either to move or to speak. So she

didn't move or speak but lay through aeons of time listening, and as she listened she knew that everybody was different. None of them were as they had been before, not Brigie or Mary or Dan, particularly Dan, Dan was quite different; Dan had turned into a lover. If she hadn't died she would have laughed at the absurdity of this, but there was no mirth in her for the dead cannot laugh.

Yet as the eternities passed she found that she could listen to Dan without irritation. His voice was not stiff like Brigie's, nor chattering like Mary's, and it wasn't the voice of the irritating youth, it was the voice of a man, it was deep and warm and kind. It was a large voice, much larger than his body, yet it lay gently on her eardrums. She had been listening to it telling of Katie's doings in the social field. . . . And then . . . then came Mary's prattle saying that Sarah had only one leg and was walking on a crutch. She was already screaming in her head when she heard the words 'Ben Taggert said they were married last Saturday.'At that moment the fact that Michael had married Sarah did not seem to matter so much, because she knew that, in a way, he would be forced to do so to compensate for her own act, her vile act of ripping Sarah's leg off. And through the screaming in her head she heard Jim Waite's voice screaming at her again, 'You're a devil! You're a bastard! You've hated her all your life.'

She knew she was a devil, and she had hated Sarah all her life. Yet at the present moment there was no hate left in her, not even for her Aunt Constance. The void that the deafness had created was lost in a greater void, for now she could not feel emotion of any kind. She did not hate, she did not love, they were emotions that belonged to another life, and in her present life, this still life on the bed, she felt she was being born again; she was emerging from a dark world. And her thoughts were new, different; but they did not help her to want to live for they were constantly stressing the fact that she was bad, because she was a Mallen she was bad, and that she would do less harm if she stayed for ever in this half world.

Faces wove in and out of her vision now, hands touched her and she pushed them away. She didn't like hands touching her. Her body was burning, she was parched, she was back in the hole on the hillside. She gasped, 'Water. Water.'

'Yes, dear. Oh yes, dear; here it is.'

Miss Brigmore supported her head as she gulped at the water.

'Are you feeling better now?'

'Yes.'

Miss Brigmore turned her head away as she now asked, 'Would you like another drink?'

'No.'

'Barbara, Barbara my darling, you can hear?'

Barbara stared up into Miss Brigmore's drawn face, but she did not answer her.

'You heard, you heard me speak. Tell me that you can hear. Barbara, Barbara, tell me that you can hear.'

'I can hear.' The words were flat, unemotional.

Miss Brigmore turned round quickly, looking for somewhere to sit, and it was Dan who pushed a chair forward, and it seemed only just in time for Miss Brigmore was evidently overcome. Her tightly buttoned bodice swelled and the buttons strained from their moorings. Her whole face was alive with love and wonder as she looked at her beloved child. When she turned her gaze on Harry he smiled at her and nodded reassuringly; then turning to Dan, he said, 'Come along, lad.'

Dan stood for a moment looking towards the bed, then turned and followed his father; Mary, the tears raining from her eyes, her apron held to her face, went with them; and Miss Brigmore was left alone with her child, her daughter, her beloved Barbara.

She leant forward and with the tips of her fingers gently stroked the hands now joined tightly together on the coverlet, but when they flinched from her touch she also flinched as if she had been stung, and the joy drained from her face as she looked into the eyes now holding hers, and she murmured, 'Oh! Barbara. Barbara, my dear, what is it? What is it now?'

What was it now? It was to stop the words which were tumbling about in her mind, leaping bridges of time and yelling, 'You're to blame, you're to blame for all that's happened. You lived in sin with that man all those years, that fat man whose flesh I am. And . . . and since I can remember you have made me think I was different, something special, rare; when what you should have done was tell me the truth and let me start life with my feet on the earth instead of my head in the clouds. I see now that the only reason you ever went to the Hall to teach was because you wanted to instal me there; you've used me as a slave on your frustrated life, you've turned me into an expensive doll, not fit to cope with ordinary living. If I had any hate left in me I would hate you, Brigie. What I want to say to you now is, don't touch me. Don't come near me, for if I am to live then I must learn to live.'

On a long intake of breath she checked the leaping words and said slowly, 'I'm going to get up.'

'Yes, yes, dear; come then.' Miss Brigmore rose hastily from the chair and went to turn the coverlet back, but Barbara held on to it, and still slowly she said, 'No, I do not want help any more; I . . . I am going to get up on my. . . .'

'You can't get up on your own, dear.' Miss Brigmore's voice was

400

quivering now. 'You're too weak, you have been in bed for months, you'll fall.'

'I am going to get up by myself, Brigie. I . . . I will sit in a chair for a while. Would . . . would you mind leaving me alone?'

The rusty scythe that had lacerated Sarah's leg could not have caused her half the pain that Barbara's words were causing Miss Brigmore. Like poisoned spears they penetrated the stiff correct façade and thrust deep into the desolate creature that lived hidden within her. Nothing that had happened in her life before had had the power to wound her as Barbara's attitude towards her now. Not the devastation of her comfortable family home brought about by her father's bankruptcy and imprisonment, which had also caused her mother's death; not the humiliating trials in those first situations as governess; not the fact that Thomas would never give her his name although she had given him everything she had in life; not the shock of his raping Barbara's mother or the shock of his death by his own hand; not the latest blow that she was to be cut off for ever from Constance; none of these things had made her feel as she was feeling at this moment.

For seventeen years she had devoted her life to this girl, she was the child she had never had. She had been mother, nurse and governess to her. In the early days she had worn herself out trying to find a cure for her deafness. She had taken on the post of educating the children at the Hall merely in order that Barbara should have advantages that the cottage could not afford. She had allowed her everything, except one thing, the love of Michael, and that she had striven to deny her whenever possible, as Constance had done. But it was she alone who was now to bear the blame for it.

Blindly, she turned about and went out of the room; in her own room she dropped on to her knees by the side of the bed and asked God, Why? *Why?*

8

CHRISTMAS HAD COME AND GONE. The Benshams had spent it at the Hall, accompanied by two guests, Miss Pearson and Mrs Florrie Talbot. Harry had hoped that Miss Brigmore and Barbara would join them. When his invitation was politely refused, he went to the cottage and tried coaxing, but to no avail. Losing his temper, he had stormed out saying that living in bloody isolation was going to do nobody any good, and that was the last they would see of him.

When the rest of the family called en masse to deliver their presents and to wish them all a happy Christmas, Barbara absented herself; the only one of them Barbara still continued to talk to was Dan. . . .

January was a bitter month. The roads became impassable and there were drifts of snow twelve feet deep. Sheep were frozen to death, and when there was a sudden thaw towards the end of the month, Ben Taggert's horse and cart got bogged down in a ditch. It took ten men to lever them out and after such an experience, the horse was no further good and Ben reluctantly let it go to the knacker's yard; nor was he himself the same afterwards.

When it froze again the roads became more treacherous than when covered with the thick snow, and no human nor animal could be sure of a footing on them. The navvies kept the railway lines clear, and the trains still ran, if not to time, but the carriage could not get from the Hall to the station, and no one but a madman would have attempted to walk the distance.

So when a madman, so rimed with frost that he appeared like a ghost, thrust open the studded door and walked through the vestibule into the lamp-lighted hall, two maids coming slowly down the stairs checked their laughter and gave a high concerted scream before running back up again.

There was no sight of any manservant, and Dan slowly made his way across the hall towards the drawing room. He did not attempt to unbutton his coat because he could not feel his fingers inside his gloves. When he thrust open the drawing-room door he was met with similar reactions, but without the squeals, as Brooks, Armstrong and Emerson drew their outstretched legs and stockinged feet sharply upwards and scrambled from where they had been reclining on the couch in front of the fire.

'Why ... why, Mr Dan! Where you sprung from?'

'Manchester.' Dan's voice was as cold as his body. He stared from one to the other of the men, then deliberately lowered his gaze to the table at the side of the couch on which stood two decanters and three glasses, not wine glasses, but ale glasses which were more than half full of whisky, and he now added grimly, 'It's evident when the cat's away the staff can play. And how they can play! You don't do things by half, do you?' He looked at the glasses again. 'I understood you have a sitting room of your own.'

'Aye, sir.' Armstrong was sidling around the head of the couch now. 'We ... we had just sat, dropped for a minute.' Emerson followed him silently, his eyes blinking, his face red with heat and whisky and he jumped when Dan barked, 'Don't lie to me!'

Dan was now tugging at the buttons of his coat and when Armstrong attempted to come to his assistance he thrust him aside with a jab of his arm, saying, 'Keep out of my way!' then he ended, 'No wonder my father's thinking about closing this rest home up. And not before time. Where's Mrs Kenley in all this?' He was now addressing Brooks, but he, showing none of the trepidation of the other men, replied surlily, 'In bed; where she's been for the past week; says she's got a cold.'

'Well, if she says she's got a cold I'd be inclined to believe her. Get going.'

Brooks now made to walk away; then turned and looked at Dan and muttered, 'Your dad would have made no fuss about. . . .'

'There you are mistaken; he's been making a fuss for a long time now about a number of things, not least the wine bill.' He pointed towards the decanter. 'And let me tell you he doesn't blame Mrs Kenley. He did you a good turn once by bringing you here, and he's done your son more than a good turn, and how have you repaid him? You've taken advantage of him for years. You're the worst of your breed, Brooks. Go on, get out! and first thing in the morning see that the outside steps are cleared of snow, and the drive also.'

The door had scarcely closed behind the butler when he bawled at it, 'Brooks!'

It was some seconds before the door was reopened, and when Brooks appeared he said to him, 'Bring me a clean glass.'

While waiting for the glass he bent forward and crouched over the fire, and the steam from his hair and face and life flowed painfully back into his limbs again.

He was sitting on the couch pulling his boots off when Armstrong placed a glass to the side of the decanter, then slowly picked up the three glasses that still held the good measures of whisky, put them on the tray and went out.

Dan took a long drink and when, like a thin stream of fire, it rushed into his body, he lay back and held his bare feet out to the blaze.

The second glass of whisky not only thawed the cold out of him but also softened his thinking. Perhaps he had come down on them a little too hard; and yet they had no right in here, they had a comfortable room of their own. And then again, it wasn't a case of having no right, it was a case of discipline and loyalty on Brook's part. He didn't blame Armstrong, or Emerson, for taking advantage, for they had received no such kindnesses from his father as Brooks and Willy had. He'd never liked Brooks. He might have been a good mill worker in his day but only because, he suspected, he wanted to ingratiate himself into his father's good books. But for years now he had also suspected him of being on the make. He was the kind of working man that got his own class a bad name, the 'You've got it, why shouldn't I have it?' type. There were a number of them in the mill and, unfortunately, these were among those who ran the unions because most of them had the gift of the gab and, like Brooks, they gloried in the fact that the bosses didn't frighten them.

With his third glass he wished he were miles away. He soon would be, he told himself; yes, he soon would be, and not only from Manchester but from here, this raving mad stretch of country that hemmed you in with its hills and mountains, that drowned you in its swelling rivers, that froze you with its everlasting snow and ice, that brought your spirit low, that made you long for warmth and sunshine with an ardour the equal of the desire for a woman.

It was the desire for a woman that had made him risk his life covering those miles from the station to here. He had met not one soul on the road, nor seen one live beast, nor bird. He could have slipped and fallen and stayed where he lay, and tomorrow they would have found him stiff. He was mad; and what for? All these weeks, all the months of talking hadn't, he knew, brought them one inch closer together; the only difference in her attitude towards him was that she argued with him no longer and did not seek to quarrel with everything he said. In fact now she listened intently to all he had to say; but it was as if she were listening to a disembodied voice. And the voice now hadn't the courage to say 'Barbara, will you marry me?' for he knew what the answer would be. The truth was, he told himself, Barbara would never marry for she had still not come alive.

Well, he had made up his mind. Or had he? Wasn't it his father who had made it up for him? 'Get yourself away, lad,' he said; 'you're wearing yourself out. The money's there for you when you want it. I'm going to give you five thousand, not all at once, and it isn't all your share. There'll be a bit over when things come to be divided; but I can tell you, lad, that's not going to be for some time, I'm not ready for me box yet. I'll see that there's two thousand in the bank for you; when you want any more you can send to me for it, it'll give me some idea of where you're at.'

Looking back now, he realized that it had been a very emotional moment. He'd had the almost womanish desire to lay his head on his father's shoulder, to put his arms about him, and to express by such action the feelings that were in his heart, but all he had been able to say was, 'It's more than generous of you; you can be sure I won't squander it.'

And now all that remained was to go along there tomorrow and tell them, tell her, and then he would pack. But he would have little to pack, for he was going to travel light. This time next week he'd be in France, or beyond. Just think of it, France or beyond.

He thought of it, and it brought him no joy.

After kicking the snow off his boots against the wall and having to lift his foot high up to do so, for the foot scraper was hidden under the snow, and knocking on the door, he entered the kitchen, as he was used to doing. Mary turned from the fire and Miss Brigmore from the delph rack, and they both exclaimed aloud much as the maids had done: 'Oh! you've never made it in this weather, Mr Dan!' Mary cried, and Miss Brigmore echoed, 'Why! Dan, Dan, we didn't expect you. How on earth have you managed to travel?'

Dan laughed from one to the other as he drew off his gloves, then took off his outer coat, and when Mary took them from him and, looking up into his face, said 'Eeh! Mr Dan,' he bent towards her and whispered with a jocularity he didn't feel, 'There isn't the weather manufactured, Mary, that could stop me coming to see you.'

'Aw! you, Mr Dan.' She flapped his hat at him, then hurried out of the kitchen, saying, 'You must have smelt the broth, that's it.'

'Is . . . is anything wrong, Dan?' Miss Brigmore came towards him now, to where he was standing holding his hands over the open fire that flared brightly between the black-leaded ovens, and he turned his head and looked at her for a moment before answering, 'No, there's nothing wrong. I . . . I only thought I'd come to see you before, well, before I leave. I couldn't go without saying good-bye to you.'

'Before you leave, where?'

'Home . . . here . . . Manchester, the mill. England. . . .'

'You're leaving England, Dan?'

As he was about to answer, he turned and looked towards the door. Mary had left it ajar and he thought someone was about to enter; but no one did and he went on, 'Well, you know I've . . . I've always meant to go; it was only a year's probation at the mill in the hope I might settle. But I knew I couldn't. I . . . I did it to please Dad. He's . . . he's been very, very good, generous.'

'Oh, Dan.' Miss Brigmore turned to the table and, with her back to him, she said, 'We'll . . . we'll miss you. Barbara, Barbara will miss you; you're . . . you're the only one she sees, in fact you're the only one she seems to want to see.'

He made a small deprecating sound in his throat. 'It's because she's house-bound,' he said; 'once the fine weather comes she'll get out and about.'

Miss Brigmore was facing him again, and now she said slowly, 'I doubt it, Dan. Barbara has changed. You know it's in my heart to wish that her . . . her deafness had never left her because she's taken her hearing as a new affliction.'

'No, no; you just imagine that. It's wonderful that she can hear again. Come on, cheer up.' He went towards her. 'You're looking very peaky yourself, aren't you well?'

'Yes, yes, I am quite well, Dan.' She moved her head in small jerks and blinked her eyes, and there was a slight tremor in her voice as she added, 'I was about to pour the soup out; we generally have it mid-morning, it warms one better than tea. Go along into the sitting room.'

As Dan moved away from her she stopped him, saying, 'On second thoughts, I won't bring it in for a while, I think you'd better tell her first.'

'Very well. Yes, yes, I will.'

He went out and crossed the hall and paused for a moment before he tapped on the sitting-room door and entered the room.

Barbara was standing near the window. She turned immediately and faced him, and as always he was aware of her height. Since her illness she had seemed to grow taller; perhaps it was because she had become thinner. He walked slowly towards the middle of the room and when she did not come towards him, he said, 'Aren't you surprised to see me, everybody else seems to be? Two of the maids nearly fell downstairs last night when I walked in, or rather, fell in. I told them not to try to bend me or I would snap like an icicle. And now Mary nearly falls into the fire and Brigie spills the soup; but you, you look as if you expected me.'

'I did . . . I heard you in the kitchen.'

'Oh! Oh!' He made a deep obeisance with his head, 'That's it, is it.

406

Still I didn't expect to surprise you; you know me so well that nothing I would ever do or say would surprise. . . .'

'Don't joke, Dan.' She came slowly towards him now and she repeated, 'Don't joke.'

'Why? Why must I not joke? Joking's part of my stock in trade.'

'Because . . . because you've . . . you've come to tell me you're going away. I heard you talking to Brigie.'

'Oh well, that's over then, isn't it?'

'Dan.' She came near to him.

'What is it?'

'Dan.' She was actually gripping his arm now, and he said, 'Now, now; don't get so agitated. Sit down. What is it?' When he had placed her gently on the couch she gripped her hands together and pressed them between her bent head and her breast bone as if she were trying to push them into herself, and then she whispered something.

He bent his head towards her. 'What did you say?'

She repeated the words and suddenly he jerked her chin from her hands and brought her face to front him, and now he whispered, 'Do you know what you've just said?'

She moved her head once.

'Take me with you, you said. You want to come with me? Barbara. Barbara!' His voice had risen from the whisper and was getting louder, and he glanced back towards the door, then lowered his tone again as he said, 'You . . . you can't mean it?'

'I do, I do, Dan. Please, please take me with you, away from here. I . . . I mean to go in any case, I mean to leave, but . . . but I'm frightened on my own.'

The light faded from his face now as he said, 'There's only one way you could come with me, Barbara, you know that?'

Her eyes were steady as she looked into his and said, 'I know.'

'You would marry me?'

Her gaze still remained steady, 'Yes, Dan.'

'Oh Barbara.' He drew her hands towards his chest; then bending his head over them he kissed the white knuckles twice, three times before looking at her again and saying thickly, 'You know I love you?'

She nodded once before answering in a low murmur, 'Yes, yes I know.'

'How long have you known?'

'Since . . . since you began to visit me.'

He smiled now, a sad smile, as he said, 'You didn't know before?'

'How . . . how could I? We always seemed to quarrel.'

'I've loved you all my life; can you believe that? Right from the first time I saw you in the nursery. I can remember the picture you made as clear as I'm seeing you now. Katie came rushing out of the nursery, crying, "The Mallen girl's hit me!" then I saw you standing straight like a young willow tree ... What's the matter? Don't bow your head.'

'I ... I hate that name, my name, my name is Farrington.'

'All right, all right, darling,' he said soothingly; 'but it won't be Farrington much longer. I ... I can't believe it; I can't believe that you want to marry me. But' – he shook his head sadly now – 'you don't really, do you, it's only a means of escape? But ... but don't worry' – he almost gabbled now – 'Doesn't matter why you want to as long as you want to. You don't love me, I know that, I don't expect you to, not yet anyway. ...'

When she lifted her head and looked into his eyes he added jocularly, 'I'm the kind that never gives up hope.' Then his voice changing, he asked seriously, 'But you like me a little, don't you?'

'I've ... I've grown to like you a lot, Dan.'

'Thank you, thank you, Barbara. That'll do for the present.'

'When ... when can we leave?'

He looked slightly surprised at her haste, then said, 'As soon as ever you're ready. But ... but have you thought about Brigie, how she'll take it, how she's going to feel about it?'

'Yes, yes I have; I've thought about it a lot; but I must say this, and I can only say it to you, it's Brigie I must get away from.'

'*Brigie?*'

'Yes, Brigie. I can't explain it. I know it's wrong. I know in my mind I am wrong to blame her for all that's happened, yet I do. I can't help it but it's her I blame.'

'Oh! Barbara, you mustn't think like that, not about Brigie; she's ... she's given you her life.'

'That's it, that's just it, Dan.' She turned away from him now. 'She's given me her life, and the weight of it is lying on me, and ... and I can see it getting heavier with the years as she protects me and turns me into a replica of herself, Miss Mallen; the spinster lady, Miss Mallen.'

'Oh! Barbara dear, darling.' Impulsively he put his arms around her, but when he drew her close there was no response from her body, and his own became still. She was looking straight into his eyes as she said softly, 'Give me time, Dan, give, me time,' and as softly he answered, 'All the time in the world, dear.'

He was not to know that another man, her half-brother, had said those exact words to her Aunt Constance in this very room.

'Will ... will you tell her first?'

'You wish me to?'

'Please.'

'Very well.' His arms dropped from around her; he turned abruptly and went out.

She stood looking towards the door for a moment; then swiftly she went to the window and, one fist tightly closed, she bit hard on the knuckles as she gazed out on to the never-ending whiteness that covered the garden, the fells and the hills beyond, and the bleak iciness of the land was reflected deep within her. Yet she strove to melt it, crying at it, 'I will love him! I will learn to love him! It can be done.'

She swung round as the door opened and Miss Brigmore entered, but neither of them moved towards the other, and when Miss Brigmore spoke her voice was so low, so distant that Barbara imagined for a moment she had lost her hearing again. 'You can't, you can't do this,' she said.

'I can, I can, Brigie, and I'm going to.'

'You mean to say you would willingly go away to . . . to a foreign country?'

'Yes, that is what I mean to say.'

Both their voices were muted now as if they were afraid of hearing not only what the other had to say, but also what they were saying themselves.

'You mean you would leave me, leave me here on my own?'

'I . . . I would have left you in any case had I married before now.

'That would have been different; you would have been in the neighbourhood.'

'Yes.'

Miss Brigmore started as the monosyllable rang out like a cry, and then was repeated, '*Yes*, in the Hall, or over the hills. You wouldn't even have minded that, would you, in the end if I'd gone over the hills, as long as you had me at hand? And then you would have had more children to mould into your ladylike pattern, the pattern that has no association with life. It's been proved, it's been proved by everyone you've touched: Aunt Constance; as much as I hated her, I realized that her life had gone awry in the first place through ignorance; and then my mother, the other Barbara, what happened to her? What happened to her, eh? And at the hands of the man you played mistress to.' She thrust out her arm now and pointed to the picture above the mantelpiece. 'I want to smash that, him that you cosseted in all ways. If you hadn't allowed his woman to come to the barn my mother wouldn't have been raped and I wouldn't have been here. You brought your pupils up in a house of sin, and you were surprised and shocked when things went wrong. You still retain the power to be surprised and shocked after all that's happened. Katie, even Katie, rebelled. . . .' Her voice was almost a scream now.

As Miss Brigmore leant back against the door it was thrust open and Dan entered. He stared hard for a moment at Barbara; then turned his attention quickly to Brigie where the opening door had thrust her against the wall, and as she was about to slide down it he caught her and, supporting her, led her to the couch. Then turning to Mary, who was now in the room, he ordered, 'Bring a little brandy.'

As Mary scampered away Dan glanced up at Barbara. His face was stiff, his eyes hard, even accusing; and now, her voice a whimper, she said, 'I'm ... I'm sorry, I ... I didn't mean all I said, it just. ...'

'Then you shouldn't have said it.'

'I ... I know that.' Her long body slumped and she sat down abruptly on a chair.

Miss Brigmore now put her hand to her head and murmured, 'It's all right, it's all right.' But when she attempted to sit upright Dan pressed her gently back, saying, 'Sit quiet.'

'I ... I would rather go to my room.' Her voice was weak, and Dan said, 'You will in a moment; Mary's bringing you a drink. Ah! Here she is.' He took the glass from Mary's hand, but when he went to hold it to Miss Brigmore's lips she waved his aid aside and, taking the glass from him, sipped at the brandy.

'I'm ... I'm sorry, Brigie.' Barbara had not moved from her chair, and Miss Brigmore looked towards her and answered simply, 'It's all right, dear.'

There was a sudden rush and Barbara was kneeling by the couch, her head buried in Miss Brigmore's lap, her arms about her waist, and, the sobs now shaking her body, she cried, 'It isn't all right. It isn't all right. I'm wicked, bad, and you have been so good to me all my life. I didn't mean any of those things, I didn't, but ... but I can't stay, Brigie, I can't, I'd die. And it isn't because of you, it's because' – she now lifted her head and looked up appealingly into Miss Brigmore's white face and, her words slow and her voice more quiet, she added, 'It's everybody all around; I'd ... I'd never be able to go into town, Allendale, Hexham, anywhere, not even walk the country roads but I'd be pointed at, the Mallen girl who caused Sarah Waite to lose her leg. And ... and I know if Jim Waite had his way I'd be publicly hounded, taken to court. I ... I couldn't bear it, Brigie.'

Neither Brigie nor Dan, nor even Mary, contradicted her in any way for they all knew that what she was saying was true, although it was something they hadn't openly faced.

As Miss Brigmore put her hand on the black shining hair and gently stroked it she turned her eyes to where Dan was sitting to her side and said, 'When will you be going?'

'There's ... there's no real hurry now.'

'You must not alter your plans; the sooner it's done the better.'

'No; as I said, there's no real hurry. What does a week or two matter? And ... and we'll be married from here, Brigie.' He now brought his eyes down and looked into those of Barbara. She was still kneeling, holding Brigie, but her head was back on her shoulders now and her mouth was open to protest, but she didn't. Something in his face cut off any protest she was about to make, and some detached corner of her mind was pointing out to her that this man who was so much shorter than herself, and so much in love with her, and always had been, to use his own words, would not be as pliable as she had imagined, and as she stared at him she thought for a moment she was gazing into the face of his father.

When her head drooped he said, 'Well, that's settled. Now Brigie, try not to worry any more; things will work out.'

'Yes, yes, Dan, things will work out. Would you excuse me now? ... Would you mind, dear?' She gently extricated herself from Barbara's arms and, her usual dignity hardly impaired, she rose from the couch and walked slowly out of the room and up the stairs and into her bedroom. Again she stood with her back to the door but now she covered her face with her hands and murmured through her fingers, 'Oh! God. Oh! God, help me to bear this.'

After a moment she walked to the bed and sat down on the chair at the head of it, and clasping her hands in her lap she sat staring straight ahead, looking as it were down the years that were to come when she and Mary would be alone in this house, cut off from the house over the hills, and cut off from the Hall, for she knew, from what Harry Bensham had said over the past weeks, that he was seriously considering selling the place, and if this were so she would never set foot in it again. So here she would be, alone with Mary, who, although a dear soul, was intellectually as companionable as an arid desert. But it would be on Mary she'd have to rely for companionship until one or the other of them died. The prospect caused her to close her eyes tightly.

And now she asked God what she had done that such justice was meted out to her; was this payment for the pleasure she had derived from comforting Thomas? If it were, it were a high price to pay. Life, she thought was a sort of madhouse. There was no reason or logic in it. You were brought into it and moulded in a certain way; the mould was termed environment, and its early years shaped your thoughts, and your thoughts dictated your actions and set your principles, and you lived up to them, except when, as she had done, you violated the laws of society and gave yourself to a man outside the sanctity of marriage.

But reviewing her life through the ideals of justice, she considered that she had paid for the liberty she had taken because she had lost her good name and become publicly known as Mallen's mistress. One time in the market she had been laughingly referred to as one of Mallen's night workers; she had actually overheard this with her own ears; and

411

so, speaking of justice, hadn't she made payment enough for her one misdeed, and she admitted to it being a misdeed?

What she didn't admit to was the accusation that Barbara had just levelled at her, that she was responsible through her teaching for what had happened to Constance and the other Barbara, and even to Katie with her radical thinking. But most of all she denied the responsibility for what had happened to Barbara herself, for from the very day she was born she had thought of nothing but guiding her aright.

She recalled the agony of the day she rode across the hills to beg Donald Radlet not to take the child from her, the child who was his half-sister. The hollowness inside of her that day when she watched him prepare to go and fetch the child himself was in her now. His death on the fell – his murder on the fell – had saved Barbara from his diabolical rule, and herself from dire loneliness. Now, almost eighteen years later, it was Barbara who was inflicting on her a future of loneliness, and she didn't know if she'd be able to bear it. Yet she must appear to bear it, if only until she was gone – married.

Dan was a kind man, and although he appeared of small stature he was in a way not unlike his father in that there was a determination in him, perhaps not so strong as was in his father, nevertheless it was there, but she wondered if he realized what he was taking on in marrying Barbara, in marrying a girl who had not a vestige of love left in her. No one who had been obsessed with a love such as hers for Michael, and who had gone through the sufferings of the past months, could scrape from the dregs of her feelings anything approaching love for another.

An overwhelming feeling of sorrow swept over her, and not only for herself, it enveloped Dan and Barbara, and Constance, and Michael, and Sarah; oh yes, Sarah. What was it about the Mallens that they should at one point in their lives do something evil? There were strange stories still current of the evil doings of the Mallens over the last hundred years or so.

During her own stay at the Hall Thomas's legitimate son, Dick, had almost killed a bailiff in the kitchen and he would have certainly killed Waite had the same bailiff not prevented him. And it was she herself who had provided the money for his bail by secreting valuables out of the house with the co-operation of Mary Peel and the children. And what had he done when he had been bailed? Run away to France, and she had heard of him no more until he had died, strangely enough within a short time of Thomas; and the solicitor had come to the house to say he had left two thousand pounds, but not to her, no, because she wasn't Thomas's wife. The money had gone to Thomas's daughter Bessie who had married an Italian Count. She thought, in an aside, should I tell Barbara about Bessie before she leaves? It may make her feel better knowing she has a relative among the foreign aristocracy.

They said the Mallen wickedness was depicted by the white streak in the black hair. Dick Mallen had carried the streak, as also had Thomas's natural son, Donald Radlet, and the cruelty in Donald had been deep and wide. Yet Thomas himself had carried the streak, and Thomas had not been evil, unless you would place his desires under that heading, and these were no worse than those of many another man of his time and postion.

Barbara had no visible streak to identify her as a Mallen; yet the streak was there, deep inside. She had always known it, and feared it and what it might lead her to. And her fears had not been unfounded.

But there were two types of cruelty; there was physical cruelty and mental cruelty, and Barbara was capable of using both. She had read somewhere that you hurt those you loved most. She did not believe this maxim; no one, unless his mind was deranged in some way, stabbed himself to death, and that is what you did when you hurt those you loved, stabbed yourself to death.

She looked across the room to where she could see the reflection of herself in the long mirror, and what she saw was a middle-aged – no, she must be truthful, an old, staid, primly dressed governess, the latter expressed by every detail of her.

She had the greatest desire, the stongest desire of her life to die at this moment, to die before her child walked out of her life, to die before the loneliness of the house and of her mind drove her mad.

9

'**D**EARLY BELOVED, *we are gathered together here in the sight of God, and in the face of this congregation....*'

There was no congregation except the four people standing below the altar steps. The church was cold and dark, it was almost like a preview of the tomb to come.

Barbara's thin body, shivering within a beautiful fur cape, that was part of Harry's wedding present to her, did not stand dazedly as one in a dream but was alert to everything about her. The old minister's voice, thin and piercing, sent each word like a steel wire through her brain.

'*... and therefore is not by any to be enterprized, nor taken in hand, unadvisedly, lightly, or wantonly, to satisfy men's carnal lusts and appetites, like brute beasts that have no understanding, but reverently, discreetly, advisedly, soberly, and in the fear of God; ...*'

In the fear of God. Did she fear God? She should fear God; Brigie had brought her up to fear God; but she feared herself more.

'*It was ordained for a remedy against sin, and to avoid fornication....*'

Was she sinning more now than she would have sinned if she had made Michael love her, love her without marrying her? And she could have done it, she could have, *She could have.* The voice in her mind was drowning that of the minister.

'*I require and charge you both, as ye will answer at the dreadful day of judgment, when the secrets of all hearts shall be disclosed, that if either of you know any impediment, why ye may not be lawfully joined together in Matrimony....*'

Yes, yes, she knew of an impediment: There was no love in her for the man at her side. And he knew that; but he would comply with what the minister was saying to him now.

'*Wilt thou love her, comfort her, honour, and keep her, in sickness and in health, and, forsaking all other, keep thee only unto her, as long as ye both shall live?*'

'I will.'

'*Wilt thou have this man to thy wedded husband, to love together after God's ordinance in the holy state of Matrimony? Wilt thou obey him, and serve him, love, honour, and keep him, in sickness and in health, and, forsaking all other, keep thee only unto him, so long as ye both shall live?*'

'. . . I will.'

'*Who giveth this woman to be married to this man?*'

Harry took a short step towards Barbara, touched her arm and mumbled something.

Dan had hold of her hand. He was repeating words after the minister; their voices see-sawed through her head. To love and to cherish, till death us do part.

'*I Barbara take thee Daniel to my wedded husband, to have and to hold from this day forward. . . .*'

He was putting the ring on her finger.

'*With this ring I thee wed, with my body I thee worship, and with all my worldly goods I thee endow. . . .*'

It was done. They were kneeling side by side, but she was in the black hole again, her body shivering as she waited to die.

They were walking over the rough stone slabs towards the vestry. Dan held her hand tightly; he was looking at her.

She turned her gaze towards him. His face unsmiling, but there was a look in his eyes that she could only describe as wonder, and in this moment, she prayed, 'God, let me love him, for he deserves to be loved. . . .'

It was over. They were back in the carriage, and Harry, aiming to break the solemnity of what he termed to himself a wedding that had been sadder than any funeral he had attended, clapped his hands loudly together as he said, 'That church; I've never felt so cold in all me life. How do the poor beggars sit through a service in there? An' him; he looked as if he hadn't thawed out for years.'

'You'll have to donate the money for a stove and coal, Dad.' Dan smiled wryly now as he looked at his father from the opposite side of the carriage where he sat beside Barbara, still holding her hand.

'What! me donate a stove and coal you say? Not on your life, lad. From what I know of those fellows they see to number one; big for their toes and laced-gruel for a nightcap. I know where the coal'd go.'

'I couldn't imagine he's seen a good fire in his life.'

'Well, whether he has or not, you're not gettin' me to donate any stove. Now, if you had brought it up afore and not rushed at this thing like a bull in a gap, and I'd been given some idea of what I was to go into this mornin', then I would have had two stoves put in there. Anyway, it's done; isn't it, lass?' He leant forward and put his hand on Barbara's knee, and her voice low, she answered, 'Yes, yes, Mister....'

'Now look, get over that an' quick. No more Mr Benshaming; you either call me Harry, or Dad, like the rest; you can have your pick. Now this one here' – he turned his head on his shoulder and looked at Miss Brigmore – 'she would sooner go to the gallows than call me Harry, wouldn't you?'

Miss Brigmore looked back into Harry Bensham's eyes. She knew what he was trying to do, but she couldn't assist him by even a smile and was grateful when he returned his attention to Dan and Barbara and said, 'What did I tell you? . . . By! I wish they'd get a move on.' He looked out of the carriage window, then added, 'But I'd better not push him else we'll all end up in a snow drift. Eeh! you're lucky, you know.' He nodded from one to the other. 'Going off into the sun. I wish I were coming with you. I never thought I'd say I was fed up with the North, but by! lad, these winters get me down. You know' – he put his head on one side – 'when you're settled some place you drop me a card. Just put on it "Sun shining, spare bed", and I'll be over like a shot.'

'We'll do that.' Dan nodded at his father. He too knew what he was trying to do, and his gratitude to him was gathering as a pressure under his smart pearl-buttoned waistcoat, a pressure that could find no release.

Of a sudden Harry sat back against the leather upholstery of the carriage and let out a deep breath. He felt tired, almost exhausted. This business of trying to say the right thing, of aiming to pass off the occasion as if it were ordinary, of wishing he could do something about Brigie's face, was more wearing than hard labour. Aye, but he had never seen any woman look so hurt in his life as she had looked these last few days. He hoped devoutly that his new daughter-in-law would show more concern for her husband should he ever need it than she had done for the woman who had brought her up and given her life to her.

There was a funny streak in that lass. They talked of the Mallen streak; he was beginning to think there was more in it than just market gossip and old wives' tales. She was beautiful, there was no doubt about that, but he would have thought a man would have wanted more than beauty. Aye, a man did want more than beauty, he wanted warmth, and if there was any in her, Dan would be lucky if he ever warmed his hands at it.

He had taken on something had Dan; but there, it was his life. You bred sons and daughters and what did you know of them? To think that Dan had loved that lass all his life and he hadn't had an inkling of it until lately. Then there was Katie who had the same warmth in her that had been in her mother; but she was freezing it, damping it down by piling the stack of causes on it; and now she was saying she wanted to marry Willy. Funny, but the more he thought of that match the more he was against it. It was odd but somehow he thought it would have less chance of survival that the one sitting opposite him. Aw, to hell! He had himself to think about, and he was going to think about it, he had done enough thinking for others. Matilda had told him: 'Don't worry about me, lad,' she had said, 'don't wear black at breakfast, dinner an' tea. And get yourself some comfort, but with the right one, you know what I mean?'

Aye, he had known what she meant. There had been depths in Matilda he had never reached. He had been a blind man in some ways, ignorant and blind. Still, he'd put a stop to that, and very shortly.

The wedding breakfast was held in the cottage; Miss Brigmore had stood out against Harry's protests. The meal was plain, almost ordinary, although Mary had done her best; as Harry and Dan were doing now in an effort to keep the conversation going. Even Barbara was forced to help them in defence against Miss Brigmore's muteness.

The meal over, the healths having been drunk, they rose and went into the sitting room, and there Harry, pulling out a heavy gold watch from his waistcoat pocket, said, 'Well now, I don't want to hurry anybody, but if you want to catch that train, an' the state the roads are in, you should give yourself an extra hour, I think you should be making a move.'

'Every ... everything is ready, I have only to put on my outer things; would ... would you excuse me?' Barbara actually ran from the room, and Dan and Harry were left looking at Miss Brigmore where she stood supporting herself with her two hands gripping the back of the couch.

Going to her, Dan put his hands gently on her shoulders and said, 'Try not to worry, Brigie; I'll ... I'll look after her. And I promise you that if ... I mean when we settle some place I will write to you and make arrangements for your coming.'

She would not speak, she could only stare at him and pray inwardly that she would not collapse, not yet awhile.

When Dan turned her gently about and went to press her towards the door, saying, 'Go up and have a word with her,' she shook her head, for all the words that had to be said had been said, she could bear no more.

Dan now asked quietly, 'Won't you come to the station with us?'

Again she shook her head.

'Leave her be. Leave her be, lad.'

Dan turned and looked at his father, and Harry made a sharp motion with his head.

When Mary's loud sobbing came to them from the hall they went out, Dan holding the door open for Miss Brigmore, and they looked at Mary and Barbara enfolded in each other's arms. They were both crying, but Barbara was making no sound.

And now Dan, going forward, took hold of Mary's arm and drew her away and towards the kitchen, and Harry followed them, and so for a moment Miss Brigmore and her beloved child were alone. Her beloved child who was now a married woman and who was going out of her life never to return into it again.

'Brigie. Oh! Brigie darling. I'm . . . I'm sorry for all I've done.'

They were clasped tightly together. 'I'll . . . I'll never forgive myself for all the trouble I've brought on you. Will . . . will you forgive me? Please, please, say you forgive me. And . . . and as Dan says, you must come to us. Brigie, Brigie, speak to me, say something.'

They were standing, still joined but only by their hands now, but Miss Brigmore did not speak, she could not. Releasing her hands, she cupped the beloved face for the last time, then leant forward and kissed it. Gently now she turned Barbara about and pressed her towards the door before turning hastily back into the sitting room.

When the men returned to the hall it was to find Barbara standing with her head bowed deeply on her chest, the sobs shaking her body.

A few minutes later they were in the carriage. The coachman had put the two valises on the rack; this was the only luggage they were taking with them. Barbara did not raise her head to give a last look towards the cottage, nor did Harry look out out of the window; it was Dan who waved good-bye to the solitary figure of Mary standing at the gate.

Mary stood and watched the carriage rumbling over the frozen road, she watched it until it disappeared around the bend, then she turned shivering and went up the path towards the front door, crying bitterly as she muttered, 'Eeh! she's gone. I can't believe it. God Almighty! What's to become of Miss?'

It was as she closed the door that the strange sound came to her. Throwing off the coat she had put on against the cold, she hurried to the sitting room and when she thrust the door open she stopped for a moment and gazed down at the figure sitting on the floor in front of the couch, her body half over the seat and her face smothered in one of the cushions, while her two hands clutched and unclutched the upholstery as if she were kneading dough.

'Oh! miss, miss.' Mary threw herself down on the floor beside Miss Brigmore, and putting her arms about her she cried, 'Don't take on so. Don't take on. Come on, sit up. I'll get you a drink; come on, come on, lass.' She so far forgot herself as not to apologize for the slip.

It was some little while before she was able to persuade Miss Brigmore to get up from the floor, and when she had her settled on the couch and had drawn a shawl around her shoulders she said, 'Now, now, just stay put for a minute, I'll get you something hot. And I'll lace it. That's what you want down you, a good lacing.'

The tears still flowed and, making no effort to dry them, Miss Brigmore sat and stared into the fire. After a while her eyes lifted upwards and came to rest on Thomas's picture. Benign as always, he was smiling at her; the watch chain across his portly figure gleamed and seemed to pick up a light in his eyes. It was as he were saying, 'Come on, come on, it isn't the end of everything. You're no worse off than when you started, in fact you're better off, much better off than when you had me to look after, for have you not got a house that is yours, and three thousand pounds in the Bank, and a friend like Harry Bensham?'

A friend like Harry Bensham? Harry Bensham would soon follow his son and Barbara. Like them he would disappear from her life, perhaps to re-appear at intervals to give her his good wishes. She looked up into the eyes that seemed alive and for a flashing moment she thought, I wish I had never stepped into High Banks Hall, for then I would never have set eyes on you, and my life might have been my own, not given to this one or that, to be thrown back at me empty, holding nothing worth living for. But the softness in the eyes looking into hers melted the thought away, and the expression on the face disappeared to take on a sadness now, and she heard Thomas's voice riding the years, saying, 'I've loved you like I've loved no one else; be content with that.'

But could one be content to live on a mere memory? Well, she'd have to, wouldn't she? She'd have to gather her forces together and face what life offered to such as she; Miss Brigmore; always Miss Brigmore.

419

10

S HE HAD GONE TO BED and sleep had come to her through a mixture of exhaustion and whisky, for Mary had, last thing that evening, laced a cup of hot milk to the extent that it had become cool.

It was nine o'clock the following morning when Mary came into the bedroom carrying a breakfast tray. After placing it on a side table she opened the curtains; then bending over the bed, she gently shook Miss Brigmore by the shoulder, saying, 'Sit up, Miss, and have this.'

'What!' Miss Brigmore turned on to her back, opened her eyes and blinked. Then she glanced towards the window and murmured, 'I've . . . I've overslept; what time is it?'

'Going on half nine.'

'Half-past nine!' Miss Brigmore drew herself up against the pillows, buttoned the top button of her nightdress, smoothed down the coverlet, then said, 'It's . . . it's still very cold.'

'Aye, and likely to get colder; there's been another three inches in the night an' it's still coming down. Here put this round you.' She brought a woollen shawl from the chair and placed it around Miss Brigmore's shoulders; then putting the breakfast tray across her knees, she said, 'Now get that down you, an' no saying you don't want it. I've been doing a lot of thinking since yesterday and what I thought was, we've got to go on livin'.'

Miss Brigmore looked up at Mary, and after a moment she said, 'Yes, Mary, you're quite right, we've got to go on living. But . . . but you must not make a practice of this; we won't have any change in our daily arrangements, I shall take breakfast in the dining room at half-past eight each morning as usual. But . . . but I thank you.'

Mary's face crumpled. She turned quickly from the bed, saying, 'Oh! miss,' and as she went out of the door she repeated, 'Oh! miss.'

Miss Brigmore could not face the breakfast of bacon, fried bread and white pudding, and so, after she had drunk two cups of tea, she carefully scraped the breakfast on to a napkin and put it in a drawer for disposal later. But first she made sure that the knife and fork showed signs of being used.

Half an hour later, dressed and trim as usual, she carried the tray downstairs; and Mary, looking at it, smiled and said, 'Well! that's it now; that's a good start. You can face any day if you've got somethin' in your stomach. That's what I say. Now the fire's blazin' and if you're going to do the accounts, it being Friday, don't you sit in that office but bring the books into the sitting room and make yourself comfortable.'

'Thank you, Mary.'

As she turned to go out, Mary said, 'You didn't say what you wanted for dinner; I could make a meat pudding which would be warmer, or there's the cold pie and odds and ends from yesterday.'

'I think we'll have the odds and ends, Mary.'

'Well, all right, please yourself, but the puddin' would have been more warmin' for you. Still, as I said, please yourself.'

Miss Brigmore crossed the hall to the sitting room. The day had started normal, except for her having breakfast in bed, and from now on she must keep it normal, but she would, as Mary sensibly suggested, bring her books from the office into the sitting room.

When she had done this and had set up the table some distance from the fire, she picked up her pen; then her hand dropped on to the open page of the household ledger and her head fell forward. This was loneliness, and no amount of routine was going to ease it, for the routine affected only the surface. Inside was a waste, as wide and frozen as the fells outside, and like the snow falling thickly beyond the window, she saw the years falling into it, yet not filling it but eroding it until there was nothing but the shell of her left.

As the tears welled up into her eyes she brought her head sharply up and her hand into a writing position, telling herself as she did so that she must practise what she had preached all these years, self-control, under all circumstances self-control. But her preaching hadn't borne much fruit, had it? Little more than a week ago her beloved Barbara had thrown self-control to the winds and told her what she thought. She had stood just there. she looked towards the window, then closed her eyes, saying sharply to herself, 'Enough, enough.' Then she bent over the account book.

2 lb sugar	1s. 6d.
¼ lb best Indian tea	1s. 6d.
¼ lb ordinary tea	1s. 0d.
¼ lb China tea	1s. 9d.

She paused. The China tea would be unnecessary in the future, it was Barbara who had liked China tea, and she herself sometimes offered the choice to visitors, but that would be unnecessary now. She scratched out the last item.

$\frac{1}{2}$ lb cheese   6d.

She went on adding items such as oatmeal, flour, yeast and finally ended up with lamp oil, half a dozen tallow candles and half-a-dozen wax candles.

Accounting for one person less in the household, the accounts should be one-third less, but they didn't work out like that, for the same amount of coal, wood, candles, and oil were needed. Yet she could cut down on oil; Barbara had kept her lamp alight well into the night.

The accounts finished, the order for the groceries made out to give to the carrier, when he could get through, she turned and looked towards the fire and asked herself what she should do now. Well, what did she do on other mornings? She had for the past few months been attending to Barbara's personal wants; prior to that period she would, at this time, have been at the Hall most weekdays certainly; week-ends she reserved for a little leisure for quiet reading and such. Now she had all the time in the world for quiet reading and such, and she hadn't the slightest desire to pick up a book.

At eleven o'clock Mary bustled in with a bowl of soup, saying, 'Ah, there now; I'm glad to see you sitting quiet for a minute.'

'You ... you haven't put anything extra in the soup, Mary?'

'No, no.' Mary shook her head from side to side. 'I wouldn't think about lacin' soup, now would I?' She smiled, then went to the scuttle, and as she lifted it to throw more coals on the fire Miss Brigmore said, 'It is quite all right, it is quite big enough for the time being. I'll attend to it when it needs it.'

Strange, she thought, that now when she had more money to spend on herself and the house than ever before, the frugal habits still held.

'Well, don't let it go too low.'

On this admonition Mary went out, and she was left alone again. She looked at the soup. She had no appetite for it, but there was no way of getting rid of it unless she opened the window. And that was impossible. Slowly she sipped at it and she had drunk only about a quarter of it when she heard the dull thumping against the outer wall, then the banging on the front door. She put the bowl down as she heard Mary go to the door; then Harry Bensham's voice came to her from the hall, saying, 'No, I'm not stayin', so I'll keep me coat on.'

When the sitting-room door opened she rose slowly from the couch, and he came straight towards her, saying, 'What a day! 'Tisn't fit for a dog to be out. Come on, get your things on.'

'Why?'

''Cos you're coming back with me, you're not staying here on your own, moping.'

'I'm ... I'm not moping, and I'm perfectly all right, and. . . .'

'Now look, I'm frozen to the marrow. I've committed a sort of crime getting those beasts out of the stables, I don't want to keep them standin' out there until they freeze to death. And another thing' – he came close to her now and looked down into her face – 'I'm lonely. There's times when I hate me own company, and it looks like I'll not get to the station for some days; they only just made it yesterday, an' by the skin of their teeth. By! that was a ride and a half. I don't know how we got back, near on ten o'clock when we got in. So come on, do me a good turn, and come and have a bite with me. An' bring Mary along. I'll tell her.'

Before she could say anything he had turned from her, opened the door and called into the hall, 'Mary! You, Mary!'

When Mary appeared from the kitchen he said, 'Get into your things, you're coming back with us.'

'Oh! oh! are we? Oh, that's good, that's good, Mr Bensham. I won't be a tick.'

He turned back into the room saying, 'No trouble in that quarter.' He was standing near her again. 'Come on,' he said gently; 'do this for me.'

He watched her head droop to the side, he watched her bite on her lip, then he watched her move slowly past him with lowered gaze and go out of the room. Turning to the fire, he parted his coat tails to let the blaze warm his buttocks while he said to himself, 'Aye! aye! well now, here we go!'

It was almost an hour later when the carriage stopped within a hundred yards of the Hall gates and Harry, opening the window and letting in a fierce icy blast, cried, 'What's it now?'

'It's the incline, sir, they can't make it, the wheels are skidding all the time.'

'Blast! Do you want help to push?'

'I . . . I doubt it would be very little use, sir, just the three of us, it'll need half a dozen or more. The back wheel looks as if it's gone into a rut.'

'Well' – Harry turned to Miss Brigmore – 'are you up to shanking it? Once we're off the road the drive isn't too bad, they cleared it yesterday.'

'Yes, yes, of course; we'll walk.'

Miss Bigmore had said they would walk, but even walking in the deep cart ruts, that had almost been filled again with the overnight snow, she found it impossible without the support of Harry's arm, and he, walking in the deeper snow in the middle of the ruts, lurched and slithered and several times fell against her, almost overbalancing them both. Mary, coming behind, was assisted by the second coachman.

When at last they reached the drive where there was but three or four inches of snow, Harry did not relinquish his hold on Miss Brigmore, but linked his arm in hers until they entered the vestibule, and there, pressing her forward into the hall, and Mary too, he cried, 'Now off with those wet boots and stockings the pair of you, and put your feet in hot water. I'll see it's upstairs afore you are. Brooks, see to that, will you? Get some cans of hot water up to Miss Brigmore's room. An' sharp now!'

Then in answer to a question that Brooks put to him he shouted back across the hall, 'No, no! not for me; the snow hasn't been made that'll get through these boots.'

He mounted the stairs behind Miss Brigmore and Mary and as they were about to disappear towards the gallery he called, 'as soon as you're ready, there'll be something hot downstairs. Don't make it too long.'

When Miss Brigmore reached the sitting room in the nursery wing she was gasping. She thought the walk through the snow had taken it out of her; she must be overtired for in the ordinary way it would have had no effect on her, she would have enjoyed it. She refused Mary's aid in helping her off with her outer clothes, saying, 'Get your own things off, your feet look sodden.'

Mary was three years younger than herself but she always treated her as if she were so much older.

When the first and second housemaids entered the room, both carrying large copper cans of hot water, she thanked them, and to Jenny Dring's remark, 'What a day for you to come out, miss!' she answered, 'Yes, it is rather wild.'

'Some bet the coach wouldn't get back to the cottage when the master left, never mind him getting back here.' Jenny poured the water into the china dish. 'But they lost their bets as I knew they would; when the master makes up his mind to do a thing he does it, I said. Like Mr Dan, they're both the same. . . .'

'Thank you, Jenny; we can manage.'

They had bet that the carriage wouldn't get to the cottage, and the master wouldn't get back here. There was nothing servants didn't know, the slightest nuance in the temper of the house was registered by them. No doubt they knew much more of what was in Harry Bensham's mind than she did with regard to what he intended to do with the Hall, yet she was certain in her own mind that he'd already decided to leave it, and his action today in bringing them from the cottage, considerate as it might appear, proved to her that he could not possibly tolerate living here alone. A man such as he, who had been used to noise and bustle all his life, would find living alone intolerable; and so, as she saw it, he would retire to Manchester and the company of Mrs Talbot, who undoubtedly would suit his requirements in many ways. She had promised Matilda that she would do her best in an advisory capacity to prevent such a liaison, but what could she do? And with a man like Mr Bensham! For she agreed with Jenny, if he made up his mind to do something the devil in. ... Really! really! Mary's sayings infiltrated one's mind, especially when one was low and off one's guard.

'Thank you, Mary; I can see to my own feet, you see to yours. But if you wouldn't mind handing me my house shoes from the cupboard and a pair of grey stockings from the second shelf, I'd be obliged. It's as well I didn't take them before.'

Ten minutes later Miss Brigmore, looking entirely herself except that there was no colour in her cheeks, stroked her hair from its centre parting and with both hands tucked a wayward tendril that was always escaping from a point near her temple to its place behind her ear; then turning to Mary, she said, 'When you're ready come down to Mrs Kenley's room, I will see her and arrange that you spend the day with her. You are not to stay up here alone.'

'Don't you worry about me, I can see to meself. I'll be down later on when I'm ready, you get yourself warmed, and food into you an' made comfortable.'

'Yes, yes, I will, Mary.'

She went out and down the nursery stairs, and then hesitated before she crossed the landing, debating whether to go down the main staircase and into the office and send for Mrs Kenley to come to her, or to go through the gallery and down the back staircase and to the housekeeper's room. She decided on the latter course because she knew Mrs Kenley would appreciate this; Mrs Kenley was a very good housekeeper and knew her place, but it was a good thing to recognize her postion with an occasional small gesture of this kind. She'd be sorry to part company with Mrs Kenley, for since the day she had chosen her from a number of applicants there had been mutual respect between them, and she herself had enough vanity to hope that wherever Mrs Kenley went after leaving this position, she would remember her with favour and as someone who knew the correct procedure in the maintenance of a large establishment.

She went through the gallery and her steps slowed before she came to the end of it. She loved the gallery. Years ago she had thought it a very romantic place; now she put the name stately to it. The deep windows were set at short intervals along one wall, each with its cushioned seat. When she was twenty-four she had likened them to lovers' seats, but when she was twenty-four she had been very young and silly. No, never silly. She had never been a silly person, she abhorred silly women.

She opened the far doors of the gallery, crossed the small landing, went through a green-baized door and into a passage, from where to the right a flight of stairs led down to the wide corridor from which doors gave off to the housekeeper's sitting room, the upper staff dining room, the servants' hall, the butler's pantry, the doors to the cellars, the door to the kitchen, and at the extreme end, the gun room.

The stairs leading to the passage were part spiral and before she rounded the curve which would have brought her in sight of the passage below and those in it, she heard Harry Bensham's voice raised in anger.

She paused with her foot halfway towards another step, withdrew it and stood undecided for a moment whether to descend or to return the way she had come. But she remained standing where she was when she heard Harry say, 'Now look here, Brooks? I've stood enough of this. You've had it coming to you for a long time, but this is the finish. I won't cut your pension 'cos I'm not a man who goes back on me word, but as soon as this snow clears you can get yourself back to Manchester. You've taken advantage of me over the years, more so of late since you've got the idea that your Willy's coming into the family. Well, that isn't clinched yet, not by a long chalk. And if he was in it already I'd still say this to you, you mind your own bloody business. I'm master in this house and when I give an order I expect it to be carried out the same as I would at the mill, an' if I was to tell you that hot water had to be carried up to Lily Rossiter's room I'd expect it to be done, and no backchat or bloody innuendoes.'

From her place around the curve in the stairs Miss Brigmore was not surprised to hear Mr Bensham use the word bloody, but she was definitely surprised that he should use innuendo. It was as she had thought for a long time, there was more in his head than he'd let out. It pleased him to play the rough, ignorant individual. He had also called the butler by his surname. His next words startled her.

'You and her never got on 'cos you, like all your tribe, you don't recognize class when it's under your nose, unless it's stinkin' with money. Well now, I'm going to tell you somethin', and you're privileged in a way 'cos you're the first one I've voiced it to, an' it's this. If I get my way she's here for life. Now put that in your pipe and smoke it, and give all the others a whiff of it. And I don't think there'll be one that won't welcome it except yourself, because as I've known from the first it was a mistake to bring you here, you were never cut

426

out for the job. An' what's more I'll tell you this when you're on, you haven't hoodwinked me all these years. You might have been going to have consumption in the first place, but there's many worse off than you who carried on workin'. Because we ran the streets together when we were nippers, you played on me, at least you thought you did, but I've had your measure, an' what I overheard you saying a few minutes ago proved I've been right in me surmise of you all along. Now, now, don't come back with anything, Brooks, 'cos I won't listen. As I said, as soon as it's cleared up you get back to your beginnings. You won't be badly off, I'll see to that, or Willy will, that's if he hasn't got too big for his boots and doesn't recognize you. And mind, I'm tellin' you this, that's something you've got to look out for an' all.'

Silently but hastily, Miss Brigmore retraced her steps back to the next landing; then quietly she let herself into the gallery again, and after walking a little way down it she stopped near one of the tall windows and lowered herself on to the velvet seat. She was here for life; he was putting her in charge, he was going to keep the place on after all and let her manage it. He had never mentioned Mrs Talbot. It didn't sound as if he were going to marry. Some of the weight lifted from her heart. Oh, this was kind of him, indeed it was. Oh yes, indeed. Doubtless he had been swayed by pity for her loneliness knowing how devastated she was at the loss of Barbara. He was a kind man; she'd always had proof of that, but now she knew he was also a compassionate man.

She looked out over the frozen landscape, and it did not appear quite so bleak and desolate now. What had Brooks said about her that had brought his master to her defence? Something from her past life doubtless, for there was nothing about it that wasn't common knowledge.

When she heard a movement outside the far door she rose swiftly to her feet, smoothed the front of her gown and walked sedately along the gallery. As she neared the door it was opened by Armstrong, and he stood hastily to the side and held it well back in order that she might pass through; and she inclined her head towards him and said, 'Thank you, Armstrong.'

Emerson, who was crossing the hall, observed her descending the main staircase and he turned sharply about and went towards the drawing-room door, and there he waited until she approached, when he opened it for her.

The servants had always been civil in their manner towards her, but in these two last encounters there had been a subtle change leading to deference. She thought wryly that lightning had no edge on the communications in a servants' hall.

'Ah! there you are. Feel warmer?'

'Yes, thank you.'

'Come and sit yourself down and drink some of this hot toddy; perhaps it'll bring some of the colour back into your cheeks, you look as white as a sheet.

'There you are.' She had settled herself in the corner of the couch opposite the roaring fire, and before handing her the steaming mug from the tray he pushed a foot stool towards her using his own foot in the process, 'Put your feet up; you might as well make yourself comfortable for it looks as if you're set for a few days.'

He now sat down on the couch, not in the far corner from her but in the middle, within arm's distance of her, and after drinking the steaming sweetened whisky and water, he lay back and exclaimed on a sigh, 'Ah! that's better. How about you?'

'It's ... it's very warming.'

'Well, don't make a meal of it, drink at all up. Talkin' about a meal, I had a word with Mrs Kenley; she thought you might like to start with hare soup, she says you're fond of that, and then some sweetbreads. For me own choice, I picked a saddle of mutton; to my mind nothin' beats a saddle of mutton, with plenty of carrots. Then she suggested almond pudding. I'm not one for puddin's as you know, give me some cheese. But will that be all right?'

'Yes, yes, indeed.'

'I thought we'd have it early, say about two o'clock. You know I'm used to having me meal around midday, habit I suppose. I never fell in with this three o'clock business 'cos around five I like me tea, and when I say tea I mean tea, not just a cup you know, like we have here, but a good spread with muffins, oh aye! toasted muffins in the winter, there's nothing like them, and a granny loaf. I'm not very fond of your fancy cakes but I like breads you know, currant or spiced, or with caraway seeds, any kind of bread. But when you have a big tuck-in around three you've got no room for anything more till supper, have you?'

'No, that's correct.'

He edged himself round on the couch now until he was looking at her squarely, and he repeated softly, 'That's correct.'

Then as she looked at him and blinked he waited a moment before saying, 'Miss Brigmore, do you think we could stop being correct just for the day, as a trial like?'

'You are laughing at me, Mr Bensham.'

He bent slightly towards her now and, his voice low, he said, 'No, lass, I'm not laughin' at you, I'm asking something of you. You know, we've known each other a long, long time, a lifetime you could say, and you've never unbent once, not in my presence anyway. Do you know that? You've never even been Brigie to me. You would be Brigie

428

to the bairns, and act like Brigie I suppose, but to me you've always acted like Miss Brigmore, and nothing seemed to alter you. I've chaffed you about it, I've even bullied you a bit, but nothing I did could make you unbend. Matilda used to say you weren't starchy with her, so why couldn't you treat me in the same way?'

Miss Brigmore drew in a short sharp breath before she said, 'Because of our respective positions.'

'Respective positions be damned! Aw' – he tossed his head to one side – 'I'm not going to apologize for swearin'. You'll hear more than that afore you're finished. Anyway, you should be used to it by now, you've heard me at it long enough. And I say again, respective positions be damned! I wasn't a Thomas Mallen.... And now-now-now' – his hand came out suddenly and gripped hers – 'don't stiffen up 'cos I mention his name, 'cos I'm casting no aspersions, because from what I can gather he seemed to be a bloke more sinned against than sinning; bit too generous in all ways I should have said. If he had his fling he paid for it. And I pity any man who goes bankrupt, and I've seen a few. I've been scared of it meself in me time. So look at it this way, if I can talk about Matilda surely you can bear that he be spoken of, because he was, in a way, your husband. Now' – he lifted up one finger and sternly wagged it at her, and his face was equally stern as he said, 'I'm goin' to get something straight, I've been wanting to put it straight for a long time. You thought I insulted you once, didn't you, because I said I couldn't understand how you'd been his mistress? Well, you didn't let me finish what I was going to say that time. It was no insult I was handing you, because having come to know you I thought this much, you weren't the kind of woman to give yourself lightly to anybody, and it wasn't your fault if you weren't married to him. He was a widower and I don't know why he didn't give you his name. But there it is; that's your business and I'm not probing into it, now, or at any other time. But what I wanted to say that time, and what you stopped me saying, but what I'm determined to say now, is that I'm not asking you to be me mistress, I'm asking you to be my wife.'

His voice had dropped low in his throat. He was holding her hand; they were staring at each other, and when she didn't speak he went on, 'You mightn't know it but I've cared for you for a long time; oh aye, long afore I lost Matilda. Matilda knew it. At least, looking back on the things she said, I think she had a pretty good idea. You see, I'd never met anybody like you in me life afore. Oh, I'd mixed with the up and ups an' their wives in Manchester, and when I say the up and ups, I mean the up and ups, from the Mayor onwards. But what were their women? If they were good looking they had nowt in their heads, and some of them were no better than well-dressed trollops. It was just to show them what I could do that I bought this place; I intended to bring them here in their cart-loads when I first set up. I did bring two parties but somehow it didn't work out. Matilda, as you know, never had the touch, an' they looked down their noses at her. By God! They did that, the snots!'

She did not wince, and he went on; 'It was at that point that I thought, well, I'll have me bairns so trained that nobody 'll look down their noses at them. And so you came on the scene; an' you know, it was from then that I began to have a different slant on life, at least what I mean is I saw there was another way to living it. But I knew it was too late for me, I was no longer pliable. I'd been brought up in the rough. And then the Manchester lot, money, money, money; that's all anybody could think about, or talk about. And it isn't a bad thing either, I'm not despising it mind; but I found it had a place, and it was only of value when you could use it to make you and them about you happy. I wanted to talk about these things. I wanted to have things explained to me, then to argue about them, and being me, to deny them while at bottom believing they were right. And I wanted to do all this with you. But you would have none of it, or me. You know you used to look at me sometimes as if I wasn't worth threepennorth of copper. And I wasn't in your eyes, and I resented it. Very likely that's why I showed you me worst side. Loosen your stays, I used to say, remember? And I could have kicked meself when you went out of the room.'

'Oh, Miss Brigmore' – he nodded at her now, a smile creeping over his face – 'you've given me a lot of food for thought. Anyway, there it is, I've had me say, or nearly. One thing more. You might not think it's fittin' that I should talk like this and Matilda not being gone a year, but Matilda would have been the first one to understand, and if the subject had come up she would have said, "Do it right away, lad; there's only one thing I don't want you to do," she would have said, "and that's let Florrie get her claws into you." Oh, she hated Florrie. An' so did you, didn't you?' He bent his face closer towards hers.

'Oh, Mr Bensham.'

'Aw! for God's sake, lass, drop the Mr Bensham.' He flung one arm outwards. 'Me name's Harry. Can't you call me Harry? Now look; I can see I've startled you; we'll leave it for a time, we'll have a meal, eh? and then a game of cards, I like a game of cards. There's something else I like, an' I bet this'll surprise you, I like to be read to. You know when I used to sit in the bedroom, supposedly reading the paper while you read to Matilda, I used to lap it up. I never had time to read; I've never read a book in me life; and that's not sayin' I don't want to, or I don't like to hear a good story. Sounds as if I'm going into me second childhood, doesn't it? But no, I think there's lots of blokes like me;

looking back from my age they're full of regrets at not having learned a little about things. But it's not too late, is it? Is it?'

He waited, and when her head fell forward and she covered her eyes with one hand, while her voice breaking, she murmured, 'No, no, it's n ... not too late,' he hitched himself rapidly towards her, and, putting his arms about her, he said, 'There, lass. There. Don't cry. I'm sorry. It must have come as a shock to you. But in any case let me tell you this.' He dared to put his hand up to her hair and stroke it. 'If you can't see your way clear to becomin' Mrs Bensham I'd still want you to run this house, take over sort of permanent like, live here. You could let Mary have the cottage. You'd be doing me a favour in that way if nothing else, 'cos I can't bear coming here and eating alone; sittin' by meself in this barracks nearly drives me mad. I could sell it. I've told meself over and over again that if you turn me down that's what I'll do, I'll sell it, but at the bottom I know it would go against the grain, selling it I mean. I would sort of lose prestige; and you know fellows in my position cling like limpets to prestige; self-made men have to have something to show for their efforts, or else what'd be the use of it all. Aw, come on. I'm sorry, I'm sorry I've made you bubble. You've never heard that word afore, have you?' He pushed her gently from him, and putting his hand under her chin, lifted her tear-stained face upwards. 'Me grandma came from the north-east, Shields way. She was always using that word. "Stop your bubblin'," she would say, "else I'll skelp the hunger off ya." I can't make you laugh, can I?'

Miss Brigmore hastily sought in the pocket of her grey woollen dress for a handkerchief; when she found it she dabbed her eyes and gently blew her nose. Then she looked at the man sitting opposite to her. His face was rugged, his hair was grey, his eyes were a clear blue; unlike Thomas's body, his was flat and, if the flesh of his hands and face were anything to go by, firm. He was a much younger looking man than Thomas, but he was the antithesis of Thomas. Thomas had been a gentleman, this man was rough; yet he was not coarse, there was a difference; and he had confessed an eagerness for some kind of culture. Yet she knew that nothing she or anyone else could do would put a veneer on him, not at this stage of his life. Yet perhaps she could feed the inward need in him, as he would help fill up the great void in her.

But as yet she could not take in the real import of his offer. He had asked her to marry him.... *marry him*. She would no longer be Miss Brigmore, she would be Mrs Bensham, and she'd be mistress of this house. It all had the quality of a dream. She who had come into this house as a governess thirty-six years ago, and had worked in the nursery for six years before Thomas went bankrupt, but not once

431

during these early years had she been invited to a meal or function downstairs, never had she sat in the dining room until the man sitting opposite to her had invited her to his table. During the ten years or more she had spent in the cottage with Thomas, she had never received a penny in wages, and times without number she had pretended loss of appetite in order that Thomas and the girls should have better helpings. She had suffered humiliation and not a little privation in serving the Mallens, and what had been her reward?

Now here was this man offering to make her mistress of the Hall. Had it come as a surprise to her? Yes, yes. Oh, yes it had. She was not unaware of her accomplishments, but she had little personal vanity, and had never, never imagined that she had been in Mr Bensham's thoughts all these years. It was something she must get used to and she would get used to it, and she would repay him for the honour he was doing her. Oh yes, yes, she would; and she began to say this.

'You are doing me a great honour in. . . .'

He cut her short. 'Now, now, Brigie, don't go into any polite palaver, not at this point. If you want to tell me now, just say yes or no, an' let's have it.'

She blinked rapidly, blew her nose gently again, then said 'I am honoured to accept your proposal, Mr Bensham.'

She watched the muscles of his face drop, she watched his mouth spread into a wide smile, she watched his hand come up and cover his brows and then his eyes. She watched his shoulder shake, and then he began to laugh.

'Aw! lass, lass, you're the limit. Look' – he was gripping her hands tightly now. 'Repeat after me: Harry I'll take you.'

Her chin dropped slightly, her eyes closed for a second, a smile hovered around her mouth and she repeated, in a voice little above a whisper, 'Harry, I'll take you.'

'There! There!' His voice was no longer quiet, it was like a bellow, and the next moment she was enveloped in a hug that jerked the breath out of her. And then his lips were on hers, right on her mouth, and his kiss was hard and warming, so warm that it seemed to melt her body right through to the void. And she was as surprised as he was when she relaxed against him and her hand touched the back of his neck.

It was some minutes before he released her. Then holding her at arm's length and with his head to one side, he said, 'There's some good years ahead of us yet, lass. And you'll be surprised to know one of the things I'm looking forward to is the things you can learn me.'

As she looked back into his face her gaze was soft, her mind gentle towards him, and she did not correct him and say, 'There is nothing I

432

can learn you, I can only teach, it is you who must learn.' But what she said and with a smile in her eyes, and on her lips, was 'I'll be delighted to learn you ... Mr Bensham.'

And at this he again pulled her into his arms and close to him, and what he said was, 'I'll Mr Bensham you afore I'm finished, Anna Brigmore, by lad! I will.'

THE MALLEN
LITTER

PART ONE

Full Circle

KATIE 1885

I

T HE NIGHT WAS HOT, and the rank, acrid smell of packed humanity hung over the narrow streets like an oppressive canopy of evil.

Miss Katie Bensham lifted her skirts as she stepped across an open drain running from the middle of a back lane, then almost skipped aside to avoid the onrush of a group of bare-foot excited boys chasing a dog which had no less than five tins tied to its tail. Turning, she cried after them, 'Stop that! Do you hear me? Stop that!' but even before she had finished speaking they had disappeared from her view up yet another narrow street, and she stood listening to the fading sound of their cries for a full minute before moving on again.

'Education!' She snorted the word aloud.

In 1880 when the Government had at last made it compulsory for all children to attend school she had thought in her enthusiastic naivety that this would solve all problems, especially with the young; but whereas some parents would react with 'Eeh! it's a good thing, it's a chance we never had; I only hope we'll be able to keep the bairns there,' too many others said, 'What they after, them up there, eh, forcin' them to school? You can't fill their bellies with readin' an' writin'. Anyway, they're havin' it too easy the day; why, me, I was in the dye works at seven.'

Dye works, gas works, mills . . . mills, *mills*. Wherever you looked, mills. But she of all people shouldn't despise mills; all the benefits she'd enjoyed during her life had been derived from her father's mill. Yet it was because her mother, like her father, had come from surroundings similar to these she was walking through now that she had turned her back on the privileged way of life.

With the death of her mother five years ago she had been thrown emotionally back, as it were, into the past, suffering for her mother's early beginnings as her mother herself never had; all her mother had ever wanted from life was enough to eat, a good fire, and the company of her man. When she had been lifted bodily from the poverty of the Hulme district of Manchester into the affluence of 27 The Drive, on the Palatine Road, and from there to High Banks Hall in the County of Northumberland, her spirit had not moved but had remained in the place where it had been born, and no amount of good living had made an impression on her; not even the presence of Miss Brigmore, the governess, had had any effect on Matilda Bensham.

For some time now Katie Bensham had been aware that she was leading a double life, at least in her mind. Three times a week she went to the Morton Rooms from half-past seven in the evening till nine to take adult classes. Some of her pupils came straight from work at eight o'clock, and there they sat learning to write their names; before they knew their alphabet she taught them to write their names: Mary McManus, Jane Gorton, Florrie Smith, Ada Wilkinson. She had twenty-seven in her class and only two with Irish names, McCabe and McManus. On Saturday nights she took a reading class for the advanced pupils; this was a mere courtesy title for in five years she had found not one person who she could say was outstanding. Sometimes she thought it was her way of teaching, for there were others in the town who could brag of their classes giving birth to scholars and orators, young men who spoke for the unions; even the Sunday schools seemed to achieve better results than she. She guessed, and knew she guessed rightly, that being a mill owner's daughter she was looked upon with suspicion; not even the fact that her father was such an owner as Harry Bensham who himself had come up from a worker, could encourage those who sought knowledge to patronize her classes; and so those who did come to her for instruction were of very low mentality. She doubted if even Miss Brigmore could have advanced them more than she herself had done.

But what troubled her even more than her failure was the realization that the work she was doing, she was doing against the grain, for she had recognized through her continual self-dissecting that she lacked the quality necessary to the pioneer; also the tenacity and selfishness, this last and very necessary ingredient that pushed every other obstacle aside but the main one, the cause, if one was truly committed.

What she had learned during her years of pressured good works wa that most of the people who lived in these warrens thought little beyond food, shelter and warmth, and it was the scarcity of these tha blighted their lives, and not the necessity to read or write.

She knew that if she gave up the venture tomorrow the little goo she was doing would not be missed. And she knew she would give it u if it wasn't for one person, and this person wasn't her father, or Mis Brigmore, her one-time governess, who was now his wife, or her elde brother, John, but Willy Brooks, the man she was going to marry the man who, like her father had worked his way up from the mill floor.

Five minutes later she emerged from the warren of the narrow streets into a neighbourhood where the houses were two-up and two-down, their high-walled back yards leading into narrow alleys. Whenever she looked up these cobbled back lanes to the endless back doors accompanied by their own particular dry lavatories and coal hatches she was reminded of Brigie's arithmetic lessons, dot and carry one, only here it was dot and carry two.

She crossed the main road, itself a barrier between classes, for beyond the accumulation of shops, public houses and churches lay the terraced houses of the upper working class, and they had to be upper for they were lying against the skirts of the lower middle class. But here again was a barrier, of open ground this time, green open ground, and leading from it the carriage road and the residences of the mighty.

No one referred to these particular dwellings as homes or houses, they were residences, and were you writing a letter to the head of a residence, you always, unless you were very stupid, added esquire after his name.

27 The Drive lay well towards the middle of this superior patch of Manchester earth. It was the house where Katie had been born and she thought of it more as home than she did of High Banks Hall in Northumberland where she had lived from when she was four until she was nineteen.

She considered it was just as well she had always retained an affection for her first home for here she was to spend her married life, at least that's how she had thought until about a year ago; or was it before that? When had she begun to change? When had she seen Willy as he really was, and as others saw him, the upstart son of her father's butler? Since she was a girl she had viewed him through a romantic vision, seeing him as someone like her father, an ambitious, brash, pushing individual, but an honest one. She had even judged him to be much more intelligent than her father, for it was her father's first wife who had brought him a mill, whereas here was Willy at twenty-nine, under-manager of one of the most prosperous mills in the town, and he had got there by his own efforts. But of late she had been asking herself whether he had achieved this position through intelligence or cunning, sucking up was the local phrase. But one thing he had made her quite sure of, he was not going to be content with being under-manager once they were married, oh no, he was for a partnership. He hadn't put it into so many words but she had acquired the power to read his mind; a look, a gesture, and she could divine his thought. He didn't need to open his mouth. She also knew that although he loved

441

her, and she hadn't any doubt about this, he naturally saw her as the key that would open the door to big opportunities.

She turned in through the iron gates and after walking half-way up the curving drive she stopped and stood looking towards the sombre, bay-windowed house and asked herself sharply, what was she going to do? There were only two months to the wedding. The presents would start coming in shortly; if she didn't do it soon, she wouldn't be able to do it at all. She wished her dad were here, or Brigie, or John or someone.

When she entered the house she was panting as if she had run up the drive. She walked through the small conservatory and opened the amber-paned glass door into the hall. It was a small hall, half-panelled, with the stairs leading up from the end of it. To the left were doors going off to the kitchen, dining room and morning room. To the right were those which led to the sitting room and study.

The sitting-room door was open, and as she stood unpinning her hat before the hallstand the voice coming from the room caused her to turn her head, stop withdrawing the hat pin, take two steps backwards and glance into the sitting room. What she saw was her future husband standing in the middle of the room talking to someone, and what he was saying concerned the furniture ... the removal of it, the scrapping of it. Pulling the second long pin quickly from her hat, she jabbed it in again before throwing the hat on to the hallstand and walking swiftly towards the sitting room. Pausing in the doorway, she looked at Willy. He had his back to her, his arm was stretched out wide, and standing near the table, a tray in her hand, was Bella Brackett, the house-parlourmaid, and Bella's eyes flicked apprehensively from the man who was to become her master to her mistress as the former said, 'Yes, that's what I intend to do, Bella, make a clean sweep of the lot.'

'Indeed!'

When Willy Brooks turned sharply about he showed no sign of embarrassment, nor did the high colour of his square, roughly handsome face heighten or lessen; quite casually he said, 'Oh, hello there.'

Katie did not answer him but walked briskly into the room, saying to Bella as she passed her, 'I'd like a cold drink, Bella, please.'

'Yes, miss. Yes, miss.'

She did not speak again until the door was closed; then casting a sideward glance at him she said very quietly, 'So that's what you intend to do, make a clean sweep?'

'Now, Katie.' He came towards her, his arms outstretched, and attempted to draw her to him, but not only did she resist his embrace, she also struck at his hands, and, her voice no longer quiet, she cried,

'Mr Willy Brooks has spoken. I'm interested to hear you've decided to make a clean sweep of this room. And, of course, that will go for the rest of the house I presume. My needs, my opinions, my tastes are of no account. You have made up your mind as to what you want. The law is passed; the master has spoken. You tell Bella. . . .'

'Now look here! Come off your high horse.' His voice was harsh now. 'What's got into you? Coming in like that. It's that blasted dung heap you insist on sitting on; you're always like this when you come back from doing your good works. All I said to her was. . . .'

'That you were going to make a clean sweep.'

'All right, all right.' He wagged his head at her. 'That's what I said, a clean sweep, an' that's what it wants, the whole bloomin' house.'

'Really!' Her tone was again studiously quiet.

'Aye, really. And don't give me any of your Miss Brigmore manner 'cos I won't stand for it, you know how it maddens me. We've been through all this. You've said yourself you were sick of antimacassars, bobbled mantel borders' – he flicked his hands towards the velvet drapes surrounding the fireplace – 'overmantels, oil-cloth in the bedrooms. You said yourself you were going to have carpets.'

'Yes, I said I was going to have carpets. And yes, I admit that I said I was tired of antimacassars, et cetera. But I said this to you, I did not say it to the maid. I consulted you, but what I didn't say was that I was going to make a clean sweep. There are some very good pieces of furniture here. This couch' – she patted the head of the couch – 'is beautifully upholstered. Do you intend to replace it with a horsehair one? Or are you going to the other extreme, is it to be chaises longues and choice Louis pieces? Perhaps you'd like to take a trip across the Channel and inspect the décor of the French salons?'

'Stop it! Stop it!' His face was flaming now. 'I've told you, haven't I, there's one thing I can't stand an' that's your High Banks manner.'

'Oh, really!' She half turned from him and looked towards the window and into the deepening twilight before she said, 'I should have thought you would have encouraged me to use it permanently so that I could live up to the style you are aiming to adopt once we're married.'

'Style? What are you getting at? What's up with you? You're the one who's preached that it's every man's duty to drag himself out of the mud. You go down town three times a week preaching just that an' rousing the women up.'

'Yes, yes' – she turned on him now, all her calmness gone, her voice as strident as his – 'so that they can better themselves, live decently, read, write, be clean, but not with the idea that they'll forget themselves and. . . .'

'Well, well! now.' His lip curled. 'That's the idea, Tory to the end. Give them a leg up, but just so far 'cos they mustn't be allowed to forget themselves, they mustn't overstep the mark an' put a foot on your level, or else. . . .'

'Don't twist my words. And don't try to tell me you advocate otherwise, because you don't. You're an advocate for just one person, and that person's Willy Brooks. Your trouble is you've got too big for your boots. And yes, your head's got too big for your hat, literally, because you're no longer content to wear a billy pot, it has to be a tall one, and silk, hasn't it? You've dropped all your old friends; you've even got your father installed with his sister in Doncaster, not for his good as you'd have me believe, but because you didn't want him under your feet. He was a servant, the one-time butler at High Banks, he could be pointed out as such and that would never do for Willy Brooks, the mill owner. Because that's what you're aiming at, isn't it? And my brother Dan's not on the scene now. Like the prodigal son, Dan has left the fold and shows no sign of coming back. There's only John, and me, and when I marry what's mine is yours, isn't it? By law what's mine is yours. . . . And what hasn't gone unnoticed by you for a moment is that John hasn't been well of late. . . .'

'Shut up! Stop it afore it's too late. You've already said things you'll be sorry for the morrow.' He grabbed her by the shoulders, and when he shook her she tore herself from his hold and, scrambling around the couch, she looked across at him and cried, 'I won't be sorry for anything I've said because it's the truth and you know it. And there's just one more thing I've got to say.' She stared at him while she pulled the ring from her finger. Then holding it out to him, she muttered, 'It's over.'

His colour changed again. It drained from his cheekbones; it left his mouth startlingly white against the day's stubble on his face. He hunched his shoulders until he looked like a bull about to charge, and his voice sounded like a growl as he said, 'Oh no. Oh no, you don't, Katie Bensham. You've led me up the garden, haven't you, right up the garden to the house door. Two months afore we're to be married an' you do this. I played fair by you an' your dad; I told him I wouldn't put it to you until you were twenty-one and here we've been almost three years engaged, and now you tell me.' His head bent lower still, his eyes became slits and he peered at her as he asked now in a demanding whisper, 'Why? why?'

She did not speak for the simple reason that she couldn't; his manner and appearance frightened her. And this was a strange experience, for having walked the slum areas of the town for years now, meeting up with every dissolute grade of humanity, she had never felt afraid; disgusted, nauseated, but never afraid. Now, as she stared round-eyed at the distorted face of the man she had once thought attractively handsome, she knew that in a way she was lucky for she was about to escape from an association that would have become unbearable. This man glaring at her was the Willy Brooks that she would surely have encountered some time after marriage, and here was a man who would stand no interference, here was one who would act not only as lord and master in his own house, or hers, but also as God.

Her voice shook slightly as she said, 'I . . . I made a mistake and I've found it out in time. It's . . . it's well for both of us that I have done so.'

'You'll not get away with this, you young bitch you! by God you won't. I'll see to that. You'll keep that ring an' we'll be married, we'll be married or I'll. . . .'

'Don't you dare speak to me like that.' Her fear of him was swept away on a gust of anger. 'And we won't be married ever. And now I'll thank you to leave. And . . . and I don't want to see you again at my house. . . . *My house*, remember, my house. Father gave me this house, this house which you have coveted since you were a boy. . . .' She stopped suddenly and stared at him; he was shaking from head to foot as if with ague. The shock had been too much, even for one of his tough character. The little empire he had pictured himself ruling had been destroyed in battle, and it had been a battle.

As if he had picked up the last word in her mind he now muttered, 'Don't think I'm beaten, don't think this is the end of me. There's mills in this town that would jump at me. And I've got influence, influence you know nowt about. If I left the mill I could halve your trade in six months, I could that. But I'll not leave, not till I'm ready, right and ready, an' then we'll see.'

As she watched him buttoning his coat as if he would wrench the material apart there came into her mind the thought, the surprising thought, that there had been no word of love mentioned. He had not said, 'But I love you, Katie,' or, 'Why have you stopped loving me?'

She had imagined it was because he was so deeply in love with her that she had these past years overlooked so many objectionable traits in his character, traits that she had not seen when, as a young impressionable girl, she had allowed her fancy to be caught by his looks, his fearlessness, and his arrogance of manner, which was so like her father's, and all which had shown themselves from his early visits to the Hall.

She realized now she was being shaken by the fact that whatever feelings he'd had for her had been used as a means to further his ambitions, and that in this moment he was not missing her as a lover should, but only as a business man might who had seen the foundations of his plans swept away through the foibles of a female. She could have been any female.

He had reached the door and had turned and was glaring at her again. His face looked blanched with bitterness, he looked years older than twenty-nine. He said now, 'I'm goin' along to see your John. This business isn't goin' to be dropped lightly, I can tell you that. But I'll also tell you that if you come to your senses I won't hold it against you.'

She knew she was doing the unforgivable thing when, adopting what he called her Miss Brigmore manner, she gave a soft laugh before saying, 'Thank you, thank you, Mr Brooks. I shall always remember your clemency, and should I in future regret the severing of our association I shall know that I have but myself to blame.'

Again she knew a moment's fear for he had taken a step back towards her, and she could see now he was striving to fight down an anger, an anger that, under other circumstances, could have brought his fist lashing out and into her face, for he had been brought up in an environment where such a reaction was natural.

Being unable to avail himself of this outlet he had to have the last word. To his mind, it was only right that a man should have the last word, and what he said sounded, to her ears, childish in the extreme but quite in pattern with an inherent part of him for he used the idiom of the mill. 'By God!' he said, 'I'll see my day with you, Katie Bensham. An' if me prayers are answered you'll never know another minute's luck. You'll remember this night an' you'll live to regret it. You'll sup sorrow with a big spoon afore you die. By Christ! you will, you bitch you.'

The banging of the front door resounded through the house and its impact seemed to take her feet from beneath her, for she stumbled, and only just managed to grab at a chair and fall on to its seat. She closed her eyes and joined her hands tightly on her lap, and her head fell forward on to her breast. She was rid of him. She hadn't done it fairly, she had taken advantage of the opportunity his conversation with Bella had provided; but what matter, it was over. It was over. She was free. There was only her father and John to face now.

446

2

H ARRY BENSHAM turned over and dropped into another valley in the feathered tick of the huge four-poster bed and grabbed at his wife who was about to rise, saying, 'What's your hurry? Lie a bit and let's have a little crack.'

'It is half past seven.'

'What of it! Look' – he pulled her round – 'this is our house, our home, we haven't got to get on the job afore the buzzer blows.'

'I always like being down to breakfast by half past eight, you know I do, and it keeps the. . . .'

'Aye, it keeps the servants on their toes. But Mrs Kenley is quite capable of keeping the servants on their toes until half past nine . . . or ten, or eleven for that matter. You know something?' He put out his hand and gripped her chin gently. 'There's a part of you that'll be Miss Brigmore till the day they carry you downstairs in a box. And I'd like to bet, as they drop you into the grave you'll push the lid up and say' – he now gave a good imitation of her voice – '"Keep me level, please".'

'Oh! Harry.'

They both lay back on the pillows now and smothered their laughing.

After a moment Harry's hand again went out to her face. And now he stroked her cheek as he said gently, 'Aye, lass. How long have we been married?'

'Long enough for you to have got over your frivolity.'

Again he was laughing, but chuckling deeply now. 'Frivolity! The words you use. Me and frivolity. Three years and eleven months, isn't it, come next Saturday? You see I know it even to a day. And you know something else? I've never known such days. You're a wonderful lass . . . that's when' – he nodded at her – 'that's when you forget you're no longer Miss Brigmore but Mrs Bensham. But I guess you'll be governessing to the end of your days. Mind you, I'm not grumbling

447

at that either. I like your governessing, except' – he now dug her gently between her breasts with his doubled fist – 'except at half past seven in the mornin'. If Matilda had even dared suggest gettin' me out at half past seven when not at the works I'd have brained her. . . . I often think of Matilda you know, Brigie.'

'I do too, Harry.'

He half turned on to his back and gazed up at the canopy over the top of the bed. 'She knew all this would happen. I keep remembering things she said afore she died, and I know now it was in her mind that we would come together. I'm lucky, I'm a lucky man.' He again turned his face towards her. 'I've been lucky all me life . . . even with the first one, 'cos if I hadn't got her I wouldn't have got the mill, would I?' He grimaced at her. 'Then I got Matilda. She was a good lass was Matilda. I used to go for her hell for leather, call her all the numskulls on the earth but she never held it against me, she loved me till the end. Do you know something?' He turned fully on to his side and faced her. 'That's something I've never asked you, but I'll do it now. Do you love me, Brigie?'

It wasn't Miss Anna Brigmore, the governess who had come to High Banks Hall in 1845 to teach Thomas Mallen's wards, who now looked back into Harry Bensham's eyes, nor was it the woman who had become Thomas Mallen's mistress and served him for twelve years after he had lost everything, nor yet the woman who had brought up his tragic daughter, Barbara. Barbara who, as a means of escape, had married Dan Bensham and gone away and left her desolate. Nor was it the woman who, at that particular stage when loneliness had enveloped her, had accepted this man's offer of marriage with gratitude but without love. But it was the woman made new by marriage, and the dignity of the title of Mrs which upheld her, that looked at him now and could say in all sincerity, and with gratitude redoubled, 'Yes, Harry, I have learned to love you.'

'Aw, lass.' When his arms went about her and he pulled her into the billowy hollow of the bed tick her body merged into his and they lay pressed close, his lips hard on hers.

When she released herself from him and said softly, 'Breakfast,' he said, 'Damn breakfast!'

Firmly lifting herself from his embrace she sat up, but when she went to put her legs over the side of the bed he caught at her gown. She remained still for a moment. Then turning her head slowly towards him she said primly, 'Will you kindly leave go of my night-gown, Mr Bensham?'

'It isn't a night-gown, it's a shift. Go on' – he slapped at her buttock while still keeping hold of the gown – 'say shift. Go on, woman, say shift.'

'If you don't let go of my night-gown, Mr Bensham, I shall . . . *shift* you on to the floor this instance.'

At this he released his hold on her, lay back on the pillows again and laughed aloud, and as he watched her going towards the dressing room he said, 'By! you can twist words about. Leave that door open mind; I want to talk to you.'

But he did not talk to her right away but lay listening to the sound of her washing. Then after a time he turned on to his side and called, 'What about going to 27 this week-end, eh? I wouldn't mind seeing one of them concerts again by that Charles Hallé fellow.'

Her voice came from the dressing room, saying, 'I don't think they will have begun yet, not until the autumn.'

'Well, there's bound to be something else going on. I remember years ago when I was a young fellow, Philip, that was me first wife's brother, he died young, he used to go to what he called gentlemen's concerts.'

'I think the present concerts were derived from those.'

'We could go to a theatre, something lively.'

'If the weather keeps like this, it would be very hot.'

'Well, it was only a suggestion. I'm content here if you are; I sometimes think you get a bit bored.'

She appeared at the open door. She was adjusting her top petticoat. Her hands behind her, she tied the strings as she said, 'Bored? You imagine I'm bored here?'

'Aye, sometimes, with the look on your face.'

Slowly she shook her head at him, then smiled softly. 'I'm never bored, Harry, never, not here, and with you. Never imagine that.'

He was sitting up now looking towards her. 'Come here,' he said.

'I'll do nothing of the sort, I'm going down to breakfast.' The voice was prim, the manner was Miss Brigmore's. She turned from him and disappeared into the dressing room as he shouted at her, 'Remember I once said I could skelp you across the mouth. Eeh! an' there's times when you madden me so much I could do it now. You know what? You're as aggravating as a young lass, you are, you are that. Sixty-four you are and as aggravating as a young lass.'

She appeared at the door again. She was fastening the buckles of a belt between her skirt and bodice now and she nodded at him as she said, 'When speaking of the conformity or non-conformity to age I would remind you that at sixty-six you should at least be showing signs of some senility, but being who you are you persist in acting as skittishly as an unbroken steer.'

A final nod and she turned from him again, and he lay still, a self-satisfied smile spreading over his face. Besides all other things she knew how to pay a man a compliment. She did that, did his Brigie.

449

When a few minutes later she came out of the dressing room and towards the bed she brought with her a fresh smell of eau-de-Cologne. With one deft swing of her arm she pulled the clothes from him and over the bottom of the bed. Taking not the slightest notice of his loud protests she now walked to the dressing table, picked up a gold watch, put it in the pocket of her bodice, then went towards the door, saying, 'Yes, I think we'll go to 27, but in the middle of next week. It is about time we had a bathroom, a proper bathroom, installed. I have seen an advertisement for one. Perhaps we could have two put in at the same time; one would be convenient for guests.'

He was standing by the bed now groping for words, and he found them only as she closed the door. 'Baths!' he yelled. 'Baths! not on your life. You'll not get me into a bath, not all over you won't.'

Baths! He stormed towards the dressing room. What would she think of next? Baths! Things had gone topsy-turvy. He was talking about wanting to hear music and she was talking about baths.

Breakfast was over. Brigie had gone to her office, there to discuss with Mrs Kenley the meals and the other business of the day, such as the necessity for new uniforms for Armstrong, the butler, and Emerson, the footman. Also this particular morning she wished to discuss the employing of a permanent sewing maid in the household, for this, she believed, would be much less expensive than the present arrangement of having the maids' uniforms made by a firm in Hexham. She had previously worked it out that she could cut this particular household cost by one-third. It wasn't that there was any need to cut down on household expenses, it was only that the habit of a lifetime prevailed with her.

She had just bidden Mrs Kenley good-morning and asked her to be seated at the opposite side of the desk when the door burst open and Harry entered, waving a letter. His face one great beam, he cried at her, 'You'll never guess, not in a lifetime. What do you think?'

Mrs Kenley had risen to her feet again, and Brigie only just prevented herself from following suit, so great was the excitement that Harry's manner and the waving letter engendered.

'Good news?' she asked. 'What is it?'

He put his hands on the desk and leaned towards her and whispered now in an awe-filled tone, 'Triplets.'

Brigie blinked at him as she repeated, 'Triplets?'

'Aye, yes, woman' – his voice was loud now – 'triplets! Dan and Barbara, they've had triplets.'

Now she did get to her feet. Her body jerked upwards, her hands went to her face. She looked from Harry to the housekeeper. Harry was also looking at the housekeeper and he shouted at her as if she

450

were at the other side of the house, 'What do you think of that, Mrs Kenley, eh? What do you think of that? Triplets! I'm a granda. Three times over I'm a granda. By! lad.' He put out his hand and gripped Brigie's shoulder. 'Come on, come on out of here.' He pulled her around the desk. 'This needs a drink all round. You, Mrs Kenley' – he turned to the housekeeper again – 'tell Armstrong to put half a dozen bottles on the table for the staff for their dinner, an' the same for them outdoors. They can pick what they like, whisky, brandy, what they like. Send Armstrong to me; I'd better tell him meself, eh?'

'Yes, yes, sir. I'll send him to you this minute. Oh, I am so pleased. Mr Dan and Miss Barbara, I mean Mrs Dan.' She inclined her head while she beamed from one to the other. 'Such good news. I'm . . . I'm so happy for you and . . . and them?'

'Thank you, Mrs Kenley.' Brigie's voice was trembling, as was her whole body. Without protest she allowed Harry to escort her across the hall, his arm about her shoulders. Her mind was a whirl. Barbara, her beloved Barbara had given birth at last. Two miscarriages, two great disappointments, and now triplets. Oh, if they had only been in England! Why couldn't they come back to England?

She said as much as soon as they entered the drawing room. Looking at Harry, she said sadly, 'If only they were here and we could go to them.'

'We could go to France.'

'No, not to France.'

'Why not? Why not?'

'You know the reason. She . . . she has never invited us. Nor has Dan. We cannot go unless we are asked.'

'Well now' – he stabbed his finger at her – 'this has put a different complexion on things. You needn't think I'm goin' to have three grandbairns an' have them brought up as Frenchies without making an effort to stop it. It was all right when the two of them were over there on their own, but this changes things. My God!' He put his head back and walked away from her down the long room to one of the tall windows at the end and, standing there, he raised his arms high above his head as he said, 'I never thought to see it; I thought it was all too late. John's Jenny has given no sign, not even a miscarriage. Then Barbara failing twice. Me only hope was Katie. I thought a year or so from now Katie might 'cos Katie's like me; she's fertile is Katie, she'll fall in the flick of an eyelid.'

Looking at the upstretched arms and listening to the words that were like an incantation to the gods, Brigie made no censorious protest. This, she realized, was a special moment in his life, as it was in hers. They were only reacting to it in their own particular ways.

He turned from the window and looked at her now and said, 'Katie

... that reminds me. I've got a letter from her an' all. Something's up; she should be here today.'

'Oh, I'm glad she's coming. But ... but what do you mean, something's' – she did not repeat 'up' but substituted, 'wrong? What is wrong?' she asked.

'I don't rightly know.' He was still smiling as he came to her side. 'She just ended her letter by saying, "I've got news for you. I hope you won't be too disappointed".'

'Perhaps she has changed her mind.'

'What!' he laughed. 'Can you see him letting her change her mind? Not Willy! No boy, not our Willy. Apart from everything else, he stands to lose too much.'

'You have changed your opinion somewhat about Willy of late, haven't you?'

The smile slid slowly from his face. He slanted his eyes at her and made a small nodding movement with his head as he said, 'Aye, aye, you're right, I have in some ways, but only in some ways. I still say he's the best man at his job in all Manchester. He's better than our John, oh aye. John's all right, but he hasn't got the ruthlessness of Willy. Willy's the right man in the right place. It would have been different if Dan had stayed on. You know I've always thought that funny about our Dan, hating the mill, hating the muck and the squalor, yet in the short time he worked there he got more work out of them and he was better liked than me or any of the rest. He was, he was. Aw, our Dan.' He now beat his fist into the palm of his hand. 'He might have disappointed me in some ways but, by lad! he's made up for it now. Triplets, eh? Triplets!'

As the door opened and Armstrong came in carrying a tray with a decanter and glasses on it he called to him, 'Heard the news, Armstrong?'

'Yes, indeed, sir. And may I offer my congratulations? And will you please convey them to Mr Dan and ... his good lady? And that is the wish of the servants' hall too, sir. We ... we are all very delighted. We ... we have only one regret, sir.'

'Aye, what is that, Armstrong?'

'That ... that they weren't born in this house, sir.'

'Aye, aye, that's my regret an' all.' Harry turned away as he spoke. 'And it's your mistress's.' He put his hand on Brigie's arm as she sat to the side of the flower-banked hearth. 'But never you fear, we'll have them here yet, won't we, eh? Won't we, lass?'

'I ... I hope so.' Brigie was looking at Armstrong now. 'And please thank the staff for their kind wishes, Armstrong. I shall convey them to Mr and Mrs Bensham when I next write.'

'Thank you, ma'am.' Armstrong bowed and withdrew.

A moment later, with glasses of wine in their hands, they looked at each other, and as Harry touched his glass to hers he said, 'Three lads. By! what you could have done for them if, as Armstrong said, they'd been born in this house.'

Brigie did not answer, because had she done so and truthfully, she would have said, 'I'm glad they weren't born in this house because never again do I want to take a child under my care. For over forty years I looked after other people's children, I infused into them my principles, I shaped their lives, and with what result? First, Barbara dead, through shame; then her sister, Constance, only seven miles away but alienated from me for ever; the second Barbara, a substitute for my empty womb, prefers a foreign land and loveless marriage rather than tolerate my company.' No, she wanted no more truck with children of any kind. That was Mary's term, truck, which reminded her she must go along to the cottage and tell Mary. She said so.

'I must go along to the cottage and tell Mary. Will you walk with me?'

'No, I won't.' His head bobbed on his shoulders. 'Why that woman wants to stay in the cottage by herself when she could be comfortable here, I'll never know. You made a mistake in saying she could have it for life.'

'No, I made no mistake.' Brigie's voice was firm now. 'She wanted a place of her own; everyone wants a place of their own, Harry. She has served me and all those connected with me all her life. I understood her needs, she is happy there.'

'Happy when she's snowed up for weeks on end, like she was last winter, an' her with a cough on her like a barking fox!'

'She's promised to come here for the bad weather this year, so let it be. Are you coming or are you not?'

'I'm not and that's flat.'

'You'll put on weight if you don't walk more.'

'I'll put on no weight' – he thumped his flat stomach – 'I'll never be fat, I'm the greyhound breed. Aw' – he flapped his hand at her – 'all right, don't look like that, I'll come along of you. You're a bully, that's what you are. Do you know that? You're a bully, a refined, educated, polished bully and them kind. . . .'

'Those kind.'

He thrust out his hand and playfully slapped her on the ear, growling, 'Those . . . them. By! one of these days I will, I will, I'll skelp your face for you. . . . Come on, get up off your backside and let's be goin'.'

She got up from her backside and followed him out of the room, and she did not wonder that such a remark, had it been made to her four years ago, would then have caused her to bridle with indignation. She was mistress of High Banks Hall, and she was loved by this man, and because she had learned to love him nothing that he could say offended her any more. But what did offend her, or rather what was hurting her at this moment, because it was bursting upwards like pus from an old sore, was the fact that Barbara had not taken the trouble to inform her personally that she had given birth to triplets. She hadn't even known that she was pregnant. . . .

It was some half an hour later that they walked the mile along the road that separated the Hall from the cottage. It was one of the rare days when the fells, and the hills, and the mountains beyond were merged in gentleness; their green, purple and brown coats, splashed here and there with buttons of yellow, denied all knowledge of their treachery. Impossible to imagine now that in a twinkling of an eye you could be enveloped in shrouds of mist that would seep into your skin and press terror into you; or a wild wind would blow up and wrap your skirts round your head and lift you bodily from the ground. But today there was neither mist nor wild wind, the air was still, the sun was hot on their faces, the sky was so high that a soaring lark seemed unable to reach it. The light all about them was pale and clear like water that had been slightly tinted with a blue bag.

It was as the cottage came into sight that Harry stopped suddenly and, looking at her, said, 'Do you know what's just struck me? . . . I'm asking you, do you know what's just struck me? It's the first we've heard of it. He never said she was pregnant; did she say anything to you?'

'No, no, she did not mention it. Perhaps because of the last two disappointments?'

'Aye, aye, you're likely right. It would have been just too much if she'd had a miss the third time.' He put out his hand and took hers, and like country lovers they walked on to the cottage.

3

THEY HAD KEPT BACK THE MEAL until the coach should arrive. Harry himself helped Katie down, restraining himself, for once, in not speaking his thoughts aloud, for he was troubled by the sight of her white face and her apparent loss of weight. The whiteness, he thought, could be put down to the heat and the travelling, but not her loss of weight. Her bust had gone and there was no hump to her hips any more, and it was only a month since he'd last seen her. She'd had a fine figure had their Katie ... but now!

On the terrace, Brigie came towards her with outstretched hands.

'Hello, my dear. I'm so pleased to see you; it seems so long. Did you have a good journey?'

'Awful. I know now what it feels like to be slowly grilled. . . . You're looking well.'

'It's nice of you to say so, Katie. I'm feeling extremely well at the moment in spite of the heat.'

And she was looking extremely well, Katie thought, younger than ever she remembered seeing her before. And her attire was surprising in that her dress was of pale mauve muslin with a neckline that showed the top of her breastbone. Wonders would never cease, marriage certainly suited Brigie! Marriage. Marriage. How would they take it? She had a good idea how Brigie would receive her news, but what would her father's reactions be? 'You've made a bloody monkey out of the fellow,' would likely be his first retort, and this would be followed by, 'I won't thank you, our Katie, if you've lost me the man with the best mill know-how in Manchester.'

Well, whatever her father's reactions, it was done, and although it was done and finally, she could put no name to her own feelings on the matter. She told herself almost every hour of the day that she was relieved – to use the local jargon concerning such matters, she had escaped a lifetime of misery – yet at the same time she asked herself, whilst scorning her weakness, would it not have been better to suffer such a marriage than never to know marriage? For maidenhood, she had discovered long ago, had its own particular tortures. When you were young, below twenty, you termed such feelings facets of love; having reached twenty-four you named them correctly as bodily needs. . . .

After she had washed herself in cold water and changed her outer garments she came down to supper which, as was usual with meals at the Hall, contrasted in all ways to those served at 27. Bella Brackett did her best, but it was a rough and working woman's best in comparison with Mrs Lovett's creations.

'You're not eating, lass?'

'I'm not very hungry, Dad.'

'Brigie here thought up all your favourite bits and pieces.'

'I'm sorry, Brigie.'

Brigie, looking across the table into the white drawn face and the eyes that seemed too large for it, said gently, 'That's all right, dear. After a few days' rest you'll regain your appetite, I'm sure.'

Harry broke in now on a laugh, saying, 'Rest, she said, she's promised you rest. That's when she hasn't got you walkin'. Believe me, if she gets her own way with you she'll pump you so full of fresh air you'll be eating like a horse. I'm speaking from experience.' He nodded at her and she smiled at him.

Her father too had changed of late; he was lighter, gayer, if she could ever apply that word to him. She had felt that in his own way he had loved her mother, yet she thought from his present attitude that he must now be experiencing a happiness with Brigie that he had never known before. She felt a sudden surge of jealousy. Here was Brigie, her one-time governess, mistress of this beautiful house – and for the first time in her life she was seeing it as a really beautiful house. 27 was a two-up and two-downer compared with it. If Brigie hadn't married her father she herself could have come back here and run the place and taken delight in it.

It was like a revelation to her in this moment that this was part of her trouble. She had been missing this kind of living. The giving of herself over to good works seemed now like the act of a silly wilful young woman, who didn't know what she wanted from life. Yet five years ago no one could have convinced her otherwise but that she wanted to give her life to improving the lot of the workers, the Manchester workers in particular. The afternoons ahead had glowed with the thought of discussions on welfare and the rights and wrongs of class, and her evenings with the soul-satisfying task of the educating and raising up of the under-privileged. Now she faced the unpleasant fact that the first year had not passed before her passion for self-sacrifice had ebbed, and it had become an increasing strain to hide the fact that her devotion to good works had, as it were, gone out with the tide.

'What did you say?' She lifted her head sharply and looked at Brigie.

'I said your father has something to tell you.' Brigie now looked at Harry and added, 'Go on, tell her. Why keep it?'

'Well, I like that!' Harry laid down his knife and fork. 'It was you yourself who said let's eat first, wait until we're sittin' down after, then we can talk about it.' He did not add 'in private like' but, casting his eyes towards where Armstrong was attending to the dishes on the side table, he sat back in his chair and said, 'All right then, all right. Everybody in the house knows so why shouldn't you. It's Dan and Barbara, what do you think?' He leant towards her now; then, his voice awe-filled, he whispered softly, 'They've had triplets, Dan and Barbara . . . triplets.'

'Triplets!' Katie sat back in her chair and stared at her father and again she said, 'Triplets?'

'Aye, that's what I said, triplets, just three of 'em not four lots of three,' he answered, thrusting out his hand in the direction of Brigie to draw her attention to his joke.

But Brigie did not join in with it, not even by offering him a faint smile; instead, she said below her breath, 'Please!' then turned her glance again towards Katie who was sitting staring at her but without, she knew, seeing her.

'What is it, dear?' She leant slightly forward and Katie, slowly rising from the table, said, 'Would . . . would you excuse me please? I'll . . . I'll go into the drawing room, it's cooler there. No. No, please, don't come with me.' She waved her hand from one to the other, and they watched her go hurriedly down the room and out of the door. But it had hardly closed on her when they, too, both rose to their feet and followed her to the drawing room.

'What is it, lass? Something's not right with you.' Harry was sitting on the couch beside her, holding her hand now.

Katie, looking at her father through a mist of tears, bit on her lip. Then glancing up at Brigie who was standing over her, she muttered, 'I'm . . . I'm so glad for Barbara. Don't . . . don't think otherwise.'

Before Brigie could make any reply Harry put in, 'Aye. Aye, I knew you'd be over the moon. And it's your turn next.' He shook the hand within his. 'This time next year you could beat her with quads, or whatever they call four of 'em.' He cast a glance at Brigie.

Brigie made no comment; instead she asked Katie quietly, 'Is it Willy?' And Katie, nodding slowly up at her now, said, 'Yes, it's Willy. I . . . I'm not going to marry him.'

There was silence in the room for a while. The hammer on the

457

open-faced clock on the mantelpiece beat out the seconds; a blackbird that should have been at roost gave evidence of its late journeying with a frightened screech as it passed the window.

Harry drew in a deep breath, then said, 'Well, lass, well; well now, this is a state of affairs.'

'I'm sorry . . . I'm sorry if you're disappointed.'

'Disappointed? Me!' Harry dug his thumb into his chest, turned his head from side to side, then exchanged a glance with Brigie before ending, 'Don't be sorry for me.'

'No?' It was a question.

'No. It's the other way about. I'm sorry for you. An' yet . . . well, I won't speak me mind on it until I know the rights. Who broke it up, which one of you an' why?'

'I . . . I did.'

'Aye, I thought it would be you, it wouldn't be him. It was a daft question to ask. Now tell me why.'

'Because' – Katie now turned her face towards Brigie but she didn't speak for a moment. When she did, what she said was, 'You're to blame you know, Brigie, because I found I was judging him on your standards, those . . . those you pumped into me. I found him more unbearable as time went on, everything he said, everything he did.'

'I'm sorry.'

'No, no, I don't mean it like that.' She put her hand out and caught Brigie's and drew her down on to the couch to the other side of her. Then leaning back, she looked from one to the other and said, 'It's . . . it's a long, long story. I just didn't give him up the day before yesterday, I only got up the courage to tell him then; I gave him up a long time ago, a year or more. Oh, much more.'

'Then I blame you for one thing, lass.' Harry's voice was stern now. 'You shouldn't have gone on, you should have come out with it and told him how you felt.'

'It's difficult, Dad, to come out with things to Willy; Willy usually only listens to one voice and that's his own.'

'Aye, aye, well, you're right there. An' you know something?' He gripped her hands now and brought his face closer to hers. 'You mightn't believe this but it's the truth, an' that one there knows it.' He nodded towards Brigie. 'I've never said it in so many words, but she's quick off the mark and she knows that at this very moment I'm right glad it's all over atween you and him, for you're worth something better than Willy Brooks. Mind your eye, there's not a cleverer bloke in any mill in the town, I'll grant him that, but like father like son, there was something there that me stomach just didn't take to.' He leant back now, and in his favourite pose looked up towards the ceiling as he ended slowly, 'It's a wonder he hasn't come down here hell for leather.' Then straightening up he said briskly, 'But me, meself, I must look slippy an' get meself back there 'cos with this happenin', well, I'll have to keep me eye on Master Willy for a bit. And make our John look out an' all. He'll need to keep on the qui vive now, if I know owt.'

Katie now asked quietly of Brigie, 'And you, what do you think?'

'That goes without saying, my dear. You knew I never thought him suitable for you. Now what you must do is take a long rest and get some colour into your cheeks.' She put out her hand and gently patted the pale face. 'And then you must think about a holiday. Yes, a holiday, that's what you need, a complete change.'

Miss Brigmore, who would always supersede Brigie, or Mrs Bensham, when it came to arranging lives, was already arranging Katie's holiday. Tomorrow, or perhaps the next day, she would bring the conversation round to the benefits of taking a holiday abroad, and she would couple this with her need to have a personal report on how Barbara was faring, and also emphasize the happiness Dan would experience at the sight of his sister.

It was strange, she thought, how things worked out, very strange. If you longed for a thing passionately enough you eventually achieved some section of it, because prayer after all was merely wanting, and working at the wanting, and oh, how she wanted to see Barbara again. In spite of all the cruel things Barbara had said to her, in spite of her desertion and leaving her alone to face old age in dire loneliness, she longed to see her, for was she not after all her child in all but birth, and it was part of a mother's role to bear ingratitude.

It was wonderful too to know that she had achieved motherhood. Perhaps her babies would soften her heart, perhaps they would teach her to love again, love Dan, and herself. Oh yes, she needed to love herself in order to forgive herself.

459

4

I T WAS ALMOST FOUR WEEKS LATER, towards the end of
August, and the evening before the day when Katie was due to
leave for her holiday in France. Letters had been exchanged
between Brigie and Barbara, cordial letters with more warmth in
Barbara's than had been previously shown. Letters had also been
exchanged between Dan and Harry, and Dan was most enthusiastic at
the news that Katie was going to visit them.

And Katie. There were moments when she felt a stir of excitement
at the prospect of going to France, not that it was her first trip abroad
for she had twice before been to France. True the trips had been short;
she had hardly been able to recover from the outward sea passage
before she was returning again. But this trip would prove different
altogether because, first, she was travelling alone, and secondly, she
was staying at an hotel alone. Apparently Dan's apartment wasn't big
enough to house her. This had surprised them all. Still, she understood the hotel was quite close to their apartment. Moreover, on this
occasion, being her own mistress, she could stay as long or as short a
time as she pleased, go where she pleased, see whom she pleased. She
was twenty-four years old, and although she wasn't married she could
be considered a matron. And it was as a matron at this moment that
she saw herself.

It was just before she retired for the night that Harry manoeuvred
her into the library just, as he said under his breath, for a word alone
with her. Now would she do this for him, would she sound out their
Dan and find out if there was any chance of them coming back? She
was to tell him that it needn't be Manchester. John had it in mind they
needed to expand and thought of setting up their own warehouse and
distribution centre in Newcastle. Also John had the idea that Willy
was working something on the side, or to put it more plainly he wasn't
working as he had done afore. Two orders had been lost in a month,
old established orders; they had gone across the town to another mill.

Why? That's what he wanted to know, and he'd find out an' all an' afore long. If Willy could play that game, so could he. And it would be the very thing if Dan would come back and take charge of the Newcastle end. Tell him, he said, there'd be no muck or grind, he'd just be a sort of head piece, 'cos we'd send a couple of good fellows with him to get started. And he had ended, 'Tell him I miss him, will you? Tell him that, Katie. Tell him I'm not gettin' any younger an' I miss him. And what's more, I'd like to see me grandbairns.'

She said she would do all he asked and more. They kissed awkwardly, and he said, 'You're a good lass, Katie.'

She had barely closed her bedroom door when there was a tap on it and Brigie came in. She, too, just wanted a word with her in private before she left. Would she give Barbara her love and tell her how much she missed her and how she longed to see her? And would Katie herself find out if there was the slightest possibility of them ever coming back to England because the years were flying? She wasn't getting any younger and she would love to see Barbara again, and, of course, her dear, dear children.

Katie promised to deliver her message too, and they kissed and Brigie said, 'I'm so fond of you, Katie.'

When at last she was in bed she turned her face into the pillow and cried, she cried for so many reasons. People, she realized, could be happy yet there were gaps in their happiness; the need of children, grandchildren. Needs went deeper than the one called love. Love had no connection with her own need at this moment. It was so physical that she even imagined that she would have welcomed Willy's arms about her. Life was made up of needs, all kinds of needs. She could never see her own being satisfied.

Finally, she went to sleep crying solely for herself.

BARBARA

I

'SHE'LL THINK IT'S VERY SMALL, tiny.'
      'Knowing Katie she'll consider it cute. And where else can
you see half Paris from your window . . . that's if you stand on a
chair?'
Dan Bensham smiled wryly and looked up towards the top of the
narrow window, one of two, that gave light to their sitting room,
which was no more than sixteen feet long and furnished with an odd
assortment of furniture ranging from a Dutch cupboard that dominated one wall, two bookcases that took up the space at each side of the
fireplace and which were packed tight with books of all sizes, and in
the middle an assortment of chairs and small tables; these holding, not
bric-à-brac but again books.
    'Are you excited?' He caught his wife's hand and drew her down the
room, across a passage and into another room, this one only large
enough to hold a small single bed and two cots.
    When they came to a stop at the foot of the cots Dan, as always,
gazed down in silent wonder on two of his sleeping sons before turning
his gaze to the third, who occupied the bed. Here lay the 'big fellow',
as he had nicknamed him.
    They'd had trouble over names; he'd had to be careful what he
suggested. He did not touch on Michael, nor yet Thomas, the first
being the name of her lost lover, and the second, the name of the father
which had been thrown at her on the day she lost her mind. Yes, he'd
had to be very careful about names. After some discussion she had
complied with his suggestion to call 'the big fellow' Benjamin, and
had accepted Harry as soon as he had mentioned it, because she
had nothing against his father who had always been very good to her;
in fact, but for his father's generosity her early life would have been
refined bread and scrape, indeed it would. Jonathan she herself had
suggested.
    As yet Jonathan and Harry were only half the size of Benjamin.

462

Benjamin grew every day more like his name, full-bodied, full-blooded. He yelled the loudest and demanded the most, and in consequence he got the most. Such was life.

Barbara now whispered. 'You must see about getting another place, we simply can't go on here. Marie can't keep taking them out for the air all day, and the concierge never lets me pass but she makes some remark about the *voiture d'enfant*, and I dislike that woman as much as she dislikes me. Dan' – she turned to him now, a plea in her voice – 'do try, please. I know . . . I know you like these rooms. It was different when Madame and Monsieur Abeille were here but everything has changed since these new ones have come. It's because we're English I suppose.'

He turned to her and gazed into her face as he said softly, 'It's because you're beautiful and she's such an ugly old hag. I could never imagine her even being born, let alone being pretty. But I promise you I'll start looking tomorrow. . . . Promise, faithfully.' He crossed his heart.

'It would have been nice if we could have lived above the shop.'

'Yes, it would; it would have solved all problems. But that was in the agreement when I took it over. The Reynauds have the apartments for life. And although Madame is nearing eighty she looks so hale and hearty she could go on for another twenty years. And' – he nodded at her – 'I hope she does. They've been good to us, we mustn't forget that, they've been good to us.'

'I don't forget it.'

Dan turned away now and, taking up a pose, he stuck his thumbs into the armholes of his waistcoat and swaggered from the room, saying, under his breath, 'Daniel Bensham, one-time Englishman, of no occupation, kept by his father.' For an instant he dropped the pose, turned his head on his shoulder, raised his eyebrows and nodded at her as he added quickly, 'And still kept by his father.' Then adopting the pose again he went on, 'Now owner of a bookshop of some repute, small, granted, but visited by not a few of the intellectuals of this city of culture. Oh indeed, yes.' Dropping his pose quickly now as she came through the door into the passage he turned and asked quietly, 'Shall I tell Katie about a certain intellectual?'

'No, no, I'd wait. Let . . . let it come about naturally.'

He nodded in agreement, pursed his lips, then went hastily into the small kitchen, and as he put the kettle on the fire he said, 'I'm glad, in fact I can say I'm delighted she broke it off with Brooks. I could never stand his father, and much less him. The only consolation I seemed to get when I thought about their marriage was that I wouldn't have to meet him, unless they decided to come to Paris for their honeymoon.

Well' – he turned to her and kissed her lightly on the cheek – 'make me a coffee, just a coffee, nothing else. Anyway, I haven't time.' He pointed to the clock on the wall. 'Good Lord! look at it. If I don't put a move on the train will be in before me, and there she'll be standing in the Gare du Nord like little orphan Annie.' He laughed as he went out of the room quoting:

'Little orphan Annie came to our house to stay
To chase the chickens from the porch and sweep the crumbs away.'

Barbara now leant forward and gripped the handle of the large black kettle that was slowly beginning to boil, and she closed her eyes and muttered to herself, 'Oh Dan, Dan,' and her words sounded as if they had been sieved through pain.

That silly rhyme. That pathetic rhyme. He always quoted it when he was troubled, and he was troubled now. Or was he just disturbed because of the coming meeting with Katie? Dan, she had found, was a complex being who laughed when he was sad and sang when he was troubled. He had said that he owed the Reynauds so much. He always thought he owed people so much, he never thought of what people owed him, of what she owed him. The sadness of it was that she could never repay him because she could never love him; like him, yes, even be very fond of him, be concerned for him, but love him, no. And not because he was unlovable, but because she had no love left in her to give to any man. At one time she had been filled with love, it had oozed out of her very pores; then it had been drained out of her, torn out of her on a hillside in far away Northumberland, on a day when she had struck a girl and maimed her for life, and a man had struck her and restored her hearing after years of silence, only to enable her to hear her loved one say, 'I never want to see you in my life again.'

She told herself, time and again, that she should not feel guilty with regard to Dan, because she gave him all she could give him and he had known when he married her that what she had to offer emotionally was but the scrapings of a barrel. Yet out of the scrapings had come the babies: the first she had carried for six months; the second had breathed and seen the light for only one day; but now she had brought him an extra one to compensate for the loss of the other two. She must look at it that way and not think as she did so often, if only they had been created in love.

Before the steam spurted from the spout of the kettle Dan had rejected 'Little Orphan Annie' for *Annie of Tharaw*. And this was evidence indeed of how disturbed he was. He always sang Long-fellow's rigmarole in his tuneless voice and to a Scottish air that went like a jig:

Annie of Tharaw, my true love of old,
She is my life, and my goods, and my gold.
Annie of Tharaw, her heart once again
To me has surrendered in joy and in pain.
Annie of Tharaw, my riches, my good,
Thou, O my soul, my flesh, and my blood!
Then come the wild weather, come sleet or come snow,
We will stand by each other, however it blow.

On and on the couplets went as she made the coffee, waited for it to settle, then poured it out. She paused a moment before lifting the cup from the table, her head back on her shoulders, her lips slightly apart, her lids lowered as she listened:

What e'er my desire is, in thine may be seen;
I am king of the household, thou art its queen.
It is this, O my Annie, my heart's sweetest rest,
That makes of us twain but one soul in one breast.

She picked up the cup and went from the room across the little passage and into the bedroom, and as she entered he turned to her as he adjusted his cravat and, his voice rising slightly, he sang, but still softly:

This turns to a heaven the hut where we dwell;
While wrangling soon changes a home to a hell.

As she handed him the coffee he bent towards her, put his lips to her cheek and said softly, 'I love you, Barbara Bensham.'

What she should have answered to this was, 'And I love you too, Dan Bensham.' How could any woman not love a man so kind, so good as this one? Only herself, spawned through rape, and known in the county of her birth as 'the Mallen girl', only she was not woman enough, mature enough to love a second time. And she did not hide the fact from herself. But neither could she blame herself.

He went from her singing the song again, only stopping to sip at the coffee. She did not follow him into the tiny nursery where he would be once more looking on his sons, as he always did before going out, and she checked herself from calling to him as she heard him come into the passage and put on his coat, 'Do be quiet please, you'll waken them,' because in the words of *Annie of Tharaw*, he was telling her once more, but more softly now like a gentle lullaby, what he would do if he lost her:

Shouldst thou be torn from me to wander alone
In a desolate land where the sun is scarce known –
Through forests I'll follow, and where the sea flows,
Through ice, and through iron, through armies of foes.
Annie of Tharaw, my light and my sun,
The threads of our two lives are woven in one.

Yes indeed, the threads of their two lives were woven in one, and must never, never be unwoven. She could think what she liked, she could suffer as she must, but never, never must she break the threads that held their two lives woven as one. This much she owed him.

2

KATIE LOVED PARIS, all of it. The hotel was good. Dan's
apartment behind the rue Nicholas Charles was the prettiest
and quaintest place she had ever stepped into. Dan's shop was
simply wonderful. And Dan having a shop was a most surprising
thing; she still hadn't got over it after a full week in Paris. Then there
were the babies. She thought of them as Barbara's babies. They were
delightful, angels. Of course, she agreed laughingly with Barbara on
this point that it was very difficult to put Benjamin into such a
category, because Benjamin yelled both by night and by day. Even
when he wasn't actually crying he was making sounds, demanding
sounds.

And then Paris itself. Paris was fascinating, and she had really seen
nothing of it as yet. She was intoxicated by the wonders that lay ahead
of her. She felt like an explorer in a strange and wonderful land, yet at
the same time slightly frustrated because both Dan and Barbara had
warned her against walking alone. She knew they were right about
this, because on her first solitary walk she had been accosted by no less
than three gentlemen, two of them with charming manners who were
desirous of helping her, and who insisted that they had been born for
the sole purpose of showing her Paris. . . .

Dan and Barbara discussed the situation in bed. It was difficult to
arrange times when one or the other could accompany her. Dan had a
young assistant, who as yet had little knowledge of the work and
whom he never left in charge of the shop for more than half an hour at
a time.

Then there was Marie to be considered, Marie who at first had been
engaged to do the work of the apartment but now spent most of her
time attending the babies.

Almost simultaneously they spoke together, then laughed quietly,
before Barbara asked, 'Does he come at any particular time?'

'No, it could be any day of the week.'

467

'But he comes in every week?'

'No, not always. Sometimes it can be a month before I see him. I think this is when he goes back to England.'

'But he's been in every week for some time now you say?'

'Yes ... yes he has, he's been in regularly since I took over. He's kind in a way; he ... he never leaves without buying a couple of books, and he's recommended others.'

'But' – Barbara paused a moment – 'you said he had, well, a name.'

'Yes, but all of his class have a reputation along those lines.'

'Class!' She snorted slightly as she turned her head sharply on the pillow. 'He's not all that high up, and your father is much better off than he is I'd say.'

He suddenly pulled her around to him, saying, 'Nice of you to put it that way, Mrs Bensham, but we must remember we're not mentioned in the Domesday Book. And when his cousin dies he'll come into the title, he'll be Sir Patrick Ferrier. It does make a difference, you know.'

His lips were moving in gentle patting kisses around her unresponsive mouth when she said, 'She's so headstrong and still has these odd ideas. Anything could happen to her wandering about the streets alone. And it isn't right. Do you think she'll stay the winter?'

'Possibly.' His voice was dreamy.

'In that case then I ... I think that you should arrange a meeting. After all he is a gentle ... gentleman....'

The last word was smothered in his mouth and she became passive and compliant as he loved her.

When it was over Dan lay back on the pillow, hoping, almost praying that she wouldn't end it as always, but she did. Slowly, silently, she turned on her side, her back towards him, and there rose in him again that infantile feeling of wanting to cry helplessly while beating his fists on something.

Dan said, 'You may be interested in this, sir.' He had never called Ferrier by his Christian name, for he had been a boy of fifteen when he first met him on Constance Radlet's farm in a valley in Northumberland, which lay seven miles across the hills from High Banks Hall. He remembered the time as if it were yesterday, not so much the meeting with Mr Ferrier but the effect he'd had on Barbara's Aunt Constance. In a few minutes this man had turned her from a dignified lady into a gay young woman. Everyone thought that Ferrier would marry her; until he started paying court to Katie. He must have been fond of Katie for it was only after she took it into her head to give up the easy life of the Hall for the harsh reality of the Manchester slums that he had returned to France.

He did not know whether or not he really liked Ferrier. He was a

468

charming man yet had an austerity about him. But by all accounts this austerity didn't prevent him from enjoying mistresses, for it was said he'd had quite a change of them over these past five years since he'd returned to France, and well before that. And so he wondered if he were doing right in letting him know that Katie was in Paris; was it right to lay her open to a man of this character? But four years ago everyone had thought it right, even desirable, and he didn't suppose his character had worsened much since then, for if a man couldn't find some one person to love, then who could blame him for spreading his company.

'Oh! It's a large tome. What is it?'

'It's called *The New British Traveller* or *A Complete Modern Universal Display of Great Britain and Ireland*. Note the print, sir, the old type of S's, and, as it says in the introduction, "It is a production of much time and indefatigable labour." And look what it covers, from the etymology of the different areas to the nature of the legislature and modes of proceedings in the various Courts of Justice ancient and modern.'

Pat Ferrier began to turn the pages of the large travel book. After a minute or so he asked, 'What year was it published?'

'That I can't quite ascertain, sir. There are a few pages missing from the front, and it's been impossible to read right through it, but from the illustrations I should say it was published about the middle of the eighteenth century. You see at the bottom it says "Printed for Alex Hogg No. 16 Paternoster Row, London".'

'Well, yes, it appears interesting.' Pat Ferrier flicked through the pages, then said, 'But I don't agree with you about its date of publication; I would say well towards the end of the eighteenth. The old S's were still in use then. But I'll take it.'

'Thank you, sir.'

'Have you anything else of interest?'

'Not this morning I'm afraid, sir, but I'm going to a house on the outskirts this afternoon so I may pick up something there. I'm also using the journey as a means of showing my sister something of Paris, besides the main streets. You remember my sister, Katie?'

Pat Ferrier lifted his eyes from the book and turned his head slowly in Dan's direction and his voice was cool as he said, 'Yes. Yes, I remember your sister, Katie, very well. And she's here in Paris?'

'Yes. Yes, she's been here over a week now.'

'That's nice. Is she staying long?'

'We're not sure; she's undecided. She may stay the winter, and then knowing Katie she may go back to England tomorrow.'

'She's travelling with her family?'

'No, no, she's alone.'

469

'Her husband is not with her?'

'Oh, she's not married.'

They stared at each other for a moment; then Pat Ferrier raising his eyebrows slightly and with his eyes cast downwards, said, 'Then I've been misinformed, I understood she was.'

'She was going to be but ... she decided against it.'

'Really!' Pat Ferrier now put his head back and laughed as he said, 'Women, women all the world over, English, French, Chinese. Ah no, I mustn't include the Chinese; they have been taught to do what they're told, and rightly.' He nodded at Dan and they both laughed now. Then Ferrier, tapping the large tome, said, 'You'll have it sent round to my apartment? I say, have it sent round, but I don't know whether they'll be able to get it in the door; the place is overstacked already. I had thought to send a consignment home and I must do so without further delay, that's if I want to visit this establishment again.'

As they parted on a laugh Dan mused, not on the fact that he had aroused, as he had hoped, Ferrier's old interest in Katie, but on the fact that the man, having lived so long in France, still referred to England as home whilst he himself never thought of either 27 The Drive or High Banks Hall as home. Home, to him, was the present, and that was wherever Barbara was. But every man's life was his own, and every man's life was strange – to the other man.

It needed a little strategy to arrange that Katie should be in the shop each morning of the following week. It was achieved by Dan's cry for help in cataloguing the books he had acquired on his visit to the outskirts of the city.

Katie offered her assistance before Dan was brought to the point of asking for it. She would be delighted to help in the shop, she had never worked in a shop, it would be exciting, wonderful, and if she could serve customers then it would help her with the language because now she was finding that Brigie's French left a lot to be desired, at least her pronunciation. Oh yes, she'd be delighted.

And Dan found that he too was delighted to have her in the shop. Laughingly, he said, 'We only want Brigie and John here, a high iron guard round the fire, a wooden table in the middle and we'd have the nursery again – with a few extra books,' he added.

It was on the third morning when she was emerging from the basement, which was used as a store-room, its only access being a trap door in the floor, to which was attached an iron ladder, that Dan, while bending down to help her up, motioned with his hand towards a customer who stood opposite a book rack. He was a tall man and was stretching upwards to the top shelf to grasp a particular book.

'See if you can help.' Dan nodded at her, and she made a slight face at him, flicked some dust from her skirt, then, head held erect, she walked towards the figure.

A moment later Pat Ferrier turned towards her, a book in his hand, and he watched her face stretch and her lower jaw drop slightly before, assuming surprise, he said, 'Miss Katie! Well, well! the world is indeed small.'

There followed another pause while they stared at each other.

'May I enquire if you are well?'

'I'm very well, thank you.'

'I am delighted to hear it. Your brother tells me you are staying in Paris for a time.'

Oh! he did, did he? Cataloguing! Help in the shop. Really! Wait till she got him alone. Barbara, too, must have known.

She looked up into the thin face. He had changed in five years; he seemed to have grown old. He was fifteen years older than herself but now he looked much more than thirty-nine. There seemed to be little flesh on his bones; she had never seen anyone so thin. He was what her father would describe as 'a yard of pipe watter'. But for all that he remained the gentleman, the courteous, charming-mannered gentleman she remembered.

They were walking up the shop now towards the counter. 'Do you like Paris?'

'Yes, very much, what I have seen of it.'

'Do you intend to stay long?'

'I . . . I'm not sure; my time's my own. I . . . I may go on.'

Go on? Where to? The only place she could go was back to Manchester, or Northumberland. One thing she had discovered, it was very difficult to travel on your own in a foreign land, and the language wasn't the only impediment.

Dan was at the counter now and Ferrier spoke directly to him. 'Have you anything new for me? Or should I say old?'

'Not so far, sir. We are busy' – he indicated Katie with a movement of his head – 'we are busy sorting them out downstairs. But I'm sure I'll find something of interest for you. It was an old house and the walls were lined with the books. If you'd care to call in sometime later in the week. . . .'

'I'll do that. Yes, I'll do that. Well' – he turned to Katie and, bowing slightly, he said, 'Good-bye, Miss Katie. This meeting has been a delightful surprise. I hope I shall see you again.'

Katie didn't answer, she merely inclined her head, then she turned it slowly and watched him as he walked up the room and out of the shop. When he had passed from sight she looked at Dan and said one word,

471

'Cataloguing!'

'What do you mean, cataloguing?'

'You didn't need my help, you planned this.'

'I . . . I didn't.' His tone was deceptively indignant.

'Well, why didn't you tell me he came here?'

'I didn't think you'd be interested. He's come here for years. He was a customer of Monsieur Reynaud, he comes in like anyone else. I never thought to tell you.'

Her face muscles relaxed, her body relaxed; she slumped a little against the counter, let out a long drawn breath and said, 'Lord! I felt awful, like a child caught at some misdemeanour.'

'Why should you?'

'Oh!' She shook her head impatiently. 'You wouldn't understand. Years ago he was on the point of . . . well, I encouraged him, I know I did. And then –' again she shook her head. 'What's the use. . . . Well, that's the end of the cataloguing, Dan Bensham.'

'Oh no, no. Now look' – he caught her arm – 'I do need help. Look at that lot down there. And Jean . . . well, you know what Jean's like.' His voice dropped as he looked to where a young man was slowly racking books at the far end of the shop. 'Numskull is his second name.'

Katie pursed her lips, drew in another deep breath, and asked, 'How often does he come in?'

'Oh, I can't say. He's unpredictable, could be weeks ahead.'

'Oh well, in that case.' She nodded at him, indicating that she had allowed herself to be persuaded.

It was on Pat Ferrier's third visit to the shop in a fortnight and on Katie's last day of cataloguing that he offered himself as her guide to Versailles, and primly, but not without a stir of excitement, she accepted.

They set out in a carriage at noon and his manner towards her could have been that of an uncle giving her an extramural lesson in history. Through the overpoweringly grand palace they meandered, to the house where the ill-fated queen and her court had played at milk-maids; round by the temple of love, through the vast gardens, up terraces and down terraces they walked, and when the tour was over and he asked, 'Did you enjoy it?' she answered politely, 'Yes, yes, indeed; it was most interesting.'

When he cast a side glance from his pale grey eyes at her she thought for a moment he had read her mind, for the truth was she had felt indifferent to all the grandeur. Everything was too large, larger than life; and the gardens, she considered, were great expanses of nothing. No wonder there had been a revolution. How they must have lived in that palace with their gold and their silver plate. How they had gorged themselves while the people starved. It was all past history but in some way it reminded her of Manchester; the grand houses at one side of the town, the slums at the other. It was ridiculous, but there it was. Her mind was a mass of contradictions. In Manchester she had come to hate the sight and smell of poverty, yet when she saw opulence and a different way of living she condemned it. What the world needed was a happy medium, and people would get that when they got Utopia. And they would get Utopia ... never.

Here she was, being handed into a carriage by an English-cum-French – because he appeared more French than English – gentleman and all she could think about was Manchester and comparisons of wealth.

'You didn't enjoy it?'

She jerked her head towards him. 'Oh yes, yes, I did.'

'You're lying, Katie Bensham.'

As they stared at each other she made a vain effort to check her laughter. Then they were laughing together.

'Why didn't you like Versailles?'

'It ... it was too much, too much of everything. As my father would say, too much of a good thing. And yet I don't think it could ever have been a good thing.'

He lay back in the carriage well away from her and after a moment he said, 'Tomorrow I shall take you to the Palais de Justice; the following day we can do the Louvre. No, no, that's Sunday, we'll leave that till Monday. On Tuesday I shall take you on the Seine.' He turned his head towards her. 'Will that please you?'

She stared at him. There was a quirk to her lips now. 'Do you really want to know?'

'Of course I do. I live to please you, my time is yours.'

'Oh!' She closed her eyes and jerked her head impatiently.

'What is it? I've annoyed you?'

'You will if you continue to talk in such a fashion. It's ... it's so artificial.'

'Really? You ... you find my conversation artificial?'

'It isn't conversation.' She imagined for a moment it was Willy sitting there and they were about to start one of their endless arguments. 'It's trifling, false. Oh. Oh, I'm sorry, I'm being rude.' She lowered her head as she shook it.

'Not at all.' His tone had changed. 'I agree with you, up to a point. I would not say my conversation is trifling and artificial because I've had no opportunity to have a real conversation with you. My remarks are definitely as you state them to be. It is the fashion of our time to communicate in monosyllables. ...'

473

'... When you are dealing with women?'

'Quite right, when one is dealing with women.'

'I object to being treated as a numskull.'

'A numskull?' He lingered over the word, and he smiled at her now as she said, 'It's a wonderful word that, so full of meaning.'

'You know it then?'

'Know it?' His tone changed again. He could have been Dan or John speaking. 'Know it? Don't forget I was born in Northumberland. I have cousins to this day who work in Palmer's shipyard in Jarrow and in our glass works; they're on the board but they're working members. I could, I can assure you, rattle off northern sayings that I'm sure you've never heard of because they would have offended Miss Brigmore's ears. Even now I am sure she would "skite-the-hunger-off-me" were she to know I was sullying your ears with such rough homely terms.'

She had her head resting against the padded back of the coach, her face half turned towards him, and she laughed gently as she said, 'I would never have believed it.'

Slowly he inched towards her until his coat touched hers; and then he said, 'We haven't as yet known each other long enough for me to convince you that I am, underneath the façade, an ordinary man, a Northumbrian. Katie' – he caught her hand and, his voice low, he said, 'It was in a carriage similar to this that we returned from Hexham one day, not all that long ago, and you promised that you would come to dinner with me in my home. And you knew then what the invitation implied. Can ... can we imagine that this is the same carriage and I'm putting the request to you again? Will you come to dinner with me tonight?'

Her face was straight, even solemn. There was a swelling in her throat and she, too, was back in the carriage coming from Hexham; and there returned to her the feeling of excitement, and something more, the feeling of being honoured, made proud.

Her lips trembled slightly as she said softly, 'I should like that.'

And so it began, their belated whirlwind courtship. She dined that night in a restaurant on the Champs-Elysées, and there were a number of things that remained in her memory for long afterwards; there was the knowledge that he was well known in this place and that his table was reserved in a secluded corner and was beautifully laid; also, that he rinsed his mouth out from the finger bowl, almost gargling in the process; another thing was the way the cream was brought to the table – the waiter served it from a brown stone jar very like the one Bella Brackett used for pickling cabbage in the kitchen in No. 27. The cream was ladled out in great dollops on to her pudding, and when Pat refused to be helped from the jar she protested gaily, 'It's unfair! It's you who needs cream, not me.'

But the main thing that remained in her mind about that first dinner was the lady who came to the table whilst they were drinking their wine. She was a woman in her thirties and beautifully gowned. She was good-looking in a brittle sort of way. The French she spoke was rapid, too rapid for her to understand, but she understood the tone of it and also the steeliness in Pat's manner as he replied.

The woman looked at her, and she looked at the woman. Pat made no effort to introduce them, and after a moment the woman, returning her cold gaze to Pat, said a few brief words and walked away, to rejoin two men and another lady at a table further down the room.

'Do you like this wine?'

'Yes, yes; it's very nice.'

He looked across the table and into her eyes and said quietly, 'The lady was angry, and rightly so; I had an engagement to dine with her tonight and I broke it. No doubt, you will understand how she's feeling.'

It was on the point of her tongue to say, 'Never having been a man's mistress you can hardly expect me to understand that lady's feelings,' but if she had she would not have said it in bitterness, for, strange to say, she didn't feel angry, rather the reverse. She felt flattered, and very mature. She understood perfectly that a single man was allowed the privilege of a mistress. Of course, if he were married then one would view the liaison differently.

He said now, 'Where would you like to go tomorrow?' and she replied without hesitation, 'Up the Seine, and to the opera in the evening.'

His eyes twinkled, his lips pressed themselves together before spreading in an amused smile, and then he repeated, 'Up the Seine we'll go, my forthright Katie Bensham, and on to the opera in the evening.'

It was a fortnight later that Katie wrote to her father and Brigie:

'My dear, dear Father and Brigie,
I don't really know how to begin. You'll be amazed at my news, it has all happened so suddenly. I am to be married on Thursday, and who to? Pat . . . Pat Ferrier. Yes, yes, I know you'll both be astounded but I hope you'll be happy for me, as happy as I am now.

We met by accident – or was it the design of Dan and Barbara? – in Dan's bookshop.

We're going through France and on to Italy for our honeymoon. We should be back in England at the end of October. I have so much to tell

475

you but there'll be plenty of time when I return home. The Manor will be much nearer than Manchester and I shall be popping in all the time.

I am happy, believe me, and I'm sorry I was such a fool and let five years go by before I could find my own mind.

My dearest love to you both. Thank you, Father, for being so generous to me all my life. And you, Brigie, for making me fit to be . . . the lady of the manor. Funny, isn't it, me to be the lady of the manor?
Katie.

P.S. I gave Dan your message, Father, and I know he is seriously thinking about it because the apartment they have is so small, and they'd have to be making a move soon, and I think he knows in his heart that he'll never make enough money out of the bookshop to support them without your help. And Brigie, dear, I passed your message on to Barbara, and I think she, too, would welcome returning to England. She didn't seem unpleased at the prospect of living in Newcastle.

P.P.S. Barbara and I are going out now to buy suitable clothes for the journey, not a trousseau, just suitable clothes.

Again my love to you both,
Katie.

Oh really! forgive me, both of you; I forgot to say the babies are beautiful, wonderful. I envy Barbara. I really do.'

3

IT WAS ARRANGED that the night before the wedding they would all dine in Pat's special restaurant on the Champs-Elysées. He was to call for them at quarter-to-eight; he arrived at seven-thirty.

'I'm sorry. I'm sorry; I apologize,' he said laughingly as he entered the apartment. 'It is most inconsiderate of me but you must put it down to my youthful eagerness, the result of a second childhood.'

After closing the door, Dan resuming the struggle with a stud in the neck of his shirt, and also laughing, said, 'Will you go into the sitting room; Katie's there, or in the nursery, and Barbara won't be long. As for me, well' – he spread one hand wide – 'look at me. I've been trying to calm the brood. I've managed two of them, but never Ben. Listen to him . . . I'll be with you in a moment.'

When Pat entered the sitting room he found it empty. He walked to the stove, stood with his back to it for a moment, then made for the door again, just as it opened, and ran into Katie. As they both laughed, she quickly reached up and kissed him lightly on the lips, and as he went to draw her tightly to him she protested still laughing, saying, 'No, no, you mustn't. . . . My dress. Come . . . come and see Ben; the sight of you might frighten him into being quiet.'

'Really! really!' Smiling tolerantly, he followed her into the room where the babies were, two of them quiet and smiling, but not the big fellow.

Ben was thrashing about in the small bed and howling his loudest.

Marie who was bending over him, turned towards them and spoke rapidly, and when Pat answered her they both laughed.

'What does she say? She talks so quickly I can never understand her.' Katie muttered under her breath.

'How can I translate?' He scratched his forehead with his finger. 'She infers he'll end up working in the gas works.'

477

'Why the gas works?'

'Oh' – he shrugged his shoulders – 'I suppose she means that with his lungs he could fill a gas-holder with wind. No, it's funnier than that.' He now bent down to her and whispered, 'The first thing I do with you tomorrow is send you to a convent, there to improve your French.'

'A convent? Oh' – she made a prim face at him – 'I should love that! ... A convent!'

Their heads came together for a moment and they shared a deep chuckle while Marie watched them.

When Pat turned to the girl and spoke in her own tongue, she let out a high laugh, then clapped her hand over her mouth as she repeated *'Couvent demain? Couvent!'* Then almost choking, she went out of the room, while Ben continued to howl.

'Oh, you shouldn't have told her.'

'Why not? The French appreciate a joke.' He did not go further and add, that particular kind of joke. And when she said, 'Joke?', he put his head back and chuckled as he said, 'Brigie to a T.'

'Oh you, really!' She turned from him and bent over the bed saying, 'There! there!' as she stroked the tear-stained crumpled face. 'Aw look,' she said softly, 'they're real, not crocodile tears.'

'Yes, they're real enough.' Pat now put out his hand and touched the fine hair on the baby's head. 'He's much darker than the other two, have you noticed?'

'Yes, but the colour of a baby's hair changes as it grows older.'

'This one's will get darker.' He gently stroked the snub nose and as he did so the child's crying eased away and he said, 'Ah! peace, peace. I've done it.' Then after a moment he added, 'I'd like to bet in a few years' time his hair will be as black as a sloe and very likely show the white streak. You know something? He's a Mallen, if ever I saw one. Do you know whom he is going to be the dead spit of? You remember the picture in the cottage of old Thomas? Well, look at the shape of his head, the face here. ...'

'Nonsense!'

'It isn't nonsense, darling. Anyway why should it be? I tell you we've got another Thomas here and he'll lead the Mallen litter. He's begun already, he's so boisterous. They should have been born in Northumberland; all Mallens belong to Northumberland. So. ...'

'Ssh! Ssh!' Katie was holding up her finger warningly to him, and with a boyish gesture of being caught in some misdemeanour he lifted his thin shoulders upwards and bit on his lip as he looked towards the door, which was partly open. Then they glanced sharply at each other as they heard Barbara's voice coming from the passage speaking to Marie.

478

Pat now moved from Katie's side and went to the door, there to meet Barbara, and before he had opened his mouth to give her his greeting he knew from the look on her face that she had overheard his remark, and he cursed himself for his stupidity. 'I'm early,' he apologized. 'I hope I haven't hurried you.' He made a movement as if to step back as he surveyed her up and down. Then he said gallantly, 'You look very beautiful, Barbara.'

When she made no reply but stared into his face he found himself disconcerted and, as was most unusual with him, at a loss for a suitable remark. He had said she was beautiful but in this moment his words could have been applied to her dress only for her face had a look of thunder on it.

He had heard that she had a violent temper, and like everybody else in the area back home he knew what it had led to, the maiming of an innocent girl, and as her gaze bored into him now he could well imagine what she might do were she to let her temper have rein.

He wondered for a moment if he should bring the matter into the open and apologize, but decided that that would only be pouring salt into the wound, for apparently she hated the fact of having sprung from the Mallens. And no wonder; for no one would appreciate being the result of a rape, and not a rape twixt youth, which might be excused, but one in which the perpetrator was a man of nearly seventy and who had been a father figure to her mother. In a way, he supposed, she must look upon herself as the result of incest. Why, oh why had he to bring up that name, and on this night of all nights! His happiness had intoxicated him and stripped him of tact, to say the least.

When she drew her eyes slowly from him and, turning about, went without a word into her bedroom, he walked into the nursery again and, standing close to Katie by the side of the bed, he bent his head and said below his breath, 'I've apparently done the unforgivable thing by mentioning that name. She is very angry with me.'

She looked at him blankly. 'She heard? Oh Pat! And tonight!'

'I'm sorry.'

Seeing that he was distressed by the incident, she smiled at him now and whispered, 'Don't worry. After all, what was that to say? Anyway, she is a Mallen and they are part Mallens, with a sprinkling of Bensham.' She reached upwards and kissed him. 'Smile, come on. We'll pass it over. I'll be my brightest, gayest, wittiest self. . . .'

Rising to the occasion, he returned her smile and, placing his fingers around her chin, he whispered back, 'Then I have nothing to worry about, ma petite Katie. The success of the evening is assured.'

. . . . . .

The evening was not a success. Barbara had a headache. It started before they left the apartment and it became worse during the evening, and they were all concerned for her.

When at eleven o'clock, much earlier than had been anticipated, Pat said good-bye to her, her headache was so severe that she could make no reply to him, not even to thank him for the splendid dinner he had provided, and of which she had eaten hardly at all.

Katie kissed her and said how sorry she was, but even to this Barbara could only incline her head.

Dan made up for her lapse in his thanks to them both. Then, 'Au revoir,' he said, 'until ten o'clock tomorrow.' He kissed Katie fondly and shook Pat's hand, and watched them drive away before he turned and followed Barbara up the stairs to the apartment.

Nothing was said until Marie had gone. Then Dan, his face grim, burst out, 'Now let's have it. What's it all about? You've got no headache. What on earth is it?'

She stood straight and stiff in the middle of the sitting room facing him. Her lips opened to speak, closed, and opened again before she ground out between her teeth, 'He ... he called them *the ... the ... Mallen litter.*'

'What!'

'You heard what I said, he called them *the Mallen litter.*'

'The Mallen litter? Why, why would he call them that?'

'Because ... because he said Benjamin looked like a Mallen, like ... like Thomas Mallen.' She spat the name out as if it were alum.

Dan glared at her, at this woman he loved, adored, worshipped in fact.

In the years together he had never crossed her. At times he had been stubborn and showed her the side of himself that had strong connections with his father, but always he had come round and been the amenable Dan, the loving, comforting Dan, and above all the understanding Dan. But now there was no evidence of any of these sympathetic qualities in his face, and the tone of his voice was cutting and almost that of a stranger when he said, 'Do you mean to say you spoilt this night for them just because of that, because he uttered a truth, because he said one of them looked like their grandfather? What you've got to face up to once and for all is that Thomas Mallen, dead or alive, is their grandfather and your father. ... Dear God!' He thrust his fingers through his thick sandy hair. 'I thought you'd got all that out of your system during your silent period back in the cottage. But I was mistaken, you're still harbouring it, and by heavens you've proved it tonight. All right' – he waved his hand at her – 'you were born of a tragedy, but I can't see any sense in carrying it on after all these years. Anyway, I should think there's enough harm and trouble

480

come out of it as it is. I don't know how it strikes you. . . .' He stopped as he saw the colour drain from her already pale skin and her eyes widen while her head moved sideways and she buried her chin in her shoulder as if seeking comfort.

Yesterday, this attitude of hers would have brought his arms about her and his mouth showering reassuring kisses over her face, but now it apparently didn't affect him, except in a reverse way, for what he did now was to cry, '*Mallen! Mallen! Mallen!* Go on, shout the name out, purge yourself of it, get it out of your system. For my part I don't care if the three of them grow up carrying the white streak; I don't care what they look like outside as long as they grow up men and have the character of my dad and John. And another thing I'll say while I'm on.' He drew in a deep breath and his tone was quieter now. 'It's Katie's day tomorrow. She's my sister, and I'm more than fond of her, so don't spoil it. And lastly, you'd better know now, because it isn't often I follow my own bent, we're going home. I'm going to take the job Dad's proposed. I've played about long enough. From now on I've got to earn my keep and yours, and that of the litter, Mallen or otherwise, until they can fend for themselves.'

As he stalked from the room Barbara lowered herself slowly down into a chair. She was shocked, she couldn't believe it, Dan to speak to her like that! Dan to act so. She had always known there was another side to him, there was bound to be, for he had his father in him, but he had never shown it to her, and she had thought he never would.

As her hands gripped each other she became aware that she had lost something tonight, and that he had gained something; in the latter case, just what she couldn't put a name to, but in the former, the fact that she hadn't seen this side of this character before was proof of the extent of his loving her. She had been difficult over the years and she must have tried his patience to the limit, yet he had never retaliated. But now he had, and all through Pat Ferrier.

It was odd how this man, whom she had met but a few times in her life, should be the means of pressing home the fact that she was a Mallen, for was it not he from whom she had first heard of her origin. Heard was the wrong word; being deaf at the time, she had read his lips. It was on the night she had danced in the farmyard with Michael, her cousin Michael, and he had almost kissed her, almost. His mother had been furious when she had come upon them, but Pat Ferrier, who was with her, had laughed and said, 'She doesn't carry the streak but she's a Mallen all right.' That was the first indication she'd had of being a Mallen.

And now, in a foreign country, far away from the farm and the valley in the Northumberland hills, here he was again reminding her of her beginnings, and not only that, but calling her babies a litter, a Mallen litter.

She hated him, she would never forgive him, not until the day she died. She didn't wish Katie any unhappiness, but him! She ground her teeth together. What did she wish him? ... That he'd never produce a litter. No! nor even one child to bear his name.

MICHAEL 1888

I

WOLFBUR FARM lay in a valley near the border of Northumberland and Cumberland.

When the people in Allendale, and those even as far away as Hexham and Haltwhistle spoke of the farmer they always referred to him as she, for Constance Radlet had run the farm for more than twenty years, and although her son, Michael, was now virtually in charge he was not looked upon as the first man in the place. In fact, it was Jim Waite who, since old Waite's death, was deferred to more than was the young master.

Michael Radlet was aware of this situation, as was his mother, but neither of them voiced their opinion on it. He could not say to her, 'You are not giving me my due any more than Jim is,' for in a way his mother, and Jim Waite, and the whole Waite family blamed him for what had happened to Sarah. That he had married her did not in their eyes lift the guilt from him, for in different ways they made it clear to him that if he had stood up to 'the other one' and told her where his real intentions lay, the climax that had led to the maiming of Sarah would never have come about.

They all took it for granted now that it had always been his intention to marry Sarah, for had he not been brought up with her, played with her as a child, protected her, danced with her at the harvest suppers? He was continually being reminded that at one time she had been able to dance. It had now reached the point that if she mentioned dancing just once again he would turn on her, really turn on her; not just growl at her under his breath as he did when they were in bed, or turn his back on her whining voice when in the kitchen, but come into the open with a yell, and bawl, not only at her but at his mother, oh yes, at his mother, 'You got what you wanted the both of you. You got rid of Barbara; once and for all you got rid of her.'

Who but his mother could have made him feel it was nothing less than his duty to marry Sarah.

'You are fond of her, aren't you?' she had said.

'Yes,' he had answered.

'Well then.' She had stared fixedly into his distressed face before adding, 'She's a sweet thing.'

Yes, she had been a sweet thing up till then, and he had been very fond of her, but when she lost her leg it wasn't only her body that became maimed but seemingly her mind. If she had been someone who had made a name on the stage through her dancing she could not have reacted more tragically at being deprived of what was after all but a twice yearly recreation, the harvest supper in the barn and the Christmas jollification in the kitchen.

And up till that time too he and his mother had been all in all to each other, but on that fateful day the bond of affection between them was broken. Barbara in her attack on Sarah had not only crippled her but she had severed the umbilical cord that had tied him to his mother.

What was more, his horror and disgust at Barbara's action and his open rejection of her had elicited in her a frenzied rage and she had spat at him his own true beginnings and the reason why his hair was fair instead of black like his father's. All the offspring of the male Mallens were black-haired, and he had thought that his father had been the fly-blow of a Mallen. But she had made it plain to him that it was no Mallen who had bred him, it was his supposed father's half-brother, Matthew Radlet, the legitimate son of the owner of the farm, the fair-haired young fellow who had died early of consumption. He had been begotten, so she had screamed at him, on the floor of the derelict house way up on the hills, the house that was used as a mean shelter for the scum of the roads.

In the hurry and anxiety of getting Sarah to the hospital that day the shock of the revelation had become a secondary thing in his mind, but a secondary thing that held shame, bewilderment and a rising resentment.

Every day in the week that followed he told himself he would bring it out in the open, yet he didn't, for he couldn't look the tall, stately woman in the face and ask her to deny or confirm this thing. Yet in a way he did confront her with his knowledge, for he had gone up into the attic in search of the photographs that used to hang in his grannie's room. It was as he looked at the photos of the two half-brothers and saw the truth staring at him from the fair-headed man that he became aware that he wasn't alone and, turning, he saw his mother standing in the doorway. She had looked from the pictures in his hand into his face, and their gaze had held for a long painful moment before she turned abruptly away. But the truth was out, even if unspoken, and it was from then that she went over, as it were, to the other side, to the side of Sarah, Jim Waite and his people. And it was from then that she too changed, and he saw her no longer as his charming mother, but as an authority, cool, distant, and ever watchful.

Soon after his daughter was born in 1883 he realized that his mother and Sarah combined were, in a subtle way, going to cut him off from his child, perhaps the only one he would ever have, legitimately, for he was finding it increasingly difficult to take Sarah. It was then he showed them that they could go so far and no further.

He would pick up the child when they said it should be lying in its cot; he would dance it up and down in his arms after it had been fed, which they prophesied would make it sick. When it was only three months old he carried it along with him on his round of the farm, and it not yet shortened and without a bonnet. It would die, they both cried, and he'd be to blame, he'd have it on his conscience, among other things, for the rest of his life.

He took it outdoors the next day, and the next, and when he saw them become fearful, he knew, in a way, that he had achieved a victory.

Against strong opposition he had called the child Hannah. There wasn't a Hannah on either side of the family. Why Hannah? Because he liked the name Hannah, and Hannah she would be.

Sensing, from the beginning, they were going to have trouble in the bringing up of the child, Constance and Sarah became even closer, and as time went on they joined in battle to subdue young Hannah's spirits and to erase in some part her foolish adoration for her father, for from the time the child could crawl, she crawled towards him, and when she could walk, she walked towards him, and as soon as she could run, she ran after him.

2

IT WAS ON A SPRING DAY, the Wednesday after Easter Monday in 1888 when, for Michael, life jumped back seven years and the longings of a boy were formulated into the desires of a man and he knew, as he had always known in that closed pocket of his mind, that his love for Barbara Mallen had not been quenched, but had been thriving in the darkness.

The day started early, at five in the morning. Hitching himself up in the bed, he lit the candle, then rose quietly from Sarah's side, thinking that she was asleep, but her voice came at him before he had put his second foot to the floor.

'Are you going to take me or not?'

There was a long pause before he answered under his breath, 'We've had it out; I told you last night.'

'I've never seen Newcastle in me life. Mam says you should take me.'

'I've told you both,' he said dully.

'You would take Hannah.'

'Yes, I would take Hannah.' The last word ended on a sigh.

'Because she can walk, I suppose, she's got two legs.'

Now his tall well built body twisted like a snake about to strike, and he was bending over her, hissing down at her, 'All right! You want the truth. Yes, because she's got two legs, and because she can smile, and because she hasn't got a nagging tongue. Now you've got it. Are you satisfied?'

They were staring at each other in the candlelight. Sarah, whose face at sixteen had been soft and pretty if somewhat pert, now at twenty-four had the hard lines of a woman twice her age. Her eyes were dry but her lips trembled as she said, 'I'll get Uncle Jim to speak to you, I will, I will.'

For a moment she cowered down deep into the feather tick away from him. His fair skin looked almost black in the flickering light. His

486

full lips were stretched wide, his big square teeth clenched and the grinding of them was audible until they opened and he said, slowly, 'Listen to me, Sarah, and get this into your head. This farm is mine, not my mother's, *mine*, and one word from me and your Uncle Jim, his mother, and his sister . . . the lot of them over there will be looking for work. Now I'm telling you, you're driving me too far, you're asking for it; but I warn you, be careful, remember what I said, this is my farm, legally mine, and I'm going into Newcastle the day to sign an agreement for that strip of land, because only I can sign it. *Me . . . me*, not my mother. And from now on it'll pay you to remember that, and you can pass it on to your Uncle Jim an' all. You can also tell him, if I hear any more of his big talk in the market about who runs this place I'll make it impossible for anybody to have any more doubts about it. Just you tell him that.'

He walked from her and went behind the screen that stood in the corner of the room and, having torn his nightshirt over his head, he pulled on his long pants and vest.

Since shortly after they were married, he had undressed and dressed behind the screen because the sight of his bare legs seemed to upset her. She didn't mind them in bed; no, she had been surprisingly free in her love-making, too free. The loss of a limb had not impaired her desires; it was her hunger in this direction that showed up his own loss of appetite. First of all he had thought it was because he had been afraid to hurt her, but now he knew it was because there was no passion in him for her. His bodily needs lacked the impetus of love. They were fulfilled on his part through a requirement of nature, that was all, and she, being a woman and a woman coached in such things by her aunt, whom she called mother, and her cousin Lily, whom she called aunt, not forgetting his own mother who had educated her, recognized the missing element in his love-making, and this, no doubt, was the cause of her bitterness as much as was the loss of her leg.

Dressed, he picked up the candle and went out of the room without speaking further.

Down in the kitchen the table was set as usual for breakfast. The fire glowed through the humped slack that had been heaped on it last night. The copper pans hanging above the mantelpiece gave out a soft warm sheen like dulled gold. The house cat, with its privileged bed near the black oven, uncoiled itself, looked up at him, stretched, moved into a new position and went to sleep again. From outside in the yard came the low murmur of the cattle, a cock crowed, then another, then another.

He brewed himself some strong tea, drank it black and sweet, then went out into the yard. The light was lifting rapidly. It was a beautiful morning; the air tickled his throat like a sharp wine. He stood for a moment and drew in a slow long breath that widened the space between his open waistcoat to three inches. Then he went past the dairy, looked in the barn where two sheepdogs were sleeping on the straw until he whistled softly, when they roused themselves and slowly followed him past the stables and into the byres.

Although it was only twenty past five Jim Waite was already there. He always felt that if he were to get up at three Jim Waite would be there before him.

Jim Waite had come to this farm when a boy. He had come with his father seeking work and a roof to shelter his mother and sister, and they had been given a shelter by Donald Radlet. That Radlet's generosity had been a form of spiting his wife, because in the early days Harry Waite had once been a footman in the home of Thomas Mallen where Constance Radlet had been brought up, made no matter, he had given them shelter, and they had repaid him well. When he died they had continued to repay his wife with hard work and long hours, until, with the passing years and the death of his own father, Jim Waite had come to look upon himself, not only as Constance Radlet's head-man but as the man who really ran the farm.

Michael had, up till the last year or so, remained a boy in his eyes, but of late, to use his own expression, Mr Michael had begun to throw his weight about. Slowly but surely he was taking the authority from him and reducing him to shepherd-handyman again, and he didn't like it, he didn't like it at all. But he knew which side his bread was buttered, and he was wise enough to realize that he would never again in his life get a place such as he had here, a house and a free supply of milk, butter, eggs and pork, vegetables and mutton. The only thing they bought were the grains. And if young Michael were to turn nasty the fact that they were now, in a way, related by marriage would, he knew, carry no weight, and he had nothing in writing, he wasn't bonded in any way. No, he knew which side his bread was buttered, and it didn't do him any harm to put on a mealy mouth. But he saw to it he got his little digs in; Master Michael didn't have it all his own way.

'A fine morning, grand, isn't it?' He had dropped the title Mr Michael a long time ago.

'Yes, it's a grand one. The winter's well past now, thank God.'

After looking around Michael came out of the byres and went into what was called the harness room, where a boiler was always bubbling with pig feed. In a few minutes Jim Waite followed him and, putting his head in the door, he said, 'I think I'd better go along the low bottoms this mornin' an' see how many have come in the night.'

Michael turned from the harness rack; he was pulling a leather strap through his hand as he said, 'It mightn't be how many have been born but how many have been pinched.'

'Oh, I don't think they'll get this far, it's scum from over the border. The last raid was miles away, up beyond Kielder Moor.'

'I wouldn't be too sure. What's forty miles to an organized band of sheep thieves? They bragged they had Roger Marden's lot killed and skinned before they reached the Cheviots, so' – he nodded – 'don't underestimate them.'

'Well' – Jim Waite's chin came out – 'we haven't lost one yet, have we? By the way, I heard a bit of news last night. I called in at The Fox on me way back. They were on about Mr Ferrier and the new herd he's startin'. A hundred guineas he's paid for a bull. That's something, isn't it, a hundred guineas? Well, as they said, he's taken up farmin' to take his mind off his troubles. And he's got troubles 'cos I don't think there can be much worse than to be saddled with an idiot son. Huh! he wanted an heir, an' he's got one. By God! I'd say he has.'

Michael stopped in the act of lifting the harness from its stand and he turned his head sharply. 'What! What do you mean, an idiot son?'

'Well, that's what they say. The few who's seen the bairn, they say he looks an idiot; Chinaman's eyes, no shape to his mouth, an' its skin stretched, you know tight like an idiot's. Of course, they've kept it dark. Ted Hunnisett said you can get little out of the servants, like clams they are, but he was delivering there, grain an' flour from the mill, an' he saw the mother, you know Miss Bensham that was. She had the bairn by the hands trying to make him walk. He shouldn't have been there, I mean Ted, not where he was at the time but he had gone round the back to make water, an' in the distance he sees a bush and it was full of blossom, pink blossom. The flowers were like cups he said, he had never seen one like it afore, and he thought he'd sneak along and pinch a branch. An' when he got to the bush he found it overlooked a part of the garden that was secluded like, an' there on the lawn below him was this bairn an' Miss Bensham. . . . I mean Mrs Ferrier. He'd had his hand on the branch he said afore he twigged them and it must have been that he moved the bush 'cos she turned and looked up, and when she saw him she must have recognized he wasn't one of theirs for she up with the child and hugged it to her and went off. Well,' he ended, 'they say God's ways are slow but they're sure.'

'What do you mean by that?' Michael was standing confronting him now, his face grim.

'Well.' Jim Waite tossed his head and assumed a slightly flustered manner. 'You could say . . . well, you could say he played the dirty on the missis, didn't he? I remember the time when he wasn't away from the door. . . .'

'That's enough, Waite, that's enough!'

The reprimand was significant in more ways than one because Michael had never before called him by his surname. It had always been Jim.

'Sorry if I've taken a liberty.' Jim Waite's voice was surly.

'I'm glad you recognize it as a liberty.'

They stared at each other through the thin haze of steam coming from the boiler.

'Things've changed.'

'Things are as they should be, and as they always should have been.'

'You mean I forgot me place?'

'You could say that.'

'Aw well, now I know where I stand, don't I?'

'Yes, you know where you stand.'

'It's come to somethin'.'

'That's your fault.'

'I've known you since you were a bairn in the cradle by the kitchen fire. It's a bit late isn't it to play the master?'

'Where you have made the mistake is that you didn't recognize me as master before.'

'Your mother was the boss.'

'She's the boss no longer.'

'Aw well, I'd say she'd be surprised to hear that.'

'Well, you'd better go and tell her, hadn't you? You're well equipped for carrying news, you've done it for years.'

Again they stared at each other, in silence now, until Jim Waite, turning away said, 'Things'll never be the same after this,' and Michael said to his back, 'That will be up to you, entirely up to you. You keep your place and give me mine and things can remain seemingly as they are. If not, well, you know the alternative.'

He swung the harness to the front of his chest and went out and across the yard and into the stables and began to prepare the horse and trap for the journey to the station.

It was turned seven o'clock when he entered the house again. Both Sarah and his mother were in the kitchen and he knew from the looks they cast on him that Jim Waite had, as usual, been before him.

He was at the sink washing his hands when his mother said, 'What's this I hear?'

'What do you hear?' He jerked his head up but did not turn towards her.

'You're taking the high hand with Jim.'

'If you care to put it that way, yes, but I would say I was merely pointing out who was master.'

'Master?' Constance Radlet's eyebrows moved upwards. Her one-

490

time beautiful face looked bony and fleshless but the skin showed no wrinkles. She was forty-four and looked every day of her age, or even more; this was caused as much by the stiffness that braced her figure as by the austerity of her features. She retained no resemblance to the gay girl she had been before she married Donald Radlet, or even to the kindly woman who had survived him.

The events of the recent years she had taken as personal insults, particularly the latest, when three years ago she had heard that Pat Ferrier had married Katie Bensham.

On the day Jim Waite had brought this news to the farm – it was only through Jim she received news of the Benshams, having now no connection with Miss Brigmore, or Mrs Bensham as she had become – it was on that day that she had gone up to her room and sat with her fists clenched as she stared into the mirror and looked down the years at her past life. On that day, if wishes could have killed, Pat Ferrier would have surely died and Katie Bensham's life would have been blighted in some way.

She had not cried at the news; instead, her resentment and anger went to join the parched tears and bitterness that had built up in her over the years.

And now this morning, as she had listened to Jim Waite's latest news, she had felt not one trace of sorrow in her, so much had life changed her, but she had thought, in the terms that any of the Waites might themselves have used, God's slow but He's sure, and indeed she knew that in this instance He was. Also that everything came to him who waited, and Pat Ferrier, in preferring a young girl to herself, had been repaid with an idiot son.

'You happy?'

'What do you say?'

'I said, are you happy?'

Michael's words had startled her. She looked at him where he stood now confronting her, a big ruddy-faced, fair-haired young man . . . but no, not young any longer, not young in this moment, simply a man. And she knew that here was another turning point in her life. Her old self, who had loved this son and who still loved him, was fearing him now. But in a way this feeling was not new for she had feared him since the day when she caught him looking at the two photographs in the attic. Yet she had the strong urge even now to appeal to him, to put her arms about him and say, 'Michael, Michael, try to understand how I feel. I've been tortured emotionally since I was a young girl. Pat Ferrier was the third man who rejected me. You can't have any idea what it is to be a woman and be rejected three times. To know that you are beautiful, attractive, and . . . and be passed over. It would have been understandable if I had been plain

491

and without personality, but I was a lively and yes, yes, a charming young woman, charming enough for your father to do murder for me. And look what life has done to me. . . . Look.' But what she said was, 'What do you mean, am I happy?'

'I thought you'd be happy, having heard of Ferrier having an idiot son.'

She did not answer for some time and they stared at each other, open enmity between them now; then slowly she said, 'Every man in the end gets what he deserves, and I would remind you to remember just that. . . . Sarah' – she turned to where Sarah was leaning on her crutch at the end of the table watching them both, and she finished, 'You can cut the bread now.'

Her head moving slowly from side to side, Sarah looked hard at her husband before swinging her body expertly around and clip-clopping to the sideboard, and there, again just as expertly, she lifted up with one hand the bread board on which reposed a loaf and brought it to the table.

Pulling a chair forward, she sat down, then leant her crutch against the corner of the table, and after cutting two slices of bread she glanced to where Michael had now seated himself at the opposite end of the table and said, 'Mam says you can drop me off at Hexham; she wants some things. Don't you, Mam?'

Constance was at the stove. She didn't turn round nor did she speak, and Sarah went on, 'I can get the carrier cart back.'

Slowly Michael placed the full spoon back in his porridge before saying, 'I told you; and that was final. Whatever you want in Hexham you can get on Friday.'

'I want to go in today.'

He shook his head slowly as he stared at her, 'Oh no, you don't. What you want is to be given the chance to cause a scene there and blackmail me into taking you into Newcastle. That's it, isn't it?'

'Why are you so set on going alone?'

As he stared at Sarah he was aware that his mother had turned sharply from the fire and was glaring at him. They were both glaring at him, seeing him in a new light, as Jim Waite had done earlier on. And he left no doubt in either of their minds that the new light was shining for good and all when, getting up abruptly from the table, he said, 'I'm going into Newcastle, and I'm going on my own. This is only a beginning. And I'm telling you both' – he looked from one to the other – 'if I want a day off I'm taking it, and on my own, or the child with me if I so need her. Now chew over that, the both of you.' And on this he marched from the room.

They looked at each other, but neither spoke. As usual, Sarah's lips began to tremble while her eyes remained dry. Then Constance, turning from her, went back to the stove. But she didn't bend over it, she just stared at the big hollow above the fire that led into the chimney, and she saw her future as black as the soot adhering to it. . . .

When Michael was dressed for the road he went across the landing and into the bedroom where his daughter lay sleeping, and as he bent down to kiss her she opened her eyes and put her arms around his neck and said sleepily, 'Hello, Dada.'

'Hello, my love.' He only used this term of endearment to her when they were alone.

'You going out?'

'Yes.'

'Where?'

'Oh, a long way off, Newcastle.'

'New-cas-sel?' She spread the word out.

He nodded at her.

'You're not takin' me?'

'No, not this time; next time I go I'll take you. What would you like me to bring you back?'

Her eyes twinkled. 'A monkey on a stick, like the one I had last year and got broken, and some sea shells.'

'All right, you'll have a monkey on a stick and some sea shells. Good-bye now.' He kissed her again, and she hugged his head to her.

'Be a good girl.'

'Yes, Dada.'

He turned from the door and looked at her. She looked fresh and beautiful to him . . . and innocent. No rancour in her face, no recrimination. But how long could she remain like that before they contaminated her with their bitterness.

When he emerged from the Central Station in Newcastle he did what he had done on his two previous visits to the city. He went across the road and gazed back at the façade. It was a mighty piece of work to front a railway station, he thought, and it was a great pity that it was being befouled with soot and bird droppings. He crossed the road again and went towards the end of the building to where unobtrusively a winged head gazed down from the side wall. He liked the expression on its face, it was kindly. But what a waste, all that stone and workmanship to front a railway station! He shook his head at it all.

He next took a walk along the quayside; then made his way up the Castlegarth steps and into the town. The sights and sounds of the city intrigued him, and all weren't beautiful. Going up a narrow alley he passed a doss-house. The door was open and he had a brief glimpse of one room where men lay huddled on the floor, some munching food, some asleep. The scene was softened by the glow from a blazing fire, but the stench from the place brought his nose wrinkling; animal dung smelled sweet compared with it. And more than once in the same vicinity he received invitations from ladies of light virtue, which made him suddenly feel the need of their services. But he did not avail himself; he was fastidious in that way.

Later, he walked past the cathedral. He had never gone inside, churches didn't appeal to him, yet he could admire the exterior, a mass of stone held a certain attraction.

Eventually he stopped in Pilgrim Street and ate, and ate well. Later, he walked along Collingwood Street where the shops had fine big windows in which to display their goods, not open casements like those in the side streets, and as he gazed into them he wished he had brought Hannah with him. She would have loved the display. He did not allow his mind to muse on the fact that Sarah might have enjoyed it equally as much.

The solicitors' offices were in Percy Street and his business there took him but half an hour. He wrote his signature to the deed of land consisting of ten acres of fertile pasture adjoining the south side of his property. The same, purchased from Lord Alvin for the sum of thirty pounds, was witnessed by a clerk.

When he asked the solicitor his fee he was told a bill would be sent to him, and he answered that he preferred to pay on the spot. The solicitor stretched his face, rang a handbell and spoke to his clerk. A few minutes later the clerk put a slip of paper on the desk before his master. The solicitor then turned it round and looked up at Michael. Michael looked down at the paper and said, 'Three guineas.' He drew the money from his pocket, handed it across the table, shook the solicitor's hand, wished him good day and went out.

There were now ten more acres of land added to the farm and it excited him not at all. He had no great love of land. He had no great love of anything for that matter. Life was a routine filled with duties, responsibilities, all to be met. There was only one thing in his outlook this day that was different from yesterday; in future he would not only be the master of the farm, but see to it that he was seen to be the master of the farm. Whether he was the bastard son of his half-uncle, or the son of his mother's husband made no difference, the farm was his, and from now on he would bring that home to them, every one of them from his mother down to the youngest of the Waites.

There was a full hour and a half before he need return to the station. He meandered down to the river again and gazed at the bridges and the bustling activity that was going on between them; big ships, little ships, coal barges, wherries. The latest one, the swing bridge, was but twelve years old; they must have been building it when he was a lad. He turned from the river and went back into the town. He went through the Haymarket and on through streets that were becoming grander and wider as he walked.

It was as he left a street called Lovaine Place and turned down a narrow passage that he saw coming towards him from the other end a tall lady accompanied by three children. They were small children only about three years old; two of them were walking one on each side of the lady and she was holding them by their hands, but the third one, who seemed older, was dancing and jumping well ahead of them. He did not know whether it was a boy or a girl, even when the child stopped in front of him; not until he stooped down and touched the black ringlets hanging from under the sailor hat and the child laughed up at him and said, 'Hello,' was he certain it was a boy.

He looked up, waiting for the mother's approach, but she had stopped. Then, for the first time in years he knew he was possessed of a heart, literally, because its beating thumped so hard against his chest wall that the sound reverberated through his ears, filling his head and seeming to blind him, for the face and figure of the woman were blotted out for a moment. He blinked once, twice, and then again. And now he could see her. She was not the Barbara he remembered, there was no resemblance to his last memory of her; before him was a woman, a fully matured woman, beautiful, so beautiful that he felt faint at the sight of her. She was standing, still as a statue, waiting. Waiting for what? He heard Sarah's voice coming at him as if from the figure before him, saying, 'I want to come with you. Why are you so set on going alone, eh?'

He must move, go forward, speak to her. It was Barbara. Barbara. But what if it got back to them in some way? They would say, 'There we knew it. We knew all along what you were up to.' His thoughts were jumbled, tumbling about in his head. What was the matter with him? He must speak to her, he must look at her close to. He must tell her. . . . What must he tell her? That he had realized too late that his love for her was as great as hers had been for him? And where would that lead him?

The child turned from him and called across the distance, 'Mama! Mama! come.' He saw the other two children tug at her hands. But still she didn't move. She was waiting for some sign, and he gave it. He turned in the narrow passage and almost ran down the length of it. He had to keep his feet in a step that could be still termed walking. He came into the main street and hurried along it until he came to a side street and he went up this, right to the end of it. There he stopped and like a man spent, he leant against the wall and looked back the way he had come, thinking that if she passed he would catch one more glimpse of her. But she did not pass.

After a few minutes he brought himself abruptly upright. He had been a fool, stupid; he had turned and run. What would she think? What could she think but that he had meant what he said that day near the copse: 'I never want to see you again as long as I live.' Yet he knew now that every day since then, that's all he had longed for, just to see her again.

Now he was running down the side street again and along the main street and to the narrow passage; but there was no sign of her or the children. He raced to the end of it and came into Lovaine Place again. It was empty. He looked at his watch. If he intended to get home tonight, he must get to the station right away. But he didn't move.

A man and a woman were coming into the square from the opposite side. He waited until they approached, then said, 'Excuse me, but . . . but did you see a lady with three children as you were coming in, I mean outside of here?' He flapped his hand widely, indicating the square. The man and woman looked at each other, then at him, and it was the man who spoke. His voice had a distinct haughtiness to it as he said, 'No, no; we have seen no lady with three children.' When they immediately passed on he felt foolish.

Her name was Mrs Bensham. He could start knocking on the doors in this square and ask if the Benshams lived there. Then what? Should Dan Bensham be in the house, what would he say? I have come to have a look at your wife?

Get yourself home.

As if obeying a command he turned about and hurried through the town and caught his train with only two minutes to spare.

It was not until he got into the trap to begin the last part of his journey home that he remembered he had not bought the monkey on a stick or the sea shells for Hannah.

THE IDIOT

I

COMPARED WITH HIGH BANKS HALL Burndale Manor was a small house, but it was a companionable house, warm, welcoming. The Manor had been in the Ferrier family for three hundred years. Even the present house was built on the foundations of the previous Ferrier home, which had been burned down one Christmas time, when a tired maid dropped her head on to the kitchen table at four o'clock in the morning and went to sleep. The guests revelling in the house and the staff in the barn had all been too drunk to fight the fire caused by a toppled candle burning into the wood of the grease-sodden table. No one knew how long the previous Manor had stood, some said three, some said four hundred years; what was known was that the timbers had been so dry and worm-riddled that by daylight there was nothing left of the place.

Although the manor house was comparatively small, the acreage was large, extending to seven hundred acres, and not all being of barren hillsides, but of gardens, fertile fields, and woods.

Katie was a bride of five weeks when she first saw her new home, and from the moment she entered its doors she knew she would love it and all therein, from the butler, McNeil, who was so old he tottered – but as Pat said would be allowed to totter until he died – to Mary Dixon, the meanest of the staff, being but a kitchen maid; she took them all to her heart. How could it be otherwise, for she was experiencing such happiness that the world and all in it appeared good and glorious.

Pat Ferrier, during his short courtship of her, had been gallant, charming and amusing, but as a husband he had been a revelation. She did not mind that his expertise in this direction was due to his experience as a lover of many women, for she knew that in his eyes she was someone unique, someone who translated joy for him. His loving was tender and exciting, and brought out in her qualities she never knew she possessed. Moreover, as the weeks grew into months and she became happier still in the knowledge that she was to bear his child, she acquired a poise that all Miss Brigmore's teachings could never have implanted in her, because it was the outcome of the fact that she was loved and honoured, and she was about to become a mother. And this, she determined, would be the first of many pregnancies, for she would give Pat, not just one son or daughter, but a family of sons and daughters.

Not least of her pleasures were the dinners she graced, some companionable affairs of half a dozen, others larger assemblies when twenty or thirty guests would be present. She preferred the smaller dinner parties, for at these the conversation became general, and she was surprised and pleased at Pat's knowledge of everyday affairs, particularly politics.

She had considered her own mind very wide when she was struggling with the social problems of Manchester, but listening at these special gatherings she recognized how colossal her ignorance of world affairs was. When she confessed this to Pat he kissed her and laughed as he said, 'Well, my darling, the more knowledge you gain of your ignorance the more you will learn.'

The depth and wisdom of his answer did not explain itself fully until she had pondered on it.

It was a humbling thought, that all the while she had been concerned with the trivialities of her good works great things were taking place beyond her horizon; jealousies were working like yeast in countries which Pat said would eventually make them rise to war.

It was at the dinner table that she learned that Germany was jealous of England, it was jealous of her colonies and the positions these afforded to the young bloods of the country. Although Germany had the biggest army in the world, and had, apparently, no need to envy England, nevertheless it did, because England, the little island, the powerful dynamic little island, was preventing the German army from ruling Europe. Moreover, England had prevented Germany from marching through Belgium in 1870, and had refused to let it attack France in 1875: France was crippled at the time; never kick a man when he's down, was the Englishman's motto.

So she learnt that the Germans, from admiring the British, had grown to hate them. What apparently annoyed them was that the English found them amusing. The working-class Englishman thought of the Germans as pork butchers, for every good pork butcher's shop was found to be owned by a German. The Englishman also considered the Germans a pompous people, for didn't they come to England and march about the country playing in bands. And they all had big bellies through drinking beer.

As Katie listened she laughed. Yet there were times when she despised herself for not putting over her point of view, particularly when the topic of conversation turned on the children of the working class and the wisdom of educating them. But then ladies didn't, not at the dinner table and in front of guests.

Her days during the first months at the Manor were joyously full with entertaining and being entertained. But one day a week she insisted on being kept free, and on this day she would drive over to her old home, accompanied most times by Pat, and there they were welcomed with open arms.

Christmas had been particularly happy for Katie that year because her father and Brigie both came and spent it at the manor house, and their stay had been prolonged by a snowfall that continued for three days.

It was during this time that she first experienced a bout of morning sickness which gave final confirmation to a hope which she had not up till then mentioned to her husband, and when she quietly and without coyness, but with a twinkle in her eye, told him the news he had taken her in his arms and held her tightly pressed against him, not kissing her, not even speaking, because his feelings in that moment could find no relief in outward expression.

During the months that followed he petted and pampered her and amused her and, as she laughingly admitted, extended her education beyond the point where Brigie had stopped. In fact Brigie's teaching now appeared to be of a very elementary quality.

The child was due in July. The layette was one that would have met the needs of royalty. Excitement pervaded the house from the wine cellars up to the set of four rooms on the second floor on which the workmen had spent three months, turning it into a nursery, complete with day nursery and night nursery with a nurse's bedroom and sitting room attached.

She started her labour pains on the Sunday afternoon when the sky was black with an impending storm. The storm itself did not break until late evening and it raged all night and did not die away until the first light, and it was with the first light that she gave a great cry that brought Pat from the adjoining room, and he saw his son born.

When, an hour later, he looked down on the child lying in the cot to the side of the bed he laughed and said, 'He's an ugly brute, he's going to be like me,' and she gazed up at him and whispered, 'All babies look ugly when they're born, but if he grows like you he'll be the most handsome man alive.'

'Katie, darling Katie, how can I ever repay you for what you have given me? How ? How?' He took her face tenderly between his hands

499

and as tenderly he laid his lips on hers, and she closed her eyes and went to sleep.

The nurse said she had never known such a quiet baby. The wet nurse said it must be her milk for the child seemed filled with happiness. He rarely cried, and there was a perpetual smile on his face which, as the days passed, lost its look of crumpled ugliness and took on a soft, wide-eyed surprised stare.

Katie could not remember exactly when she first began to worry about the child. Was it when he made no movement to pull her finger into his mouth and suck it, but just held it limply while staring up at her? Or was it when she noticed that the contours of his face did not drop in as a baby's should?

He was three months old when the nurse said, 'He's lazy. You get them like this; they want a smacked backside now and again to rouse them.' And when she went to apply the remedy, even gently, Katie almost sprang on her and, grasping the child from her knee where he lay on a towel being dried, she glared at the woman and cried, 'Don't you ever raise your hand to him, ever!'

In one flashing moment the nurse, who had been thinking that this particular mother was easy, the child being her first, and her knowing nothing about babies, discovered that she was being confronted with a parental passion such as ladies never showed; you expected and got this reaction from the lower classes, but never from those in manor houses and the like. She was huffed, and she showed it.

When the child was four months old Katie changed his nurse. The new one was a widow from the village. She had been a mother six times, but four of her children had died, the remaining two being now married. She was a kindly soul and wise, so from the beginning she never proffered an opinion on the child, and since her mistress never put questions to her regarding it she kept her opinion of her new charge to herself.

When the child was a year old it had not yet said either mum-mum or da-da, nor had it made any attempt to pull itself to its feet or even to crawl. Katie would sit him on a rug and hold out her arms and say, 'Come. Come, darling,' and the child would look at her and smile, a wider smile than the one which usually turned up the corners of its straight lips, and after what seemed to be a great effort would turn on to its hands and knees with a flopping movement, and with its head up and gazing at her it would crawl slowly towards her. And she would lift it into her arms and press it to her breast, and control once more the great tide of fear that over the past months had been rising towards her brain and threatening to overwhelm her.

But her emotions did find vent before they reached the stage that would have caused her to have a mental breakdown. It happened one night as she stood by the cot and looked down on the sleeping child. Thinking she was alone she pressed her face so tightly between her hands that she inflicted pain on herself; and it was as she shook her head in a despairing movement that she was startled by Pat's arms pulling her around roughly and his voice saying, 'Let us talk. Let us talk, Katie. We must face this. Come.' And he led her downstairs to their bedroom.

Her crying had been audible, verging on hysteria, she had cried and wailed for a solid hour. Only when he said, 'I'll call the doctor,' did she calm down; then choking and spluttering, she gasped, 'What have I given you, Pat? He is not right, far from right. I've . . . I've known it for a long time. He . . . he could be an imbecile. *Oh, Pat, Pat. Oh I'm sorry. Oh, my dear, my dear.*'

When he held her closely pressed he did not contradict what she had said, for she had voiced what was not just his fear but his certainty that his son was abnormal.

As Katie half feared the child did not alienate Pat's feeling for her; rather he became more attentive, if that were possible. The only time he left her to travel alone was, first, when he went to London to see a doctor who had been recommended to him and the second time, when for a period of two weeks he returned to France, there to visit a specialist.

After his visit to London he had brought back with him Doctor Cass. The doctor was an old man, blunt and seemingly unfeeling. He spoke in short sharp sentences saying that he had seen hundreds of babies such as this, but this one was fortunate, if you could call it so, for he wouldn't be smothered on the quiet, or chained up in some cell, or at best relegated to a garret in the top of the house. On the last words he had turned and looked from Pat to Katie as much as to say, Well, the last is up to you.

It was evident, he went on to say, that the child had just missed being a mongol; and they could hope that he would not grow up an idiot, merely an imbecile. There was nothing much one could do, he informed them, until the child was a few years older, five or six. It might turn out then that he would show a certain amount of intelligence, which could be developed with training, constant specialized training. He emphasized the latter. He had, he said, known cases where a child like this had in later years even been able to earn its living at a craft, a simple craft, a handicraft; but that was all they could hope for.

Of course, he had ended, his was only one opinion, there were others they could consult. And he showed that he wasn't really unconcerned when he suggested that Pat might find it worth while to go to France, for there a psychologist by the name of Binet was doing interesting work with the mentally retarded.

Who knew, he said finally, while he shook their hands and thanked them with softened courtesy for their hospitality, who knew but that Binet could help them. New methods were being discovered every day. It all had to do with the metabolism; when acids couldn't be metabolized they passed out in the urine and deficiency occurred, mental deficiency.

'Yes, yes.' He was still talking as he got into the carriage. 'It's all to do with the metabolism. If you decide to see Binet tell him what I have said, and I'll send him a note if you so wish. He might say I'm quite wrong in my diagnosis and the child will grow up simply to be a moron. And there are a lot of them about, by God! yes; half the country is composed of morons. Well, good-bye. Good-bye. And let me say this. If you feel I can help in any way just drop me a line and I'll be up.' He had put his head out of the carriage window and looked up at the sky and around the drive and exclaimed in his abrupt fashion, 'Lovely country. Lovely country,' and then he was gone, leaving them both devastated.

Patrick went to France and saw Monsieur Alfred Binet, and Monsieur Binet said he could do very little but pass an abstract opinion on the child, not having seen it. But it seemed that Doctor Cass had been right in his diagnosis, except in one aspect; Monsieur Binet could hold out no hope from the description that had been given him of the child's behaviour that he was as light a case as a moron. But one never knew. If, as Doctor Cass had said, his features were not completely mongolian but just tended that way, and his reactions were not completely static, then there was a possibility that he would grow to be merely a mongolian imbecile, not an idiot; and if this were the case he could turn out to be quite intelligent, in fact, of even a higher intelligence than a moron. He had known such cases, there was hope.

Such dubious hope had a devastating effect on both of them, yet they made the child the focal point of their lives, which changed the pattern to almost a sombre ritual. The gay dinner parties came to an end; only those who were close friends or relatives were invited to the house; and the staff, after being lectured by McNeil in the servants' hall, became like a loyal clan in that they did not chatter to anyone outside the estate, and they allowed no one to enter the house except those known to be close friends or relatives.

But even the visits of the close friends and relatives upset Katie for she insisted that the child should not be hidden away in the nursery, she would not be guilty of Doctor Cass's assumption. Yet when she saw the pity in the eyes of those who looked on her son her whole being was rent with pain. And no one had caused her more pain than her father, for he reacted from the first as if she herself were to blame. She had the suspicion that he imagined her child would not have been as he was had she married Willy. And she was right, for this, Harry thought, was what came of high breeding – the Ferriers went so far back that their line had been weakened.

2

LAWRENCE PATRICK CHARLES FERRIER was three years old on the fifth of July, 1889, and hadn't yet walked, not even with stumbling step, but could say 'Pop-a' and 'Mar-a.' He could say 'fow' for flower, and 'de' which meant drink, and 'Bri-Bri,' which stood for Brigie.

This progress had come about within the last six months and the effect on Katie had been as if she had discovered that her son was showing signs of genius. If he had sat at the piano and composed a sonatina she could not have been more delighted, and it wasn't only that he was attempting to speak, and walk, but that he was also showing a preference for people and things. He liked cakes but didn't like meat; he liked milk but wouldn't drink soup.

Only yesterday when he had taken his hand and swiped from the table a bowl of soup his nurse had placed before him Katie had laughed, and she had gone running to Pat and told him. And he had come up to the nursery to view the evidence of his son's independence.

Putting his arm around Katie's shoulders, Pat had pressed her to him and they had looked at each other and the smile they exchanged was winged on hope.

But the child showed his greatest advancement in his preference for certain people. When some of the maids spoke to him he would make no response whatsoever, just stare at them out of his wide blue eyes; but others he would touch, or even extend his arms towards them. This latter he always did with Brigie, and Brigie would take him to her heart and hold him close and call him 'My lamb'. And Katie loved her for it while at the same time almost hating her father for the fact that he never touched the child, did not even extend a finger to him.

The day was hot, and the garden was heavy with the scent of roses. Katie had tea served in the shade of the oak tree. There were only herself, Brigie and Harry present, together with the child. Katie held him on her knee and she interspersed her conversation with her father and Brigie to talk to him in short, repetitive, stilted sentences. Lawrence like some milk? Lawrence like some cake? No, no! Lawrence must not touch that. This is for Lawrence. ... Cake. Cake.

'My dear.'

'Yes, Brigie, you were saying?'

'I wasn't, but I'm going to. And don't become annoyed with me, please, for what I am about to suggest, but I think it would have more effect if you were to talk to him in a natural fashion.'

'I do, I do.'

'No, my dear, I'm afraid you don't. What you say is: Lawrence have cakie. Lawrence have this. Lawrence can't have that. To begin each sentence with his name is not natural, it will penetrate his mind in this stilted fashion and the result will be that when he does talk it will be in a similar manner.'

Katie stared at Brigie. She wanted to say, 'What do you know about it? All waking hours of the day and sometimes of the night I am with him, talking, coaxing, playing.'

Brigie was not slow to realize how Katie had taken her suggestion and she sipped from her cup before saying, 'I'm sorry, my dear, you must forgive me. I forget I'm not still in the schoolroom.'

Katie let escape a deep sigh; then tracing her finger through the short, thick hair on her son's head, she murmured, 'You're right. I know you're right. I've got into a habit. I'll ... I'll do as you say.'

When the child wriggled on her knee she put him on to the grass. Then, with a look of wonderment on her face that was painful for Brigie to witness, she pointed to him as he pulled himself to his feet and began a stumbling walk as a baby might who was taking its first tentative steps, testing one foot forward before lifting the other, and she cried, 'He's walking! That's ... that's the first time.'

When she rose to her feet and went to follow the child Harry's voice came at her flatly, saying, 'Sit down, lass, and leave him be.' And she sat down, and the smile of happiness slid from her face as she looked at her father, and he, breaking a piece of cake and chewing on it, did not return her look but said, 'Is Pat likely to be back afore we go?'

'Unless he gets talking to someone in the market.' She turned her glance on Brigie and ended, 'He's become very interested in the farm.'

'That's good,' said Brigie.

'He'll never make it pay.' Harry took another bite of the cake. 'He'll never get his money back on all those buildings. Putting up stone byres and runnin' water miles across the land when there's a good well there that's served him for years; he'll never get his money back.'

Katie and Brigie exchanged glances and Brigie made an almost imperceivable movement of her head which said, 'Take no notice.'

'Our Dan's a surprise.'

'Yes?' Katie raised her eyebrows in polite enquiry as she looked at her father.

'Aye, I should say he is. I always knew he had it in him; it just needed to be brought out an' this Newcastle end has certainly done it. By! Aye, he pushed orders up almost forty per cent last year. Now that's something, and from our Dan mind, him that wanted nowt to do with business. It must have been that little bookshop he had over there that set him going. Anyway something did it. They're going to move to a bigger house, up Gosforth way. Did you know? At least he's talking of it. Barbara's not so keen, 'cos she wants the bairns near the school she said. I think she's looking forward to it, I mean seeing them off to school. And I can understand it an' all, 'cos by, they're a handful! Talk about little devils! It's Ben that's the trouble; he's the leader, the other two just follow. Eeh! the tricks that one gets up to.'

Every word her father uttered was like a paean of praise, and she turned her sad eyes and looked to where her son was now crawling on all fours towards a rose bed in the middle of the lawn and she got up quickly and went towards him.

Brigie, looking straight ahead and speaking under her breath, now said, 'Please don't talk about the boys.'

'What? What's that you say?'

'I said please don't talk about the boys; you are hurting her.'

'Aw, God in heaven! Can't I open me mouth?'

'Not on that subject and not on this occasion.'

Harry looked at her. She was still gazing straight ahead. It was Miss Brigmore who had spoken, not his Brigie, or Anna. And he knew she was right, but God in Heaven! he couldn't sit here and not open his mouth. And what could he talk about if not about his grandbairns? He couldn't talk about that thing crawling over there. My God! How had that come about? Not from his side, he'd swear. They'd gone barefoot and empty-bellied over the last three generations afore him but there had never been an idiot among them. And now their Katie to give birth to one. Why, it was unbelievable. Now if it had been their John's Jenny he could have understood it. Or again, if it had been Barbara, her with her temper and the background of them whoring, raping Mallens. Yes, he could have understood it if she had given birth to a flat-faced idiot; but not their Katie. He had always considered their Katie was as virile as himself. An' she was, it wasn't her fault, it came from the other side. But she had to bear the brunt. By God! she had to bear the brunt all right. That thing in her arms now would cripple her for life. It was a pity after all that she hadn't married Willy Brooks.

When he next spoke it was debatable whether or not he was endeavouring to make amends for his tactlessness, for as soon as Katie sat down again, the child on her lap, he said to her, 'You'll never guess who I ran into the other day, and in Newcastle an' all mind.'

'No, who?'

'Your friend, Willy, Willy Brooks. By! there's a pusher if ever there was one. And it's paying off. I'll say that for him, it's paying off. Member of a swank club he is now. That's his father-in-law's doings. There's money in cotton, an' who should know better than me about that. But when you make it up into shifts and the like, well; as the young snot said to me, "There's coppers in cotton but there's gold in shifts. Aye, an' in more ways than one." That last was a dig at you, our Katie.' He nodded at her, then went on, 'Fourteen draper stores he said they've got along the river now, one in every town, and he's managing the lot. On the board of directors an' all. I nearly asked him was the price worth it. You haven't seen his wife.' He jerked his chin at her and laughed now. 'Talk about dribble at the lips an' dry at the groin, that's her. . . .'

'Harry!'

'Aw, give over chastising me. Katie's married, I'm not talking afore bairns.'

'You're talking before me and I don't like the flavour of your conversation.'

'By!' He sat up and pulled himself forward in the basket chair. 'You're on your high horse the day, aren't you? Well, I'm not listenin' to any more of it, here's me going for a stroll out of it.'

Both Katie and Brigie watched him walk away. Then Brigie said softly, 'He's your father and he can't change; he doesn't mean to hurt you in any way, he loves you very very dearly.'

'I know that, but nevertheless he does hurt me.'

'I know he does, dear.'

'Bri-Bri.' The child was holding its arms out to Brigie, and she took him from Katie and stood him on her knee and looked into his face. His eyes appeared to be laughing but she knew they weren't, for if you looked into them and did not take into account the other features of his face you saw that their expression was laden with a peculiar sadness, not a vacant sadness but a sadness that was full of awareness; it was as if in his brain there was a pocket of knowledge that made him aware of his plight and the futility of struggling against it. It was his mouth that gave the impression of a constant smile. His lips were shapeless but full and over wide for the size of his face, and they turned up at the corners.

As Brigie stared from one to the other of the child's features she realized that just a little less of one and a little more of another and he would have had facial proportions that would have taken him into manhood with the stamp of handsome on him, nay beautiful, for in some strange way there was even now a hint of beauty in his face. She pulled him to her and held him closely, and over his small shoulder she looked at Katie and said, 'Don't worry. Don't worry, my dear, I have the feeling that he'll bring you comfort yet.' But she doubted her own words as she watched Katie bow her head and the big slow tears roll down her cheeks and drop from her chin before her blind groping could produce her handkerchief.

Bring her comfort. She would forgo comfort, and happiness, and yes, even the love of Pat in exchange for her son's normality. She could bear that he turn out to be the biggest rogue and scoundrel in the county so long as he was able to recognize that he was a rogue and scoundrel.

Why, she asked yet again, had this to happen to her and Pat? Did curses carry their weight? Willy Brooks had cursed her on the night she gave him back his ring; and Barbara, from her attitude, the fury of which kept her silent during a whole evening of supposed celebration, had surely cursed Pat because he had called her babies 'the Mallen litter'. And then there was Constance Radlet. Mrs Radlet had been in her thoughts a lot of late. Had she, like Willy Brooks, cursed Pat when he failed to realize her hopes? But it didn't need a curse to pass on evil, just a wish would accomplish it, a wish oft-repeated, and from the heart, especially if the heart had suffered the pangs of being spurned, as these three had.

PART TWO

====

The Years Between

I

THEY HAD MOVED INTO THE NEW HOUSE in the awful weather of January, 1890. The house was situated on the outskirts of Gosforth, standing back from the road that led to Morpeth. It was called Brook House, the name taken from a tiny stream that meandered at the bottom of the two-acre garden.

From the outside the house itself looked like a big red-brick square box but inside the rooms were spacious and well designed. The hall was large; three reception rooms went off one side of it, and a kitchen, dining room and morning room from the other. The stairs rose straight from the hall to a large landing, which gave access to four bedrooms and two dressing rooms.

At the end of the landing another flight of stairs led to the second floor. Here were four more large rooms, but all had sloping ceilings and small windows. At the end of this second landing a ladder, attached to the wall, went straight up into the roof and to the topmost room in the house which was under the eaves and lit by a skylight.

This was Ruth Foggety's room and had she been asked what she thought of it she would have answered, 'Heaven could be no better.'

Ruth was the third nursemaid Barbara had engaged in as many months. The other two had left in tears, both saying almost the same thing, 'It isn't the place, ma'am, it's a good place; leastwise it would be if it wasn't for Master Ben.'

Ruth Foggety had survived a fortnight and showing no sign yet of tears or hysterics at finding a dead rat in her bed, or worms wriggling around her toes, or being tripped up when carrying a tea tray to the drawing room.

Ben Bensham, not yet five years old, looked at least eight and had the mind of a precocious ten-year-old. Everyone agreed on this, as they agreed that his two brothers were angels, or at least would become angels if left to their own devices and not led into mischief by their brother, their elder brother, as people not acquainted with their birth thought of Ben, and even those who were found it hard to believe that the three boys were of the same age.

It was as Barbara was arranging some early daffodils in the drawing room that she heard the screams, and as the sound of screaming was anything but unusual in the house and when penetrating down from the nursery floor could mean anything from glee to anger she took no immediate notice because her mind was concerned with making everything look just right for the arrival of Mr Bensham, as she still thought of Dan's father, and Brigie.

Mr Bensham, on his monthly visits to the warehouse accompanied by Brigie, stayed overnight in an hotel in the town, but always on the afternoon of their arrival they came for tea . . . at Dan's. And always Barbara became agitated by their coming, not so much at the thought of seeing Mr Bensham, in fact he mattered not at all to her, but it was Brigie's presence that always disturbed her. Brigie still occupied a place of guilt, coupled with condemnation, in her mind; this woman who had loved her, brought her up, cared for her, cosseted her, and on whom she should in return have lavished her gratitude reminded her only that in the main she had been the means of depriving her of the one love of her life, and she knew, deep in her heart, that Brigie could never forget that it was because she had wanted to escape from her that she married Dan.

Yet when she should arrive they would put their arms about each other and they would kiss, and on the outside it would appear like the meeting between the beloved mother and her adored daughter.

The scream came again, more prolonged this time, causing her to lay down the flowers and turn swiftly around and go into the hall and look upwards. It was only then she realized that the cries were not coming from the nursery but from the first landing. She lifted the long trailing skirt of her green corded dress and ran up the stairs, only to pause at the head and gaze in righteous indignation at the scene before her. She could scarcely believe the evidence of her eyes, she had never witnessed such a scene. There, kneeling back on her hunkers, was the new nursemaid, Ruth Foggety, and across her knees lay Ben, his little trousers pulled down to his ankles, his under-drawers too, his shirt pulled upwards and covering his head. His bare bottom, exposed and already of a scarlet hue, was being slapped; no, not slapped, struck by the flat hard hand of the nursemaid, and with each blow she was saying something. 'That's one for the worms, an' that's another for the black-clock, an' that one's –' the hand came down with terrific force on the small buttock – 'for murderin'. . . .'

'*Stop that at once. How dare you! How dare you!*'

Barbara grabbed Ben upwards away from the small, plump figure kneeling on the floor. 'You wicked creature, you!'

'I'm no wicked creature, ma'am; he's the wicked one, if you're talkin' of wicked.' Ruth Foggety had risen to her feet. 'He nearly murdered me, he did. A string across the top of the stairs of all things. I'd have gone down head first an' that would have been me end if I hadn't caught sight of him beyond the banisters there. I knew he was up to something. I've had enough of him. It's either him or me. . . .'

'Don't you dare talk to me like that, girl. And you listen to me once and for all.'

And Ruth Foggety listened to her mistress, she listened so intently that neither of them was aware of the front door being opened by Ada Howlett, the daft daily as Ruth had christened the maid who wouldn't sleep in, preferring rather the three mile tramp back to town in all weathers.

Not until Harry came up the stairs saying, 'What's all this? What's all this?' did Barbara become aware of anyone else but this girl and her son, who was now leaning against her side sobbing, for it was many years since she had allowed her temper full rein; in fact, not since she had heard Pat Ferrier call her children 'the Mallen litter' had she felt such indignation, such rage.

As Harry, puffing from his exertions – for at seventy-one he was beginning to feel his age – said again, 'Well, what's up here, eh? What's up here?' Brigie without any show of exertion passed him and went straight to Barbara's side and immediately took in the situation. She knew all about it before Barbara, her breast rising and falling with her indignation, said without any preliminary greeting, 'She . . . she thrashed him. Look, took down his trousers and thrashed him with her bare hands.'

'Yes?' Brigie looked from the girl to the black-haired boy, whose face was hidden against Barbara's side, and she thought, Well, someone had to do it sooner or later, and the someone should have been yourself. But what she said was, 'What is it all about? What caused it?' She cast a glance towards the new nursemaid. She saw that she was a girl of about sixteen. Every part of her gave off signals of youth, round breasts, round buttocks, round face, even her eyes were round, blazing in her head now, even more so than Barbara's. When she's forty, Brigie thought, she'll be a fat little woman; now she epitomizes the fullness of youth, fresh and, as Mary used often to say, blue-mottled-soap-washed fresh.

Indeed the girl was blue-mottled-soap-washed fresh.

Brigie looked at Barbara again and said, 'Come, let us go downstairs.'

Barbara did not answer but, glaring at Ruth, she cried, 'And you, get your things together and go this very day, now!'

'*No!* . . . *No!*'

513

Every eye was turned on the boy now. He had released himself from Barbara's side and had taken three steps back from her and, with his eyes still running tears, he gazed up at her and again he said, 'No!'

'What do you mean, Benjamin, no?' Barbara addressed him as she would an adult.

'No! You're not to send Ruthie away.'

All the faces looking at him underwent a change, and he stared from one to the other until finally, bringing his gaze back to his mother, he said, 'I like Ruthie.'

Barbara's lips opened to say, 'But . . . but she has just thrashed you'; instead, she restrained herself and stared back at this son of hers, the son whom she could not love, the son whom not once had she willingly taken in her arms, cuddled or petted. She could caress the other two, oh yes, particularly Jonathan, for although Jonathan was similar in looks to his brother, Harry, his nature was different from Harry's, and poles away from Benjamin's. She had never said to herself that she didn't like Benjamin, that even to look at him hurt her, for he was her son, and she must do her duty by him. And this was foremost in her mind now as she stared down on him. She imagined, as she often did, that she wasn't looking at the face of a four-year-old boy, but at that of a man, a black-haired man, black hair that was invaded by a foreign streak of fair hair running from the crown of his head down to his left temple; and eyes that were already old with knowledge; and a mouth, a sensual mouth, an experienced, kissing mouth.

'Be quiet, Benjamin. Pull your trousers up and go to the nursery. You'll do what you're told.'

'I'll not, I'll not, Mama.' He backed from her. Then with a swift movement he dived towards Ruth. And now he was clinging to her.

The colour that had drained from Barbara's face returned at a rush. Again indignation swept over her, but a different kind this time. She felt she was being affronted, pushed aside. Her child openly preferred a nursemaid to herself, a nursemaid who had whipped him.

'Don't go, Ruthie, don't go.'

Ruth Foggety looked down into the boy's face and her own broke into a smile and it acted like a soft wind stilling a rough sea, and her voice added oil to the water as she said, 'Well, now, Master Ben, what did I tell you? You brought it on yourself. I warned you, didn't I?'

The oil on the water was suddenly engulfed as the storm rose again and enveloped her as she ended, 'I told you what I'd do, didn't I, I warned you. Any more of your fiddlefartin' and I'd skelp your backside for you and I. . . .'

'Enough! Go upstairs this moment. This very moment.' As Barbara went to grab her son from the contaminated presence of the nursemaid Harry literally stayed her hand by catching hold of her arm and

514

pulling her about to face the stairs. 'Come on. Come on,' he said. 'Storm in a teacup. Let's talk this over.' Then over his shoulder he looked to where the girl was standing, her face once more showing defiance, and he said, 'You take the children upstairs, girl, and wait there.'

Barbara, preceding both Harry and Brigie down the stairs, allowed her indignation to dash along yet another channel. How dare he! This was her house. He had taken the authority from her hands. It was too much, too much. One thing and another, she couldn't stand much more. She was tired, depressed, bored. Yes, yes, *bored*. Life was almost like being back in the cottage again, closed in by the hills, the mountains. What was life for anyway? She lifted the daffodils from the table and thrust them into the vase before she rang the bell. And then she made an effort to calm herself down when she heard Harry say, 'Get your things off. Get your things off, lass, 'cos you're not goin' to be asked.'

'Oh, I'm sorry, I'm sorry, Brigie.' She now went towards Brigie and they kissed and enfolded each other. Then she said, 'Sit down, sit down. But ... but you see what I mean.'

As Brigie sat down and smoothed her grey serge skirt over her knees she said, 'But if you let her go, will the next one be any better? The last two were nincompoops. In your letter last week you said you were very pleased with her. She was clean and bright and the children seemed to have taken to her. That's what you said.'

Barbara sighed as she answered, 'Yes, that's what I said, but you've seen for yourself.'

She looked from Brigie to where Harry had flopped down in the winged chair to the side of the fireplace, and what he said was, 'Get us a cup of tea, girl, an' then I'll tell you what I think.'

When Ada Howlett, answering the bell, was given the order to bring in tea, Harry remarked, 'Well, of the two I know which one I'd put me money on. That one looks about as bright as Manchester mud. With all the unemployment and empty bellies in the town I'd have thought you could have done better than that.'

He was an aggravating man was her father-in-law. Every word he said to her had, she felt, a thread of criticism running through it. She replied primly, 'When they're near the town I understand they like to live at home. If they live further out in the country they are quite willing to live in, although they can demand less money.'

'What you payin' her?'

'Five shillings a week.'

'Aye, well, I suppose that's fair for this kind of work. But my lot would spit in your eye if you offered them that, I mean in the factory in Manchester.'

515

'You can't compare factory workers with domestic servants, Harry,' Brigie put in sharply.

'No, I'm not sayin' you can' – he bobbed his head at her – 'but I think it's about time you did, for some of them work just as hard, except those back home. My Manchester lot work like blacks, but you and Kenley between you, you ruin that lot back at the house. The money! Eeh! the money I've to pay out. It's nobody's business.'

'Be quiet, Harry.'

And when Harry became quiet Barbara looked at him and wondered at the power her adoptive mother had over everyone who came in contact with her.

They had their tea, and they discussed the situation regarding Ruth Foggety, and two hours later when they left Barbara was much calmer and she had promised to consider Harry's advice on the matter before sending the girl packing.

Just before Brigie stepped up into the carriage she turned to Barbara and, looking straight into her face, she asked, 'Were . . . were you expecting a visitor today, dear?'

'A visitor? No; only you. Why? Why do you ask?'

'Oh, no . . . no reason. No reason at all. Perhaps it was because everything in the house looked so inviting. You have made it very lovely, dear.'

Barbara returned Brigie's stare for a moment, then said, as a daughter might to a mother, 'Well, I always take special care that things are just so when I know you are coming. You don't think I could forget you have eyes in the back of your head?'

They exchanged tight, prim smiles; then Brigie climbed into the carriage and waved Barbara good-bye.

The carriage had hardly turned from the drive on to the main road before Brigie gave her whole attention to looking out of the window.

'What is it? What you looking for?'

'I'm looking for the hired carriage that I'm sure followed us here.'

'You're daft, woman.'

'That's your opinion, and you are entitled to it.'

'Because you saw him in the town, you think he came on your trail?'

'I'm sure of it.'

'Well, well, I hope you're wrong 'cos if you're right I'll have to tell our Dan.'

'No.' She turned sharply from the window. 'You must never do that.'

'Oh now! You look here, woman, look here. There's nobody going to make a monkey out of our Dan and me stand by and watch it. Oh no!'

516

'Please.' She was sitting close to him and had taken his hand now. 'Please,' she repeated, 'do as I ask, at least for the time being. I . . . I know Barbara. She has been slighted, spurned; she would never dream about looking his way again, she's over full of pride.'

'That's as may be, but don't forget what the rumours say. That Jim Waite of theirs has a big mouth apparently and he doesn't keep it closed in the market. He gets talking to Watts.'

'Watts's work is to drive the coach, not to gossip.'

'Ssh! ssh!' he pointed towards where the coachman sat on the top of the box outside, and Brigie said, 'If he can't hear what you say then he can't hear what I say. But I repeat, he's a gossiper.'

'Well, I find a bit of gossip handy at times; it's well to know what goes on roundabout. An' from what I can gather Michael Radlet's a morose man with no thought for anybody but his daughter, and when a man's unhappy things can happen. You should know that.'

Brigie turned slowly from him and looked out of the window again. Then she started visibly and only stopped herself from exclaiming aloud as she saw the hired cab standing in a narrow side lane, and beside its door a tall man with his back to her. But she knew that back as well as she would have known the face.

Her mind worked rapidly before she turned to Harry and, her tone soft with no semblance of Miss Brigmore or even of Brigie in it, she said, 'Don't do anything. I mean don't mention anything to Dan about our suspicions until we are sure, will you not? Please, please, Harry; do this for me.'

'How can you be sure, you're not here often enough?'

'I'll . . . I'll know the next time I see her, and we'll make it soon, next week.'

He stared at her for a moment before saying, 'And you'll tell me, you'll tell me the truth?'

'I'll tell you the truth, or what I know of it.'

'Fair enough.' He nodded at her. 'But we're going to the warehouse now to see our Dan and put him wise to what's happened this afternoon. That young lass is the best thing that's hit that nursery yet, I should say. What do you say?'

She smiled at him now, 'I agree with you.'

'Fiddlefartin's an' all.'

'Harry!' She was Miss Brigmore again.

He leant his head back against the leather upholstery of the coach and his body shook with his chuckling. 'Eeh! By! I thought I'd fall downstairs when she came out with that, and so natural like. But' – he brought his head upwards – 'what do you think of young Ben clinging to her like that after she had skelped him, and right well for his backside was blazin'. There's something funny about that, odd in a way, don't you think, and a bit frightening, a child turning from its mother to a maid?'

'Most children of today are more acquainted with the nursemaids than they are with their parents. You know that.'

'But not in this case. Dan's never had the bairns imprisoned upstairs. He's like me, he wouldn't be for it. No, that little scene went deeper, there was more in it than met the eye. Aye, much more.'

Yes, there was more in it than met the eye. Brigie knew this. She could give a full explanation of it in a few simple words: the child realized his mother didn't love him.

She had watched Barbara with her three children but she had never seen her stroke Ben's black hair as she had done with the others'; comb it, yes; dress him, yes; feed him, yes; but never love him. At first she had thought that she shouldn't judge because she wasn't with them often enough, but as time went on and the visits became monthly affairs she knew that the first-born of the triplets was like a thorn in Barbara's flesh; although he was but a child, she saw in him a reflection of the portrait that hung above the mantelpiece in the cottage. Ben was a constant reminder that she was the daughter of Thomas Mallen.

That the boy would grow up like his grandfather, Brigie had no doubt, and in her heart she was both glad and sorry. Glad that Thomas would live once more, but sorry that Ben was being deprived of love when he most needed it.

It was eleven o'clock at night on the same day. Ruth Foggety sat in the kitchen on a straight-backed chair at the corner of the bare wooden table and awaited her fate. The mistress had spoken to her only once since the rumpus on the landing, and that to say, 'You will wait till the master comes in, he will deal with you.'

She hadn't been long enough in this establishment to know who was the real master. In the place she had been before it was the missus who had ruled, and she thought it was the same here. But now she wasn't quite sure. She considered the master was a kindly little bloke, a man who would do anything for peace she would say. And yet she didn't know. Look at the way he had gone for Mrs King last week, her who called herself a cook. Cook indeed! God! she couldn't even skin a rabbit, it went to the table with half its coat still on. And the cabbage she dished up. Honest to God! you would think it had been boiled in the dock water itself. The master had said as much, but in his own way of course. She had been surprised to hear him talk so, stiff, quiet, but right to the point. 'I want no excuses,' he had said. 'If you haven't improved by the end of the month then I'd advise you to look for another post.'

When she thought about it, it had surely been the mistress's job to complain about the meals. And, of course, she had. Oh yes, she had heard her. But it was himself who came out of the dining room that night, a plate in his hand and, pushing it under the cook's nose right in the kitchen here, had said, 'Mrs King, would you mind explaining to me what this is?' Sarky he was, right sarky. Old Ma King hated his guts. But she herself liked him. Yes, she did.

She nodded to herself at this point of her thinking. She must admit she liked him, but she didn't suppose she'd be able to keep it up when he gave her the push. She wished he would hurry up and get it over with. He had been upstairs a good half-hour; he hadn't got in till after ten. He had been to a meeting, or some place such as business men attended in the City.

Although she was waiting for the door to open, when it did she was startled and jumped to her feet.

'Sit down. Sit down.' Dan pointed to a chair. Then he himself pulled another chair from the far wall and brought it to the table and sat down opposite to her before he said, 'Well now, what's this I'm hearing?'

She looked at him straight in the eyes before answering, 'I don't know what you've heard, sir, but whatever it was, it was likely the truth. The top an' the bottom of it is I skelped your son's backside. An' I'll tell no lie, I'm not sorry I did.'

'What had he done?'

'He put a string across the top of the stairs, looped it round one of the banisters so that he could pull it and trip me up. And where would I have landed but at the bottom, with me neck broke and me past knowin' a thing about it?'

Dan looked into the round bright eyes, into the round open countenance, and the fearlessness of it evoked in him an admiration, while at the same time the thick North Country voice and the idiom of her language that brought colour into everything she said made him now want to laugh, as it did whenever he heard her.

He had found difficulty in understanding some of the men he had set on in the warehouse when he had first come to Newcastle, especially those from further down the river. There was one in particular who hailed from Shields who, to his mind, needed an interpreter. At times the rapidity of the men's speech irritated him, and this, coupled with the dialect words made it almost as unintelligible as a foreign language. Only of late, as he had listened to this girl, had he put the word colour to their speech.

He said now, 'That was very naughty of him. As you say his action could have caused serious consequences, and I can understand that you are angry. . . .'

'Oh, I wasn't angry.'

'You weren't?'

'No.'

'You mean, you slapped him without feeling angry, you did it, one could say, in cold blood?'

'If you put it like that, sir, yes. At first, that was. You see I promised it to him, 'cos he'd stuffed everything in me bed but the rabbit, and the only reason that wasn't there was 'cos it wouldn't stay still.'

'You mean he tried to put a rabbit in your bed?' Dan widened his eyes but kept his features straight.

'He did, he did. And how in the name of God he got it up the ladder into the loft I don't know, sir.'

It was too much. Dan bowed his head. His eyes became bright, he made a sound in his throat. He had a mental picture of Ben, assisted, of course, by his two lieutenants passing the rabbit up that steep ladder.

A sound from her throat brought his head upwards and he looked at her under his lids to see her fingers to her lips, her eyes sparkling; and then she said, with laughter breaking her words, 'Oh sir, he's a caution, a joker. He'll grow up to be a joker. There's never a night but I find something in me bed. If it isn't anything alive it's something that nearly makes me jump out of me skin. Last night it was a bunch of holly leaves. God! they felt like a bucket of Irish snakes.'

As Dan's head went down again her hand pressed more tightly across her mouth, and so together they smothered their laughter.

A moment later, his eyes blinking, Dan rubbed the water away from the corners of them as he said in a voice that he now tried to make sound sober and correct, 'He climbs that ladder unassisted?'

'Oh, aye sir, like a lintie. An' he must have done it for some time 'cos he goes up and down it quicker than I can.'

Dan rose to his feet and with an effort he kept his face straight as he said, 'Well now, Ruth, the mistress is willing to give you another chance but you must be careful of your treatment of the boys.'

Ruth drew in a long breath that extended her full breasts further, before saying, 'Oh, I will sir, I will.' She nodded at him politely. 'An' I don't think I'll have the same trouble again 'cos I got the better of him. He knows now I can give as good as he sends. Did the mistress tell you he stuck up for me? . . . He did, as young as he is he did. Mind you, sir, I can't believe he's just on five, not like the others. But there he was, stickin' up for me on the landin', saying he didn't want me to go. I got a gliff, in a nice kind of way though. Oh, I don't think I'll have much trouble with him in the future, sir.'

Dan now nodded back at her before saying, 'I hope not, Ruth. And just one thing more. The mistress would like you to. . . .' How could he put this? Could he say, 'Stop using such terms as fiddlefarting'? Barbara had not uttered the word. It had been his dad who had told him, what Barbara had said was that the girl had used abominable language. He coughed and went on, 'What I mean to say is, the mistress would like you to be careful of how you speak in front of the children. You know what children are; they pick up all kinds of words and repeat them in front of their elders – and guests. You understand?'

She stared at him for a moment before she replied, 'Aye, sir. Yes, yes, I understand. An' I'll try.'

'That's a good girl. Now get yourself off to bed; you've had a long day and you must be tired.'

'Thank you, sir. Thank you very much, sir.'

He had reached the door when he turned, and his head slightly to the side he asked, 'Why must your father call on a Sunday morning for your wages, Ruth? Why can't you give them to him during your leave time?'

'Oh.' She smiled a half sad, half wise smile as she replied, 'He couldn't wait a fortnight, sir; he'd skin a louse for its hide would me da. But that's not the real reason. He wants to be sure I've been to Mass.'

'To Mass?'

'Aye. You know when I came, sir, I . . . I told the mistress that she could dock the time off me leave, but I had to get to Mass on a Sunday.'

'Oh yes, yes, I remember.' He smiled slowly at her now as he asked, 'Do you like being made to go to Mass?'

As slowly, she smiled back at him as she answered, 'Oh, it isn't a case of likin', sir, it's a case of needs must when the devil drives. An' as me dad says it's either that or spend the rest of me life in hell after I'm dead.'

He said quickly. 'Good-night, Ruth.'

And she said again, 'Good-night, sir, an' thank you.'

As he went up the stairs he bit hard on his lip. Needs must when the devil drives, it's either that or spend the rest of me life in hell after I'm dead. Oh, that was wonderful, wonderful. He must tell that one to Barbara, spend the rest of her life in hell after she was dead.

Before he had reached their bedroom he knew he wouldn't repeat the gem of Irish Catholic Geordie confusion to Barbara; Barbara hadn't the mind for such things. He drew in a long breath.

When he entered the room Barbara was asleep. He walked quietly to the bed and stood looking down on her, and his love for her, which nine years of marriage had been unable to level off into comfortable acceptance, brought his heart beating faster as if he were a young groom awaiting the consummation of love on the first night of marriage.

He put his hand over his eyes as he turned from the bed and went into the dressing room.

As he got into his night-shirt he heard a slight creak of the floorboards above his head and he looked upwards. She was going into the nursery to have a last look round. She was a good girl, the boys would come to no harm under her, and she'd manage Ben. And she'd be the first one who had been able to do so. Moreover, he had a strange idea that as young as she was, she'd be able to give Ben what he needed, love, motherly love, and the discipline that went with it.

THREE DAYS LATER the letter came. It was fortunate that the post did not arrive until after Dan left for the city in the morning – it was his one complaint about living so far out. When they had lived in Bolton Square the mail was put on the table with the breakfast, but now it could be nine o'clock in the morning before it arrived.

Remembering to put the letters on a salver, Ada Howlett brought them into the breakfast room and placed them at Barbara's hand where she was sitting lingering over a final cup of tea. She was wondering what she would do with herself this morning; this afternoon she had an appointment to visit Miss Ferguson's Day School. The school had been recommended to her as an excellent place for five-year-olds. Both she and Dan were in agreement that it would be much better to send the children out to kindergarten than have a nursery governess in the house. But they agreed for different reasons. Dan because, although he admired Brigie and now realized that her instruction had at the time been outstanding, he felt that he and John had been lucky to escape her influence so early. She was an excellent instructor of little girls, but whether boys would have fared so well under her tuition he doubted; boys to his mind needed a different approach, a stronger, sterner, wider approach.

Barbara's reasons were personal. With the children at school she'd have the house to herself, and herself to herself, for most part of the day. She'd be able to take stock, think; perhaps she'd further some of her accomplishments, such as the piano, or painting and embroidery. She might make a study of English literature. There were so many things she could do if she had more time.

She was asking herself the pertinent question, But would she do them when she had the time? when the salver with the letters on it was placed to her hand, and she said, 'Thank you, Ada. You may clear now;' and, rising from the table, she picked up the letters and went out of the morning room, across the hall and into the drawing room.

There was a small desk set to the side of the drawing-room window on which she wrote her correspondence and kept her household accounts. Sitting down in the chair, she looked at the top letter. It was from Brigie; no one wrote in such a copper plate hand as Brigie. She laid the letter aside. The next one was addressed to Dan. The post-mark was Manchester; that one she surmised was from John. The following three were also addressed to Dan, Daniel Bensham Esquire. The last one was addressed to her. She did not recognize the writing. She turned it over, then back again and looked at the postmark. It said Newcastle. Taking a paper knife, she opened it and withdrew a single sheet of notepaper and she had got no further than unfolding it when her hand went to her throat and gripped it hard, for the letter began, 'Barbara, Barbara.'

She closed her eyes for a second in order to clear the mist from them. When slowly she opened them, they lifted each cramped word from the page and before she had come to the end of the letter she knew she was being born again.

'Barbara, Barbara,
   Please bear with me, I beg you to bear with me. I have been searching for you since the day we met in that narrow passage and I turned from you and fled. But . . . but believe me – and you must believe me – it was not because I didn't want to see you, for you have never left my thoughts since that tragic day on the farm. I know now, Barbara, that all that happened was my fault. I acted like a weakling, I should have stood up to them, all of them, and told them what it was, who it was, I really wanted. Now it is all too late, I know that, but all I want you to believe is that in turning from you that day it was in fear of the consequences of standing close to you and looking into your face. I may tell you that no sooner had I rounded the corner than I knew that I was once again running away from reality. And so I came back. But you were gone. Since then I have endeavoured to find your home address, and it was on the very day that I found the name Bensham on a warehouse in the town that I also espied Brigie driving in a coach towards the outskirts.
   Barbara, I have been like a demented man these past few years, and more so since I last saw you. If I could only hear from your own lips that you have forgiven me then I think I can go on. You, I know, have at least three children, I have only a seven-year-old daughter whom I dearly love, and if it wasn't for her I would

have left the farm and emigrated long before this. But she needs me and so I stay.

Will you allow me to see you, just once? That's all I ask, just once. You should receive this letter on Wednesday. There is a wood at the end of the lane beyond your house. I shall wait there on Friday; I shall be there about noon and shall not leave until about four in the afternoon. Come and speak to me, Barbara, please, please.

Michael.'

As she sat gazing before her she actually imagined herself being born again. She had, as it were, been living in a womb during the past nine years, not consciously aware of what life could mean, loving could mean. The ice that had encased her heart was melting, after all these years her heart was beating again, beating so hard and fast it was choking her.

She held her two hands to her throat. She was back on the stepping stones, she was slipping, and he was holding her and they were clinging together; his face was above hers and he was laughing down on her. That was another time he had almost kissed her.

There was passing in procession before her eyes the countless, countless times she had inveigled and bullied Brigie into going over the hills to the farm. Since the time she could recall anything, she saw herself demanding to be taken over the hills to the farm to see Michael.

She had been born with the passion in her for Michael. At first it had been the demanding passion of a child, and then it had been the painful, tormenting passion of a young girl of fourteen, but at seventeen it had been the passion of a woman, in the mind of a girl, but all the time it had been passion, passion that considered nothing but itself and its consummation.

So on that memorable day when she was a woman, the day when truth was spoken by everyone concerned, when he had scorned her, her passion had taken its broken bleeding self into the refuge of silence, and the silence had led her into paralysis of body and mind. Only with the shock of his marriage did she regain her faculties. . . . And now! *And now!*

She took her hands from her throat and picked up the letter from the desk as if it were something of great weight and with a swift movement she crushed it between her breasts, only as swiftly to drop it on to the desk again.

She rose to her feet and walked down the room. When she reached the door she turned and walked swiftly back. Six times she did this before stopping and muttering aloud, 'No, no, it's too late, years too late – years and years too late.' She spoke the last words aloud, then turned sharply towards the door as if she had been overheard. Going back to the desk again she put her hands on the back of the chair and supported herself against it as she looked downwards. He loved his daughter he said, he couldn't leave his daughter, she needed him. If he could have left his daughter would she have left her sons? And Dan?

Again she was walking up and down the room. Dan, Dan. She mustn't hurt Dan. She had sworn never to hurt Dan. Dan had brought her out of the house of bondage into the land of Egypt. Oh, why must she quote Mary's mis-quotation of the Bible? Brigie used to laugh at Mary's mis-quotations. Brigie, Brigie, Brigie again. If it hadn't been for Brigie she would be with Michael now. No, no, that wasn't true; it was Aunt Constance. Oh yes, Aunt Constance. How she had hated her Aunt Constance, and still did if the truth were known, still did. But then she couldn't put the entire blame on her Aunt Constance; neither Brigie nor her Aunt Constance could have done anything if Michael had cared to defy them. But Michael had loved his mother and wanted to please her. Did he still love her? What would Aunt Constance say now if she knew her beloved son was trying to pick up the threads that he had snapped when they were young, so young. Love was for the young. Love like theirs had been the essence of youth. Yet she was now but twenty-six, and beautiful, more beautiful than she had ever been; but if she were to believe her mirror, it was a vacant beauty, a cold unwarmed beauty, with no fire about it.

She stopped and held her tightly joined hands to her breast. She mustn't go on thinking, because thinking would only lead her to the wood, and she must not, *she must not* obey his whim. Yet the cry in that letter did not spring from a whim, more from a tortured mind. Michael, poor Michael. She could pity him as she had pitied herself over the years, but she could not go to him. She would not go to him. She must destroy this letter.

She went to the desk now and smoothed the single sheet out and read it once again; then lifting it between her finger and thumb as if it were contaminated, she walked slowly with it towards the fireplace, hesitated for a moment, then thrust it into the flames. The next moment, full of regret, she closed her eyes and bit hard down on her lip. She should have kept it; if she wasn't going to see him again it would have been something to treasure. She could have hidden it. But where? Where? She hadn't a room to herself. Dan held the old-fashioned idea that he must share not only her bed but also the amenities of the bedroom. He was for ever putting suits into her wardrobe and she was for ever taking them out and placing them in his own. When he couldn't find anything immediately, a handkerchief, a collar or a stud, he rifled her chest of drawers like a dog unearthing a bone. And Jonathan was almost as bad, but in a different way. When he was allowed into the bedroom he made straight for her handkerchief drawer because he said he liked the smell. He seemed to find pleasure playing with her handkerchiefs, sorting them into piles. Where could she have hidden anything? She put her hand to her brow. Her mind was in a whirl. What had she to do this morning? Nothing, nothing. Nothing till this afternoon when she went to the school. Well, she must find something to do. She'd give cook the orders for the day, go up to the nursery and see the children – and that girl. She wasn't at all happy about Dan's decision to keep her on but she agreed with him that she was the best yet and, reluctantly, that she had got the better of Benjamin. For this at least she should be grateful to her. Nevertheless she didn't like the girl, she was a forward young miss, too ready with her tongue, too apt to forget her place. Anyway, she would go up and she would force herself to talk to her and tell her what was required of her today. Then she would go out for a walk, a brisk walk in the fresh air, and when she returned her mind would be more at ease.

It was an hour later when she left the house. She walked down the drive and turned to the right, and a quarter of a mile along the country road she came to the entrance to the wood.

It was an open wood. She did not know to whom the ground belonged but there were no barriers separating it from the road. She walked some way along its length until she saw a narrow path leading into it from the road, and she took it and walked through the wood. In parts it was thick with holly and scrub, and she made her way round these clumps and eventually came out at the far side and on to open farmland. Here the land was tilled almost up to the roots of the trees; there was no road across it. She took another zig-zag path back towards where she judged should be the road, but on emerging from the wood she found that she was at the far end of it and almost a mile from her home.

As she walked back towards the house her mind was clear on one point: she knew why she had visited the wood.

3

IT HAD RAINED INCESSANTLY all morning. Ada Howlett said to the cook, it had been coming down whole water before six and she'd got soppin' coming, but rain before seven dry before eleven. But the rain did not cease before eleven, if anything it increased towards noon.

Barbara had been in a state of high agitation all morning, and now as she stood looking through the window of one of the guest rooms at the end of the house, from where she could see through the gate on to the road beyond, she told herself that she mustn't do this thing, she even prayed that something would happen to stop her doing it, yet she knew that she was going to do it, whatever the consequences she must do it, if only this once.

By one o'clock her eyes were stiff with staring and her legs ached with standing. She could not sit, for then she would be unable to see the road because of the bushes that edged the drive.

It wasn't until she heard Ada's voice coming from the landing saying to Ruth Foggety, 'Have you seen the missis? She hasn't gone out has she an' her snack's on the table?' did she move from the window and go out of the room.

'Oh, Missis,' Ada bobbed her knee. 'I just wanted to tell you your din . . . your meal's on the table.' She never knew what name to give to the tray meal that Barbara ate at midday.

'Thank you. I'll be down in a moment.'

As she went towards her own room Ruth Foggety followed her, saying, 'Excuse me, ma'am, but I'd better tell you, I put Jonathan to bed 'cos he's got the croup.'

'The croup?'

'Well, he's coughin' like, an' it could turn into the croup. Better be safe than sorry I said to meself, so I put him to bed.'

'You . . . you did quite right, Ruth. I'll be up in a moment.'

She went into her room, stood before the mirror, stared at herself in it, then closed her eyes before turning away and making for the nursery.

As always, Benjamin was the first to run towards her to speak, 'Thinnen's got the croup, Mama.'

She paused and looked down at him, saying stiffly, 'What have I told you, Benjamin? You can say Jonathan's name if you like. . . . Say Jonathan.'

His head back on his shoulders, Ben stared up at her. The smile had gone from his face, and he now said, 'Thinnen.'

Barbara knew it was no use persisting further, she would lose the battle and the girl was looking on. She said, 'Jonathan hasn't the croup, he has a cold.' She passed him and took hold of Harry's extended hand and went into the night nursery.

Jonathan was lying in his small bed and immediately he put on a display of coughing for her.

'Now, now, you mustn't do that.'

'I have a cough, Mama. Ruthie says I have the croup.'

'You have not the croup, you just have a cough. Now be a good boy and stay in bed. I shall come up again and see you shortly.' She tucked the clothes round her son's chin then felt his brow. It was hot, but not feverish.

'Be a good boy now.' She turned from the bed and went from the room, followed by Harry.

In the day nursery Benjamin seemed to be standing exactly where she had left him. He looked at her but didn't speak. She looked at Ruth, where at a table under the window she was sorting a pile of the children's freshly laundered clothes. Instead of calling the girl to her she went to her side and in a low tone said, 'You must try and give things their correct names. We talked of this the other night, remember?'

'Yes, ma'am.'

As Ruth looked up at her, as she had to do because of her height, but without any trace of subservience in her manner, Barbara thought, she's bold, really bold, and she turned abruptly, passed Benjamin without glancing at him, and went downstairs.

She remained in the dining room for ten minutes and she ate hardly anything from the tray.

She returned to the spare room and stood at the window again. She was greatly agitated now; he could have passed during the time she had been away. It was now almost half past one, what should she do? Why ask? She knew what she must do. Why else had she gone to the wood? But look at the weather, she would be drenched. And was it likely that he would come on a day like this? *Yes! Yes!* Hail, snow or blizzard wasn't likely to keep away the man who had written that letter.

She swung round from the window and almost ran out of the room across the landing and into her own room, where she went immediately to the wardrobe. She must put on a thick coat. And there was a waterproof cape in the hall cupboard; she'd put that on too.

As she pulled the coat from the hanger the bedroom door opened and she had to grab for support at the open wardrobe door.

'What's the matter, aren't you well?' Dan came towards her and led her to a chair. 'What is it?' Now he was on his hunkers before her, her two hands grasped tightly between his own. 'You look as white as a sheet. What is it, tell me?'

She tried to speak but found it impossible. Her mouth opened and closed like a fish gasping for air.

Suddenly his grip tightened and he said on a whisper, 'You're not . . . you're not?'

Now she did speak and almost vehemently. 'No, no, I'm not.'

'No.' The syllable was soothing, yet threaded with disappointment. Of course he knew she wouldn't be; if will power on her part could prevent a pregnancy she'd never give him any more children.

'Well, what is it, what's wrong, do you feel ill?' There was a slight edge to his tone now.

'I . . . I felt faint.'

'What were you doing with your coat?' He looked towards the coat where it was lying on the floor.

'I . . . I was going to clear the wardrobe, put in my summer clothes.'

'Clear the wardrobe? Ridiculous! What you want to do is to rest. And also, what I think you need is a change, a holiday. Why don't you go down to Brigie's for a few days?'

'Brigie's?' She pressed him aside and rose to her feet. 'What a stupid thing to put to me! You know I hate that place.'

'It was the cottage I thought you hated, not the Hall.'

'It's all the same, it's the vicinity.'

His head drooped and he looked down at the floor, and the nearness of it made him aware that he was still on his hunkers. As he pulled himself upwards he thought, Everything I do is symbolic. He lifted his eyes to the ceiling now as a shrill cry came from the nursery, and the feet bounding across the floor could have been those of a donkey. Ben again with Ruthie in pursuit.

He gave a half smile as he said, 'You can't rest with that going on. Come on across to the spare room.'

There were three spare rooms but only one in particular was called *the* spare room, for it was the one in which he sometimes slept should he return late from a business dinner in the city at which he had imbibed well but not wisely. This was not a new pattern. He had adopted it in the old house when in a less than sober state he had got into bed one night only to have her get out at the other side, saying with disdain, 'You are nauseating.'

Now she allowed herself to be led across the landing and into the room and helped on to the bed. He arranged the pillows behind her head and drew a light cover over her, then stood looking down at her and said, 'There.'

'Why are you home at this time?'

'I wanted some papers and' – he sat down slowly on the edge of the bed – 'I wanted an excuse to see my wife. . . . What is it? What's the matter?'

'Nothing, nothing.'

'Have you a pain in the heart?'

Had she a pain in the heart?

She took her hand away from below her breast and shook her head as she said, 'No, no, it is only a little flatulence, I swallowed my meal too quickly. Are you . . . are you staying long?'

'As long as you need me.'

She pressed her head into the pillows and closed her eyes. 'I'm all right, really I am. It . . . it is only my usual monthly indisposition.'

'Oh. Oh.' He patted her hand now, then rose from the bed, smiling almost a happy smile. She had spoken openly to him about a natural function; it was almost the equivalent of her standing naked in front of him.

'You rest,' he said; 'just rest. I'll get them to bring you a cup of tea up, eh? And I'll look in before I go. If you should be asleep I won't disturb you. All right?'

She made a motion with her head, then watched him walk softly across the room as if she were already asleep, and this last evidence of his consideration made her want to spring from the bed and cry at him, 'Stop it! Stop it!' His solicitude was a torture in itself, and, added to all that he had done for over the years, it redoubled the feeling of guilt that was already weighing on her.

Well, it seemed that God or providence, or whatever it was that ruled people's existence, had spoken. She had been stopped from doing something foolish. Her mind became silent for a moment, until a voice broke into it, crying loudly, 'Not foolish, not foolish, something wonderful.' Before she had received Michael's letter her life had been dull, monotonous, but just bearable. The same existence would never be bearable again, and now she wondered how she was to endure it. She had but to stretch out her hand and there was love, love for which she had been born to experience, love that she had been deprived of.

531

Her mind became blank, until she asked herself, and quietly now, would she have actually gone if Dan had not put in an appearance at that moment? Up till then she had wasted almost two hours, why hadn't she gone to the wood straightaway if she had been going at all? She had prayed for something to prevent her and her prayers had been answered. She should be satisfied.

What time was it now? She looked towards the mantelpiece. Ten minutes to three. Another hour and he'd be gone. 'From noon till four,' he'd said. But who but a madman would stand for four hours in a wood in this weather? She turned her eyes towards the window where the rain was running down in an unbroken sheet. No one but a madman, or a man who had been given a second chance to love.

There was a tap on the door and Ada came in with a cup of tea. She thanked her and gratefully drank the tea, after which she lay back and closed her eyes.

When the door opened without a tap and the foot steps came softly towards the side of the bed she feigned sleep. She could hear Dan's breathing and she knew that he was bending over her when his breath fanned her face. She would not be able to bear it if he kissed her. He didn't. The door closed and she was alone. She lay rigid, waiting for the sound of the front door closing, and the fifteen minutes before it did seemed like an eternity.

As if it had been a signal, she rose swiftly from the bed and went to the window which looked on to the side of the house, and from there she saw the carriage leaving the yard.

It was now twenty minutes to four. Before the pointer touched the quarter to she was down in the hall and pulling the waterproof cape from the cupboard.

'You going out, ma'am?' Ada was standing looking at her with mouth agape.

'Yes, yes, Ada; I feel I need air.'

'But it's teeming heavens hard, ma'am, you'll get soaked.'

'Oh, a little rain won't hurt me. I . . . I shall not be long.'

'But ma'am, the Master said. . . .'

'I know, I know, Ada.' Her voice was unusually gentle, her tone even friendly. 'It's quite all right. Don't worry, I'll only be gone a short while. But . . . but I feel I need air, I need to walk.'

'Yes, ma'am.' Ada Howlett opened the door for her and she went out, her head bent against the slant of the rain.

When she reached the beginning of the wood, her face was running with water and she couldn't see very far ahead, but far enough to know that there was no man waiting on the road. Well, she knew it would be madness for anyone to stand four hours in this downpour. Her step slowed and almost stopped, but she kept moving.

532

It was at the moment when she was about to turn and make her way back that a figure emerged from the path that she had used the other day. He had his head bent and he didn't look up until he stepped on to the road, and even then it was merely a glance before he turned right and away from her. And then he was standing still, his shoulders back, his head up; he swung round but he did not move towards her.

The rain washed him from her vision time and time again before simultaneously they moved towards each other. And then they were standing within arm's length, blinking, peering, their eyes drawing their images back into the empty years.

His hand came slowly out towards her. He did not speak, nor did she when she placed hers in it; then like two children who had died and were meeting again in another existence, they walked back to the path that led into the wood, and then on into the wood proper. Their hands still joined but their bodies were well apart.

When they stopped it was under a large oak. The rain was coming through the branches in great plops and the light was dim.

'Barbara. Thank you. Thank you.' His first words were low and husky.

He released her hand and they still stood apart. What she replied was, 'I'm sorry I . . . I couldn't get before; there were things. . . .'

'I understand.'

'You . . . you must be very wet.'

'It's nothing.'

'How did you get here?'

'By cab from the city. It's due to return at four o'clock at the end of the road.'

'Oh.' Her chin moved upwards.

Their mundane pleasantries ceased. The rain hissed and spat. The wind whistled through the tops of the trees. The dismal dreariness that only a sodden wood can give off was all about them. They stood gazing at each other.

She was more beautiful than ever he had imagined.

He looked older, so much older. His face had hard lines on it; there was no semblance of Michael the boy; here was a man, a big, strong, blond man. And he was Michael, her Michael. Oh, Michael, Michael, what must I do?

'How are you?'

'I'm quite well.'

'That wasn't what I meant. I . . . I meant, are you happy?'

How did she answer this question? Well, however she answered it, it must touch on the truth. She said, 'I have three sons, and . . . and Dan is very good to me, very, very good. Are you happy?'

'No.' The straight simple answer was their undoing. She said softly, 'Oh, Michael.'

Their hands instinctively clasped again, tightly now; the distance between them lessened. He gazed into her face as, his voice breaking, he said, 'I . . . I meant just to see you. I just wanted to tell you I was sorry, sorry for everything, but most of all that . . . that I didn't run away that time. As I explained in the letter, I scurried because I . . . I was afraid, afraid of this moment. But it had to be, Barbara. I know it had to be.'

'Oh, Michael.'

That's all she could say, 'Oh, Michael.' Her heart was bursting. Nothing in the world mattered but this moment and the fact that she was standing here with him and that he was declaring his love for her with every part of him, for his whole body was trembling. But when he said, 'It's too late, isn't it, it's too late,' she shivered. She did not know whether it was a statement, or a question, but she answered it as a statement, saying, 'Yes, Michael, it's too late.'

'You . . . you wouldn't leave Dan and the children?'

She gulped but said nothing for a moment. When she did speak she reversed his question. 'You wouldn't leave your child either, would you?'

'They . . . they would break her, with bitterness and recrimination they would break her.'

'Then there's nothing more we can do, Michael.'

'Yes, there is. Yes, there is.'

She could scarcely hear his voice above the hissing rain. 'We could meet now and then, just now and then. I . . . I must see you, Barbara. If it's only once in six months I must see you. I can't live with the thought of never seeing you again. I . . . I could have gone on I suppose if I hadn't caught sight of you that day. But from then, oh!' – he shook his head – 'you've no idea of the agony. It's as if a disease had got into my blood. . . . No, I didn't mean it that way, I meant. . . .'

'I know what you meant, Michael.' Her voice was soft, her manner simple. 'I was born with the disease. I'll carry it till I die.'

They fell against each other, and for the first time in their lives their lips touched, gently, reverently at first; then, all restraint washed away, their entwined bodies swayed as if they were locked together in combat.

The long moment of passion finally spent itself and they leant against the tree trunk. Their arms still entwined, they gazed at each other, and Michael, each word coming out on a gasp, said, 'It's done, there's no going back. I . . . I can get away now and then, once a fortnight perhaps.'

She wanted to say, 'It will be difficult,' but the words stuck in her throat; she felt tired, utterly spent. For years and years she had waited for this moment, and it had to come like this, furtively in a wood, and both of them wringing wet. What would it have been like if . . .?

'I . . . I could come here once a fortnight, on a Friday. I've been round the wood, it's very isolated. Could you get away then?'

She did not answer, she simply made a small motion with her head, and he drew her towards him again, but gently now.

'It must be past four.' She looked towards his chest and he un-buttoned his coat and drew out his watch. 'Ten past,' he said.

'You must go.'

They stared deeply at each other again.

'Barbara, Barbara, I'm so happy, you haven't any idea, you never will have.'

'I have an idea, Michael.' Her head moved slowly up and down.

'There are so many things I want to tell you.'

'And I want to hear them.'

'I'll always tell you everything, Barbara, the truth. From now on everything, and the truth. It must be the truth.'

'Me too, me too, Michael, only the truth.'

It was she who took his hand and led him away from the tree. Where the path joined the road she glanced to right and left, and in a voice that was an imitation of Brigie's, she said, 'We must be circumspect.'

He gave a slight understanding smile. 'Indeed we must be circum-spect. Oh, my love! My Barbara, my dear, my very dear.' They were embracing once again.

'I'll . . . I'll be here next Friday.'

'Next Friday?'

'Yes, next Friday. Good-bye, my love.'

She did not reply, but she smiled at him softly, and as softly touched his cheek with her fingers, then turned away and hurried down the road. And she did not look back.

When Ada helped her off with her cloak she said, 'Why, ma'am, you're sodden and right through, your coat an' all.'

'Oh, I'm all right, Ada. I enjoyed my walk.'

Ada looked at her mistress and thought, She must have; she looks heaps better than when she went out, the air's done her good. She should walk more often. If she did my tramp of a mornin' she'd be like a fightin' cock in no time. . . .

And Barbara took to walking more often and it seemed to do her the world of good in all ways.

4

BARBARA DID NOT HAVE ANY VISITS from Brigie and Harry during the next few weeks because Mary was ill, and one Thursday morning there came a letter to say Mary had died and would Barbara be coming for the funeral.

That evening Dan said, 'Of course you must go for the funeral, Mary was like one of the family. You needn't go anywhere near the cottage but you must go back for the funeral. You could leave first thing in the morning.'

'No,' Barbara said, 'I, I can't go until Saturday.'

'Why?' asked Dan.

She hesitated before replying, 'It's the fitting. I have a fitting in town, and Miss Brown doesn't like it if I alter my time, she's much in demand. What's more if I'm to attend the funeral I'll need to get a black coat, ready made, I've nothing black.'

'Well, you'd better send a letter by express and tell Brigie you'll be there on Saturday. And if I were you I'd make up your mind to stay for a few days, you need a change. The boys won't come to any harm, not as long as they've got Ruthie.'

She ignored his last remark and said, 'Perhaps you are right. I'll see;' but she didn't look at him as she spoke.

Everything seemed so easy; everything seemed to be working towards. . . . What was it working towards? She didn't allow her mind to probe the future.

She took a walk on the Friday before going into Newcastle for her fitting; and on the Saturday morning Dan himself put her on the train and he walked along by the carriage until she was out of sight.

She felt little sense of guilt now, agreeing with Michael that they were hurting no one; as long as they could keep their meetings secret things could go on as they were.

It was she who had planned where their next meeting should be, and when she had told him he had held her tightly and whispered, 'Oh Barbara! Oh Barbara!'

She had arranged for it to be on the day following Mary's funeral, and if anything should happen to stop her coming then the day following that, and so on until at last they would be together. She did not question what effect his excursions would have on the occupants of the farm, she left it to him to make his own alibis.

At one point in the journey, as she sat thinking quietly, she suddenly became overwhelmed by a sense of quite another kind of guilt as there came to her the reason why after all these years she was going back to the Hall. She recalled how good Mary had been to her, putting up with so much from her; and how little thanks too she had received from her. She had been in service since she was a child of eight. She had been at the Hall long before Brigie put in an appearance there. Poor Mary. She should be feeling a deep sorrow at her going, and all she could think was that she was old, sixty-six, or more.

It was strange, she thought, that she should look upon Mary as old yet not consider Brigie old, and Brigie was near seventy now, but Brigie seemed to defy age. Her body was slim and she still had a presentable bust, and the skin of her face was taut. Brigie would never be old. As Dan laughingly said, they would have to shoot her.

Dan, Dan. The wheels of the train beat out his name. She mustn't dwell on Dan. Dan belonged to her other life, her life of duty and loyalty, and he was, she knew, happier than he had been for some time, for she had shown him a great deal of kindness and consideration over the past weeks. Yes a great deal of consideration, especially with regards to his needs. At such times, in a twisted way, she considered that she was paying the price for Michael. But how she would be able to suffer him on her return she did not know, for after her next meeting with Michael she would be a changed woman.

Brigie was delighted to see her, her pleasure was evident. But not so Harry's. His reception of her appeared cool, so much so that, immediately they were alone, she asked Brigie, 'Is anything wrong, I . . . I mean with Mr Bensham?' She always gave him his title.

'No, no. Why do you ask?'

'I felt he wasn't quite well.'

'You think he doesn't look so well as the last time you saw him?' There was no anxiety in Brigie's voice.

'Perhaps it's just my imagination.'

A short time later Brigie chastised Harry for his reception of Barbara. 'She noticed,' she said, 'you made it very evident.'

'Aye, well, I can't help it; I've got me doubts about that young madam still. Oh I know' – he jerked his head at her – 'she's the sun that shines in your sky, she could cut your throat an' you wouldn't stay her hand. You said, mind, you would tell me if you twigged anything. Well, have you?'

'There is nothing to worry about, I can assure you. She has just confirmed what Dan said in his letter. She's only been twice in the city since we last saw her, and the second time was yesterday when she went for a fitting and to buy a suitable coat for the funeral. The previous time was when Dan took her to the Theatre Royal. So you see your suspicions are most unjust.'

'Aye, well, I'm sorry if I'm wrong, but I wouldn't have our Dan hurt for all the world. He's been good to her. By God! he has. An' I'm going to say it again whether it vexes you or pleases you that the men are few an' far between who'd have taken her on in the state she was in, and after what she had done to that lass. . . .'

'Harry!'

'Oh aye, you can feel hurt, but me memory's long an' you wouldn't have got me doing what I did, no, by God! you wouldn't. And what you want to consider an' all is that he saved you some heart scald, because if he hadn't taken her off your hands God knows what she would have got up to. There's a deep well in her, say what you like.' At this he rose and stamped down the room.

'Where are you going?'

He turned towards her from the door. 'I'm going for a walk. You're always yarping on about walking doing you good; well, I want a bit of good done to me at this minute.'

'Harry.' She went swiftly towards him. 'Please, please, don't be annoyed. I promised you, and you can believe me, that if I suspected there was anything untoward happening I . . . I would tell you, but I can assure you there's not.'

'Aye, you can assure me, but can you be sure? If that fellow was round there once he'd come again, an' he wouldn't waste his time. No man wastes his time if he feels compelled to go looking out a woman like he did.' His tone changed, his expression changed, and he said quietly now, 'I'm worried, Brigie, very worried inside. It wouldn't matter if our Dan didn't worship the ground she walks on, but he's besotted by her, an' I don't want to see him hurt 'cos I'm very fond of our Dan. And Dan's the only one who's given me anything, I mean worthwhile. John there, he's good in the works, nobody better, but he hasn't proved himself otherwise. Perhaps it's not his fault, I don't know. And our Katie, God help her, look what she's thrown up. Aye' – he shook his head – 'look what she's thrown up. But Dan, he's given me three fine grandsons.'

'She played some part in it you know.'

'Aye, I know. I'm not belittling her in that way, but it's funny – now

538

I've got to tell you this – when I saw her the day I had the most strange feeling. An' you know me, I'm not given to fancies, never have been. Feet flat on the earth Harry Bensham, that's me, that's how I've got where I am the day, no fancies. Yet when I looked into her face, into her eyes, I had the kind of feeling she drew a blind down over them an' she was hiding something. I can't explain it, but I sensed something.'

'Harry. Harry.' She put up her hand and touched his red-veined cheek. 'This is prejudice, you know it is prejudice. And if you sense something in her she senses something in you, you know you can't hide your feelings. And it's going to be very awkward if you continue to adopt this cool manner towards her because Dan has persuaded her to stay on for a few days.'

'Aw, well' – he jerked his head to the side – 'she can stay as long as she likes, you know that. I'm glad to hear she wants to stay, an' I'll write our Dan and tell him to give himself a holiday, and this'll be a chance to bring the bairns over.' He nodded at her now, smiling. 'I'd like that, aye, I'd like that, I'd like to see them running about here. You know, she's never brought them, she's never allowed them to come. I suppose I've held that against her an' all. I'll go down right now and I'll write to our Dan.'

'Do that,' she said. 'Do that.' When she was alone she remained standing where she was and she repeated to herself, 'No man wastes his time if he feels compelled to go looking out a woman like he did.'

They buried Mary on the Monday. She had no living relatives left to attend her funeral. Brigie and Barbara were the only two women present, the rest were the older male members of the staff, those who had known her over the years.

A high tea was served in the servants' hall for the staff mourners. Brigie, Barbara and Harry had their ordinary tea in the drawing room.

The butler was still present in the room when Harry said, 'What are we going to do about the cottage?'

'What do you mean, what are we going to do?' asked Brigie.

'Well, it's no use to us. I can't see the use in keeping it; it isn't in the grounds, a mile along the road and on the other side an' all. It's no use to us.'

'It's eating no bread, as Mary herself would have said. Poor Mary,' Brigie added softly, shaking her head. 'I'll miss her so; indeed I will. It seems that she's been with me every day of my life.'

'Aye, well, her time had come, like it'll come to all of us. But about the cottage eating no bread. I don't know so much. It'll need keeping up; inside and out it'll need keeping up. If a place is not tended it moulds. Anyway it's full of old rubbish.'

'It is not full of old rubbish.' There was indignation in Brigie's tone now. 'The furniture is made up of good, solid pieces. It's only the floor coverings and drapes that need renewing.'

'The place looks cluttered to me, always has done.'

'Because you have always compared it with this.'

'No, that's not the reason at all, too many falderals about it. And Mary was like that an' all; she went around like a bundle of duds.'

'Oh, Harry.' Her Miss Brigmore tone told him that she was shocked, but it did not seem to affect him for he flapped his hand at her as he said, 'Aw, I meant no disrespect, but when you're dead you're dead and you can't be hurt one way or t'other. I consider it's a lot of nonsense all this speaking well of the dead. Not that anyone would speak bad of her. But in the main when folks die they suddenly become angels; the blackest rascals are given white gowns, folks speak about them in whispers. Speak no ill of the dead, they say. Well, for my part, I would say speak no ill of the livin' and we'd all be better off.'

'Yes, indeed, indeed, I agree with you.' She was nodding at him now. 'Speak no ill of the living. Oh yes, I agree with you.'

He stared at her, his face half turned away, his eyes slanted. He knew he had tripped himself up. He drank deeply from his cup and as if to please her and to show he was aiming to practise what he preached, he turned to Barbara and said, 'I'm glad you're staying on, lass, and I'm looking forward to having the bairns here.'

'Thank you.' She inclined her head slowly. 'I'm sure they'll love it, it will all be so new to them, so large. You'll likely have trouble with them scampering about, especially Ben.'

'It won't trouble me, lass, it'll put me in mind of when I had mine all young. By! aye, it'll be something to see them scampering about. How is that young Foggety piece coping?'

'Oh ... oh very well.'

'No more smacked backsides?'

'No. I ... I don't think there's been any need for her to resort to such treatment.'

'Well, that says something for her. I'll be interested to see how she handles the tribe here. She has something that lass. Aye' – he rose from the chair nodding to himself – 'she has something. If she had been in my mill I'd've picked her out. Oh' – he turned and with a half smile looked down on Brigie – 'not in that way. No, not in that way. But I would have put her in charge you know, 'cos I think she has the makings of a natural born manager.'

Barbara made no comment on this. She watched her father-in-law go down the room and out into the hall, leaving the door open behind him. It was an irritating habit he had of never closing a door. He was an irritating man in many ways. She wondered how Brigie, the precise, pedantic individual, had tolerated him all these years, and she

540

was amazed that she had any feelings for the rough, bumptious, coarse individual.

At this point she reminded herself that she was forgetting it was the rough, bumptious, coarse individual who had provided her with the niceties of life and that without his help both she and Brigie would have fared little better than the woman they had buried today. Years ago she had liked him, why didn't she like him now?

She knew why she didn't like him now, she didn't like him because he saw through her. He had always been able to see through her, and his kindness to her all those years ago was not because he liked her but because he liked and wanted to please Brigie.

'I'm going to the cottage tomorrow to tidy up. And he's right, you know.' Brigie nodded now at Barbara. 'There is a lot of stuff that could be dispensed with. But I still maintain there are some good, serviceable pieces. You ... you wouldn't care to come with me?'

'No, if you don't mind, no.'

'It's all right, it's all right. Will you have another cup of tea?' Brigie lifted the silver teapot and Barbara answered, 'Yes, please, I would like another.'

As Brigie refilled the cup she said, 'It'll be like old times having the children in the nursery.'

Barbara nodded her head. 'Yes, I suppose it will.'

'He's looking forward to them coming so much, it means a lot to him.'

'I can see that. I'm ... I'm very sorry I've deprived him of the pleasure all these years.'

'Oh, he understood, he understood. But ... but from now on it would be nice if you could bring them now and again.'

'I'll do that.'

When Brigie's hand came out and caught hold of her arm in a tender grip she stilled the wave of shame that threatened to envelop her. The means justified the end; she knew she would sink to any form of duplicity in order to be alone with Michael.

It was strange but her life seemed to have revolved a full circle, for tomorrow or the next day or the next they'd meet in the vicinity of where it all began so long ago, and they'd come together as they should have done when they were young. And that was all that mattered – nothing else.

5

THE DAY WAS FINE. Brigie went to the cottage about noon, to decide on the furniture she meant to dispose of, but before leaving the Hall she asked Barbara what she was going to do, and Barbara had replied that she might take a walk around the grounds, or might go up to the nursery and supervise the preparations for the children coming, she hadn't really made up her mind. The best thing would be to do both.

When Brigie asked Harry what he intended to do, he said he intended to walk over to the farm and see what they were up to. Then, if she kept her nose clean, he would call at the cottage and escort her back home in case she was attacked on the road. Or failing that, he would help her to carry the rubbishy furniture back to the house.

Brigie laughed and left the house in a happy mood because Harry was in a happy mood.

Shortly afterwards Barbara came down from the nursery, took a light coat from her room, and went for a walk through the gardens. She had known the gardens well, and nothing had been altered that she could see over the past nine years or so.

When she finally emerged from the park she crossed the coach road and walked over the open ground that led to the foothills. These she skirted and took the road Dan had taken on the black winter's night he had spent searching for her, and eventually she came to the broken gate. Here she stopped and looked about her and a memory stirred in her. She gazed towards the hills where they slowly mounted upwards like a chain of beads, and to where, beyond one of them, was the mouth of the lead mine in which she had lain down and prepared to die, and would have died but for Dan. *Dan. Dan.* She forbade herself to think of Dan.

Carefully stepping over the rotten wood of the gate that was embedded in the grass she took the narrow brush-bordered path to the right of her.

When she came to the shell of the house and the tumbledown barn there was no figure standing outside to welcome her. She looked towards the barn and sniffed disdainfully at the smell of decay, then stood gazing about her. The place was eerie, frightening. The flags of the courtyard were almost obliterated by grass and beyond there was a dense wall of tangled gorse, bramble and bracken. She remembered she had once come here with Brigie and Mary to pick blackberries and later their cottage had been filled with the pungent smell of boiling blackberries and they'd had jelly for tea for weeks afterwards.

A crackling in the undergrowth startled her, and when the crackling became a crashing sound she stared fearfully towards the hedge. When there emerged from an unseen path a sheep followed by a sizeable lamb, she drew in a deep breath, put her hand over her mouth, and laughed softly.

The sheep was as surprised by the sight of her as she by it and it turned tail and scampered away along the path towards the gate.

After she had waited half an hour she looked at her watch. She could wait another half-hour, there was plenty of time, dinner wasn't until three. But her legs were tired with standing. She moved towards the house and sat down on a pile of broken masonry that was almost covered with weeds.

When she next looked at her watch it said twenty past one. She was sighing deeply and rising to her feet when she saw him. His approach had been silent. She remained still for a moment, then she was running towards him, and he to her.

'Darling. Oh Barbara, Barbara. Darling, darling.' He was smothering her face with his lips and she was gasping and talking at the same time.

'I'd almost given up hope, but I said there'd be tomorrow and I'd come again, and again. . . . Oh Michael, Michael, it was only Friday, but it seemed years. What did they say, I mean, where are you supposed to be?'

'Oh' – he shook his head – 'oh, I'm on a round. I'm calling in at Hewitt's, the blacksmith's you know. No questions, you see I'm working.' He pressed her away from him in order that she should see his working clothes, corded jacket, moleskin trousers and black gaiters.

'Then you'll soon have to go back. Come and sit down.'

When she went to draw him towards a grassy patch he said softly, 'No, not here, in the barn.'

'Barn?' She raised her eyebrows at him.

'Come.' His arm about her, he led her through the gap and to the extreme corner of the barn above which the roof still held, and there he pointed down to the floor and she stared at the carpet of dry grass

543

that covered about three square yards of it. Then she looked at him and he said, 'I came yesterday and gathered it.'

She gazed at him and he at her and she whispered, 'Oh Michael, Michael,' before pressing herself against him.

Without a word he gently drew the pins from her hat. Next he took off her outer coat, and then his own, after which, his arms about her, he drew her on to the bed he had made in preparation for what they both desired and longed for, and had dreamt of since they were young.

There were no words spoken, the only sound in the barn was their unintelligible murmurings.

It was half past two when they rose from the floor, and gently now he hooked and buttoned her clothes and helped her into her coat, smoothed her hair, then handed her her hat.

When he led her to the opening she stopped and leant against the rotten stanchion and gazed up into the sky. There was a look of peace on her face that had never been there before. She said softly, 'I want one thing more.'

'What is that, my love?'

'To die, to die right now at this moment.'

'Don't say that.' His arms were about her again. 'If you died I would die. I know I couldn't go on without you, not now, not now.'

They stood in silence looking into each other's eyes; he then said, 'You couldn't be as happy as I am but . . . but you are happy, aren't you?'

'Oh Michael, Michael, I have no words to tell you, and if I tried I would spoil it. It was the most wonderful, wonderful happening of my life.' Again they gazed at each other.

She did not see the incongruity of the situation. She did not think in this moment that she had just done what she had scorned her Aunt Constance for doing, and that once she hadn't failed to throw this fact in Michael's face. Nor did she wonder if the oddity of the situation had struck him. The past was forgotten, nothing mattered to her now, only that she'd had him at last, and he her, and she knew that she would do anything, even leave her sons should he raise his finger. But regretfully she knew also that that price would not be asked of her because he had a daughter.

He said now, 'When are you going back?'

'Oh, it'll be some time. Mr Bensham wants the children here. Dan is bringing them at the week-end. . . .' When her voice trailed off he said, 'I'm sorry if I'm hurting Dan but . . . but I can't help it.'

'I know.' Her head was down. 'I'm sorry too that I'm hurting him, but I can't help it either. And . . . and I should say at this point' – she raised her head and looked into his face – 'I should say that I'm sorry I'm hurting Sarah, but . . . but we said we'd always be truthful to each other, and I can't say I'm sorry for her because ... because she has you.'

'She hasn't me, Barbara. She never had me. She had to be compensated. ... I'm sorry, darling.' He caught her hand.

'Oh, I know, I know. What I did was dreadful. We must speak of it, bring it into the open. And I say again it was dreadful, but I paid for it, almost in a way as much as she did. I lost my mind for a time. Did you know that, Michael?'

'Yes, I heard you were ill.'

'It was your marriage that brought me to life again.'

He shook his head.

'Yes, yes, it was. And Jim Waite gave me back my hearing.'

'I heard in a roundabout way that you could hear again. You know I've grown to dislike Jim Waite. I think it began when he kept on bragging about lathering you. I know it did. I really hated him.'

'Don't. It was a day of truth all round. ... Does Sarah hate me?'

He could not answer that, but his colour rose and she looked away from him and said, 'It's no wonder. In her place I'd feel the same. But, oh Michael' – she was clinging to him again – 'if only I were in her place; I wouldn't mind losing both my legs if I were your wife. ...'

Some minutes later, their arms entwined, they walked along the narrow path. As they neared the broken gate she asked softly, 'When will you be able to come, tomorrow?'

'Oh, I only wish I could. Oh, how I wish I could, and every day, but I promised to take Hannah into Hexham.'

... 'The following day?'

'Yes, I'll be here Thursday, the same time. Yes, Thursday. Oh, my dearest, my love. ...'

They had gone a little way further on when he said, 'I'd better leave you here.'

'No, walk with me to the bend, no one can see us from there. And anyway, no one ever comes this way.'

'Oh, yes they do.' He nodded at her cautiously. 'They must, or the path wouldn't be as open as this. But mostly at night, I suppose, poachers on their way to the estate.'

'Oh yes, yes, of course.'

They walked to where the path began to widen and give on to open ground, and here they kissed passionately again and clung to each other.

Their hands were still joined as they left the path, but after a moment they separated, pausing only to gaze at each other, before he started back towards the foothills whilst she made towards the road which she would have to cross before she entered the grounds again.

So steeped in her happiness was she that she looked neither to right nor to left at the point where she left the moor and crossed the road. If she had she would have seen Harry Bensham standing in the shadow of the hedge open-mouthed, gaping at her. . . .

He knew it, he knew it. By God Almighty! he knew it. He was no fool; he had never been taken for one in his life until now. She wouldn't believe him. Brigie wouldn't believe him. Had she known about it all the time? By God! he'd soon find out. Poor Dan. Poor bugger. And after all he had done for her. As soon as he got back to the house she'd go; she'd be out of there in a brace of shakes if he knew anything; he'd kick her backside down the drive himself, he would that.

With each step he took towards the cottage his temper rose and his heart beat faster. Their Dan was being made a monkey out of. He could see it all now, he could see why she had given in so easily about bringing the bairns here; after her refusing for years to let them near the place. The scut! the whoring young scut! But she wasn't young, she was no longer a young lass, she was a married woman with three bairns, and a husband who had always been a damned sight too good for her. Oh, the whoring bastard! And that was no understatement.

He had never liked her, he had seen through her even when she was a bit of a bairn. He had said to Brigie once, 'You worry too much about that one, she'll go her own road and to hell with everybody who stands in her way.' Well, here was one she wouldn't send to hell, and by God! he would get in her way, Michael Radlet's and hers! After all that had happened: his wife crippled, his mother estranged from Brigie, and after Brigie having brought her up and slaved for her; and that blasted Mallen bloke for years afore that. It was as everybody hereabouts said, there was a rotten streak in the Mallens, and that bitch was a Mallen all through.

When he crashed open the kitchen door of the cottage and stalked into the hall, yelling, 'Where are you? Where are you?' Brigie came to the top of the stairs and cried in concern, 'What is it? What's the matter? What has happened?'

'Come down here and I'll tell you.'

When she reached the foot of the stairs she said again, and in deep concern now, 'Oh, what is it, Harry? What is it?' She saw that he was unable to speak; his face was scarlet, even his scalp, where his hair receded, was scarlet. She watched him straining his neck up out of his collar, which he then began to pull from his throat as if trying to get air.

When he did speak there was froth around his lips, and his head wagged as if on a spring before he brought the words out, not rapidly as was his usual form of speech, but slowly, and punctuated with gasps. 'That . . . that one of yours. . . . A bitch she is, a brothel . . .

546

bitch.' His head was still wagging. 'On the hills with ... with the farmer ... Radlet.'

When her head moved in denial he thrust his hand out to her, his forefinger stiff and stabbing. 'It's true. Just seen her ... them.' He gulped now and pulled harder at his collar. 'Lovers. Lovers. Do you hear?' He stammered now, 'K ... kissin', kiss ... kissin'. Him one road, her the other. Goin' for walk she said. By God! I'll walk her, walk her out of the house. Sh ... show her up. Our Dan ... our Dan.'

As he dragged out the name he pressed his two fists into his chest and his body doubled, and she gripped him, crying, 'Harry! Oh! Harry.'

When he fell slowly to the floor she knelt beside him and tried to straighten his bent body, crying all the while, 'Harry dear. Oh, Harry, what is it? Speak to me. What is it?' But even as she asked she knew the answer, for Mary's death had been preceded by a similar seizure. 'Oh, Harry. Harry. Oh, my dear. My dear man. Oh, Harry.'

When she got him on to his back he lay still, his eyes wide, staring up at her, and she still beseeched him to speak, saying, 'Harry. Harry.' Then she looked around her as if searching for someone to ask for advice, but there was no one, and she was a mile from the Hall and alone here, and he could die at any minute.

He mustn't die, he mustn't. She'd nurse him. Oh Harry. Her Harry. Her dear Harry. She must not give way like this. She mustn't.

She regained control of herself and, her voice endeavouring to be calm, she bent over him and said slowly, 'Lie still, perfectly still, don't move. I'll ... I'll be back with help.' She nodded at him while she rose to her feet, and she backed slowly from him and opened the front door. She looked at him once more, then turned, and lifting her skirts high up to her knees, raced down the path and into the road.

She did not stop and look either up or down the road to see if anyone was coming, so few people travelled this way except the carrier cart at stated times, and a carriage now and again. As she ran she thought, There must be a curse on Barbara Bensham – no, not Bensham, Mallen, for she was a Mallen through and through and like all Mallens she brought trouble to everyone she touched, disaster, heartbreak and trouble. But if this time she brought death she would never forgive her, never, not as long as she lived.

6

DAN CAME WITHOUT THE CHILDREN, and John and Jenny came, and Katie and Pat came, and for three days one or another crept into the room and stood by Harry's bed.

Dan would hold the hand with the two twitching fingers and thumb which, other than the eyes, was the only sign that there was any life left in his father's body. He found it unbearable that this man who had been so vital, who had bawled and thrust his way through life, who had been fearless in his opinions and steadfast in his loyalties should now be reduced to two pain-filled eyes and three twitching digits.

On the night of the third day they all tried to persuade Brigie to go to her room and rest. She had not even changed her clothes, she was wearing the same dress she wore on the morning she had gone to the cottage. The only time she had left the bed-side in three days was to go to the water closet. She dozed at intervals in the chair by the bed, even in the day-time now.

In a family conclave in the drawing room they said to Barbara, 'You go up and try to persuade her. You're nearest to her, she's more likely to listen to you. If she doesn't rest soon, well. . . .' They left their thoughts unspoken.

So Barbara went up to the bedroom. She tip-toed past the nurse and towards the bed where Brigie was sitting, and she bent over her and put her hand gently on her arm and said, 'Let me take your place just for an hour. Please, please, Brigie.'

What Brigie did was to lift the hand from her arm and push it aside, and she did not look up at her once beloved Barbara, but she kept her eyes on the man who had given her the dignity of marriage, who had made her mistress of the house in which she was once a servant, and in whose company over the past years she had known an enjoyment of life she hadn't experienced before, and she saw that he was agitated, and the cause of it was evident. She bent forward and took hold of the twitching fingers and looked into the live eyes moving restlessly in the dead face and said softly, 'It's all right, my dear. It's all right,' and without moving her head she added, 'Will you please leave us, Barbara?'

Barbara did not feel repulsed by Brigie's words, nor had she been by her previous attitude; Brigie was greatly distressed, she was at the end of her physical resources. And so she went downstairs and told them she had failed.

When Dan next went into the bedroom he drew up a chair beside Brigie's, and after looking at his father for a moment he said under his breath, 'He seems to be wanting to say something.'

Brigie did not answer Dan, she made no movement, but she thought, Yes, yes, he wants to say something, and say it to you, Dan, and I will in no way prevent him should he recover enough to do so, even knowing it would mean the end of your happiness.

She was amazed at the clearness of her mind, at the calmness of it. Her body was very tired, but her mind was clear and working, motivated as it were by a light, a light that was showing her the true values of those around her. She, who had prided herself on her perspicacity, had, she knew now, been blinded by her own selfish needs of frustrated motherhood and had endowed her adopted daughter with all the qualities she would have wished a child of her own flesh to possess. But Barbara had not been born of her flesh, she had within her the flesh of a Mallen, and though Thomas himself had not been a really bad man he had undoubtedly passed on the traits of viciousness and weakness that had always smeared the Mallen name. Yet, such was her reasoning, she knew that later when all this was over, her mind would say to her, what had Barbara done after all but turn to her first love, the man she should have married. Well, if her mind said that to her, she told it now, it would be talking to deaf ears.

'I ... I feel sure he wants to say something, Brigie. Look at his fingers. It's as if he were writing. Do you think he could write?'

She did not take her eyes from Harry's as she answered, 'I don't know.'

'I'll get some paper.'

When he had gone from the room Brigie said pityingly to herself, 'Oh Dan, Dan; you're digging your own grave.'

He was only gone a minute before he returned with a leather bound writing pad and a pencil, and holding it above his father's face he said slowly and with compassion, 'Do you think you could write, Dad? Is this what you want?'

He put the pad on the coverlet and placed the pencil between the twitching finger and thumb, and when he saw them grip on to the stem he cast a bright look at Brigie and said, 'This is what he wanted.'

Brigie said nothing. This was to be the one time, the very first time

549

that she wasn't prepared to sacrifice herself and those around her for her beloved Barbara.

'He's writing, Brigie. Look, he's writing. That's an M. Yes, it's an M.' His voice was excited. 'I . . . C.' He repeated each letter slowly as the finger and thumb guided the pencil erratically over the paper. 'K. No, an H. I don't know whether it's a K or an H. What do you think?'

The fingers dropped heavily on to the paper. Harry's eyes pierced those of his son's. The lids blinked, then closed. When they opened again the pencil moved once more.

'He's starting over again. M . . . I . . . C . . . and now an R. Or is it an H? M again. But this is an N. Now . . . what is this? What is he trying to do now? Look, Brigie. Is that a T?'

Brigie moved her head once before she said, 'Yes, I think it's a T.'

Harry now showed clear signs of acute agitation. His eyes blinked rapidly; he was irritated by their stupidity. Once more the pencil moved.

'He keeps doing that M,' said Dan. 'And now this looks like H . . . I . . . L. I can't make it out.'

The pencil suddenly dropped from between Harry's finger and thumb. He closed his eyes and Brigie, leaning towards him, said, 'Rest, dear, rest. You can do more later. You'll feel better tomorrow, and then, then. . . .'

She stopped as Harry's eyes looked straight into hers. They were willing her to complete what he had begun, and now with tears in her voice she said, 'It'll be all right. Don't worry, my dear, dear Harry. I'll see to it. I promise you, on my word. . . .'

'What is it?' Dan had come round to her side again. 'Is there something on his mind?'

When she didn't answer but continued to stare at his father, he said, 'Look at this. What do you make of it?' and she looked at the paper and the scrawl. The jumbled letters spelt MICK MOUNT then HIL. He whispered now, 'Do you know anyone called Mick Mount?'

Slowly she shook her head.

His voice a mere whisper, he said, 'It must be somebody at the works. I'll go down and ask John.'

When Dan had left the room she leant over the bed and said softly, 'Oh, my dearest Harry, that you should be troubled like this. And you have been so good, so good to everyone, but especially to me. And I thank you, Harry, I do, I do thank you from the bottom of my heart. And I want you to know I love you as I've never loved anyone. Believe that, will you? Please believe that. You are my very, very own dear Harry, and don't worry any more about this, this other business. I shall clear the matter up. I promise you. I give you my word.'

His eyes were glazed with water and when his fingers gripped hers she repeated again, 'I give you my word, Harry. I do.'

Now, hand in hand, they remained looking at each other until his eyes closed. After a time he made a vain attempt to open them, but found he was being overwhelmed by a great tiredness; being the man he was, he fought against it; he wasn't ready for the long sleep yet. There was something he had to do, or see to it that his Brigie did it for him.

As the rain of Brigie's tears fell on his face he finally gave in and went into a coma. It was four days later when his spirit left him.

7

HARRY WAS BURIED in the same grave as Matilda. Brigie had not waited for the family to propose this, she herself had made it clear that it was her wish even before the funeral arrangements were discussed.

Afterwards the family gathered in the library to hear the reading of the will. It was to the point, as Harry had been in life. No mucking about, as he would have said. The mill in Manchester and the warehouse business in Newcastle were to be divided equally between his three children, leaving Katie's share in trust with reversion to her brothers or their descendants on her death. To his wife he left High Banks Hall for her lifetime and three thousand pounds a year for its upkeep, this amount to be found from the profit of the mill, and on her death the estate would pass to his three grandsons, Benjamin, Jonathan and Harry Bensham, to be divided equally, either through sale of the same, or in agreement reached through the trustees. Should any of the three die before marriage, his share would go to the surviving brothers or brother.

There was no mention of Katie's son, and the will had been made out only last year.

Katie showed no rancour about this, nor about the reversion clause. If not quite inured to pain she accepted it as something inevitable. Moreover she had understood her father; like most of his type abnormality in any way frightened him. He could accept people so affected outside the family. Armless and legless monstrosities being pushed around in barrows with tin mugs around their necks imploring alms aroused his compassion, but when such touched on his family they frightened him. They brought alive old wives' tales of evil, and of spells and curses handed down. She knew that he had looked upon her son in this way.

But Pat did not take the omission as she had, and as they drove home he said so. 'It was very small minded of him,' he said. 'Thank

God the boy will never need financial help, but apparently it would have been all the same had he done so.'

She put her hand in his and looked at him softly as she said, 'Don't let it worry you, it isn't worrying me.'

'Are you sure?' The question was gentle.

'Yes, yes, I'm sure. There's only one thing that worries me.'

'And that?'

She looked fully into his eyes as she said in all seriousness, 'That you should ever stop loving me.'

'Oh Katie! Katie!' He shook his head at her. 'Then I can assure you you haven't a worry in the world.'

She leant against his shoulder and they both looked at the upholstered back of the carriage seats opposite, and their thoughts ran along the same channel, repeating the same words: Not a worry in the world. Their son, four years old, who could walk only with stumbling step, and talk as an infant, and who looked strangely inhuman, not ugly or frightening, just strangely inhuman, and who was already classified under the heading of 'mongolian imbecile', and they could speak of not having a worry in the world.

Why, Katie wondered, was one never allowed to be happy? She had married a wonderful man, she had a beautiful home – no, a magnificent home – yet God had made it His business to deform her son both mentally and physically. Why? Why?

The streets of Manchester were swarming with children, the majority of them underfed, barefoot and lice-ridden, but they were normal, in most part they were normal.

Yet, she asked herself as the carriage turned into the drive of the Manor, would any of them be as lovable as the child waiting patiently for her there in the house? No, for whatever was lacking in Lawrence it wasn't the capacity to love. His whole aim seemed to be bent on loving, and showing it.

If only her father had accepted her child's love. But her father, like her mother was gone; the family was broken. There still remained John and Dan, but she saw little of either of them and less of their wives. Jenny lived in an entirely different world; as for Barbara – well, Barbara was a strange creature. She wouldn't mind if she never met Barbara again. Although they had at one time, when girls, been close they had now nothing in common, no nothing, for Barbara had three healthy sons.

Life was unfair, cruel and unfair. . . .

Five minutes later she was holding her son in her arms and he was hugging her tightly around the neck while his shapeless mouth spread kisses over her face. And when he stopped and lisped, 'Bri. Bri,' she laughed as she looked at Pat and said, 'He expected Brigie to come back with us. I told him we were going to Brigie's. Isn't that amazing?' And Pat nodded in confirmation.

As she put the child to the floor she thought, 'But there'll always be Brigie, as long as she's alive. And she'll need an interest now – she's always liked Lawrence. I'll bring her over. It'll be good to have her here . . . and, and I need her.'

There came to her mind a saying of her mother's: When one door closes another one opens to let both stink out and fresh air in.

She couldn't analyse how it actually applied to the present situation, only that without her father dying she could never have hoped to have the comfort of Brigie; and it surprised her at this moment how much she needed the comfort of Brigie; in spite of the love of Pat she needed the comfort of Brigie.

8

JOHN AND JENNY had returned to Manchester; the mill could not be left for long. As John had said in his quiet, even dull way, his dad would have been the first to say, 'Get back to work, life's got to go on,' and Jenny had endorsed this. Jenny endorsed everything that John said.

Although he was very fond of his brother, Dan found John heavy going. Already, at thirty-one, John was a stolid settled man. It was hard to believe he was childless for he had a slightly pompous air like that which a father of a grown family could have been excused for adopting.

Dan said as much to Barbara and she answered, 'Oh, I don't know, I don't find him pompous. I've always found him nice and kind. Jenny's a little dull; she hasn't changed much from when I first met her, but she adores John, and that's everything.'

'Yes,' he said, 'that's everything.' His voice was flat, he looked weary. He was going to miss his father. Yet the sight of her sitting before the dressing-table mirror had the power to turn his thoughts away from his loss. There was no one to equal her in the whole world; her skin looked like thick cream, he likened her eyes to bottomless dark pools, turbulent pools, but wherein he was happy that his very soul should sink and be lost forever; and he could never find words to describe her hair, crow-black but with a sheen on it that no crow possessed. Her figure became more beautiful with the years. She represented a constant ache to him, and always would. He said, 'I'll put Ruth and the children on the twelve-ten on Thursday. You do want them here, don't you? They won't be in the way?'

'Of course not, of course not.' She turned her head quickly and looked at him.

'What I meant was they'll be all right with Ruth if you think they'll not upset Brigie.'

'No, I'm sure they won't, they'll likely help to bring her out of herself. She's taken this to heart much more than I ever imagined she would.'

'We forget that she's an old woman, she's sixty-nine.'

'You'd better not let her hear you say that, she doesn't consider herself old.' She smiled at him, and he smiled back at her as he said 'I won't mention her age,' then went out.

In spite of the sadness that filled him he was experiencing a new phase of personal happiness because Barbara had been kinder and sweeter to him these past few weeks than ever before, and her sympathy since his father's illness had touched him greatly. He considered himself very fortunate when he compared his life with that of John, and also of Katie . . . poor Katie.

Brigie showed no enthusiasm when it was proposed that the children should come to the Hall yet she did not voice anything against it. She had spoken very little to anyone since Harry's death. As Barbara had said, she had taken his going to heart.

At intervals during her life she had been acquainted with deep loneliness. In her early years when loneliness had struck her she had longed to be old for then she imagined one didn't feel things so vitally, emotions wouldn't tear at the heart in old age. But the years had taught her that age did not harden the senses but made one more vulnerable and stripped one until one's sensitivity lay on the surface of the skin like an open wound.

In the night she cried for Harry, for they had shared so much. Strangely, it was the uneducated man who had kept her mind alive in these later years, for he had become avid for knowledge and she had been happy to supply it. This often meant that she herself had to read up the subject first. Yes, he had kept her mind alive. And her body too, for although they had come together late in life they had come with a vitality that many would not have experienced in youth.

Oh, she missed Harry Bensham; more, yes, if the truth were told, more than she had ever missed Thomas Mallen.

But now her period of silence was over and she must talk. She must talk as she had never talked before. But she couldn't do it until Dan had left the house.

Dan set out for Newcastle early on Wednesday morning. From her bedroom window, Brigie watched Barbara see him to the carriage; she watched her receive his warm embrace; she watched her wave her hand in farewell in answer to him; and the bitterness in her rose.

She took a seat at the little desk to the side of the window and waited for the knock on the door. It wasn't long in coming. 'Come in,' she said.

Barbara came in and straight to her side, saying, 'Dan has just gone.'

'Yes, I saw him.' Brigie continued to sort the bills on the desk.

'Can I assist you in any way?'

'Not in my present work.'

'In what other way?'

Brigie now turned and looked into the pale beautiful face and she said slowly, 'If you will come up into the nursery I will tell you.'

'Is it not arranged to your liking?'

'What I have to say has nothing to do with the arrangement of the nursery, but I'd rather we were not overheard, should you be inclined to raise your voice.'

Barbara stared at Brigie, her face slightly screwed with enquiry. 'I don't know what you mean, raise my voice. Why should I raise my voice?'

'You will know shortly. I'll thank you to accompany me to the nursery.'

It was the old Brigie speaking, the governess, the goddess of the upper floor, and Barbara followed her out as if the years had rolled away and she were a child again, defiant but forced to be obedient.

When they reached the nursery floor Brigie led the way across the landing into the room that, at one time, had been her sitting room and which had now been prepared to receive Ruth Foggety. Once inside and the door closed, she turned to Barbara and said, 'Will you be taking a walk today?'

Barbara's face slowly stiffened. Her lips scarcely moving, she said, 'Yes, I shall be taking a walk today.'

Their eyes held.

'I thought you might. And you will be meeting Michael?'

Barbara seemed to grow in inches, her chin moved upwards, her neck stretched, yet at the same time she looked as if she might collapse, such was the hue of her skin. Her voice was a muffled murmur as she said, 'Well. Well, now you know.'

'I'm not the only one who knew. Harry knew, that is what caused his collapse.'

Brigie restrained herself from going to Barbara's support. And she needed support. She found it by reaching out and holding on to the high back of a chair; she rested against it, her bust almost pressed flat; and now she gasped as she said, 'Oh no! No you don't! You won't. I won't accept the blame.'

'Nevertheless it was because he saw you together that he had the seizure.'

'No! No! I tell you no! Those things can happen at any time. He was

557

an old man, his high colour indicated heart trouble. No! No! I tell you. *No!*'

'If it eases your conscience you may think that way.'

'I must; I'm burdened with enough, I can't bear any more.'

'That is your own fault.'

'It isn't my fault. Don't let's go into all that again. It isn't my fault. I didn't ask to be born, and of such a father. Don't say it's my fault. . . .'

'We are up in the nursery, but I still suggest that you keep your voice down. Now' – Brigie turned about and walked to a chair and sat down, and not until after a full minute while she looked at Barbara where she stood, her body still pressed against the back of the chair, did she say, 'This thing must stop.'

'Oh. *No, Brigie! Not this time!*'

'You have a husband and three children and, besides having a child, he has obligations that he must meet.'

'We both know that, and we'll both meet our obligations, but we won't be parted.'

'It can't go on. It isn't right.'

'Huh!' Now Barbara pushed her body back from the support of the chair but continued to grip the top with outstretched hands and she laughed mirthlessly as she said, 'You to talk about right or wrong!'

'When I did wrong it was to myself alone, I injured no one.'

'You injured my mother. If you hadn't arranged that Thomas Mallen should be kept on my mother's and Aunt Constance's income he would never have been in the cottage; a man like him would have found some work, or friends; so, no matter what you say, you won't convince me that you are without guilt in the shameful disastrous affair that resulted in me being born, and carrying within me the Mallen streak as they call it, and which I have passed on to my sons, visibly to one. . . . The name of Mallen is a curse in itself; people never seem to forget it. Pat Ferrier called my children the Mallen litter and I've hated him ever since. And he's been repaid in kind.' She paused for breath, and now, her voice a tone lower but holding even more bitterness, she said, 'I hate myself for being the offspring of a Mallen. Do you know that? I hate myself. But being so, I know what I am and I know that I'm capable of going to any lengths to keep the only thing in life that I've ever thought was of any worth, my love for Michael and his for me. . . . So, Brigie, whatever schemes you've got in your head you can forget them if they're concerned with parting us, as I'm sure they are.'

Brigie's face was almost as white as Barbara's now, and when she spoke her words were thin and icy. 'What if I inform Dan?'

'The only result of that would be unfortunate for Dan because I'd leave him.'

558

'And the children?'

There was a pause before she replied, quietly but firmly, 'Yes, even the children.'

Barbara had moved from the support of the chair and was standing in the middle of the room now as if out in the open facing an enemy. She waited for Brigie to speak while their eyes held in deep bitterness.

But it was some minutes before Brigie said, 'Do you imagine that Michael would ever leave his mother and his crippled wife . . . and his daughter for you?'

Barbara should have come back immediately with, 'Yes, yes, I know he will,' but there was a telling pause before she said, 'If I ask him he will. He'll do anything I ask of him.'

'I doubt it. I know Michael Radlet better than you do. He's a big man in bulk, but he was a weak youth, his only strength lay in stubbornness and I cannot see that in these last few years his character will have changed much. If his love for you had been so strong he would have defied Constance years ago. There was only one obstacle in his way then, and it was her, now there are three, his wife and his child . . . and his mother. So I shouldn't count on the fact that he'll sacrifice anything at all for you. He'll carry on the clandestine meetings. Oh yes, because he always struck me, even as a young boy and in spite of his charm, as one who'd want to eat his cake and still have it.'

'You're just being spiteful now; you know it isn't true; you don't know Michael.'

'You are not a stupid woman, Barbara; you know what I'm saying is true. However, we won't discuss his character any further, but we will come to Dan. I never thought I would say this, but Dan is much too good a man for you. You took advantage of him in making him marry you. . . . Yes, yes, you did.' She lifted up her hand. 'You made him marry you, partly, as you informed me in no mean manner, in order to get away from me and my authority. And I can only guess how little you have paid him in return. You may point to your sons as a form of payment, but a child can be born through indifference or rape, as we only too well know, don't we?' They stared white-faced at each other before Brigie ended, 'The conception of children is not dependent on love. . . .'

The nursery became silent, yet the silence vibrated with the emotions emanating from them both.

'Do you hope to go on keeping Dan in ignorance?'

'Just that, since you ask, because he is happy in his ignorance. Were I to leave him he'd be devastated. Michael and I have talked this out. We want to hurt no one, but we want each other, we need each other, and we mean to have each other. We are discreet; we shall go on being discreet. . . . So there you have it. If you bring this matter into the

559

open you will wreck a number of lives; if you leave things as they are no one will be hurt. It isn't up to me, it's up to you.'

Brigie began to cough. Her breath had caught in her throat, she felt for a moment she was going to choke. She was beaten.

Her coughing eased, she looked at Barbara who was staring at her, not a trace of shame or repentance on her face, and in this moment, and for the first time in her life, she felt hate towards her. She had never experienced hate, for never before had she allowed her emotions rein; she had disliked some people, despised others, while people like Harry's cousin, Florrie, had aroused her contempt, but never had she known the feeling of real hate, and that it should be turned on her beloved Barbara caused a feeling of sickness to rise in her. She felt ill.

As she rose slowly to her feet she knew that with her next words she would sever the last link with the only human being she had considered really her own; for if Barbara had been born of her flesh she could not have been more her own child. So once again, as it had done so often in the past, her life stretched lonely before her. Although she'd be visited by Harry's children, Katie, John and Dan, she did not look upon them as kin; Barbara she had considered her only kin.

She stopped on her way to the door and said, 'I am breaking my word to my dear husband, and will have to answer to my conscience for it, because you have forced me to remain silent for Dan's sake and that of the children. I would like to add I wish for no further connection with you whatever, but this would require an explanation to Dan, therefore I'd be obliged if you would refrain from visiting me again unless accompanied by your husband. . . . You will have to resort to your previous venue in order to continue your intrigue.'

One last look, a long pain-filled exchange, then Brigie continued to the door and went out.

Barbara stared at the door's blank surface, then her head drooping to her chest, she covered her face with her hands and, turning, she leant against the wall and audibly cried, both in voice and tears, 'Oh Brigie. Brigie. Oh, Brigie, Brigie. Why don't you understand? Can't you understand? I can't help it. I can't help it.'

After some time, bringing herself upright, she dried her face with her handkerchief, smoothed her hair back and then, with her hand on the door handle, she paused for a moment as she thought, Thank God I beat her.

And in this moment the heart-felt utterance wasn't made because now she could still continue to see Michael but because the thought of having to face Dan, should he ever know the truth, filled her with a sickness that was a mixture of fear, pain and remorse.

9

NOTHING UNTOWARD HAPPENED in the Bensham family between the years 1890 and 1893, nor was there a great deal of turmoil in the world.

England was all right. She was holding more than her own in commerce. Of course there were a few who said Lord Salisbury was mad for ceding Heligoland to the Germans. Didn't he know what the Germans were up to? They were out to challenge our naval supremacy.

Nonsense, nonsense. England ruled the waves and had always ruled the waves and would continue to do so as long as God managed the tides.

And women? Women were causing a ripple here and there. It was said that in London and in one or two big cities they had clubs, just like the men. Of course in general, few people believed this, but what was believed, and with concern in some quarters, was that more women were reading, and not only those in the middle classes. Why, it was even understood that women from the working class, the upper part of it, of course, were asking for books by George Eliot, but so ignorant were they that they thought the author was a man. Dickens, of course, was more commonly read, but not so Mrs Gaskell, or Trollope, and Thackeray wasn't to the working-class taste; too sarky was Thackeray, he took the mickey. As for John Stuart Mill; if they had heard of his 'Subjection of Woman' the majority would have scorned to read it because they knew all about it, they lived it. Who knew better than they about the subjection of women.

But neither the events of the world nor the struggles of the working class towards emancipation touched Brook House and its inmates during these years. Mrs Dan Bensham occupied herself mostly with reading the works of the Brontë sisters, never Dickens or Mrs Gaskell. For poetry, she preferred Byron to Wordsworth, and sometimes she read Donne, but only those poems written in his early years when his love emanated from nature and not from the spirit.

Dan's taste in literature went much wider. He read anything and everything in the spare time allowed him. Sometimes the gaslight was still burning in the spare room at one in the morning. These were the times when he would return home late, or when Barbara felt indisposed, and she had been feeling indisposed more frequently of late.

However, Dan was not always reading when the light was on at one o'clock in the morning. Often he was sitting propped up in bed, his hands behind his head, staring before him, and always when he sat thus he was reviewing the past years.

There was a short period about three years ago when he had imagined that Barbara was really beginning to love him. At long last he felt he had won through, for during this time she had shown him a tenderness and a consideration that had been lacking in her feelings before. But this period had come to an end; exactly when he could not pin-point, it had just seemed to trail off. There had been a cooling down until for the past year, there had been practically nothing between them but polite, everyday chit-chat: the weather, how the business was going, the children . . . and Ben, particularly Ben.

Ben was a handful. He was a great source of irritation to Barbara. She told Dan frequently that something must be done about Ben. To this he answered again and again, 'I'm not sending him away to school. I've told you, they are not going to be separated; where one goes they all go.'

Dan longed to tell her that the root of Ben's trouble lay with her. She had never taken to the child because he was a daily reminder of the source from where she had sprung.

As the boy grew older the intruding streak of hair to the side of his head grew wider. It had earned him the name of 'piebald' at school, and the nickname had taught him to fight. Hardly a week passed but he came home with the scars of battle on him. He never needed to relate his exploits, this was done for him by his adoring brothers. He was by far the biggest of the three, he was by far the best looking of the three, he was by far the most intelligent of the three, and he was the least happy of the three.

Dan worried about Ben and endeavoured whenever possible to give him his attention, but this he knew was not enough to fill the void in the boy. He often wondered how his three sons would have fared if it hadn't been for the kindness and attention of Ruthie.

Ruthie, he considered, was a godsend, but he knew he stood alone in his opinion of her, for Barbara would have dismissed her long ago had she not been aware that the girl took from her shoulders practically all the responsibility of rearing the boys. Moreover, Dan knew that if Ruthie were to go there would be a void in his own life, for never did he come in late at night, cold, sometimes tight, and nearly always tired, but there she was in the kitchen, her round, plump, comfortable young body giving off a mother feeling, her round cheery face smiling, her round keen eyes, that were full of an alert intelligence, prying into him and anticipating his needs.

That her wisdom was put over in cliches, not at times unmixed with strong language that would have brought Barbara's hackles rising had she heard it, appeared all the more true to him. He once said to her, 'You know, Ruthie, at times you appear like my mother to me,' and this had caused her to throw her head back and laugh and say, 'My God! sir, if I was, that would have beaten the immaculate conception, a bloody miracle wouldn't have been in it, 'cos you must have been all of twelve or more when I was born, add another sixteen on to that afore I could have had you. Lor! I don't think elephants take that long.'

Often now he found he wanted to talk seriously to her, confide in her; for, being Ruthie, she knew quite well how the situation upstairs stood. But no, he told himself, this would never do. He must never discuss Barbara, particularly with a servant, it was unthinkable. Yet he wanted to discuss her with someone.

He had thought of going to Brigie. Two or three years ago he would have, but since his dad died Brigie had changed. He had never imagined that the loss of his father would have affected her so; she had grown old of a sudden, and odd in a way. He understood she scarcely left the Hall or grounds except to go and visit Katie. She and Katie had become very close, likely because of the child, he thought. Brigie was fond of it. She never came into Newcastle now to visit them.

On the few times they had taken the children to see her, she had welcomed them warmly.... Or had she? He had imagined she was pleased to see the children and himself but not Barbara. Yet how could that be, because Barbara had been the king-pin of her life for so long? For her the sun had revolved around Barbara. Yet there was something, something he couldn't put his finger on. There were a number of things he couldn't put his finger on. At times he felt he was living outside a locked and barred house, and there was no visible means of entry....

He had been suffering from toothache for the past week and although he wouldn't admit it to himself he was afraid to go to the dentist, but so bad did the pain become on this particular Friday that he was forced to leave his office and go and seek relief. The tooth was difficult to extract and when it finally came out he reckoned that the cure was infinitely worse than the disease.

Getting into a cab he went back to the warehouse, saw his manager and told him he was going home for the rest of the day. His manager, Alec Stenhouse, was a capable, reliable man, and an outspoken, thick-tongued northerner. 'Best thing, sir, best thing,' he said. 'An' my advice to you is to have a bellyful of whisky and knock yourself out. I've only been to them dentists once and I'm tellin' you I'd rather have a leg off than another out. An' you stay home a day or two, there'll be nowt perish here. And if you ask me, you need a change, for you've been goin' around lately more like a wet week-end than a dry Sunday.'

Before the cab reached home Dan had decided he would take Stenhouse's advice and go to bed with a bellyful of whisky.

When he entered the house, however, he was met not with concern and sympathy but with consternation among all those present. Ada Howlett and Betty Rowe were both in the hall, as were Jonathan and Harry, who on the sight of their father both rushed to him, crying, 'Oh! Papa, Papa, Ben has run away.' As they clutched his arms he opened his swollen lips and, looking at the two girls, said, 'What's this? What's all this about?'

'Well, sir' – Ada Howlett dropped her voice to a conspiratorial whisper as she leant towards him – 'there's been ructions on, sir, ructions. The mistress wouldn't take Ben with her for a walk. He kept on and on, an' she lost her temper and slapped him and sent him up to the nursery. Then she went out for her walk like she does, sir, an' then a short while ago Ruthie came runnin' downstairs asking where Master Ben was. And none of us knew. We ... we've looked all around the garden, sir, an' up and down the road. ... Oh, an' look at your face, sir. Eeh! they've made a mess of you. ...'

'Ben's gone. He's run away, Papa.'

Dan put his hand on Jonathan's shoulder and turned him about towards the stairs as he said to Ada, 'Where's Ruth now?'

'She's out lookin', sir. Run ... run like a hare she did. Betty here says he couldn't have gone down the drive, sir, for she was in the backyard bath-bricking the window sills and such, and she could see the drive. Couldn't you, Betty?'

'Aye, sir. Yes, sir.' Betty bobbed as she spoke. 'He didn't go out that way, sir. I was in the yard all the time.'

'It's my opinion, sir,' said Ada now with authority, 'that he went down the garden an' climbed the railin's into the field.'

Dan now looked at Harry and said, 'Go upstairs with Jonathan and stay there until I come back.'

'Couldn't we look, Papa?' asked Harry.

'No, no. Stay upstairs so at least we'll know where you are. Now do what you're told, go on.' He pushed them both forward, then put his hand up to his face, and Ada said again, 'Eeh! they have made a mess of you, sir. You got it out then, sir.'

'Yes, Ada,' he said flatly, 'I got it out.' He turned from her and went across the hall and into the kitchen, where the cook was standing at the table making pastry. She looked up as he came towards her, and she said, 'He's a lad, sir. Lads always go off on their own. I don't know what the fuss is all about. He's likely gone up to the wood. They were all up there last week on the quiet, although the mistress forbade them the place 'cos of tramps 'n things. But lads are lads all the world over. Oh, you've had your tooth out, sir?'

He made no answer, merely nodded his head.

'By! your face's in a mess, sir. I wouldn't bother me head goin' out after him sir; as I said, lads are lads. Why, mine have gone off for days on end. They'll come back when they're hungry, that's what I say. Their bellies if nothin' else pull them back home.'

He went out of the kitchen, across the yard, and through the privet-arch that led into the garden.

The garden was long and narrow. Half its length was covered with lawns and rose beds, and was bordered by a rose trellis; beyond was a section given over to vegetables, and further on was a rough piece of ground where the children played. There was an old summer-house standing to one side, and the tiny stream cut across the opposite corner of the land, and the boundary was bordered by a four-foot wooden fence.

It was as he passed through the trellis arch, thick now with the tangle of roses, that he saw Ruth. She had just climbed the fence and was now pulling Ben over. Ben's head was down and he was crying.

He went to raise his hand and shout when he saw Ruth put her arm around the boy's shoulder and lead him into the summer-house and close the door. Swiftly now he hurried down the path between the high fronds of staked beans and stepped on to the rough grass, only to stop when he came within a few feet of the summer-house door. Something Ruth was saying brought him to a standstill: 'You never saw nobody kissin' anybody, d'you hear? You were dreamin'.'

Ben's voice, high and angry answered, 'I did, I did. I tell you I did. And she never kisses me, never, not once. She kisses Jonathan, and sometimes Harry, but never me, never, never. She never kisses me. . . .'

The voice was cut off as if it had been smothered; and it had been smothered.

Ruth had pulled the child to her. Burying his face between her breasts, she pressed his head into her as she said, 'Listen, Ben. Now listen to me.' She paused a moment, bit tightly down on her lip, looked round at the small space of the summer-house which was littered with the children's toys, then pushing him from her none too gently, she gripped him by the shoulders and squatted down on her hunkers till her face was level with his, and she said to him, slowly and clearly, 'Now listen to me, you hear me, Ben Bensham. Now pin your ears back an' listen ... you've got to forget what you thought you saw....'

'But I....'

'Listen, I tell you, just listen. Now I'm gonna ask you a question. Do you want to lose your ma, your mother? Do you? Do you want to lose her? Do you want her to go away an' for you to never see her again? Now answer me, do you?'

The boy stared back at her, his eyes black and deep with a pain he could not understand, and Ruth went on, 'Well, I'm tellin' you, you open your mouth and go round shoutin' about what you think you saw in the wood, an' that'll be the finish, you won't see your mother ever again. She'll go; she'll leave this house an' she'll go. And what's more, and now I'm telling you this straight an' from the horse's mouth, an' no eehing or awing about it, if she goes I go an' all. Now, now just think on that. I'll leave the lot of you. An' where would you be then? You'd have somebody like Ada or Betty, an' God help you. So I'm tellin' you, you breathe one word of what you said to me, open your big mouth an' repeat just one word to either Jonathan or Harry or' – she paused – 'anybody else in the whole wide world an' boy, you'll be on your own, a shipwrecked sailor'll not be in it. You know the story of Sinbad the Sailor? Well, I'm tellin' you, he'll be having it cushy compared to you and the rest of them 'cos I'll be gone like the divil out of hell. ... Well, there it is, it's up to you.'

'But ... but Ruthie, I ... I saw Mama, I tell you I saw Mama with a strange gentleman, and she kept calling him Michael, Mich....'

'All right, all right!' Ruthie swung round from him and made for the door. 'You want trouble? Well, Benjamin Bensham, let me tell you, lad, you're goin' to get it. Just say that once more to anybody else and you'll bring the world about your shoulders.'

She swung round again and almost dived at him, and pulling him into her arms she hugged him to her, saying, 'There now, there now, don't cry. 'Tisn't like you, 'tisn't like you to cry. You're the big fellow, Ben, the big fellow, you're twice the size of the other two, an' you could buy them at one end of the street and sell them at t'other. You're clever, Ben, you've got it up top, so try to understand. Something's happened. All right, all right, I'll give you that, something happened an' you saw it. I believe you, but if you speak one word about it you'll create murder, you will that. I know it in me bones, you'll create murder.'

She held him close in silence for a time; then looking into his face

566

again she said, 'Promise me on your honour – Cross your heart. Go on, cross your heart an' swear you won't say a word. . . . Aw, that's it, that's it. Now we know where we stand. This is just atween you and me, eh? Just atween you and me, the two of us, a sort of secret, eh? 'Cos . . . 'cos if we let it out your da . . . father would get hurt, an' badly, and of course your mother . . . Eeh! she'd get into big trouble.' Her voice trailed off as she thought, An' the divil's cure to her for she deserves her nose rubbed in the clarts, the bitch, the upstart bitch that she is. An' if it wasn't for him I'd let the lad yell his head off. I would that. But it would finish himself if he knew, the fool of a man that he is. Why do the likes of her get the likes of him. They have it all ways women like her.

Again she made for the door but absent-mindedly now, and when she reached it she turned to the boy and said, 'Give me a few minutes' start, then come up to the house. Just walk in as if you'd been out for a dander, an' I'll go for you like I usually do, you know; it'll make it all natural like. When I ask you where you've been just say you were rabbitin'. An' afore you come up swill your face in the rain bucket round the corner; come up fresh like an' jaunty, eh?'

He nodded slowly at her, sniffed, took the remaining tears from the end of his nose with the side of his finger, then watched her go.

She was no sooner outside and had closed the door behind her when she stopped, her mouth agape. A man was disappearing between the bean canes, and it wasn't old Rogers for it wasn't his day for the garden. And anyway she couldn't mistake that figure, although what he was doing here at half past three in the afternoon God knew. And God help her if he had been anywhere near the summer-house.

This was a nice kettle of fish. The mistress was a trollop that's what she was, a trollop. For some time now she had wondered about her walks, wondered what drove her out almost every Friday, rain, hail or snow. The weather had to be very bad before she didn't take her trot on a Friday afternoon. How long had she been taking her Friday afternoon walks? Dear God! it must have been years. But then she walked at other times an' all. Aye, but only if it was fine. And so nobody had twigged. Well, who would? She wasn't painted like a whore.

There were whores all over Newcastle, nobody but a blind and deaf saint could miss them. But they were working-class whores, not ladies. By God! the next time she went for her she'd have to put a tight rein on herself not to turn on her and give her a mouthful.

When she went into the kitchen the cook said, 'The master's back.'

'Is he? What's brought him at this time of day?'

'He's had a tooth out, he's got a face like a suet puddin. He's gone out lookin' for the boy.'

'Oh, that boy! We're wastin' our time runnin' about like loonies; he'll come back when he's hungry.'

'The very words I said to the master, the very words; his empty belly 'll bring him back.'

'Is . . . is the mistress in?'

'No, she's not back from her walk yet. An' it's to be hoped that Master Ben's in afore she is, or he's likely to get another skelpin'. And serve him well right; he's a young rip is that 'un.'

When she reached the hall she saw Ada Howlett standing by the front door, and Ada turned to her and said, 'The master's home. He's got toothache. He went scootin' down the garden looking for that imp, then he came in like the divil in a gale of wind an' went as quickly out again. But here he's comin' back again. Likely his face is givin' him gyp.' She turned from the door and went towards the dining room, saying, 'I don't suppose he'll be able to eat, but since he's home she'll want the dinner put forward.'

Standing at the foot of the stairs, Ruth had planned in her mind what she was going to say to him. 'I shouldn't worry, sir,' she was going to say; 'he'll be back, he likes to cause a sensation does Master Ben.' But she said nothing. She looked at his face as he came through the door. True, one cheek was swollen and his mouth was out of shape, but having a tooth out could never have brought that look into his eyes. He looked wild . . . mad, out of his mind. Her breath caught in her throat as she thought, God Almighty! he must have heard every word. If he'd been outside the summer-house he could have heard it all, 'cos me voice is like a corn-crake.

When he came up to her and stopped at the foot of the stairs and stared into her face for a moment before going on up them with never a word, she knew without doubt there were now three in the secret, and if she knew anything it wouldn't remain a secret for much longer.

He had almost reached the top of the stairs before she moved, and he was opening his bedroom door when she called softly from the stairhead, 'Sir! Sir!' When she reached him he was in the room, the door in his hand, and he turned and looked at her as she muttered below her breath, 'Oh sir. Sir.' He blinked as if trying to get her into focus; then he lifted his hand and pushed her away and banged the door.

With the flat of his hands now against it and his two arms stretched taut he stood as if about to do an exercise. The next minute he had pulled the door open again, his head down as if he were about to run but he stopped when he saw Ruth still standing on the landing.

'Whisky,' he said. 'Bring me the decanter and . . . and a glass.'

'Yes, sir. Yes, sir.'

She ran down the stairs, and returned within a matter of minutes, and went straight into his room without knocking and placed the decanter and the glass on a side table. Then looking at him where he was standing now, his back to her, gazing out of the window, she said softly, 'I . . . I would lie meself down if I were you, sir.'

He didn't answer until she moved; then he turned and said, 'Tell . . . tell your mistress I' – he stopped, blinked, gulped, then ended, 'I have gone to bed with' – he patted his cheek.

'Yes, sir. Yes, sir, I'll do that. I will, I'll do that.' She nodded at him as she backed away, then she went out and closed the door gently after her.

It was more than half an hour later when Barbara entered the house and was informed by Ada that the master had come home with a bad face-ache after having a tooth out and had gone to bed. She said nothing about Ben's escapade; Ruth had warned her to keep her mouth shut. Ruth Foggety, Ada knew, as also did the cook and, of course, Betty, had a standing in the house and the ear of the master, if not the liking of the mistress, who put up with her merely because she could manage the tribe in the nursery. The mistress might rule the house but Ruth Foggety was the power on the top floor.

Barbara went straight to her room and took off her outdoor things. But before leaving the room to go and see how Dan was she stood thinking for a moment. She regretted having been out when he came home; but he had never been home in the afternoon for years, not on a week-day at any rate. She remembered vividly the last time he had appeared unexpectedly in the house in the afternoon. It was on the day she had met Michael in the wood for the first time.

She went out and across the landing and tapped on his door, then gently opened it. She saw that he was lying on his side; on closer inspection she imagined he was asleep and had been helped there by a generous dose of whisky – she had filled the decanter herself that very morning.

She stood looking down at him. His face was very swollen, his mouth distorted. He had a nice shaped mouth, wide, the lips full, yet she had never been able to feel its contact without experiencing a slight revulsion, whereas Michael's mouth. . . . She mustn't stand here thinking such things. Yet she couldn't help but make comparisons for her body was still warm from Michael's embraces.

She wondered she had not become pregnant. She told herself she must remember this as a possibility and not spurn Dan's advances completely. How long was it since he had been in her bed? Eight weeks? Ten weeks? She must allow him there again. She didn't know how she'd be able to suffer it but that was another of the penalties she must pay for Michael. She was already paying through Brigie.

She had never imagined Brigie's displeasure would have affected her so much. Nowadays Brigie looked at her as if she despised her, as she likely did. Brigie's look made her feel unclean, and she wasn't unclean. In going to Michael she was fulfilling a function that but for Brigie's interference in the first place would have been her natural right.

She moved slowly away from the bed and out of the room. She felt tired, she would like to go to bed herself at this moment, and if she did she knew she would fall into a deep, deep relaxed sleep. She wanted to sleep in the wood; oh, how she had wanted to go to sleep in Michael's arms. They had found a secluded spot in the depth of a thicket, and even when the few frequenters of the wood passed near them they could not see them, and the undergrowth of leaves and twigs always heralded anyone's approach.

Their meeting today had been ecstatic for they hadn't met for three weeks. Last Friday and the Friday before that he had been unable to come, and she had felt desolate. The reason, he said, was that Hannah had been very ill. She had caught a fever and at one time he had despaired of her life, but now she was out of danger and no protests had been made by the other two when he proposed his fishing trip, for he had sat up the best part of a fortnight with the child.

She had suggested today that it might be expedient in the future if they were to find some little place in an isolated spot that they could rent. She did not tell him that with this in mind she had made a friend of a Mrs Turner, whom she had met casually at the dressmaker's. She had cultivated Mrs Turner's acquaintance when she had heard that the lady had a cottage, lying on the outskirts of Hexham which she let to summer visitors. She was quite entitled to a day out and the journey from Newcastle would be quite simple. It might not be so simple from Michael's end but nevertheless she knew he would undertake it.

Oh, how she wanted a long, long day with Michael, a long day that she could turn into a long night. How wonderful would have been their life together if they had married, something beautiful, exquisite, exciting. He had merely to put his lips on hers and her body would respond immediately. Her passion not only equalled his but went beyond it; she thought of it as giving completely of herself.

Following her line of duty, she now went up into the nursery and there found Ben in the sulks. He would not speak to her, not even raise his head to look at her because she had refused to allow him to accompany her on the walk. Because she felt happy she acted gently towards him, and put her hand on his shoulder and said softly, 'I'm sorry, I'm sorry my dear. Tomorrow; I promise you we'll go for a walk tomorrow.'

When he shrugged his shoulder from her touch and turned his head still further away she exclaimed sharply, 'Now you're acting childishly, like a little girl.'

She was actually startled by the way he turned on her. His head came up as his body swung round and brought him to his feet, and his face scarlet and his lips trembling, he shouted at her, 'I don't want to come tomorrow, I don't want to come with you tomorrow or any time. I don't! I don't!'

'That is enough, Ben. You are being rude; I shall tell your father.'

When Ruth hurried from the other room and made towards Ben, she said to her, 'See that he goes to bed, and at once. And . . . and don't give him any pudding with his meal. Now that is an order; he's not to have any pudding with his meal.'

Ruth looked up at her mistress. Her eyes unblinking, she stared at her until Barbara said, 'What is it? What do you wish to say?'

'Nothin,' madam.'

'Well, if you don't wish to say anything I will thank you to take that expression off your face when you are looking at me.'

When the girl continued to stare at her in the same fashion she found herself blinking. She couldn't put a name to the look on the girl's face; she was, she supposed, telling her, in the only way she dared, that she disapproved of her slapping Benjamin. At this moment she had the desire to slap her as well. When people annoyed her she always wanted to strike out at them. It was an urge she had to conquer and to remind herself frequently that her present way of life was the result of just one such urge. Nevertheless she would dearly love to be rid of this girl. But she was too valuable in her services, and it had to be admitted that she cared for the children.

She turned about and went into the day nursery where Jonathan and Harry were sitting at a table drawing, and with no small art on Jonathan's part.

They both looked up as she came towards them and said, 'Hello, Mama.'

'Hello, dears.' She touched first one head and then the other. 'What are you drawing?'

'I'm drawing a ship,' Harry said.

'Look what I've done.' Jonathan held up the block to her and she exclaimed, 'Why! that's splendid. I . . . I seem to know the face, who is it?'

'Mr Purvis.'

'Of course, of course, Mr Purvis.' She put her head down until her chin was resting on Jonathan's hair and she laughed gently as she said, 'Poor Mr Purvis, with his drooping eye. You must never let him see it.'

'His lid twitches when he gets excited,' put in Harry.

'And he sniffs,' said Jonathan. 'Like this.' And when he demonstrated, Barbara, assuming disgust, said, 'Oh dear. Oh dear. How dreadful.' Then she stooped and kissed first one and then the other before saying, 'Be good boys now,' which was her usual form of farewell.

As she made to go Jonathan asked, 'Will you come and see us in bed, Mama?'

'Yes, yes, I'll be up later.'

The moment Barbara left the nursery floor, Ruth came into the day room and, going to the table, she said, 'Good lads,' and they looked up at her and laughed. And when Harry, pulling a face, said, 'We're going to share our pudding with Ben, we heard Mama,' she put a hand on each head and rumpled their hair, and as they laughed together she said, 'You'll do, the pair of you. Go on in now and cheer him up. . . .'

Barbara looked in on Dan again about nine o'clock. He was still asleep. She went to her room and by ten o'clock she too was asleep.

It was around this time that Dan awoke. His head was bursting; his mouth was full of blood and tasted vile. His face was swollen even more now, and his lips were so stiff he could scarcely move them.

Painfully he pulled himself up in the bed. The gas mantle was turned down low; someone had been in and lit it. He tried to collect his thoughts. Something awful had happened, something dreadful. Life had exploded, but how? Why? He couldn't think. The pain in his head and jaw was excruciating. He wanted a drink. He turned his head slowly and looked towards the table. The decanter was still there, but it wasn't that kind of a drink he wanted; it was a hot drink, something warm and soothing.

God! what had happened to him? He brought his legs over the side of the bed and as they touched the floor he remembered; not that the dentist had made four attempts before he got his tooth out and then had broken it in the process, but that his son had seen his mother kissing another man in the wood.

He remembered too that she had come into the room and he had feigned sleep and had only just stopped himself from springing up and grabbing her by the throat and choking her until he should feel her life slowly ebb away, as his had done this afternoon when he stood outside the summer-house and listened to a servant remonstrating with his son to keep his silence and so save the boy from losing a mother and the husband from losing a wife.

But he had lost his wife, that is if he had ever had a wife. Yes, that was the question, if he had ever had a wife. For her he had been but the means of escape. And let him face it; he had known what he was taking on, and he had been glad of the chance to take it on because he

572

imagined that no man could love a woman as he did her, and as he had done from a very young boy, and in the end fail to gain her love in return. Love bred love. . . . But not in this case. . . . Annie of Tharaw. He'd never sing *Annie of Tharaw* again.

How long had it been going on? Oh, a long time. Yes, yes, a long time; definitely since they came to live here, and that was almost four years ago. She had hoodwinked him all this time. She had lain in his own arms, let him love her, when perhaps that very day, that very afternoon, during her *walk*, she had lain with him the big fellow, the blond farmer. . . . God Almighty! if only he had him here. As big as he was, as strong as he was, he'd drive a knife into him. It was a pity he didn't possess a gun. But he could hire one and go to the farm tomorrow and shoot the swine dead. . . . That's if he were that kind of a man; but he wasn't that kind of man, was he? No, he was the kind of man who was made weak through love.

Well, was he just going to sit back and take it?

What would happen if he brought it into the open?

He would lose her. She would go to Radlet like a homing pigeon. And he couldn't bear the thought of that, could he?

No, no, anything but that. He dropped his aching head into his hands. Why hadn't she left him? Was it because of concern for him, or was it because of the children?

Whatever had stopped her from going to Radlet had been through concern of some kind; she hadn't been callous enough just to walk out and leave them.

But there was another side to it. Perhaps Radlet was obliged to stay where he was; perhaps his conscience would not allow him to leave the wife whom Barbara had crippled, nor his mother who doted on him, nor his daughter, for he understood he had a daughter.

He rose from the bed and staggered to the door and opened it. The landing was dimly lit. He looked across it towards the door of the room that was rightly his, and there swept over him a feeling of such rage that his mental and physical pain was blotted out. For a moment he was his father and raging against duplicity and the fact that he was being made a cuckold.

He had never held himself in high esteem, he was aware that he possessed no exceptional talents, he was the offspring of ordinary parents, and had his father not made money he would likely have married an ordinary woman of his own class. But his father had made money, and had bought a mansion, and had sent his sons to a school where they had learned the manners of those who lived in mansions; yet he knew that all he had learned merely formed a cloak, a façade, to cover his real self, for all the education in the world could not penetrate a man's real being, the being that was the core of him. He also realized that in spite of his rage there wasn't enough of his father in him to burst open the door and drag her from the bed, and leave his mark on her with his fist. He only wished there was, for at least then he would have added to his meagre store of self respect.

Although he was sober his step was that of a drunken man as he went down the stairs, across the hall and into the kitchen.

The light was still on and Ruth was sitting by the table.

She'd had her head down on her arms until the door opened; now she raised it, peered towards him and blinked the sleep out of her eyes; then she was on her feet, saying. 'Oh my! sir. My! look at that face. Sit yourself down.'

She pulled a chair forward, and he gripped its back and lowered himself onto it. Then putting an elbow on the table he rested his brow on his hand.

'You want a drink, something hot? Hot milk? That's it, hot milk.'

'No.' He shook his head. Then, his lips moving stiffly, he said, 'Coffee, black, strong.'

She hurried from one side of the kitchen to the other, and no more words were spoken until she placed the steaming cup of coffee, not on the table, but into his hand, and as if she were dealing with a very old man, or a young child, she guided his other hand towards the handle, saying softly, 'Drink it up now. Drink it up.'

Not only was the coffee too hot for his tender mouth but he found he couldn't open his lips wide enough to take the cup. Swiftly now she took it from his hands and, pouring some of the coffee into the saucer, she blew on it, then held it to his mouth, and he sipped at it, then gulped, and in that way he finished the cupful.

The next thing she did was to bring a bowl of hot water to the table and dip in it a flannel cloth, which she wrang out, waved in the air for a moment, then gently applied to the side of his face.

As the soothing warmth penetrated his skin he gave a small sigh and relaxed against the back of the chair.

'That better?' Again and again she wrang out the cloth; then renewed the water and continued with the applications.

After a while he put out his hand and, his lips moving easier now, he muttered, 'Thanks. Enough for ... for the time being. Thanks.'

As she went to the sink and emptied the dish and hung up the flannel she talked. 'By! whoever did that job on you the day wants to go back and learn his trade. I've never seen anything like it in me life. You look for all the world as if you'd been hit by a crane. If he had used a grapple on you he couldn't have done more damage. They say salt and water's a good thing, hot salt and water. I'd keep washing it out, sir.' She came to the table now and, bending down to him, she said, 'If I made you some hot toddy do you think you could manage it?'

He shook his head.

Slowly she slid down into the chair opposite to him and, her forearms on the table and her hands joined, she looked at him sadly before saying, 'You should be in bed, sir.'

He raised his head. 'I've been in bed, Ruth.' The words came out of the side of his mouth.

'You want to go back again, sir, and stay there for a day or so.'

They stared at each other for fully a minute; and then, turning from her, he dropped his face into his hands and although he felt he was sinking to the bottom of self abasement he could not still the rising tide of tears that swept up through his body and gathered in his throat before pouring from his eyes, nose and mouth.

He had cried when his mother died and he had cried in private but with joy when his sons were born, and he had cried at the loss of his father, but this was crying such as he had never experienced before. It was a tidal wave of anguish which swept away the remains of his self-respect and his manhood.

When he felt Ruth's arms going about him he did not thrust them off but turned towards her and held on to her, and, his face pressed between her young breasts, he tried to quell the avalanche that had been let loose in him.

'There now. There now. Aw, me dear, me dear, let it out, let it out, It'll ease you.' She moved her hand over his hair and went on talking as if it were one of the boys she was holding. 'Don't mind nothin'; you'll be all right. There now. There now.'

By the time his crying eased, the dampness had penetrated through her cotton dress and her shift. When he finally raised his head he gazed up at her and muttered, 'I'm ashamed, Ruthie, I'm ashamed.'

'What of?' Her voice was a trembling whisper now. 'You've got nothin' to be ashamed of.' She did not add 'sir'. 'No' – she shook her head – 'you've got nothin' in the wide world to be ashamed of. Your only trouble is you're too good. But don't worry, you'll come out on top, you'll see. D'you want my advice?'

His silence was his answer and she said, softly, tentatively, 'Let things lie. You can do no good by causing a rumpus. There . . . there's the boys to think of. And given time who knows but that she'll come to her senses.'

He withdrew his arms from her waist but, still looking at her, he murmured, 'You're a great comfort, Ruthie; you always have been. It'll be a lucky man who gets you.'

'Huh!' She turned abruptly from him and went to the stove, and it was as if there had been no emotional scene as she said lightly, 'Lucky, you say? I only hope he agrees with you for I'm likely to lead him a hell of a life. I'm one for me own way, an' as stubborn as an Irish donkey.'

575

There was a pause before she ended, flatly, 'I'm goin' to fill you a hot water bottle, then you're going to bed.'

After a moment, while he sat with his head bowed looking at his joined hands pressed hard down on his knees, he made a statement. 'You think me a poor specimen, don't you?' he said.

When she made no answer he lifted his head slowly. She was over by the sink; she had her back to him and some seconds passed before she turned around. She did not move but she looked at him across the space, and then she said, 'I think you're the finest gentleman I've ever met in me life, or I'm ever likely to, an' I'll be content to serve you as long as you want me, an' in any way you want me. Any way....'

10

I T WAS IN FEBRUARY 1894 that Michael rented the cottage
from Mrs Turner, at least he supplied the money, but it was rented
under the name of Mrs Bensham. Barbara was greatly excited this
morning and had difficulty in containing it. At breakfast she had
informed Dan that tomorrow she was going on a shopping expedition
with Mrs Turner.

He raised his eyes and looked at her for a moment and said, 'Oh!'
while he continued to stare at her. His reaction was slightly disconcerting; he had been disconcerting in many ways of late. He was drinking
more heavily than he had done before but it hadn't caused him to
make extra demands on her; in fact, it was months since he had been to
her room. He hadn't seemed himself following the tooth extraction;
he had been in bed for a week and she'd had to call the doctor when a
secondary bleeding occurred from his gums. It was from then that he
had changed. He appeared older, and at times very strange.

More than once it had occurred to her that he might have knowledge of what was going on. But then she waved the idea aside;
knowing Dan as he was, he wouldn't be able to keep that to himself,
he would have brought it into the open and begged her to give
up Michael; or perhaps he would have reacted like his father might
have done and sworn and cursed and threatened. But one thing
she was certain of, he would not have ignored the matter and kept
quiet.

Yet there was something. But whatever it was it didn't trouble her
much. She did her duty, she ran the house well, and saw that the
children were looked after, and she attended to their schooling,
inasmuch as she went to see the headmaster when there were any
complaints about Ben and his behaviour.

Ben was a constant worry; he caused her more concern than Dan
did. Whereas she saw Dan only at meals, twice a day, breakfast, and
dinner in the evening, and not always then, the children were home

577

from four o'clock in the afternoon, and, of course, she had them on top of her all the time during the holidays.

It was on this particular morning as she said good-bye to them in the hall that she noticed the shape of Ruth Foggety's stomach. The girl had her hands on her hood, pulling it over her head, her cloak was open. Instead of her starched apron forming the usual slight mound over her print dress, Barbara's astonished gaze took in the particular bulge, and immediately she connected it with the girl being sick. She remembered Harry telling her that Ruthie was sick. She recalled the incident vividly because he hadn't used the word sick, he had said 'thrown up,' and she had rebuked him sternly. And she had thought yet again, That girl, how can one expect them to speak correct English listening to that. Thrown up, indeed!

Now, as indignation flooded her, she thought, The chit's pregnant. But I'm not surprised. Not at all, not at all. Really! Just wait till she comes back, just wait.

Immediately Ruth entered the house after seeing the children to school, Ada gave her the message that the mistress wanted to see her in the morning room, and at this they exchanged a knowing look. Then Ruth, taking off her hooded cloak handed it to Ada, saying softly, 'Stick it in the kitchen for me for a minute, will you?' after which she smoothed her hands slowly down over her apron, went towards the morning room, knocked on the door and when the order came for her to enter she went in.

Barbara was standing in front of the china cabinet rearranging a set of figurines. She carefully closed the glass doors before she turned to face 'that girl', as she had always thought of her, then seating herself in a straight-backed chair she laid one hand over the other, palm upwards on her lap before she said sternly, 'Well! have you anything to tell me?'

'What about, ma'am?'

'Don't prevaricate, girl. You're in a certain condition, aren't you?'

'If you put it that way, yes, ma'am.'

The nerve of the creature, the insolence. If she put it that way! Her voice was touched with her anger as she said, 'Don't be insolent, girl. And remember whom you're talking to.'

'I do, ma'am.'

Barbara rose to her feet. She knew from the heat of her face that her whole complexion had turned red. She had the greatest desire to strike the creature.

'You know you will have to leave?'

There was no response from Ruth, but she held Barbara's eyes and waited for her to speak again.

'You understand what I'm saying to you, girl?'

'I understand well enough, ma'am.'

'The man, is ... is he going to marry you?'

'I should hardly think so, ma'am.'

Really! Really! She said now, 'I'll allow you to stay until the end of the week, by which time I will have replaced you. This will also give you sufficient time to make fresh arrangements.'

The girl stared at her, her round eyes seeming to bore into her, and then she said in an even tone, 'As you say, ma'am, as you say,' and with that she turned on her heel and walked out.

It was on the point of Barbara's tongue to call her back and tell her to stand there until she gave her leave to go, but instead she drew in a deep breath, sat down again and repeated, 'I should hardly think so, ma'am.'

The similarity of their situations did not strike her. She herself was a married woman, circumspect in all her doings except in one thing; even about this she had been most discreet. That girl had always annoyed her; she'd be glad to see the back of her. But now here she was faced with another problem: a new girl would need supervision for some time to come, and what was more, with the departure of that brazen piece she would have more trouble with Ben, because the boy, and she had to admit this, would take no notice of anyone but the girl. Well, from now on he would have to be brought into line, and if he couldn't be handled at home she would insist, really insist, that Dan send him away to school, and to one noted for its discipline, for if ever a child needed discipline he did.

She was glad that she had told the girl she could remain until the end of the week, otherwise she doubted if she would have been able to get away tomorrow, and she must get away tomorrow.

She rose to her feet. The girl had said it wasn't likely she could marry the man. This must mean he was already married. He was likely some friend of that awful man, her father. What would he say when he knew? Her jaw dropped slightly when she realized that he must know already, although he no longer came to collect her wages; this procedure had ceased over a year ago when he had hurt his foot in the docks; instead, she returned home on her half-day once a fortnight.

Well, she'd return home for good at the end of the week, on this she was determined. This was one thing Dan could not overlook. He had been on the girl's side since she had first come here, and instead of chiding her for the way she answered back he laughed and called her cute. She wondered if he would put her present condition down to cuteness?

When Dan came home at six o'clock he followed his usual procedure. He went to his room and washed himself, changed his coat, then went on up to the nursery where he talked with the boys, sometimes for ten minutes, sometimes for as long as half an hour. Afterwards he came downstairs and went straight into the dining room. The meal was set for seven o'clock; supper, cook called it, Barbara gave it the name of dinner.

Barbara was already in the dining room when he arrived. He inclined his head towards her and, as was also his rule of late, he did not address her first.

As she took her place at the table he went to the sideboard and poured himself out a drink which he threw off in one draught.

As the door opened and Ada entered carrying a tray, with Betty behind her carrying another, he took his seat at the table. It was then that Barbara said, 'It has been a dreadful day, so cold.'

'Yes, yes, very cold.'

'Have you been busy?'

'About the same as usual.'

'I ordered Scotch broth, I thought it would be warming tonight.'

'Scotch broth? Yes, yes; it's always warming, Scotch broth.'

When the plates of soup were put before them, they both began to eat, and by the time Ada had arranged the main course on the table they had finished their soup. She had placed the joint of lamb before the master and the three vegetable dishes before the mistress. As she took the soup plates away Barbara said to her, 'Thank you, Ada; we'll manage.'

'Will I bring the iced pudding on to the table or will I leave it on the sideboard, ma'am?'

'Leave it on the sideboard, Ada, thank you.'

Alone once more, they made no pretence at conversation. When the main course was finished, Dan, rising from the table, muttered a mumbled excuse, and she said to him, 'Don't you want any pudding?' and to this he answered, 'No. No, thanks.'

Her indignation rose when she saw that he was going to leave the room, leave her at the table with the meal unfinished. She said sharply, 'I want to speak to you.'

He stopped, his back towards her; then he slowly turned round and looked at her fully in the face for the first time since he had come in.

'It's about the girl.'

'The girl?' The expression on his face changed, his eyes screwed up as if he were at a loss to know to whom she was referring.

'The girl, Ruth.'

'Oh. Oh, Ruthie.' His head nodded, he closed his eyes, then walked towards the fire. Again he had his back to her.

'She's in a certain condition.'

His head came slowly round on his shoulder, his eyes slanted towards her and there was a half smile on his face as he said, 'Yes, isn't it interesting?'

'What! What do you say? Surely you heard what I said.'

His head remained in the same position. 'Yes, yes, I heard what you said. And I said, isn't it interesting? The only thing is I wonder you haven't noticed before.'

Her whole face drooped, her mouth opened, her bottom lip protruded, and then she said in genuine amazement, 'You mean to say you knew that she was pregnant?'

'Yes, of course, I did. She must be four months or more.'

'You stand there and tell me that you have known this, the girl who is looking after your sons, and you condone. . . .'

She actually jumped as he swung round and bawled, 'Shut up!'

They were staring at each other when the door opened and Ada appeared, saying, 'Did you call, ma'am?'

She had to drag her voice from her throat and use all her control to say with some semblance of calmness, 'No, no, Ada. Leave the clearing until after. I'll ring for you.'

Ada flashed a keen glance between them before going out and closing the door, then Barbara, the colour flooding her face and her eyes blazing now, hissed, 'Don't you dare speak to me in that fashion.'

'I'll speak to you in what fashion I like.' He had taken a step towards her, and now as they glared at each other everything was clear to her, but being who she was, she had to pretend, she had to defend herself. 'You're mad,' she said. 'The . . . the drink is having an effect on you. Anyway' – she stroked down the white ruffle that edged the front of her dress and, her head moving upwards, she said, 'I've given her notice; she goes at the end of the week.'

'She doesn't go at the end of the week.'

It wasn't only his tone, it was something in the look on his face that took the stiffness from her carriage. Her shoulders drooped, her body seemed to shrink. A moment ago she had thought everything was clear to her. What had been clear was the fact that he knew about her and Michael, but now what she was faced with was something else, something he was telling her. In his defence of the girl he was telling her. . . . Oh no, no! He couldn't. Not in this house with that girl, that common creature – she still could not see any similarity between their cases. Her voice rose and her words came out almost on a squeak as she cried, 'I . . . I won't have her looking after my sons.'

'No? Well, she'll continue to look after *my* sons. What is more, her child will be born here.'

'I . . . I won't allow it.'

'You what! What did I hear you say?' He was laughing at her but there was no mirth in his laughter, rather he looked like a devil, a compact small devil. Then, the grim laughter sliding from his face, he said, 'This is my house, I give the orders. Remember that. I'll repeat it, this is my house and I give the orders. You said you had something to say to me. Was that all, to tell me that Ruthie is going to have a child?'

He waited and he watched the emotions pass over her face and he willed himself to feel no compassion.

For her part she could not believe that this was the same man who had begged for her favours for years and been grateful for the scraps she had offered him. She felt that if she stayed another moment under his malevolent stare she would collapse. She turned slowly about and went from the room and up the stairs into the bedroom, and she did not sit on the bed, she lay on it, fully dressed she lay on it and gripped the coverlet.

Well, it had to come. This was the end, and thank God for it! She'd be seeing Michael tomorrow.... After a moment, during which she lay with her hand across her eyes, she thought, I'll miss the children, Jonathan in particular. Yes, I'll miss Jonathan. But nothing will matter once I'm with Michael. I can have more children, Michael's children, *Michael's children.*

II

BARBARA WAS LYING ON A BED in a strange room in a cottage she had seen for the first time an hour ago and she didn't care for it, either inside or out.

But here she was in Michael's arms, her eyes closed tight, her head buried in the bare flesh of his shoulder, her lips pressed tightly together, but her ears wide open to what he was telling her.

'I can't, I can't, Barbara. Oh God in heaven, you know it's the only thing I want in life just to be with you, but I can't. Hannah has never been right since the fever. She needs me . . . she demands to go with me everywhere, she hardly lets me out of her sight. And . . . and the others, Mother used to do a lot about the place, now she hardly lifts her hand outside the house. Since I put my foot down and told her who was master she's taken the attitude of letting me get on with it; she used to see to the dairy, now she does it only when it pleases her. And Sarah, well, she finds it awkward.' The last words were mumbled; then on a loud tone he ended, 'A whole day's cream went sour yesterday, only fit for the pigs. There was hell to pay last night. . . . Barbara, my love.'

He tried to look into her face but she turned it away from him, and her head came from his shoulder and on to the pillow and his voice sounded distant now as it came to her, muttering, 'If . . . if you feel this way about it, sure about it, then do it, leave him. You can live here – we can fix it up better than it is now – and I'll get across whenever I can. You know that, don't you?'

He moved his lips in her hair. 'All I want is to be near you, close, close, like this.' He pressed his body tight against hers. 'But there are so many things, responsibilities. . . . Barbara, Barbara, look at me, say something.'

She turned on her back and looked at him but she couldn't say anything. She felt that she had been turned into a dumb animal, a trapped, dumb animal. If she were to speak her thoughts at this

583

moment she would have cried at him, 'I can leave Dan and the children, I can step out into the world with hardly a penny for I have little of my own, I'll even lose the respectability of being a married woman, and what do you offer? This dreadful, mean cottage, without gas, or water, except what water can be carried from the brook, and you would expect me to live alone here, day following day, just waiting for you coming once a week. And then one hour, two at the most, and you'd be gone. And so great is my love for you that I would suffer it if you really wanted that, but you don't. You don't want me to leave Dan or the children, for then I would be another responsibility. Oh Michael, Michael, don't let me think that Brigie was right; you're not a weak man, you're not, you're not. Brigie has been proved wrong so many times; dear God! let her be proved wrong again.'

'Have . . . have you said anything at all to him?'

'What?' She had difficulty in hearing his voice, it was as if she had gone deaf again.

'I said, have you said anything at all to Dan?' He was sitting away from her now on the side of the bed, slowly filling his pipe. 'I mean did . . . did you admit anything, anything at all?'

'No, no, I didn't.' Her voice was unusually loud and he turned swiftly to her and, laying down the pipe on the side table, he bent over her again. 'I'm only asking because I want to work out what's best for you.'

'I know what's best for me, Michael.' Her voice broke.

He stared down into her face and nodded his head before saying, 'I know, too, darling. I know too, and I'll make it as soon as I can. When Hannah is just a little older and can stand on her own feet.'

'In the meantime you expect me to stay in that house with that girl and see her carrying Dan's child. I can't do it, I won't suffer it.'

He sat back from her again but took hold of her hand now and said softly, 'I've got to say this, Barbara, I must say it. You can't blame Dan. If he has known about us, as you think he has for some time, you can't blame him. The only wonder to me is that he hasn't brought it into the open. It . . . it points to one thing in my view, he doesn't want to lose you, he can't bear to lose you, and . . . and I know how he feels. It appears to me he'll be quite willing to let things go on as they are. It's all up to you from now on.'

'What did you say?'

'I said it's all up to you, Barbara, from now on. . . . What's the matter?'

She put her hand across her mouth, and then her two hands were covering her ears and her eyes were wide and filled with fear as she whispered, 'I . . . I had to read your lips, Michael, I had to read your lips; I didn't catch your last words. Two or three times today you . . .

your words have faded away. I'm . . . I'm going deaf again. I'm going deaf again, Michael. *Michael, I'm going deaf again.*'

He was holding her and rocking her, speaking above her agonized crying now. 'You're not, you're not. It's just that you're upset, it's emotional. It must have been in the first place for you to recover, and now, now you know what it is you can control it. Don't . . . don't get yourself so upset. Dearest. Dearest. There now. There now.'

After some minutes she sat up against the back of the bed and dried her face, and as she looked at him she said between gasps, 'Michael, I . . . I couldn't bear to be deaf again, not . . . not like before. I'd . . . I'd kill myself rather. . . .'

'Hush! hush! Don't ever say such a thing because if you were to die I'd die too.'

'Would you, Michael?'

'Yes, yes I would, Barbara.'

'You really would?'

'I would, because I couldn't live without you, you should know that.'

She believed him because she wanted to believe him. Oh, she wanted to believe him, because if she stopped believing in him. . . . Well, then. . . .

PART THREE

Ben

WAR

I

ENGLAND WAS AT WAR. The terrible Germans were massacring the poor Belgians, raping nuns and cutting off babies' hands, but as everybody in England knew they would soon be avenged because the British Expeditionary Force had crossed the Channel to put an end to it.

Everybody said they had seen it coming. Why, look at the number of German bands that had been going about these last few years. And where did they go? Not into the country towns. Oh no, but into the industrial areas where there were shipyards, and mines, and foundries. German bands! They weren't German bands at all, they were spy bands. And then there were all those German pork-butcher shops. Why weren't the pork-butcher shops run by Englishmen? No, the Germans had inveigled themselves in through the Englishmen's bellies. Feed them, fatten them and then slaughter them was their method. Did you ever know a German pork-butcher who didn't want to talk, who didn't make himself pleasant? Oh, they had seen it coming for years. Anyway it would soon be over. So they couldn't really see the point of them taking the golden sovereigns off the market and dishing out paper money instead. Fancy a paper pound, and a paper ten shillings? But that wouldn't last long either.

On August 19th Kitchener sent his fifth division to France, then in September he sent the sixth. Some people couldn't see why because the British Expeditionary Force was out there, wasn't it? And it was the best equipped army in the world, wasn't it? Well, as far as the newspapers went it was, for they said that there were as many as five thousand six hundred horses and eighteen thousand men to a division. Well, just think what they could do. Of course, they admitted to snags here and there. For one thing the army hadn't wireless, like the navy, but still they had all those horses, hadn't they?

The British Expeditionary Force ran into the advancing Germans at Mons, and had to retreat.

The men covered two hundred miles in thirteen days, many of them sleeping as they walked. There was muddle and arguments in high places; midnight meetings between Kitchener and Asquith and the Cabinet, with the result that Kitchener crossed to France and told Joffre, the French Commander-in-Chief, who was boss.

By November men were digging a maze of trenches in France and preparing to settle in them for the winter. By now the ordinary English family knew it was at war; and the postman knocked on thousands of doors and handed bewildered women telegrams, headed: ON HIS MAJESTY'S SERVICE.

The Bensham brothers met at the end of August. By prearrangement they entered their home en masse, so as to get the shock over in one go, for all had enlisted in His Majesty's Forces. They were going to fight for King and Country, and what they had all agreed upon was that they weren't going to wait for conscription, not they.

They were now twenty-nine years old and not one of them was married. Harry alone had come near to it. Two years ago he had been engaged to a Miss Powell, but Miss Powell's character hadn't been strong enough to cover her dislike of his mother, and when she had openly expressed her feelings to her future husband he had used it as the opportunity for getting out of an awkward situation.

The Bensham boys weren't the marrying kind, people said, but that wasn't to say they didn't like women, especially that Ben. Benjamin's escapades with the ladies offered food for gossip, not only among the female workers in the warehouse and wholesale rooms of Bensham & Sons Ltd., but also among a certain section of the ladies in Newcastle. These might not be counted in the upper stratum of the city's society, nor yet did they belong to the bottom layer. Benjamin Bensham was known to be choosey; it was also said that he never had to lift his finger twice.

Benjamin was the tallest of the three brothers by some inches. He was also endowed with broad shoulders, narrow hips and a head of thick shining black hair, distinguished, as it had been almost from birth, by its white streak, which, now that he was in the army, he laughingly remarked to his brothers, he would have to live down. Generally a white streak came out in one, but his had been planted on him; it wasn't fair. They all laughed about his white streak.

Ben's skin too seemed to have taken its hue from his hair, for it was dark; at times it looked as if he were deeply sun-tanned. No one seeing the three together could have taken the other two for his brothers.

Yet Jonathan and Harry were often taken for twins. Their height was no more than five foot eight, their stature was slight, very like their father's, as was their hair, a sandy, nondescript colour. Their complexions were fresh and youthful, and they looked at least three years younger than Ben, and whereas they were of similar temperament to each other they varied from Ben in that they were of a sunny, easy-going nature, which showed little variation either up or down. As people said, you always knew where you had them, whereas Ben's countenance when he was not in the presence of the ladies looked sombre, and nearly always there was a deep frown line between his heavy brows. Yet at times he could express a gaiety that was unknown to his brothers, while at others fall into despondency that was equally unknown to them. Ben was one apart and always had been.

Yet in spite of the differences in their make-up, they had been good friends from childhood, Jonathan and Harry remaining firm in their loyalty to Ben.

When they decided, as Ben said, to honour the nation with their services they determined to do it together, so they gave out they were going on a joint fishing holiday. Only on one point did they differ, into which service each meant to enlist. Both Jonathan and Harry were for the navy, but Ben was for the army. He tried to persuade them into his way of thinking, whilst they combined their efforts to influence him. Neither side prevailed, and so it was into the navy that Jonathan and Harry went, and Benjamin joined the army.

Ben could have been home two days ago but he had waited until he heard from the others that they were getting a brief leave.

They stopped in the porch, and it was Jonathan who said, 'As soon as we get into the hall let's all sing "God Save the King", that'll bring them running. Well, I mean if Dad's in, and the girls.'

'Oh, the girls.' Harry put his hand on his heart and swayed. 'Wait till Ada sees us.'

'What do you bet?' Ben was pointing from one to the other now. 'Twenty-to-one Betty cries.'

Harry jerked his chin upwards with a scornful movement. 'Come off it, lad, who d'you think you've got on? Now if you'd said twenty-to-one she doesn't, then I'd take you on.'

'We'd better go to Mother first.'

The bantering ceased; they looked at Jonathan and nodded, then entered the house.

As they crossed the hall, Ada came from the direction of the kitchen and she stopped dead for a moment; then lifting her apron she held it across the bottom of her face, and as she watched the three young masters come to attention and salute her she put her hand up and grabbed the streamers of her starched cap and exclaimed, as if in prayer, 'Eeh! Dear God!' then moved slowly towards them, and they, as always when teasing her, repeated in chorus, 'Eeh! Dear God! . . . and Ada Howlett.'

'Oh, Master Ben. And you and you.' She pointed to Jonathan and Harry in turn. 'What you been an' gone and done? Eeh! the missis'll have a fit, she'll pass out. Eeh! you had no call to go and do it, not right away you hadn't. And all of a bunch. Eeh, by God!'

The kitchen door opened again and Betty Rowe came into the hall, a different Betty Rowe, a plump, middle-aged Betty Rowe, and she, too, stopped and lifted her apron to her .face. But when the three young men saluted her she ran towards them, beaming now, and what she said was, 'Eeh! well I never! Don't you look a sight for sore eyes. Eeh! well I never.'

Benjamin exchanged a quick glance with Jonathan and Harry. Then looking at Betty again, he demanded, 'Why aren't you crying? Why aren't you blubbing your eyes out?'

'Cryin'?' Betty's face stretched. 'What've I got to cry for? You look grand, all of you. We'll have to chain the lasses up 'cos now they'll be after you like cats in. . . .'

Betty's descriptive phrasing of girlish pursuits was cut off by Ada's elbow in her ribs, and Ada, now on her house-parlourmaid dignity, said, 'The mistress is in her room, sir.' As usual when the three young men were together she had addressed Ben, and laughingly they turned away as one and bounded up the stairs.

They did not knock on the door but opened it slowly, as was their custom before entering, thus giving them time to close it again if it wasn't convenient for her to see them. But when it was wide open they saw her standing in front of the wardrobe mirror, and they entered one after the other, Jonathan first, Benjamin coming last. This, too, was usual.

Barbara had her hands to her hair, and she kept them there and she looked for a moment as if she had been turned into stone. Then swinging round, she faced them. And now her head moving from side to side, she said, 'No! Oh no! No!'

'It's all right. It's all right, dear.' It was Jonathan who came forward and put his arms about her and, mouthing his words slowly, he said, 'It had to come. Just as well sooner as later; we've got it over with.'

She looked from his beloved face to Harry, whom she liked, then on to Ben, whom she disliked with an intensity that neared hate. His uniform was different. It would be, he would have to be different; he had always been different, and indifferent, obstinate, moody, unfeeling, selfish. The only thing she was glad about at this moment was that he'd be separated from the other two and no longer have any influence over them. But oh, oh, her Jonathan, her dearest Jonathan. He was her only comfort, at least in this house; this house that had become enveloped in silence with the years, this prison wherein she was provided with food and clothing. The only thing that had made it bearable for her all these years was Jonathan, the kind, dear, understanding Jonathan, loyal Jonathan.

She did not know how much he knew. He had never probed and she had never proffered any information on the situation that existed between herself and his father, but always he had been loving towards her.

It was he, and he alone, who had talked to her from the time all those years ago when he and his brothers had been allowed to take their meals in the dining room. It was after Ruth Foggety had left the house, and she had not left until her stomach had protruded like a barrel before her. She thought it was only Jonathan's childish conversation and attention, childish but understanding attention, that had saved her reason during those days when Ruth Foggety had unashamedly carried Dan's child; and when Dan himself had taken on a succession of images, the first being a drunken one. Scarcely a night passed for months when he didn't sit downstairs and drink himself stupid, and not once during that time had she gone to sleep until she had heard his bedroom door bang. It was impossible to lock her door for there was no key to it, there were no keys to any of the bedroom doors, and there was no bolt inside.

When this image slowly faded, it was taken over by the one who spent nights away from home. The last image, which was his present one, he had assumed some fifteen years ago, when he had picked up again his hobby of collecting old books. Most of the nursery floor was now like a miniature library.

It was from the time that he had renewed his interest in books that he had also adopted a more civil manner towards her, it was impersonal but correct. He never enquired into her doings, not even as to the state of her health. Even when the deafness had come fully on her again he made no reference to it but resumed his finger language when he wanted to communicate with her, as if he had never stopped using it.

Some years ago she had worked out a strategic pattern for herself. Some days she did not dine at home but had something to eat in town. And so when she decided to stay away all night he could not be sure whether or not she were in her room, unless he asked the servants, which she was sure he did not. This worked very well when Jonathan and Harry were at college, and Ben as usual about his nefarious business.

But of latter years there had been few times when she had been away from home all night.

She was sitting now on the dressing table stool and they were standing before her in a half circle, and she shook her head from side to side as she said, 'But . . . but why the navy and . . . and without a commission?'

'Oh, that'll come.' It was Harry who answered her in his rapid fashion, both his mouth and his fingers moving. 'Johnny here has told them he wants to be an Admiral and I said I wouldn't mind being Rear, just as long as it was all in the family.'

When Jonathan pushed him and they both flung their heads back and laughed, she said without a smile, 'Don't . . . don't you understand what you've done? This . . . this is a shock.'

'But, Mother' – Jonathan was bending over her – 'you knew we would do it, we've said as much for some time. We told you if war came we would go?'

'But . . . but not like this. It could have been done in a different way. Will you be home for long?'

Both Jonathan and Harry looked at her, their faces unsmiling now, and Jonathan spoke on his fingers, saying, 'We've got to report back tonight, and . . . and we're for Scotland tomorrow. But where's Scotland!' He shrugged his shoulder. 'We'll be back at the week-end plaguing you again.' He smiled. 'And Ben here, he'll be near, he's stationed in the town, because they said they wanted someone to man the defences. Lucky devil as usual.' He turned and grinned at his brother. But Ben didn't answer the grin, nor did he look at Jonathan, he was looking at Barbara. And Barbara, turning her troubled gaze from Jonathan, met the defiant, sullen look without comment, while he took in her loveless stare and knew the feeling of rejection as fresh again as he had done when he'd first recognized it as a boy.

If only once she had put her hand out to him, if only once he could have remembered her touching his hair, if only once she had kissed him, not just held that pale cheek out to be kissed, but kissed him. For years he had wondered why she hated him so, and then his dad had told him.

It was on the night he was sent down from college. There had been no reprimand from Dan about ruining his career, just a quiet understanding of his unsettled state; then had followed the baring of souls.

'I don't want to act like I do towards her,' his dad had said, 'but she's made me what I am, as she's also made you what you are.' He had then listened to the story of how his mother had come into life, and why, because he himself was a replica of the man who had sired her, she could not look on him without being reminded of her ignoble beginnings.

From then on he had understood her more, yet he had been unable to forget her years of neglect which at times had been cruel because of the open love she had shown to the other two. He still longed for some sign of affection from her, the touch of her hand, a kind look from her eyes. Sometimes he thought he would bring it all into the open and say to her, 'I'm not to blame for being born; and remember I'm of your flesh too.' But he could never bring himself to take that step because if she still rejected him after that his second state would be worse than his first and life would really become unbearable.

He often wondered how he and his father would have fared if it hadn't been for Ruthie. The only comfort his father had had for years had come from Ruthie and the only mothering he had ever known had come from Ruthie. But Ruthie wasn't his mother; this tall, beautiful being looking at him now was his mother. If only she wasn't so beautiful. She was turned fifty and there wasn't a line on her skin, and if she had grey hairs she had them well hidden. Yet in spite of her beauty she had the unhappiest face he had ever seen on a woman, and this was like salt to his wounds, for, in spite of what she had done to him, she had done equally as much harm to herself, for her lover, the farmer in the Northumberland valley, could not have given her much satisfaction over the years or else there would have been times when her expression would have shown some sign of pleasure if not delight; but even when she must have thought she was unobserved it remained the same.

Once when on a visit to Brigie he had gone along the road to the cottage and, having forced a window, he had gone in. Although it was kept aired by the Hall staff it smelt musty and full of decay, and everything looked old-fashioned.

When he had stood before the picture that still hung over the mantelpiece in the living room and had looked at the old white-haired man with the bulbous stomach smiling down from out of the frame, he had thought, My God! will I come to that? Yet he could see a resemblance to himself in the face, and the way the hands were placed on the knees; he nearly always sat like that himself.

He had gone from room to room thinking that this was where it all started, the love and the hate, and only the hate remained. And then, since the day was fine, he had walked over the hills, seven miles over the hills to Wolfbur, and he had gone down into the farmyard and asked for a cup of milk, and a woman on a crutch had given him a large mug full and offered him some bread and butter. But he had refused it. He thanked her, and touched his hat but hadn't raised it; he did not want the streak to give him away. An older woman had come to the door and looked at him hard. She must once have been tall but was now slightly stooped, her hair was white and her face was lined, and he had thought, That's Constance, and the other is Sarah. But where was he, his mother's lover?

They met as he was leaving the farm. In the gateless gap in the wall they both stopped and looked at each other, and although the man had changed he recognized him as the person he had seen kissing his mother in the wood and he knew he should take his fist and bash it into this man's face by way of repayment for the hurt he had done both to himself and to his dad. But as he continued to look at the man he thought, If people hadn't interfered he would have been my father and my mother would have kissed me.

The man said, 'Where are you from?' He lied and said, 'Hexham,' and when he turned from him and walked away, the man called after him, 'There's a nearer way than that,' but he took no notice and walked on.

Life was crazy, the world was crazy, mad crazy; war was crazy and he was going into it. He didn't want to go into it; no, he wanted to stay in the warehouse. He liked the business; he liked travelling back and forth between Newcastle and Manchester; he liked staying with his Uncle John and his Aunt Jenny. And there was a woman in Manchester who was good to visit, and there was another in Newcastle who was good to visit. He didn't want to join the blasted army. Let the politicians do their own damned work because that's all wars were for, to clear up the mess of politicians.

'Where will you be going?' She was speaking to him.

He answered very coolly, 'I'm not sure; it's they to command, me to obey from now on.'

Jonathan and Harry laughed, and Harry said, 'That'll be a change. But it won't remain long that way, I bet. What d'you say, Jonathan?' and Jonathan replied, 'I'll lay my bet with yours.' Then they both grinned at Ben.

As Barbara rose hastily from the seat they all moved back, and when she said, 'You'd better have some tea, don't you think?' Jonathan and Harry, as if they were still young boys, answered, 'Yes, yes, we'd like some tea,' and they followed her out of the room and downstairs, Benjamin coming last.

2

BENJAMIN WAS THE FIRST TO LEAVE the house. He put his head round the drawing-room door, called, 'I'm off then. Be seeing you,' and left. But he got only as far as the steps leading down to the drive when Harry caught him up and, pulling him round by the arm, demanded, 'Look! what is it?'

'What do you mean, what is it?'

'Something's up.'

'Nothing more than usual. You saw what happened, you were there. Has she spoken one word to me except to say, "When will you be going?" since I came in?'

Harry sighed, gave one shake of his head and said 'It's a special night. You could have stayed your time out.'

'She's much easier when I'm out of the house.'

'Aw, man' – Harry was again shaking him by the arm – 'when are you going to get over that? Look, it's because of her deafness. . . . And look. . . .'

'No. Now don't let's go over it again, boy. I've lived with it since I can first remember and I don't mind now, I don't, honest.'

'She doesn't mean it.'

'What do you mean, she doesn't mean it? Can you tell me what she means?'

They stared at each other in the deepening twilight and Harry said, 'I'm going to miss you; we're all going to miss you.'

'All?'

'Aw, hell's flames!' Harry flung his head from side to side. 'Come off your perch. You know, you're as bad as she is, you are, you are; you get on your high horse and there's nobody can do anything with you. You've got no room to talk. And tonight was special. We agreed before we came in, in a sort of unspoken way, that it was special. And you know something, you know something, Ben?' Harry's voice now dropped to a whisper and took on a note of deep sadness. 'This might be the last time we'll see each other for God knows when. I don't know what'll happen to us when we get up there, I only hope we're not separated. I asked if we could be together and you know the answer I got from a big-mouthed ignorant slob? "Aye," he said; "you'll have the same nurse to put your nappies on you." I could have belted him, I could.'

Ben put out his hand and gripped Harry's shoulder, saying, 'You'll be all right. You'll likely be in dry dock until it's over. And that won't be long so they say. If I don't see Jonathan before we're off give him a dig in the ribs for me. Bye, Harry.'

'Bye, Ben.'

'Bye.'

They shook hands, stared at each other for a long moment, then Ben turned and walked briskly away down the drive. But he hadn't reached the outer gate before Jonathan's voice came at him now shouting, 'Hie you!'

Ben stopped, and when Jonathan came up with him he demanded, breathlessly, 'What do you mean, going off like that?'

'Duty calls.'

'Well, she can wait.'

'You're barking up the wrong tree. I'm going to Ruthie's.'

'Oh!'

'She'd be pleased if you'd drop in.'

'Well, time is running short.' Jonathan looked at his watch. 'But I'll put it to Harry; we'll see.'

They stood, as if slightly embarrassed, looking at each other until Ben said, 'Take care of yourself. And mind what I told you; ask to be put on a painting job, preferably doing the captain's portrait.'

Jonathan's head went back on a laugh. 'I'll say those very words. Chief, I'll say, I ain't goin' to slap no paint on no ship's backside, no sir, not me. Cap'n's portrait or nothing, that's what me big brother said. Take it or leave it, Chiefie, take it or leave it.'

They thrust at each other with their fists; then their hands clasping, their gaze held.

'Look after Harry,' said Ben.

'And you, give those girls a break,' said Jonathan.

Then Ben was walking out into the road and Jonathan back up the drive.

Ruth Foggety lived in the corner house of Linton Street on the outskirts of Jesmond Dene. It was a respectable neighbourhood. All Jesmond Dene was respectable. But in Linton Street the houses were small, two down and two up, self-contained yard with its own tap, and gas in all the rooms, not merely downstairs. Some people called Ruth Missis, and some called her Miss, generally she was known as Ruthie, but no matter by what name they called her she was known to be a kept woman. As, however, the man was said to be a gentleman, and he was the only one who called, a lot was forgiven her.

Very few people had ever seen her man, for he rarely visited her in the daylight, even in summer.

She had an enviable life of it, had Ruthie, so the neighbours said. Who else, even in this street that supported an insurance agent, a chemist's assistant, a shopwalker, and four clerks, who among them could take their family away, two or three times in the summer, for a week at that?

She had only the one child, and she had grown up into a fine girl. Everybody had a good word to say for Mary Ann Foggety, and Mary Ann had a cheery word to say to everybody she met.

Few people had been invited into the end house of Linton Street but those who had said that it was better and more tastefully furnished than any other in the street; in fact, some said that Ruthie had her house furnished quite a bit above her class.

There was never any speculation about the young man who came to the corner house for he had called there since he was a young lad in short trousers. Sometimes he had brought another two lads along with him, but mostly he came on his own; and he had continued to come as he grew older. Some said he was a distant relation of Ruthie's, others that he was her fancy man's son. But then, surely, it wasn't likely her fancy man would let his son visit her an' all, was it now, and him just a little boy?

No one dared to ask Ruth outright who her young visitor was, or, later, the young man, or the big fellow as he grew to be, because they knew she had a tongue that would clip clouts and they might get more than they bargained for by way of answer.

When Ben knocked on the door Ruth opened it to him, stared at him for a moment, then her head moving at first in small nods was soon bouncing on her shoulders and she turned from him, leaving the door open, and walked through the sitting room into the kitchen, saying loudly, 'Well! you've done it then?'

'Yes, I've done it.'

In the kitchen she turned and faced him and her head now shaking slowly from side to side, she said, 'And of course the other two have gone into the navy?'

'Right first time. . . . Have you a drop of anything in?'

'Did you ever know the time I hadn't? Sit yourself down. By the look of you, you won't do the British army much good. You're a fool, you know that, don't you?'

599

'Yes, yes, Ruthie, I know that. If I remember rightly, you've told me the same thing at odd times before.'

'An' it won't be the last time either.'

From a substantial rosewood sideboard flanking the wall opposite the open fireplace she brought out a bottle of whisky and two glasses, and as she handed him a good measure she asked, 'What did she say?'

'What do you think?' He looked up at her.

'Nothing?'

'Next to it. She got out of it by saying, "Shall we have tea?"' He took a sharp gulp of the whisky; then, putting the glass on the table he smacked one lip over the other before looking towards the fire and saying, 'You know, she frightens me at times, she's so calm.' Now his body swung round to her and he ground out, 'So bloody calm.'

Taking a chair opposite him, Ruth sipped from her glass and sighed, 'It's all on the surface; she's no more calm than you are. There's a volcano inside of her I would say, always has been. Anyway, don't expect me to sympathize with you, either about that or' – she dug her finger towards his uniform – 'the mess you've got yourself into. You could have waited, couldn't you?'

'And be conscripted?'

'Where you bound for?'

'They didn't tell me. They haven't started to confide in me yet.' He grinned at her. 'It's early days but rumour says down south somewhere. I wouldn't mind seeing France again. It's hard to believe I was born there. I'm a French citizen by rights.'

'Parly voo frongsay? An' that's not all you are....'

He put his glass down so quickly on the table that the remains of its contents sprayed over the edge, and he flung back his head and let out a roar. Her Irish-cum-Geordie accent mouthing the French tongue was too much.

'Aw you!' Laughing with him, she rose to her feet and made to pass him on her way to the scullery to put the kettle on, but paused, her face just a little above the level of his – for she had developed, as she had promised in her teens, into a round, comfortable little woman – she gazed at him and their laughter suddenly stopped and instinctively her arms went about him and his head fell on to her breast, as it had done all those years ago in the summer-house. And they held each other tightly for a moment, until she said thickly, 'I'm gonna miss you.'

It was some seconds before he mumbled, 'And me you Ruthie.'

He disengaged himself from her embrace – she was never the first to break away, a rule she had made over the years – and turned to the table and, looking at the glass, said, 'I can see the bottom again,' to which she replied, 'Well, you're not getting any more, not yet anyway. We're having a cup of tea and a bite to eat. I've got some finny-haddy in the oven, can't you smell it? an' I've baked the day.'

He called to her now in the scullery, 'Where's Mary Ann?'

'At a dance.'

'With Joe?'

'Well, I'm not sure. It could be Tom, Dick or Harry now, anything in uniform. She's got no more sense than all the rest. I told her the night if she wasn't careful she'd get more than her eye in a sling. She said they'd all be gone soon. What I said to her was, there was still no need to lay herself out on the butcher's slab, there'll always be flies around to settle on the meat.'

Oh, Ruthie! He rubbed his hand hard across his chin. Always be flies around to settle on the meat. What would he have done without her all these years? She had been the one person who had kept him from going really sour; and not only him. He asked now, 'Are you expecting Dad?'

'I expect him when I see him.'

She expected him when she saw him. Her retorts, as always, were colourful, taken from the esoteric language of the Tyne. He had listened to it – and her – more than to his parents. Oh yes, because as far back as he could remember the conversation between them had been almost nil, as had his own conversation with his mother.

'Does your dad know you've gone and done it?'

'Yes; I could hardly have left him in the lurch. But he's got Alec Stonehouse. He's a good fellow is Alec.'

'What about Jonathan an' the school, and Harry an' the office, will their jobs be kept open?'

'I don't suppose it'll matter much to Jonathan if he never sees the school again. I think he was going to branch out on his own in any case. He's good you know, Ruthie, very good, especially with portraits.'

'Aye, I know.'

'And Harry's place will be all right. If it isn't, he won't worry; they'll always want accountants. . . . Ruthie.'

'Aye, I'm listenin'.'

'I was thinking last night, if I was to peg out who would mourn me, I mean besides you?'

She appeared at the scullery door, a plate of bread in her hand, and she stood there looking at him as she cried, 'Now you look here, you great big galloot. Now you snap out of it. Who'd mourn you? Your dad for number two, or I'd say number one, and meself second, and Mary Ann, and the lads. You don't realize how much those two think of you.' She walked towards the sideboard, put the plate down on it, opened the drawer and took out a cloth, and as she swung it across the table she said, 'You're a big outsized numskull. You can see nowt beyond her, nowt or nobody beyond her, can you? What you want to get into your head, lad, is that you're not the only fellow whose mother hasn't broken her neck over him. You go on like this simply because she hasn't made a fuss. . . .'

'Shut up, Ruthie.' He had risen to his feet. 'For God's sake don't you give me that line, not at this stage. It isn't that she hasn't broken her neck over me, but that she hates me. All my life I've asked myself what I'd give for one kind word from her, and the truth is I would have given anything, everything, Dad, you, the lads, aye even at times life itself, if she had once put her hand on *my* head as she did on the others. If she had once said to *me* "What are you doing, Ben?" as she did to the others. If she had once taken an interest in anything I was doing, any damn thing. But no; no. Do you know what it's been like living with the other two thirds of yourself, seeing them comforted and cosseted while you had to look on? She started a canker in me years ago, even before the day I saw her with her fancy man. The only thing I'm grateful for is the other two never took her side against me.'

Ruth brought the plate from the sideboard and put it in the middle of the tablecloth, then she went back into the scullery and from there she said, 'You should have left years ago, I told you.'

'Yes I know. I know you told me; but I'm my father's son, we're masochists.'

'You're what?' She was at the kitchen door again. 'You're what-did-you-say?'

He sighed and smiled faintly as he said, 'We both enjoy pain. How else would we have stayed there, how else would he have put up with it? When I view his life and the wasted years I keep asking why? Why? And yet I've only to turn to myself for the answer. You keep hoping she'll change and that one day she'll smile at you. You tell yourself that something will happen to break her crust, and you want to be there with both hands outstretched waiting for a crumb. Christ Almighty!' He closed his eyes now and swung round.'Men are bloody idiots. They look on their women as the weaker sex. Huh! that's funny when you think about it, for they have hides like rhinoceroses and the tenacity of gorillas. They're animals, that's what women are, primitive animals. . . .' He turned again and looked at her, small, plump, motherly and above all kind, and he said contritely, 'I'm sorry, Ruthie.'

'Don't you be sorry for speaking the truth, 'cos we are just that, just what you said, animals, gorillas and rhinos, the lot. How else do you think we'd get through life? How else do you think a woman would suffer the maulin's of men, 'cos men's hunger's got nowt to do with love? And how else do you think we'd be able to stand a head pressing itself through delicate private parts if we weren't animals? It's as you said, we're animals, tough, with hides like rhinos. Aw you want to think of something new to tell us what we are, lad.' She flung her arm outwards across the table as if swiping a lot of rubbish from it and was about to go back into the scullery when his laugh stopped her.

When she turned and looked at him, he said, 'You know what you are, Ruthie? You're a witch doctor, a bloody fat little witch doctor. Let's have another drink, eh?'

'Aye, after you've had your tea an' something to eat.'

'Aw you!'

'An' you.'

'You do me good. You always did.'

'Aw, away with you.'

She disappeared into the scullery and he sat down again, stretched his legs out towards the fire, put his hands behind his head and leant back.

Away with you! she said, and he was going away. He hadn't fully realized it until now, but he was breaking away, snapping all the threads. He was going to war.

PEOPLE WERE GETTING USED TO SEEING Kitchener's head on a poster, his right arm out, the fist doubled, his forefinger pointing, cutting off the end of his moustache. Above his cap was the word 'BRITAIN' in outsize letters, under his black collared neck was the word 'wants' in small print, and under it an enormous 'YOU'. The bottom of the poster read: 'Join your country's army. God save the King.'

And most men obeyed the command. Many who didn't were sent white feathers; sick men received the feathers, men who were in specialized jobs received the feathers. In some cases it was just a way of getting your own back on someone you disliked.

There was talk everywhere about the Eastern Front strategy and the Western Front strategy. People said how terrible, how sacrilegious when a German shell hit Rheims Cathedral in September 1914. But there was rejoicing when Sir David Beatty succeeded in sinking or damaging a number of German cruisers off Heligoland with the loss, in dead or prisoners, of over a thousand Germans. Then, less than a month later, there was dire consternation at the wickedness of the Germans when a U-boat sank three British cruisers within an hour.

Neither Jonathan nor Harry *was* in the *Aboukir*, the *Cressy* or the *Hogue*, and Barbara for the first time in years went to church and offered up her thanksgiving.

In October when the battered and bloody army made its retreat from Antwerp and Dan received a letter from Ben to say that he was safe and, if not quite sound, still had all his extremities, Barbara did not go to church.

Those who had said the war would be over before Christmas ate their words, together with the usual Christmas fare.

It was at the beginning of February that Ben came home on leave and for the first time Dan heard he had been mentioned in despatches and been given a commission.

The man who walked in through the door of his old home on the biting, low-skied February day had no resemblance to the one who had walked out alone in his stiff new private's uniform the previous August. This man had lost a great deal of weight; his face looked angular and bony, and he seemed to have grown taller than his six-foot one, or perhaps it was the way he held himself.

He came in unannounced, and when Barbara, coming down the stairs, saw him standing in the hall, she stopped, gripped the rail of the banister tightly, drew in a short breath, then came on towards him. Holding out her hand, she said, 'Why, this is a surprise. Why didn't you let us know? Oh' – she withdrew her hand and stepped back from him – 'you ... you have been commissioned! Well, well. How are you?'

Her voice had the high sing-song note to it that he remembered so well. 'Your ... your father's in the drawing room. He ... he has a slight cold.' She moved still further back from him, her arm outstretched towards the drawing room as if he were a stranger and she had to show him the way.

He had not yet spoken to her, he had just looked at her. As he took off his greatcoat, Betty Rowe came running from the kitchen, crying, 'Master Ben! Master Ben! What a sight for sore eyes! Eeh! Ada! Ada!' she called over her shoulder, knowing that the mistress, who had her back to her, was unable to hear, and Ada came into the hall and right up to Ben. And they shook hands like old friends, and she too stood back from him and exclaimed, 'Eeh! Master Ben, you're an officer? Well, don't you look a bit of all right.'

'Ada!'

'Yes, ma'am.' Ada moved aside and made way for Ben to follow his mother, but before he did so he winked, first at her and then at Betty, and they giggled and Ada said, 'We'll get the tea, we'll get the tea. Eeh! who would believe it?'

Dan was sitting in a high-backed chair drawn close up to the fire. When the door opened he did not turn towards it; he had been dozing and wakened to the sound of a commotion in the hall. But he often heard Ada and Betty nattering in ordinary tones; they had the house so much to themselves they found it difficult to lower their voices when he was at home.

When Barbara came into his view he saw that she was smiling and her hand was held outwards, and he turned and looked round the side of the winged chair.

'Why! Ben! Ben!' He was on his feet and clasping his son to him. Their arms remained tight around each other until Dan cried, 'Well! talk about a shock. Where have you sprung from? Come on, come on, up to the fire. This is weather to bring with you. How are you?' He

605

stopped his embarrassed chatter and looked at his son and realized he shouldn't have asked.

When he had last seen Ben he had been a bit on the heavy side; now there was scarcely a pick of flesh on his bones. He looked smart in his uniform, grand, but he was too thin, too thin by half. 'Well, this calls for a drink, four o'clock in the afternoon or not four o'clock in the afternoon.' He was smiling widely as he turned towards Barbara and his words were wide-spaced as he said, 'A drink, we'll have a drink.'

She moved her head downwards and not only did she smile at him, but she smiled at Ben and said, 'Of course, of course,' and hurried from the room.

Ben sank back into the chair. Of a sudden he felt very tired. It was a different kind of tiredness from what he had continually experienced during the past months; that had been a weary, dirty, mud-clinging, freezing, death-stinking tiredness. This was a warm relaxing tiredness. He was home and being given a homecoming. She had smiled at him and called him by his name. He wanted to fall asleep; just sitting here, he wanted to turn his head to the side and go to sleep.

'How you feeling? Are you all right? How's things?'

He drew in a long breath before answering, 'Quite good at the moment.'

'At the moment?' Dan nodded quietly now. 'How about other times, is it rough?'

'Pretty rough.'

'You didn't tell me you were in for a commission?'

Ben's old grin came through for the moment as he said, 'Some have greatness thrust upon them.'

'No! No! How did it come about? Come on, come on, tell me.'

'Oh. . . . I did a bit of dirty work, more by sheer fright than bravery. Nobody's brave out there. I knew a fellow who used to say fear was a tin opener. I didn't realize what he meant until he stopped being afraid one day and became foolhardy, and he wasn't there to open his bully-beef tin that night.'

When Ben stopped talking Dan did not ask any further questions but he sat looking at his son. Ben had changed. He wasn't as morose as he had been; perhaps the things he had worried about when he was at home had been put into perspective against the greater issues he was combating over there in the icy mud of the trenches.

When Barbara brought in the tray with the decanter and glasses on it Dan rose from the chair and with an 'Ah! well now' he poured out the drinks. Then they stood with their glasses in their hands and raised them silently to each other. It was like a fitting gesture of celebration.

Both men remained standing until Barbara was seated; and then it was she who spoke. Leaning towards Ben, a smile on her face, she said, 'How long are you on leave?'

'Three days.' His fingers fumbled with unuse at the words, but he mouthed them for her, then added, 'I've already been here four.'

'You have been here four! You mean in England?'

'Yes.' He nodded from her surprised face to his father; then touched his uniform as he said, 'Officialdom.'

'Did it take four days to get you into your uniform?' Dan was laughing now, and Ben answered, 'Much longer than that. I . . . I was due to come over last month but there was a hitch. But tell me, how are the others?'

'Oh, we heard last week. They're very well and both together. They're due for leave after the next trip so they say. Their letters are very funny; they seem to be enjoying life.'

'I'm glad. They're still up in Scotland?'

'No, no.' Dan shook his head. 'Well, not now. They were in Portsmouth before Christmas.' He turned his head away and picked up the poker and stirred the fire as he added quietly, 'I think they're at sea now.'

Dan did not make any reference to his father's remark but looked at his mother now and asked, 'And what do you do with yourself?' Although she could not hear it his tone was polite as if he were making enquiries of an acquaintance.

'Oh, me? Knitting, sewing; I help Mrs Turner. You remember Mrs Turner? Well, I help her in organizing this and that. We have an entertainments committee and also allocate homes where the young men, away from home, those in the Forces you know' – she inclined her head with another smile – 'are invited for a meal or a week-end.'

'Very nice, very good, nice for them.' He nodded at her but did not add as at one time he might have, 'You'll have to get them to invite me, I need a home from home.'

The conversation flagged for a moment, until Ben asked, 'How is Uncle John?'

'Oh, fine.' Dan pursed his lips. 'The mill is working nearly twenty-four hours a day now, and it's almost the same this end. Stonehouse has turned out trumps.'

'I thought he would.'

'What do you think about putting him on the Board?'

'A very good idea; he's worth it and it'll be a means of keeping him.'

'Yes, yes, I'll do it then, I'll put it to John. But John will be for him; he knows a good man when he sees one.'

'How is Aunt Jenny?'

'Oh, she's still Aunt Jenny. Nothing moves her, floods, storms or tempests, wars or famines, nothing moves Aunt Jenny.'

They both exchanged a smile; then Dan said, 'I don't know what you'll think about it but you'll be surprised to hear that Brigie wants to turn the Hall into a convalescent home for soldiers. She's amazing. You've got to hand it to her, ninety-four and her mind's still as clear as a bell. She had it all planned out before she put it to us. I said you and the boys were the main ones concerned and I would write to you, but as it stands, you know, she can do as she likes with the place until she dies. Anyway, what do you think?'

'I think it's an excellent idea. Oh yes, I'm for it, and I'm sure the others will be too. But ... but isn't it too far out and off the beaten track?'

'That seems to be the beauty of it she says, quiet and peace. She's already had a medical opinion on it, Doctor Fuller from the Infirmary. I think he's in the process of contacting the military authorities. Anyway, you know Brigie, the world's organizer.'

'But where's she going to live? Back in that cottage?'

'No, no; she proposes to live on the nursery floor.'

'All those stairs?'

'No, no. She said there could be a lift made out of the servants' staircase with access to the first floor and the nursery floor.'

Ben now gave a small laugh and he said, 'She'll never get that, not in wartime.'

'If she passes it over to the military she'll get it.'

'Yes, yes, she may at that too. Well, well, Brigie, she never ceases to astound one, does she?'

Barbara had remained silent during this discourse and now, her expression still pleasant, she looked at Ben and said, 'What would you like for dinner? There is some pork, we could have roast pork. Would you like that? There is cold chicken from yesterday, but I'm sure you'd prefer roast pork.'

He stared at her. She had remembered he loved roast pork, with the crackling done so crisp it shot off your teeth when you snapped it. Again he felt that warm, relaxed feeling coming over him, and he nodded as he said, 'I'd love that, roast pork and crackling, and stuffing.'

As she got to her feet she repeated, 'Oh yes, and stuffing.'

After she left the room they sat looking at each other as if they were both experiencing a feeling of guilt. If they had spoken on the subject nearest their hearts at that moment Ben would have said, 'She's changed,' and Dan would have said 'No, nothing has altered. Don't delude yourself, nothing has altered.'

The meal was a happy one, the evening was a happy one.

When, just turned nine, Ben almost fell asleep in his chair, it was

Barbara who said, 'Wouldn't it be wise if you went to bed and had a good night?' and he answered, 'Yes, you're right. It would be wise for that's what I need more than anything, a good night.'

When he stood before her she offered him her hand, and he took it, but when her head and shoulders remained still he couldn't bend towards her and kiss her. He shook hands with his father too. Theirs was a tight grip. And then he went upstairs to his room, which, he had found earlier on, was just as he had left it. Undressing quickly, he got into bed, stretched to his full extent, heaved one long, deep sigh, said to himself, 'No thinking, nothing, go,' and just as he had trained himself to sleep while standing up, so now he went straight to sleep in the first comfort he had known since he put on his uniform.

The following morning Betty brought his breakfast up to bed, and he woke reluctantly, pulled himself upwards and peered at the bed table set across his knees. It was daintily laid out with everything he required and all he could say was, 'What's this?'

'What does it look like, Master Ben? Your breakfast. The mistress said you had to have it in bed.'

Now he opened his eyes and stared at her and said, 'Did she now?'

'Aye, she did.' She lifted the cover from the plate and exclaimed, 'Two eggs, four slices of bacon, two sausages and two slices of fried bread, eeh! Now get that down you.' Then standing back from the bed, she said, 'I'm glad to see you, Mr Ben. We all are.'

'Thanks, Betty. And I'm glad to see you too.'

'We have a new cook.'

'Oh, I didn't know. What happened to May?'

'It was her legs, they gave out.'

'But they've been giving out for years.'

'But they really did this time an' she had a pan of broth in her hand. Lord! you should have seen that floor. It was a good job it wasn't very hot, she was just putting it on the stove. But this one's all right; she's Annie. She's a good cook. . . . Well' – she backed from him, jerked her head at him, and ended, 'Make the best of every minute, Master Ben, an' we'll see to all you want.'

For the first time a semblance of his old self came through as he leant towards her and whispered, 'Will you, Betty? Honest, all of you? How old is the cook?'

Her hand to her mouth, Betty turned round and ran to the door, saying, 'Eeh! Master Ben, you don't change, you don't change. The war couldn't change you.'

He sat looking at the tray for a moment and repeating to himself, You don't change, the war couldn't change you. Ah well, make the best of it, she had said, and that's what he meant to do. He'd go round and see Ruthie first thing. Then he wondered if Miss Felicity

Cartwright still lived at the same address and was still Miss Felicity Cartwright. Well, he'd find out, and if she were vacant they'd go to a show, then have something to eat, and then – then. . . . He'd better warn them not to wait up for him.

Three days he had, three days before he had to return to hell. Ruthie had a saying that God was good and the devil wasn't bad to his own. Well, the devil she knew and the devil he knew must be running two different establishments because the gentlemen over there had been less than kind to him, and a few others too during the past months. Yes and a few others. . . . Aw, for God's sake eat, eat man.

And he ate.

4

I T WAS THE MORNING OF THE THIRD DAY. He was to leave at twelve to catch the one-fifty-five from Newcastle. His father was coming back in order to drive him to the station in the automobile he had acquired.

He had his breakfast in bed, as he had done on the previous two mornings, and, as usual, he joked with Betty. Then he got up and soaked himself in a bath, dressed slowly and went downstairs.

He found his mother in the drawing room. The fire was blazing, the room looked beautiful, and so did she.

'Did you sleep well?'

'Like a top. You mightn't believe it but I've learned to sleep standing up. If anyone had told me this time last year it could be done I would have laughed at them.' He sat down on the couch within an arm's length of her, and when he stared at her her eyelids flickered and she asked softly, 'Have you enjoyed your leave?'

'I'll say. It's been like heaven.'

Her face was straight, her eyes sad as she asked, 'Is it so terrible out there?'

'It isn't good.'

After another moment she asked, 'Have . . . have you no idea when it will end?'

He smiled wryly, shook his head and said, 'Nor have they. A child playing with tin soldiers could make a better job of it than some of them out there.'

Her voice was very soft now as she said, 'It's a pity you didn't go with Jonathan and Harry.'

'I've thought that myself more than once; at least there would be no mud.'

She turned from him and looked towards the fire as she asked, 'Would you mind if I came to the station with you?'

He gazed at her profile. She had asked would he mind if she came to the station with him.

When she looked at him he said slowly, both on his fingers and verbally, 'I'd like that very much.'

'Your . . . your father said he'd be home about eleven.'

'Yes. Yes, he told me.'

He was experiencing that warm, relaxed feeling inside again, and he told himself he'd experience it again and again in the weeks to come, when he remembered this moment. Of a sudden he was glad that a war had come upon them; nothing but a war could have changed her attitude towards him. How was it that no mistress, and not even the prospect of a wife, a beloved wife, could fill the void in a man who had craved mother love all his life. What were men after all but overgrown boys, children, babies still hanging on to the breast. He had never known her breast, he had been wet-nursed; he had never known any part of her until these last two and a half days. He was happy as he had never been happy before. He had an overwhelming desire to fall against her. But that would likely scare her; he must let well enough alone. They would go on from here.

She looked at him fully in the face now as she said, 'It would have been nice if you'd all been together once more,' and he said without any rancour 'Yes, it would; it would have been just fine. But there'll be another time.'

'Can I pack you something? I mean is there anything you would need on the journey besides what we spoke of yesterday, woollens and such like?'

'No, I think you've covered everything, thanks.'

The sun was shining, she looked towards the window. 'It's not so cold. The . . . the spring will soon be here. It . . . it will be easier for you in the finer weather.' She paused, then asked, 'Won't it?'

'Yes. Oh, much easier in the finer weather.'

In the awkward pause that followed there came the sound of a commotion from the hall. She didn't hear it, but the sound brought his head round towards the door as he heard Ada exclaiming highly, 'Oh my God! Oh No! Oh my God!' then Betty saying, 'What is it? Eeh! no! no!'

He said, 'Excuse me a minute,' and got up from the couch and went down the room and into the hall, closing the door behind him. The front door was open, the telegram boy stood there. He had something in his hand which was extended towards Betty, but Betty had her apron to her face and her grey head was shaking and she kept repeating, 'Eeh! no! no!'

'What is it?'

'Look! Look!' Ada who was standing further back in the hall

pointed towards the boy, and Ben said harshly, 'Don't be stupid, woman, it could be anything. It could be for me. Give it here.' But even as he took the telegrams from the boy's hand he knew they weren't for him, they were addressed to Mr Daniel Bensham and headed ON HIS MAJESTY'S SERVICE.

He felt terribly sick, he was actually going to be sick. He gulped in his throat, swallowed a mouthful of spittle, then even as his mind yelled, 'No! no! not this', he knew it was this.

He opened the first telegram. He saw nothing but the name of Harry Daniel Bensham. He opened the second one. He could see nothing now. Then his vision cleared and he saw disjointed words: It is with deep regret . . . Jonathan Richard Bensham. Oh Christ Almighty! no! no! Oh Johnny, Harry. Johnny, Harry. No! No! Oh Jesus Christ! why have you done this? Why? The question was bawling in his head when the door opened and he turned. They all turned and looked at the woman standing there. She was staring at the telegrams that Ben was holding before him, one in each hand, like prayer books. Then she seemed to leap across the distance from the drawing-room door right to Ben's feet and she tore them from his hand and stared at them.

No one moved. The girls had stopped their crying. Ben held his breath, and it was as if Barbara had long since died. Her face was ashen, her body straight and stiff. There was no flicker of her eyelids as she stared into Ben's face; no muscle in her body moved until the scream erupted that brought them all into moving, shouting life.

For the first time since he was eight years old Benjamin put his arms around his mother. He held her tightly to him and shouted above her screams, 'Don't! Don't, Mother! For God's sake!' Then his hands were mixed with those of Ada's as she tried to unloosen her mistress's grip from her hair. The neatly plaited black coils were hanging loose and the hair pins were dropping on the polished floor of the hall, their pinging sounds lost in the screams. Ben tried to close his ears against the sound, yet in his head he was screaming too.

Struggling as if with a maniac, it took him all his time with the help of Ada and Betty to get his mother into the drawing room, and when once they had forced her on to the couch, her screaming and struggling stopped so abruptly that they all lay for a minute in a huddled heap over her. Then Ben, pulling himself back on to his knees, looked up at Ada and gasped, 'Send . . . send for the doctor. And Betty, go . . . go down to the village post office. Get them . . . get them to phone my . . . my father.'

Why . . . why in hell's name hadn't they got the telephone in the house by now!

Oh God! The two of them. There'd only ever be a third of himself

613

left now. They had been one, they had been born as one, and they had grown up as one. She hadn't been able to divide them; her love and her hate hadn't been able to divide them. Oh God in heaven, look at her; was she going too? In sudden fear he put his hand on her breast, then dropped his head to it. There was a faint beat. He gently lifted her eyelids. She was unconscious.

His mind began repeating his brothers' names in agonized fashion: Oh Harry; oh Harry, oh Jonathan; oh Jonathan; Harry, Harry.

He dragged himself to his feet. His head was bowed, the tears were raining down his face. If anybody had to go, why couldn't it have been him? He had been near it a dozen times these past months; twice he had been surprised when he had come to and found himself alive. Once he thought he had been buried alive. When they dragged him from the mud and from amidst the four German bodies, the bodies from which he had taken life, they'd had to scrape the mud from his face and out of his mouth. They'd had to pour the thick hot tea down his throat because he thought he'd lost the use of his arms, and he had until the shock wore off. But had he died, and a single telegram had come, the shock she would have received would not have made her scream.

He turned to the fireplace and, resting his arms on it, he lowered his head on to them. The world had been created by a madman; God was a madman; no reasonable thing or power would create torture for no purpose. The experience of the past months, the chaos in which the world was drowning was not, to his mind, the result of either a country's greed, or the ambition of nations; politicians of their own volition could not, he reasoned now, create such havoc, for the human mind could and would think, dissect, reason and then act in the end to preserve its own survival. No, there was a malevolent power, a mad God playing with the universe, and he was so powerful, so indiscriminate he directed his attention equally to families as to nations; he inflicted special torture. . . . 'Aw' – he tossed his head from side to side – 'stop it! stop it.' This business about God and pain. It wasn't the mud that sent you mad, nor mangled bodies, it was deep inner personal misery. . . . And now he was really alone. No more Jonathan or Harry. No more than the other parts of himself. It was unbearable, unbearable.

The long shuddering breath turned him swiftly towards the couch and he was kneeling by her side again. He watched her whole body quiver. He caught hold of her hands and waited for her to open her eyes.

It was some minutes before she did, and he looked down into them, his own shining, seal-black with tears, compassion and love. She stared straight up into them and, as if remembering a nightmare of which he had been part, she shrank against the back of the couch and, her hands snapping from his, joined themselves between her breasts and there appeared on her face such a look of hate and condemnation that he literally drew back from it.

Plainly, as if written there, he read the condemnation in her eyes. She was condemning him for being alive; her beloved Jonathan and her dearest Harry were dead, but he, the scourge of her life, the reminder of her beginnings, still breathed, and he groaned inwardly and deeply, No, no!

There now came over him the dreaded feeling that he had experienced once before when, during the retreat, he found himself separated from the others. As the night lifted and the dawn came up, he saw that he was lying on some kind of plain and he was afraid to get off his belly and crawl, much less to stand up, for he got the weird idea that once he took a step forward he'd fall off the edge of the earth.

Now he was standing on the brink again and all he desired was to fall over, but such was the weight of despair in him that it kept him riveted to the spot.

It was the doctor who, entering the room, pushed him back and into sanity ... for the time being.

THE EDGE OF THE EARTH

I

'I'M BEING SENT, I've got no say in the matter. I've told you.'
'You can object.'
'But what if I don't want to object?'
Hannah Radlet looked from her mother to her grandmother, where they stood like a combined force behind the kitchen table. Hannah was thirty-two years old, and of those years she had memories that took her back for twenty-eight of them, and they always conjured up the picture of her mother and grandmother standing together whenever they were doing battle. Her father would be on one side of the table and there they would be, not shoulder to shoulder, because her grandmother, although stooped, was much taller than her mother, but side by side, and nearly always their expressions would be similar, as if their thoughts were being projected from one mind.

She had thought of late that a war was nothing new to her, for she had been brought up in the midst of a private war. When she was very young she had stood on the outside and watched, but as she grew older she was drawn into it.

She was twenty-two before she escaped the battlefield of the farm. She knew now that her sole reason for her marrying Arthur Pettit had been in order to get away from her mother and grandmother. But she hadn't been married a week before she realized she had jumped out of the frying pan into the fire, for then her own daily fight, and it was a daily fight as well as a nightly one, was to prevent her body from being ravished by a man who, when it came to satisfying his needs, had no idea of tenderness.

Arthur Pettit had been an auctioneer and estate agent, and part of her misfortune, she considered, was that their flat was over his office.

She often wondered too what she would have done eventually if he hadn't died within three months of their marriage. He died a heroic death, everybody said so; he was trampled to death right outside his own home by two huge-footed brewery horses pulling a dray. He had been entering his office when he saw the child aimlessly crossing the road and the horses frantically galloping down from the other end, the dray swaying madly while the barrels rolled off it.

The two horses, placid creatures, pets of many of the townsfolk, had been shot into an hysterical gallop by simultaneously being stabbed in their haunches with hatpins in the fun-seeking hands of two gormless youths.

Both he and the child had died, and the town had mourned him and pitied Hannah, and she had cried openly, and in secret she had cried, with not a little shame that she could feel nothing but release at being free once more. And she wasn't only free from the marriage, she was free from her mother and her grandmother, and she was determined to stay free.

After having refused their pressing offer to return home she took up nursing. But things didn't work out here for her either; it was, she imagined, as if the two women on the farm were willing her back to them, for she suffered recurrent attacks of rheumatism. The rheumatic fever she'd had when a child had fortunately left her heart intact, but inflicted, from time to time, severe bouts of rheumatism on her, particularly in the lower part of her back, and these could leave her incapacitated for weeks.

When her father had collected her from the hospital on this particular occasion she had said to him, 'I'm not staying, mind,' and he answered, 'I don't want you to,' and she knew he didn't. As much as he needed her comfort he would let her go without a restraining word.

She had lain on her back five weeks, but it was almost five months before she was fully recovered, and during that time she was once more drawn into the private war. So again she left them. Tears, recriminations, admonitions did not deter her once she was able to look after herself.

She was stubborn. She was spoilt. Her father had spoilt her. They both said this, but, as always, her mother finished, 'He hasn't only ruined my life and made your granny's a misery he'll spoil yours an' all. You'll see. You wait and see.'

When she was very young she had thought, Poor Dad. Poor, poor Dad. That is before she knew about the woman, and that they on their side had a case. It was her mother who had screamed the facts at her one day when she was fifteen. 'Fishing!' she had yelled. 'Fishing! You want your eyes opened, girl. You want to see him as he really is. Your dear, dear dad has been leading a double life for years, keeping two houses. Yes, yes, keeping two houses. He's got a fancy bit, the fancy bit that took this off.' She had beaten her hand against the empty dress. 'A devil from hell if there ever was one. And her a married woman with a good man and three sons. But she's not satisfied. She never was satisfied; she wanted everything; nothing but the world would suit that Mallen piece. By God! if she gets my prayers her death will be long and slow, and her mind clear. . . . Where do you think he was last week when he was out all night? The rim was supposed to come off the wheel, remember? And Shankley only had the cart in a few weeks afore. The rim came off the wheel! Huh! And his day off a week that he insists on. How many times has he taken you into town of late? Answer me that.'

She had stood amazed looking at her mother and, with a strange pain in her heart, had thought of all the excuses her father had made not to take her into Hexham or Newcastle or wherever he was going, and on that day she recalled with surprise that she had already seen the fancy woman, she had met her. It was in Hexham on a market day. How old had she been? Ten or eleven? She had gone to the shops for some errands and had left her father in the market place. It was when she was making her way back that she saw him standing up a side street talking to a lady. When she went to him, he had put his hand on her shoulder and the lady had stared at her, and he had said, 'This is Hannah.'

She remembered that the lady had been very pretty – she hadn't put the word elegant to her in those days but now she could. She had recognized her as class, but her face had been white and strained, and it almost appeared to her as if her father was in the middle of yet another row, and with this smart lady.

He had pressed her away, saying, 'I'll catch up with you. Go on down to the market.' And when he did catch up with her he was quiet and looked worried. It wasn't until they were on their way home that he said, 'Hannah, will you do something for me?' and she said, 'Yes, Dad, I'll do anything for you.' He had then stopped the trap and taken her hand in his and said to her, 'Don't say a word to either your mother or your grannie about the lady you met today,' and she had said, 'No, I won't.' And after a while she had forgotten about her. That was until she was fifteen.

Now there was nothing she didn't know about the Mallen piece or the family connection between her and Grandmother Radlet. Moreover, she knew all about Brigie, the governess, who had been old Thomas Mallen's kept woman, and who was now mistress of the Hall over the hills; the Hall that had been turned into a hospital-cum-convalescent home, where she was going to work.

'Do you know it's full of loonies?'

She came back at her mother sharply now, saying, 'Oh, for God's sake! Mam. Don't be stupid.'

'Don't you take that tone with me, girl.'

'Well, don't talk about things you know nothing about.'

'They're loonies. Your Uncle Jim said you can hear them yelling from the road.'

'Me Uncle Jim! He should have been writing stories, me Uncle Jim, or running a daily gossip column. He's an old woman.'

'That's enough. That's enough, Hannah.' It was Constance addressing her now. 'Don't speak like that about your Uncle Jim who has worked so hard and who cared for your mother long before she came into this house.'

'Well, to my mind it's a great pity he did, and then he wouldn't have made me and everybody else feel we owed him the earth.'

The two women were so shocked that for a moment they were deprived of speech, and they remained indignantly silent as Hannah went on, 'Those men over there are no more loony than you are; some of them are the result of shell-shock, others have been gassed, and some just couldn't stand any more.' She now leant slightly forward and stuck her chin out towards them as she said, 'And you know what happens to people who can't stand any more? They explode ... up here.' She tapped her head twice with her finger. 'That's what they do. . . .' She paused, then ended, 'But them over there, they're just ordinary fellows who one way or another have had more than enough.'

'You seem to know a lot about them.' Constance narrowed her eyes at her granddaughter and Hannah, looking back at her, said, 'No, I don't know a lot, not yet, but from what I've seen. . . .'

'From what you've seen?' Sarah's crutch made two dull taps on the drugget-covered stone floor as she took a step forward, and now she was leaning over the table as she cried, 'You haven't been over there already?'

'Yes, I've been over there already. And what's more, I've seen the wicked old witch herself, Mrs Bensham, the one you used to call Brigie.' She turned her head and nodded towards her grandmother. 'And how you can keep up a feud against an old woman like that beats me. Not that she needs your sympathy. From what I've heard she may look like a little wizened nut but her mind's still intact and everybody there knows it. And she's respected, highly respected. . . .'

'That's enough.' Constance stared at her granddaughter for a moment, then turned from the table. The mention of Brigie, the mention of 'the little wizened nut' caused an ache, like a homesickness that she often experienced at night when her memories took her back to days which, over the distance, now seemed to have been gloriously happy, when Michael was young, and Barbara was young, and they had harvest suppers in the barn and everybody danced. Sarah had danced, the niece of the farm labourer, she had danced with the young master of the farm, and even Brigie had danced. She had been light on her feet, had Brigie.

The early jealousies, the rejections, even her disastrous marriage to Donald Radlet, appeared from this distance all part of a peaceful time compared with these latter years. These years that covered nearly half her lifetime and had been fraught with nothing but bitterness and recrimination.

She would never admit to herself that if Barbara had come into this house as Michael's wife she could not have suffered more, in fact she knew she would have suffered much less, for then she would not have lost her son. Then she would not have been forced to stand by the side of a daughter-in-law whom she had trained from ignorance into some semblance of literacy, but whose basic thoughts and attitudes still remained those of the lower-class farm workers from whom she had sprung.

Her years spent instructing Sarah would have undoubtedly borne fruit if the girl, and then the woman, had been happy, but the crippling of the girls' body had also crippled her mind, until now she was nothing more than a shrew, a small, loud-mouthed, deformed shrew. Yet she allied herself to her for years; for after all, she had told herself Sarah was only human, she had to have someone on her side, at the same time arguing that she herself was morally defending right.

Time and again it amazed her that anyone like Michael, who fundamentally was not strong minded, for at one time she could sway him as she wished, could keep up this intrigue over what had been a lifetime, and hold them to ransom as it were. Years ago he had given them an ultimatum. In this very kitchen he had faced them both and said, 'I'll give you a choice and this is my last word on it because I'm sick to death of you both; leave me to go my own road, as I'm doing now, and things stay as they are; keep on and tell me just once more I've got to stay home, then I'll tell you the date when we'll all leave because I'll sell up ... like that!' He had snapped his fingers and the sound had been like the crack of a gun reverberating through the kitchen. And it could have been a gun, for his words, like bullets, pierced her heart. 'I'm seeing her. Aye I'm seeing her. Let's bring it into the open. And I'm going on seeing her. Get your heads together as usual and decide. You needn't worry, I won't see you left in a field. There's Palmer's cottage down the road; it's been empty this while back. It's more than a cottage it's a house, and has six good rooms. I've already enquired the price of it. It has two good acres of land to it; you could both be self-supporting. As I said, it's up to you.' And on that he had walked out, leaving them speechless. And from then, daily, without let up, she had prayed that something would happen to that sperm of hell, because that's all she was, that's all she had ever been, she had come from a hell raiser, and a line of hell raisers, and she had been a she-devil ever since.

But the reasons came and went, the years came and went, and her prayers weren't answered. She did hear a faint rumour that Barbara had lost her hearing again but it was never confirmed. But it was confirmed that she had lost two of her sons, drowned at sea, and together. On that day she had thought, Now she'll know what it feels like. But she has still one son left.

Now Jim said he was in the Hall and as mad as a hatter. One of the orderlies had told him he was the worst one there. They had given him a room to himself, not because he owned the place, or would when the old girl went, but because he lashed out right and left on the slightest provocation.

And Hannah was going there.

Constance could not actually sort her feelings out with regard to this move; the only thing she was sure of was her concern wasn't entirely caused through fear for Hannah's safety. Hannah was a self-possessed, self-willed individual and in the main could take care of herself. Part of the feeling was resentment at the fact that her grand-daughter was going into her old home, and that she had already recognized Brigie as the owner of it.

Brigie, Constance considered, had come out of all this very well. When one came to think about it there was really no justice, for all their misfortunes had begun with Brigie. If she hadn't become their Uncle Thomas's mistress none of the tragedies, with the exception of their Cousin Dick almost killing that bailiff, would have happened.

Her thoughts were cut off when the door opened and Michael entered.

Michael at fifty-three looked every year of his age. The hair that had been corn-coloured was now completely white. Although his body was still straight, it was heavy. His face was lined, and jowls were showing beneath the chin. Yet overall he still appeared an attractive man.

As soon as he stepped over the threshold he took in the situation. But in any case he wouldn't have been left in ignorance of it for long for Sarah turned on him immediately, crying, 'Do you know where this one's going?'

He went to the sink that stood under the window and, gripping the pump handle to the side of it, he worked it two or three times before he said, 'Yes, I know where she's going.'

'Oh, of course you would. And you agree with it. In fact I shouldn't be surprised but you put her up to it, felt she was ready for a family gathering. . . .'

He had the soap between his palms when he turned round and looked at her, stared at her, and then he said one word, 'Careful,' before turning slowly about and finishing the business of washing his hands.

As he dried them on a towel he stood staring out of the little window above the sink. 'And you agree with it,' she had said. He had been floored when Hannah told him where she was going, because even to his mind it didn't seem right somehow, piling insult on top of injury, as the saying went. But there, Hannah was an individual, she would go her own gait. And he was glad of that; oh yes, he was glad of that. But nevertheless he couldn't say he was happy about her decision to take up work in the Hall. Apart from it being sort of enemy ground to those two back there, Ben was there, Barbara's one remaining son, and although he felt, in fact he knew, she had no feeling for him, she was likely to take it amiss that his daughter – and Sarah's daughter – was going there to work, to live there, and could come in contact with him. There was no knowing. He made a slight movement with his head against his thoughts: the whole thing, the whole business seemed like a web with some giant spider going round and round dragging them like flies to the centre and to some final conclusion as it were.

His head now jerked as if tossing his thoughts aside, for his thoughts troubled him these days. So many things troubled him these days. He never imagined the time would come when he would think Barbara troubled him, but she did. She had become a sick woman. She had one focal point in her life, and that was himself. It was one thing to love, and be loved, and they had both done that, oh yes, yes, the stolen days with her had been all that made life bearable at one time, but of late even before she lost the boys there had been a change in her. He sometimes thought that behind her loving she was constantly condemning him. And there was every possibility that she was, for he had broken his promise to her, more than once.

He should have left those two behind there when Hannah became able to take care of herself, but he hadn't, because he had realized, and he had tried to make her realize, that they too had to be looked after. His mother had grown old rapidly; she was old even ten years ago; and Sarah, well, Sarah had to be provided for, he owed her that. He couldn't say to Barbara that he was being forced to stay with his wife by way of payment for the injury she had inflicted on her.

It was all so complicated, so brain wearying, so hellish at times.

He turned and looked at his daughter now and said, 'What time are you leaving?'

'Any time.'

'Have you any bags?'

'No; they went from the Infirmary straight up there yesterday.'

There was a combined catch of breaths expressing indignant astonishment from both his mother and his wife, and without looking at them he said, 'I'll get the trap ready then,' and turned on his heel and walked out.

Hannah looked at her mother and grandmother and they stared back at her; then her mother, flouncing ungainly around, hobbled towards the door leading into the hall muttering unintelligibly, and Constance, after shaking her head sadly at Hannah, exclaimed through twitching lips, 'Girl! Girl! You don't know what you're doing,' then turned and followed her daughter-in-law.

Left alone, Hannah rested her head on her hand and closed her eyes tightly. Oh, those two; they always managed to make her feel in the wrong, so that every time she left them she was overwhelmed with guilt and torn with pity for them. But she mustn't let them break her down. Once she did that she too would be finished. She must get away, even if the Hall did turn out to be a mad-house, it would be preferable to this one.

6

ANYONE WHO HAD KNOWN THE HALL before the war would not have recognized the interior if they had entered it now. Beyond the lobby was what appeared to be a hotel reception area in that it had a long desk to the left of the staircase and a number of easy chairs in groups of three, each with its own small table, placed in set positions to the right of the stairs.

The drawing room had the word 'Private' nailed to a panel, and it was private inasmuch as it held, stacked almost from floor to ceiling, most of the pictures and the best pieces of furniture from the first floor. The dining room remained almost as it had been, a place in which to eat; but the cutlery was no longer silver and the china was that issued for the use of Army officers.

The library was the only room in the house that had not been changed; it was known now as the rest room.

The morning room was now the matron's bedroom and sitting room combined, and the rooms off the kitchen corridor had been utilized as small dormitories for the staff, while the servants' hall had become their dining room.

The first floor bedrooms had all been turned into dormitories, with the exception of the smallest which was at the far end of the landing and near the new set of stairs leading to what had been the nursery floor.

The gallery, too, was a dormitory, but the doors giving access to it from the main landing and those at the far end leading onto the wide passage, from where the lift now rose, were kept locked. The gallery was known by the patients as the 'Bonkers Bunker'. Most of the men who came to the Hall had their introduction to it through the 'Bunker'. After a few days, or a few weeks, or a few months, when they were no longer afraid of the bars across the lower parts of the windows, and could look up and appreciate the painted ceiling, they left the Bunker and went into E dorm, and some quickly, others not so quickly, graduated through D, C, and B, until one day they happily found themselves in A. That was the time they shook hands all round, laughed, joked, thanked the sister, kissed some of the nurses and got into the coach and were driven to the station; the coach because Mrs Bensham didn't like motor cars, although she allowed them into the grounds in the form of ambulances, staff cars, and food trucks.

Ben did not pass through the Bunker. Since he first came he had been given a room to himself, which arrangement was considered 'a bit thick' by some of the officers; everybody who came there went through the Bunker, and if anybody needed to go through the Bunker it was the new admission, because he kept the whole floor awake for nights running.

It was the matron who finally answered the complaints with, 'Gentlemen, Captain Bensham, I think, is entitled to a small room in what is virtually his own house.'

The grumblers apologized and said they understood and that she would hear nothing more from them.

But in the days that followed it was difficult for them to keep their promise, for the Bensham fellow seemed to wait until midnight before starting his pranks. First he would talk, and then he would yell, and then he would scream, and what he screamed burned their ears, until he was quietened with a jab in the arm. And again they said it was a bit thick and, what was more, it wasn't right that the nurses had to put up with him; he should be in the Bunker where the orderlies could take it. In fact the general opinion was that he should have had an orderly to himself both night and day, but then as most of them knew they hadn't enough orderlies to staff the Bunker.

But Captain Bensham remained in the end room. Special nurses were detailed to him and the door was locked whenever they left him alone.

Hannah had been three weeks in the Hall before she saw Captain Bensham.

It came about that Nurse Byng, who was a hefty fifteen stone, developed tonsillitis and was ordered to the sick bay. Her relief was Nurse Conway, who although not so big, was well equipped to hold her own, at least she had a pair of lungs that she could use with some force if she ever needed help.

The only nurse at the moment available for relief work was Nurse Pettit, who as a not fully-trained nurse had been put on 'breaking in duties', which meant seeing to the chair patients, keeping an eye on those in D and trying to get coherent answers from those in C. So Matron Carter told Sister Deal to take Nurse Hannah Pettit along to Captain Bensham's room and to introduce her to Nurse Conway who would show her what must be done.

The first thing Hannah noticed about Captain Bensham was the white streak of hair. Her father had told her about that, the thing that singled out the Mallens. Then it had become of little or no interest as she took in the rest of the man.

He was sitting in a chair by the side of the window and she had never, not in all her life, seen anyone so still, not even in death.

She had washed and laid out a number of dead but there had remained a softness about them. Although their hearts had stopped beating there still seemed some life left in their flesh. But this man had about him the stillness of stone.

He was a big man, at least she thought he would be if there was flesh on his bones. His face looked deathly white against the blackness of his hair. His eyes too looked black, but it was a dull blackness, devoid of sheen, like spent coal. His hands lay palm downwards cupping his knees. He reminded her of someone she had seen sitting just like that. The Sphinx? Abraham Lincoln? He didn't look human.

Nurse Conway said to her without bothering to lower her voice, 'He can sit like this for hours, but don't take anything for granted, he can come out of it like the crack of a whip, and with just such a sound. It's as if something snaps, and then he'll start, talk, talk, talk. He'll start telling you everything as if he knew who he was talking to. It'll all be mixed up, but' – she stopped and jerked her head and, looking at him, she smiled. 'The other day he did know who he was talking to. I nearly fell over backwards; he called me by name. Poor devil.' She went to him and drew her hand gently over the top of his hair; it was as if she were caressing a child.

She turned now and looked at Hannah, saying, 'You can go about your usual stuff; tidy up, put fresh flowers in when they send them along, but just keep your eye on him. Remember if you hear that snap, I don't know where it comes from, his mouth doesn't move, it seems as if something goes click inside him. Oh, there's another thing, he may not talk at all, he may just stare at you. You'll have to put up with that. Don't move away, it seems to agitate him when you move away, just go on with whatever you're doing, knitting, reading, anything. All right?'

'All right.'

Hannah wanted to keep looking at the man, this man who was the son of her father's mistress, or woman. Whichever way you looked at it, it amounted to the same thing. But she made herself attend to the requirements of the room.

It was a pleasant room, not clinical. There was a bow-fronted chest of drawers, a rosewood wardrobe and dressing table, only the bed was similar to the furniture in the dormitories, it was the usual hospital iron-framed bed.

When at last she allowed herself to sit down, she took a chair at the opposite side of the window and once again she looked fully at the patient, and her mind emitted two words, and they were almost verbal: Poor devil. And again she thought, Poor devil.

He must have been a good looking man at one time, his height, his hair, the bone formation of his face, his mouth; his mouth was wide and the lips full. She only just in time stopped herself from visibly starting and getting to her feet when he moved. Although it was just the slightest movement of his head in her direction it was as if she were watching a granite statue being impregnated with life. For a moment she felt as fearful as if she were actually witnessing such a spectacle.

When his gaze became fixed on her face she looked back into his eyes and she smiled shyly while asking herself uneasily whether she should talk or remain quiet. Nurse Conway had given no instructions along these lines. She decided to talk.

Her voice faltered slightly when, nodding towards the window, she said, 'It's a beautiful morning.' She paused. 'The gardens are looking lovely.' Another pause. 'It's . . . it's a pity they've dug a lot of them up for vegetables.' Now she swallowed, or rather gulped, then she said, 'It'll . . . it'll be nice when you're well enough to take-a-walk.' Her voice trailed away as she imagined she saw the skin of his face move. It was like a faint ripple; it was there one second and then it was gone, she must have imagined it. She did not talk any more but tried to assume a calmness under his vacant stare.

It was with genuine relief that she rose to answer the tap on the door, and when the young ward maid pushed a tea-trolley towards her she said, 'Oh thanks, thanks. We can do with that.'

After closing the door she drew the trolley towards the window. He was still looking straight ahead as if she had never left the chair. She talked now as if to herself, saying, 'Oh, toasted tea-cakes. I must say they do you well here. Can't grumble about the food. Bread and butter, jam. Ah! strawberry. I wonder if the pips are wooden.' She glanced towards him, smiling, then shook her head at herself.

She poured out the tea, brought the trolley close to his side, then, lifting his hand from his knee, she placed the cup and saucer in it. He could feed himself, they said, which was odd she considered, for why, when he could move his muscles, did he assume a rigidity that made him appear paralysed for hours and hours on end? She stood watching him as he drank the tea. He did not sip it, but poured it down his throat, hot as it was, almost at one go. The action was rough, almost uncouth.

'You're thirsty,' she said and took the cup from his hand and refilled it, but before she gave it back to him she put a plate into his hand with half a buttered tea-cake on it. Now his eating took a different form; he nibbled at the tea-cake and then chewed slowly before he swallowed. When she offered him the other half of the tea-cake he made no attempt to lift it to his mouth, and so she began to coax him. Her hand on his shoulder, bending forward, she looked into his face and said, 'Come on, try. Just have this other bit. It's very nice. You must eat. You're a big fellow you know, you've got to get some flesh on those bones.' At this point her mind chided her for treating him as a child, but what else could she do, she asked herself, he was a child.

'All right then, if you don't want it.' When she went to take the plate from him his fingers formed a grip on it, and then he was lifting the tea-cake to his mouth, and as if she had achieved a victory she laughed gently as she said, 'There now, there now. You wanted it after all, didn't you?'

When he had finished eating she said, 'I won't press you to any bread and butter, and really, I always suspect the jam.' She leant towards him, her face smiling again. 'You know my father swears he knows of a factory where they make wooden pips to put in raspberry and strawberry jam.'

She felt slightly silly and not a little guilty at mentioning her father to him. As his eyes surveyed her, she turned to the trolley and, picking up a piece of currant loaf, she said, 'Try this, it looks nice.'

When her hand and the plate were pushed slowly but firmly aside and he reached out to the trolley and picked up a piece of bread and butter, she stood gazing at him. Well, well; he knew what he wanted. There must be times when his mind worked in an ordinary fashion; could that mean he understood what was being said to him? She'd better be careful, they should all be careful and not treat him as a mental child. Poor soul. Poor soul. He reminded her in some ways of the stories of her childhood. He was like the giant who was locked away in the fortress of a bigger giant, and was being slowly starved to death.... But he had put his hand out and taken that bread and butter. She must tell Nurse Conway about that.

An hour later she told Nurse Conway about it, and Nurse Conway said, 'Did he really? Are you sure?' and she answered, 'Yes, he pushed the currant bread away and put his hand out and took half a slice of plain bread and butter.'

'Oh, I'll report that to Sister and she'll tell Matron. The doctor will likely be interested to hear that an' all....'

But the great news didn't get as far as the Matron, for the sister informed Nurse Conway that Captain Bensham had shown such signs as this in hospital, but they hadn't lasted, in fact according to his record he had regressed after such an effort; efforts tired him.

.   .   .   .   .

Every afternoon for the following week Hannah relieved Nurse Conway, and it was on the Friday afternoon that she met his father and Mrs Bensham.

She hadn't seen 'the old lady' since the day she came for interview, and then she had only caught a glimpse of her going to the lift, and she hadn't needed to be told that the shrunken little woman with the straight back was Brigie. Even without the attention being meted out to her, she would have recognized her.

It was around three o'clock in the afternoon when the matron herself heralded into the room the old lady and a slightly built man, who looked about fifty and who bore no resemblance whatever to the patient sitting by the window.

The matron had a loud and cheerful voice. 'Here we are then, Captain Bensham, here we are, two visitors for you, your father and. . . .' The matron never knew what title to apply to Brigie when connecting her with this man, so she ended still on a loud note, 'Mrs Bensham.'

The figure in the chair didn't move; it was as if he were stone deaf, like his mother.

Matron now turned from Brigie and Dan towards Hannah, saying, 'This is Nurse Pettit. Nurse Conway is off duty, and I'm afraid Nurse Byng has gone down with tonsillitis, and the winter over. Dear, dear! one doesn't expect such things.'

As Matron motioned her, with a discreet movement of her hand, towards the screen, indicating that she make herself scarce Hannah thought, What a stupid thing to say. And her a matron and all. And the winter over. But then, likely she was embarrassed in her own way. It must be very difficult ushering the owner of a house into one of her own rooms as if she were nothing more than a visitor.

Matron was saying now, in a low voice, 'The nurse will be on hand should you need her,' then she made her adieu and left.

Hannah sat behind the screen in the far corner of the room; she opened a book and attempted to read. Then after some moments, curiosity getting the better of her, she made no further pretence at reading but strained her ears to catch what was being said, and as she listened she shook her head, for the father was talking to his son like everyone else, as if he were addressing a child.

And this was exactly how Dan did see Ben, as a child. As always, he was finding it difficult to talk to him. If he had been called upon to speak the truth he would have admitted that he hated to come into this room because, when he looked at his son, this son who had been 'the big fellow', tears seemed to ooze out of every pore in his body.

Poor Ben! Poor fellow! It would have been God's mercy if he had gone with the other two; oh yes, yes. Yet he was selfish enough at times not to wish him gone, because he was all that was left of his own flesh and blood; besides John, of course, but John was a different sort of flesh and blood.

It was hard at times to believe that this was his son he was looking at, this great shell of a man who had twice been mentioned in despatches but whose mind had eventually been burned out in the fires of war, shell-shock they called it, on top of slight gassing. Ironically the gas from their own lines had turned back on them, driven by a contrary wind on a day in September 1915. Minutes later a shell had burst which should have blown him to pieces, but it had left no physical mark on him, it had just turned him into a living corpse. Yet he was much better, if one could use the word better, than he had been some months ago in that hospital. God! that hospital. He would have gone mad himself if he'd had to visit there just one more time. The agony of seeing grown men rocking themselves like babies and, like babies, crying with the same whining, frustrated cry of a hungry infant was too much.

The doctor said Ben's case wasn't unusual; withdrawal symptoms he called them. He said he had frozen and had placed a wall of ice between himself and reality as it were, but he would gradually thaw – he hoped.

And he had thawed, but his second state was worse than the first, for, unless heavily drugged, he continued to talk, wail, and shout for hours on end, and not only that but he would also attack anyone who went near him.

His thawing caused him to be put under stricter confinement, until gradually he took up the pattern of immobility for much longer periods and his outbursts became verbal only.

Dan had had to pull a lot of strings before he could get him transferred to the Hall, for the military had passed it to be used only for what they surprisingly termed mild cases of shock and recuperation.

He had begun, as he always did, 'Can you hear me, Ben? Can you understand me? You ... you are much better. You-are-doing-fine. The doctor's report is-good.' He looked into the unblinking eyes and nodded. 'Brigie is here. Aren't you going to look at her? She has come all the way from upstairs to see you.' He still spaced his words.

'Oh! Don't put it like that, Dan.' Brigie's voice was low and thin; but it had no tremor to it, it still retained the timbre of the Miss Brigmore tone. Still low, she went on, 'Treat him normally. I'm ... I'm positive he understands; behind it all I'm sure he knows and understands.'

She recalled that Katie used to talk to Lawrence like this. Katie. Dear, dear Katie. She would miss Katie.

There was a movement behind the screen as if a book had dropped and they both looked towards it. Then Dan said, ' Yes, yes, perhaps you're right.' He coughed before resuming, and slowly and sadly now, he said, 'Your Aunt Katie died yesterday. Poor dear Katie. You remember your Aunt Katie?'

Their eyes were drawn to Ben's knee on which his first finger was tapping, and Brigie muttered, 'There, there, what did I tell you! 'I'm sure he wants to say something. He's trying; look at his face.'

Brigie now put out a thin wrinkled hand and turned Ben's face towards her, and as she did so there was a sound as if he had clicked his tongue forcibly against the roof of his mouth, yet his lips hadn't moved. The sound was repeated louder this time, and now his lips did open and as the words tumbled from his mouth Hannah came quickly from behind the screen.

'Murphy! - Murphy! - Hell's - flames - Murphy - bleeding - guts - over - you - go - High Command - High bloody Command - Hell - Imbeciles - Imbeciles - Imbeciles - Over - you - go - Murphy! - Murphy! . . .'

Hannah, who was now holding his hands which were twitching as if from slight electric shock, turned her head to where Dan was assisting Brigie to her feet and said quietly, 'If you wouldn't mind.'

Dan nodded at her, and the expression on his face was almost as sad as that on his son's.

When the door closed behind them, the agitation in Ben's hands lessened a little and his words were spaced more evenly. As he talked his head nodded, but all the while he kept his eyes on her face as if pleading with her.

When big slow tears spilled over his lower lids her own blinked rapidly and she murmured, 'It's all right. There, there, it's all right,' and she put her arms about him as she would have done with a child, and pressed his cheek tight against her shoulder trying to still the flow of his words, but all the time he went on talking. From what sounded like gibberish she recognized here and there place names, battle place names; then he began to repeat words that sounded like poetry. Over and over again he kept saying, 'Swimming-in-the-womb-like-a-tadpole-in-a-jar, held-by-a-string-in-the-hand-of-God.'

He must have repeated it ten times when she lifted his head away from her and pressed him back into the chair, and the movement checked the rhythm of his words. His voice less agitated, he began chattering about Murphy again, and she sat by his side and took his limp hand into hers and asked gently, 'Who is Murphy?'

'Murphy. Murphy – towards his dissolve – Murphy – dissolve –'

'Who is Murphy?'

'Murphy. Murphy – all guts, Murphy.'

'Who is Murphy? Tell me, who is Murphy? Your friend, another officer?'

'Murphy. Wise Murphy, wise Murphy.'

The door opened and the Sister entered.

'Having trouble?'

'No, Sister, just . . . just a little spasm.'

'People are so thoughtless, people who should know better, they should never have told him about his aunt. His father said he thought that's what brought it on.'

Sister Deal now looked at her watch and said, 'You'll be relieved in half an hour, and it's your day off tomorrow isn't it, Nurse?'

'Yes, Sister.'

'You're lucky you live so near and can go home.'

. . . 'Yes, Sister.'

'There now, there now.' She flicked a thread from the front of Ben's dressing gown, saying, 'Dear, dear; it's untidy we are;' then went straight on, 'It's a pity Mrs Bensham has an antipathy towards motor vehicles or else someone could have driven you over the hills tonight.'

'That's all right, Sister. Jacob's van will get me across first thing in the morning.'

'Is it very far?'

'About seven miles.'

'Your people have a farm, I understand.'

'Yes, Sister. Wolfbur Farm.'

'Do you like these parts?'

'Yes.' She paused. 'Yes, I like them very much.' And she did. If her home had been happy she would have been content to stay among the hills for life.

'I wish I did.' The Sister now looked at her and, the dignity of her position slipping from her for a moment, she was just one young woman talking to another as she said, 'I've never been in such a benighted place in my life. What . . . what did you find to do, I mean before the war?'

'Oh' – Hannah lifted her shoulders – 'everything. At least, looking back it seems that there was never a spare moment; and the highlight of the week was going into Hexham with my father. . . .'

'Oh dear. Oh dear, he's off again.'

They both turned towards Ben who was now yelling unintelligibly at the top of his voice, and the Sister said, 'I think we'd better get him back to bed. I'll give him a shot to quieten him down; it's been too much for him. I still say they should never have told him about his aunt.'

·   ·   ·   ·   ·

Up on the floor above, Brigie, watching Dan walking back and forth, said suddenly, 'Stop that and sit down. It won't get you anywhere.'

Dan sat down; then he leant forward, put his elbows on his knees, and dropped his face into his hands.

Brigie did not speak for some moments. Her tongue flicked in and out over her wrinkled lips until she stopped it by sucking them inwards as if pressing them down on some emotion, which was exactly what she was doing.

At ninety-five she knew that her heart could not stand the pressure of too much emotion, emotions wore one out, and of late years she had been grateful for the habit that she had been forced to acquire during her governess days of disciplining her emotions. She could count on one hand the times she had allowed them to get the better of her. Now, it was imperative to her very life that she did not allow old age to weaken her defences. Her voice was calm as she said, 'He is better than he was; you should be grateful for small mercies.'

'Sometimes I think I would rather see him dead.'

She endorsed this statement whole-heartedly but she didn't voice it; what she said was, 'He's in good hands, he's getting every care, but the one we must think about now is Lawrence. What's going to become of him? Poor, poor Lawrence, one won't be able to say of him he's in good hands and he's getting every care, if he goes into one of those homes. With all the money in the world, you'll never get the right people to look after him.'

Dan straightened up and passed his hand tightly over his chin before he said, 'Well, there's nothing you can do about Lawrence, Brigie. You have to make your mind up on that.'

'I don't agree with you.'

He turned his head and looked at her.

'I've been thinking, and now, Dan.' She raised her finger and moved it once in his direction before going on, 'Before I tell you what's in my mind, I must ask you not to condemn it out of hand. I may be old in years and I admit my body, although not decrepit, is not what it used to be, but my mind is still as clear today as it was thirty or forty years ago, and, I consider, much wiser than it was at that time. Now.' She folded her bony hands on her lap, put her head slightly to the side and continued, 'I've always been very fond of Lawrence. I . . . I could communicate with him long before anyone else could and as I've said many times, and to you yourself, there is wisdom in Lawrence that would not shame some professors. If it hadn't been for one of the doors in his mind closing, he would, I am sure, have done great things. As it is we have a five-year-old boy in a thirty-year-old frame, so what I propose, Dan, is to . . . to bring him here. Now, now.' She lifted her

633

finger again. 'I know I may die soon, next week, or this very night, but I may live for a year or two, in fact I may even reach a hundred if I give my mind to it.'

'You certainly won't if you take on Lawrence.'

'Sit down, sit down, Dan.... Why, you speak as if the poor boy were obstreperous. He's as gentle as a....'

'I know all about that side of him, Brigie; but he's a man, he's a six-foot-one man.'

'And a puff of wind would blow him over.'

'That isn't the point. Don't be purposely blind, Brigie. Face facts; he's a man.'

'He's a boy, Dan, a boy.'

'You can't expect a housekeeper like Mrs Rennie to put up with him. Have you thought about that?'

'Well, if Mrs Rennie doesn't put up with him then somebody else will.'

'Brigie, be sensible.' He sat down and pulled his chair towards her. 'It would be a problem if you had the run of the whole house, as before, but you're up on this floor, the space is limited. Just think of the mess he made with his whittling at the Manor; you could hardly get in the door for wood shavings.'

'I'll control his whittling, I'll keep it confined to the night nursery. He'll do what I tell him. And anyway, I won't be like Katie, I'll put his whittling to use. I'd told her for years she should sell his animals and give the proceeds to charity; but no, no, there are two rooms over there almost chock-a-block with them. It's a great pity to my mind they weren't short of money; she would have seen some purpose in his life then. As it was, she just looked upon it as childish pastime. I could never understand her on that point. It was the only weakness in her training of him.'

Dan, sighing heavily, began his pacing again, saying, 'Well, it's up to you; after all, Brigie, it's up to you. When you've got to fight your way out through wooden dogs, cats, horses and goats, not to mention ducks, hens, partridges and pheasants, don't say I didn't tell you what to expect.' Then coming to a halt, he asked, 'What'll happen to the Manor? He's the next in line. Sir Lawrence Ferrier – what a tragedy. And old Sir Francis could drop dead any day. I wonder if she ever visualized this possibility. She must have. Her will should be interesting.'

'Yes, it is.'

Dan narrowed his eyes at her. 'You know what's in it?'

'Yes, yes; she discussed it with me.'

'About Lawrence, and his future?'

' Yes, about Lawrence and his future.'

'What did she plan? Not what you are proposing, I'm sure.'

'No, no; she never thought of that. She decided that the Manor should be sold and that either you or John would take care of Lawrence . . . in your homes.'

'Oh my God!' He bowed his head, then turned away. After a moment he looked at her again and said, 'So that's what's made you take this step?'

'No, not really. I would have proposed it in any case because I knew that no matter how John looked at it, Jenny would have collapsed at the very thought of the suggestion. As for Barbara, well, if she cannot bear to look upon her own son, I wouldn't expect her to care for a boy like Lawrence. I said as much to Katie, but she imagined that you, Dan, would override Barbara's scruples in this case. . . . She was very fond of you, Dan, you were her favourite brother.'

'Oh Brigie, don't make me ashamed.' He bowed his head and shook it from side to side.

'I'm sorry; that wasn't my intention. But when we're on the question of Barbara, have you ever put it to her pointedly that it is her duty to come and see Ben no matter how she feels?'

'No, I haven't, Brigie, because I know it would be useless.'

'Is she still the same?'

'Still the same, only worse. She becomes more withdrawn; I don't think we've exchanged half a dozen words in a month.'

'I'm deeply sorry, Ben.'

'Oh, don't worry, Brigie. I'm so used to this way of life that if it changed I wouldn't know how to deal with it.'

'Dan.'

'Yes, Brigie.'

'Will you allow me to bring up a delicate subject?'

'You can say anything you like Brigie, you know that.'

There followed a pause.

'Is she still seeing him?'

There followed another pause before he answered, 'As far as I know. Day after day she goes off, and sometimes she takes an overnight bag, but not so often of late years.'

Brigie's white head gave an impatient jerk. 'Years and years! Yes, a quarter of a century and more this has been going on. And it is against all the facets of her temperament as I knew it. I mean for her to put up with such conditions. I should have imagined that when he made the decision not to leave his family – and he must have done this at one time – she would have broken it off; she wouldn't have suffered the indignity of remaining his hobby as it were, and the knowledge that he wasn't a god after all but simply a man should have been enough to make her see reason. . . . Yet, I blame myself for a lot that has happened; I should not have been against her marrying him in the first place. I'm sorry, Dan, but I shouldn't.'

'What's done's done, Brigie. It's all over a lifetime ago, two lifetimes in fact. You mustn't blame yourself, you were just part of the whole sorry mess, as I was.'

'You have been very good, Dan.'

'What does one mean by goodness? Boil it down and what do you get? Selfishness. I was good, as you call it, because I wanted her, I wanted her more than anything else in the world. And I went on wanting her; even when this business began I went on wanting her. I think the turning point forced its way through the day she knew Ruthie was pregnant and she was going to turn her out. The self-righteousness, the unreasonableness of it, the fact that she took me for such a damned fool, a gullible damned fool, got home to me. From then on I didn't ache so much.'

'What's going to happen to her, Dan?'

'I can't give you that answer, Brigie.'

Brigie looked down at her hands. The fingers were twitching, and she joined them together tightly before she said, 'Locked in her deafness again, no boys, no you, or me. She must be very unhappy, Dan, so very, very unhappy.'

'She's got all she wants, Brigie . . . at least I hope she has. It's odd that I should say that, but I mean it. I hope that in having him still she has all she wants from life.'

And as Brigie looked at him she knew he was speaking the truth. Such was love. And if ever a man had loved he had, and still did. Poor Dan. Poor Dan.

636

3

ON JULY 1st, 1916, it was estimated that nineteen thousand British men were killed and fifty-seven thousand wounded. More died on that one day than on any other single day during the war. The men had gone over the top in wave after wave, and in wave after wave the German machine guns had mowed them down like rows of skittles. The Somme was the cemetery of Kitchener's army, and it had its repercussions on the Home Front. Yet people still sang, still laughed; they laughed at 'Old Bill', Bairnsfather's creation of a walrus-moustached middle-aged soldier, whose face expressed endurance and defied death. The caption read, 'If you knows of a better 'ole go to it.'

And how many men in France would have paid the price for the 'better 'ole' with a bit of shell-shock or an amputation, or even gas, if the better 'ole meant home.

As on land so on sea. The German and British fleets played tig at Jutland. Where was Britannia, why wasn't she ruling the waves? But the nation rallied. Are we downhearted? 'Keep the home fires burning'. 'It's a long, long way to Tipperary'. 'Sister Susie's sewing shirts for soldiers'. 'Down at the Old Bull and Bush ... Bush, Bush'.

Then Christmas was upon them.

And nowhere were spirits higher than in High Banks Hall. During the autumn fifteen officers had packed their bags, shaken hands all round, kissed the nurses, thanked Matron most warmly, and gone back to Headquarters – to see where they fitted in now. A year ago every one of them would have longed 'to jump the ditch', as they called the English Channel, but even those in the highest of spirits did not now express any wish to cross the water again.

The Bunker had been especially busy during the past months and the number of beds in it had doubled. But the atmosphere in the Hall in this Christmas week of 1916 was that of a country house preparing for the festive season.

The day before Christmas Eve every patient, with the exception of those in the Bunker, and the lord of the manor, as the man in the end room had been jokingly, but not unkindly, dubbed, were engaged in some Christmas activity, cutting down holly, or sawing wood, or making paper chains; or climbing steps to hang the decorations.

Some of the decorations were already in place. Not only on the mantelshelf, but in all odd corners of the entrance hall were to be seen wooden animals of all species, shapes and sizes. Some were roughly hewn, some you could say were finely sculptured, but all had about them a movement that suggested life.

There was a notice board attached to the wall at the side of the inner hall door. On it was pinned a bill headed 'Pantomime Extraordinaire: "The Sleeping Beauty".'; then followed a list of characters taking part. The first one read, 'Princess Sweetface, Major Andrew Cornwallis-Stock'.

Below this was a typewritten form giving information about the times the bus – in this case the ambulance – would meet the train to bring visitors to the Hall on Christmas Eve, and also the time it would leave for their return journey.

And below this, still on the board itself, printed in chalk, and one could say affectionately, were the words: 'Lawrence's Animal Fund for Red Cross, December 17th, £88.14.0d. We are hoping Father Christmas will bring the total up to £100. Thank you. . . .' Brigie had once said to Katie not to worry about Lawrence for he would be a great comfort to her. And her prophecy had come true, more than ever after Pat died. But never had Brigie imagined he would bring comfort to anyone else, particularly to a group of men who had arrived at the Hall via a valley of physical and mental hell, yet without exception every man, from the major down to the swill orderly, had taken to Lawrence. Perhaps in some cases their affection could be put down to relief that their stay in limbo had been of a limited duration, whereas this man's, this tall, thin, ever-smiling, unaging man was condemned for life.

Yet no one actually pitied Lawrence, for you couldn't pity someone, no matter how mentally crippled, who continually emanated happiness; in fact the wise among them envied his state. Lawrence had not been given a free run of the Hall, he had simply taken it. His movements in his own home had never been restricted, and so Brigie did nothing to change this pattern; except for one thing, and this had been difficult for him to understand, for he had always roamed about the Manor whittling at his pieces of wood, and the servants cleared up the debris.

When he first came under Brigie's care, he had cried pitifully, as a child might cry, for the loss of his mother and he had cried also when he was forbidden, strictly forbidden, to whittle in any place but in the room connected with his bedroom. But as time went on he conformed; and he was helped greatly by having a new interest; he was among men, lots and lots of men, and he liked that.

It would seem to the casual observer that Lawrence gave a similar attention to everyone who spoke to him, but his manner was misleading for he had his favourites, and the man in the room on the first landing just beyond the bottom of the nursery stairs became his first favourite.

Their meeting had come about quite by accident. He liked Nurse Pettit, or Petty, as some of the patients called Hannah, because she always had time to listen to him. Moreover, she knew about horses; she could say, 'Oh, you have done a shire!' or, 'What a lovely hunter!' or, 'Now that's a fine Shetland.' And he was capable of appreciating this. He could neither read nor write but he could copy any animal he saw in a book.

Coming along the landing one day he watched Hannah disappear into a room at the end of it, and so in his uninhibited way he opened the door and went in after her. And there he saw the man sitting by the window.

Hannah, in some agitation had cried, 'Oh, Laurie! Now you mustn't come in here,' and when she went to turn him about he had resisted her. Gently but firmly he had pressed her aside, and then he had gone to the window and sat in the chair opposite to the man and held towards him a wooden goat he was carrying. And Ben, after looking at him for a long while, slowly lifted his hand and took the animal from him.

Hannah had stood looking at the two of them, both men of about the same height, both about the same age, but one a man, even although he looked emaciated, and the other, what name could you put to Lawrence, a child, a boy, someone who at times did not appear quite human, more of spirit than flesh and blood? And these two men were full cousins. It was weird when she thought about it.

Perhaps it was deep blood calling to deep blood, but from that meeting there was between them a bond, and its impression as time went on showed itself on both of them, for it was Lawrence who first elicited a straight question from Ben.

Lawrence had been a regular visitor to the room for over two months when, of a sudden, one day Ben moved in his chair and asked, 'How old are you?'

'Old am I?' Lawrence had a habit of repeating what was said to him. He had then cast a glance at Hannah and said, 'I'm big, more than ten, aren't I, Petty? Aren't I, more than ten?'

639

'Oh yes, Lawrence,' she had said; 'you're more than ten, more than twenty,' while keeping her eyes on Ben.

'I am more than twenty,' said Lawrence, and Ben repeated as Lawrence had done, 'More than twenty.'

Hannah, not able to contain herself, had exclaimed aloud, 'Oh! that's marvellous, marvellous.'

And it was marvellous. Everybody said so, his father, Mrs Bensham, Nurse Byng, Nurse Setter, who had taken the place of Nurse Conway, for Conway had said that another winter here and she'd be in the middle bed of the Bunker, Sister Deal, the doctor, because everyone knew that the question was a breakthrough. As the doctor had smilingly said, 'He has started to use a pick on the ice wall.'

Hannah had been very glad when Nurse Conway decided to leave for she had taken over full duties in the private room, and each step the patient made left her with the feeling of personal triumph, for as she told her father, whenever they met on the quiet, she had known from the beginning he would come through.

Hannah didn't always go home now on her day off; sometimes she would allow three weeks to pass before she put in an appearance, and when she did there were the usual recriminations, the usual sly digs, and always without fail, particularly on her mother's part, the raking up of the black past.

Sometimes she arranged to meet her father in either Hexham or Allendale and they'd have a meal together and she would talk freely, and more than once she talked very freely, even angrily, when she brought the taboo subject into the open, and asked him why *she* didn't come to see her son. He was her son; what kind of a woman was she?

Always Michael met her onslaughts with bowed head and tight lips and always he said the same thing: 'I've told you. You ... you don't understand, I can't expect you to understand, This ... this is not a surface thing, Hannah.'

Once she replied that no emotion was a surface thing, and what she couldn't understand was that he could care for someone enough to make their own home unhappy for years; and that's what he had done, let him face it, and because of a woman who was so devoid of compassion that she wouldn't even look upon her own flesh when it needed her most.

On that occasion, which had taken place only a month ago, he had risen from the table in the restaurant and she had to follow him out into the street, where, his face white and drawn, he had looked down on her and said, 'We have never quarrelled, Hannah, you and I, and I don't want to quarrel with you now. It would be no use trying to explain everything to you because you wouldn't understand. I couldn't expect you to. I'll only say this. Ben represents for her someone she has disliked since she was a child, just through seeing his likeness hanging above the fire-place in the cottage where she was brought up. He appeared to her, this man, as a gross, nasty old man, and when she discovered that it was he, this old man, who was her father, then her world exploded. And I was present that day and I helped to blow it up. And . . . and Ben. From the moment he was born he was for her a replica of her father as he once had been.'

'That isn't his fault; her reason should tell her that, if she's got any. So why does she hold it against him? By what I can gather she's a. . . .'

'Don't say it, don't say it, Hannah.' His voice had been stiff, his manner one that he had never before shown her, and then he had turned about and walked away from her.

She had been home only once since then, and like two witches, her mother and grandmother had sensed that there was a breach between her and her father and, as she put it to herself bitterly, they had been all over her; their welcome could not have been warmer. But because they had been unable to get anything out of her their farewells had been as usual.

At times now she felt very alone, lost and tensed up; and her work, instead of taking her mind off herself, and them, seemed only to bring them all closer, for when she was in the private room she felt, in some strange way, that she was at the centre of the turmoil again. And that was, after all, understandable.

'Look, come on, come and see them pulling the logs.'

She took his arm and raised him from the chair by the side of the fire, and then suited her step to his shuffling until they reached the window; then pointing down, she said on a laugh, 'How on earth do they expect to get that one into the house? And what are they going to do with it when they get it in? It can't be for the fire.'

Ben looked down on to the end of the courtyard where it opened out into the sweep of the drive, and he said in thick fuddled tones, 'Never-get-that-in.'

'No, you're right. Well, I wonder what they're going to do with it. But that's anybody's guess because Captain Raine and Captain Collins are among them, and you never know what's going to happen when they're around. . . . Isn't the snow beautiful? But that lot that came down in the night might have put paid to the ambulance getting through to the station; it's certainly put paid to me getting over the hills. There might have been hope yesterday, but not today.'

He turned to her. 'Can't . . . go . . . home?'

'No.'

'S-sorry.'

'Oh' – she turned him from the window – 'I'm not, not really; there'll be much more going on here than there would be at home, I can tell you that. Hospitals are the most cheerful places in the world at Christmas. I've always marvelled at that.'

After lowering him down into the chair again she straightened up and, looking into the fire, said, 'It is amazing, isn't it, the feeling of good will that people rattle up for Christmas. Huh!' She shook her head. 'There must be something in it after all. Well, I'm off now.' She turned and looked down at him and her hand went slowly forward and touched his cheek. 'Be a good lad. See you this afternoon.'

His head moved as if on a swivel and he watched her disappear behind the screen for a moment then reappear swinging a short navy blue cloth cloak over her shoulders. And now she nodded towards him, saying on a laugh, 'The first thing you must do after the war is to line all these corridors and landings with hot water pipes, not to mention all the rooms in the kitchen quarters.'

She stared at him for a moment, then pulled a face at him and went out.

Ben turned his head slowly towards the fire, and like his speech his thinking came slowly and disjointed: Be a good lad – First thing he must do after the war – she expected him to take up this house after the war. Put hot water pipes in the corridors. There was a blind faith in her; she was a stubborn kind of young woman. He had first come up against it in that other world. Her stubbornness had been like a hand thrust out groping for him in the darkness; he had known it was there but wouldn't touch it. And her voice had come out of the great vast open dirty blood-stained space of No-Man's-Land, coaxing, wheedling, not strident like the other voices, the voice he put to the big one and the voice he put to the pretty one. She was neither big nor pretty, but she had a nice voice, and she called him lad; always when they were alone she called him lad.

In a way she was not unlike Ruthie. Ruthie had come to see him last week. Or was it the week before? But then she came to see him often. His father brought her. But she disturbed him. They both disturbed him; Ruthie because she always became so choked she couldn't speak. She no longer came out with quips of earthy wisdom, and his father's face looked so set in despair that he had wanted for a long time, even during the time he had lived in the small windowless room of his mind, to bawl at him, 'Don't look like that, don't keep telling me I'm an imbecile.'

At such times Murphy would say, 'Hold it, laddie.' Murphy always kept making excuses for everybody. About his father he would say, 'He doesn't think like that, he's just worried.'

But Murphy had gone mad, when they had locked him in that cage he had damned and blasted the souls of doctors, nurses and orderlies, particularly orderlies. But since they had come here, Murphy had said, 'Rest easy, laddie, you'll be all right. Rest easy.'

Murphy called him laddie, like she called him lad; Murphy too had liked her from the beginning. Best one in the bunch he had said. Nothing much to look at except for her eyes, but there's one thing sure, laddie, she'll never bore you that one. Now Conway, you get tired of her face; and Byng, oh boy! Byng. Somebody mixed up the sexes when they fashioned Byng. Light heavy-weight champion of the world, Byng. Muscles on her like four pounders. 'No,' Murphy had said, 'your bet is Pettit, laddie.'

But he had resisted even Pettit. He wanted to be beholden to no one. . . . And then the boy had come; the boy who was of the same blood. The boy hadn't remembered him, for it was years since he had seen him; but he had remembered the boy. He had recognized him instantly; this was his cousin, and he understood, without knowing he understood; moreover, he recognized in the boy someone exactly like himself, someone locked up in a cell; the only difference was that the cell wherein the boy lived had bright windows in it.

A log of wood burned through, snapped, and one end slipped slowly on to the hearth. It wasn't burning but he knew he should bend forward and pick up the tongs and put it back. But there was no effort in him.

That was the thing he had to manufacture now, effort, because he had used up the effort of his whole life in one great leap, in one love-propelled leap to save Murphy, as Murphy had saved him twice before, and for a second of a second he had held death in his hand. Then, their arms locked about each other like lovers searching for sublimity, they had rolled down the slope into the shell hole; for a matter of about sixty seconds they lay until the ground settled back and there came a lull in the air above them as if a great ethereal hand had clamped down on the antics of a maniac. And when the epoch-long seconds had passed he had spat the dirt from his mouth and growled, 'Now!' and they had scrambled up the other side of the crater, there to be met by a poisoned wind.

They were flat on their stomachs and some yards apart when the earth exploded again, and this time it took with it all the other planets in the universe; everything disintegrated as Murphy was disembowelled.

When he came to himself he was standing up and quite some distance from what was left of Murphy, and all about him there was nothing but sky, no earth except the narrow ledge to which his feet were fixed, the rest was one great empty void. He had reached the end of the earth and although he wanted to step over and join Murphy he had found it impossible to move.

When they whipped his feet from beneath him and brought him flat on to his face and dragged him into a trench infinity was blotted out and he went into the small dark cell; and from then on whenever anyone tried to open the door he fought them.

He had loved Murphy. He could use the word love now in relation to him because it was akin to the feeling he'd had for Jonathan and Harry, only more so, because Murphy had known what it was to feel deprived.

He had first met Murphy when he joined up; they had done their training together, such as it was. He soon learned that Murphy was a highly intelligent man and his own worst enemy, for he was a rebel. He hated the working class from which he had sprung, and he despised the upper class; he had read more than any other person he knew.

After four months together they were separated, then, when he joined his unit as an officer, an officer who had just lost two brothers and had been finally rejected by his mother, it was some comfort to find that his sergeant was Murphy.

He had previously become imbued with many of Murphy's ideas and antagonisms, officers and men being one of them; the fact that they could fight together but weren't allowed to drink a glass of beer together now became theory forced into practice. Murphy, he considered, had more knowledge in his little finger than all his brother officers put together.

They had decided that after the war – they were both going to come through, of that they were positive – they would start a magazine, a magazine that dealt with new thought, new values, that in short asked the question, Why officers and men? Apparently everybody knew the arguments for ... but their job would be to put the reasons against.

Murphy could write, he could use words.

I swam in the womb like a tadpole in a jar held by a string in the hand of God.

That was the end of the piece he had written when they were resting after the previous bloody massacre they had come through.

> So fast flows time,
> So slow flows pain
> Pressing upwards against the current
> Like the salmon to its end.
> When I dissolve
> Will I remember the nest
> Of water in which I swam

Like a tadpole in a jar,
Held by a string
In the hands of God?
The salmon,
The tadpole,
and me,
All spermed,
What are we?

Murphy's parents left him with a courtesy aunt, when he was five years old. They went off to dig holes in Greece; then they forgot to come back, so great was the attraction of holes. Of course they sent money regularly for his support, which means went a long way towards supporting the aunt's weakness for the bottle. He never saw them again until he was eighteen, by which time he hated the sight of them.

It was strange that Murphy had to die crawling out of a hole. He was always writing about holes or wombs.

And she said that he would have to put pipes all round the house after the war.... What would she do after the war? Go back and live on the farm? He knew who she was. His mind wasn't so slow that the connection between her and the farm over the hills had escaped it. She was Michael Radlet's daughter, the man who had robbed his father of his wife's love. But he hadn't really robbed him; you couldn't take away what wasn't there.

His father came at half past one and Nurse Pettit came back on duty at two o'clock. When his father said to her, 'We had a Christmas like this in '76; we were home from school. I remember it well, it's just like yesterday,' he looked out of the window and said, 'Nur ... Nurse-won't-be-able ... to get home over ... over the holidays.'

Dan looked from Ben to Hannah as he said 'No? But they've cleared most of the road to the station.'

'Sh ... she....'

'I don't....'

Both Ben and she had started to speak together, and when Ben remained silent but looked intently at her she went on, 'I don't live that way, I live over the hills.'

'Oh' – Dan fixed his attention on her – 'You do? Which part?'

'In the first habitation where the valley opens out, Wolfbur farm.'

'Wolfbur Farm?' Dan repeated the words slowly, it was as if he were copying Ben's way of speaking. His eyes had narrowed, but now they widened and his mouth dropped open before he said, 'I ... I know Wolfbur Farm. Has ... has it changed hands?'

'No.' Hannah's face was straight and her voice stiff as she looked

645

back at him. 'No, it hasn't changed hands. My name was Radlet before I married.'

It was on an intake of breath that Dan said, 'Oh!'

'Yes, Mr Bensham, I am Michael Radlet's daughter.'

Dan's eyelids blinked rapidly in confusion. Then his face stiff and his voice harsh, he said, 'You should have made us aware of this.'

'Why?'

'Why? I don't think that needs an explanation.'

'I think it does; I'm a nurse. I am, in a sort of way, on national service, I go where I'm sent. I was sent here and . . . and part of my duties was to attend to your son.' She moved her head in Ben's direction but did not look at him.

'You could have explained.'

'Explain what? That I objected to carrying out this part of my duties when the whole world was disintegrating because I had been caught up in a stupid feud between two families? You would expect me to complain that my sensitivity was being shocked by the intrigue between my father and your wife? Well, Mr Bensham, it may surprise you to know that it has never shocked me. Distressed me, yes, that two people could be so selfish as to create such havoc. Yes, that distressed me, because one of them I idolized. But times change, and if one's lucky one grows up and is enabled to look at such things objectively. And don't think the news will distress your son.' Now she did look at Ben as she added, 'The Captain has been well aware of my identity for some time. Will you excuse me?'

With the strongest show of temper Hannah had allowed herself for some time she left the room; yet she had closed the door quietly after her, and Dan stood looking at it for a moment before turning to Ben. And now he asked quietly, 'Is that so?'

'Yes-yes, that's-so.'

Dan sat down and, leaning forward, he asked gently, 'But why didn't you tell me?'

'Was. . . . Was-there any need? As she said . . . a victim of a feud. . . . And she's not alone . . . is she? We're . . . we're all victims.'

Dan rose to his feet again and went and stood by the side table and stared at the wall. 'I don't like it,' he said; ''tisn't right somehow.'

'That . . . that . . . isn't you. I . . . I always thought your second name . . . your second name . . . was tolerance.'

'This has nothing to do with tolerance, Ben, and you know it.'

'I wouldn't say-say that, I would say it has. . . . You've . . . you've tolerated the sit-tuation half your life. . . . Now . . . now because her son and . . . his daughter meet in a hospital it strikes . . . strikes you as improper. I can't see that, and if you're worrying that . . . that anything should come of it, a repeat of the present situation in . . . in reverse, then set . . . set your mind at rest. If . . . if I would ever be fit for a woman again she . . . she wouldn't be my type.'

Dan turned his head and met Ben's eyes and he smiled wryly as he said, 'No, as you say, I don't think she'd be your type.' He sighed, then said, 'I'll slip upstairs now. I'll see you in a short while.'

'Dad.'

Dan turned from the door.

'What . . . what is that Mrs Rennie like?'

'Capable; a very good woman I'd say.'

'Why doesn't she-she like Lawrence?'

'For a number of reasons if you ask me. She wasn't engaged to look after a fellow like Lawrence, nor to change a wet bed, if only occasionally.'

'Oh. Oh, I see.'

'It . . . it isn't often though, I must admit, only when he gets over excited or worried.'

'Well, I should say it's-it's her that worries him, so-so she brings the bed business on herself.'

'Yes, yes, I suppose she does. But she's got her hands full up there as it is. Brigie's body might be frail but her mind is anything but; Brigie demands things done her way or else.'

'There . . . there could be a sol-solution. I . . . I was thinking about . . . about the cottage.'

'The cottage? What about the cottage?'

'Well, what's . . . what's going to happen to him when Brigie goes-and that could be any-any hour of any day? If . . . if the cottage was made hab-itable and you could get some young fellow who . . . who was no use for . . . for the war, you could in-install them there; there's many would . . . would be glad of the job.'

'That's a thought. That's a good thought.' Dan nodded, half smiling now.

'He could still come along here and see Brigie, and-and the stable and-and barn could be made into a sort of work-shop for him, because the house wouldn't be big enough to hold his clippings.'

Dan's smile widened and he nodded as he said, 'Yes, indeed, you have something there. It never struck me. I'll put it to Brigie.'

But once he was outside the room his mood changed. There was something he was going to put to Brigie at this moment and it didn't concern Lawrence.

When he reached the nursery floor his face was set and having greeted her and asked how she was, he told her in tense terms about the identification of the nurse whom they both considered had been of great help to Ben.

Brigie's reaction remained characteristic of her. She stared at him,

647

remained silent for a full minute, then said, 'Well, well, you surprise me, Dan. And yet more than once I've had the idea that she and I had met before but I was unable to recollect where. Now I know. And yet she bears no resemblance to either Sarah or him. Sarah was pretty, and he, well, we know what he looks like. But there was something familiar about her. Yes, yes' – she nodded her head – 'that could be it. Neither in looks nor character does she resemble her parents, but her grandmother. Constance. There I have it.' She nodded again. 'Constance always had a way of holding herself, a sort of proud, slightly defiant way. But then' – her withered lips pouted slightly – 'Constance was beautiful and one couldn't say that that young woman takes after her in that way. She has a strange face in that it is neither beautiful, pretty, nor yet plain. I suppose today they would describe her features as interesting.'

She lay back in her chair and now she nodded towards Dan as she said, 'I wonder how she feels living in the kitchen quarters in the one-time home of her grandmother, not forgetting the fact that I, her grandmother's one-time governess, now own the place? It's a strange situation, don't you think?'

'It's an unpleasant one, and I'm not referring to who owns what.'

'Then why so?'

'Now need you ask, Brigie.'

'Yes, yes, I do, Dan. If, as you say, Ben has been aware of this for some time and it hasn't affected him adversely, and she has been aware of the situation all the time, and looks at it . . . how did you say she looked at it?'

'Objectively.'

'Objectively. Dear, dear, the way they use language today; one word and they convey to you the reactions of a lifetime. . . . But I shouldn't let this trouble you, Dan, unless you are afraid of further developments, I mean complications that might arise between them. Are you?'

'Oh no! No!' He laughed now. 'Not from what Ben said. He made it pretty clear, and, to use his own phrase, she's not his type.'

'Well, I'm glad to hear it. Yet I would question that phrase. One can never judge what a man sees in a woman, nor yet what a woman sees in a man for their outward appearances . . . and tastes. For example, take Mrs Norton-Byers. She has extremely prominent teeth and an over-large nose; she's over-tall for a woman, being almost five foot ten I should say, and he is undersized for a man, a man of quality that is, being nothing more than five foot four, yet look at them and their brood of nine children. I think they're the happiest couple I know, so happy that I would like to have seen more of them over the years, and wish they had not lived so far away in Hexham.'

'There are always exceptions.'

At this point Mrs Rennie entered the room with the tea tray, and Dan turned to her and said cheerfully, 'Hello there, Mrs Rennie. How are you?'

'Oh middling, thank you, sir, and busy.' With a slightly offended air Mrs Rennie set about pouring out the tea, and Dan said, 'Well, you could say that of us all.'

'Are you staying for Christmas, sir?'

'No, I'm afraid I can't. In fact I'll have to be off very shortly if I'm to catch the train.' He glanced at his watch. 'But by the look of things downstairs I feel I'll be missing something; the jollification seems to have started already.'

'Noise!' Mrs Rennie almost snorted the word.

'Well, you must make allowances, it's Christmas.'

'Christmas!' Again the snort. 'They're acting like children. Pantomimes!'

Ignoring Mrs Rennie, Brigie inclined her head towards Dan as she said, 'This is all because I have expressed a wish to go down to the pantomime tomorrow night.'

'And quite right too; the noise and excitement could kill you.'

'Nonsense! Anyway' – Brigie still did not look at Mrs Rennie – 'what better way to die. And by doing it that way I would likely achieve something, for I'm sure I should be the first one to have fulfilled the expression "died laughing".'

In open admiration Dan looked at her. She wouldn't die tomorrow, not if she could help it. If will was anything to go by she'd live for many a year yet. But unfortunately will wasn't all; she had a heart, and her breathlessness pointed to its weakening.

When Mrs Rennie had left the room Brigie asked, 'What are you going to do with yourself over the holidays?'

'Oh, I shall find plenty to do.'

'I mean for relaxation and entertainment.'

'For that, Brigie, I shall go as usual to Ruthie's.'

'How is your daughter?'

'Well' – Dan cast his glance ceilingwards – 'the last thing I heard of her she had broken off her fifth engagement.'

'She sounds a very flighty girl.'

'She may sound it but she's not; she's very like her mother. To my mind she's being sensible, she's looking round. As Ruthie says, when she meets the first man who'll make her lose her temper that'll be the one she'll marry. Up till now she's just laughed at them.'

Dan looked at his watch again and there was a moment's silence between them before Brigie asked, 'What will Barbara be doing?'

'Oh.' Now his gaze was directed towards the floor, first to one side of him and then to the other, and he answered softly, 'Same as usual.'

'She must be desperately lonely, Dan.'

'That's her fault.'

'If only she'd come and see me. I . . . I long to see her, just once again. Couldn't you ask her?' Brigie's voice was trembling now.

'I did. I did, Brigie. I told you, and I told you the response I got. She just stared at me as if I were an imbecile.'

'Did you . . . did you make it plain to her, I mean in both ways' – she moved her fingers – 'that she needn't see Ben?'

'I made it all very explicit, Brigie, very explicit, and . . . and I did it kindly.'

Brigie drooped her head now, and shook it slowly; the tremor in her voice increased and her tongue flicked in and out of her mouth in the pattern of the aged before she muttered, 'She didn't even answer my letter.'

'You mustn't worry, Brigie. You have done your utmost, you can do no more. What . . . what I think you've got to realize is that she's as sick in her mind as Ben, I mean as Ben was, in fact more so, for there's hope for Ben, but I can't see any for her.'

Brigie raised her head now and there was a faint blue mist of tears in her eyes as she said, 'Love is a terrible thing, Dan. No one should ever say that love is beautiful, it's a crucifixion.'

'Yes, I agree with you there, Brigie. Oh yes, I agree with you there. It's a crucifixion all right.'

4

'WON'T YOU TRY and show willing?'
'And fall . . . fall down the stairs? It's "Sleeping Beauty"
. . . you tell me. We . . . we don't want to-to turn it into . . .
"Humpty Dumpty", do we?'

'You won't fall down the stairs; Nurse Byng and Sister will be with you.'

'Where will you be?'

'I'll be off duty, I'm really off till Boxing Day.'

'What . . . what will you be doing till then?'

'Well, there's one thing I won't be doing and that's sitting in my room; there'll be lots going on.'

'Enjoy yourself.' He now reached over and took an envelope from the table and handed it to her, saying, 'A Merry Christmas and . . . and my thanks.'

'Thank you.' A little puzzled she slit the envelope open; it was too soft to hold a card. She drew out the double sheet of blank paper and a cheque which read, 'Pay Hannah Pettit the sum of twenty pounds', and she looked at it for a moment; then folding it up, she returned it to the envelope and slowly handed it back to him, saying, 'It's very kind of you, Captain Bensham, but I'm afraid I can't accept it.'

'Why . . . not?'

'Well, because . . . because it's money and I. . . .'

'And you don't take mon . . . money from strange men?' There was a shadow of a smile on his face.

'No, it isn't that either. And at the same time, yes it is. But you're not a strange man, and although it's very kind of you I'm sorry I can't accept it. If it had been some little gift now, a box of chocolates or. . . .'

'I'm sorry . . . I'm sorry I couldn't get out this week to . . . to get you any chocolates.'

'Don't be silly.' Her voice had an edge to it now. 'You know what I mean. Anyway, thank you all the same, I appreciate the gesture. No hard feelings?'

'No . . . no hard feelings, Nurse.'

'Well, I'm off. Happy Christmas.'

'Happy Christmas.'

'Be a good lad until I see you again, Boxing Day.'

He didn't answer but watched her go as usual behind the screen for her cloak, come out, pause, smile towards him, say, 'Take plenty of water with it, mind;' then go out.

He had never known a woman to refuse money before. And there had seemed to be no exceptions here. Nurse Byng hadn't turned her nose up at the envelope, nor had Sister; nor did he think would the night staff.

He reached out for the envelope again, took out the cheque, looked at it, tore it up, then began to tremble.

Happy Christmas. Happy Christmas. Happy Christmas. Boxing Day. Boxing Day. Boxing Day. And all the days ahead, never ending, never ending. Oh Christ! He was off again, going back to the edge of the earth. Murphy. . . . Murphy. Our Father, who art in Heaven. . . . Don't forget to take water with it. Nurse. *Nurse. Nurse.*

5

WHEN 1917 DAWNED England had a new Prime Minister, Lloyd George. But would he, people asked, make a better job of it than Asquith?

There was trouble on the labour front; the coal industry had been nationalized for the duration of the war; and coal wasn't the only thing that was short, the food queues grew longer. Looking back to 1914 it appeared to almost everyone that the war had been on for endless years, nor did there seem any prospect of it ending until mankind was wiped out; that is, all except the occupants of High Banks Hall, for here life went on most days as it had done since 1915. Patients left, more came; more and more came, and it was said that they needed another Bunker. Yet there remained in the house a feeling of permanency and peace, engendered no doubt by a certain discipline and continued routine.

Many of the men leaving expressed the sincere desire to remain, for there was the secret fear in them that the way things were going they might once again be sent to France.

It was now April, and the weather had been as other Aprils, sunshine and showers; but during this, the third week of the month, there had been three days of uninterrupted sunshine, which had brought patients out of the Hall and into the grounds and encouraged them to turn their faces upwards.

Ben, having taken ten paces from the bottom of the terrace steps, stopped abruptly and his head down, his gaze directed towards his feet, he muttered thickly, 'They're betting on me again.'

'Well, some of them have lost their bets this morning, haven't they?'

'That's questionable, I can't go any further.'

'You want to go back?'

'Yes, please.'

They walked back up the steps into the main hall, up the staircase, along the corridor and into the end room without exchanging further words.

It wasn't until Ben lowered himself into the chair that he spoke. Drawing his hand tightly down over his face, he said, 'It's still there, the drop. If ... if I was to walk a hundred miles it would open up. I'll never be able to span it.'

'Don't talk nonsense. It used to be at every step you took outside the room, and now just look what you've done in these last few months. You've left this room, you've gone down the stairs, out on to the terrace, then down to the drive. . . . And now this morning . . . ten steps.'

'I'm ... I'm still afraid, Petty.' He looked at her pleadingly.

'Of course you are.' She came and stood in front of him. 'But you're not half so afraid as you used to be, are you now? Now are you?'

He smiled wryly. 'You'd flog a dead horse, wouldn't you?'

'Well, I've known a lot of dead horses that have got up and walked out of this place, and you're far from being a dead horse, let me tell you. I told you yesterday if you ever hope to carry out your plan about the cottage and Lawrence, you've got to face up to *it*. Look that gap straight in the eye and say, all right, I've come to the edge of the earth but I'm not going to slip off, I'm going to walk down it.'

'And into what?' Ben's pallid face looked childishly pathetic for a moment. 'That's ... that's what I'm afraid of, into what? If when the fear's on me I force myself against it, will ... will I drop back into what I was? That's what terrifies me.'

'You won't, you won't go back. I'll tell you something.' She bent towards him. 'I've got a bet on you an' all.'

'You?' His tone was now indignant.

'Yes, me.'

'And what have I to do to win your bet?'

'Get to Byng's wedding on June 20th.'

He now relaxed against the back of the chair and laughed. 'That's a long shot, Petty.'

'I'm good on long shots. I told her she could get Captain Collins up to scratch if she tried, and she's done it. And you can an' all.'

Slowly now he reached out and took her hand; then he lifted it, not to his lips, but to his cheek, and he pressed it there for a moment. And when he let it go she turned from him and went behind the screen for her cape.

The action meant nothing to either of them; they both understood this. It was merely a gesture between a grateful patient and his nurse.

He looked towards the screen. 'Where you going on your day off?'

Her answer was brief, 'Home.'

'Oh, that's nice.'

She came from behind the screen.

'You think so?' Her face was straight as she looked at him. 'Well, that's where you're wrong, so don't sit there envying me a warm home-coming. You have your burden, I have mine. I'll have to tell you about it some day.'

Of a sudden her voice had turned bitter, and as she tugged the strings of her cape around her waist it was as if she were wrestling with herself. And she was, for she was having to prevent herself from blurting out, 'Your mother's causing hell on earth in our house. It's getting worse. I don't want to go home, and I never see my father on his own now. What kind of a woman is she anyway?'

The look on his face now caused her to bow her head and mutter, 'I'm sorry.'

'So am I,' he said. 'So am I.'

She went hurriedly out, asking herself what had come over her. Why had she to turn on him like that? He wasn't to blame but he had known to whom she was referring when she had spoken of a burden. Blast that woman! Blast her! For one person to cause such havoc! Look at the lives she has ruined. She wished she was dead. She did. She did.

6

I T WAS ON A THURSDAY in the middle of May. Barbara
shivered as she pushed open the wooden gate of the cottage garden.
She noticed that the grass hadn't been cut, which meant that the
gardener hadn't been for a week or more. This was surprising because
Mr Brown was very regular in his attendance; he had looked after the
small garden for years.

She opened the door and went inside, and the smell of must came at
her like a wave from a bog. The place was damp. Yet what could you
expect when it was only opened once a week for a few hours.

Before taking off her coat and hat she went into the bedroom and lit
the gas fire. She did the same in the small sitting room. Then she lit the
oil stove in the kitchen, after which she put the kettle on the gas ring
and made herself some tea.

The cottage had changed with the years. It was now comfortably
furnished. In 1904, Michael had bought it from Mrs Turner. He then
had water piped in and gas laid on. It was when the innovations were
complete he had suggested again that she come and live there, and
again she had realized how little Michael knew of her and her needs.

It was true that she had been born in a cottage, and in the main
brought up there, but it was an eight-roomed cottage and the smallest
room would have encompassed both the bedroom and sitting room of
this place. Moreover, what he had forgotten, and what she didn't
remind him of, was that she had spent most of her young days in the
Hall; in fact it could be said she had been brought up in the Hall, and
in both the cottage and the Hall she had been accustomed to being
waited on by servants.

And he had suggested that she should sit in this tiny cottage and see
to its requirements while waiting for his coming once a week – and
sometimes not that!

She hadn't seen him now for three weeks, and if he didn't come
today – well, she didn't know what would be the outcome. There was

something building up inside her that was frightening her. It had been growing with the years, but since Christmas it had become like a great live thing gnawing at the inside of both her body and mind, and she was afraid of it, afraid that something would happen to cause it to break out.

It had nearly broken free at Christmas.

Christmas.

She had been alone at Christmas, alone with the great buzzing silence inside her head. Really alone; no Jonathan, no Harry, not even Dan. If she had been aware of his presence in the house on Christmas Day it might have helped a little. It was strange that on that particular day she had needed to know he was there, as he had always been. It was strange too that she had been thinking a lot about him lately. His face would keep intruding on that of Michael's; even when he wasn't there she'd see his face imposed on Michael's. And her thoughts too were changing in the most troublesome way for they were putting her in the wrong, and when she asked them what could she have done, loving Michael as she did, they gave her no answer, and their silence was condemning.

She was lonely. Oh dear Lord, how lonely she was. She covered her eyes for a moment with her hand. If Michael didn't come today. . . . But he would come today, he must come today. There was no letter in the box and that was a good sign. Last week and the week before a letter had awaited her; he'd had a cold and been forced to take to his bed, but he was better, much better and would be with her soon.

She took the tea into the sitting room and, pulling a chair close to the fire she sat down. She had removed her hat but not her coat; the place was like death. But would death be cold? Lately, she had thought a lot about death. She would go into death happily if it wasn't for Michael. Yet at times it was as if Michael were already dead; it was as if he had been and gone. She had to make herself cling to the thought that she still had him, and would always have him until they died. Yes, but where and when would she have him? She was fifty-three years old and there would come a time when neither of them, particularly herself, could make the journey to this place. What then? And what of Dan then, too? Before that time should come, would Dan leave her? She often wondered why he stayed. But then it was his home and she was the intruder; and she remained only for the comfort it gave her and the prestige it afforded her. She was Mrs Bensham, she could still be waited on by maids, she could still ride in a carriage. Yet, after all, these were only compensations, poor compensations. If she'd had Michael to herself every day and every night she would not have needed compensation and this cottage would have been a palace.

She did not hear the door open. She knew nothing until he was standing in front of her. And then she sprang up like a young girl on the verge of love and threw herself on him, and they held each other tightly and kissed long and hard. And to an outsider it would have appeared that the liaison was starting but that very day.

'Oh Michael! Michael!'

'You're cold.'

'No, I'm not, not now. Oh, let me look at you.' Her voice came to him in a high cracked sound almost like a whine, and he said slowly, 'How are you?'

'I'm ... I'm all right now. Oh yes, I'm all right now.'

She took his coat from him, then took her own off and hung them on a peg in the passageway between the two rooms, and, putting her head around the door, she said, 'I've made some tea, it's still hot.'

He followed her into the kitchen and stood with his arm about her shoulders as she poured out the tea. When they returned to the sitting room and sat closely side by side on the couch he drew his head back from her and said, 'Aren't you feeling well?'

'I'm ... I'm never well when I'm away from you, you know that.'

They leant together again, but he did not kiss her, he just laid his cheek against hers, and the expression on his face was sad.

When of a sudden he yawned she exclaimed, 'You're tired,' and he nodded at her and spelled out on his hands, 'I've been up most of the night. A cow had trouble calfing. She lost it, but she's all right.'

'Oh, Michael, Michael. Come and lie down, come on!' She pulled him to his feet, and when they were in the bedroom she undressed him, and then herself, and ignoring his tiredness, and shameless in her need of him, she made him love her, and love her again.

When it was finally over and they lay looking at each other he saw that she was relaxed and happy, and he considered this a good time to give her a piece of news that he felt she should know. Softly he mouthed, 'Barbara.'

'Yes, Michael?' She was moving her fingers gently in small circles around his face. Her eyes looked dreamy.

He pressed back a little from her and began to speak; then changed his mind and spelled out on his fingers, 'There is something I think you should know.'

'Yes, Michael.' Her eyes were fully open now, staring at him.

He waited a moment, pushed his thick white hair back from his forehead, then again on his fingers, he said, 'It's to do with Ben.'

As if controlled by a switch her whole face changed. A dark shadow spread over it, and her voice was high and sharp as she cried, 'Michael! Michael! You know I don't want to hear anything about him. I'm ... I'm sorry he is the way he is but ... but if you're asking me to go and see him you know it's impossible. I would have gone to see Brigie after she wrote to me, I would, I would, but he was there, and I can't explain it to you. I've tried, haven't I? But not even you understand. The other two, I loved them, and they me, but he ... he never did. Right from the beginning there was something between us. My fault, yes, I admit, my fault, because I kept seeing that ... that Mallen man every time I looked at him. And he grew up to be like what I imagined Thomas Mallen was, big, brash, a woman raper!'

'It's all right. Please, listen. Now be calm, Barbara.' He was holding her hands tightly while shaking them. 'Listen. I'm ... I'm-not-asking-you-to go and see him.'

'You're not?'

'No; I ... I just want to tell you something. He's ... he's ...'

'Dead?'

'No, he's not dead, he's very much better.'

She lowered her eyes from his lips for a moment, then looked at them again as they moved and said, 'What I haven't told you is that Hannah, my Hannah, has been nursing at the Hall for some time, and he is one of her charges. . . . And now listen, Barbara. This might seem very strange to you. And yet why should it be? What I mean to say is. . . . Oh' – he shook his head – 'I may be imagining all this, yet I think there's something in it.'

Her expression checked his speech; then, her voice a faint whisper, she said, 'You mean? You can't mean!' Her face screwed up in visible protest.

'Now, now. Don't get upset. It was just something she said when she was over last week. It might have meant nothing, but on the other hand it might have meant a lot. Anyway, it caused a row in the kitchen as usual. They had referred to him as . . . Oh' – again he shook his head – 'it doesn't matter. But it was in her defence of him that I imagined. . . . What is it?'

'No! No, Michael.' She was pressing back from him. 'I couldn't bear it. Your daughter and Ben!'

'Why?' He leant on his elbow and looked down at her. 'I should have thought that it would have given you some comfort, that two people who were part of us were going to have some happiness out of this sorry business. I . . . I thought they could have been you and. . . .'

'Don't, don't say any more about it. It isn't right.'

'Why isn't it right?'

'It just isn't, I couldn't bear the thought of. . . . Oh!' She jerked herself from his hold and got up from the bed and pulled on her dressing gown.

He dropped slowly back on his pillows and looked at her. He had never imagined her taking the news like this. He had thought she might be a little sad to think that her son and his daughter were reaping the happiness that had been denied them, that was all. But . . . but she was furious. She was right, he couldn't understand this feeling that she had against her own son.

He sighed deeply. He was tired, physically and mentally he was tired. He had of late wondered how much longer the situation could go on. But then he had harboured the same thought back down the years. And look how long it had lasted, more than twenty-five years. And for nearly all that time the short hours of their life together had been spent in this cottage, and the payment he had been called upon to pay was hell on earth back there.

The farm that had been the place of wonder and joy to him in his youth had turned into a cage. Yet he had never ceased to love the cage and its setting; it was his gaolers who had made his life unbearable. And where was it going to end, where? They were getting worse, both of them. His threats to sell up were losing their effect. They knew he wouldn't have the courage to carry them out.

His life as he saw it now had been wasted, utterly wasted; he hadn't done one good thing with it, except breed Hannah. But would Hannah be able to stand up against them, if what he imagined was growing between her and Ben Bensham should come to anything? She was strong was Hannah, but those two had ways of breaking down strength. If only he had been as strong, really strong, not just stubborn. He had faced himself long ago and he didn't like the look of himself.

He glanced towards where Barbara was sitting huddled over the gas fire and a wave as of shame swept over him. It was true he loved her, and had always loved her, but he hadn't loved her enough to walk away from that valley, and them. At first he had made the excuse he couldn't leave his child, and then when his child no longer needed him he fell back on the old tags of duty, the duty that she herself had placed upon him when she had maimed Sarah.

Oh, he was tired, so tired, weary. Where would it end? They were neither of them getting younger. Yet her passion burned as fiercely as when they had first come together, too fiercely for him at times. He was tired, in more ways than one he was tired. He turned slowly on to his side and closed his eyes.

The blood was running down the side of Barbara's lip where her teeth had broken the flesh. She couldn't stand any more, she could not stand one more thing. This was the limit of her endurance: Sarah Waite's daughter – she did not call her Radlet, for she still thought of her as the cowman's niece – Sarah Waite's daughter and her son! It made no difference that her son was already dead to her, another insult was being heaped upon her.

She was very much aware that Ben would, on Brigie's decease, become master of the Hall, besides which, being Dan's son and a partner in the business, he was already a rich man, and all this would go to benefit Sarah Waite's daughter.

That the girl was Michael's daughter also was merely an accident, so her troubled brain told her. She had always been jealous of his love for his child because, she imagined, it lessened his love for herself. The next thing he would be telling her was that his resurrected moral code would not allow him to carry on their association any longer! Men did this kind of thing, she had heard of it, they used the woman for years under the cloak of love, then got religion, or cold feet or whatever name you cared to put to it, and the association was ended. And what happened to the woman? What would happen to her if . . . *if*?

She was so alone she was going mad. She couldn't go back home with her mind in this state, she couldn't, she couldn't. And then there were the days ahead thinking of Ben and that girl. He had said there might be nothing in it. Then if he thought that, why had he brought the subject up?

Oh, there was something in it. Oh yes, yes, there was everything in it. And that girl. Once she was married to Ben, what would she do? She'd bring her mother, Sarah Waite, and her grandmother, Aunt Constance, dear Aunt Constance – Aunt Constance whom she had hated all her life – she'd bring them all over to the Hall and there they would live in comfort and grandeur. She saw it all; it passed like a cinematograph picture before her eyes. She saw her Aunt Constance walking leisurely about the grounds, a parasol held nonchalantly across her shoulder. She saw Sarah Waite, not walking with a crutch but being wheeled by a servant through the rose garden towards the lake; and that girl, Sarah Waite's daughter, dispensing tea on the lawn; then to the side, the picture showed her Dan and his woman, Ruth Foggety, and their daughter, all happy together and laughing like a family; and she was standing outside the gate looking in. She was gripping the iron bars; she could feel the cold seeping through her body. Now she saw Michael in the picture, Michael accepted, forgiven. She saw him take his mother's arm and walk towards the woman in the wheelchair. Everyone looked happy, contented, prosperous. The only person not present was Brigie; Brigie would be dead.

She stared at the fire. No, no! she couldn't bear this. She had stood all that it was possible to stand. She would break the picture, the contented happy picture. She could do it. Oh yes, she could do it. This was one thing she could do. How? How? Well, if Michael and she were to die here, now, this very day, there would be no coming together of her son and his daughter, not after that. Oh no, not after that. But it must be done now, now, no waiting. She had waited too long. Oh yes, far too long for Michael to be her own.

Pulling herself up from the chair she went quietly to the bed-side. He was asleep; he was so little concerned about her feelings that he could sleep. Such was the make-up of men, even of her Michael, her beloved Michael. Oh Michael, Michael. Oh my love, you will understand. Shortly you will understand because we'll be together for ever. No more separations, never again, never again.

She stood staring down at him for a full minute; then slowly and deliberately she walked to the fire-place, turned the gas out, waited until the flame had entirely disappeared, then turned it on again, and to its full extent this time. Then walking swiftly she went to the door and closed it and placed a mat against it, and from there she turned and came back to the bed, and slowly and quietly she lowered herself on to the floor beside it. Putting her arm out across the bed until the tips of her fingers touched those of his, she laid her head to the side and waited. And strangely her last thoughts were not of her beloved Michael, nor yet of her husband, nor of her hated son, but of Brigie, the only mother she had known, and as she drifted into sleep she thought, The shock will kill her, and she'll be with us too. I'll like that, for after all I loved her. And she won't try to separate us again.

7

IT WAS AROUND HALF PAST TWO on the Friday afternoon and Hannah was again about to go off duty, and again she wasn't smiling and had no pleasant word for her patient. At this moment she was feeling anything but pleasant. 'There's a Chinese proverb,' she said, looking at him from the corner of the screen, 'and it says, "The journey of a thousand miles begins with but one little step."'

'I know it. And now I'll tell you one, and I'm sure you haven't heard it. It goes like this: "Nerves are like guerrilla warfare. You get them out of one sector and they spring up in another." That doesn't go as far back as the Chinese, it was coined in France. . . .'

'By one Murphy?'

'Yes, by one Murphy.'

'So you know something, Captain Bensham?'

'No, but I'm willing to listen.'

'I'm tired of your Murphy and his philosophy and his poetry. I've listened to him for months. What you should do is let Murphy drop over the edge of the earth.'

'He did, Nurse Pettit, he did drop over the edge of the earth.'

'Well then, he's gone, and you should forget about him because I can't see that Mr Murphy's great philosophy did you or him any good.'

'His name wasn't Mr Murphy, Nurse. Believe it or not his name was Gerald Pertwee Featherstone-Gore, but he retaliated against it, and because of his inordinate love of potatoes he went by the name of Spuds or Murphy; I preferred Murphy, and he was a very dear friend of mine.'

'Well, he's dead, and as I see it there's nothing so dead as death; it's final, it's finished. And I'm as much against those who spend the rest of their lives weeping over the dead as I'm against those who make saints out of sinners once they are dead. Anyway, I'm off duty now and I'm wasting no more of my time persuading you one way or the other to go along that drive and out of that gate. But there's one final thing I'll tell you and it's this. If your Master Lawrence isn't moved from upstairs shortly, Mrs Rennie is for the road, and the whole place knows it. If I'm right, your idea was to spend the rest of your convalescence in the cottage, right?'

'Right, Nurse.'

'Well, as far as I can gather Lawrence would go there quite willingly with you, or Mrs Bensham, and as things stand now I don't think Mrs Bensham is likely to take up residence in the cottage again, so that leaves you. And don't forget, although you've already had two offers of a manservant, they're not going to hang around for ever. . . . Oh, why am I bothering! After all it's got nothing to do with me.'

'No, you're quite right, Nurse, it's got nothing to do with you.'

They stared at each other, each face showing hostility, until Hannah's became scarlet. Then she swung round and marched from the room.

Ben sat perfectly still in what, from outward appearances, looked as if he had returned to the closed room of his mind. But his mind was working and at a furious rate. She was an aggravating woman – girl – miss – missis – or whatever you could call her, really aggravating; she always had to be right. Had he talked so much about Murphy as all that? Had he spouted poetry? He couldn't remember doing that, but he must have. Murphy had been a great one for poetry. He was going to put them all into book form had he survived.

> So is my need of you so great,
> So great your loss inside my breast,
> That void to void so deep a hole
> For ever in it sank my soul,
> And time, and solace, makes no quest
> To draw it back to life's fast spate,
> For what is life without you.

'So is my need of you so great' . . . No, no, it wouldn't do. There were enough complications in this family already, but that would put the tin hat on all of them. He, his mother's son, and her lover's daughter coming together? Oh no! No! not if he could help it.

But one thing she said was right; he must get out of that gate and along to the cottage. And once he got back into life, into 'life's fast spate', there'd be all the women he needed. He'd never had any fear of being without a woman. Yet of late he had not felt the need of one, not as he used to. But it would come back. Oh yes, it would come back. As she said, once he made himself go outside that blasted gate.

But outside the gate the land was bare and wide, stretching into infinity; inside the grounds, there were still many trees left and they bordered the edge of the earth, but beyond the gate were fells, and hills, and all slipping downwards, toppling for ever downwards. . . . If the road to the cottage had been sunken it would have helped, but as he remembered it it ran along level ground, and in parts it rose above the level of the fells.

When the door opened he realized that Nurse Byng was somewhat late in making her appearance, he also realized she was in some kind of a state and the bearer of bad news.

'Eeh! poor Petty. You'll never guess what's happened, Captain Bensham.'

He became stiff. He felt sick. A dizziness rushed into his head and his voice sounded like a squeak when he said, 'Nurse Pettit? Something has-has happened to her?'

'No, no, not to her.'

The sickness subsided, his head cleared.

'What then?'

'A man's just come over from the farm, her uncle I think he is, and he's brought terrible news. Eeh! it's awful. Her father, her father's committed suicide.'

'. . . *No!*'

'Yes. He was found in a cottage with a woman. They had gassed themselves.'

He was in the void again. Everything in him had stopped; there was no beat from his heart, no breath in his body; space, space all about him. He heard a distant voice crying, 'Oh! Now Captain Bensham. Come! Come! Captain Bensham.'

So was my need of you so great, so great your loss inside my breast . . . what is life without you? He was mourning, his whole being was mourning. But who was he mourning? Her? Whose loss? His own? Or Hannah's? But why should he mourn her? For if she had taken a hatchet and come over here and killed them both before she put an end to herself and her fancy man she couldn't have severed the unspoken hope that lay between him and Hannah more cleanly. But it was her he was mourning, her in whose womb he'd swum along with the other two . . . like tadpoles in a jar held by a string in the hand of God. The other two she had loved. Yet he was her first-born; it was he who had broken her water and made way for the others – and made way for the others – and made way for the others –. Here he was going again, slipping away over the edge, and there was no lifebelt to cling to, she had gone back over the hills – over the hills – over the hills. The thin thread between them could not stand the strain of that distance. It was ended, finished.

8

THEY BURIED THEM BOTH on the same day, and by accident, certainly not by design, at the same time but in cemeteries far apart.

There was only one mourner following Barbara. It was impossible for Brigie to attend and for Ben also; John unfortunately had suffered a slight heart attack, and could not travel; and so Dan stood at the grave-side alone but for the minister and the grave diggers. And there was in him a loneliness that was fathomless.

Yet over the hills, in the far valley, a long cortège followed Michael; farmers from all around, business men from the town, and those he'd had dealings with in the market, they all came to pay their respects, and offer their sympathy to the widow who, God knew, had had it rough all her life. That she'd had to suffer this last indignity was, in their concerted opinion, a bit bloody thick. Yet on the other hand when all was said and done a man's life was his own.

It had been common knowledge for years that Radlet kept a woman on the side, and those of the older generation said it was the very one who had taken his wife's leg off. But the younger ones said they didn't believe that; no man as nice as Michael Radlet had been would carry on with a woman who had maimed his wife; oh no. And besides, he came from a good family, his mother had been a lady. Even when she had taken over the farm and run it as good as any man she had remained a lady. No, she would never have put up with her son doing that.

At least that's what they had said before it all came out in the Sunday paper and named the woman as Mrs Bensham.

Now Mrs Bensham had been the Mallen girl, daughter of that old scoundrel who had left more white streaks around the countryside than a seven-year old buck rabbit.

There was a tale that had gone round years ago about the Mallens and that streak; it was said that no real Mallen died in his bed, and it had been proved right with her, for it said in the paper she was lying on the floor and there was little question of who had turned the gas tap on for he had been found stark naked in bed while she had a dressing gown on. Knowing what they knew about the Mallens, the older ones said they weren't surprised in the least. But what had her husband been thinking about to let it go on?

Eeh! what some people got up to, especially the gentry. But then they weren't really gentry, the Benshams. They had owned the Hall for years, but old Bensham himself had come up from dirt, so they said, and, keeping to pattern, what had he done at the end but marry his bairns' governess? And she was no better than she should be, for wasn't it known that she had been old Mallen's fancy bit for years before that when he owned the Hall? And now she was mistress of it, and in her dotage. Lived upstairs in what was the nursery, because she had given the house over to the military. Again some said that that was because old Bensham's grandson had gone wrong in the head after being blown up over there. And to cap it all, his other grandson by his daughter was in the Hall an' all, and him an idiot.

By, did you ever know such a set-up! It was a pity the war was on because this last event would have set the place on fire on market day.

As it was it only supplied food for gossip in the public houses and the village inns for less than a fortnight before it was overtaken by the war again.

667

9

'**U**NCLE DAN.'
    'Yes, Lawrence?'
    'Couldn't you take me to see Petty?'
'No. No, I'm sorry, Lawrence, I don't think I could.'
'You don't think you could?'
'No, Lawrence.'
'No, Lawrence.' Lawrence shook his head. Then looking straight up into Dan's face, he asked simply, 'Why?'
'Oh, because. Well, because it's a long way, it's away over the hills. I mean the place where she lives.' Dan's voice held impatience.
'On a farm with cows. Petty told me she lives on a farm with cows, I like cows. I made a cow today, Uncle Dan.'
'Did you? That's good.'
'People like my cows.'
'Yes, yes, they do.'
'Yes, they like my cows. They pay money for my cows.'
'Yes. It says on the board that you have totalled up to two hundred and seventy-five pounds. That's a lot of money you've made for the Red Cross.'
'I like making cows. When will Petty come back?'
Dan drew in a sharp breath. 'I'm . . . I'm not sure. Look, I tell you what to do. Take that cow, the one you've just made, and go down and show it to cousin Ben.'
'Cousin Ben's away.'
'*Away*?' Dan turned his head quickly and looked to where Brigie was sitting in the big leather chair. Her body seemed to have shrunk during the past weeks and her voice was small and her eyes sad as she looked at him and said, 'He means he doesn't talk so much.'
'Oh.' Dan drew in another sharp breath. 'I looked in his room as I came up. He . . . he wasn't there. I thought he'd be in the grounds.'

'Yes, that's where he'll be. I . . . I see him out and about quite a lot these days.'

'But he hasn't been to the cottage?'

'Not yet, not yet. But give him time. It's early days, it's really early days yet. You should be thankful.' She turned to Lawrence now and said, 'Go down and see if your Cousin Ben has returned to his room.'

Lawrence got up from the floor, where he had been sitting, but he did not move immediately towards the door; instead, he bent his tall thin body down towards Brigie and said softly, "I could go over the hills; I could walk to Petty and bring her back.'

'It's too far away, Lawrence.'

'Too far away. I can walk a long way.'

'I know you can, dear. But go down now and see if Cousin Ben has come back.'

Obediently now, Lawrence went out of the room, and Dan, looking at Brigie, asked, 'Have you talked with him lately?'

'Yes; he came up yesterday.'

'What do you think?'

'I don't think he has regressed, it's just that he hasn't gone forward.'

'Is she coming back?'

'I . . . I wouldn't know that, Dan. But speaking personally, I hope she does.'

'You were hoping something would come of it, weren't you?'

'Since you ask, yes. Yes I was, Dan. She's a very fine young woman. Nothing to look at, I grant you, but she's got something, spirit, something, something that he needs.'

'I can't see eye to eye with you about this, Brigie. It didn't seem right to me then, it seems less right now. You know I've had the idea lately that Barbara got wind of it in some way and if she had she . . . she would have done exactly what she did in order to put a final spoke in their wheel.'

'You're too hard on her.'

'I'm sorry, Brigie, but don't misjudge me on this, I'm holding no animosity against her.'

'No? Exactly how do you feel about her, Dan?' She laid stress on the 'do'.

'Well.' He sighed deeply. 'It's odd but at first I felt lonely, so lonely it was unbearable. I'd been without her for years yet her going left me desolate. I was back in my youth longing for her, craving for her. . . . But gradually the feeling left me, and now . . . well, I feel free. It's strange when you think I could have been free of her years and years ago, but I wouldn't let her go. If she had gone off on her own bat that would have put a different light on things, but I couldn't release her. Now I feel like a gaoler would feel when an unruly prisoner has

669

finished his time. And you know, Brigie, she was a prisoner, like a bird in a cage. No, more like a tiger in a back yard. I made the mistake of trying to tame her by kindness when I should have used the whip.' He took out his handkerchief and wiped his face with it.

'What are you going to do now?'

'Oh, something, something. One thing I'm not going to do, I'm not going to rot. I'm fifty-six but I still feel sort of young inside, and I haven't done anything with my life. Once the War is over I'm going to pick up where I left off all those years ago; you remember when I wanted to roam the world? Well, I feel I'd like to have a shot at it before it's too late. I may only cover a little bit of it, but enough to satisfy me.' He paused a moment, then said, 'May I ask how you feel about her?'

'So sad, Dan, so hopelessly sad. She's with me constantly, she never leaves me. It's as if I could put my hand out and touch her. She had a wasted life and I must take a big share of the blame for that.'

'No. No. I don't see it, Brigie. Even if she had got him in the first place there would have been trouble of some kind. She was born to create trouble; as sure as the sparks fly upwards. Some people are made like that. Barbara was poison to everyone she touched.'

'Oh, don't say that. Poor Barbara. Poor dear Barbara. She was the only child I ever had.' The tears rolled quietly down her wrinkled cheeks and she dabbed at them in the refined way that had ever been part of her. Then after a moment she looked at him and said, 'Will you marry Ruth now that you're free?'

'No! No! Never, Brigie.'

'Why?'

'Why?' He jerked his head to the side as if throwing off something unpleasant. 'There's never been any question of it. Ruthie has always understood this.'

Brigie's pale watery gaze was fixed on him. Men, they were all alike, at the core of them they were all alike. God must have set in the heart of the first man an unthinking selfishness and his sperm had passed it down through the ages. Thomas Mallen could have married her, but he didn't, he wouldn't. Not that she thought that Ruth would make Dan a fit wife. The common girl had grown into the common woman. A kindly woman granted, a cheerful one too, but not the wife for Dan. No, it was merely on the matter of principle that she had put the question.

She said now. 'You know best.' Then a tired smile spreading over her wrinkled features, she said, 'The question of what I'm going to do doesn't arise, does it? It's quite settled for me, isn't it? There's only one thing I can do now, sit and wait. But' – she moved her head slightly – 'after all that's what I've done all my life, at least for more than sixty-six years of it, sit and wait for one or the other of you to see what you're going to do. . . .'

'Oh no, you haven't, Brigie; you've never sat and waited for anything.' He wagged his head at her. 'You've willed it to happen. Now haven't you?'

'Ah well, Yes, yes, I suppose you're right, too much so, and to my sorrow. But now at ninety-six, I haven't any choice, have I? I'm obliged now to wait for the inevitable. I suppose I could force the pace and make that happen too, but I won't. This time I will sit and wait, at least until I've seen Ben and Lawrence settled in the cottage. . . . You must do your best in that quarter, Dan. Try and persuade him; he's been in that room much too long. He will never get rid of his fear of space there, he's got to move out into it.'

'I'm afraid it doesn't rest with me, Brigie. When I mention it all he'll say is, "Time enough, time enough." He's in God's hands and . . .'

'Don't talk rubbish, I'm surprised at you.' It was as if the years had dropped from her. She pulled herself well back into the chair and her old head bobbed on her shoulders as she cried at him, 'God helps those who help themselves, and He helps those who try to help others to help themselves.'

Dan stared at her open-mouthed for a moment, then on a gentle laugh he said, 'I seem to remember someone saying they were going to sit and wait for the inevitable.'

'I did, but it doesn't mean that I'm going to waste time while I'm doing it.'

'Oh, Brigie, you'll never die, not you. They'll have to shoot you.'

'Quite possibly.' She did not smile but went on, 'Yet, I won't put them to that trouble for a little while. Being a woman, or the shrivelled remnants of one, I still claim the privilege of changing my mind. . . . And' – her voice dropped back into thinness again – 'it will pass the time.'

Yes, it would pass the time, fill in the loneliness. There was only one thing to feel grateful for, this would be the very last time in her life when loneliness would assail her. Her darling Barbara had left her devastated once again and nothing could alleviate it until they met as they surely would in the great beyond. Until that time she would, as usual, put a face on things.

Training told. Oh yes, training told.

10

IT WAS A WARM DAY. Nurse Byng had got her charge as far as the lake, which was the longest distance he had walked yet, and she felt triumphant, but was wise enough not to show it, for the Captain was of uncertain temper these days, not that she'd ever found his temper good. She wasn't very fond of the Captain, so without reluctance she left him seated by the water's side while she went to attend to her other duties.

Strangely, the rim of the lake held no fear for Ben, although there was a drop of almost three feet down the bank to the level of the water. He bent forward and sat gazing down at the water, his thoughts on his problem. If he could pass through those gates, just once . . . that's all it would need, just the once. He could have done it by now if she'd been here, he was sure of it. She would have pushed him through, for she had reached that stage of irritation with him where she was substituting action for persuasion. That very last morning they had fought nearly all the time. 'You have learnt to talk properly, so you can learn to walk properly.' If any of the others had spoken to him in that fashion he would have put them in their place; he was sufficiently recovered not to stand any nonsense, or rudeness.

Why hadn't she come back? Was the scandal too much for her and she couldn't face it? Here it was forgotten; old patients going, new ones coming; every day new ones coming. As for the staff, they were too concerned with the shattered young lives about them to keep talking about a couple, well past middle age, who had committed suicide together. . . .

'Hello, Cousin Ben.'

'Hello, Lawrence.'

Lawrence lowered his gangling length on to the seat beside him and, holding the wooden object in his hand, he said, 'Look, Uncle Ben, a cow.'

'Oh, that's a fine cow.'

'It's a fine cow. Brig said, make cows 'cos there are cows on the farm ... Petty's farm.'

'Yes, Lawrence, there'll be cows on the farm.'

'Lovely day, Cousin Ben.'

'Yes, it's a lovely day, Lawrence.'

'Petty won't come from the farm, Cousin Ben.'

He turned his head sharply towards the flat smiling face and said abruptly, 'Who said she won't?'

'Brig. Brig says she won't come back, Cousin Ben. I said I could go an' fetch her; I'm quite big, aren't I? Aren't I, Cousin Ben?'

'Yes, yes, you're very big, Lawrence. When did Brigie say that Petty wasn't coming back?'

'Oh.' Lawrence's attention was caught by a moorhen on the lake and he pointed to it scurrying across the surface leaving an ever widening arrow behind it, and he cried excitedly, 'Look! Cousin Ben. Look, it's swimming. I can swim, I can swim, Cousin Ben, like this.' He made excited flapping movements with his arms.

'Yes, yes, I know you can, Lawrence.'

'Brig says it's a long way over the hills. But I can walk over the hills 'cos ... I want Petty, Cousin Ben. Petty's nice. My mama was nice.'

Ben stared into the pale blue eyes that lay level with the cheeks, the flat face now drooped with a sadness that brought an added ache into his chest, and he said softly, 'Yes, your mama was very nice, Lawrence. I called her Auntie Katie. I ... I liked your mama, Lawrence.'

'I like Petty, Cousin Ben. I could go over the hills because they won't let her come.'

'Who won't?'

'Them.'

'Them?'

Lawrence nodded. 'Brig said them. Them are over there on the farm with the cows, and they won't let her come. But I could go and ...'

'All right, all right, Lawrence.' He put his hand on the boy's to silence him. Then after a moment he turned and looked towards the lake again.

If he could only get through that gate. He ... he would try tomorrow.

No. No. This afternoon.

What about now?

No! He couldn't go now, he ... he felt tired.

The endless death of enforced ease.

Where had he heard that? Another of Murphy's? No, no; he remembered. It was a line he had written himself years ago, after he

673

had seen a group of workless men standing on Newcastle quay. He had thought it good. 'Work, the only resistance against the endless death of enforced ease.'

He was experiencing an endless death sitting in these grounds, in that room back there, the room which a relief nurse had tactlessly suggested could hold three beds. It was his house, he was entitled to a room to himself. He'd always had a room to himself back home, no not back home, in the house in which he was brought up. She had given him a room to himself when he was quite young, but she had let Jonathan and Harry share.

But this was his house; he could have a room to himself, all the rooms to himself if he wished.

The endless death of enforced ease. Oh for God's sake! shut up. Shut up!

'What did you say, Cousin Ben?'

'Nothing, Lawrence.' He was standing on his feet looking back towards the house. He wouldn't go in there again, he wouldn't go in there again until he had been through those gates. But going through the gates wouldn't get him over the hills.

'Where are you going, Cousin Ben?'

He turned to Lawrence, 'Just for a little walk. You stay there. No.' He came back to him again and, bending over him, said, 'You go up to Brigie and tell her your Cousin Ben has gone for a walk up the road. Can you remember to say that . . . up the road?'

'Cousin Ben has gone for a walk up the road. Yes, Cousin Ben.'

'That's a good fellow. Go on now.' He patted his shoulder and pushed him forward, then watched him going off at a shambling trot.

Get going. You said you were going, so get going.

He looked down at his feet, they were clinging to the earth, held there as if by a magnet from its centre. 'Damn you! blast you!' He addressed each foot in turn, then looked up towards the house again as there came to him the sound of a car being revved up.

That was it. *That was it*. He could ride through the gates. Once through the gates he'd be on the road; there'd be nothing for it, he'd have to either walk back or go forward. His feet moved, his knees bent, his hips swung and he almost went into a trotting run.

When he came to the courtyard the beads of perspiration were running down his face. There was an army transport truck in the yard. Two men were unloading stores from it. He went up to it.

'Who's driving?'

'Oh, the driver's in the kitchen, sir, having a cupper.'

He went to the kitchen door. It was open and laughter greeted him, until he said, 'Excuse me,' and then a khaki-clad man rose quickly from a chair by the table, put down a mug of tea, paused a moment, then said, 'Yes, sir?'

He realized the man knew who he was, and so for the moment he took advantage of his position. 'When are you returning?'

'Any minute, sir.' The soldier looked past him. 'They've cleared the truck. Any minute now, sir.'

'Will you give me a lift?'

Again Ben was made conscious that the man knew all about him because the surprised look on his face gave place to eagerness as he answered, 'Yes, sir. Yes indeed, sir.'

Ben turned from him and went towards the vehicle, took a deep, deep breath before pulling open the cab door, then clambered up. It appeared to those who were watching as if he had thrown himself into the seat.

A minute later the driver was at the wheel, the truck was turned, and they were passing the house; now they were going down the drive, down, down, down, until there in the distance were the gates. They were open, pushed well back, and the grass growing from the verge through the bottom bars said they had been open for some time. There was no division between the inside and the outside world.

They were going through the gates when the driver stopped the truck.

His heart began pounding against his ribs. He wasn't going to make it. His eyes stretched wide, he looked at the man, and the man said, 'You didn't say where you wanted to go, sir. Was it the station way?'

His mouth opened and shut twice before he answered, 'No, no; over towards Alston. Not as far as that really, just, just over . . . over the hills.'

'Over the hills, sir? It's a tidy way.' He looked at his watch. 'I'm due back in half an hour, but I tell you what, sir, I . . . I could take you some of the road, half way or more. But then that could leave you stranded up there in no-man's-land like. . . . Aw.' He pursed his lips, looked thoughtful, then asked tentatively, 'Are you sure you want to go the day, sir?'

'Yes, yes, I'm sure I want to go today, corporal,' and his tone said, 'Don't treat me like an idiot!'

The man, in no way offended, grinned and said, 'Well, sir, if you want to go the day you'll go the day,' and he started up the engine and drove out into the road and towards the hills.

Ben looked hard at the cottage as they passed it. It looked small, and almost derelict. How would he like living in the house in which his mother was born and brought up? Enough! One thing at a time. He was out, wasn't he? He was out on the road. Yes, but he was in the safety of the truck and there was a man by his side. What when he was on his own . . . up there?

Wait – wait – wait – wait. His heart beat out the word to the rhythm of the engine.

They were mounting upwards. The truck bounced over the rough ground like a solid ball, on and on, up and up. Now he was looking at the world. It stretched out on both sides of him, dropping away into deep valleys, spreading into moors, then rising again to hills, fold on top of fold to wider and higher hills.

'Grand sight, sir.'

He could not answer the man but he moved his head.

'Only been this way twice before, once in a fog. God! it was frightenin'. But it's different the day, grand sight, grand, see for miles, almost to the ends of the earth you could say.'

To the ends of the earth . . . the edge of the earth. 'Even though I walk in the valley of the shadow of death I shall. . . .' Oh, for God's sake! 'I lift up mine eyes unto the hills.' Shut up, will you! *Shut up*, for Christ's sake! 'I come, I come, my heart's delight, I come my heart's delight. . . .' He was going over the edge again, and he was here in the safety of the cab with this man by his side. 'It's a long way to Tipperary'. 'I pursued a maiden and clasped a reed. Gods and men, we are all deluded thus! It breaks in our bosom and then we bleed.'

He was pursuing a maiden, with Shelley he was pursuing a maiden, and when he clasped her to his breast would he bleed? His mother had made him bleed, all his life she had made him bleed, but he wouldn't have minded that if only she had clasped him to her breast. Quiet! stop it! She's gone, and all past memories with her. You worked it out, you worked that one out at least, for if she couldn't go on living for the man she loved, or show a little kindness to the man who loved her, and who had given her her two beloved sons, than how did you expect her to love you, you, who carried the white streak, a Mallen.

The view became wider. He closed his eyes tightly for a moment against the great expanse of earth.

'We're nearly at the top now, sir. There's the old ruin. I remember that. We went in there that day in the fog and a lot of good it did us; there's hardly any roof left on. But the stink, God! it was awful; you've no idea, sir.' He turned and grinned at Ben. 'All the king's horses and all the king's men couldn't have created a smell like there's in there.'

They passed the house; another mile and another mile and now they were going downhill.

It was just as they came within sight of the farm lying like a huddle of black stones in the far valley, that the man stopped and asked quietly, 'Where exactly do you want to go, sir? Or did you only want a run?'

'No, no, not just the run. That ... that farm down there.'

'Oh, well, the way the road goes it's only a mile or so. Will I take you on, or will I drop you, sir?'

The man was leaving the initiative to him, while at the same time saying, 'Get out here, sir, if you don't mind, or else I'll get it in the neck when I get back.'

'I'll ... I'll make it on foot. It was very good of you to come so far, as it is. . . .'

He was standing on the road. The truck had backed over a low ditch and on to the fell land. Now it had turned in the direction of home. The driver leant out of the cab.

'You be all right, sir?'

... 'Yes. Yes, thanks. Thanks.'

The head was withdrawn, then popped out again. 'How do you aim to get back, sir?'

How did he aim to get back? 'I'll ... I'll get back.'

'It's gone eleven o'clock now, sir.' The man was looking at his watch again. 'I'm making the run again this afternoon between three and four; I could come this far and pick you up.'

'Th ... thank you, but ... but I don't think it will be necessary. I hope not. Still it's ... it's very kind of you. I'm ... I'm very grateful. Well, on second thoughts, yes, yes, you could. If I'm not back by then, you could. It's very kind of you.'

'Anything to oblige, sir. So if you're not back then, I'll pop over. Good-bye, sir.' The man gave him a smart salute, which he returned; then he stood watching the truck bobbing away back up the long slope into the distance – and his feet wouldn't move.

He turned his head as far to one side as he could and then to the other. He was alone, utterly, utterly alone. The edge of the earth lay an inch from his toecaps; there was nobody in sight or in shouting distance of him. He could stand rooted here until his heart gave up the uneven battle against fear, or he could take the step forward and fall over the edge; it was up to him. He had only himself to rely on now, no Nurse Pettit, no Nurse Byng, no Nurse Taylor, no Matron, no doctor, no father, no Brigie, not even such a one as Lawrence. Why did he say not even such a one as Lawrence, for it was Lawrence who had forced him so far.

The journey of a thousand miles begins with but one little step.

He drew in a great draught of air, then another, then another, and he stepped over the edge of the earth. And he didn't become rigid and fall flat on his face. His feet were moving, left foot, right foot, moving faster with each step, faster, faster. Now he was running, running by himself out in an open space. The tears poured from his eyes and streamed down his face like an overspill from a dam.

When he stopped he was off the road and leaning against a dry-stone wall, gasping and sobbing aloud for there was no one to hear, no one to see, there was only himself to watch himself, and he had watched himself step over the edge of the earth, and he had not fallen into the abyss, he had not crawled on his belly and choked on muck, and his mind hadn't leapt back into that dark mad cell. He was alive.

It was some time later, after he had dried his face, smoothed back his hair, and adjusted his coat that he walked on to the road and down the last slope to Wolfbur Farm. . . .

The yard looked smaller than he remembered it from that one visit. Everything looked smaller, the farmhouse, the barns, the whole place seemed to have shrunk.

He moved slowly towards the back of the house. Going down the middle of the yard he looked from right to left. There was no one about yet he was conscious of voices coming from the house. The byre doors were open, so were the stable doors, but there was neither cattle, men nor women to be seen.

He turned towards the kitchen door and knocked. And now his heart began to pound again and a new fear seized him as he waited. But there was no response to his knocking.

The fear subsided just the slightest; he could still hear the voices in the distance.

He walked back up the yard and round the corner, and as he approached the front of the house the voices became louder as if the door had opened, but the front door remained closed.

Yet a door had opened. They came out of the sitting room: Constance, Sarah, and Jim Waite, all following Hannah, who was crying, 'All right, all right, I admit it. It was unfair of Dad to leave the place to me, but he did. And you know the proviso, you can both stay here for life, unless . . . unless there is any disagreement. And then I am authorized to provide you with alternative accommodation. Those were the words in the will, remember, alternative accommodation. And it wasn't written the day he died but three years ago . . . three years ago! And why he didn't say anything about you, Uncle Jim, is because you were a thorn in his flesh for years. You spied on him and tittle-tattled, and you caused as much trouble as he himself did in the family. Oh yes, you did.' She stabbed her finger at him. 'I would say more, for you aggravated it. And I'll say again, I don't care a damn what happens to you, Uncle Jim, because I know, and he knew, that you feathered your nest out of this place. It got to be an almost quarterly thing for a sheep to stray, didn't it? And where did they stray to? Ratcliff's butcher shop. Oh, you weren't as cute as you thought. . . .'

'Don't you dare talk to your uncle like that or I'll . . .'

'I'll talk whichever way I like, Mam, because you know what I'm saying is true. And I'll have you remember I'm no longer a child, not even a young woman, I've been married, I've been out in the world. And that's where you should have been pushed years ago.'

'Did you hear that? Did you hear that?' Sarah appealed to Constance. 'The injustice of it after what I've....'

'Oh, for God's sake! Mam, don't start on that tack again; you've lived on your crutch long enough....'

'Hannah!'

'All right, Grandma. And you can say *Hannah* like that, but don't tell me you haven't thought the same thing. But you decided to hide it behind that superior façade of yours, simply because you wanted an ally.'

'Girl! Girl! what's come over you?'

'I'm speaking the truth, Grandma. For the first time this house is hearing the truth, this miserable house, because we've all led miserable lives, everyone of us....'

'And whose fault was that, I ask you?'

'Yours in the first place, Grandma, for not letting your son marry the woman he wanted. You cashed in on an accident. That's how I see it.'

'My God! I never thought I'd live to see it, or hear it.' Jim Waite put his hand to his head.

'Well, you have, Uncle Jim, and the truth must sound very strange, particularly to you.... And when I'm on, Uncle Jim, get it into your head that I'll know everything that's going on here, you're not the only one that can use spies, and if the place goes down ... well, then as the will said....'

'Shut your mouth, shut your mouth this minute. God in heaven, you're brazen, that's what you are. You've turned into a real brazen hussy.'

'Yes, Mam, just as you say I've turned into a real brazen hussy.'

'And shameless into the bargain. You're utterly shameless if you go back there. And I'll tell you something, the whole countryside will talk; your name'll be mud – your father, now you, whoring from the same stock....'

'Sarah! Sarah! be quiet. Be quiet, I say! ... Hannah.' Constance turned and looked into Hannah's face which from being red was now as pale as lint. 'Let me put it to you this way. You claim the farm is yours. All right, all right, he left it to you. Then why don't you stay and work it? I'd be quite willing to take alternative accommodation.'

It was some seconds before Hannah could answer and her voice was much lower but trembling as she said, 'Aw, Grandma, the subtlety of you; anything to keep me from going back there.'

'Yes, yes, Hannah, anything to keep you from going back there.'

'And . . . and it's not because I'll be seeing Brigie or I'll be nursing poor creatures, but because I'll be in contact with Captain Bensham, to whom Mam so generously referred to a moment ago, as "that barmy bastard". Well, I'm going back, and yes I'll be in contact with him. . . . And now I'm going to tell you all something.' She looked from one face to the other, and there was a catch in her voice as she went on, 'I wish to God things were as you all imagine them to be, I wish he could say to me, "Come and live with me, Hannah, and be my love." And let me tell you, if he did I'd jump at the chance. But for peace of mind I'll be charitable and tell you that he doesn't know I'm alive, not in that way. I'm a nurse, I'm one of the staff, that's all I am to him, and I'll say again, more's the pity.'

They were silent, all of them, until Constance murmured, 'Don't do this, Hannah. Don't do this. Don't go back.'

'I've got to, Grandma. In any case I could never live here again, not with you all. There's been too much said, none of us could ever forget it, and it had to be said, it's been festering for years. All I say now is, you let me live my life and I'll let you live yours . . . here in peace.'

'Oh Hannah! Hannah!'

'It's no good, Grandma, and tears won't help, the time's passed for tears. I've shed all the tears I'm going to shed over this business. I thought when Dad went that was the finish of me, but life's tenacious. I'm going, and I'm going to live. I don't rightly know how but I'm going to live. . . .'

In the pain-filled pause that followed there came a sharp knock on the door and it startled them all. It was Jim Waite who went forward and opened it, but without exception they all gaped at the man standing there for he had become instantly recognizable to the others, and it wasn't only by the white streak that ran down to the left temple in his black hair; if by nothing else they would have recognized him from the expression in his eyes as he stared fixedly at Hannah.

Hannah had never fainted in her life, but she knew she was on the point of it now. So great was the shock at seeing him at this particular moment, and here on the doorstep of all places, that she was incapable of either speech or movement, she was almost in the same state as he had been when they first met, that was until he said, 'Hannah!' like that, different, firm. 'Hannah!' Then she was lifted towards him, and as she gripped his hands and cried, 'Oh Ben! Ben, you did it!' Sarah let out a sound that spiralled to a scream. 'Nothing between them! Doesn't know you exist! You to talk about speaking the truth!'

Hannah turned her head towards her mother now and, her voice almost as loud as hers, she shouted, 'I didn't, I didn't know.'

'You're a liar! Do you hear? A bare-faced liar. And you think you're clever with it. You're nothing, but your father over again. To think I'd see the day. Don't you realize that I've been put through enough without having her son coming into my very house. *Her son and you ... Get out! Get out ... you! You! ...*'

'Be quiet! Sarah.' Constance spoke with authority, but Sarah took no heed. And now Jim Waite joined his voice to hers. Stepping through the door, he growled, 'Look, Mister, get yourself away afore I ...' He got no further. The eyes that glared at him were as black as the hair above them and the voice that came through the tight lips was one of authority. 'I'd advise you not to come any nearer and to keep a civil tongue in your head.' They were looking at each other like wrestlers about to grapple. 'By what I have inadvertently overheard during the last few minutes I would also remind you that you are dispensable, and it would be well for you to remember that.' He did not add 'my man' for it was not necessary, it had been conveyed in his tone.

Ben now looked at Hannah, where she was standing gazing at him, her eyes wide and bright with tears, her lips apart, and he said briefly, 'Get your things.'

When she turned and went upstairs, Sarah using her crutch as swiftly as any leg, bounded forward and, blocking her way, cried at her, 'No, you don't! You'll get your things and go with him over my dead body. The son of that, that Mallen bitch. It's indecent, filthy. You're not clean.'

'Sarah! ... *Sarah!*' Constance came forward and, gripping Sarah by the arm, pulled her away from the foot of the stairs; then looking at Hannah, she added grimly, 'If you're going, go and be quick about it.'

Hannah paused on the bottom step, and looked at the faces turned towards her, her family and each expressing hate in some form. Her head drooped, she stepped down into the hall and quietly she said, 'It doesn't matter. I don't need anything; most ... most of my things are over there anyway.' Then going to a cupboard she took out a coat and put it on her shoulders before moving towards the door, only to be pulled to a halt by Sarah's voice again crying, 'You'll regret this day as long as you live, my girl. If you get my prayers you'll. ...'

Hannah swung round towards her mother. 'Don't ... don't say it, Mam. Remember, curses come home to roost.' Then turning to Constance she said, 'Good-bye, Grandma.'

Constance gave her no answer, she made no response whatever. She was watching the wheel of life as it came to the end of its circle. Her granddaughter was going back to High Banks Hall with a Mallen – *with a Mallen.*

Ignoring the fierceness of Jim Waite's stare, Hannah went past him and over the threshold and, without looking at Ben, went down the steps.

681

They walked side by side along the front of the house and out through the gap in the stone wall on to the road. And they walked almost half a mile without either glancing at the other or speaking. When, simultaneously they stopped, their gaze held in muteness, until Hannah swallowing deeply, asked softly, 'How long had you been standing there?'

'Long enough.'

Her eyes did not waver from his but her colour rose; and then she said, 'The main thing is you made it.'

'Yes, I made it.' He reached out and took her hand and they walked on again, silent once more.

When they stopped it was almost exactly at the place where the driver had dropped him shortly before, and he said, 'I got a lift up to here.'

'You came by motor-car?'

'In a truck.'

'How, how did you do it? I mean, what . . . what made you do it?'

'It was Lawrence. He . . . he said if I didn't come and get you he would.'

'Lawrence?' She smiled gently. Then again she said, 'Lawrence?'

'He missed you.'

They glanced at each other. 'That's nice to hear.' Her voice was small.

They walked on again, more slowly now as the hills became steeper. The sky was high, the sun was warm, the light was thin and clear, the world about them looked wide, empty and wide, space everywhere, no people, nothing only clean space. They gasped, now and again paused, but didn't really stop until they reached the summit and were opposite the ruined house. Then they sat down.

They sat on the grass verge with the ruins behind them, the ruins of the old house wherein her father had been conceived. They sat in silence looking away down into the vast bowl of the valley until, after a time, he brought his gaze down to his hands which were joined and hanging between his knees now, and he asked softly, 'Did you mean all you said back there?'

She looked into the distance as she replied, 'Yes, I meant it.'

'You'd . . . you'd come and live with me, just like that?' He lifted his eyes towards her, and now hers were waiting. 'How . . . how long have you felt like this?'

'I . . . I don't really know. It . . . it must have been practically from the beginning. . . . And you?'

'Since you put your hands into the void and pulled me out, all the time I think, but . . . but I wouldn't give it daylight. There . . . there was my mother's rejection and others; fickleness, no depth . . . and then there was the situation. Your father, my mother, No, I wouldn't give it daylight until, well, I realized I couldn't make it without you, I'd never make it without, I didn't want to make it without you.'

'Oh Ben! *Ben!*'

They were locked together, not kissing, just holding tight, their faces on each other's shoulder as if in shyness, as if they could not face the enormity of the thing that was happening to them. When their heads moved and once again they were looking at each other, Ben, from deep in his throat, asked, 'Do you realize that this is how it would have been with them if they had been given the chance?'

Dumbly she nodded her head.

'You'll always want me, Hannah?'

'Always Ben.'

'You'll have to be sure.'

'I am sure.'

'I need you, Hannah.'

'I love you, Ben. I love you ... oh, I love you ... *I love you.*' She hugged him to her with each declaration.

That was what he wanted to hear, not for him to say it first, but for some woman to say 'I love you, Ben, I love you, *I love you.*'

It was strange but no woman had ever said those words to him.

As he put his mouth down on hers and drew her into him he knew he had reached home; he was on solid ground, and the earth had no edge to it.